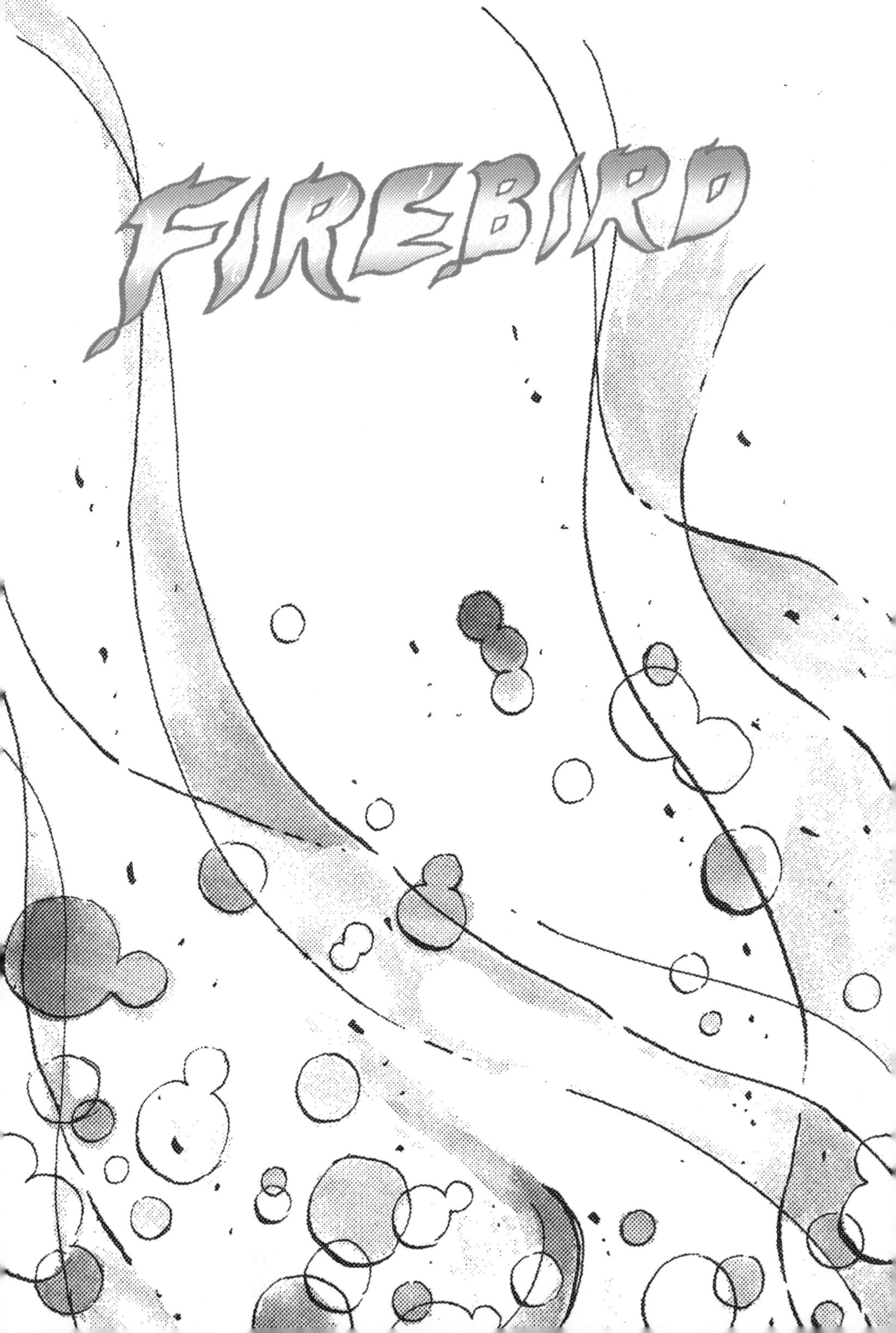
FIREBIRD

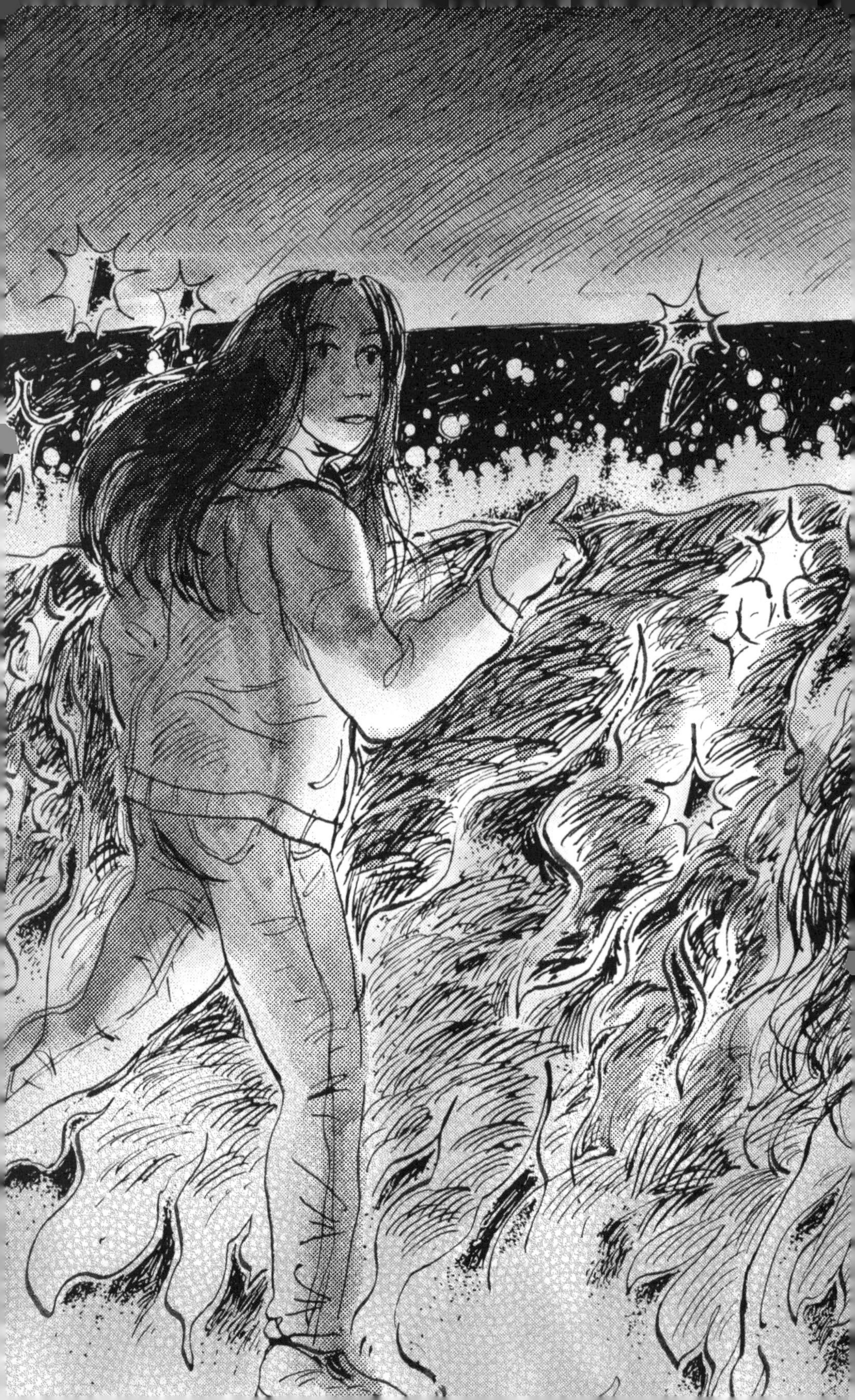

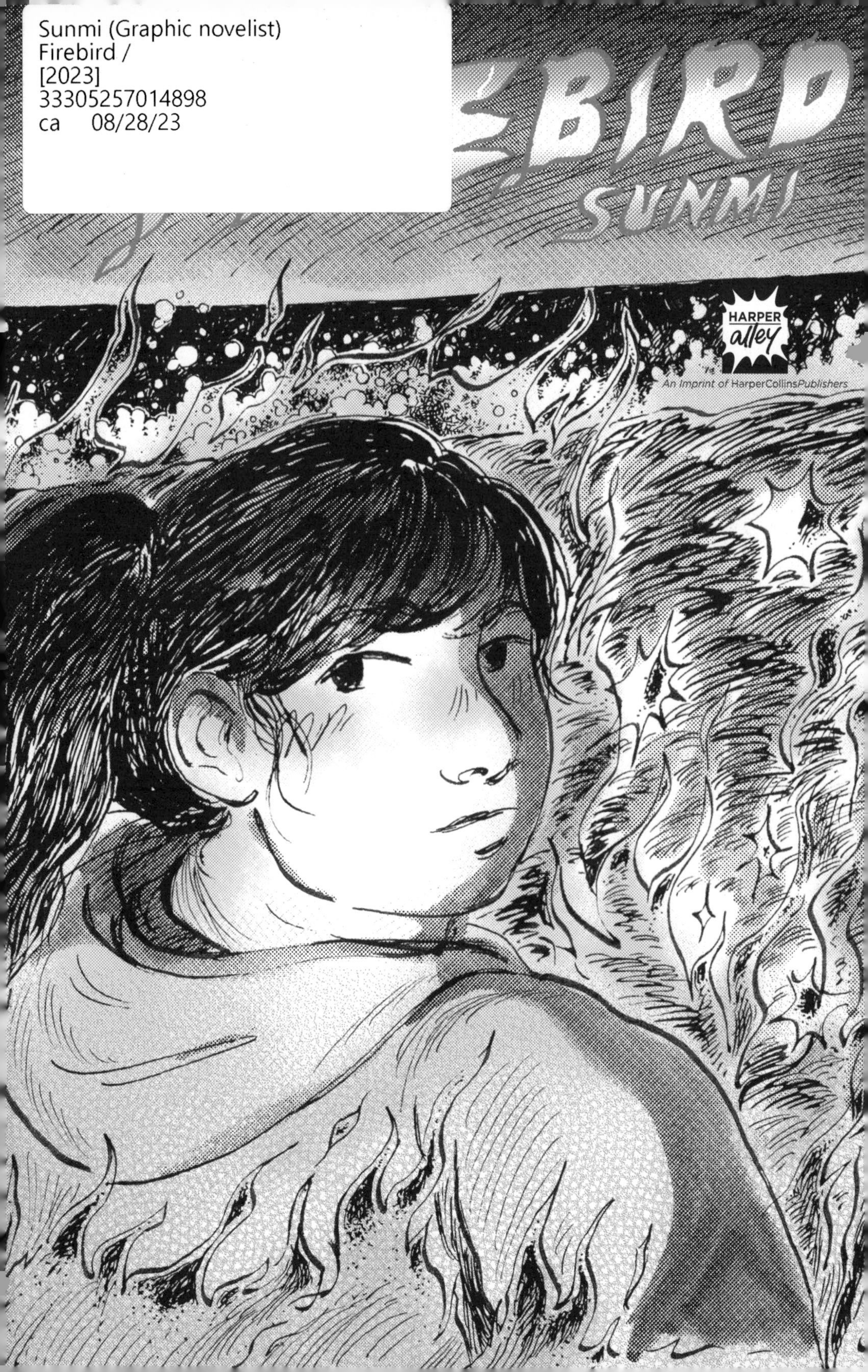
BIRD
SUNMI
HARPER alley
An Imprint of HarperCollinsPublishers

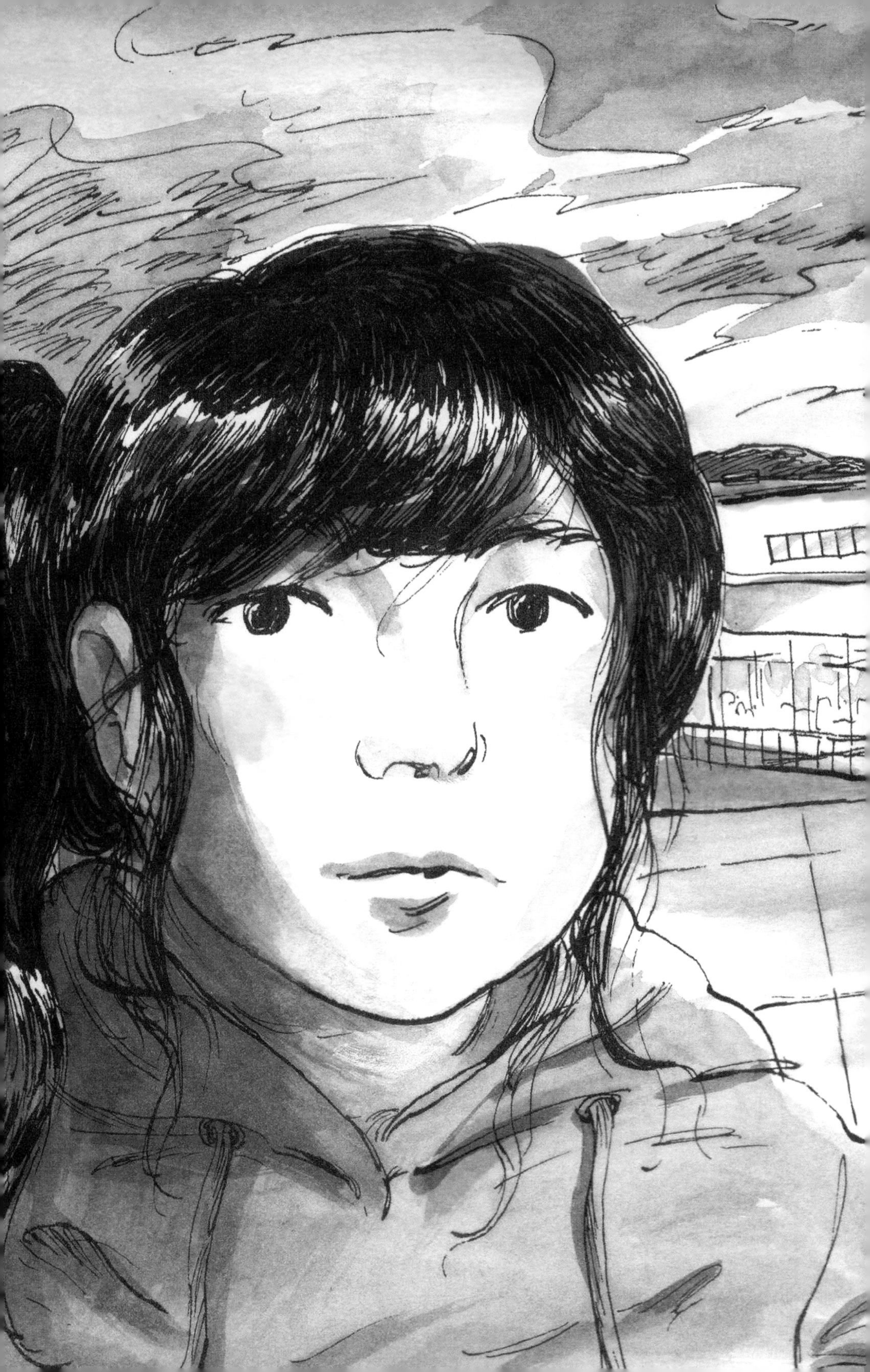

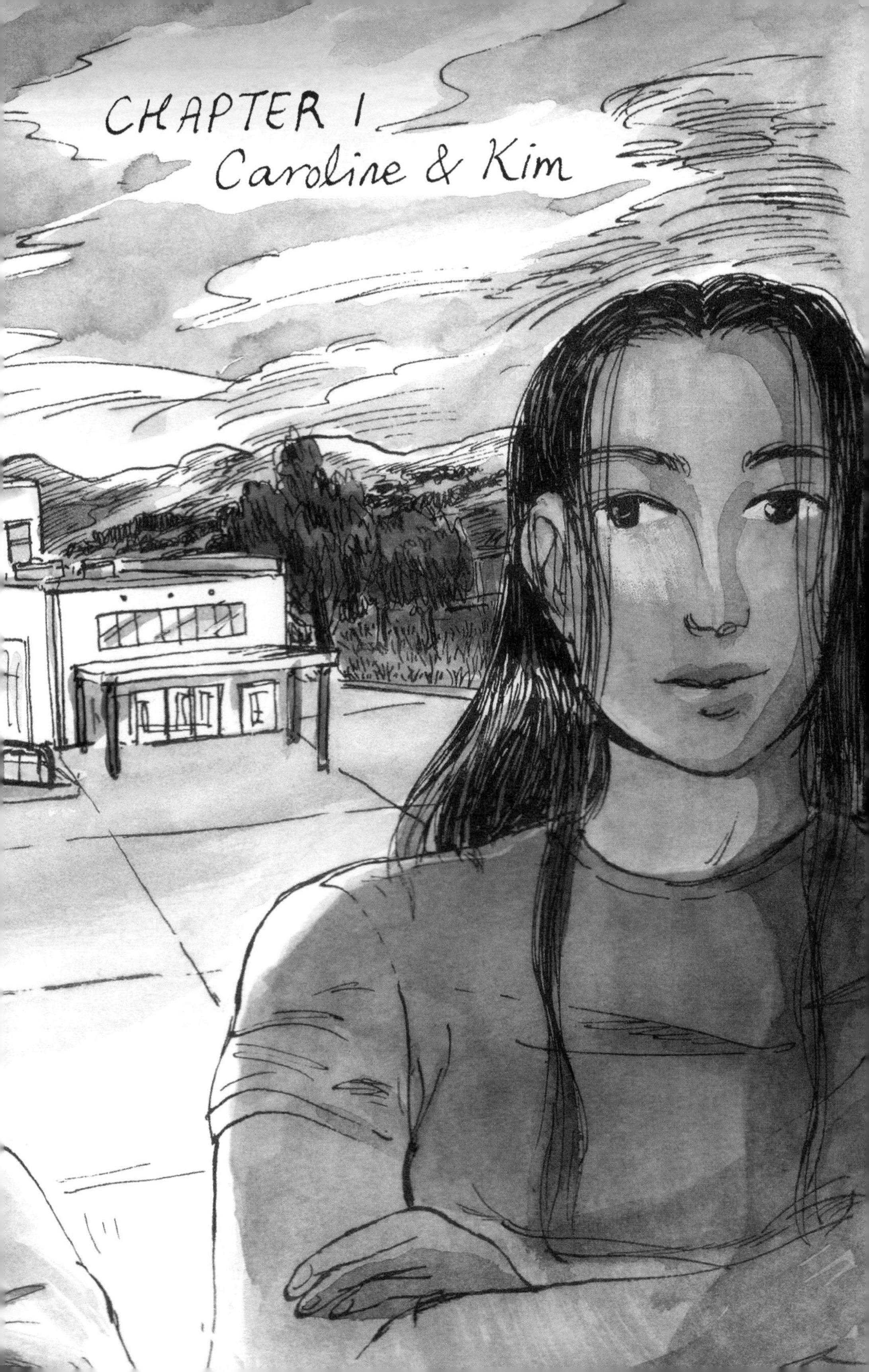
CHAPTER 1
Caroline & Kim

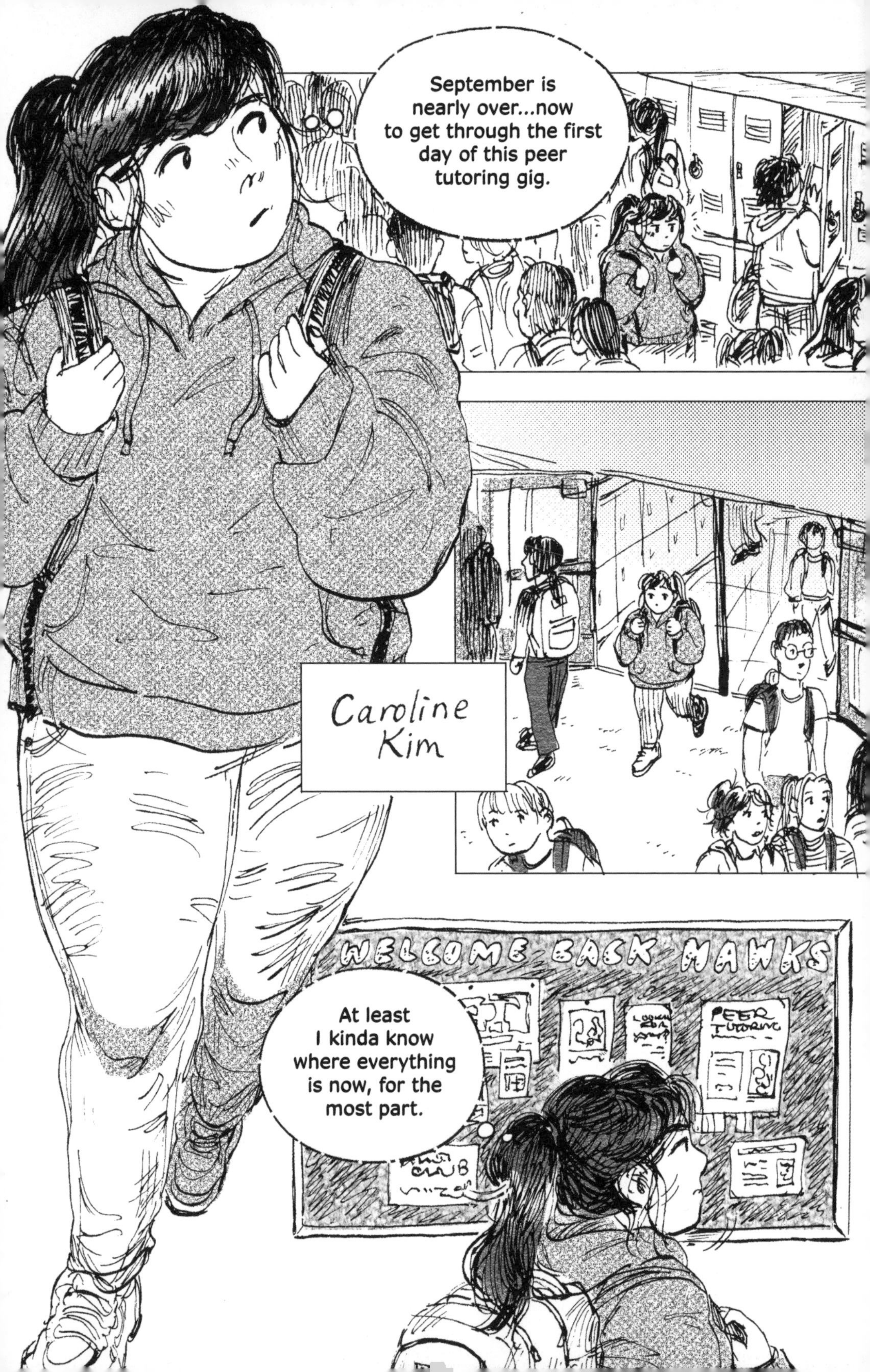
September is nearly over...now to get through the first day of this peer tutoring gig.
Caroline Kim
WELCOME BACK HAWKS
PEER TUTORING
At least I kinda know where everything is now, for the most part.
CLUB

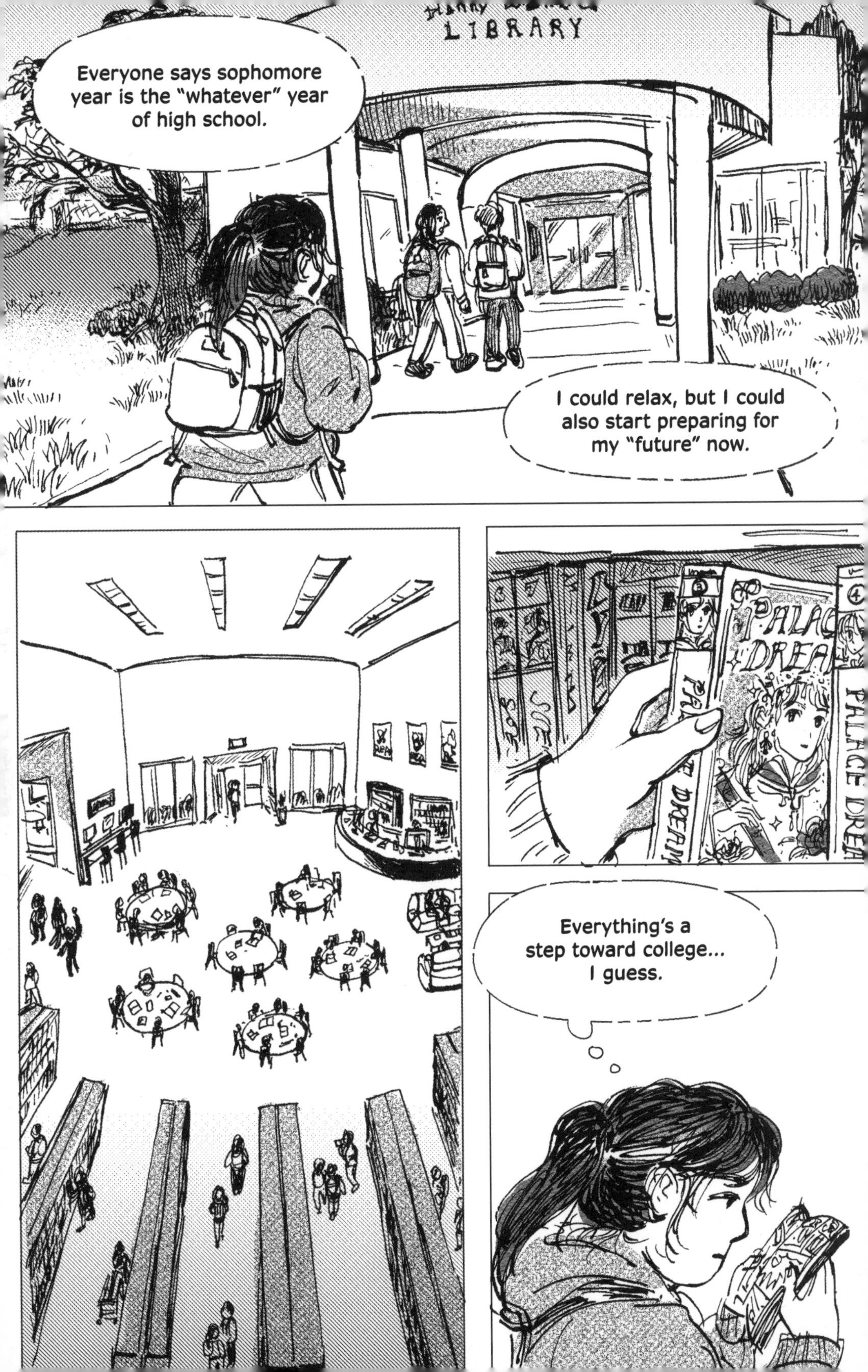
LIBRARY
Everyone says sophomore year is the "whatever" year of high school.
I could relax, but I could also start preparing for my "future" now.
Everything's a step toward college... I guess.

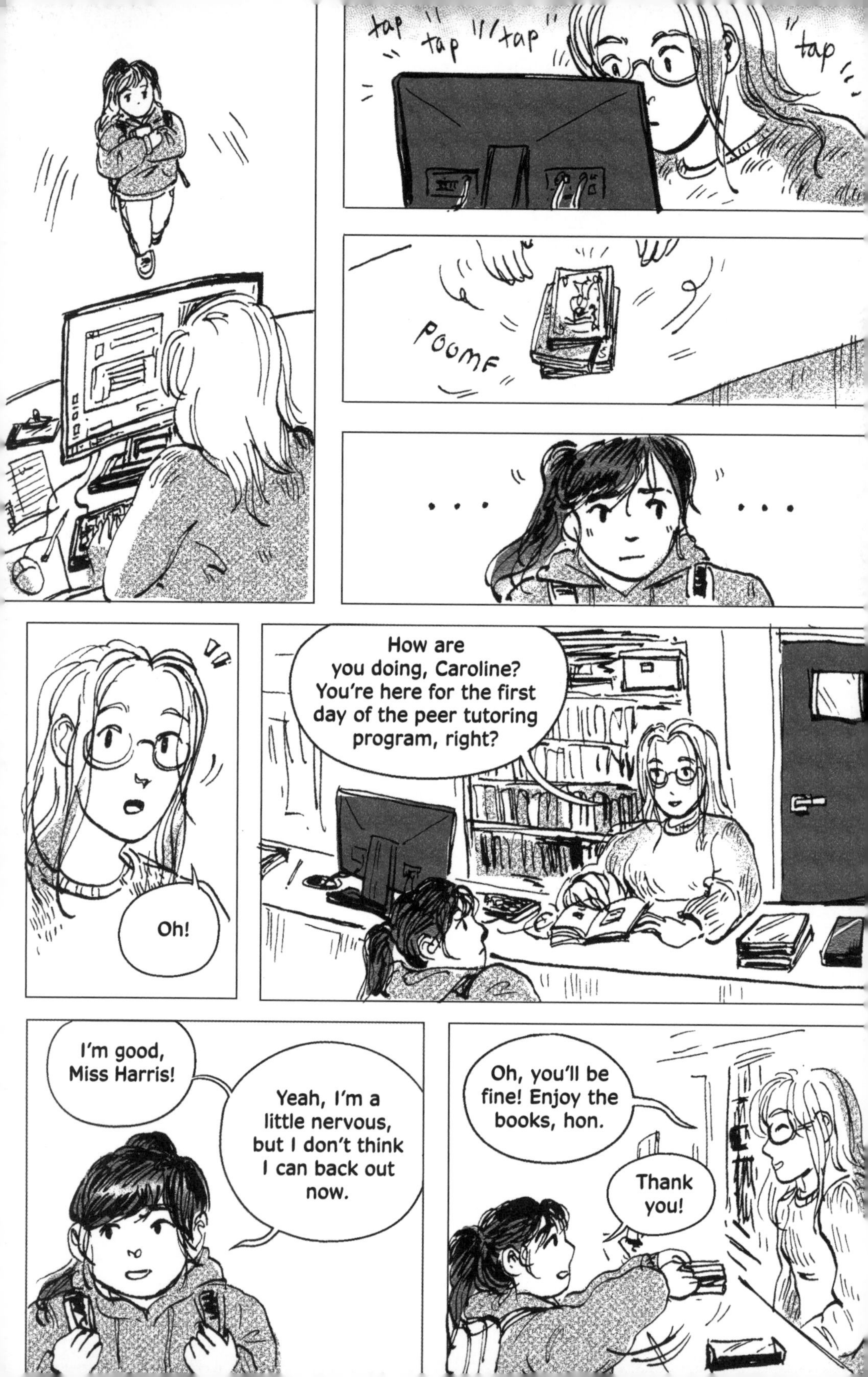
tap
tap
tap
tap
POOMF
. . .
. . .
Oh!
How are you doing, Caroline? You're here for the first day of the peer tutoring program, right?
I'm good, Miss Harris!
Yeah, I'm a little nervous, but I don't think I can back out now.
Oh, you'll be fine! Enjoy the books, hon.
Thank you!

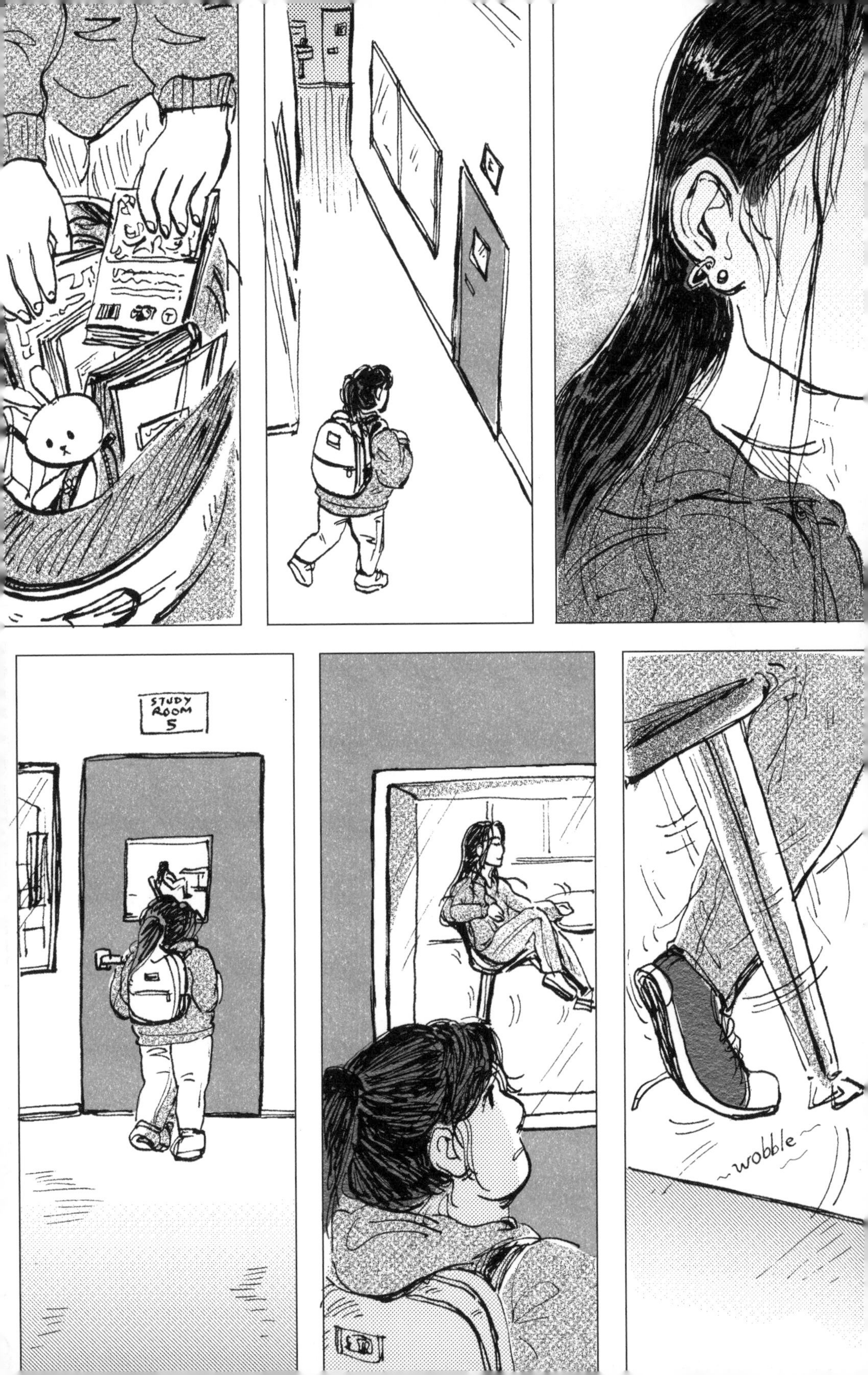
STUDY ROOM 5
~wobble~

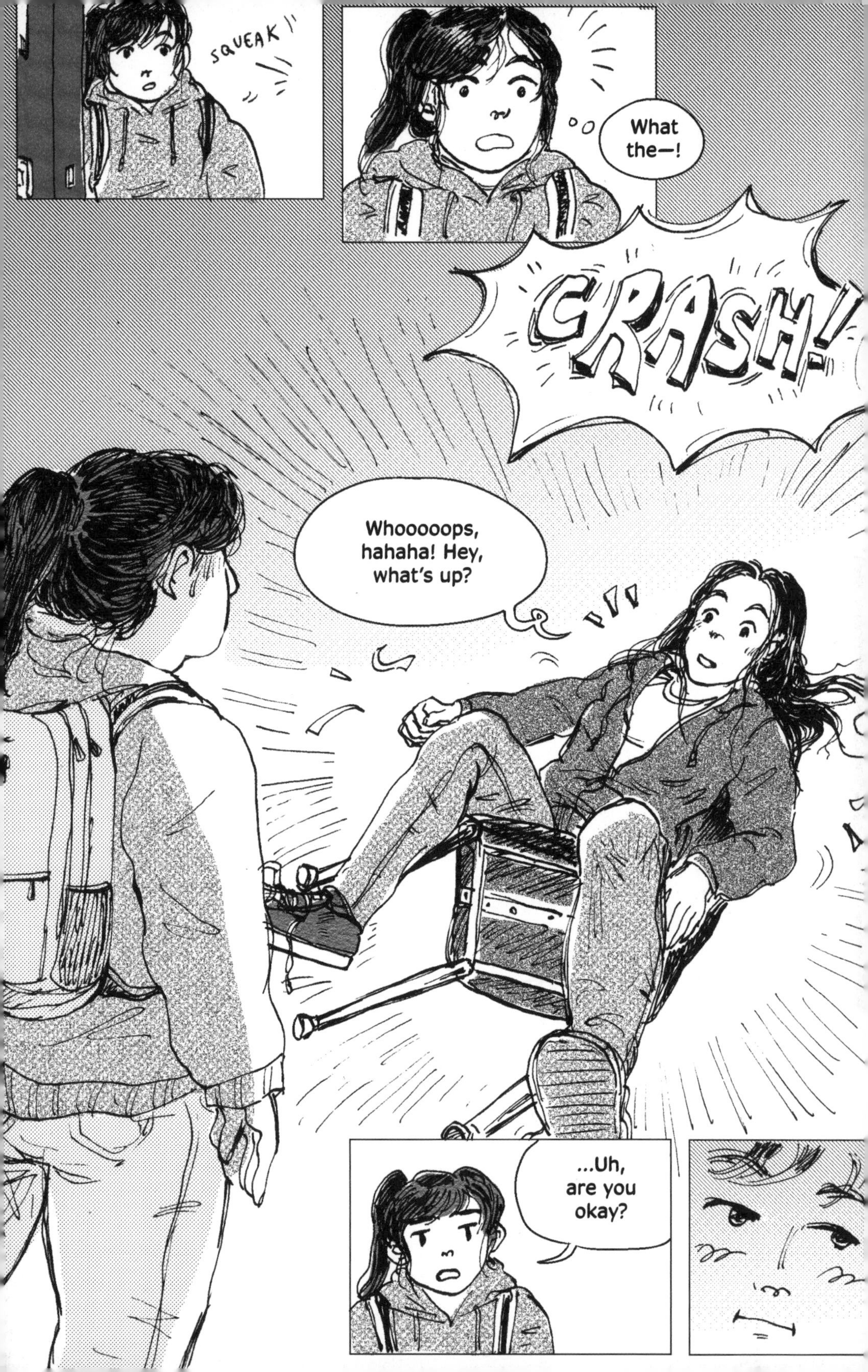
SQUEAK
What the—!
CRASH!
Whoooooops, hahaha! Hey, what's up?
...Uh, are you okay?

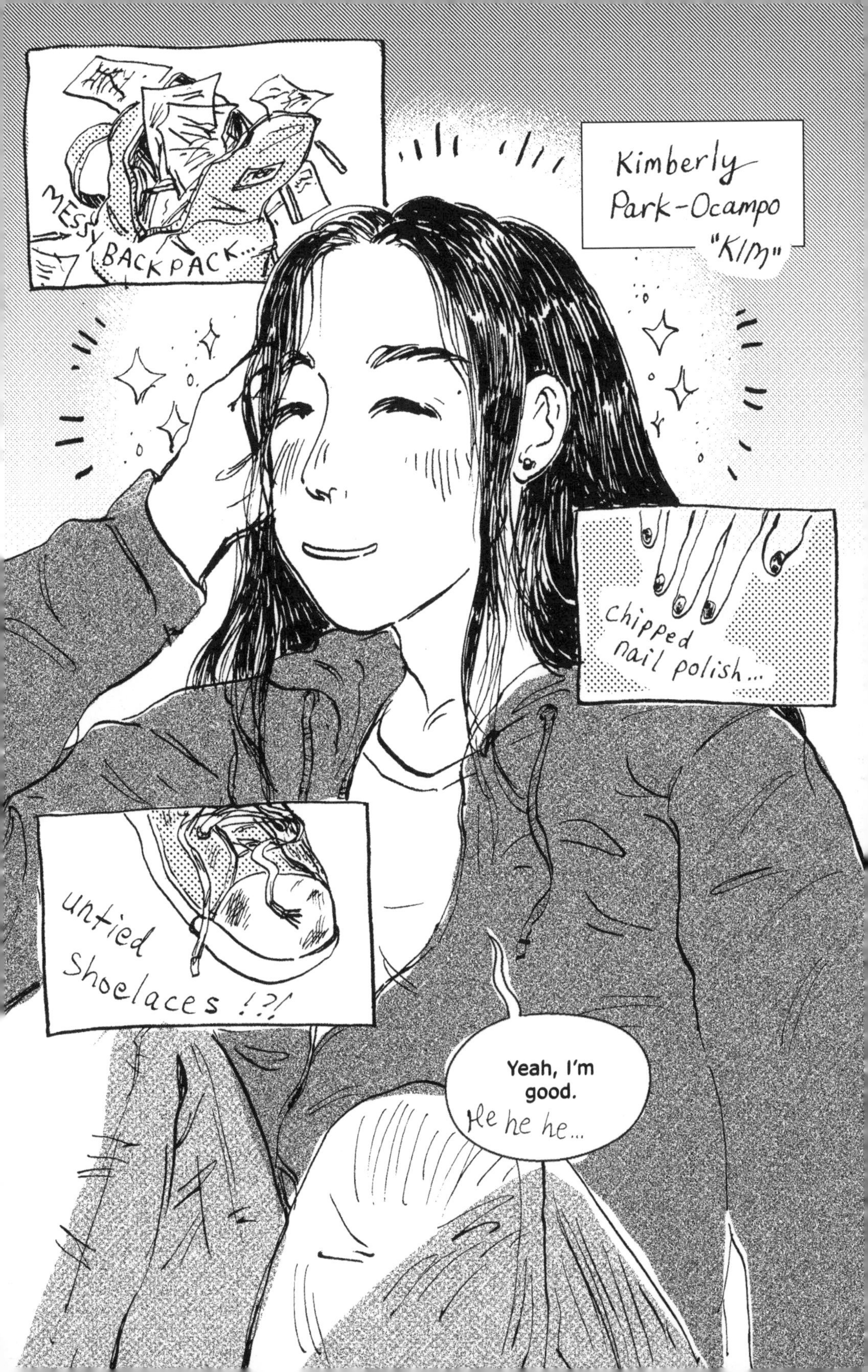

MESSY BACKPACK...
Kimberly Park-Ocampo "KIM"
Chipped nail polish...
untied Shoelaces !?!
Yeah, I'm good.
He he he...

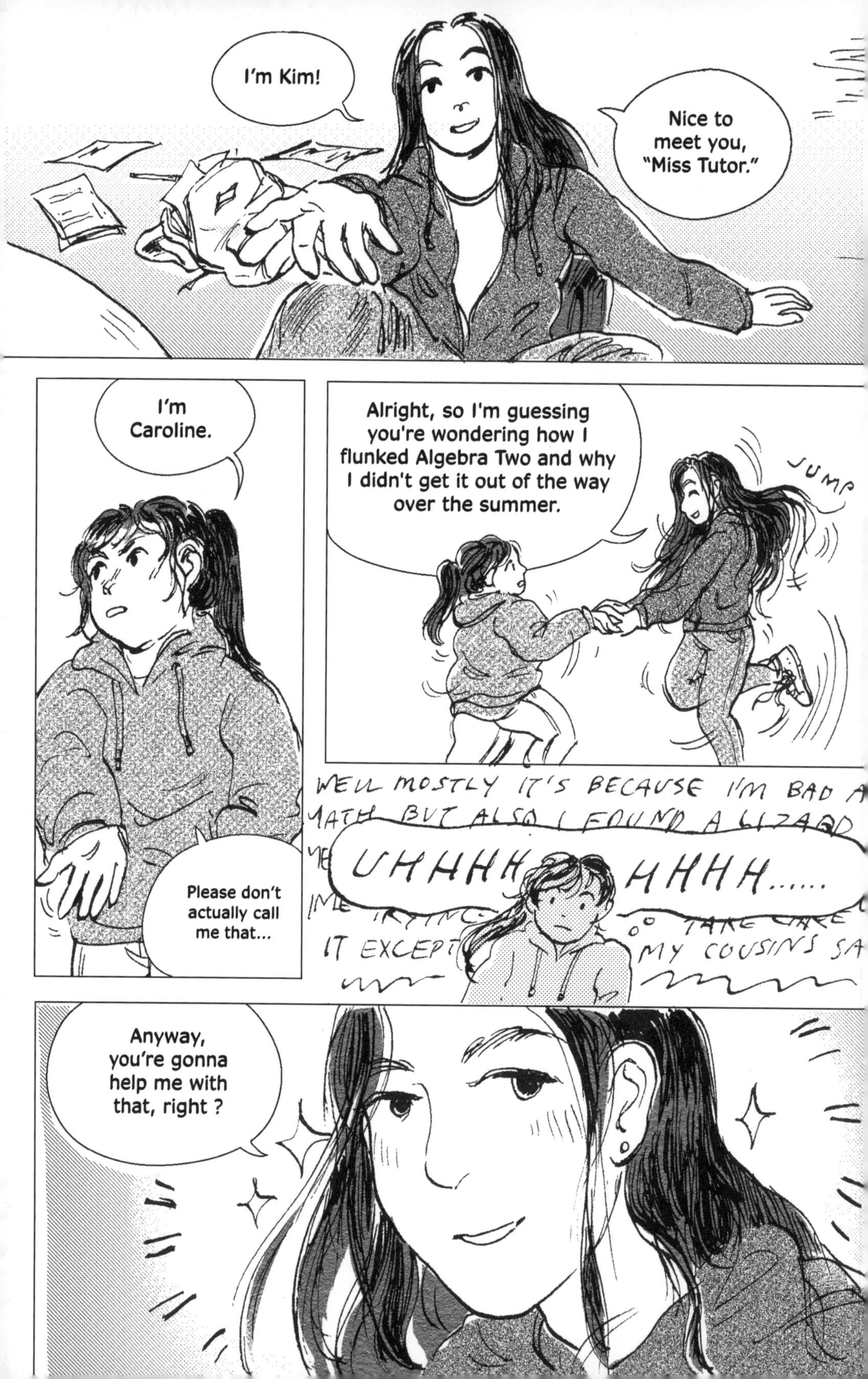
I'm Kim!
Nice to meet you, "Miss Tutor."
I'm Caroline.
Please don't actually call me that...
Alright, so I'm guessing you're wondering how I flunked Algebra Two and why I didn't get it out of the way over the summer.
JUMP
WELL MOSTLY IT'S BECAUSE I'M BAD A
MATH BUT ALSO I FOUND A LIZARD
IT EXCEPT
MY COUSINS SA
UHHHH HHHH......
Anyway, you're gonna help me with that, right ?

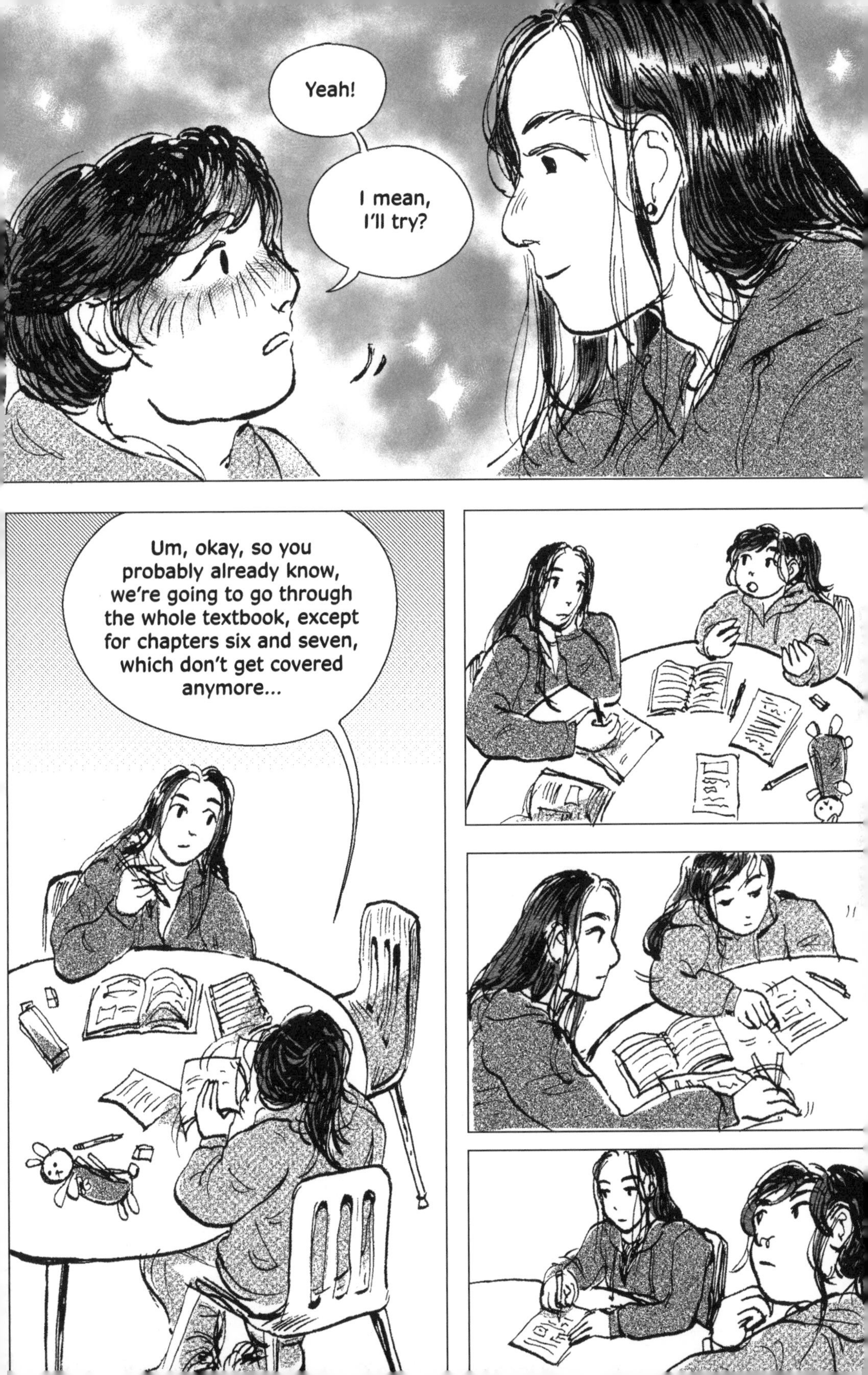
Yeah!
I mean, I'll try?
Um, okay, so you probably already know, we're going to go through the whole textbook, except for chapters six and seven, which don't get covered anymore...

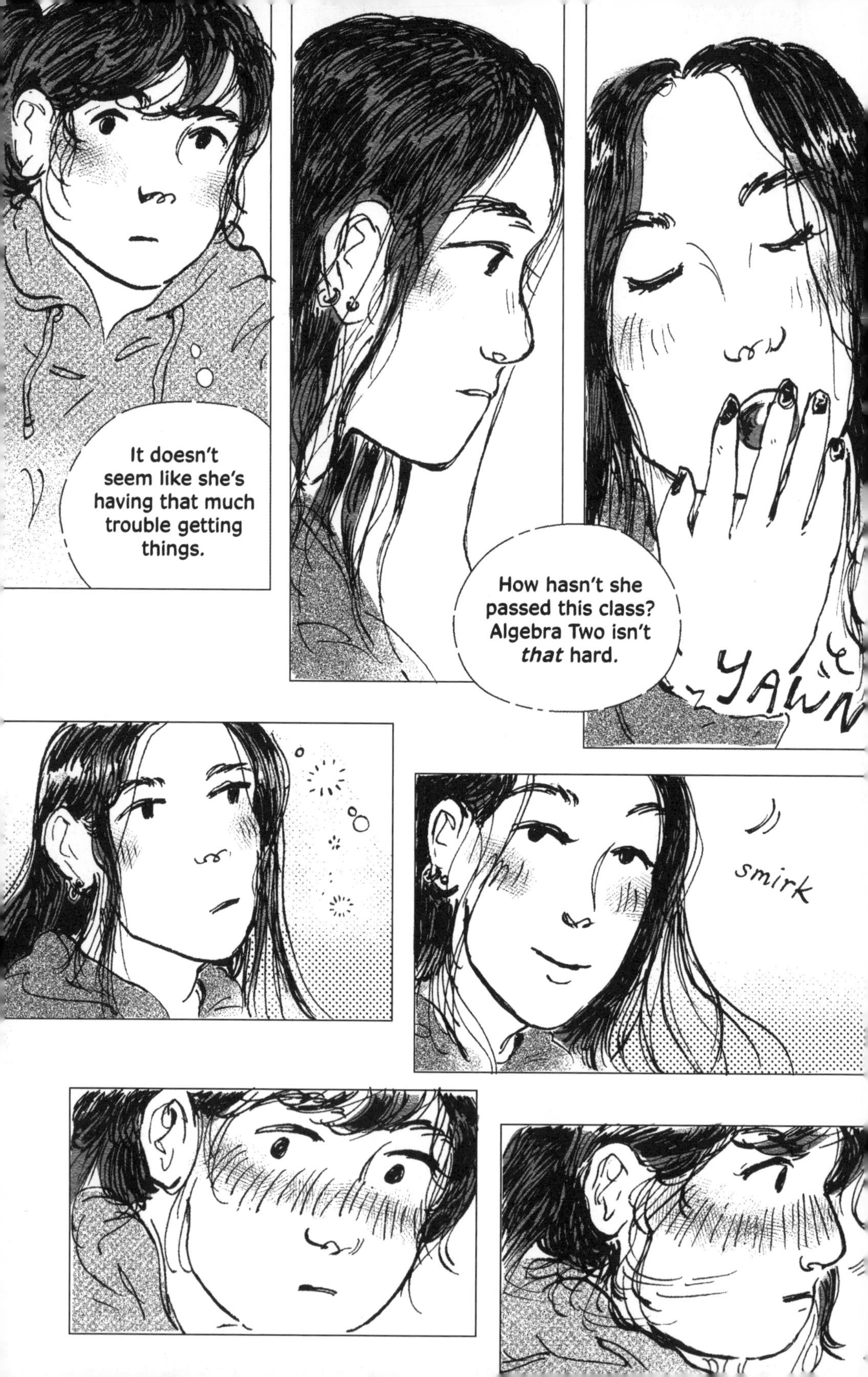
It doesn't seem like she's having that much trouble getting things.
How hasn't she passed this class? Algebra Two isn't *that* hard.
YAWN
smirk

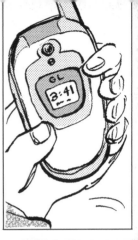

Uh, so you got everything right? No questions about polynomials or anything else in chapter one?

POKE

No-ope!

I'm all good, Miss Kim~

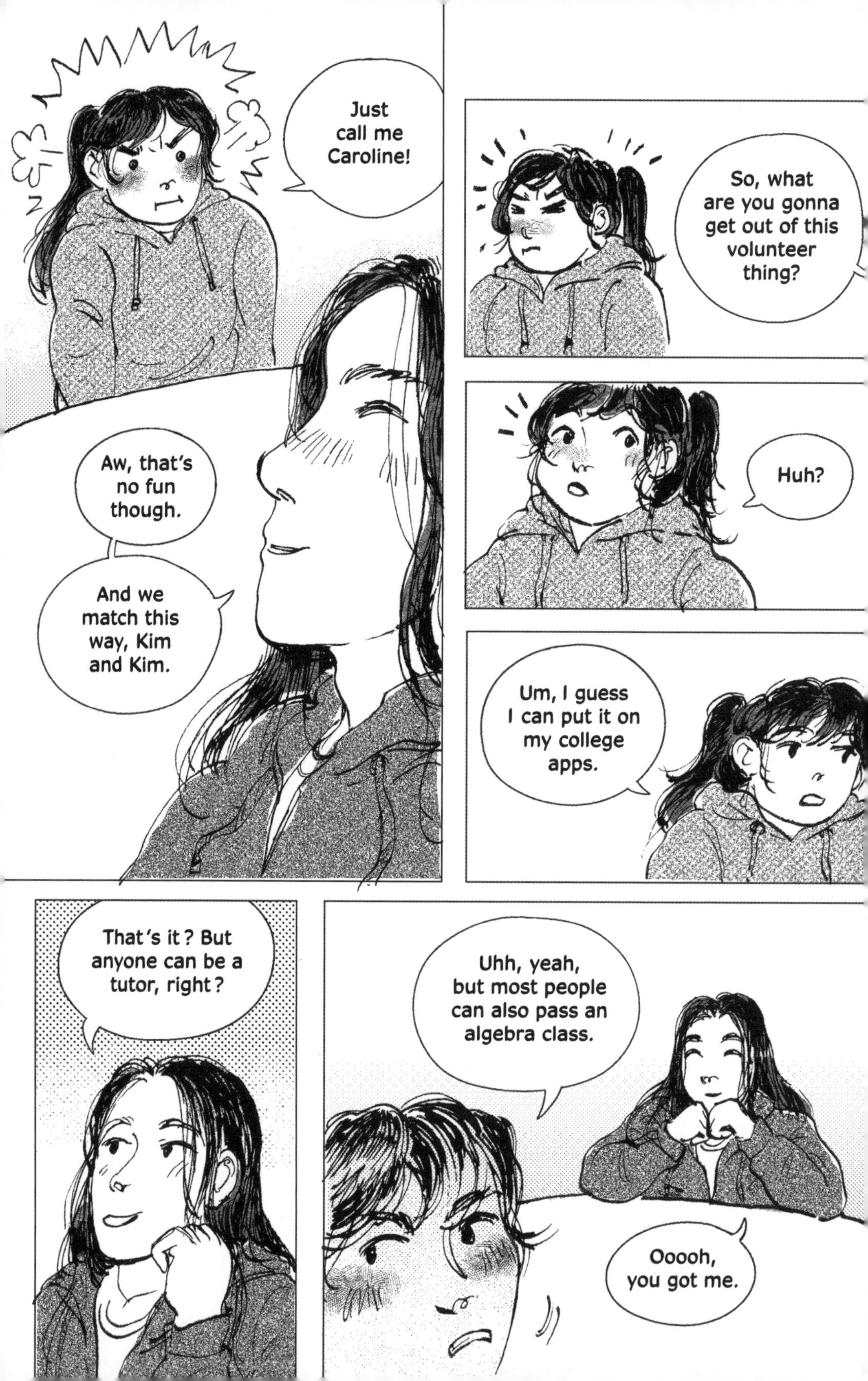
Just call me Caroline!
So, what are you gonna get out of this volunteer thing?
Aw, that's no fun though.
And we match this way, Kim and Kim.
Huh?
Um, I guess I can put it on my college apps.
That's it? But anyone can be a tutor, right?
Uhh, yeah, but most people can also pass an algebra class.
Ooooh, you got me.

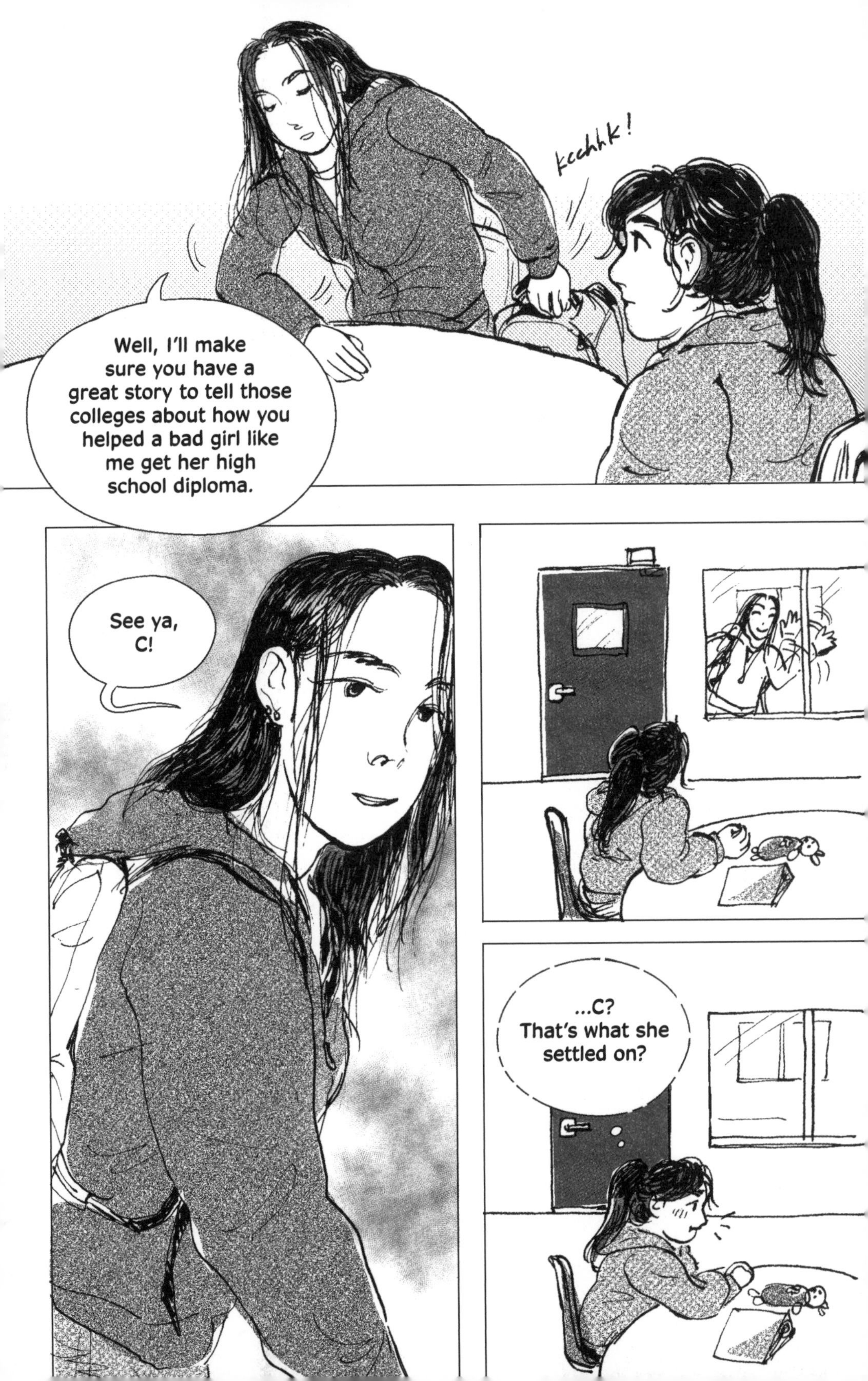
kcchhk!
Well, I'll make sure you have a great story to tell those colleges about how you helped a bad girl like me get her high school diploma.
See ya, C!
...C? That's what she settled on?

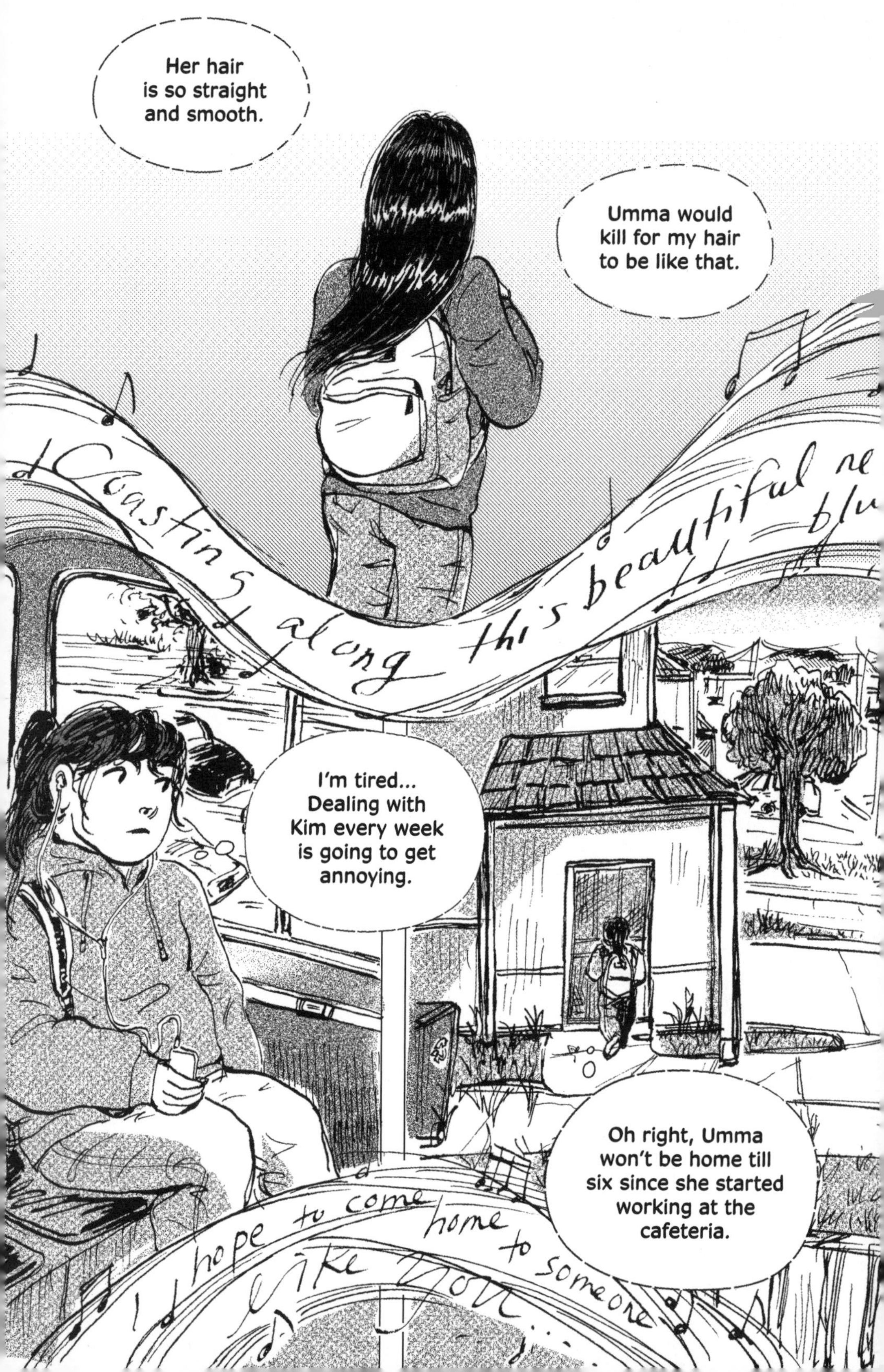
Her hair is so straight and smooth.
Umma would kill for my hair to be like that.
Coasting along this beautiful
I'm tired... Dealing with Kim every week is going to get annoying.
Oh right, Umma won't be home till six since she started working at the cafeteria.
I hope to come home to someone like you...

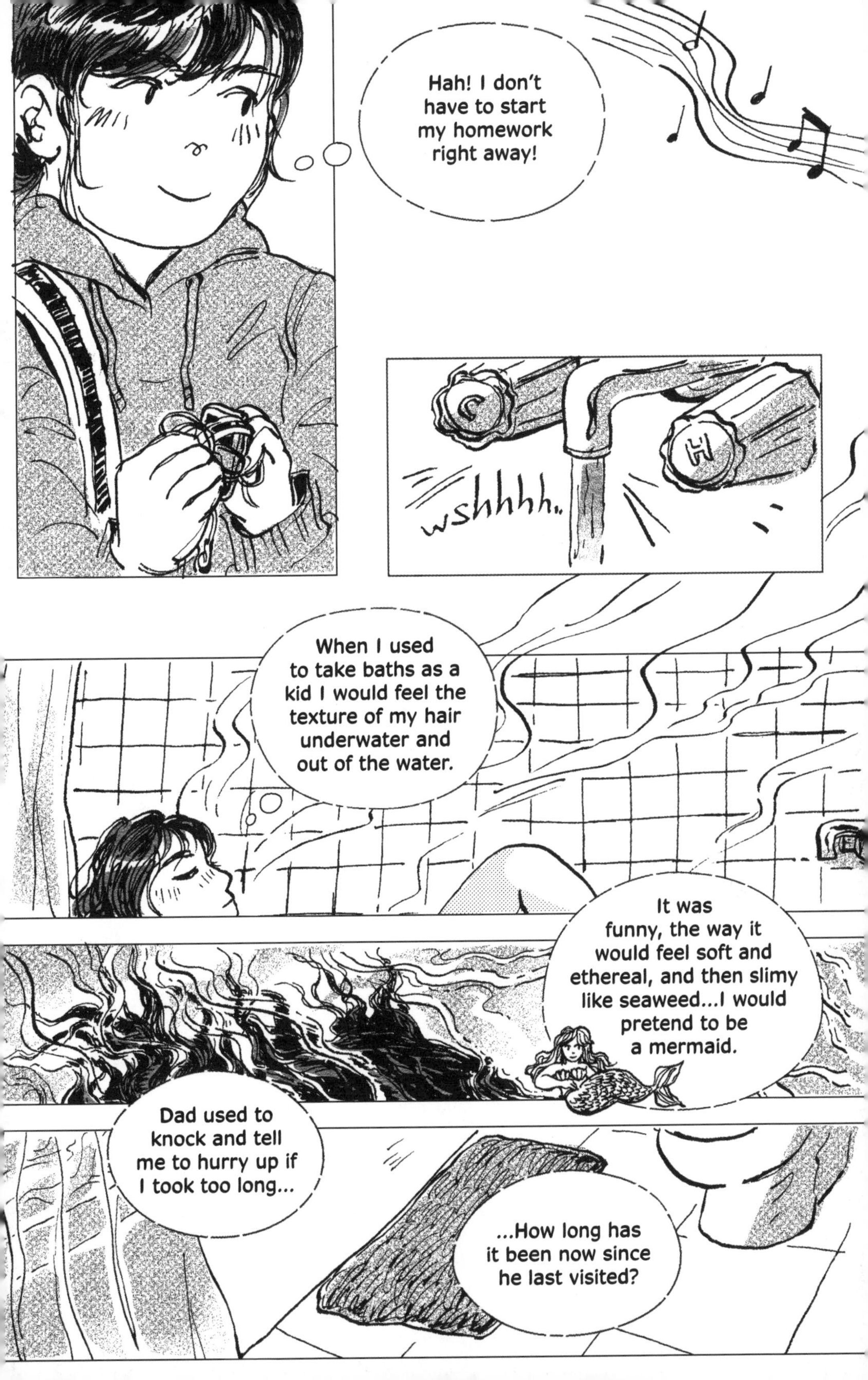
Hah! I don't have to start my homework right away!
wshhhh..
When I used to take baths as a kid I would feel the texture of my hair underwater and out of the water.
It was funny, the way it would feel soft and ethereal, and then slimy like seaweed...I would pretend to be a mermaid.
Dad used to knock and tell me to hurry up if I took too long...
...How long has it been now since he last visited?

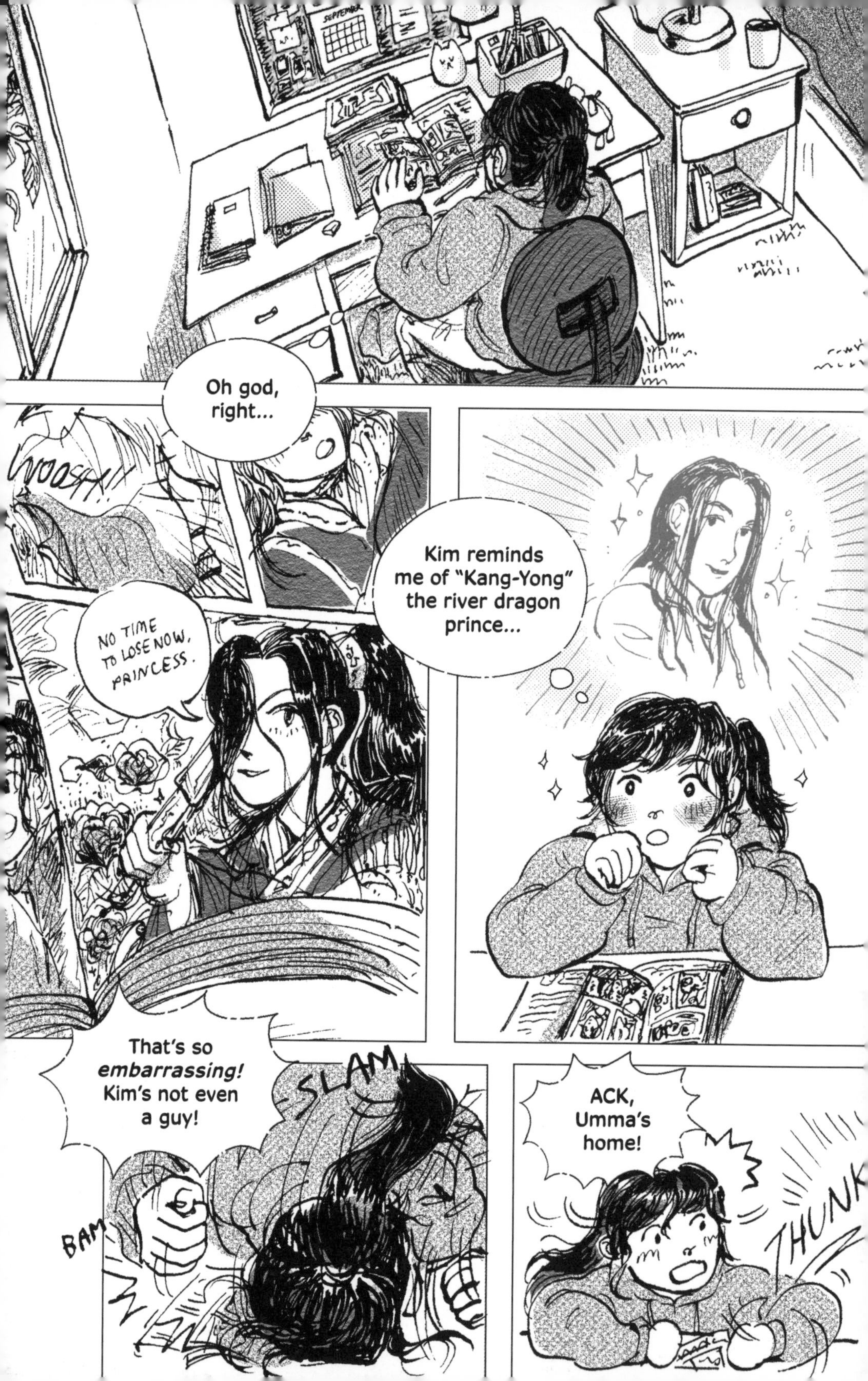

SEPTEMBER
Oh god, right...
WOOSH!!
Kim reminds me of "Kang-Yong" the river dragon prince...
NO TIME TO LOSE NOW, PRINCESS.
That's so *embarrassing!* Kim's not even a guy!
SLAM
BAM
ACK, Umma's home!
THUNK

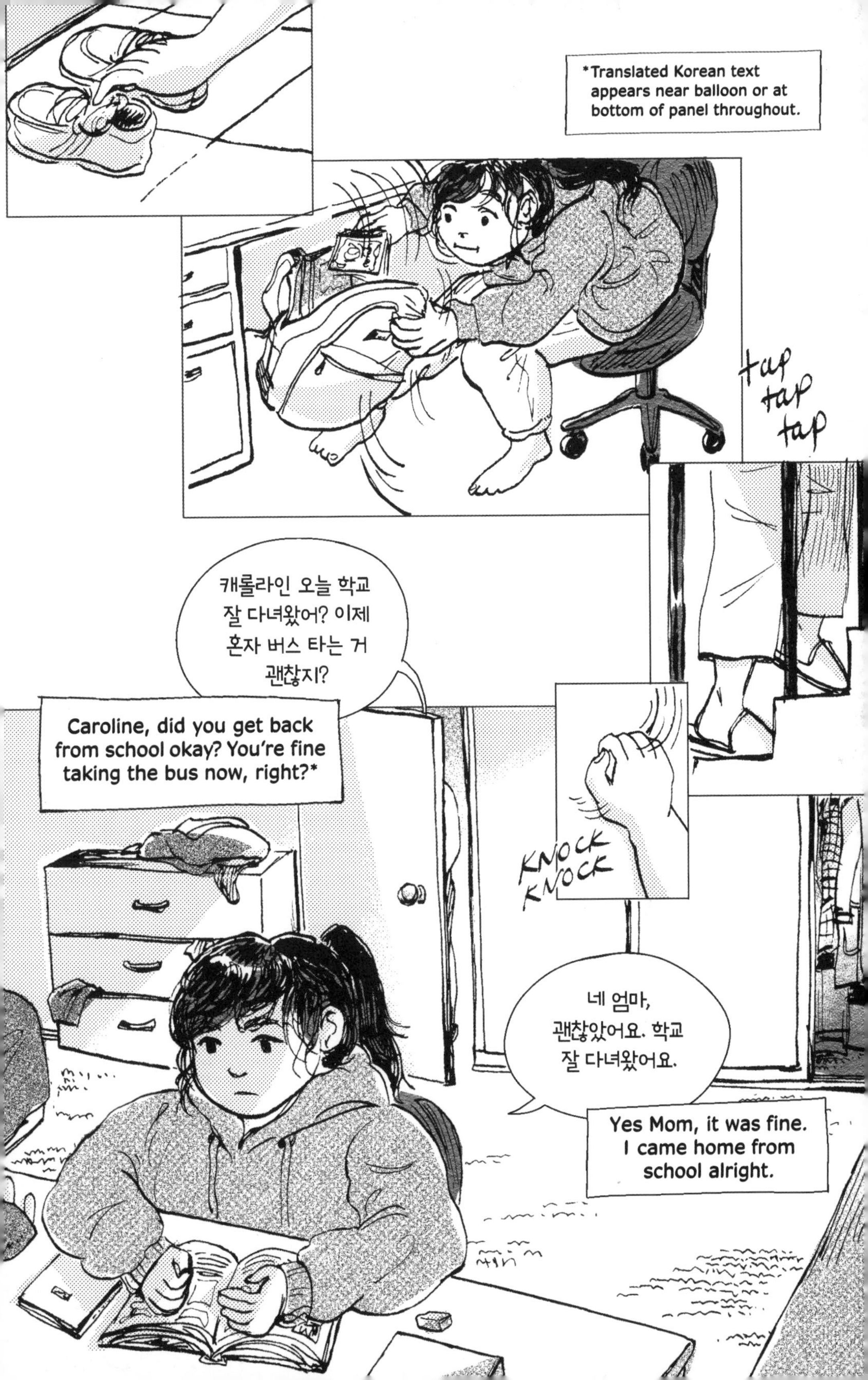
*Translated Korean text appears near balloon or at bottom of panel throughout.
tap tap tap
캐롤라인 오늘 학교 잘 다녀왔어? 이제 혼자 버스 타는 거 괜찮지?
Caroline, did you get back from school okay? You're fine taking the bus now, right?*
KNOCK KNOCK
네 엄마, 괜찮았어요. 학교 잘 다녀왔어요.
Yes Mom, it was fine. I came home from school alright.

그래, 무슨 일 있으면 전화 좀 하고. 공부는?

열심히 하고 있어요 엄마.

Right, if something comes up, please call me for once. And your studies?

I'm studying hard Mom.

오케이~ 좀 쉬고 저녁 해 먹자.

Okay~ I'm going to rest a bit, then let's have dinner.

Phew, she's in a good mood.

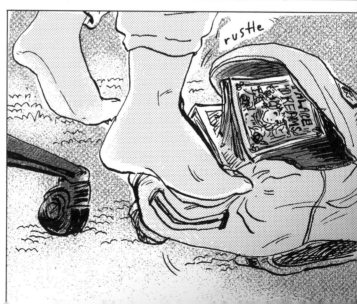

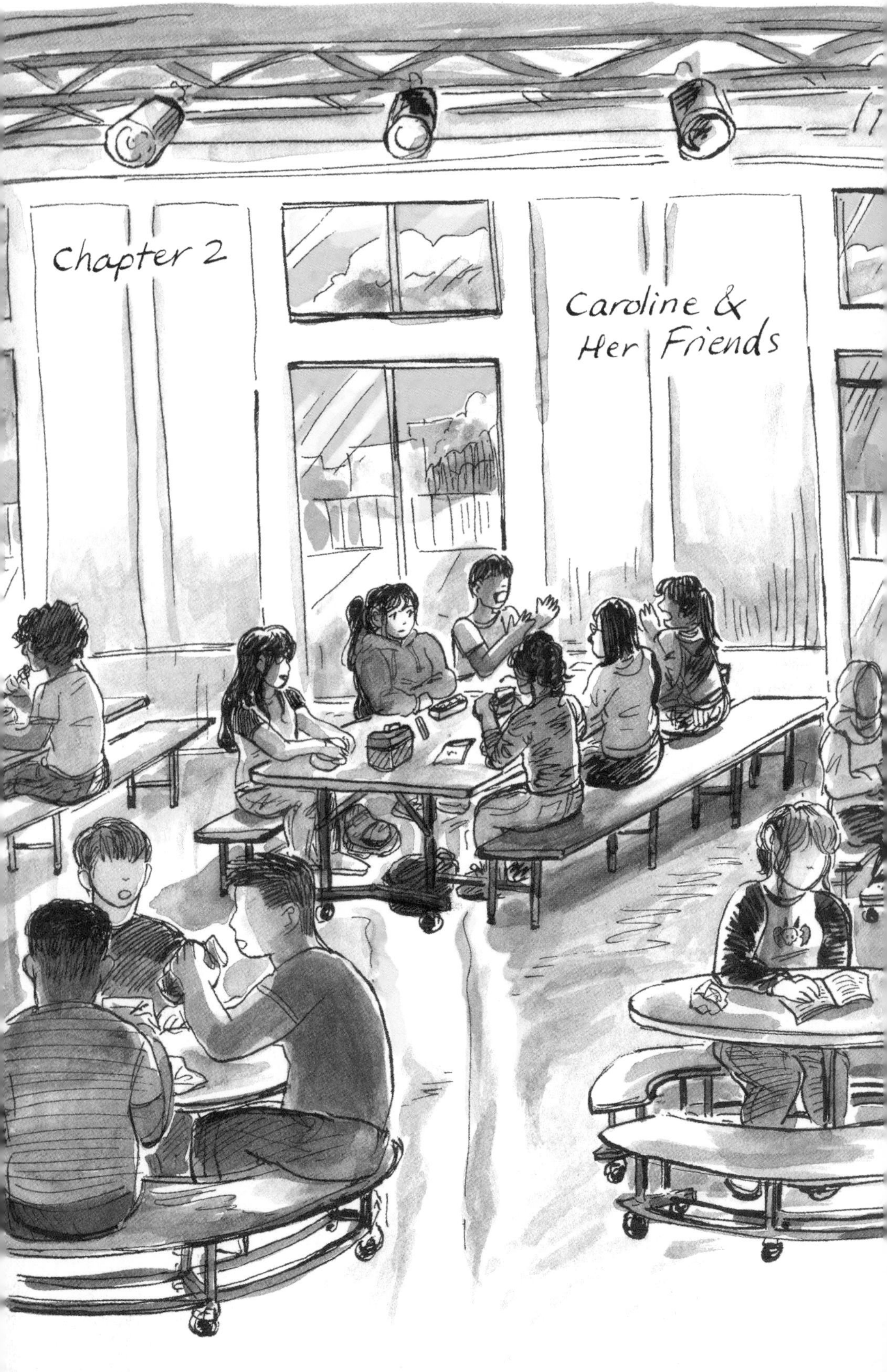
Chapter 2
Caroline &
Her Friends

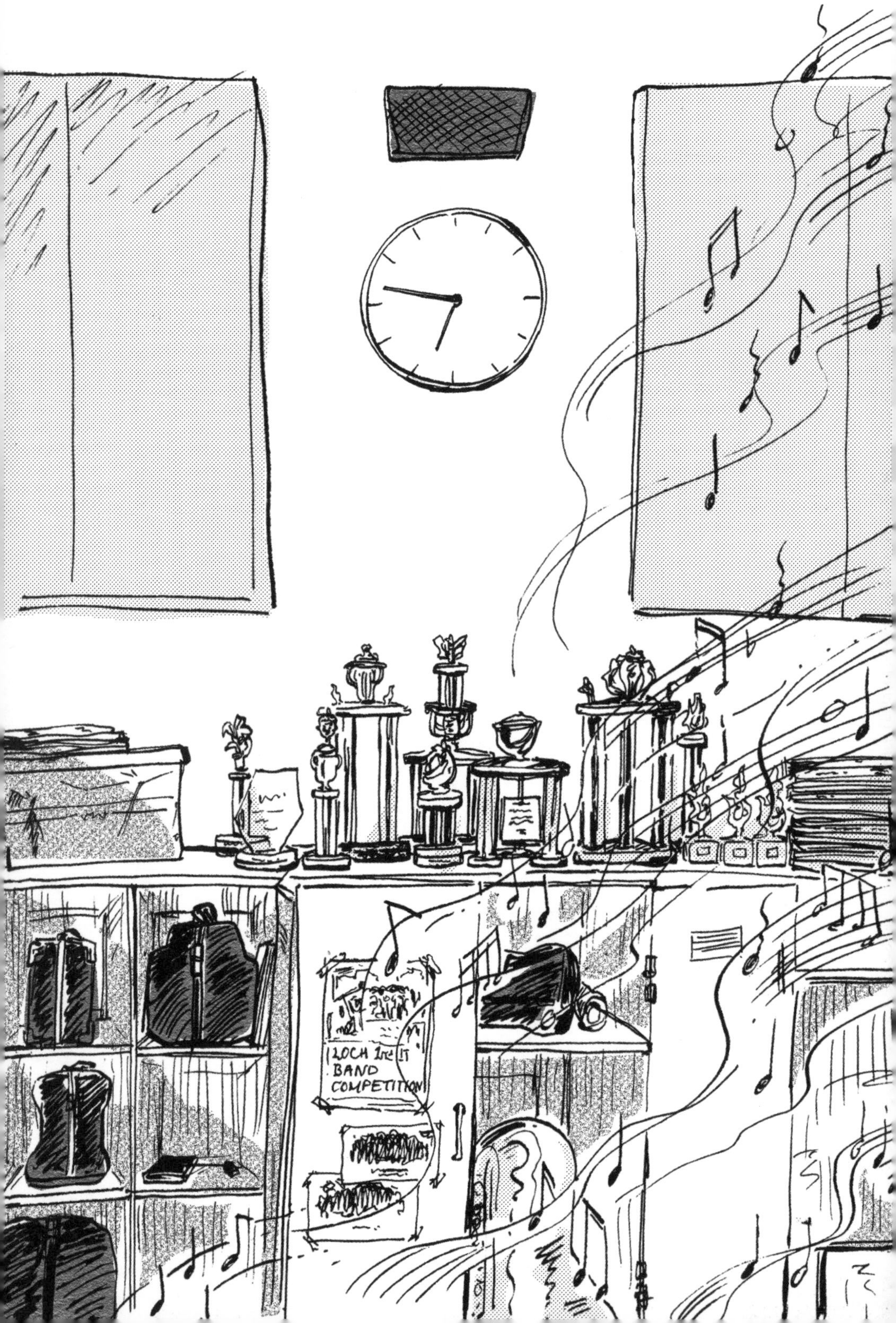
BAND
COMPETITION

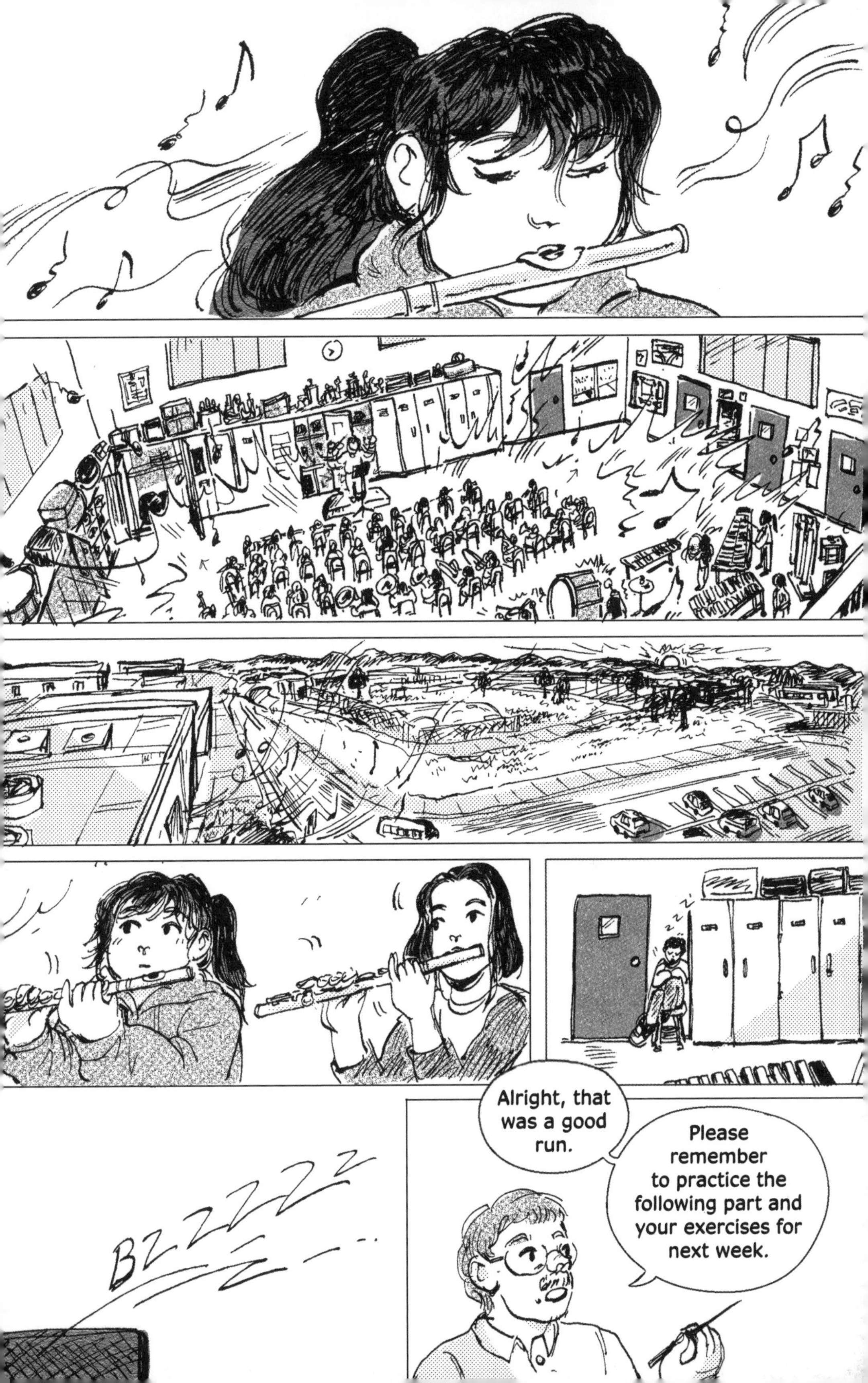

BZZZZZZ
Alright, that was a good run.
Please remember to practice the following part and your exercises for next week.

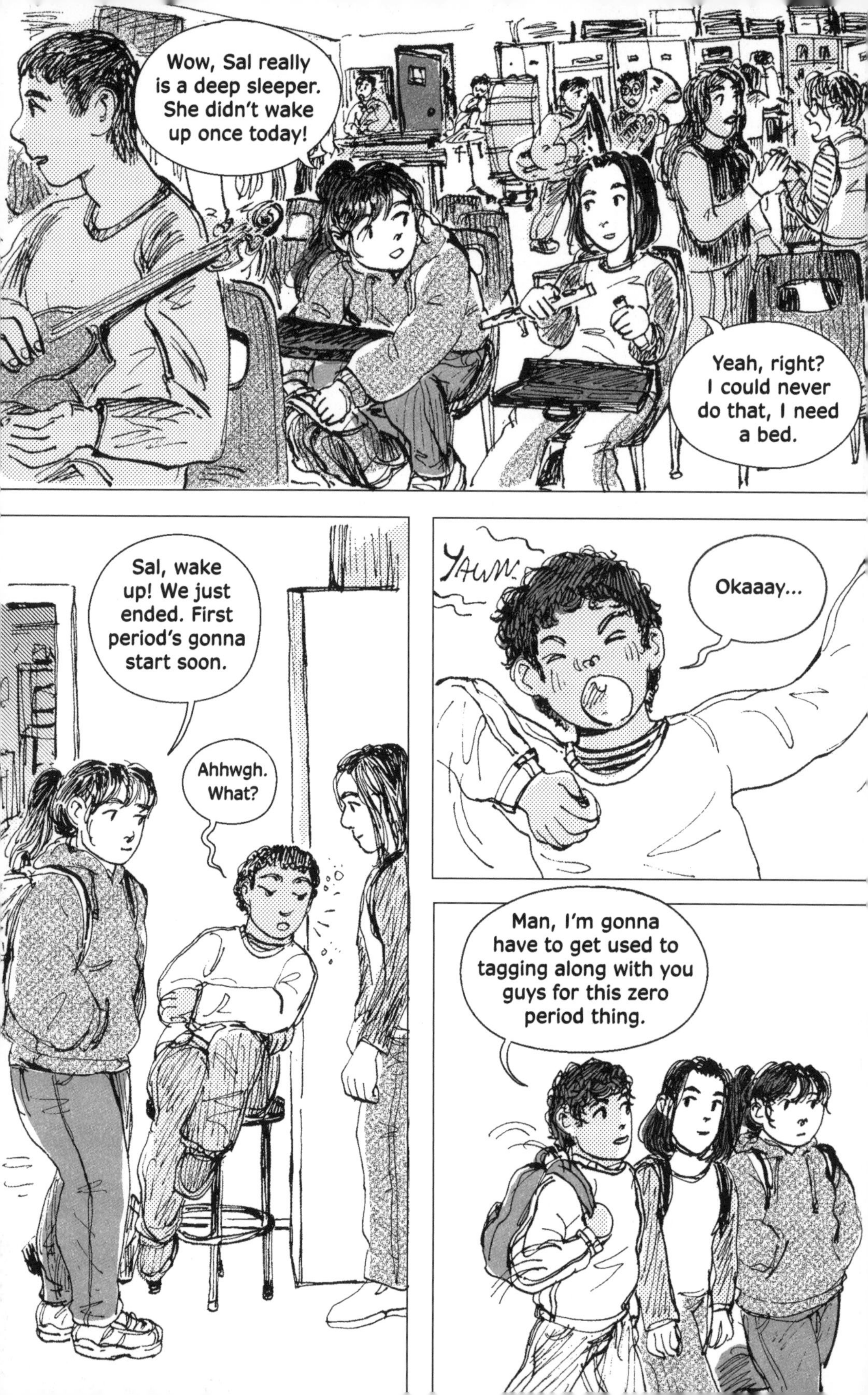
Wow, Sal really is a deep sleeper. She didn't wake up once today!
Yeah, right? I could never do that, I need a bed.
Sal, wake up! We just ended. First period's gonna start soon.
Ahhwgh. What?
YAWN!
Okaaay...
Man, I'm gonna have to get used to tagging along with you guys for this zero period thing.

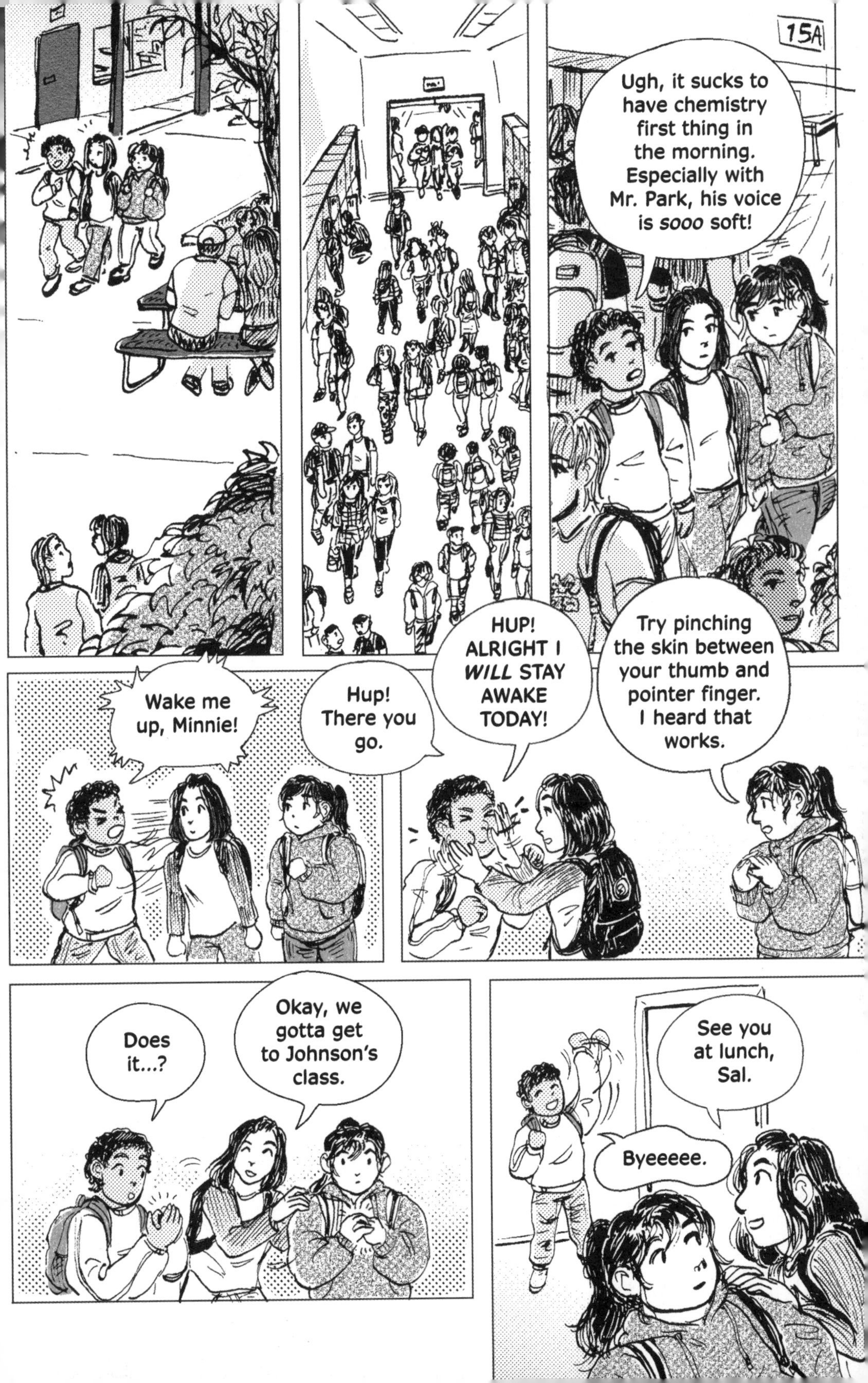
15A
Ugh, it sucks to have chemistry first thing in the morning. Especially with Mr. Park, his voice is *sooo* soft!
Wake me up, Minnie!
Hup! There you go.
HUP! ALRIGHT I *WILL* STAY AWAKE TODAY!
Try pinching the skin between your thumb and pointer finger. I heard that works.
Does it...?
Okay, we gotta get to Johnson's class.
See you at lunch, Sal.
Byeeeee.

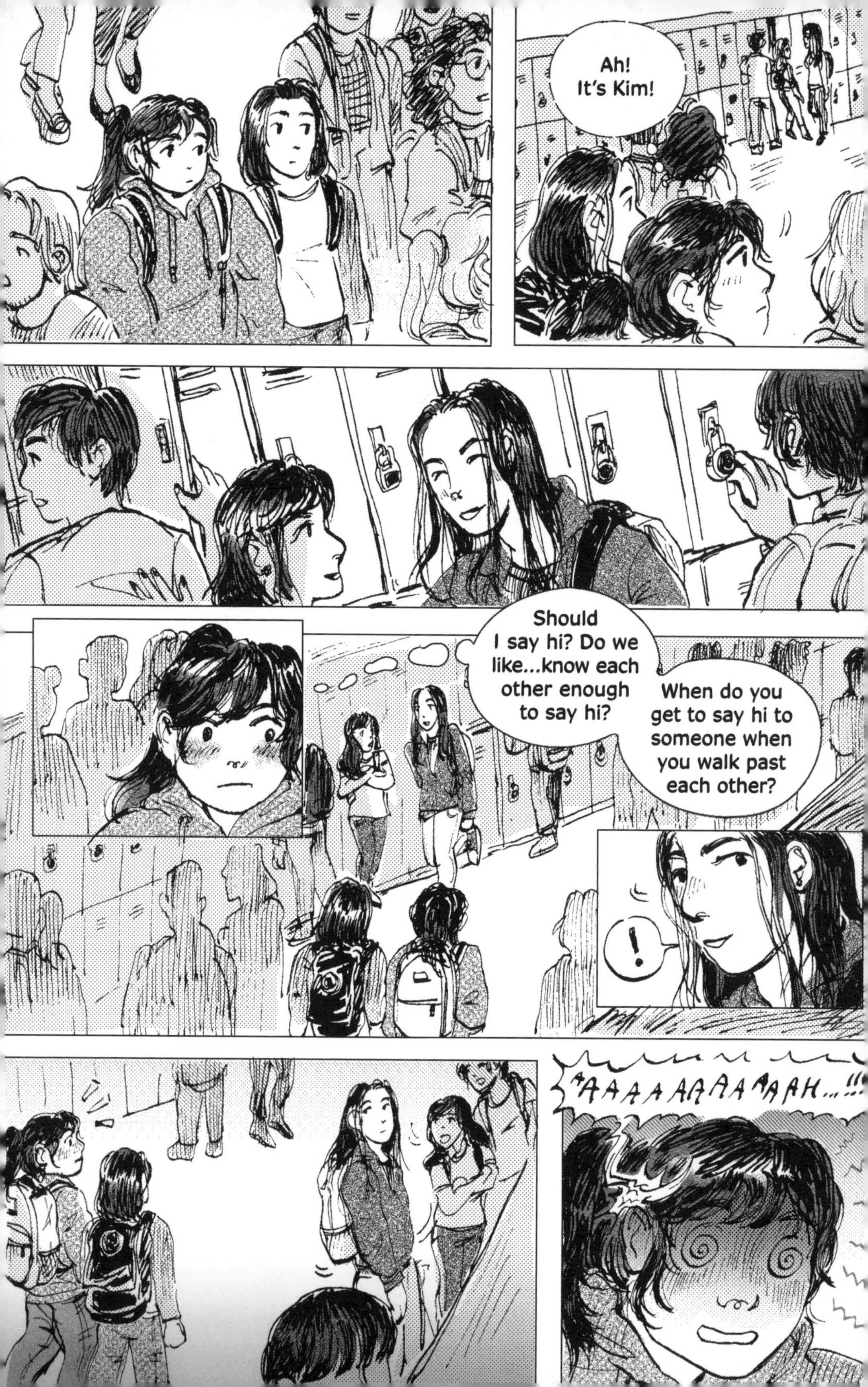
Ah! It's Kim!
Should I say hi? Do we like...know each other enough to say hi?
When do you get to say hi to someone when you walk past each other?
!
AAAAAAAAAAAH...!!!

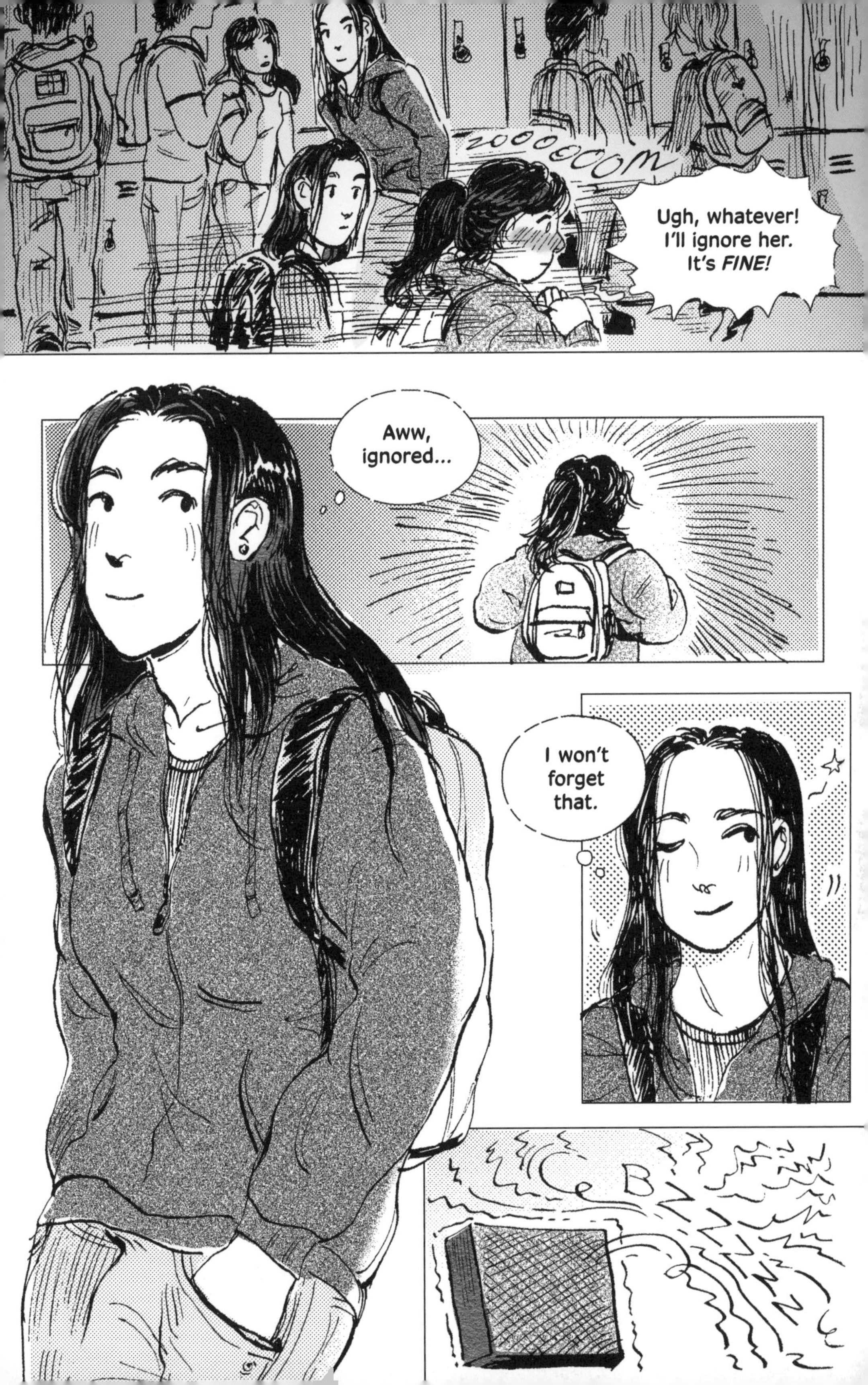
ZOOOOOOM
Ugh, whatever! I'll ignore her. It's *FINE!*
Aww, ignored...
I won't forget that.

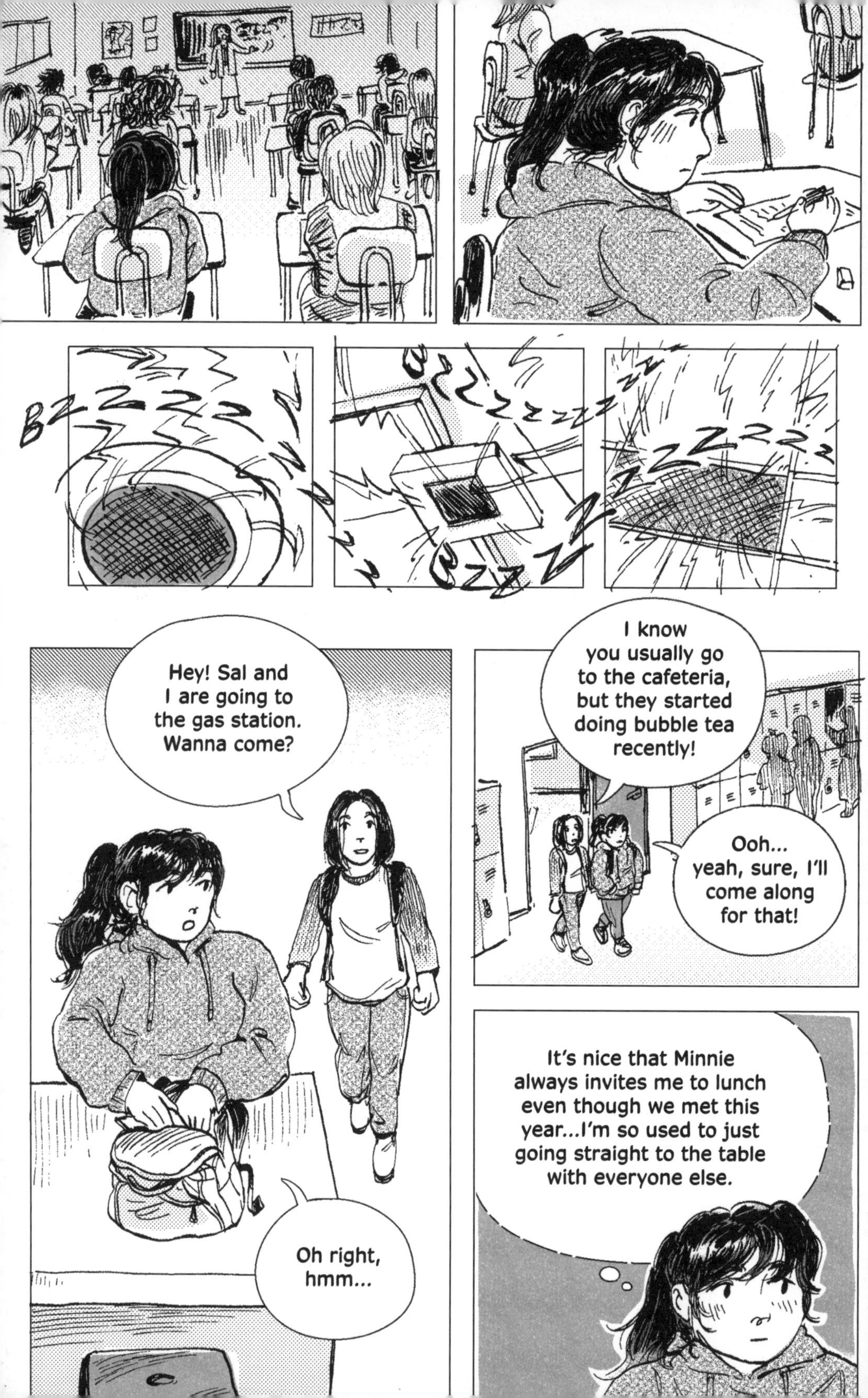
BZZZZZZ
ZZZZZZZ
ZZZZZZ
Hey! Sal and I are going to the gas station. Wanna come?
Oh right, hmm...
I know you usually go to the cafeteria, but they started doing bubble tea recently!
Ooh... yeah, sure, I'll come along for that!
It's nice that Minnie always invites me to lunch even though we met this year...I'm so used to just going straight to the table with everyone else.

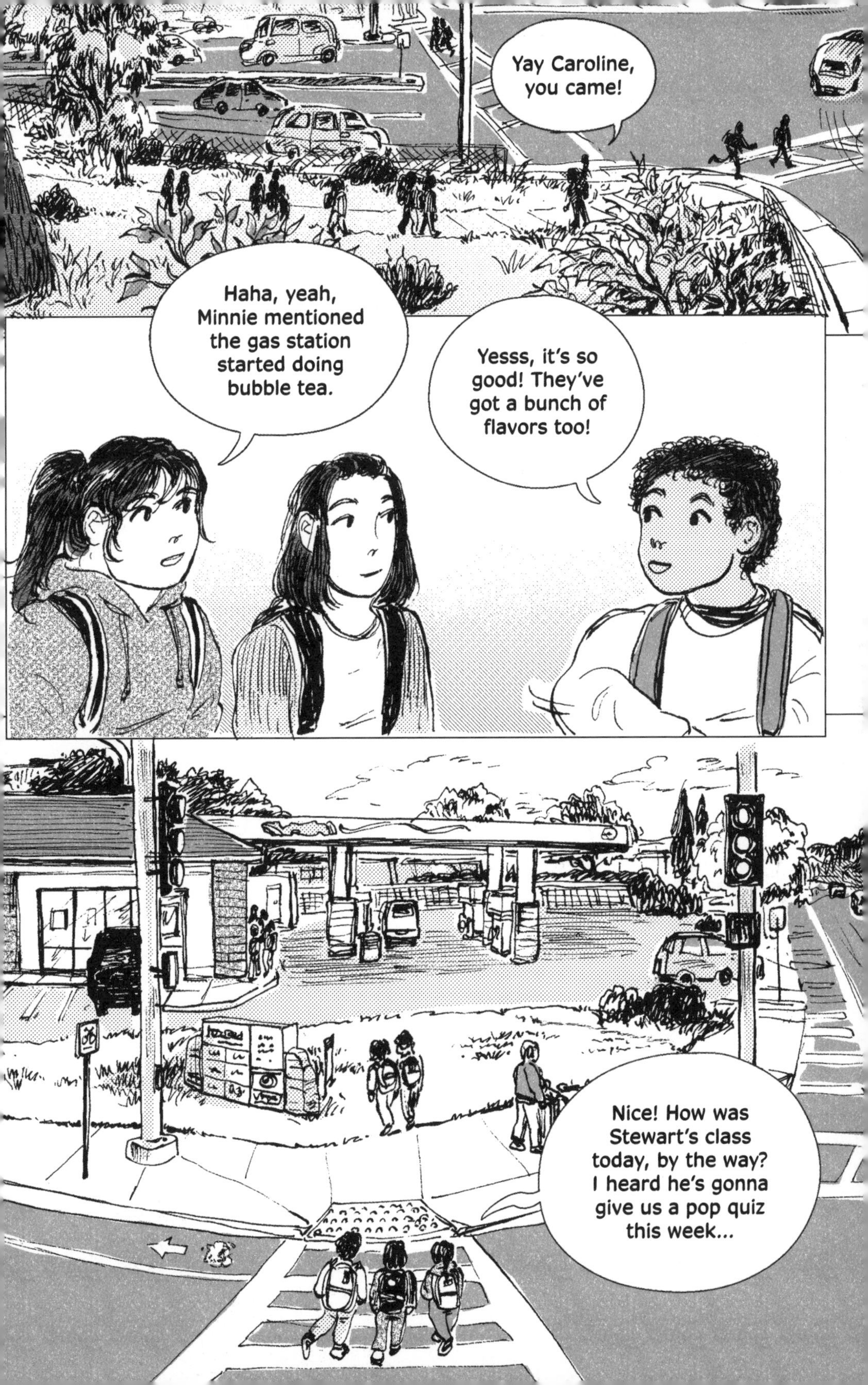
Yay Caroline, you came!
Haha, yeah, Minnie mentioned the gas station started doing bubble tea.
Yesss, it's so good! They've got a bunch of flavors too!
Nice! How was Stewart's class today, by the way? I heard he's gonna give us a pop quiz this week...

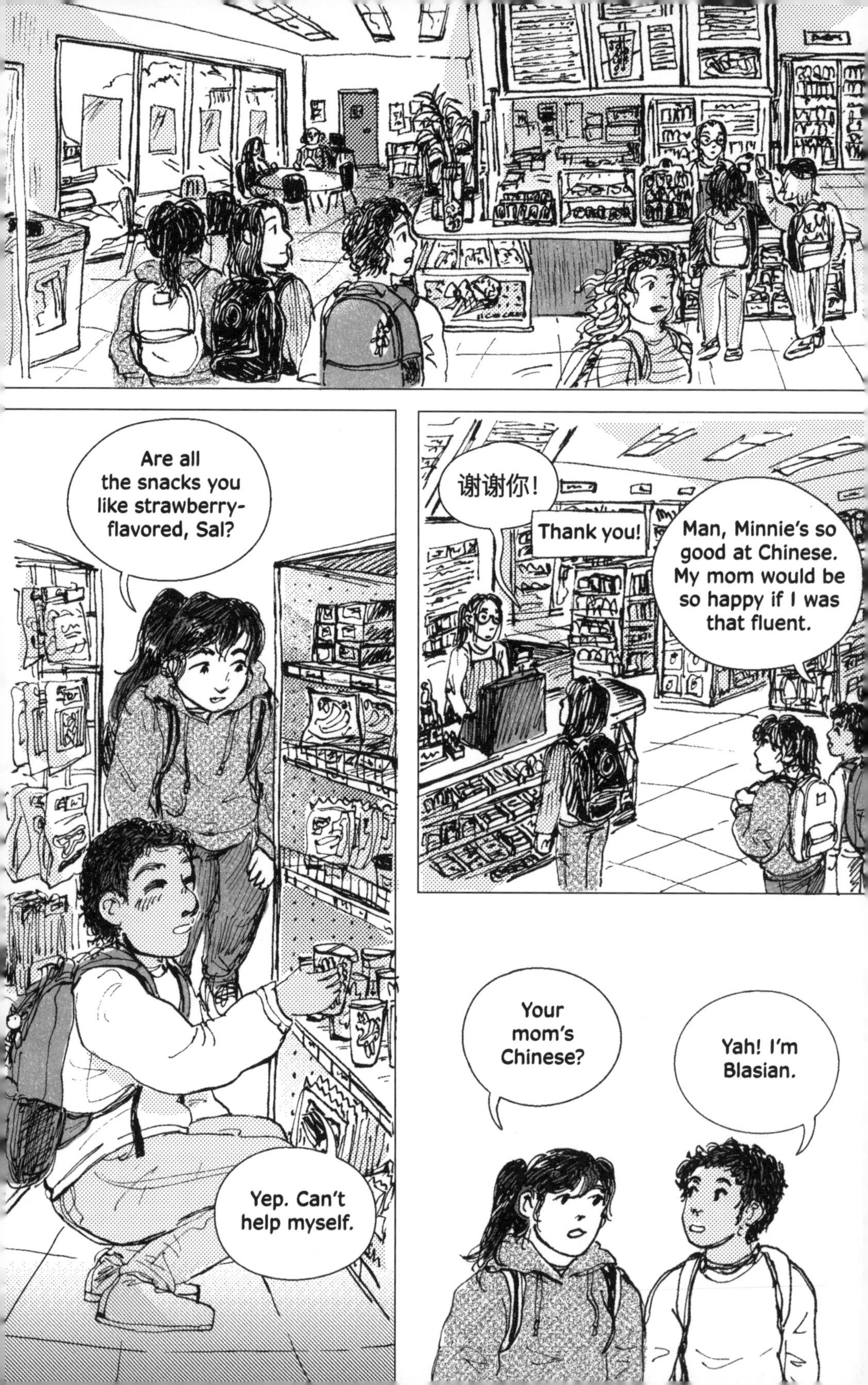
Are all the snacks you like strawberry-flavored, Sal?
Yep. Can't help myself.
谢谢你!
Thank you!
Man, Minnie's so good at Chinese. My mom would be so happy if I was that fluent.
Your mom's Chinese?
Yah! I'm Blasian.

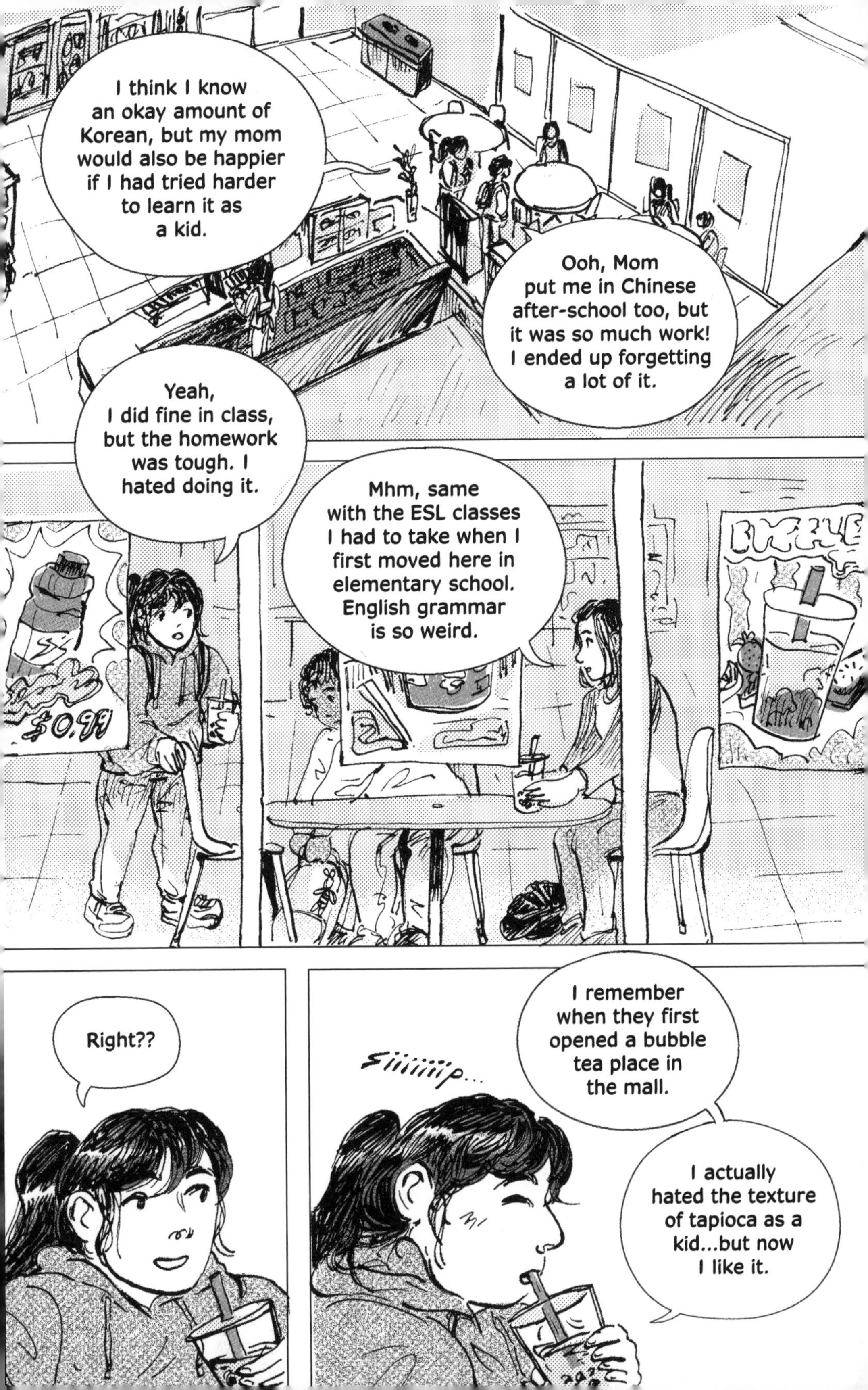
I think I know an okay amount of Korean, but my mom would also be happier if I had tried harder to learn it as a kid.
Ooh, Mom put me in Chinese after-school too, but it was so much work! I ended up forgetting a lot of it.
Yeah, I did fine in class, but the homework was tough. I hated doing it.
$0.99
Mhm, same with the ESL classes I had to take when I first moved here in elementary school. English grammar is so weird.
Right??
Siiiiiiip...
I remember when they first opened a bubble tea place in the mall.
I actually hated the texture of tapioca as a kid...but now I like it.

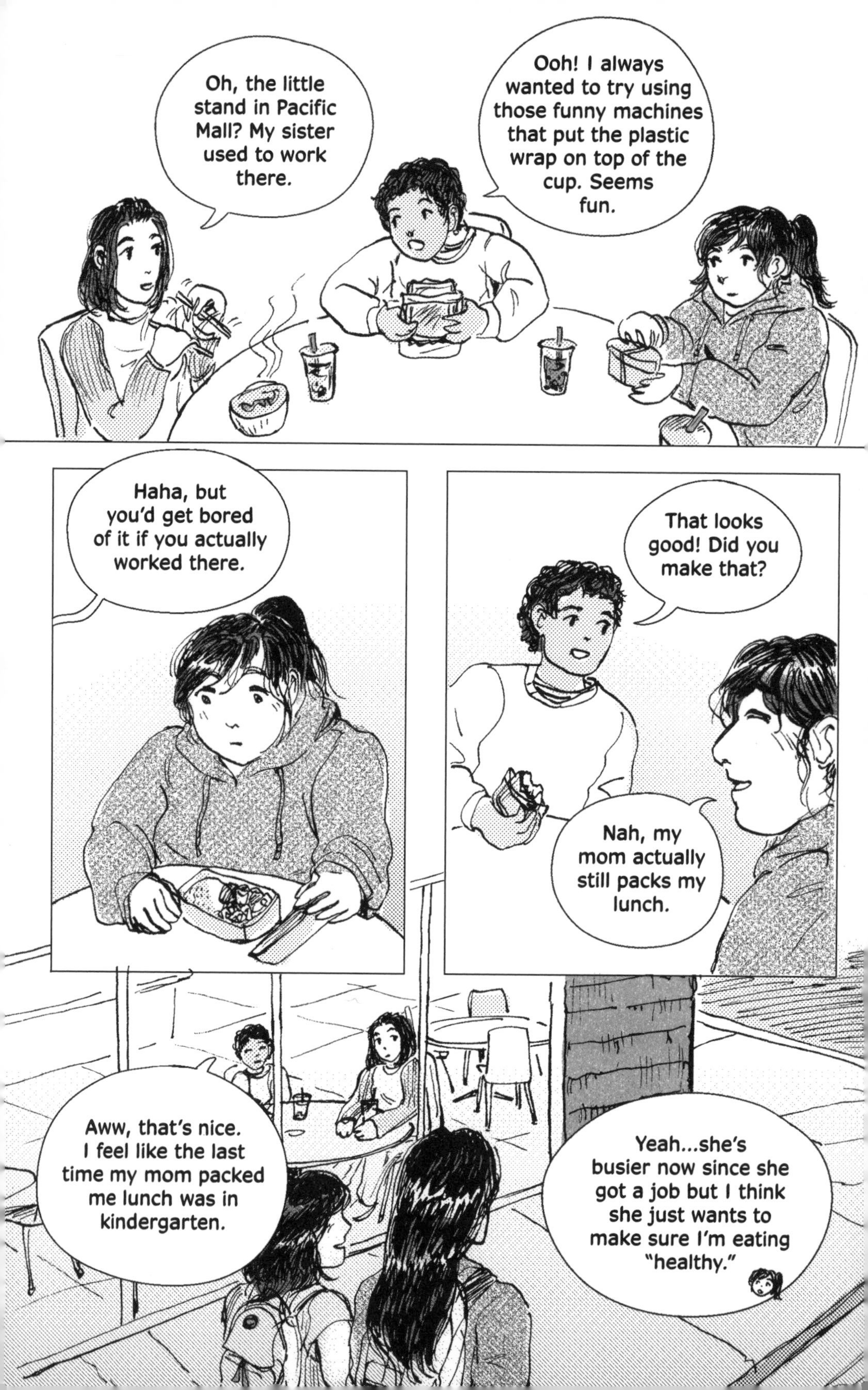
Oh, the little stand in Pacific Mall? My sister used to work there.
Ooh! I always wanted to try using those funny machines that put the plastic wrap on top of the cup. Seems fun.
Haha, but you'd get bored of it if you actually worked there.
That looks good! Did you make that?
Nah, my mom actually still packs my lunch.
Aww, that's nice. I feel like the last time my mom packed me lunch was in kindergarten.
Yeah...she's busier now since she got a job but I think she just wants to make sure I'm eating "healthy."

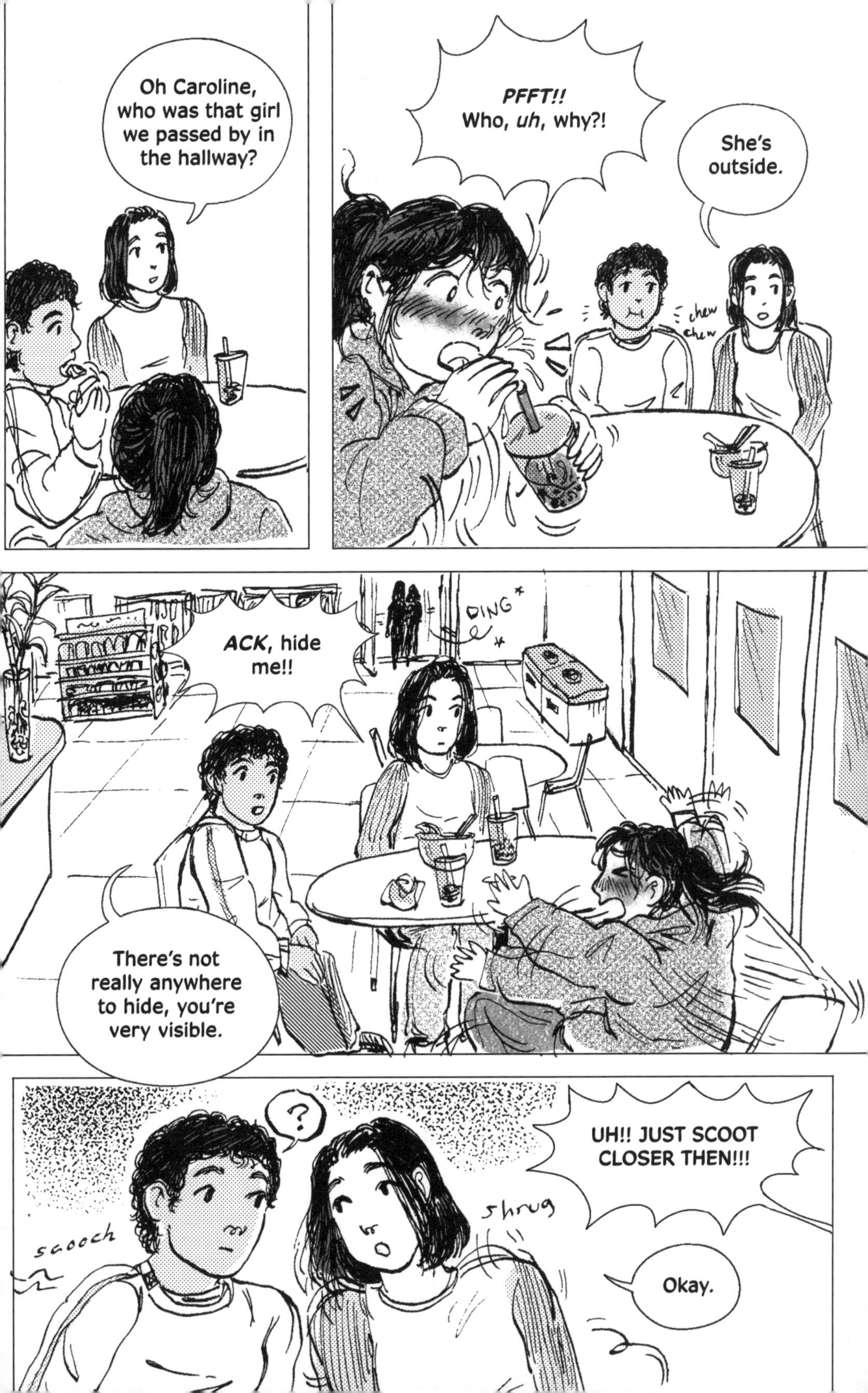
Oh Caroline, who was that girl we passed by in the hallway?
PFFT!! Who, *uh*, why?!
chew chew
She's outside.
DING
ACK, hide me!!
There's not really anywhere to hide, you're very visible.
?
scooch
shrug
UH!! JUST SCOOT CLOSER THEN!!!
Okay.

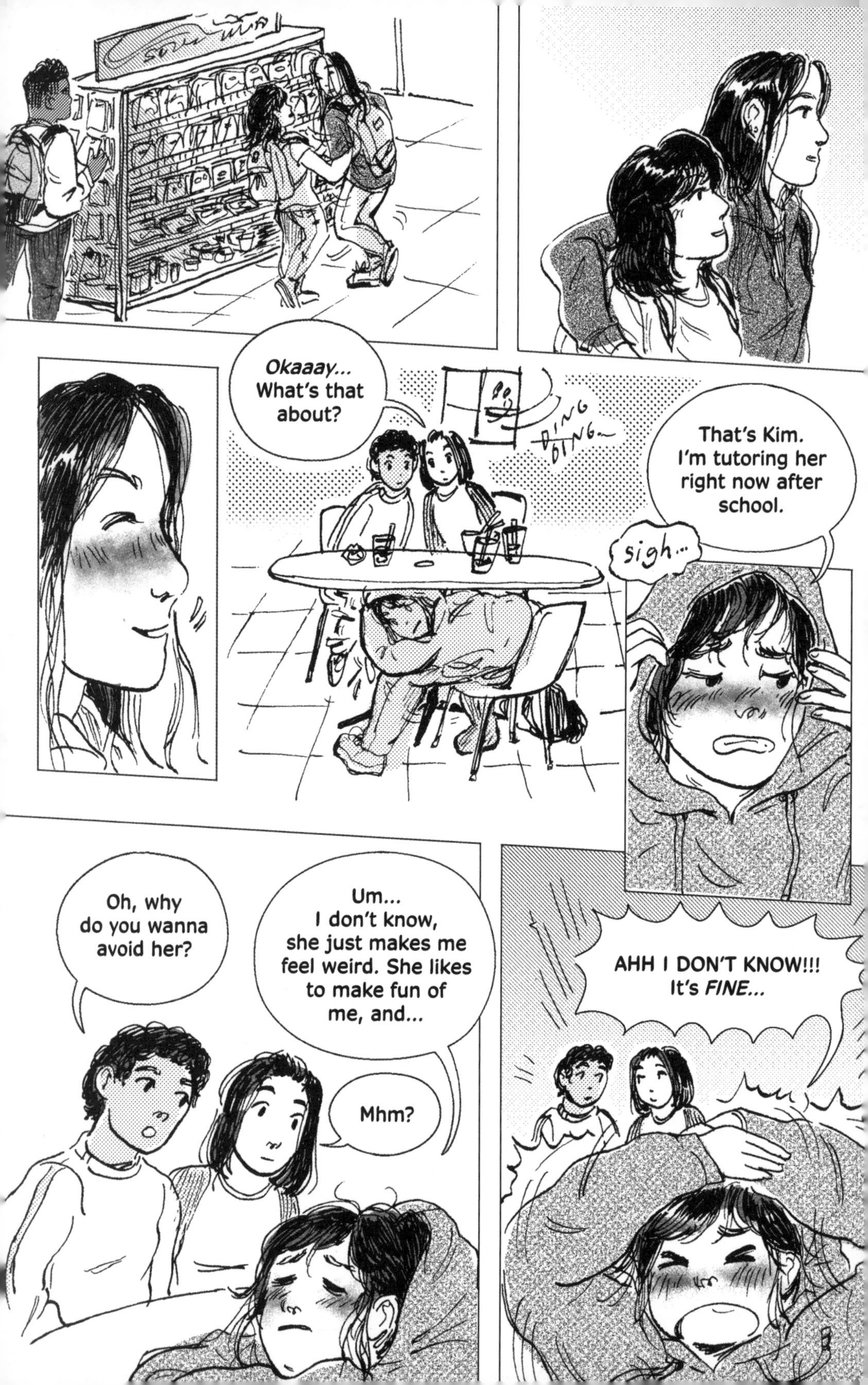
Okaaay... What's that about?
DING DING
That's Kim. I'm tutoring her right now after school.
sigh...
Oh, why do you wanna avoid her?
Um... I don't know, she just makes me feel weird. She likes to make fun of me, and...
Mhm?
AHH I DON'T KNOW!!! It's *FINE*...

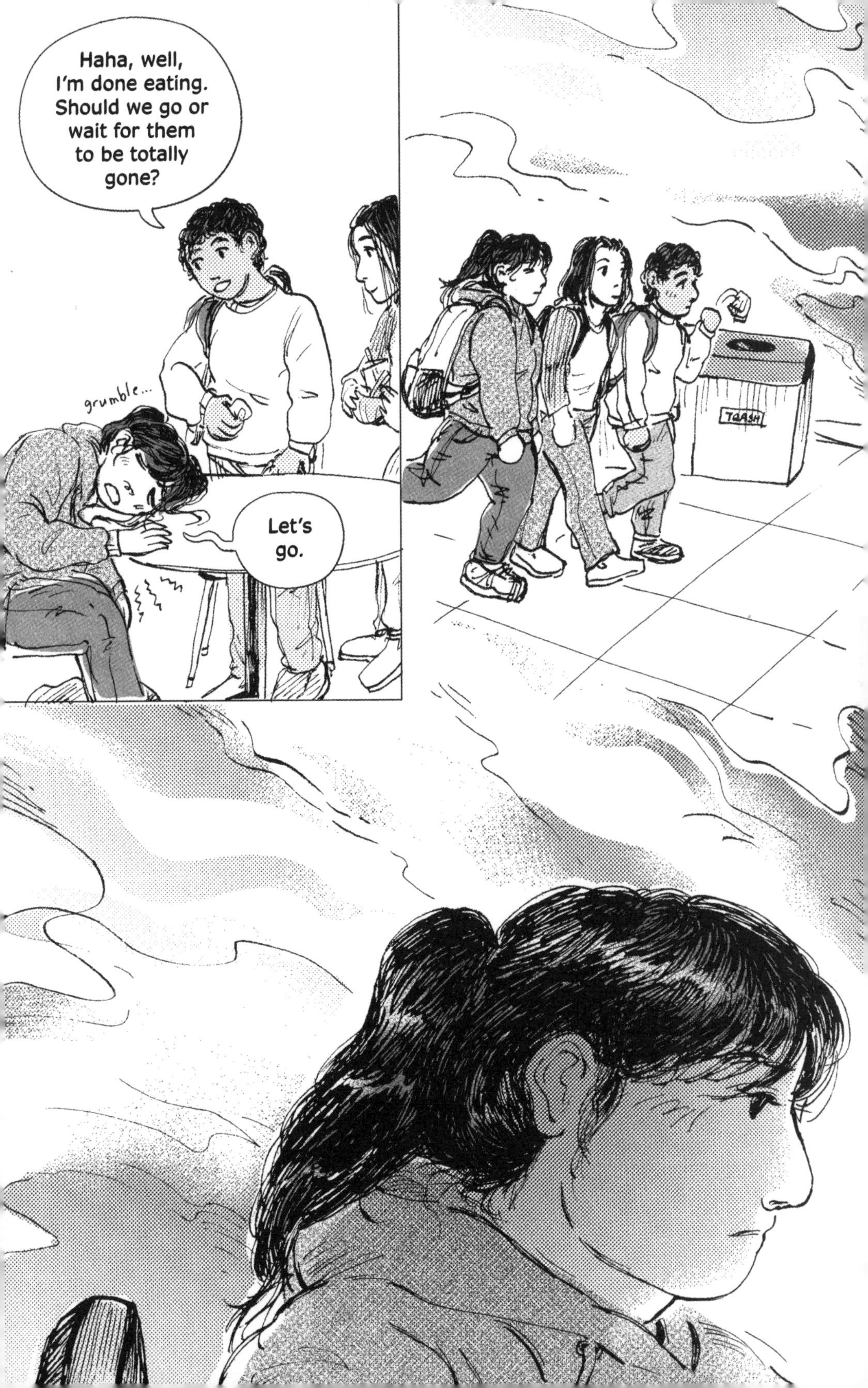
Haha, well, I'm done eating. Should we go or wait for them to be totally gone?
grumble...
Let's go.
TRASH

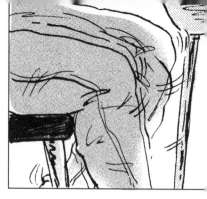

There was that thing said at the cafeteria yesterday...

Kim?

Like Kimberly Park-Ocampo?

Oh, my sister says she's wild. She's friends with both the like, super rich kids and the punks. They get into all kinds of shit.

gulp

Huh.

I heard she even goes to college parties and hooks up with girls there.

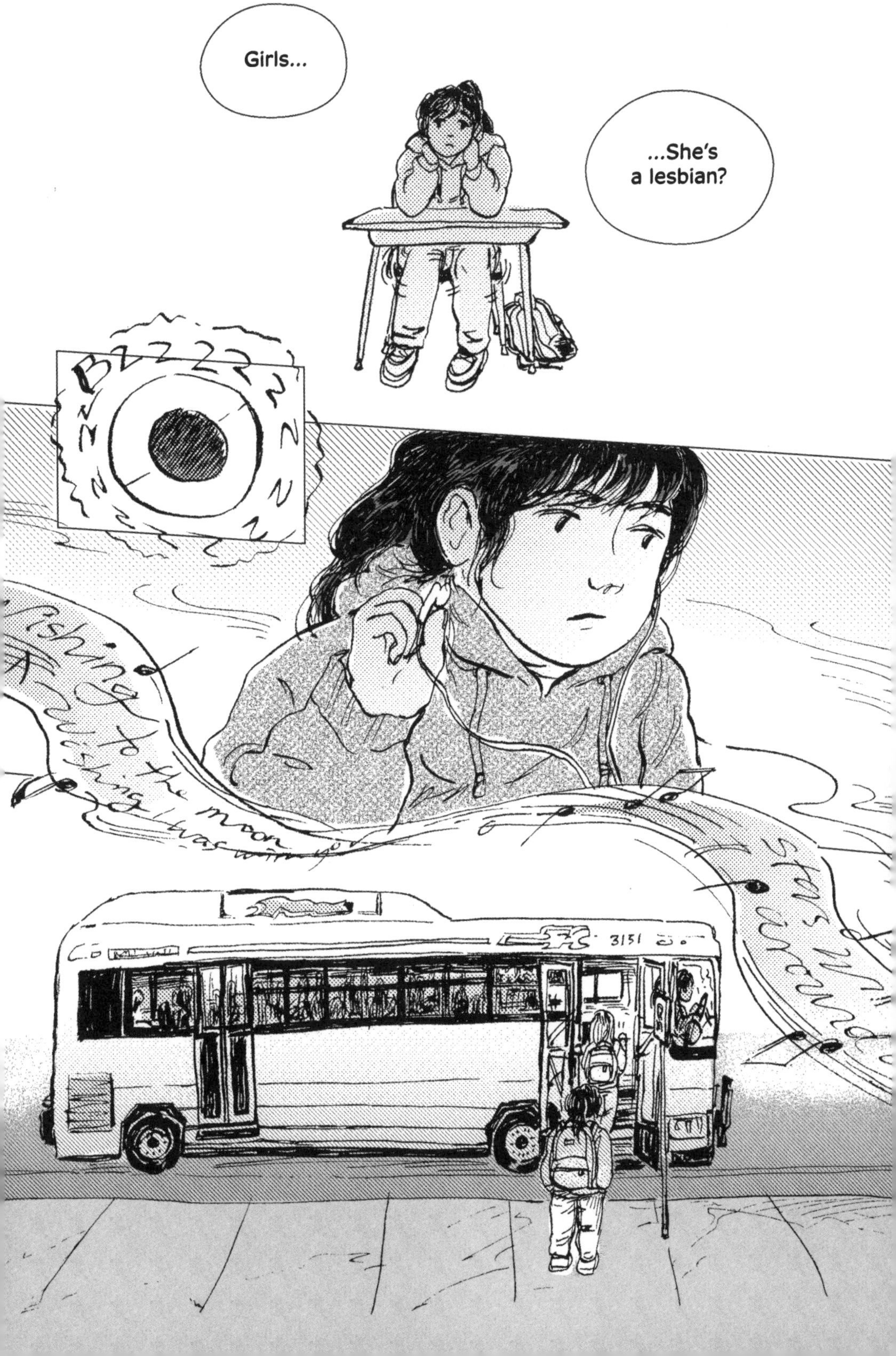
Girls...
...She's a lesbian?

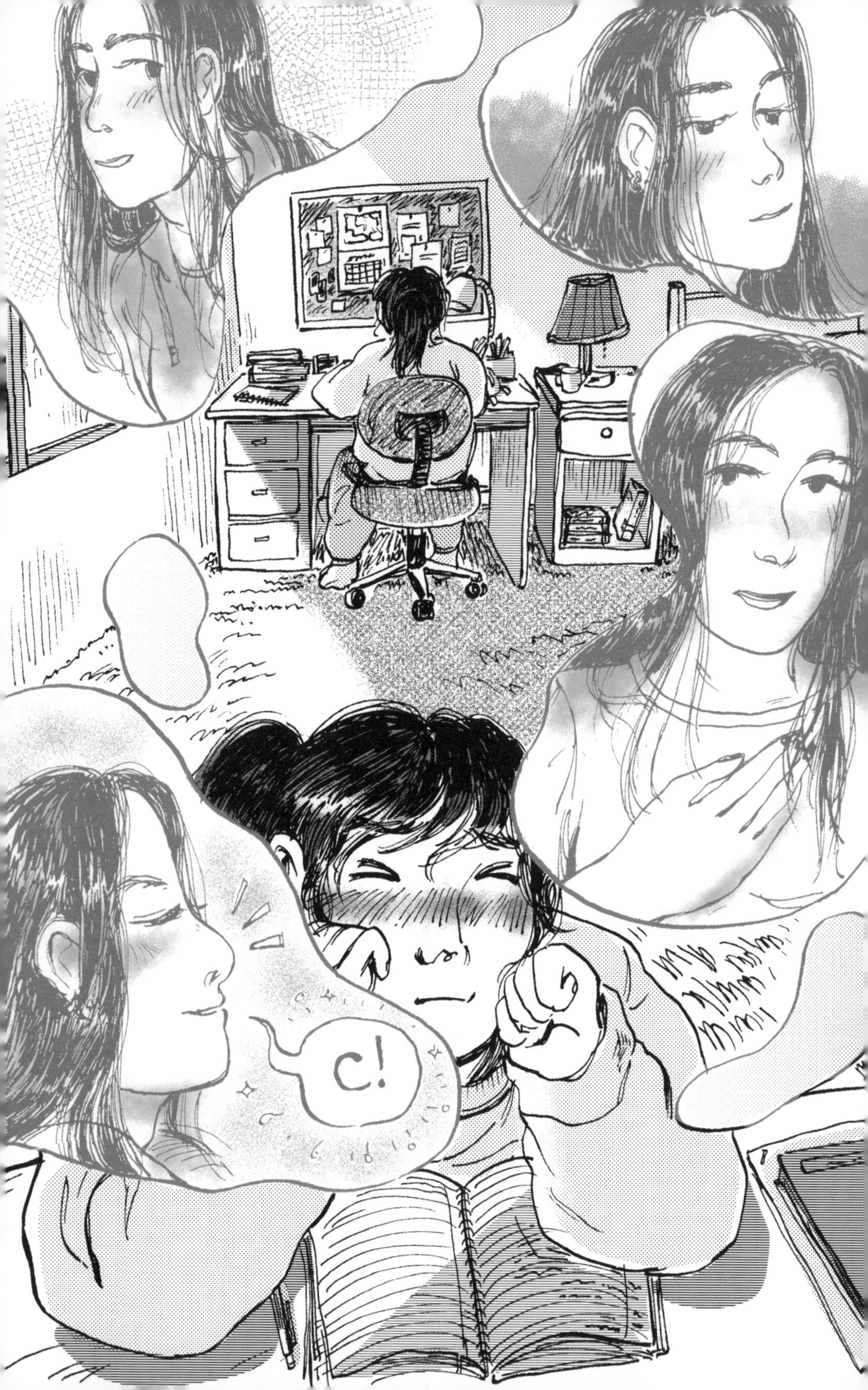
C!

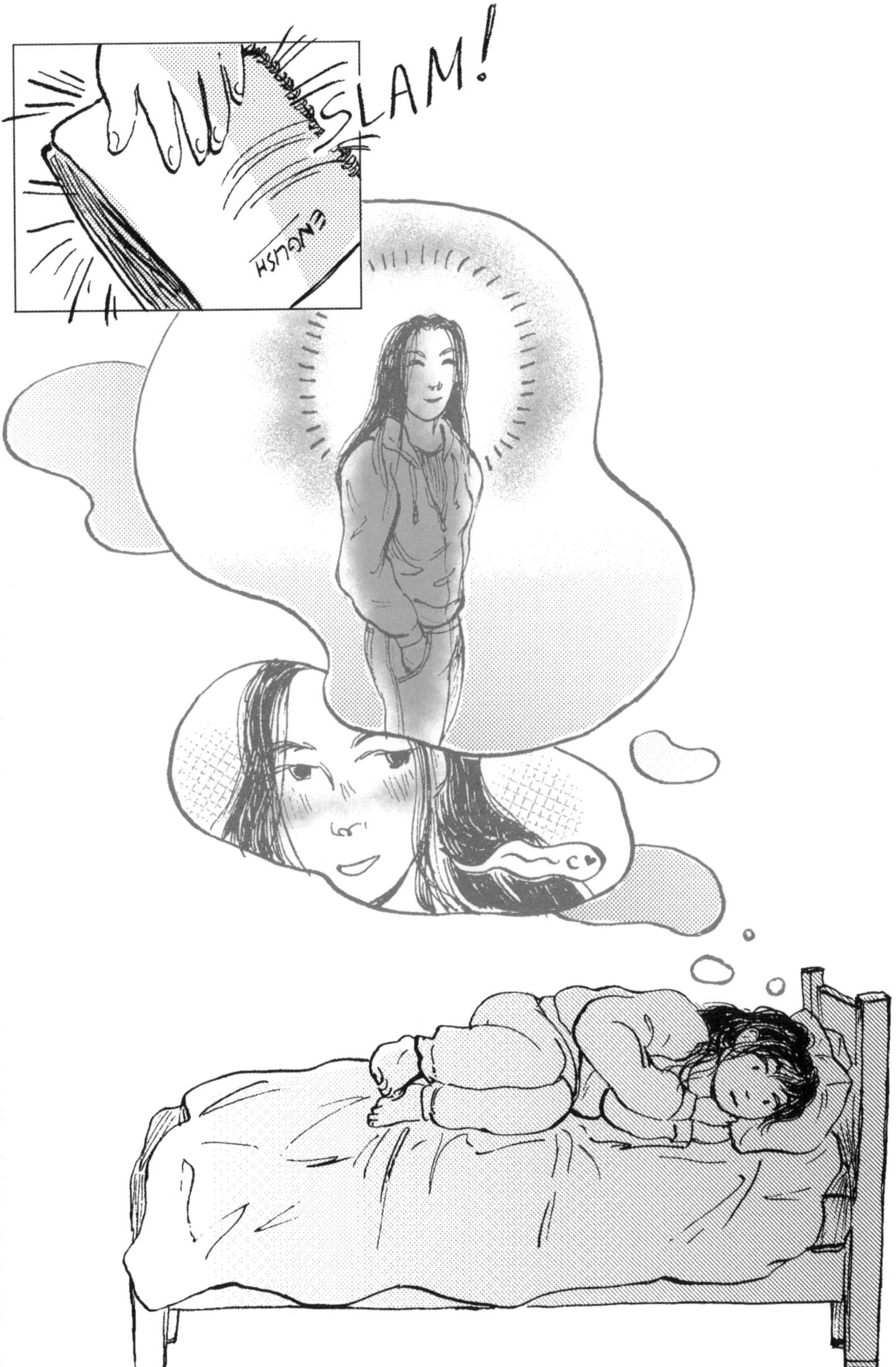
SLAM!
ENGLISH

Chapter 3

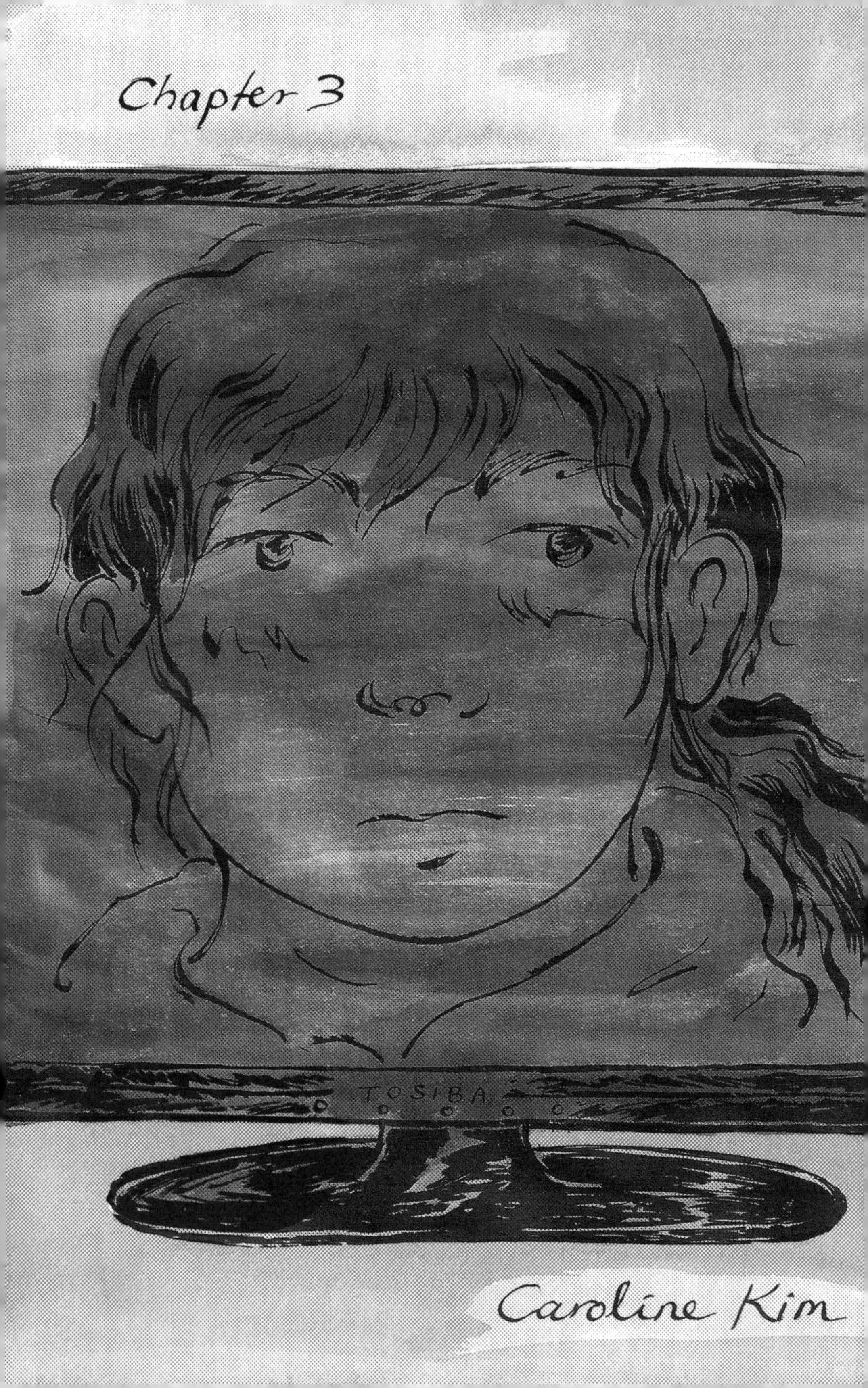
TOSIBA

Caroline Kim

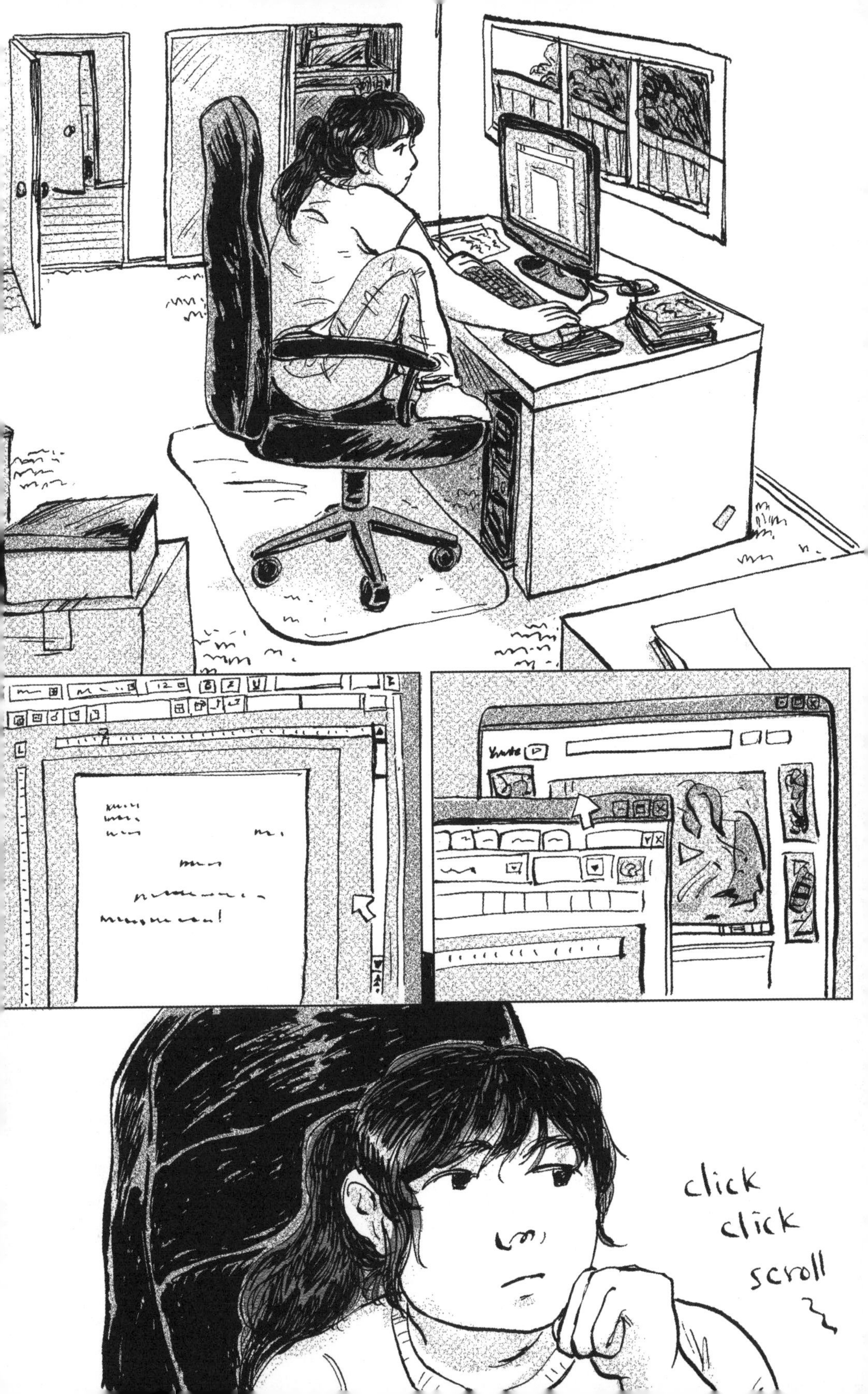
click
click
scroll

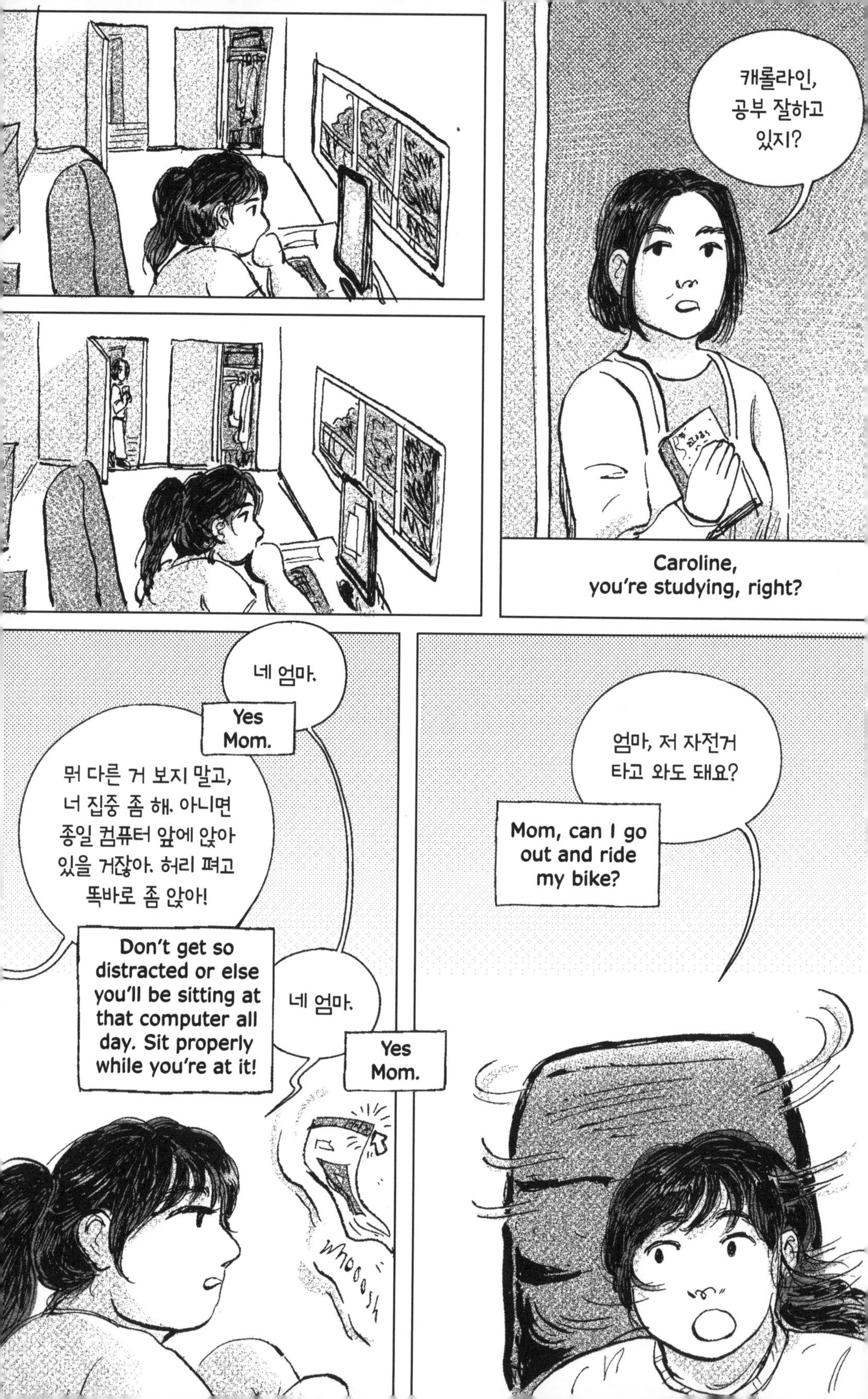
캐롤라인, 공부 잘하고 있지?
Caroline, you're studying, right?
네 엄마.
Yes Mom.
뭐 다른 거 보지 말고, 너 집중 좀 해. 아니면 종일 컴퓨터 앞에 앉아 있을 거잖아. 허리 펴고 똑바로 좀 앉아!
Don't get so distracted or else you'll be sitting at that computer all day. Sit properly while you're at it!
네 엄마.
Yes Mom.
whoooosh
엄마, 저 자전거 타고 와도 돼요?
Mom, can I go out and ride my bike?

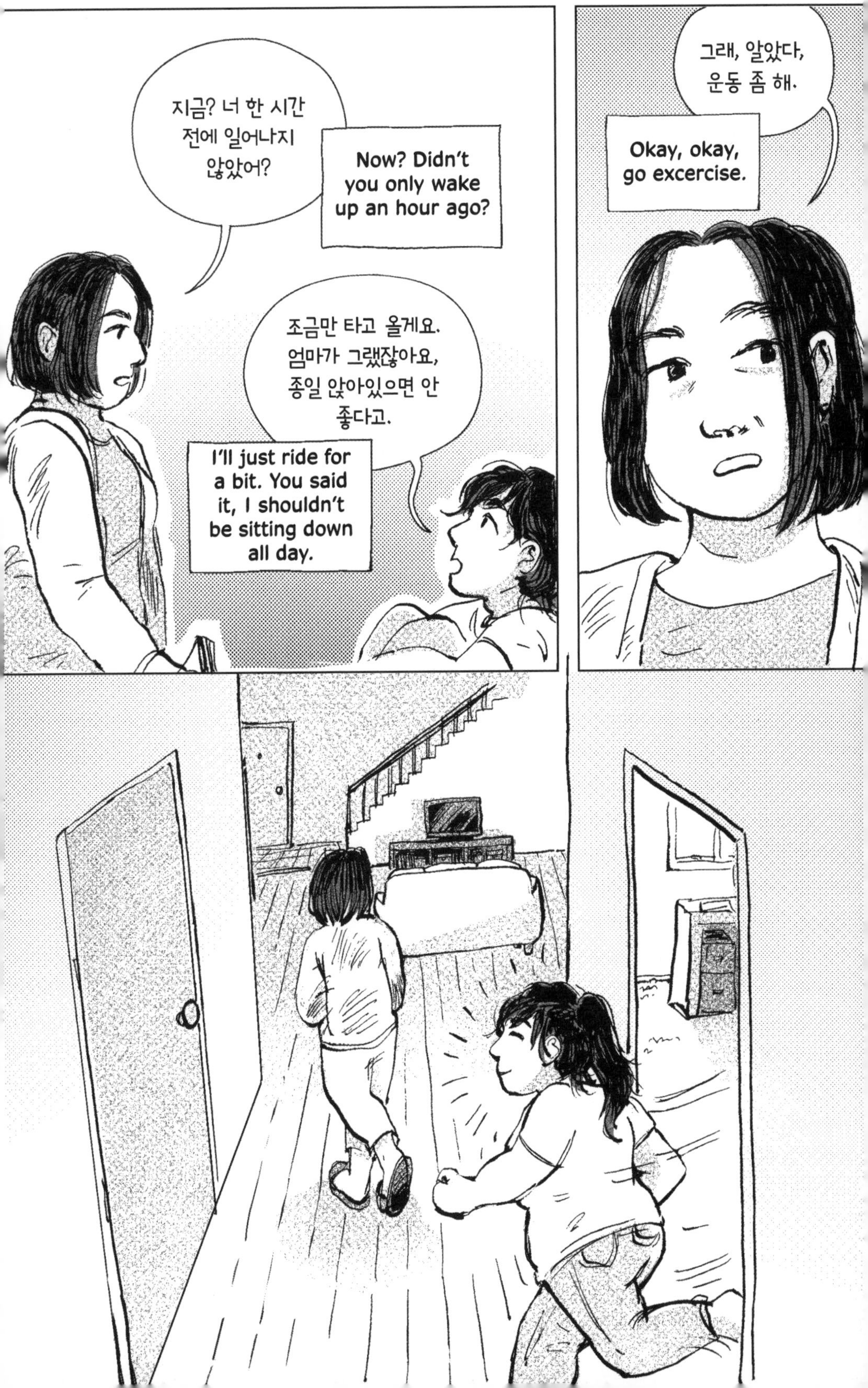
지금? 너 한 시간 전에 일어나지 않았어?
Now? Didn't you only wake up an hour ago?
조금만 타고 올게요. 엄마가 그랬잖아요, 종일 앉아있으면 안 좋다고.
I'll just ride for a bit. You said it, I shouldn't be sitting down all day.
그래, 알았다, 운동 좀 해.
Okay, okay, go excercise.

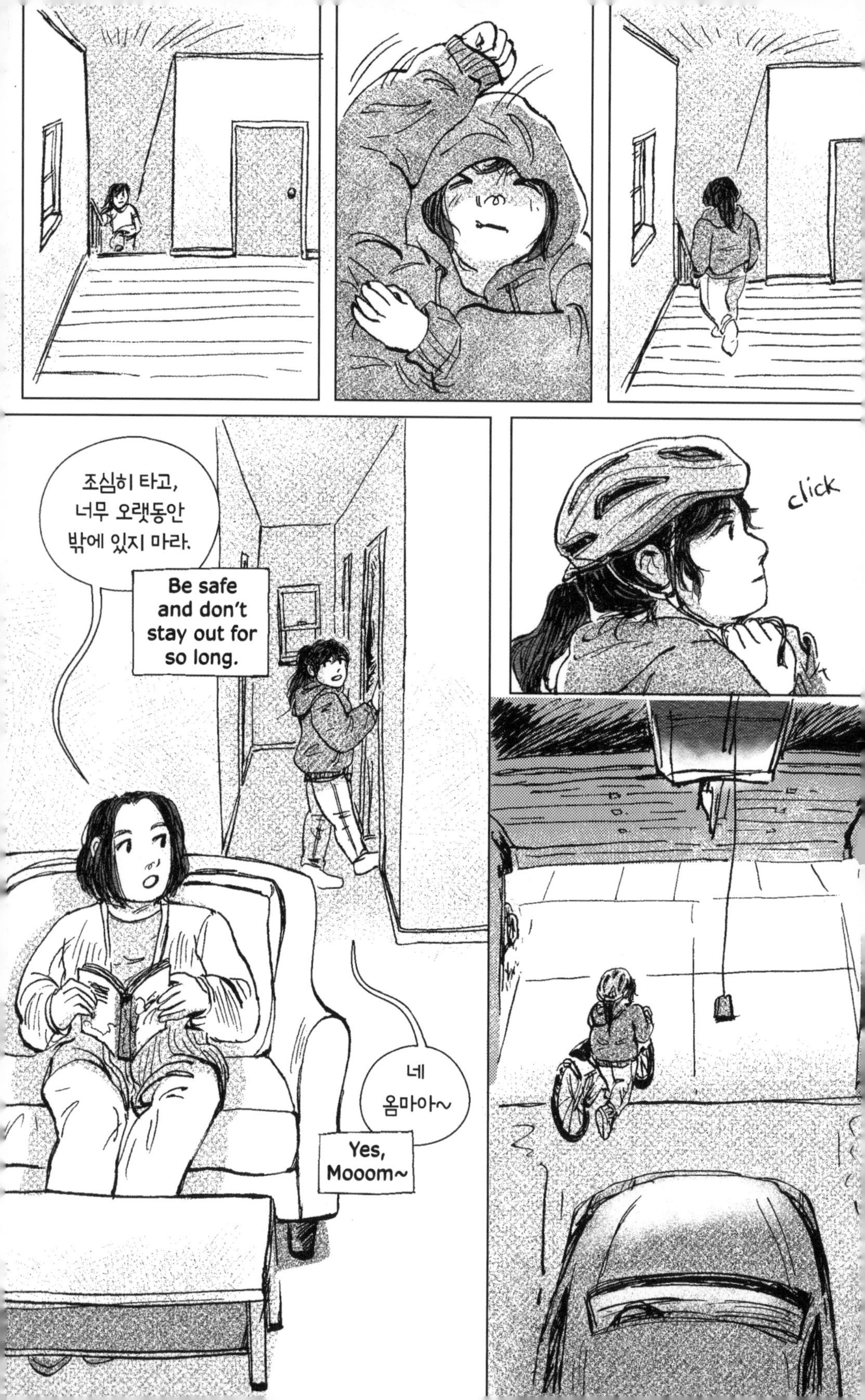
조심히 타고,
너무 오랫동안
밖에 있지 마라.
Be safe and don't stay out for so long.
네
옴마아~
Yes, Mooom~
click

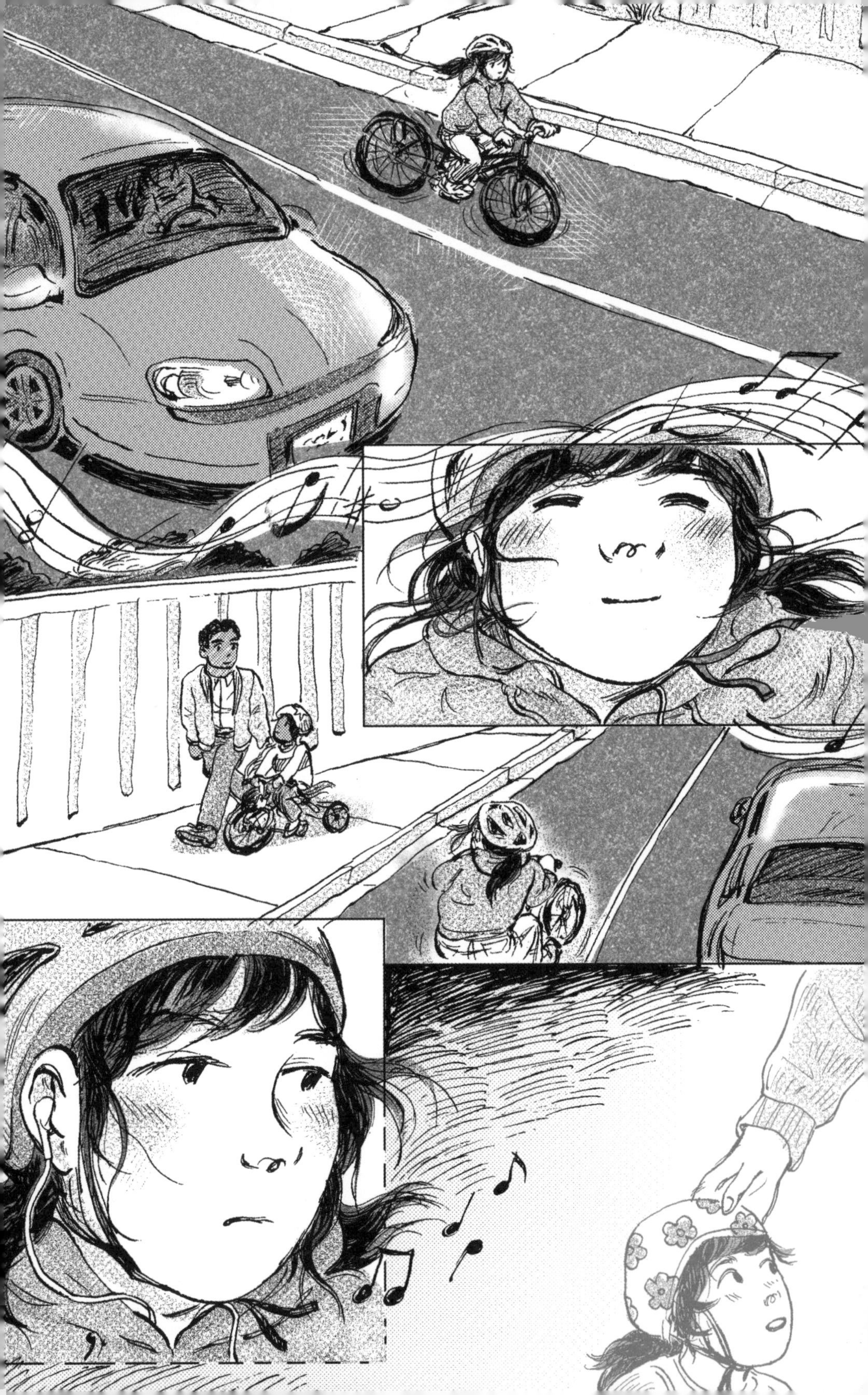

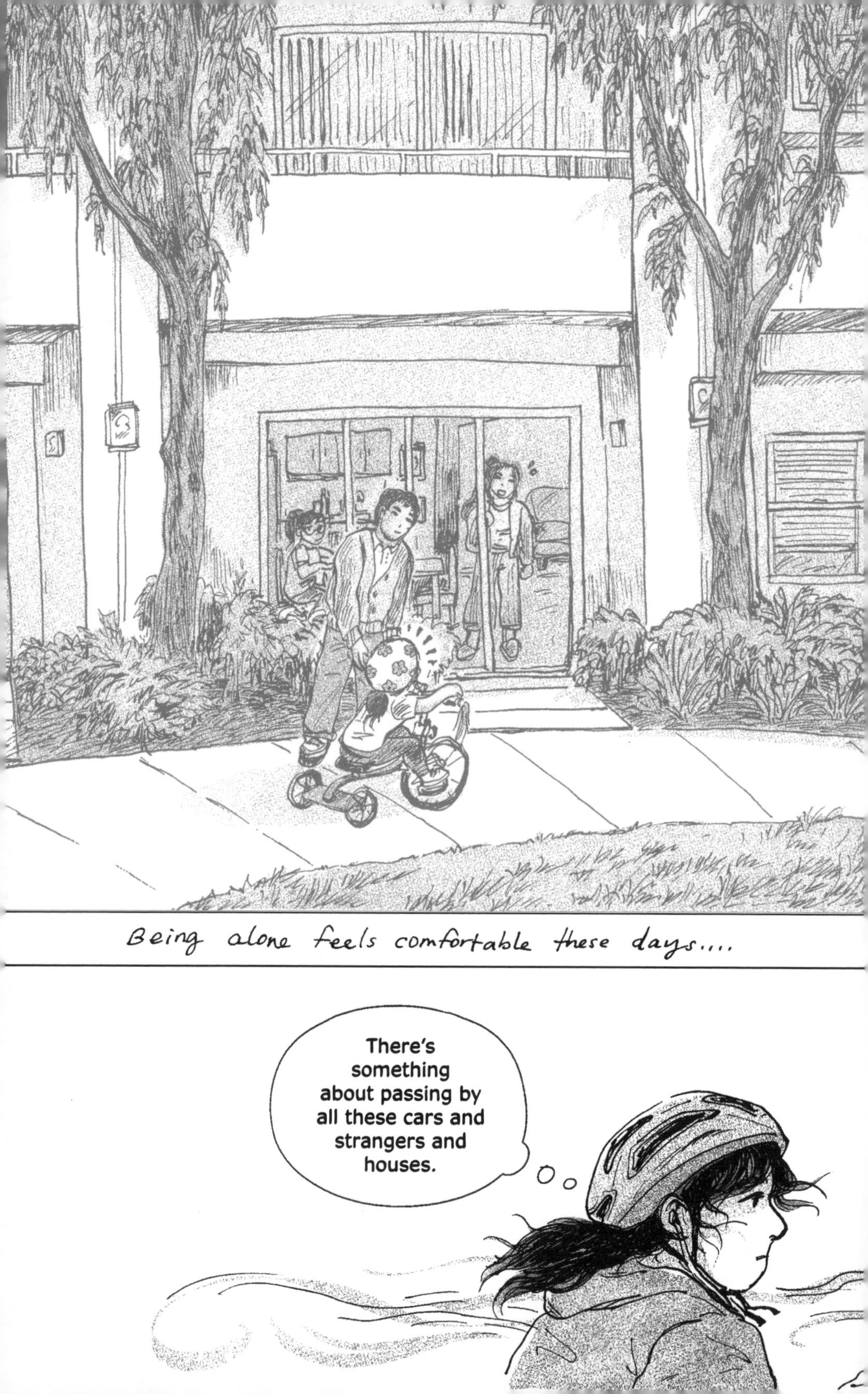
Being alone feels comfortable these days....
There's something about passing by all these cars and strangers and houses.

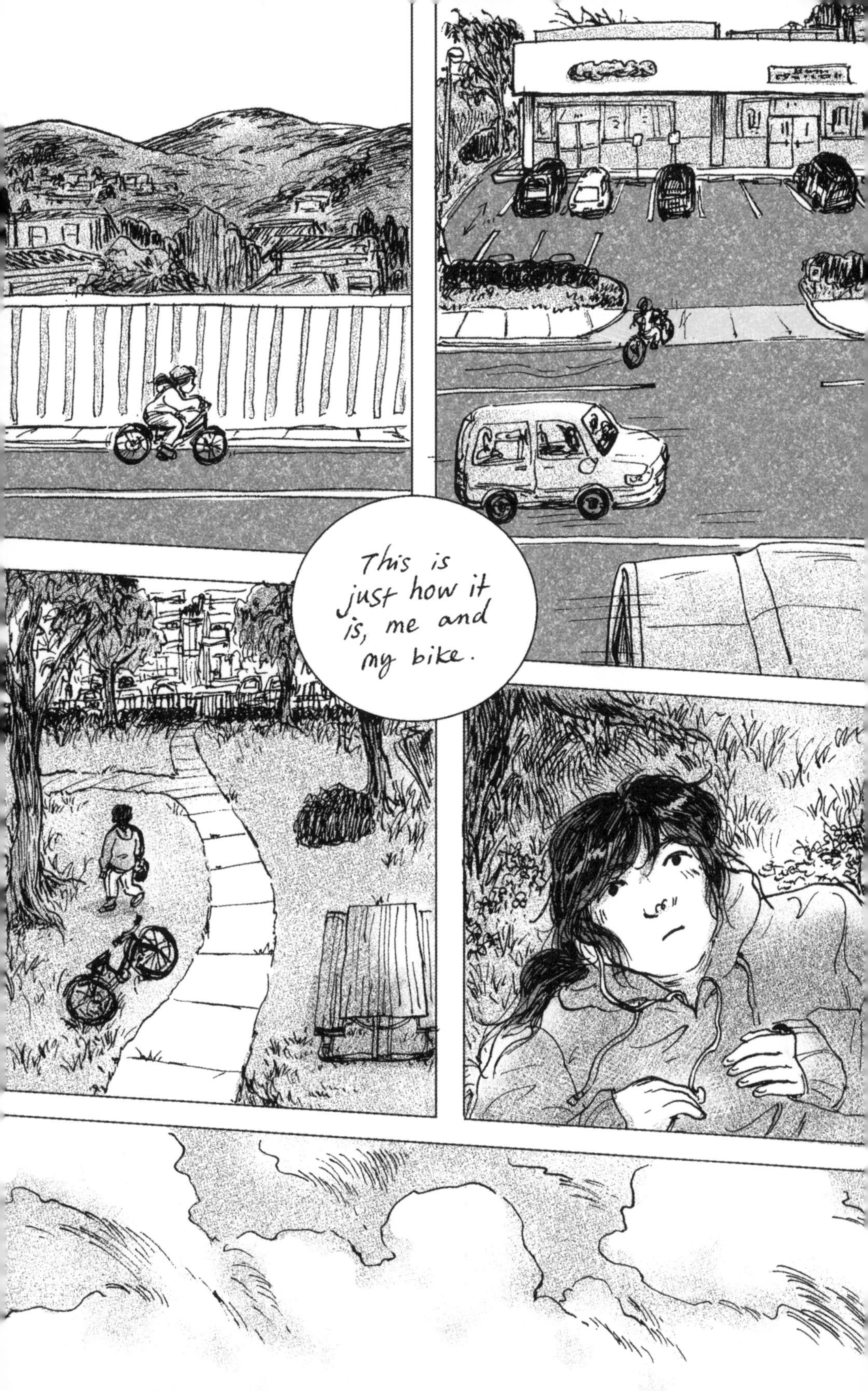
This is just how it is, me and my bike.

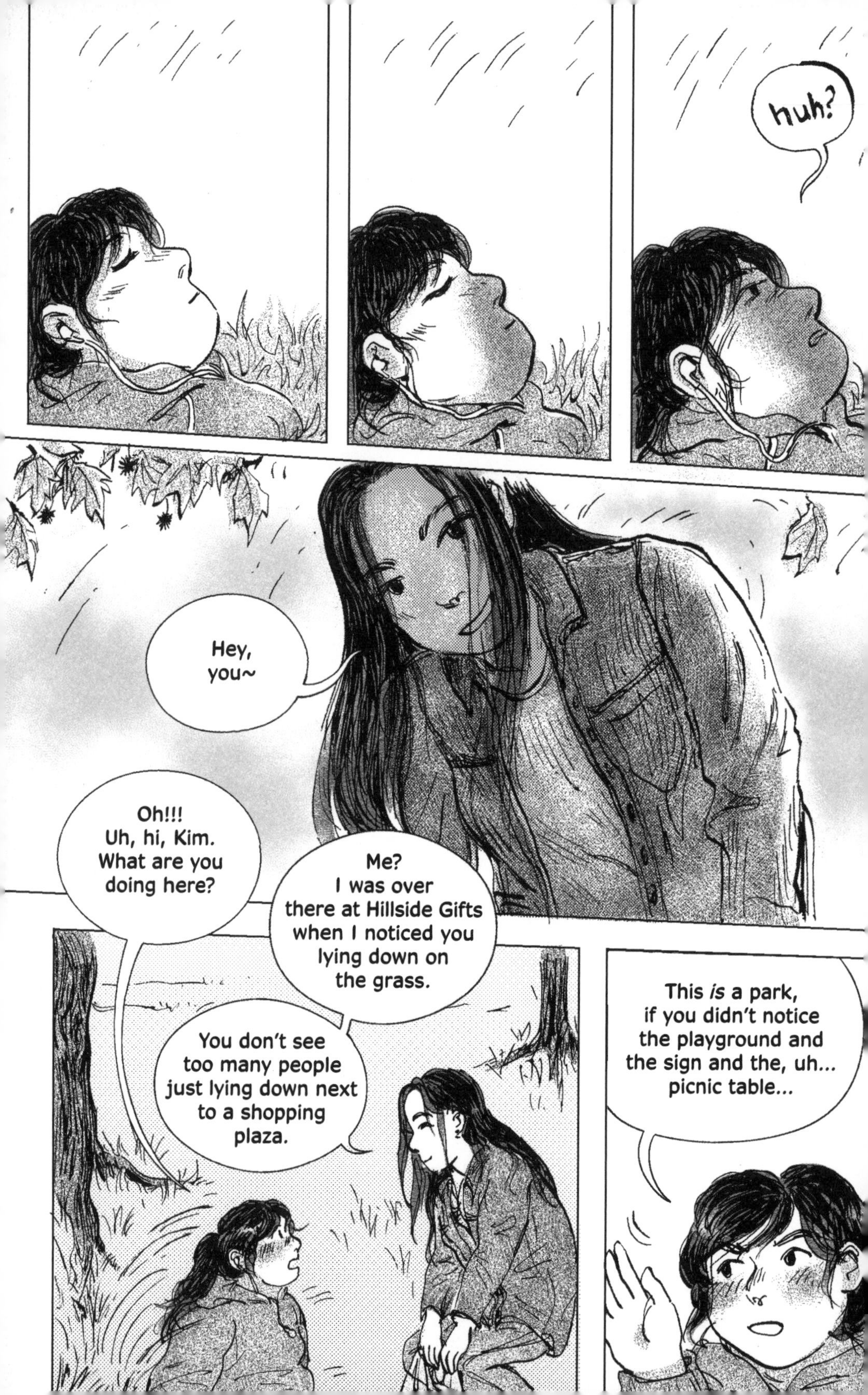

huh?
Hey, you~
Oh!!! Uh, hi, Kim. What are you doing here?
Me? I was over there at Hillside Gifts when I noticed you lying down on the grass.
You don't see too many people just lying down next to a shopping plaza.
This *is* a park, if you didn't notice the playground and the sign and the, uh... picnic table...

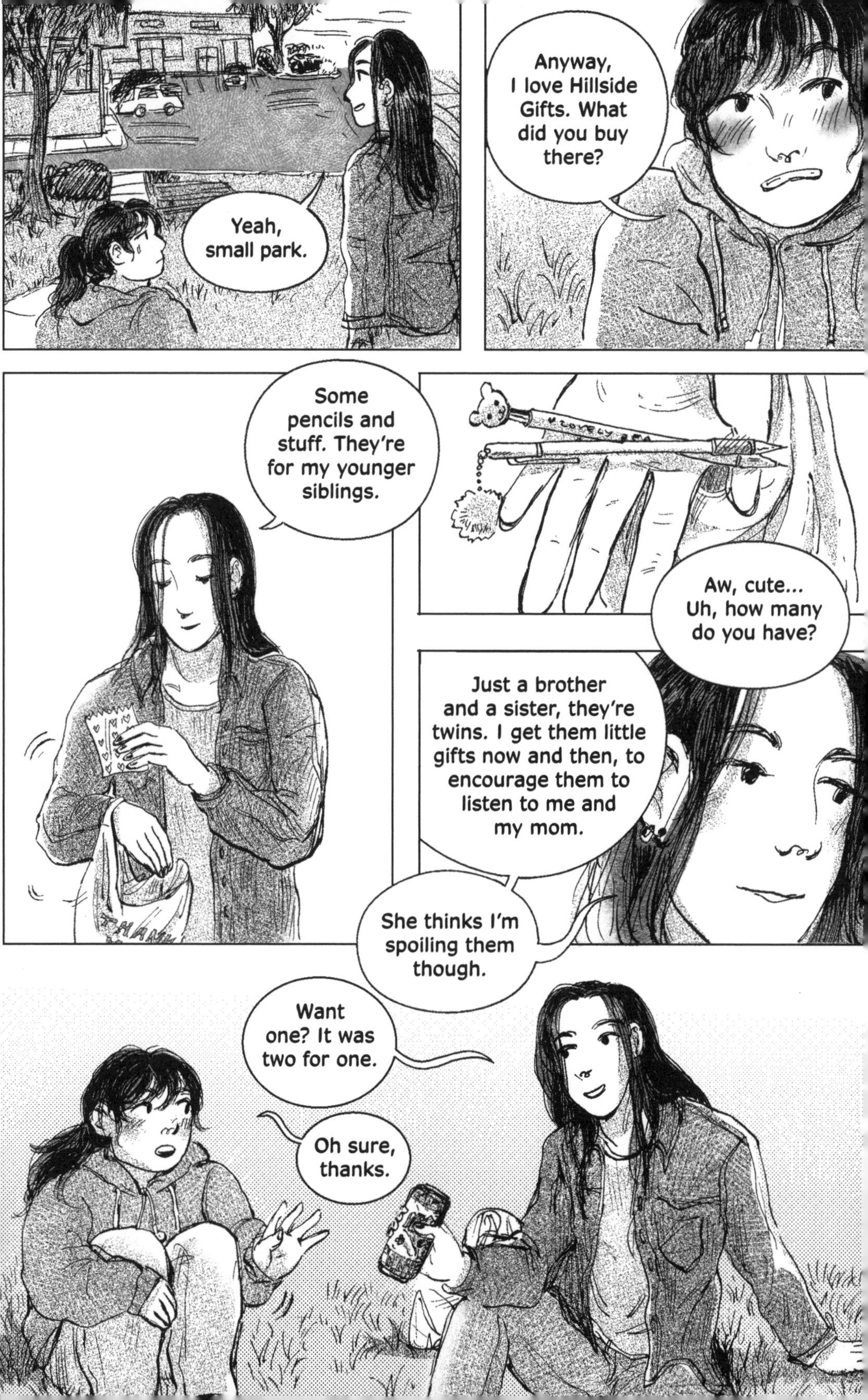
Yeah, small park.
Anyway, I love Hillside Gifts. What did you buy there?
Some pencils and stuff. They're for my younger siblings.
Aw, cute... Uh, how many do you have?
Just a brother and a sister, they're twins. I get them little gifts now and then, to encourage them to listen to me and my mom.
She thinks I'm spoiling them though.
Want one? It was two for one.
Oh sure, thanks.

You got a cute bike there. We've been looking to get some for them actually, from Walmart.

Yeah, we got this from one when I was in middle school.

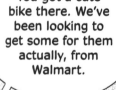

Ooh, so you haven't grown much taller since then?

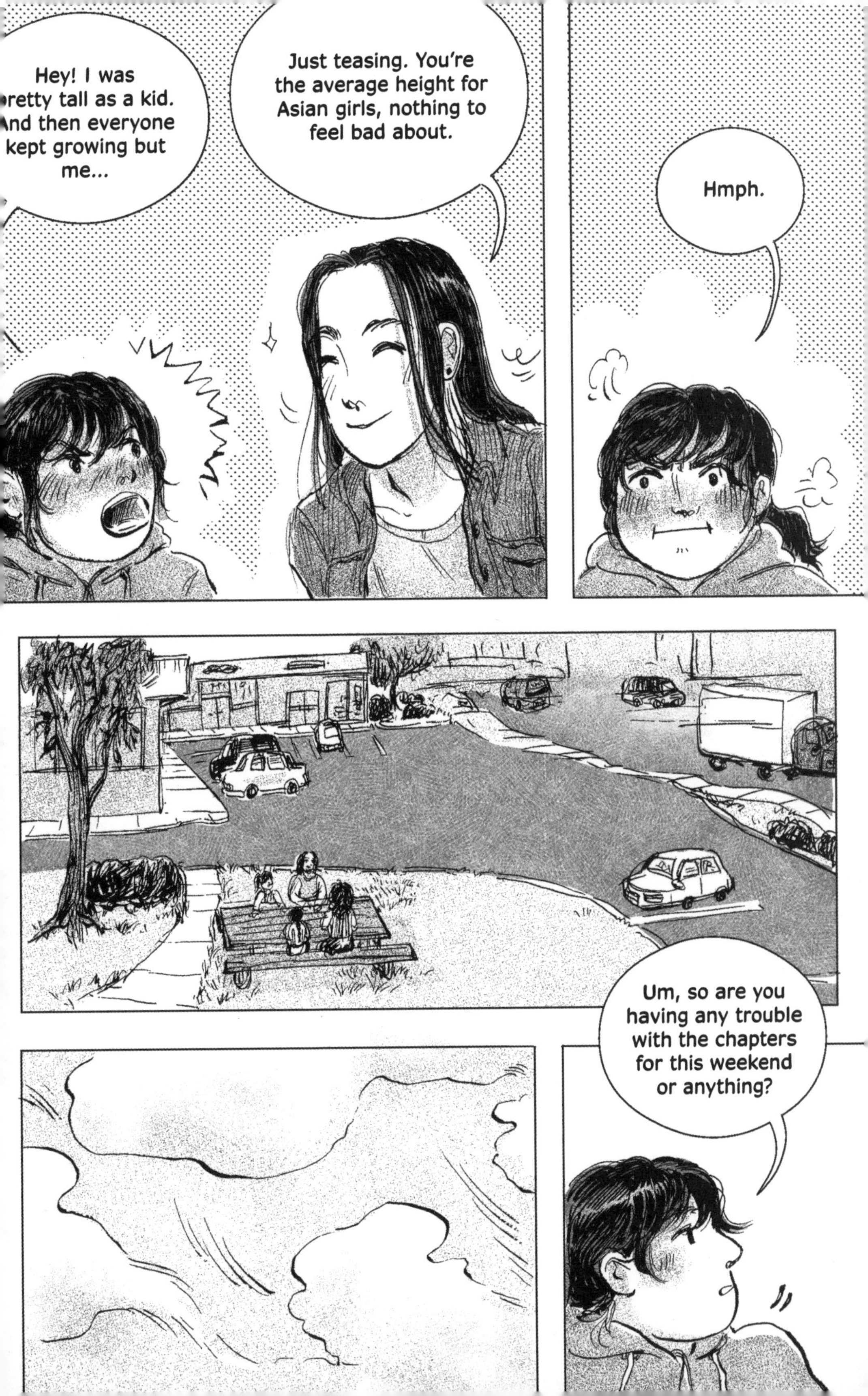
Hey! I was
retty tall as a kid.
nd then everyone
kept growing but
me...
Just teasing. You're the average height for Asian girls, nothing to feel bad about.
Hmph.
Um, so are you having any trouble with the chapters for this weekend or anything?

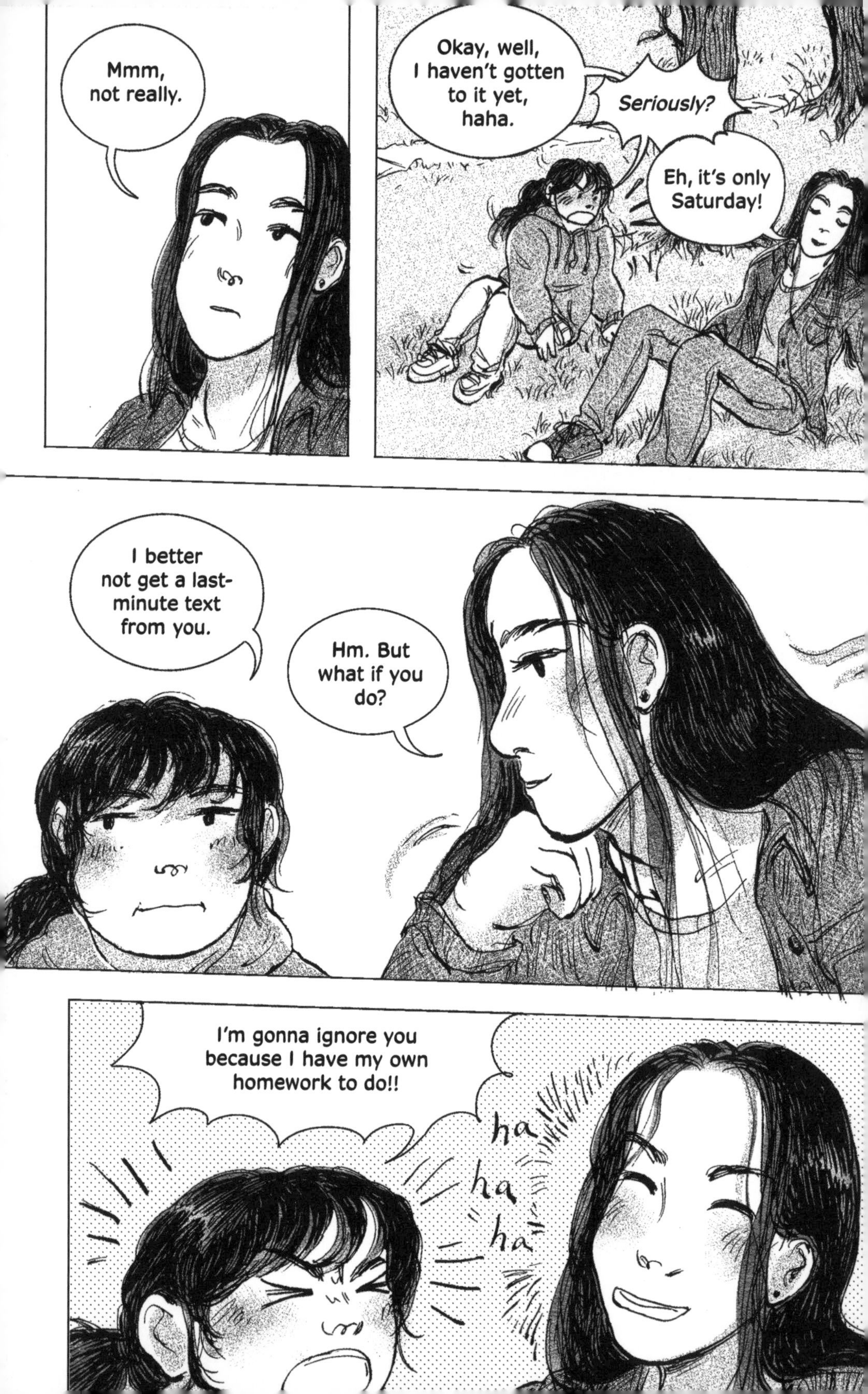

Mmm, not really.
Okay, well, I haven't gotten to it yet, haha.
Seriously?
Eh, it's only Saturday!
I better not get a last-minute text from you.
Hm. But what if you do?
I'm gonna ignore you because I have my own homework to do!!
ha ha ha

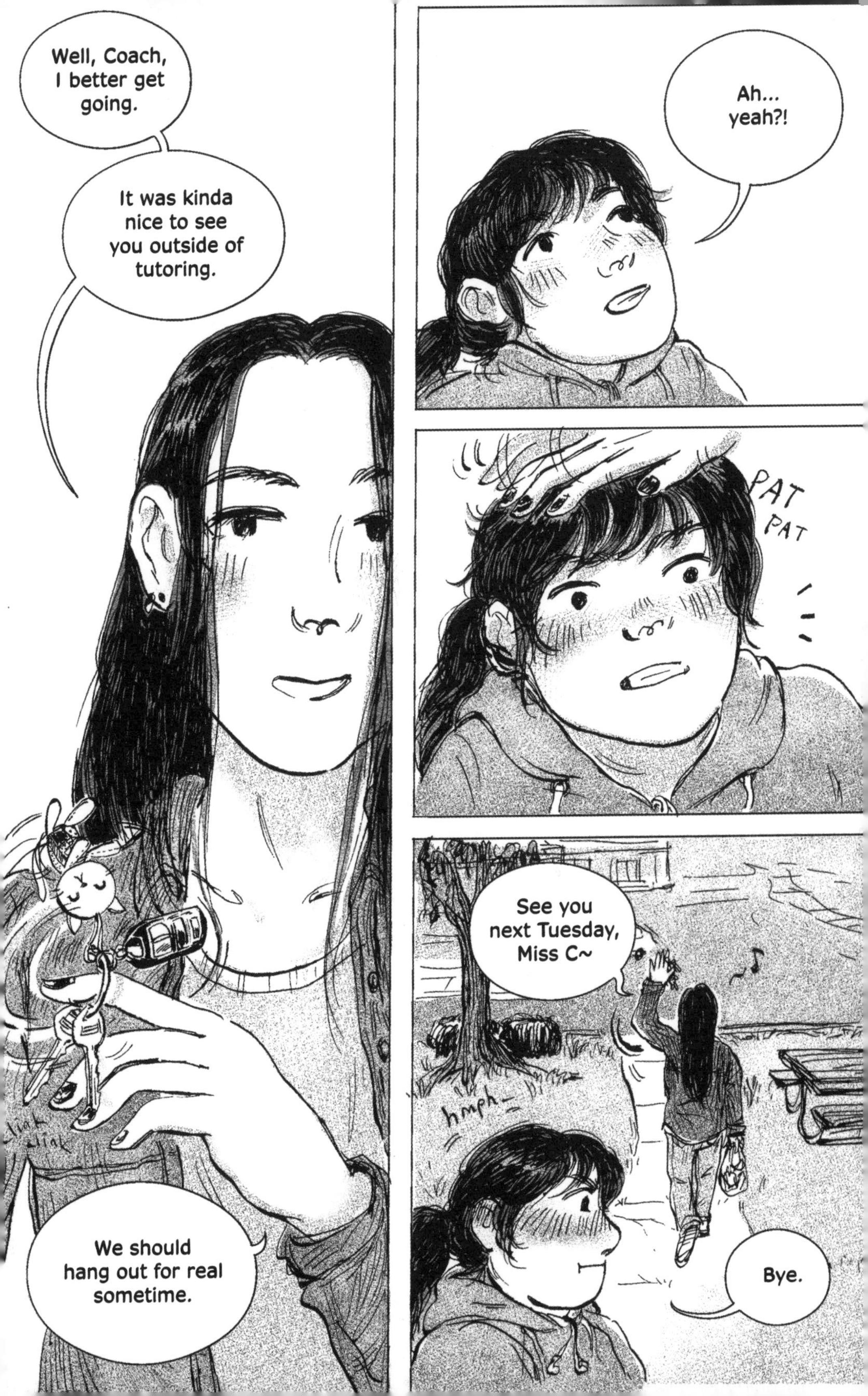
Well, Coach, I better get going.
It was kinda nice to see you outside of tutoring.
We should hang out for real sometime.
Ah... yeah?!
PAT PAT
See you next Tuesday, Miss C~
hmph
Bye.

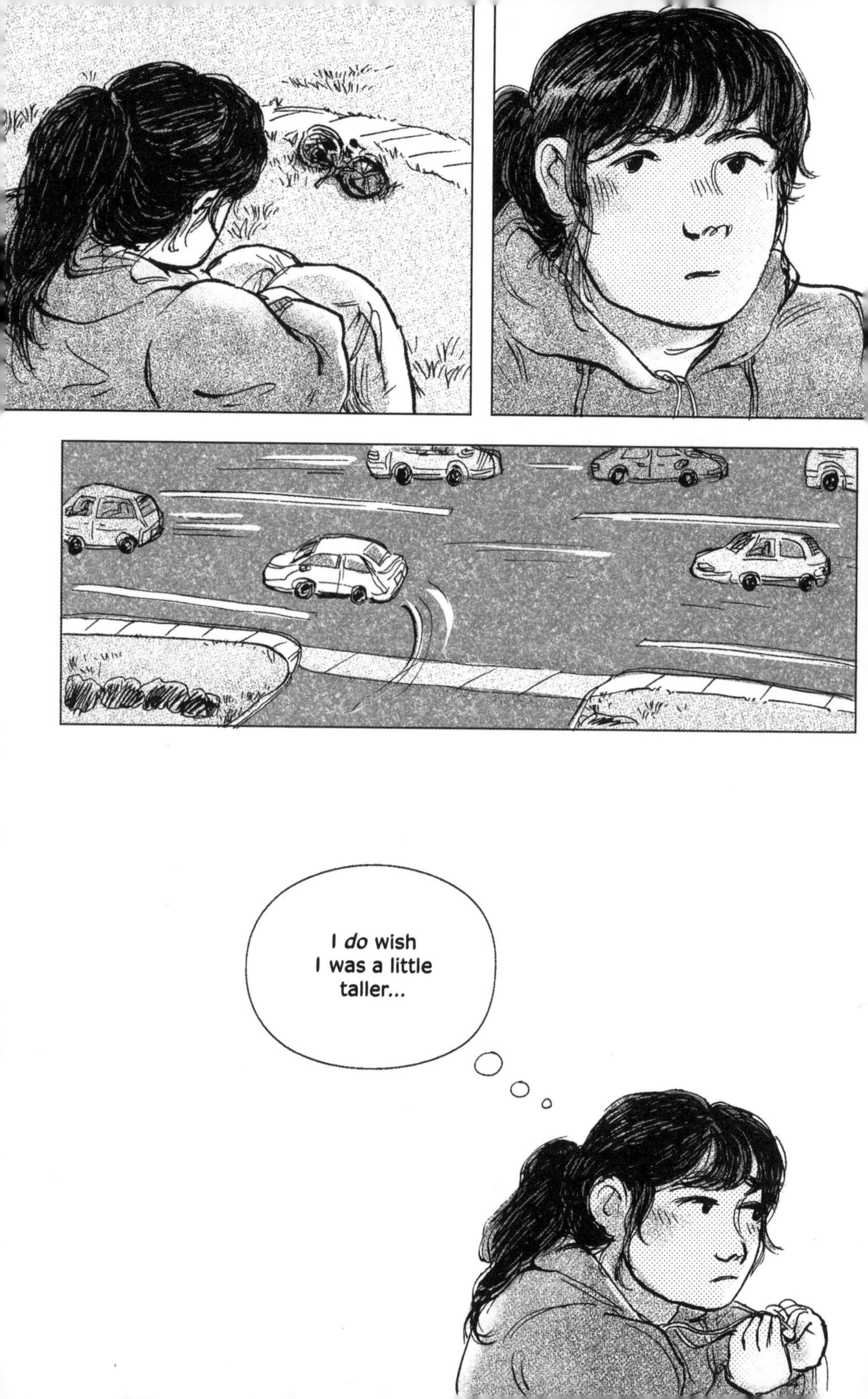
I *do* wish I was a little taller...

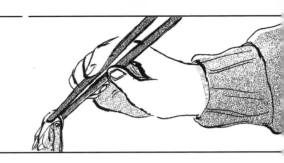

캐롤라인, 밥 다 안 먹어도 돼. 조금 남겨도 괜찮아. 밥 너무 많이 먹으면 안 좋아.

Caroline, you don't have to finish all your food. It's fine to leave a little anyway, too much rice isn't good for you.

그럼 처음부터 그냥 밥을 적게 주세요…

If I should leave some, just serve me less rice then...

It's just rice. Don't worry about waste, if you're full, you don't have to finish it, okay?

그냥 밥이야. 버리는 거 신경 쓰지 말고, 배부르면 남겨, 알았지?

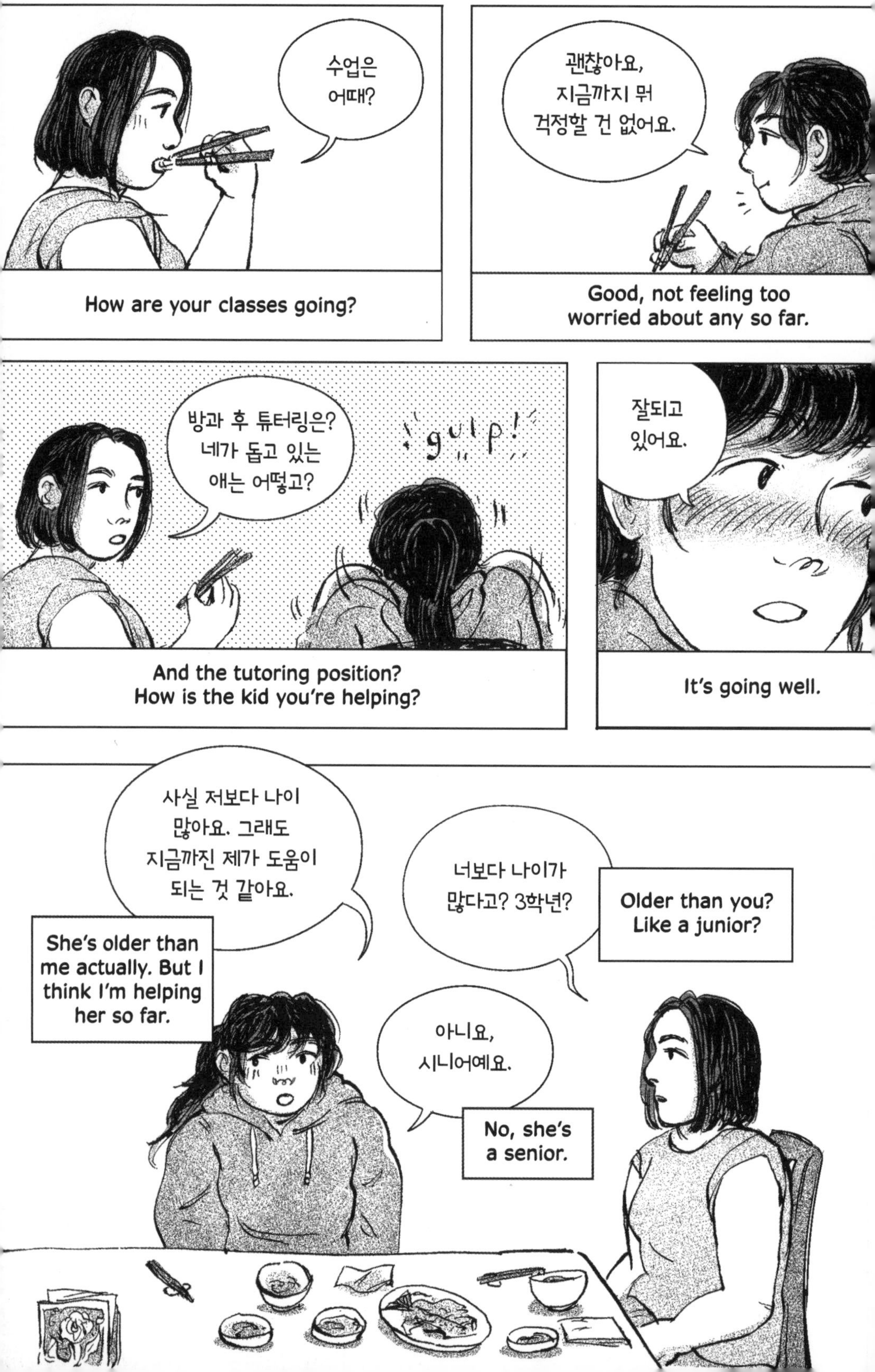

수업은 어때?
How are your classes going?
괜찮아요, 지금까지 뭐 걱정할 건 없어요.
Good, not feeling too worried about any so far.
방과 후 튜터링은? 네가 돕고 있는 애는 어떻고?
gulp!
And the tutoring position? How is the kid you're helping?
잘되고 있어요.
It's going well.
사실 저보다 나이 많아요. 그래도 지금까진 제가 도움이 되는 것 같아요.
She's older than me actually. But I think I'm helping her so far.
너보다 나이가 많다고? 3학년?
Older than you? Like a junior?
아니요, 시니어예요.
No, she's a senior.

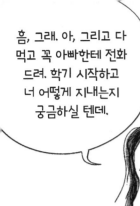

흠, 그래. 아, 그리고 다 먹고 꼭 아빠한테 전화 드려. 학기 시작하고 너 어떻게 지내는지 궁금하실 텐데.

네 엄마.

Yes Mom.

Huh, okay. Well, make sure to call your dad after you're done eating. He'll want to hear how you're doing since school started.

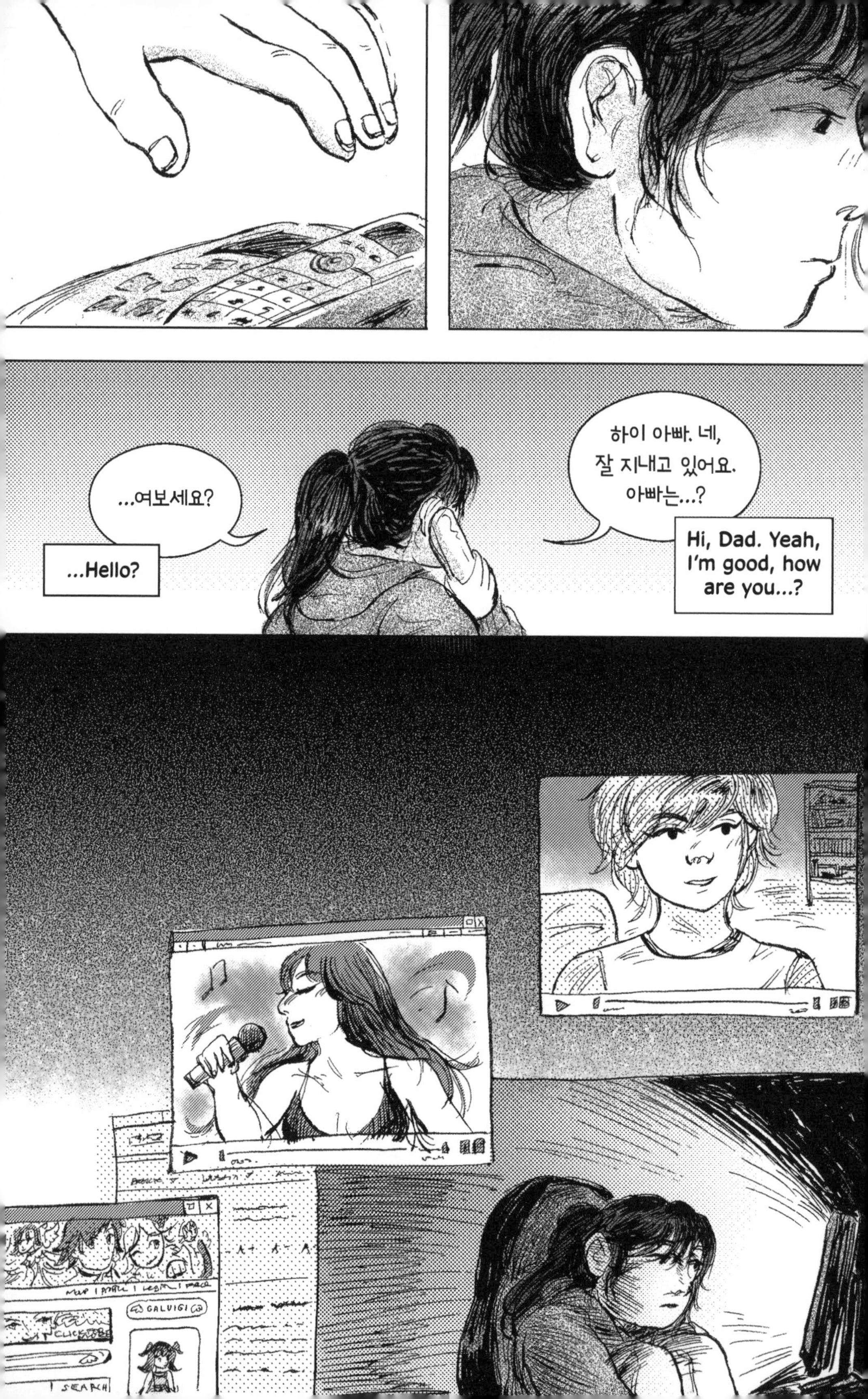
...여보세요?
...Hello?
하이 아빠. 네, 잘 지내고 있어요. 아빠는...?
Hi, Dad. Yeah, I'm good, how are you...?

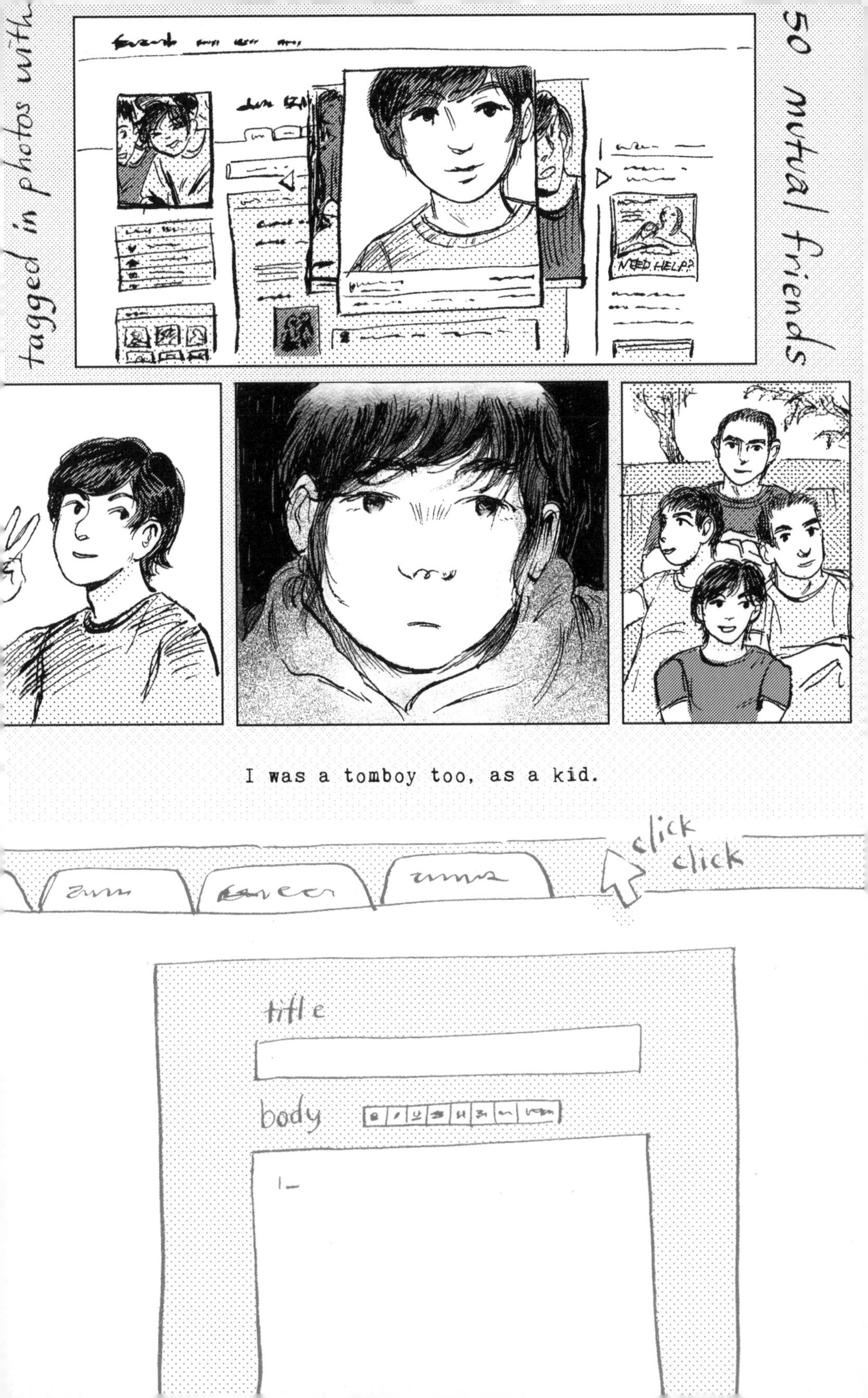
tagged in photos with
50 mutual friends
NEED HELP?
I was a tomboy too, as a kid.
click
click
title
body

I wanted short hair and baggy pants and for people to treat me like a person and not a "little girl."

I envied the other boys, in school and at church. All of the Korean families we knew had boys and we were the only one with two sisters.

When I played with them, I wanted so bad for them to accept me, regard me as one of them.

It wasn't that I hated feminine things though. I still liked them, but kept it secret.

...And I argued with my mom constantly about my hair.

Mom used to do my hair every day, in the same style. She pulled back my hair so tightly I felt like my head was in a vise. She'd tie it up in a half ponytail with a cute hair tie. I liked the hair ties but hated the feeling, the tightness on my head. I remember the headaches at the end of the day...

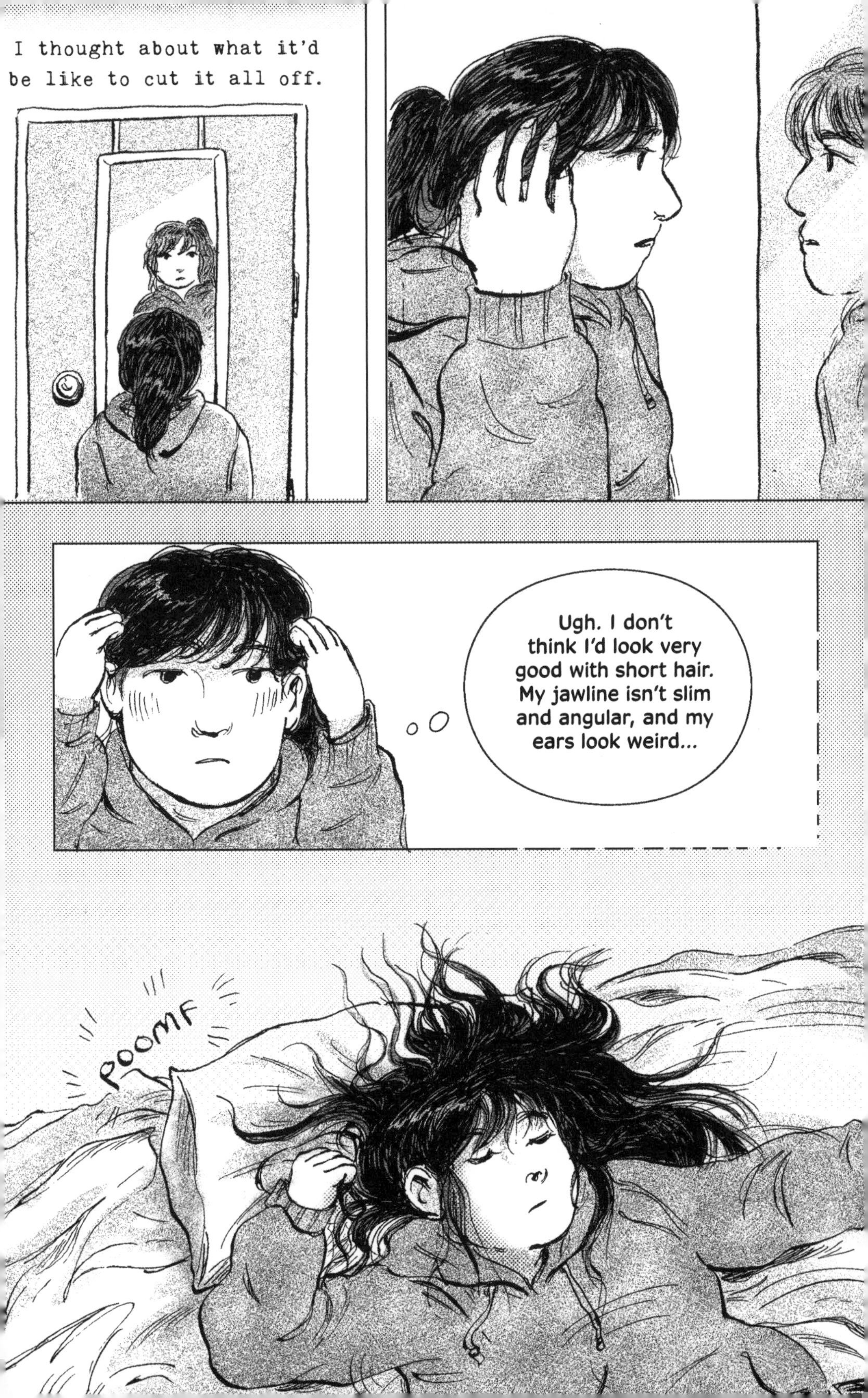
I thought about what it'd be like to cut it all off.
Ugh. I don't think I'd look very good with short hair. My jawline isn't slim and angular, and my ears look weird...
POOMF

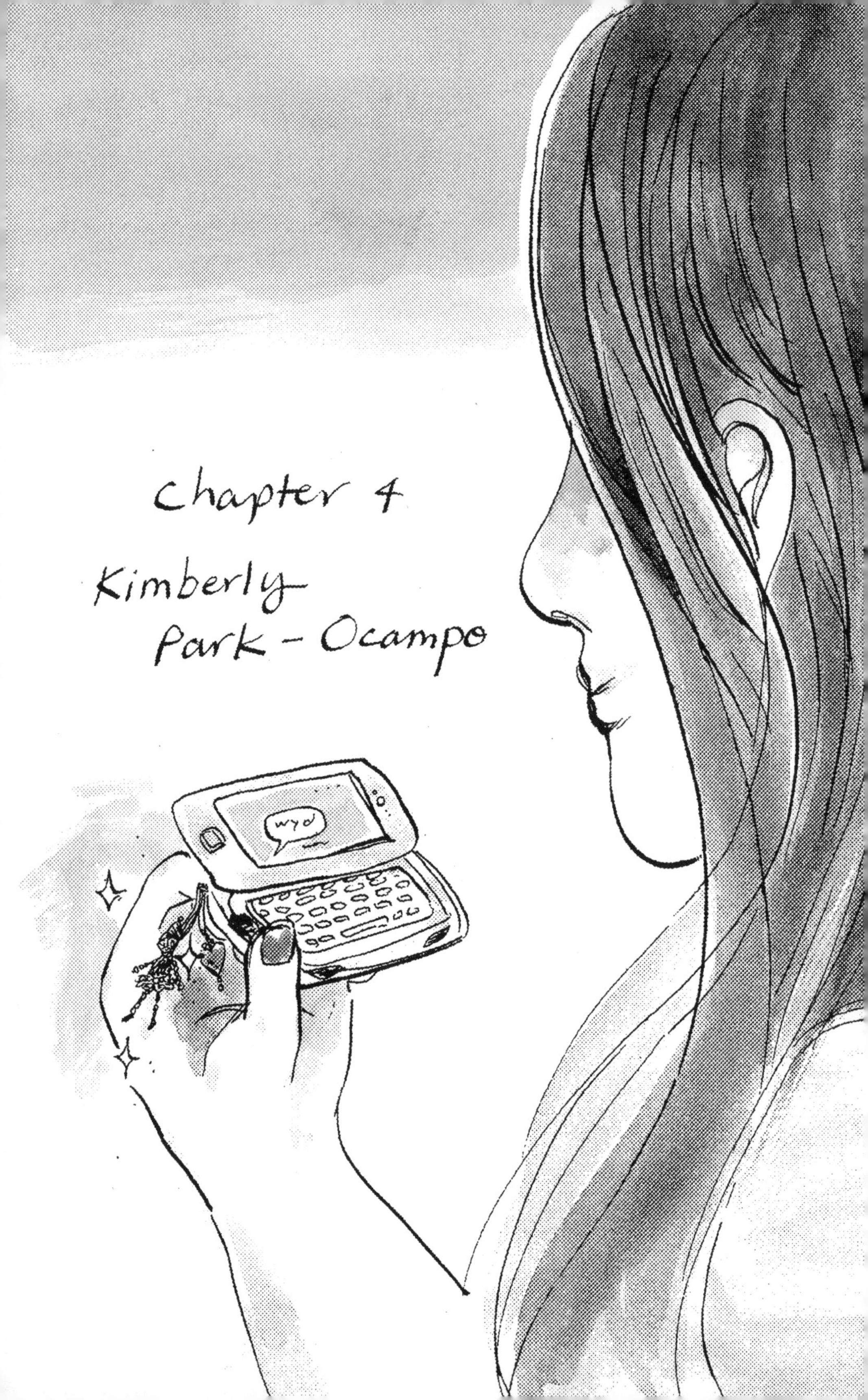
Chapter 4
Kimberly Park-Ocampo
wyd

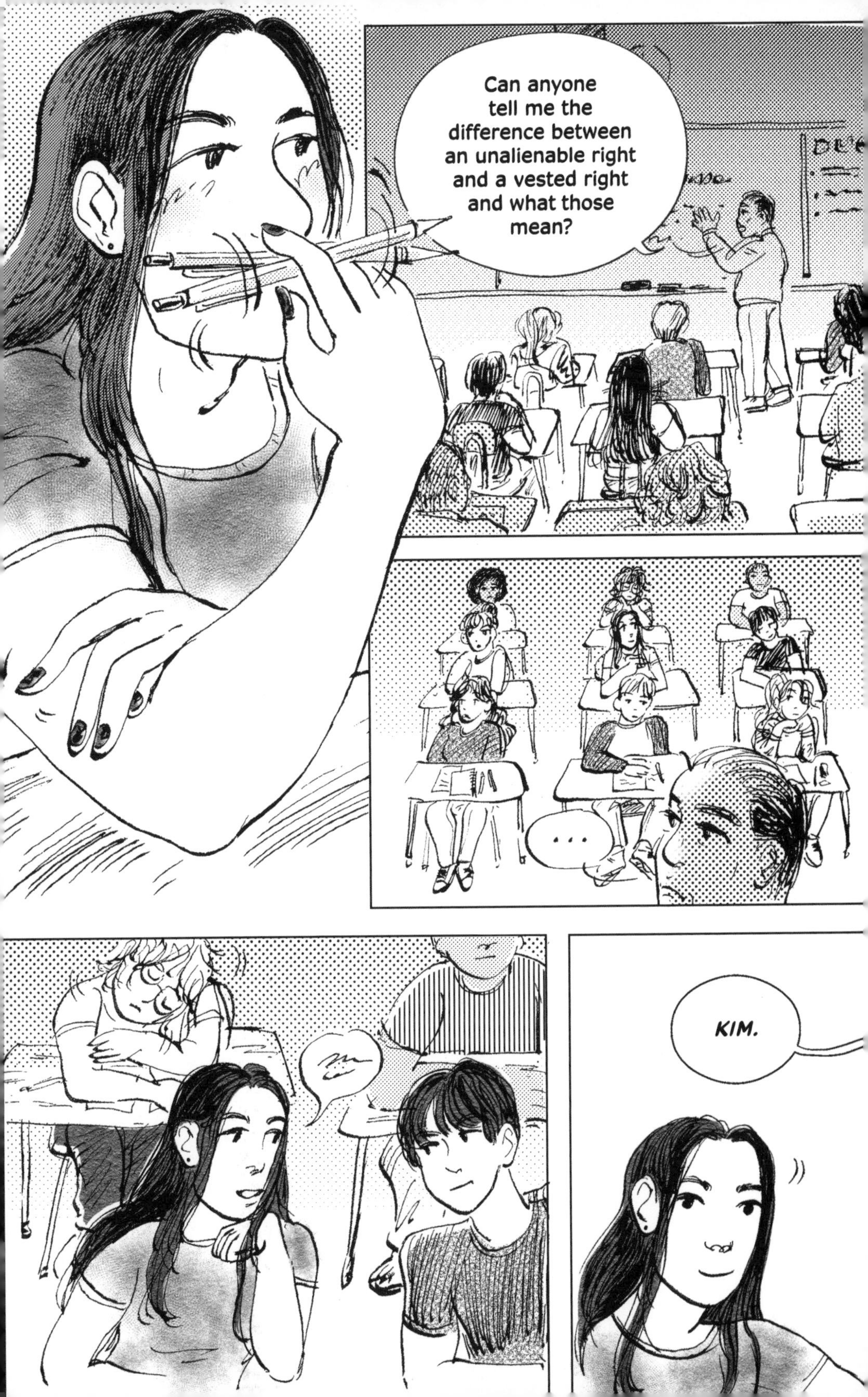
Can anyone tell me the difference between an unalienable right and a vested right and what those mean?
...
KIM.

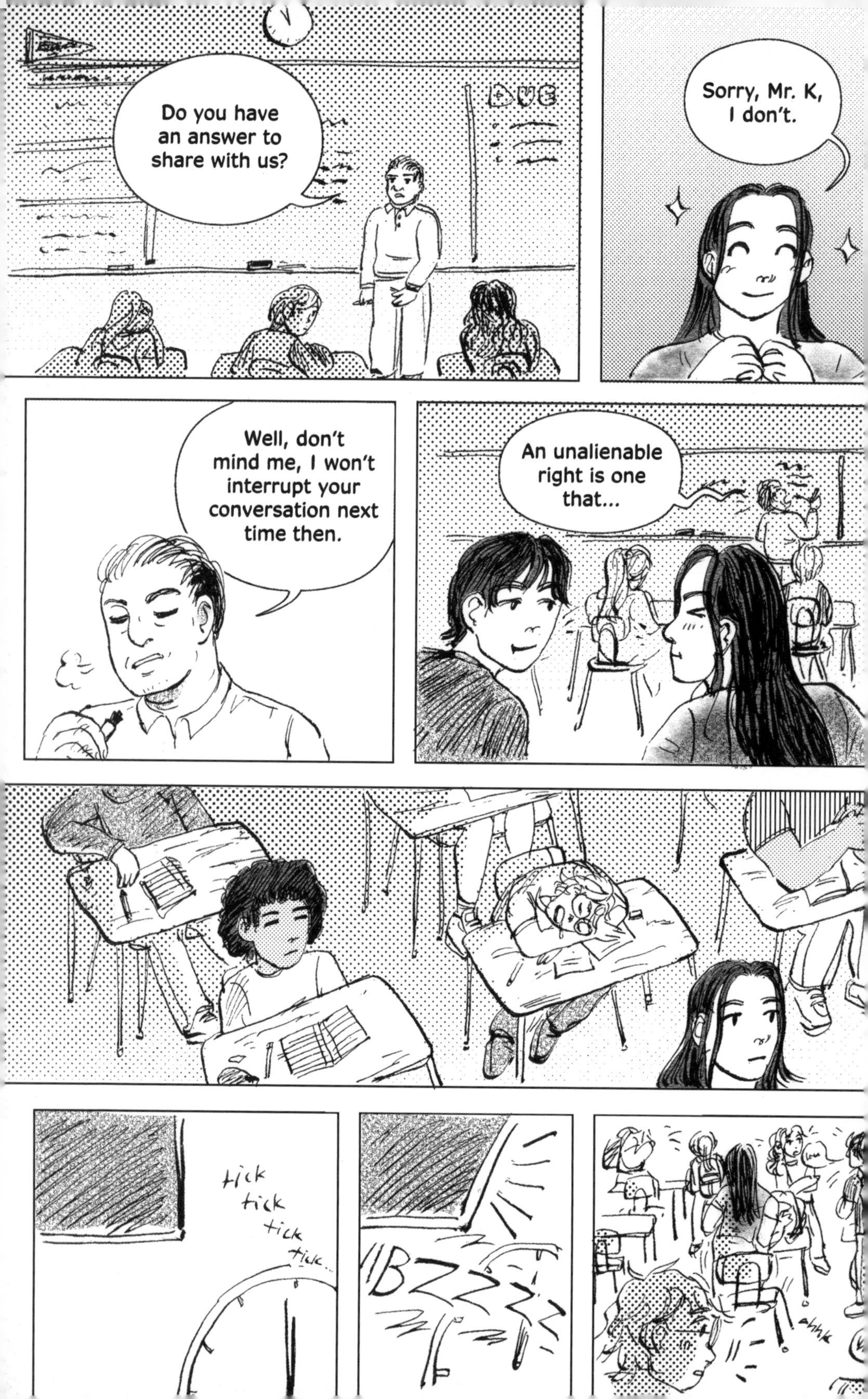
Do you have an answer to share with us?
Sorry, Mr. K, I don't.
Well, don't mind me, I won't interrupt your conversation next time then.
An unalienable right is one that...
tick
tick
tick
tick...
BZZZZ

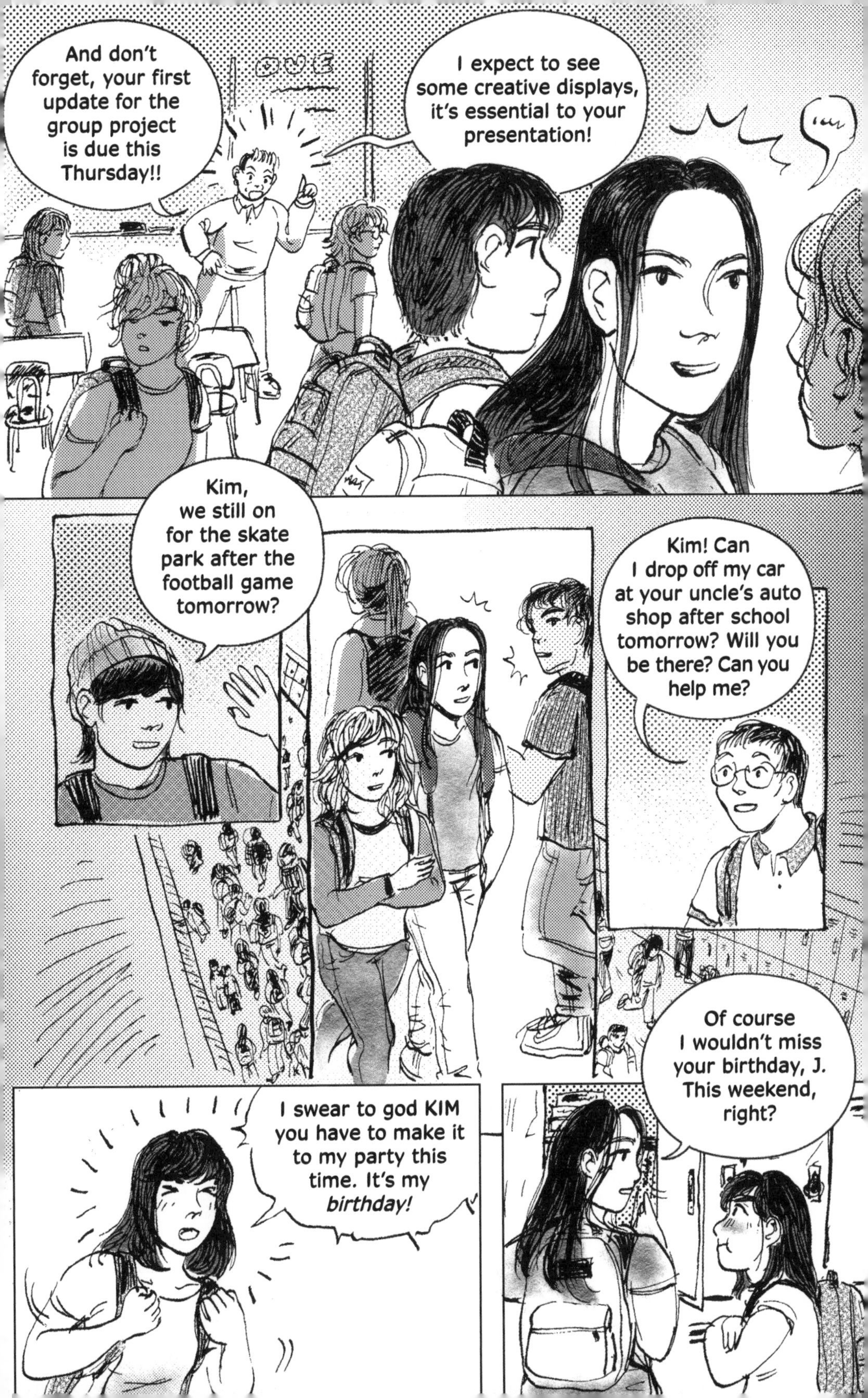
And don't forget, your first update for the group project is due this Thursday!!
I expect to see some creative displays, it's essential to your presentation!
Kim, we still on for the skate park after the football game tomorrow?
Kim! Can I drop off my car at your uncle's auto shop after school tomorrow? Will you be there? Can you help me?
I swear to god KIM you have to make it to my party this time. It's my *birthday!*
Of course I wouldn't miss your birthday, J. This weekend, right?

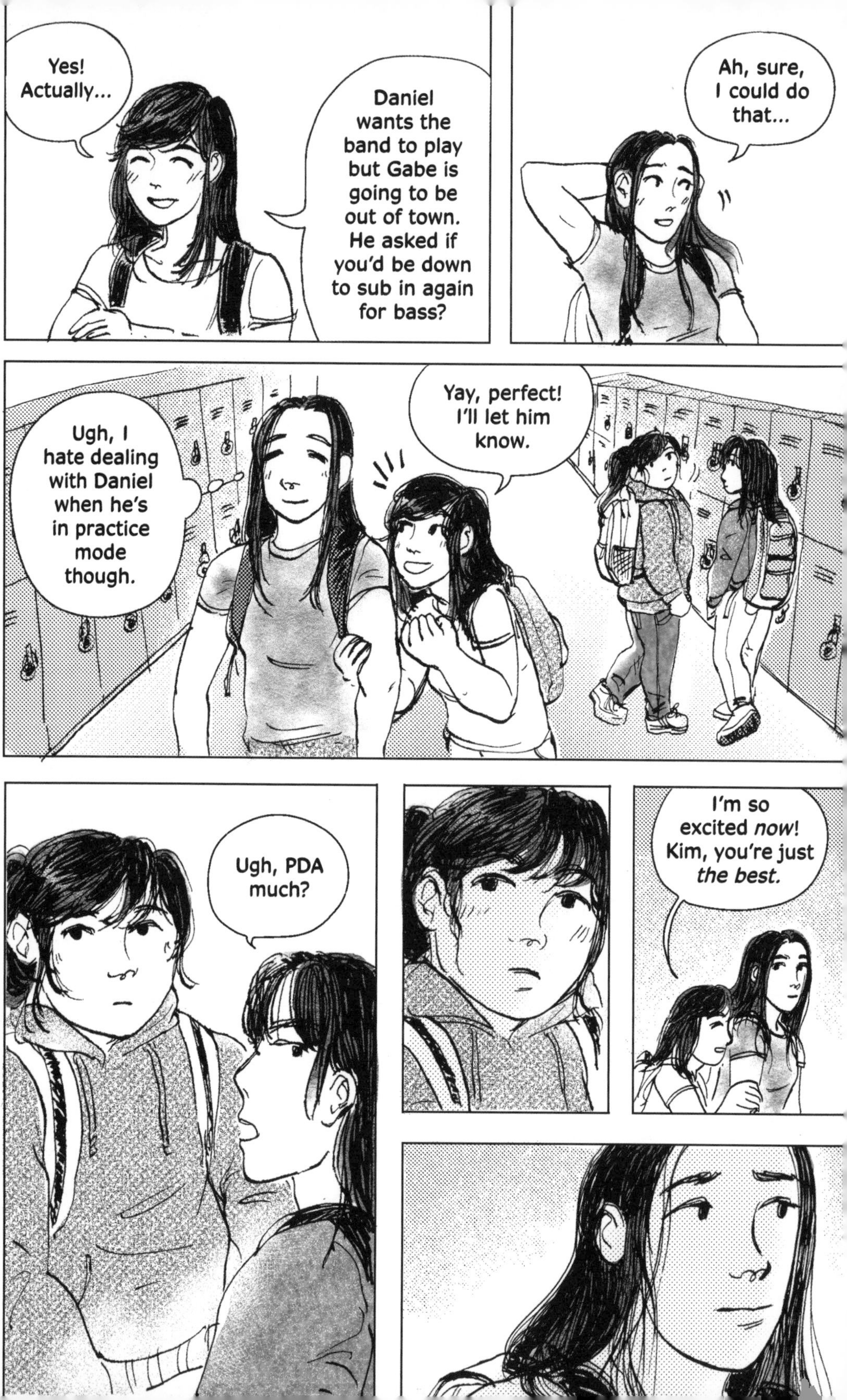
Yes! Actually...
Daniel wants the band to play but Gabe is going to be out of town. He asked if you'd be down to sub in again for bass?
Ah, sure, I could do that...
Ugh, I hate dealing with Daniel when he's in practice mode though.
Yay, perfect! I'll let him know.
Ugh, PDA much?
I'm so excited *now*! Kim, you're just *the best.*

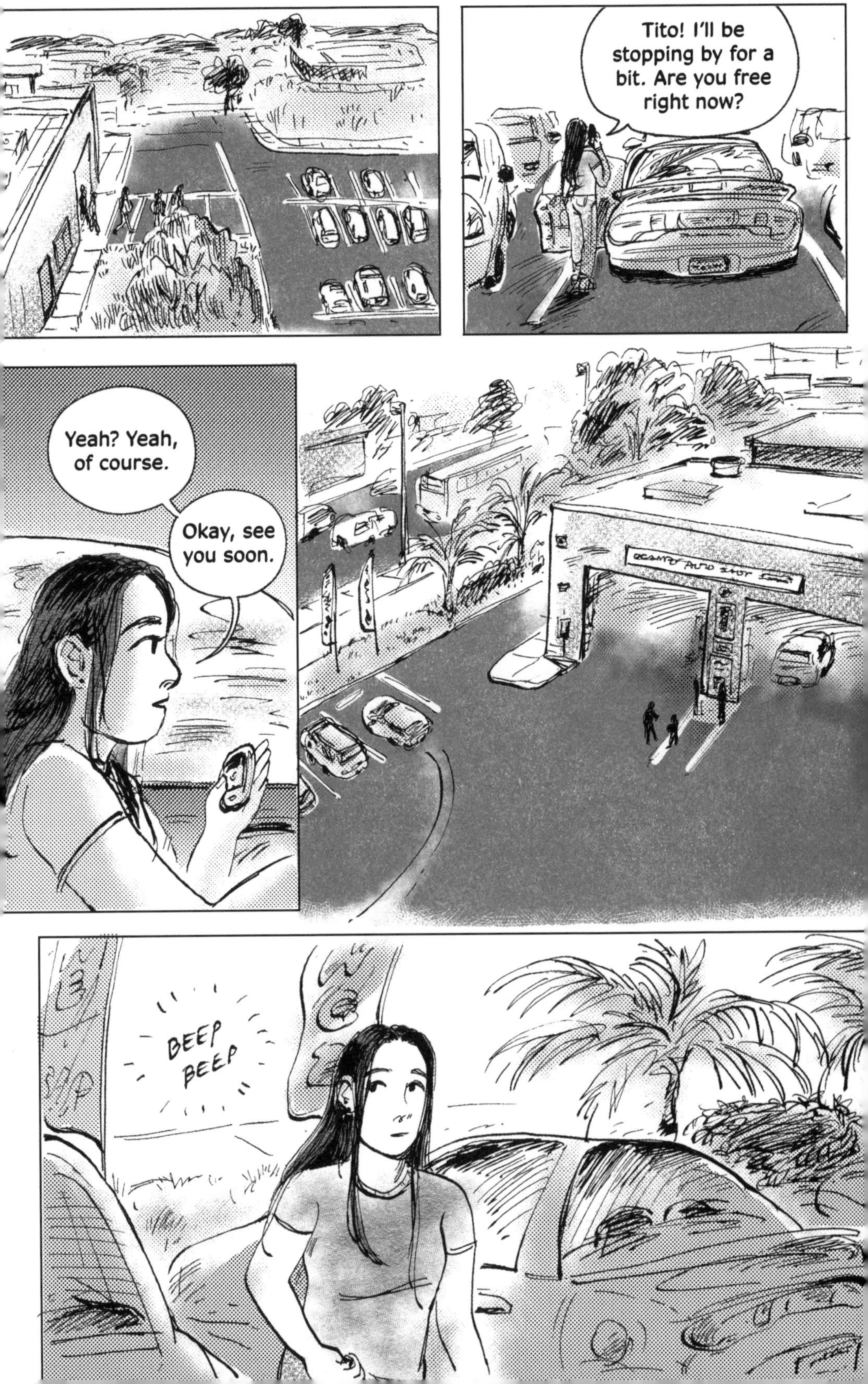
Tito! I'll be stopping by for a bit. Are you free right now?
Yeah? Yeah, of course.
Okay, see you soon.
BEEP BEEP

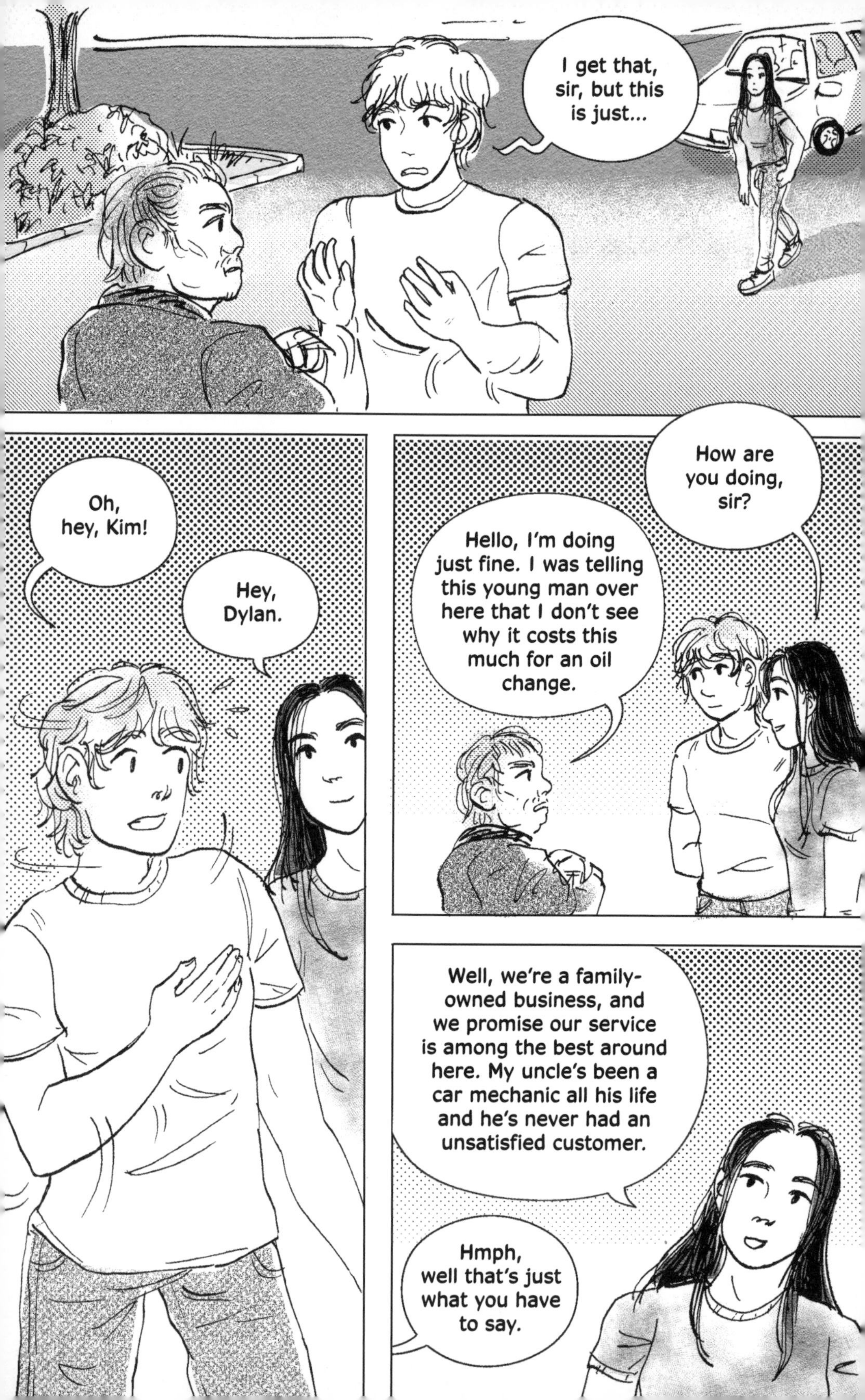
I get that, sir, but this is just...
Oh, hey, Kim!
Hey, Dylan.
How are you doing, sir?
Hello, I'm doing just fine. I was telling this young man over here that I don't see why it costs this much for an oil change.
Well, we're a family-owned business, and we promise our service is among the best around here. My uncle's been a car mechanic all his life and he's never had an unsatisfied customer.
Hmph, well that's just what you have to say.

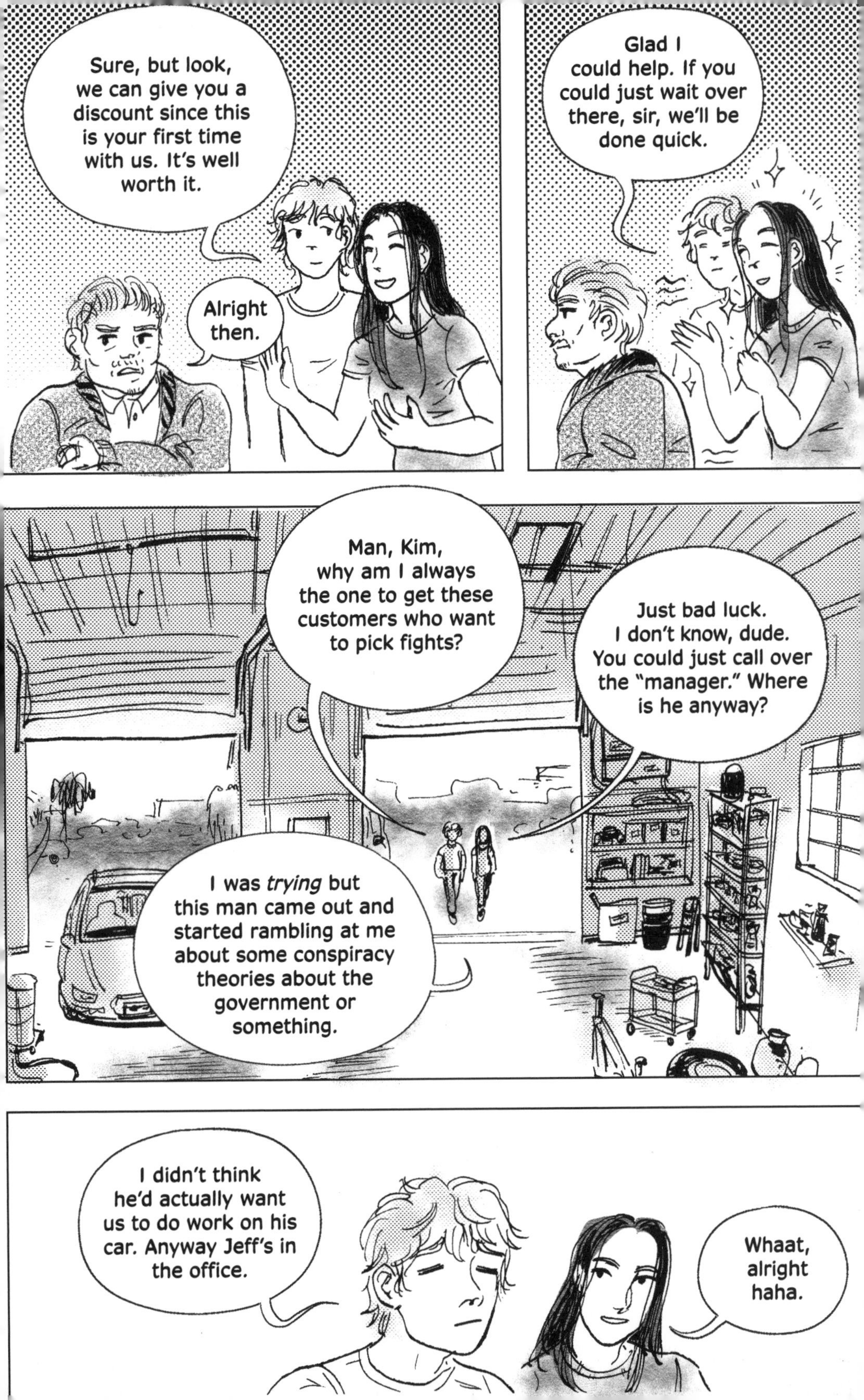
Sure, but look, we can give you a discount since this is your first time with us. It's well worth it.
Alright then.
Glad I could help. If you could just wait over there, sir, we'll be done quick.
Man, Kim, why am I always the one to get these customers who want to pick fights?
Just bad luck. I don't know, dude. You could just call over the "manager." Where is he anyway?
I was *trying* but this man came out and started rambling at me about some conspiracy theories about the government or something.
I didn't think he'd actually want us to do work on his car. Anyway Jeff's in the office.
Whaat, alright haha.

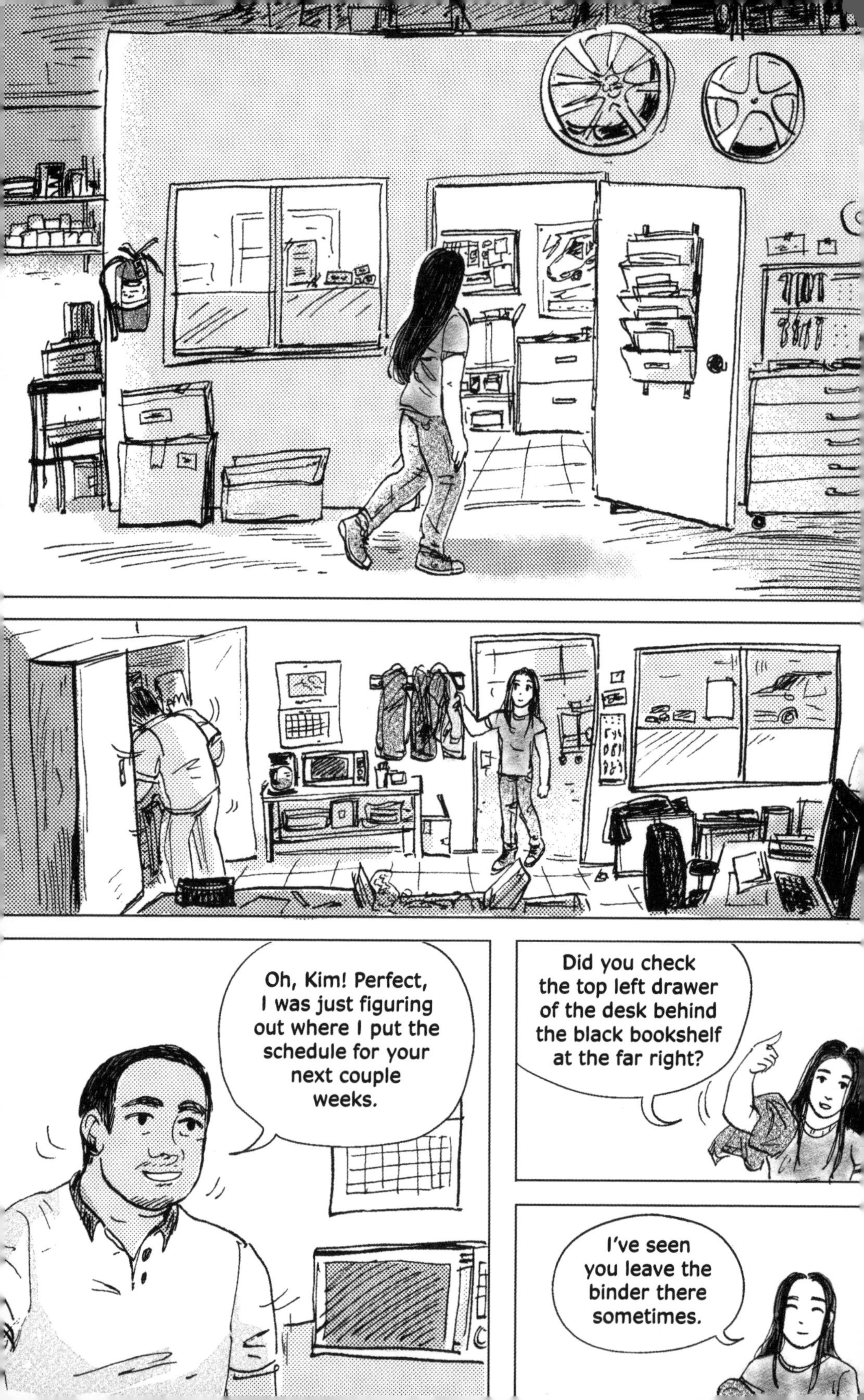
Oh, Kim! Perfect, I was just figuring out where I put the schedule for your next couple weeks.
Did you check the top left drawer of the desk behind the black bookshelf at the far right?
I've seen you leave the binder there sometimes.

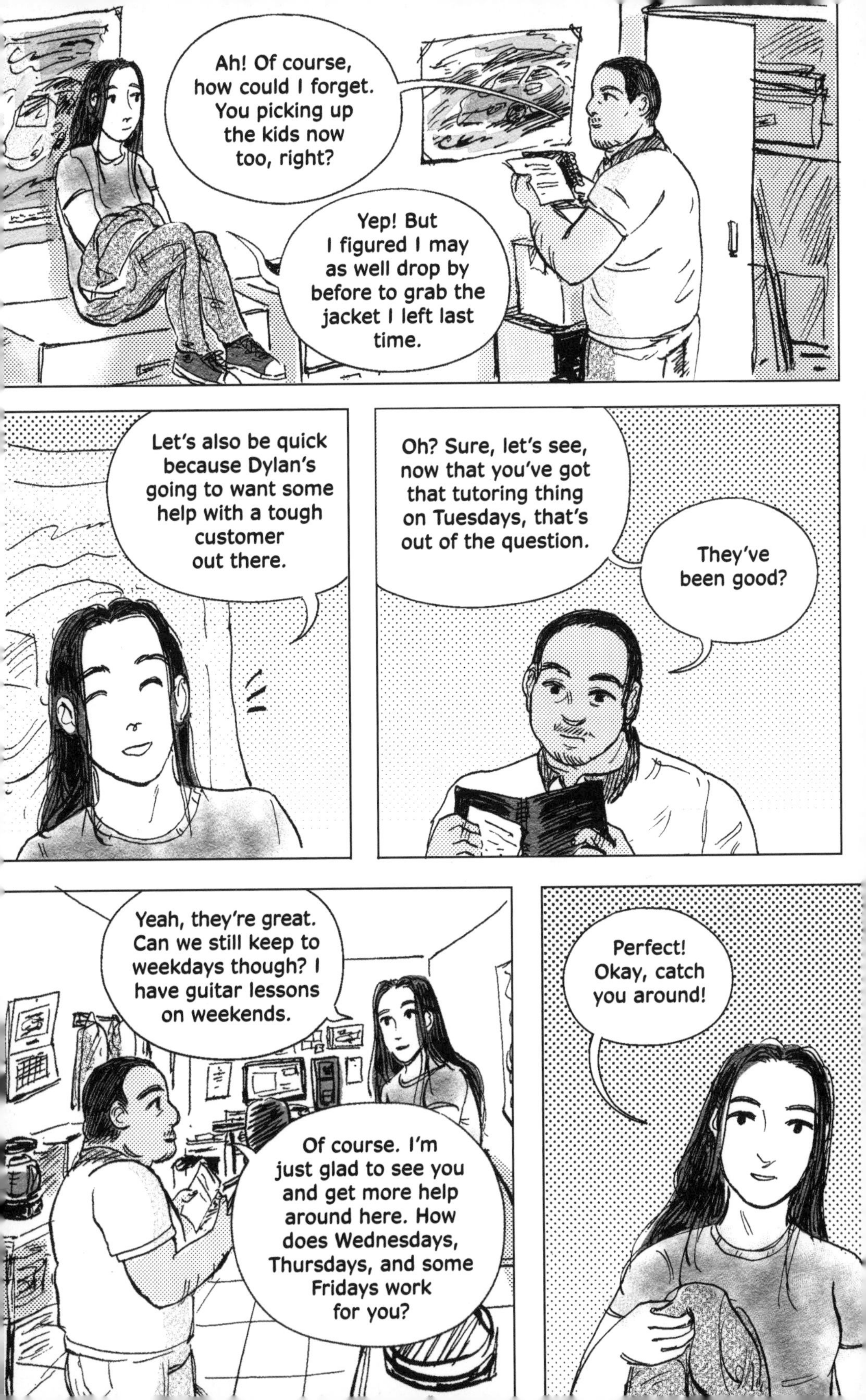
Ah! Of course, how could I forget. You picking up the kids now too, right?
Yep! But I figured I may as well drop by before to grab the jacket I left last time.
Let's also be quick because Dylan's going to want some help with a tough customer out there.
Oh? Sure, let's see, now that you've got that tutoring thing on Tuesdays, that's out of the question.
They've been good?
Yeah, they're great. Can we still keep to weekdays though? I have guitar lessons on weekends.
Of course. I'm just glad to see you and get more help around here. How does Wednesdays, Thursdays, and some Fridays work for you?
Perfect! Okay, catch you around!

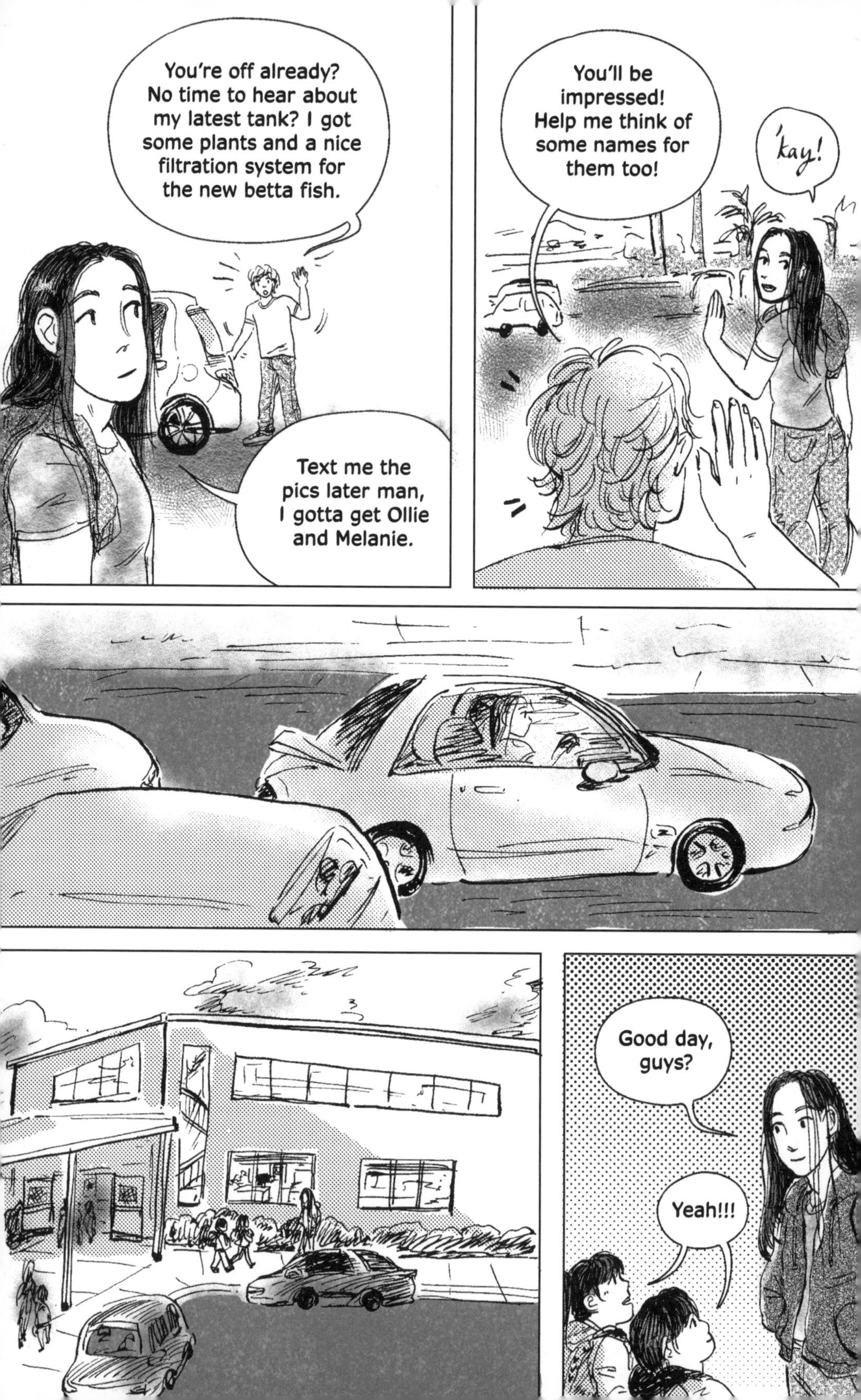
You're off already? No time to hear about my latest tank? I got some plants and a nice filtration system for the new betta fish.
Text me the pics later man, I gotta get Ollie and Melanie.
You'll be impressed! Help me think of some names for them too!
'kay!
Good day, guys?
Yeah!!!

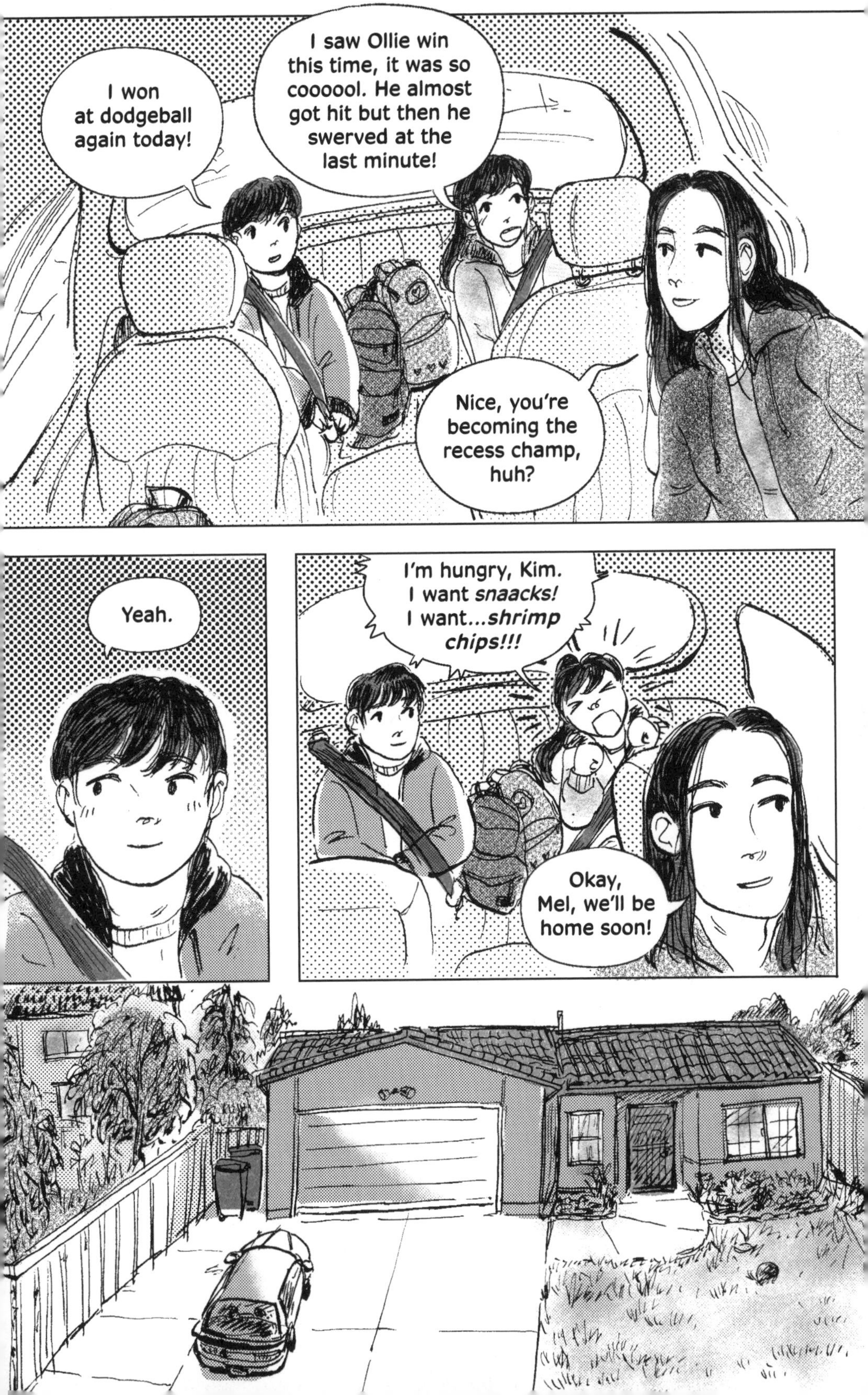
I won at dodgeball again today!
I saw Ollie win this time, it was so coooool. He almost got hit but then he swerved at the last minute!
Nice, you're becoming the recess champ, huh?
Yeah.
I'm hungry, Kim. I want *snaacks!* I want...*shrimp chips!!!*
Okay, Mel, we'll be home soon!

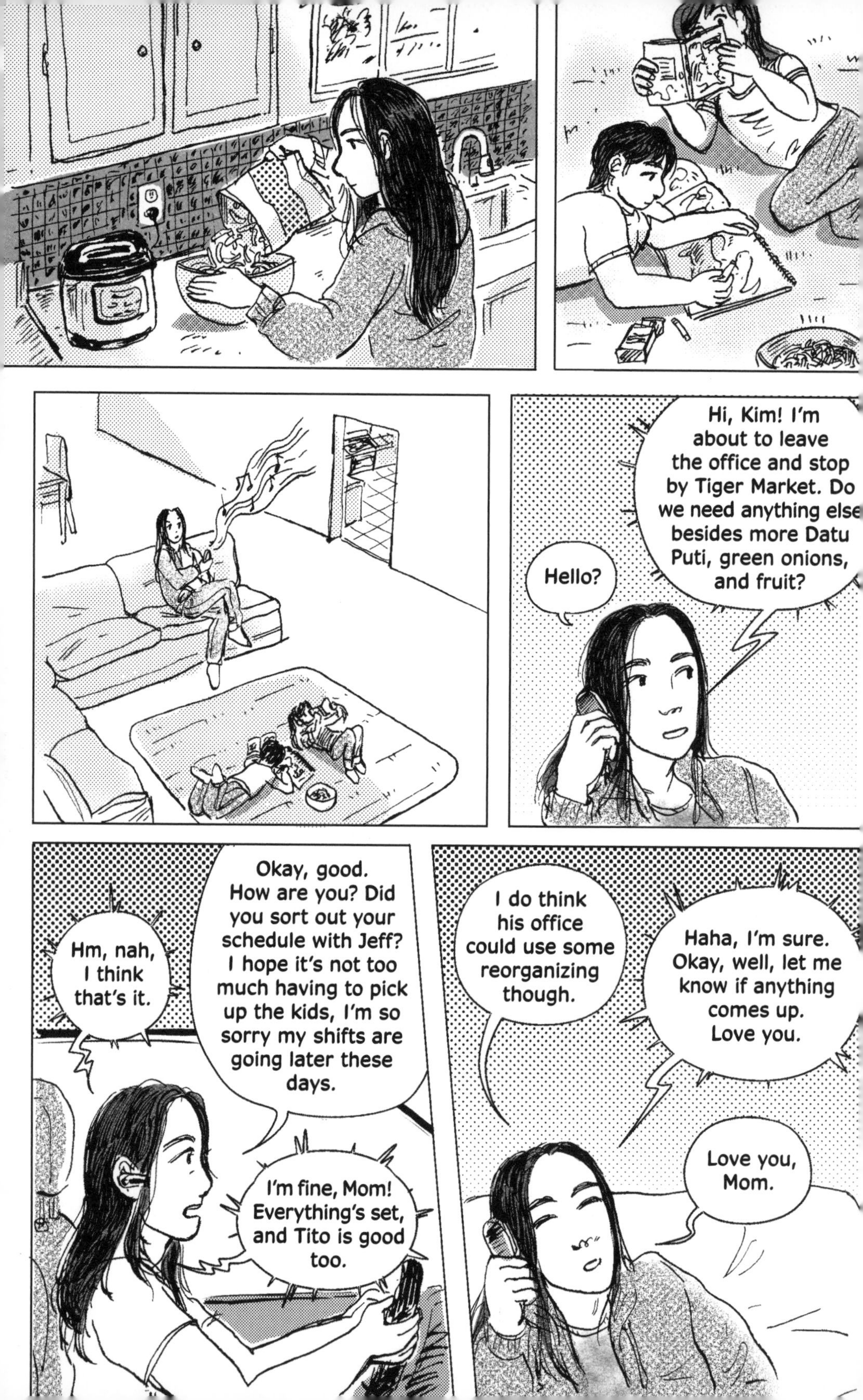
Hello?
Hi, Kim! I'm about to leave the office and stop by Tiger Market. Do we need anything else besides more Datu Puti, green onions, and fruit?
Hm, nah, I think that's it.
Okay, good. How are you? Did you sort out your schedule with Jeff? I hope it's not too much having to pick up the kids, I'm so sorry my shifts are going later these days.
I'm fine, Mom! Everything's set, and Tito is good too.
I do think his office could use some reorganizing though.
Haha, I'm sure. Okay, well, let me know if anything comes up. Love you.
Love you, Mom.

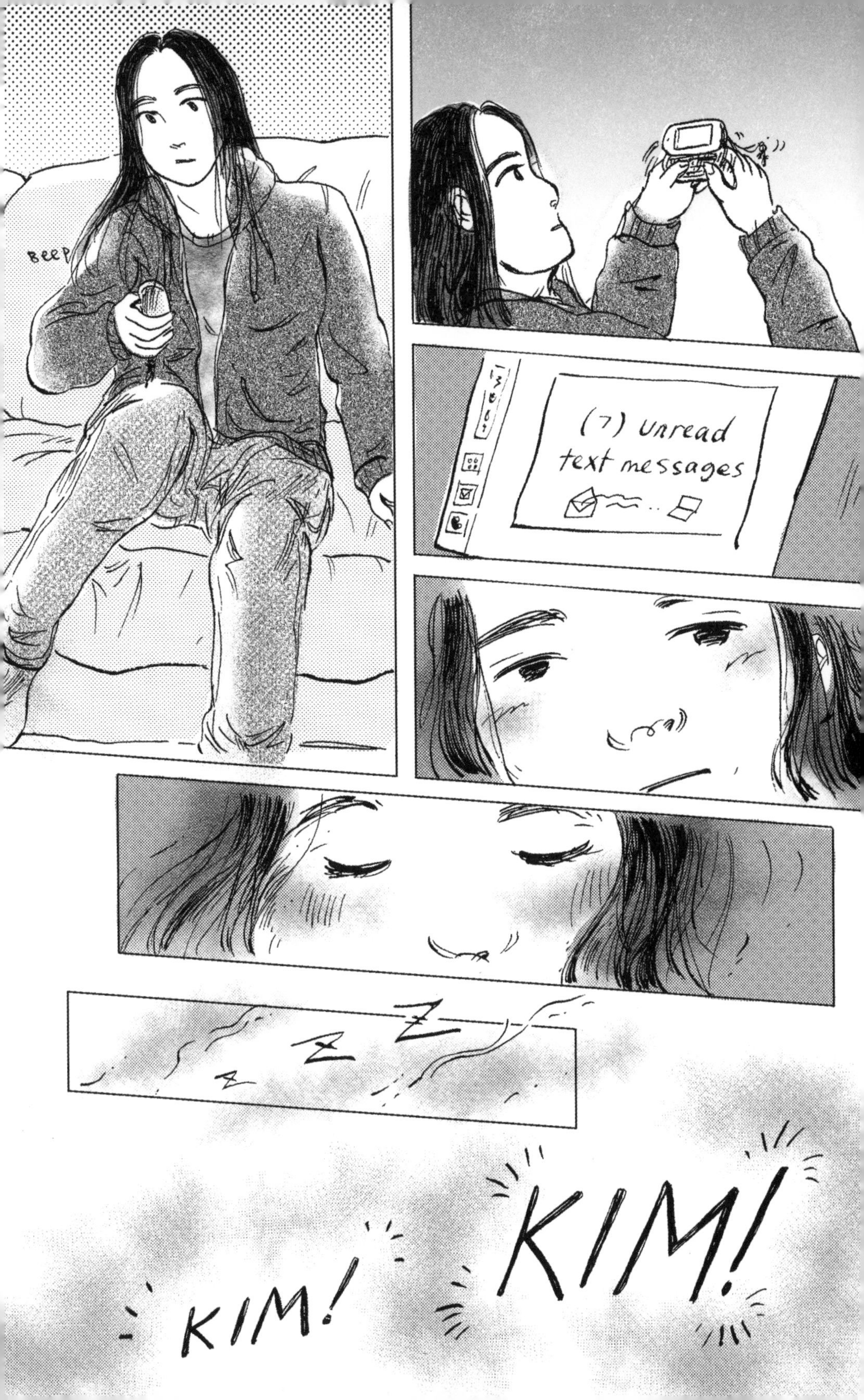
BEEP
(7) unread
text messages
KIM!
KIM!

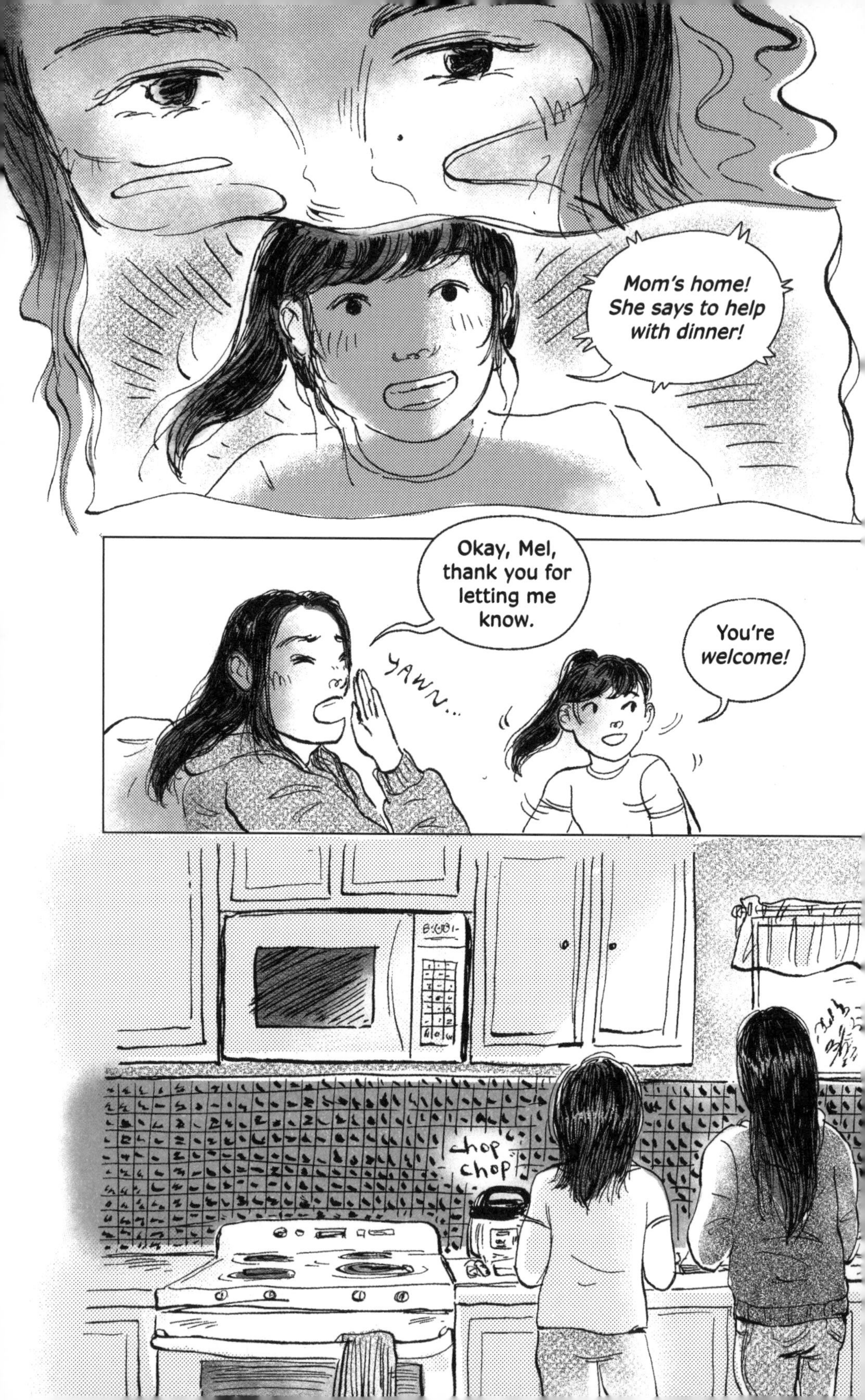
Mom's home! She says to help with dinner!
Okay, Mel, thank you for letting me know.
YAWN...
You're welcome!
chop chop

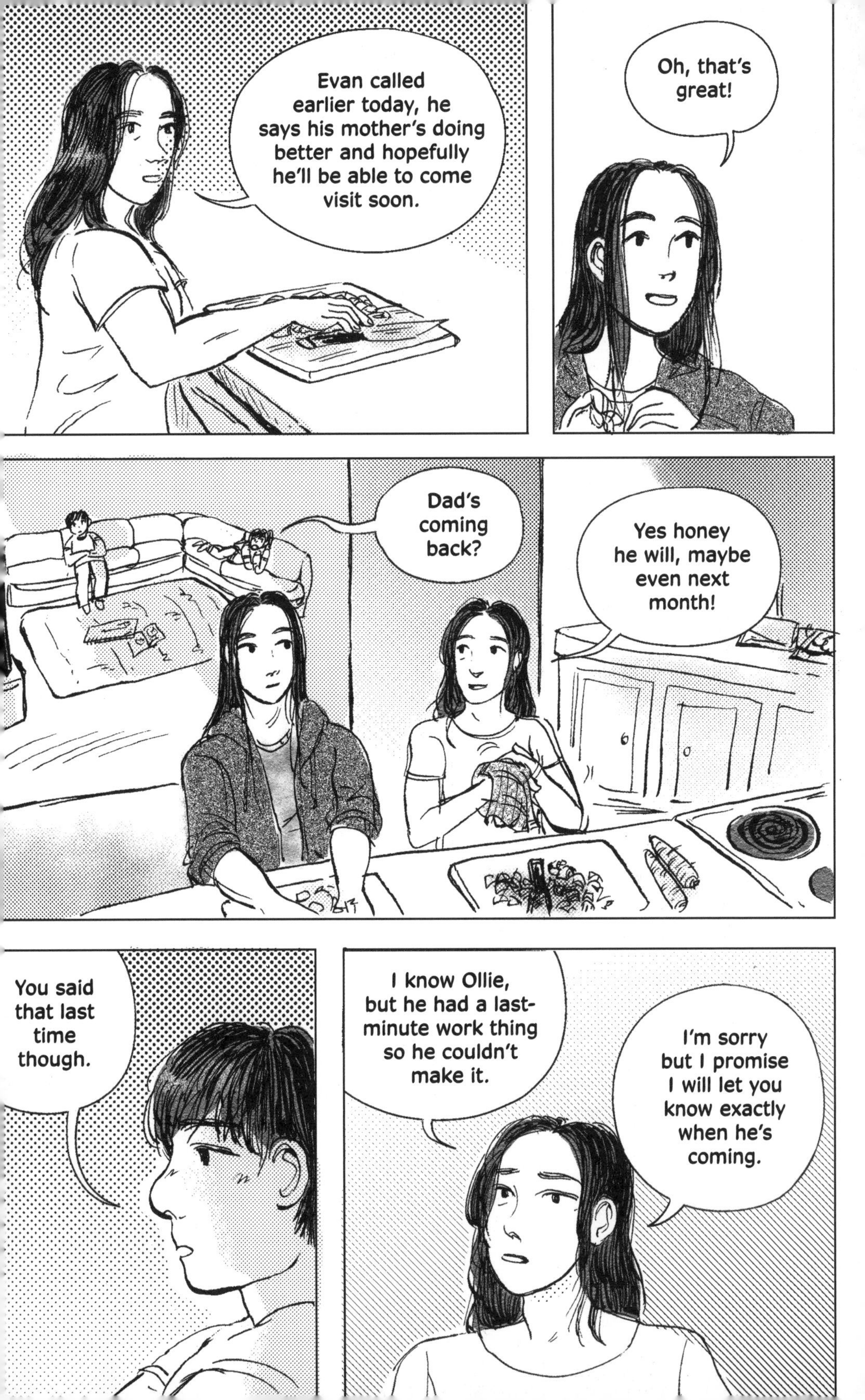
Evan called earlier today, he says his mother's doing better and hopefully he'll be able to come visit soon.
Oh, that's great!
Dad's coming back?
Yes honey he will, maybe even next month!
You said that last time though.
I know Ollie, but he had a last-minute work thing so he couldn't make it.
I'm sorry but I promise I will let you know exactly when he's coming.

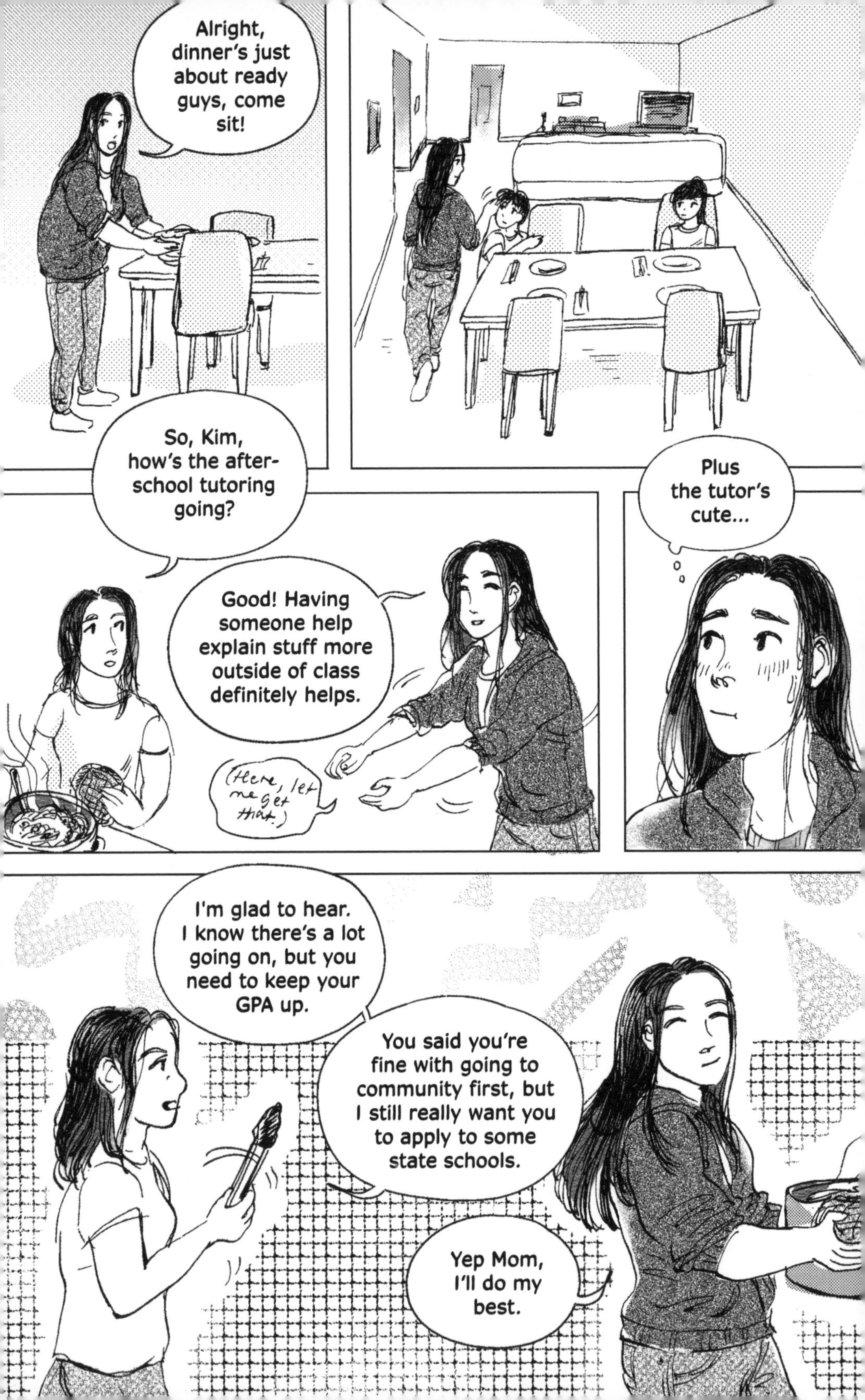
Alright, dinner's just about ready guys, come sit!
So, Kim, how's the after-school tutoring going?
Good! Having someone help explain stuff more outside of class definitely helps.
(Here, let me get that.)
Plus the tutor's cute...
I'm glad to hear. I know there's a lot going on, but you need to keep your GPA up.
You said you're fine with going to community first, but I still really want you to apply to some state schools.
Yep Mom, I'll do my best.

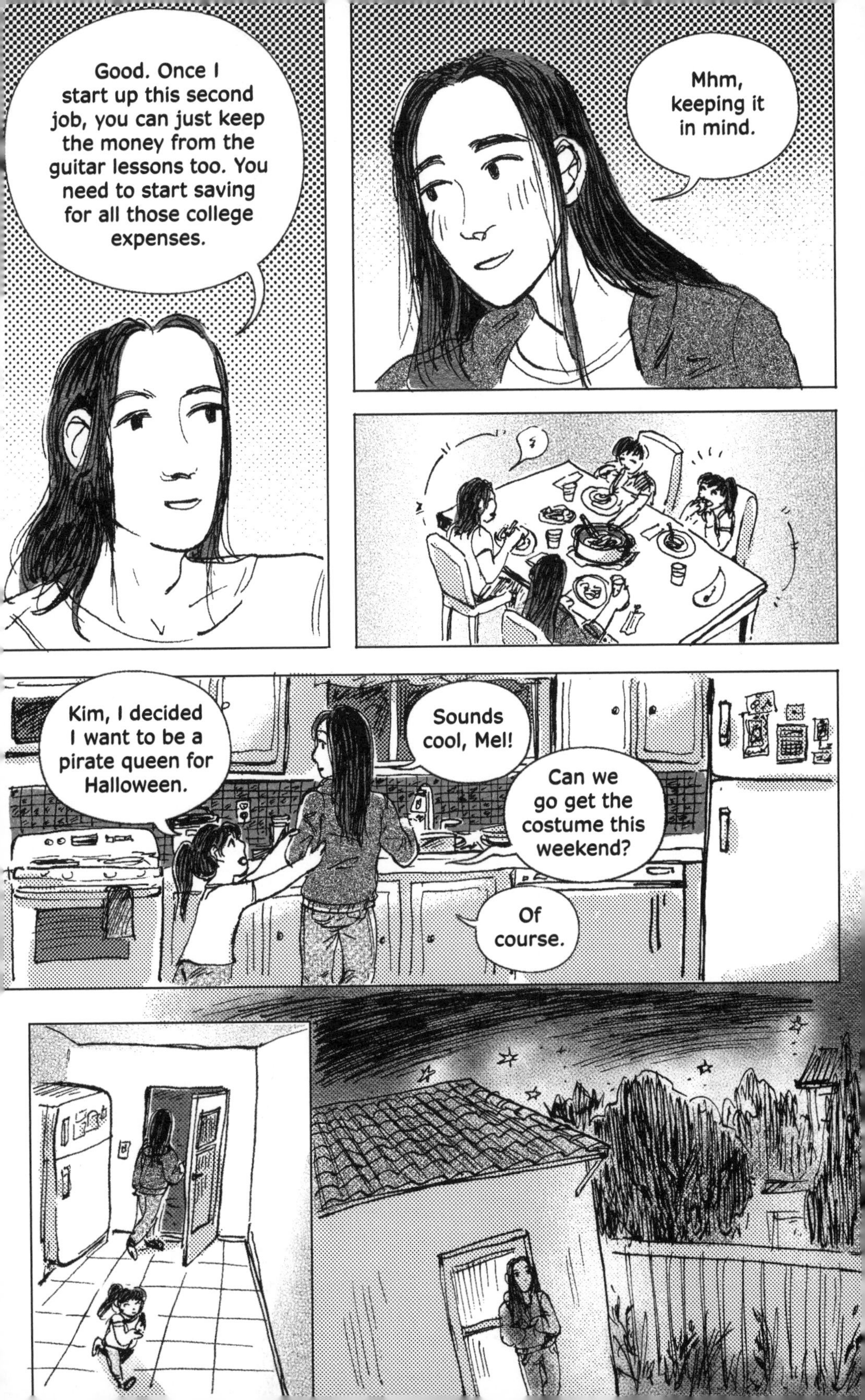
Good. Once I start up this second job, you can just keep the money from the guitar lessons too. You need to start saving for all those college expenses.
Mhm, keeping it in mind.
Kim, I decided I want to be a pirate queen for Halloween.
Sounds cool, Mel!
Can we go get the costume this weekend?
Of course.

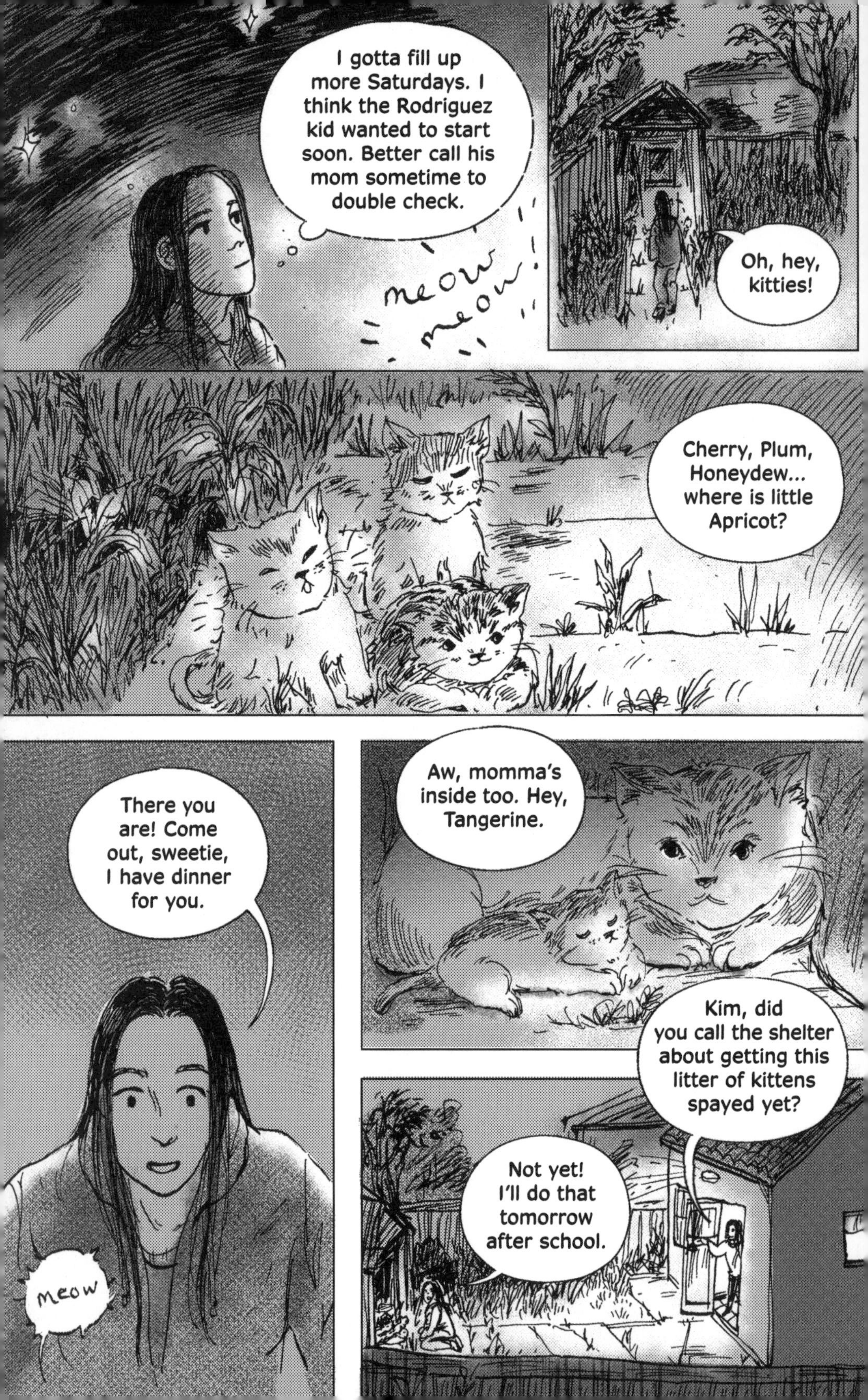
I gotta fill up more Saturdays. I think the Rodriguez kid wanted to start soon. Better call his mom sometime to double check.
meow meow!
Oh, hey, kitties!
Cherry, Plum, Honeydew... where is little Apricot?
There you are! Come out, sweetie, I have dinner for you.
meow
Aw, momma's inside too. Hey, Tangerine.
Kim, did you call the shelter about getting this litter of kittens spayed yet?
Not yet! I'll do that tomorrow after school.

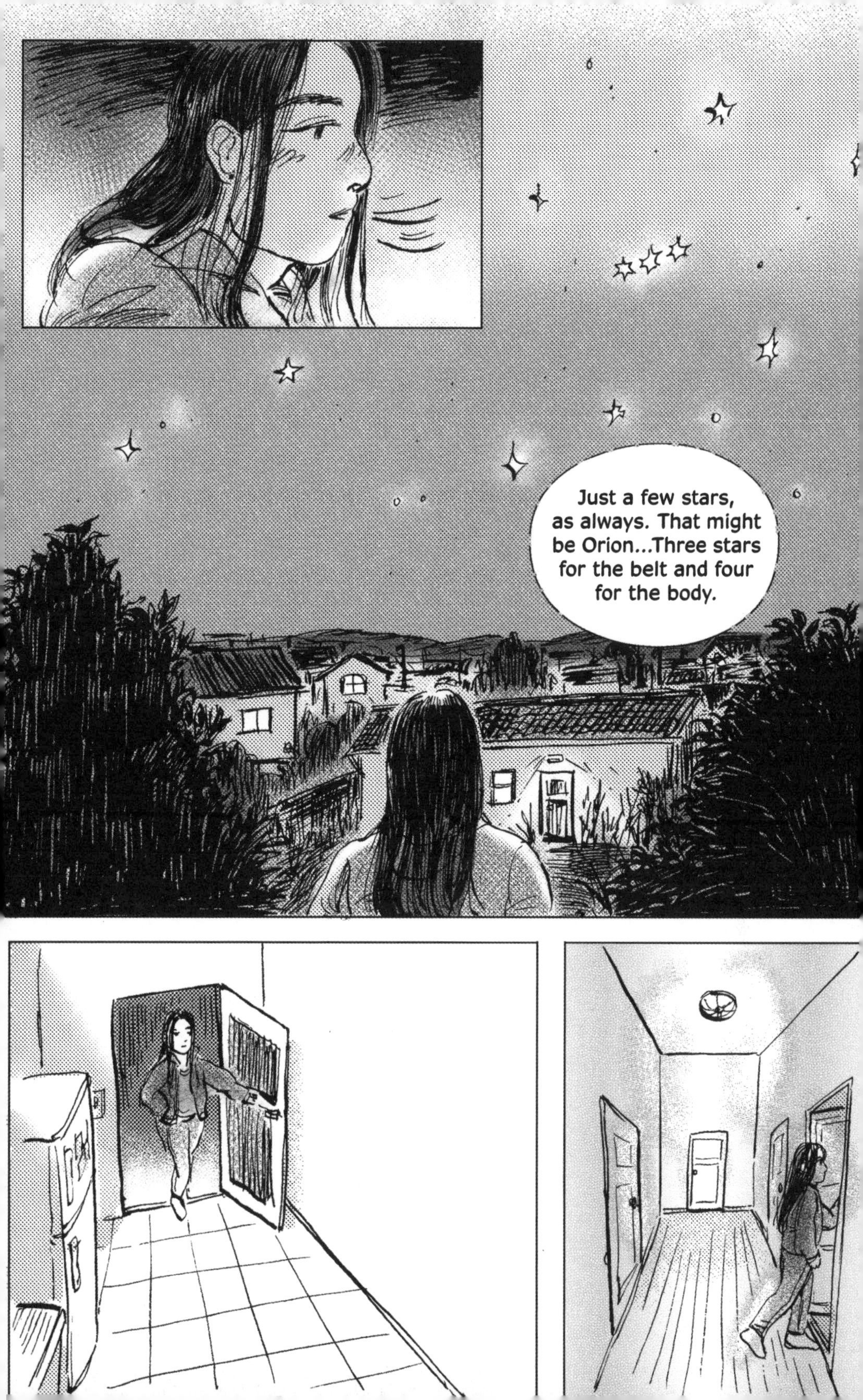
Just a few stars, as always. That might be Orion...Three stars for the belt and four for the body.

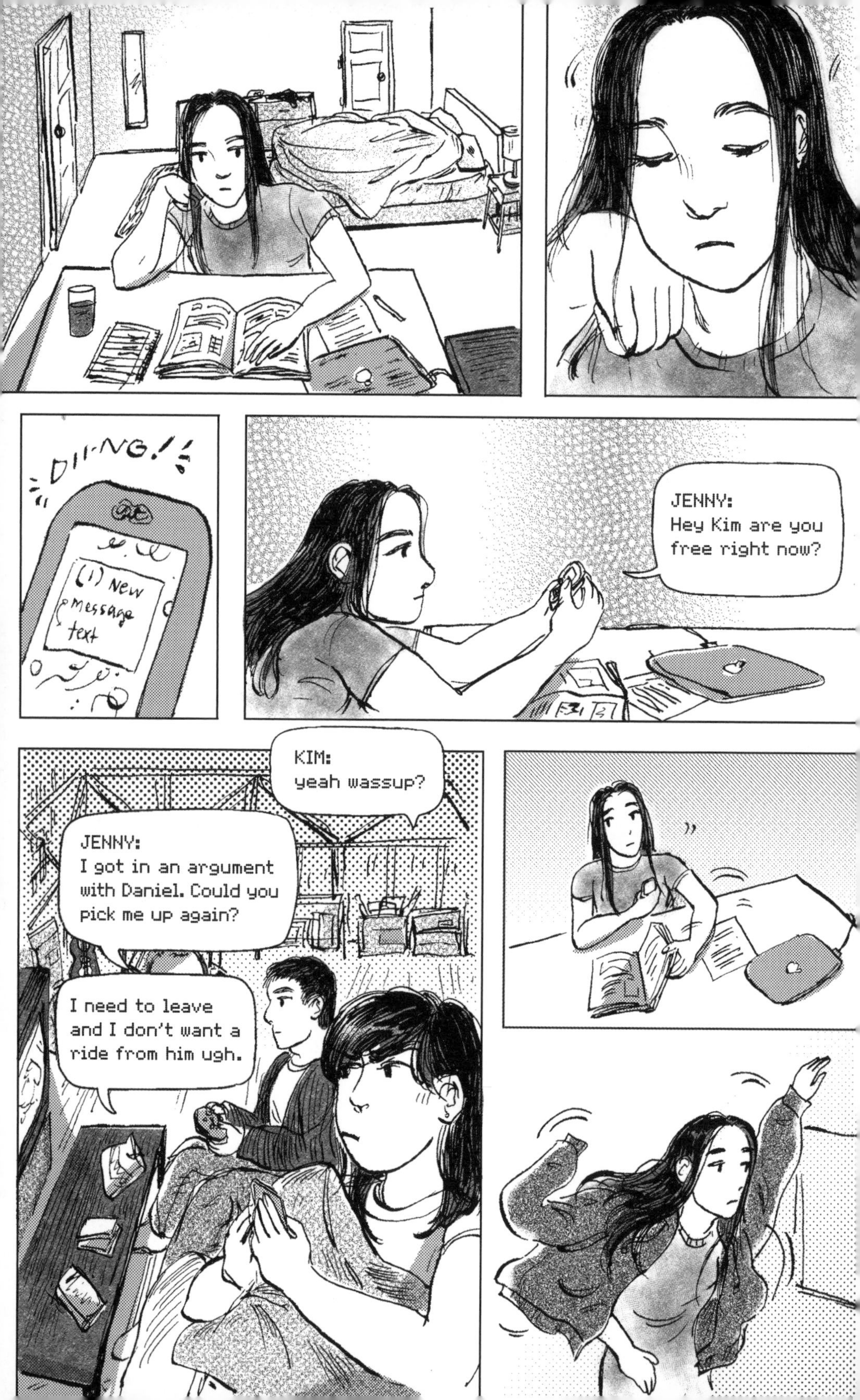
DIING!!
(1) New message text
JENNY:
Hey Kim are you free right now?
KIM:
yeah wassup?
JENNY:
I got in an argument with Daniel. Could you pick me up again?
I need to leave and I don't want a ride from him ugh.

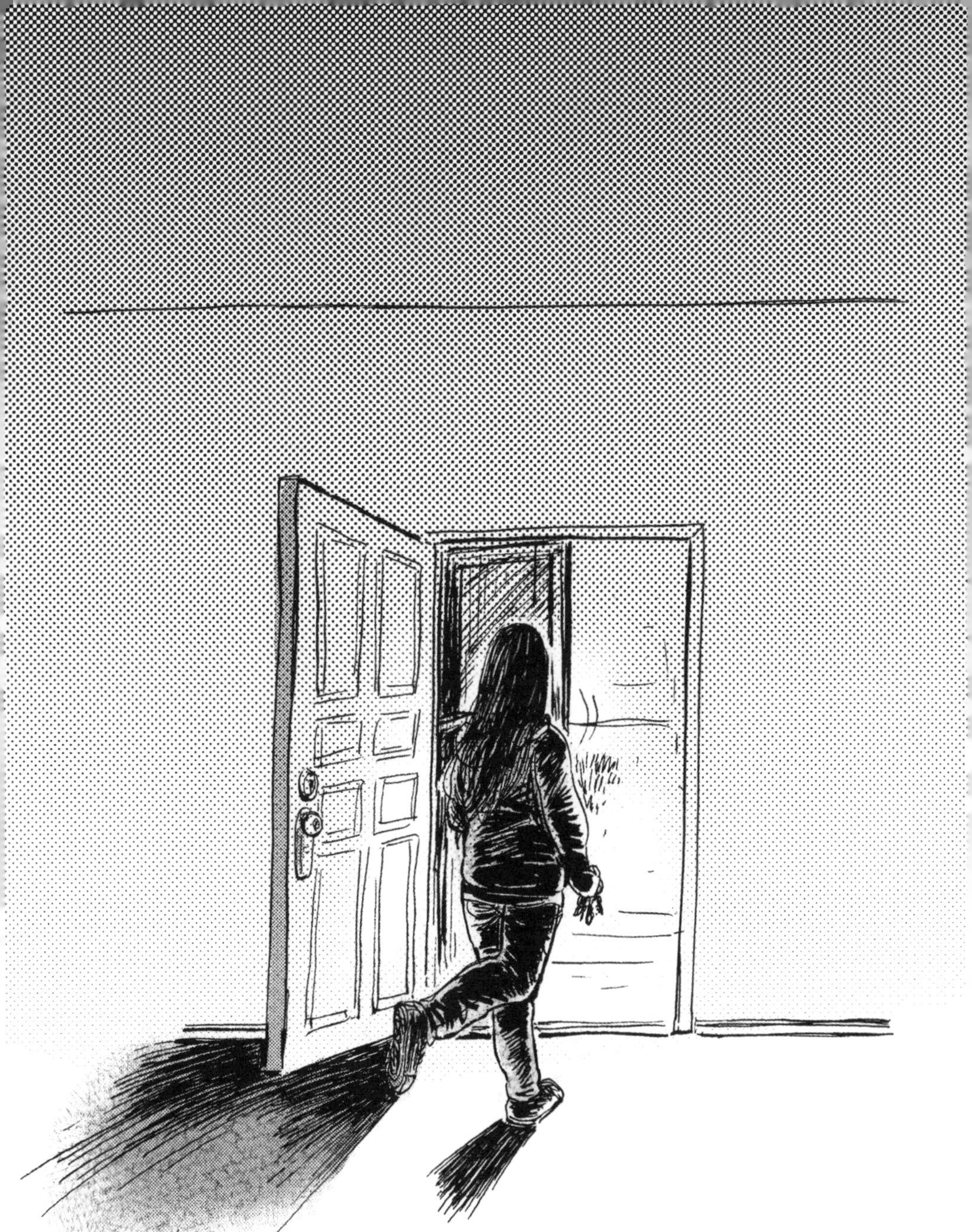

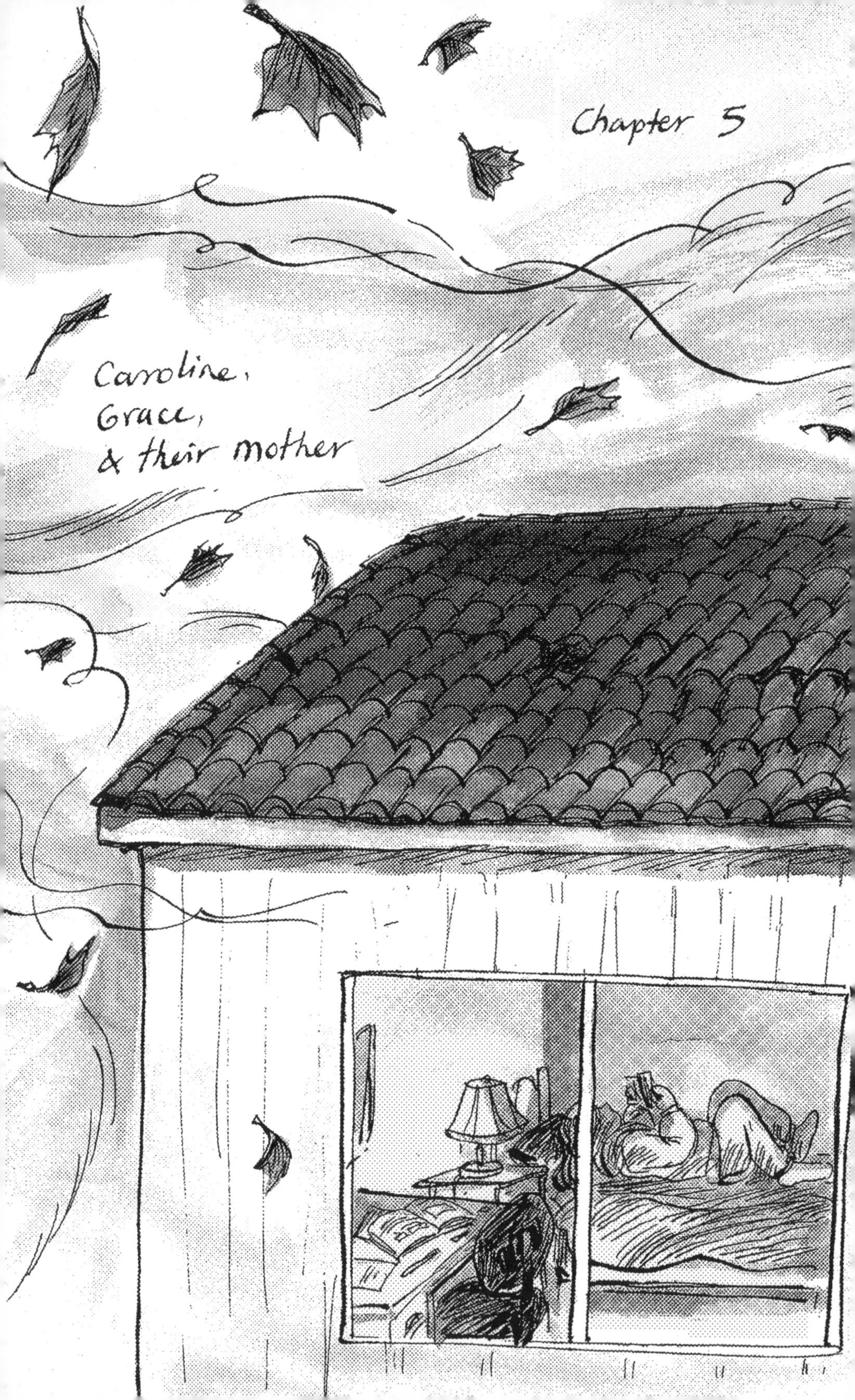
Chapter 5
Caroline,
Grace,
& their mother

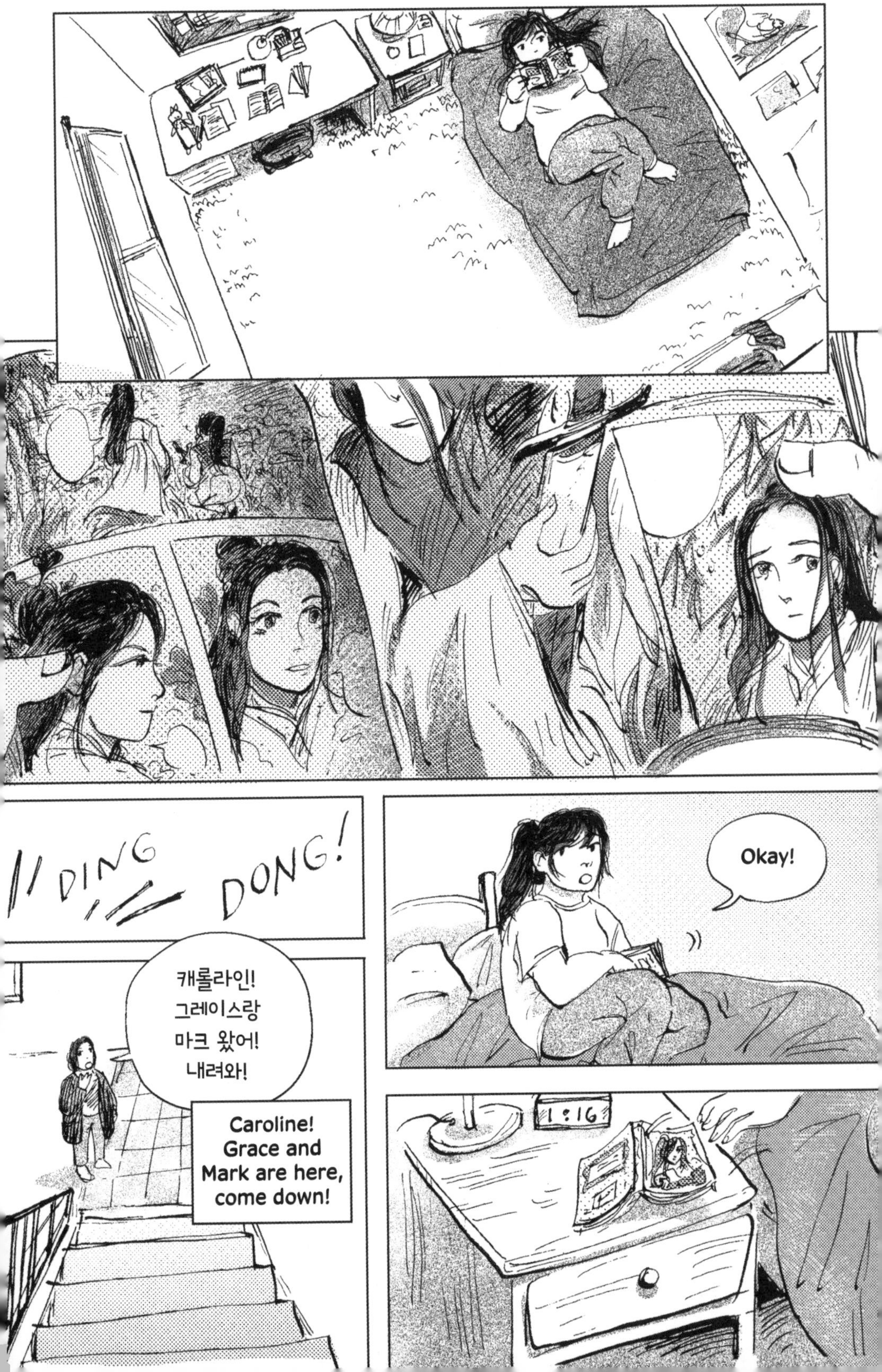
DING DONG!
캐롤라인!
그레이스랑
마크 왔어!
내려와!
Caroline!
Grace and
Mark are here,
come down!
Okay!
1:16

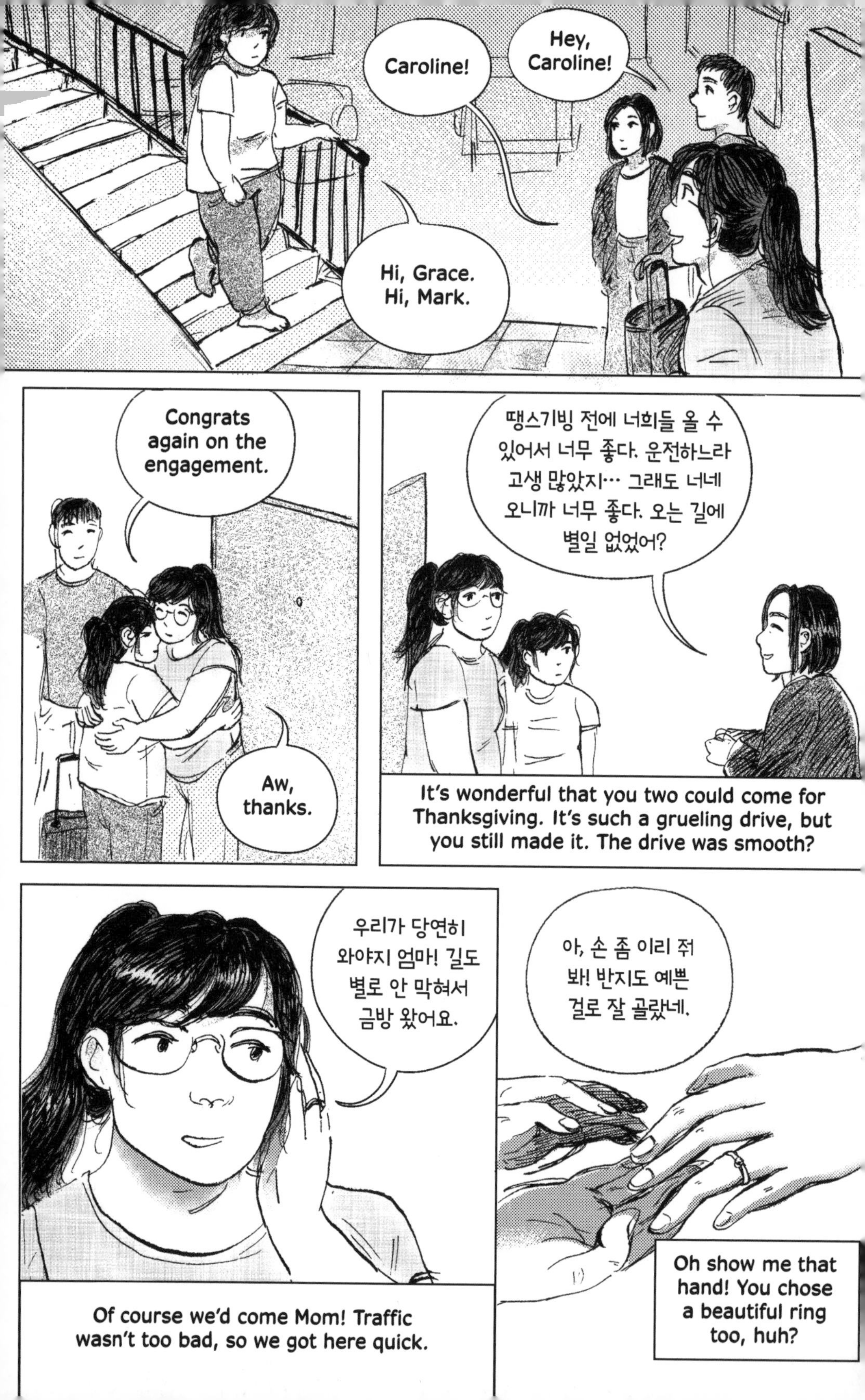
Caroline!
Hey, Caroline!
Hi, Grace. Hi, Mark.
Congrats again on the engagement.
Aw, thanks.
땡스기빙 전에 너희들 올 수 있어서 너무 좋다. 운전하느라 고생 많았지… 그래도 너네 오니까 너무 좋다. 오는 길에 별일 없었어?
It's wonderful that you two could come for Thanksgiving. It's such a grueling drive, but you still made it. The drive was smooth?
우리가 당연히 와야지 엄마! 길도 별로 안 막혀서 금방 왔어요.
Of course we'd come Mom! Traffic wasn't too bad, so we got here quick.
아, 손 좀 이리 줘 봐! 반지도 예쁜 걸로 잘 골랐네.
Oh show me that hand! You chose a beautiful ring too, huh?

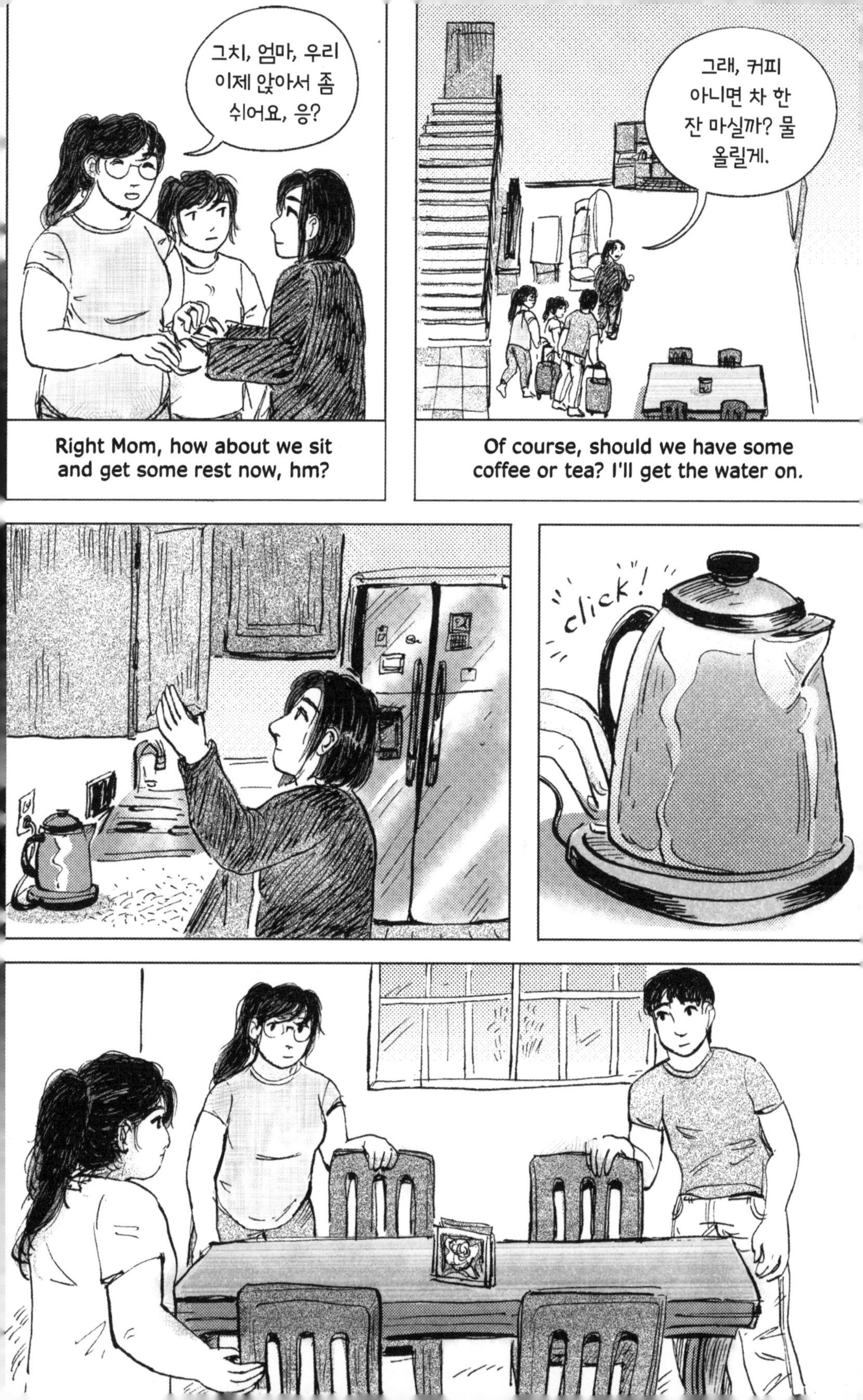
그치, 엄마, 우리 이제 앉아서 좀 쉬어요, 응?
Right Mom, how about we sit and get some rest now, hm?
그래, 커피 아니면 차 한 잔 마실까? 물 올릴게.
Of course, should we have some coffee or tea? I'll get the water on.
click!

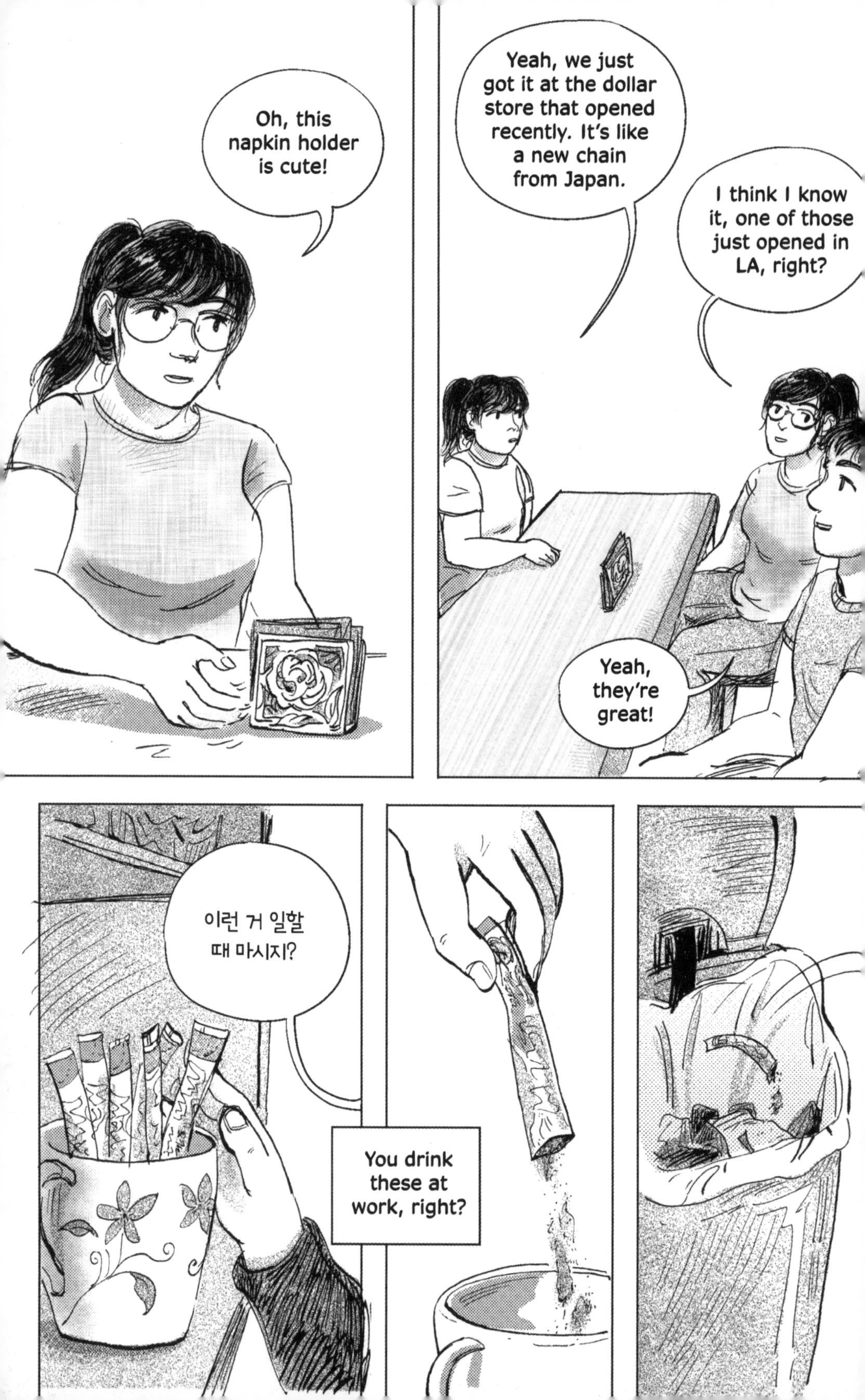
Oh, this napkin holder is cute!
Yeah, we just got it at the dollar store that opened recently. It's like a new chain from Japan.
I think I know it, one of those just opened in LA, right?
Yeah, they're great!
이런 거 일할 때 마시지?
You drink these at work, right?

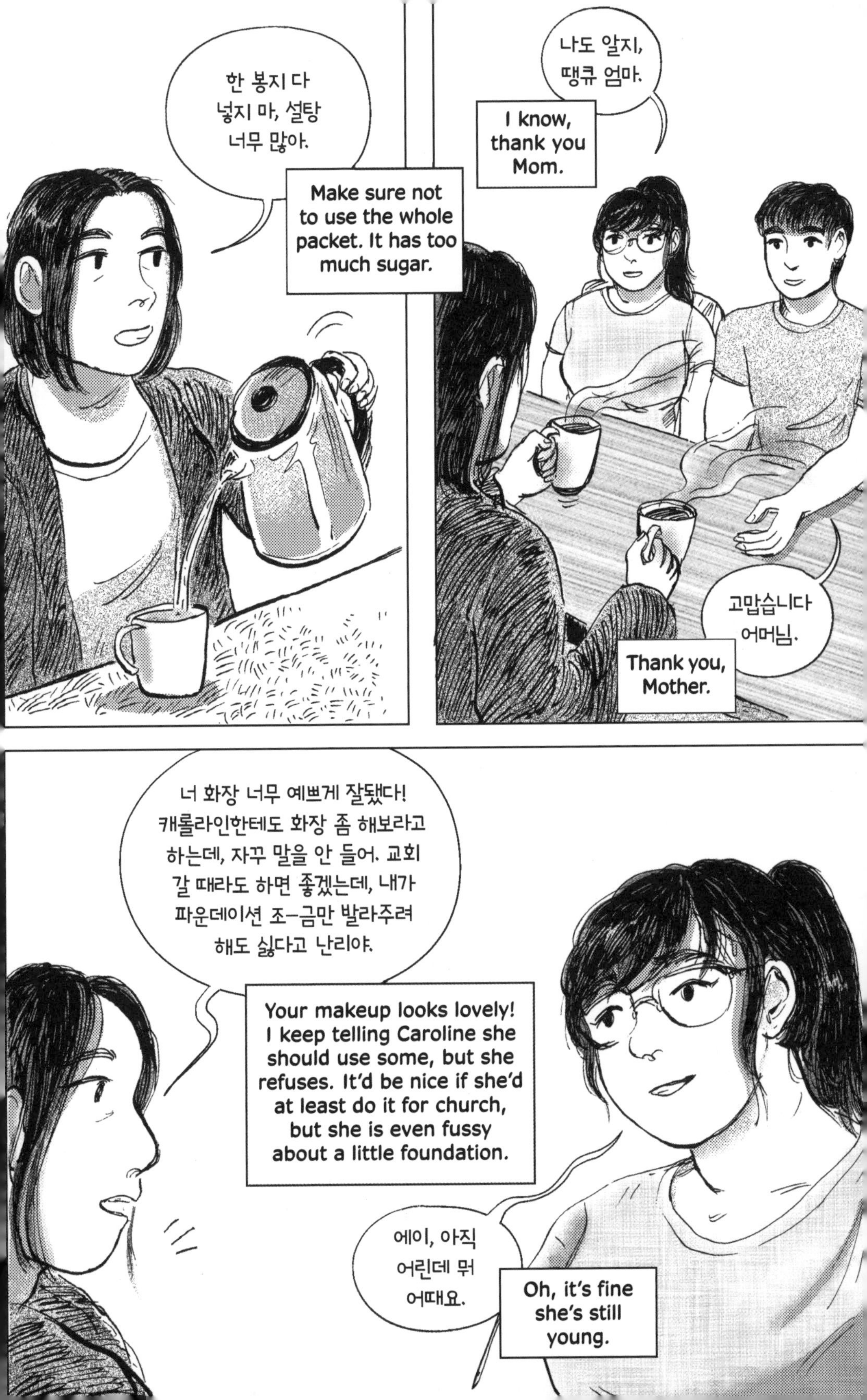

한 봉지 다 넣지 마, 설탕 너무 많아.
Make sure not to use the whole packet. It has too much sugar.
나도 알지, 땡큐 엄마.
I know, thank you Mom.
고맙습니다 어머님.
Thank you, Mother.
너 화장 너무 예쁘게 잘됐다! 캐롤라인한테도 화장 좀 해보라고 하는데, 자꾸 말을 안 들어. 교회 갈 때라도 하면 좋겠는데, 내가 파운데이션 조--금만 발라주려 해도 싫다고 난리야.
Your makeup looks lovely! I keep telling Caroline she should use some, but she refuses. It'd be nice if she'd at least do it for church, but she is even fussy about a little foundation.
에이, 아직 어린데 뭐 어때요.
Oh, it's fine she's still young.

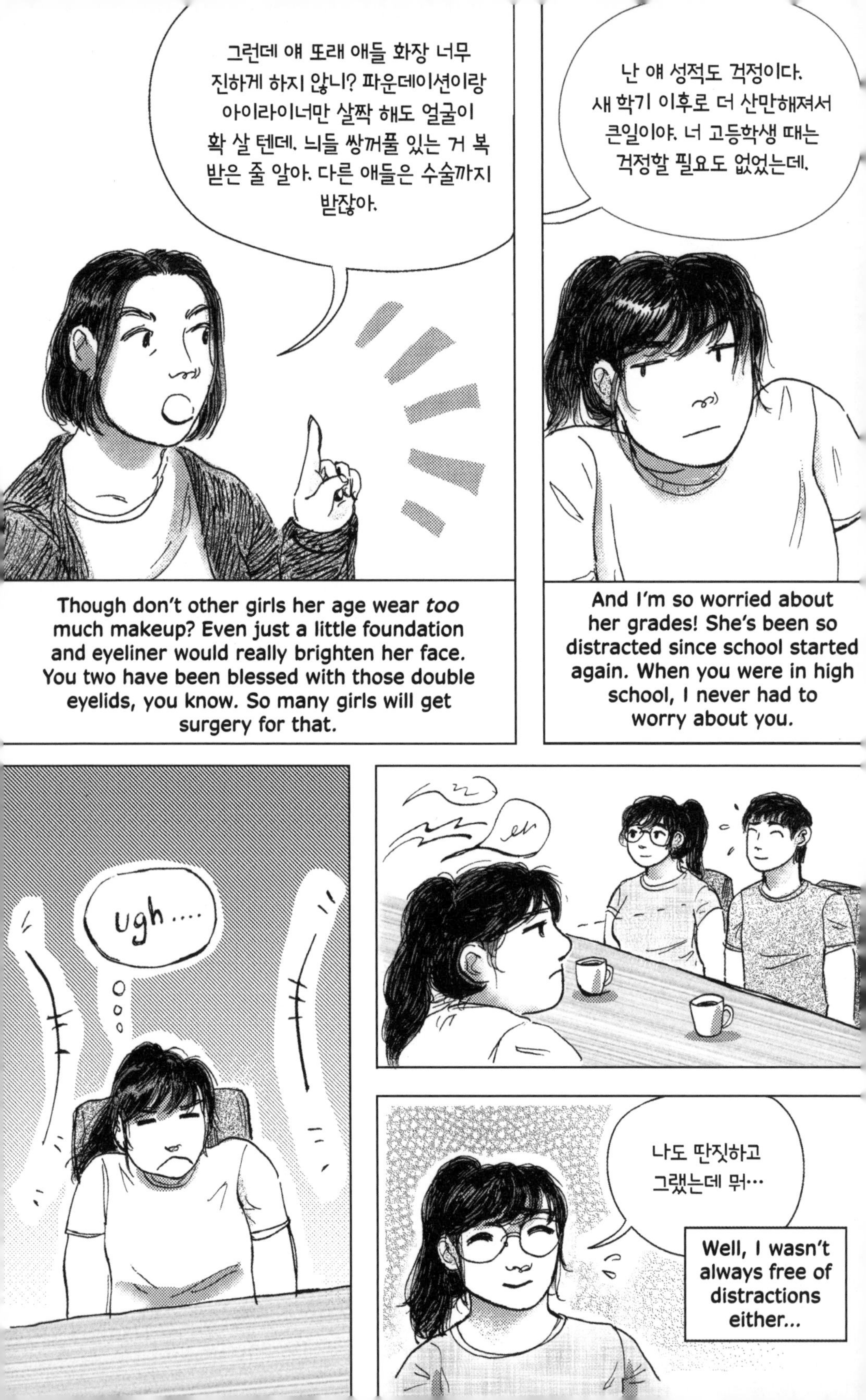
그런데 얘 또래 애들 화장 너무 진하게 하지 않니? 파운데이션이랑 아이라이너만 살짝 해도 얼굴이 확 살 텐데. 늬들 쌍꺼풀 있는 거 복 받은 줄 알아. 다른 애들은 수술까지 받잖아.
Though don't other girls her age wear *too* much makeup? Even just a little foundation and eyeliner would really brighten her face. You two have been blessed with those double eyelids, you know. So many girls will get surgery for that.
난 얘 성적도 걱정이다. 새 학기 이후로 더 산만해져서 큰일이야. 너 고등학생 때는 걱정할 필요도 없었는데.
And I'm so worried about her grades! She's been so distracted since school started again. When you were in high school, I never had to worry about you.
ugh....
나도 딴짓하고 그랬는데 뭐…
Well, I wasn't always free of distractions either...

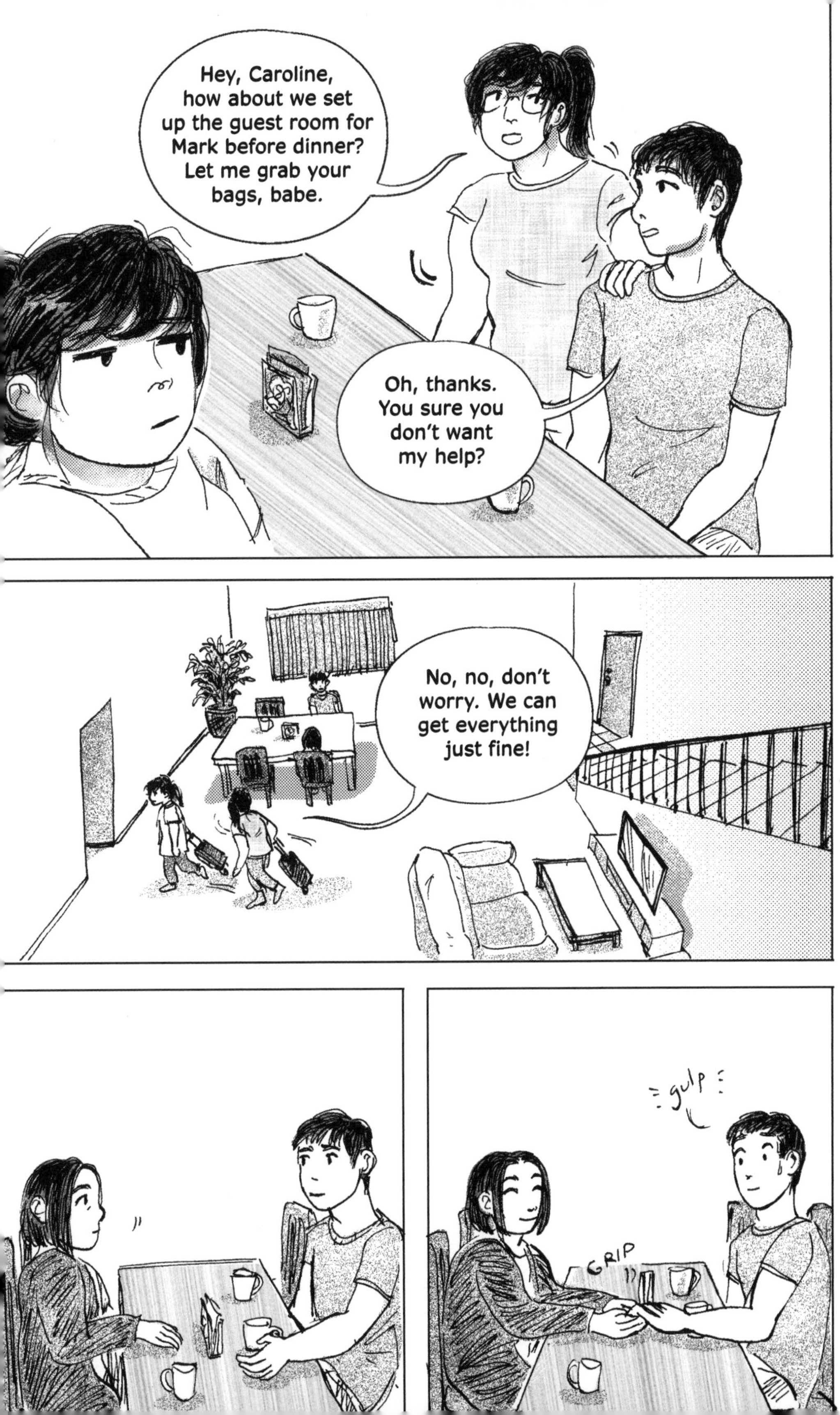
Hey, Caroline, how about we set up the guest room for Mark before dinner? Let me grab your bags, babe.
Oh, thanks. You sure you don't want my help?
No, no, don't worry. We can get everything just fine!
GRIP
gulp

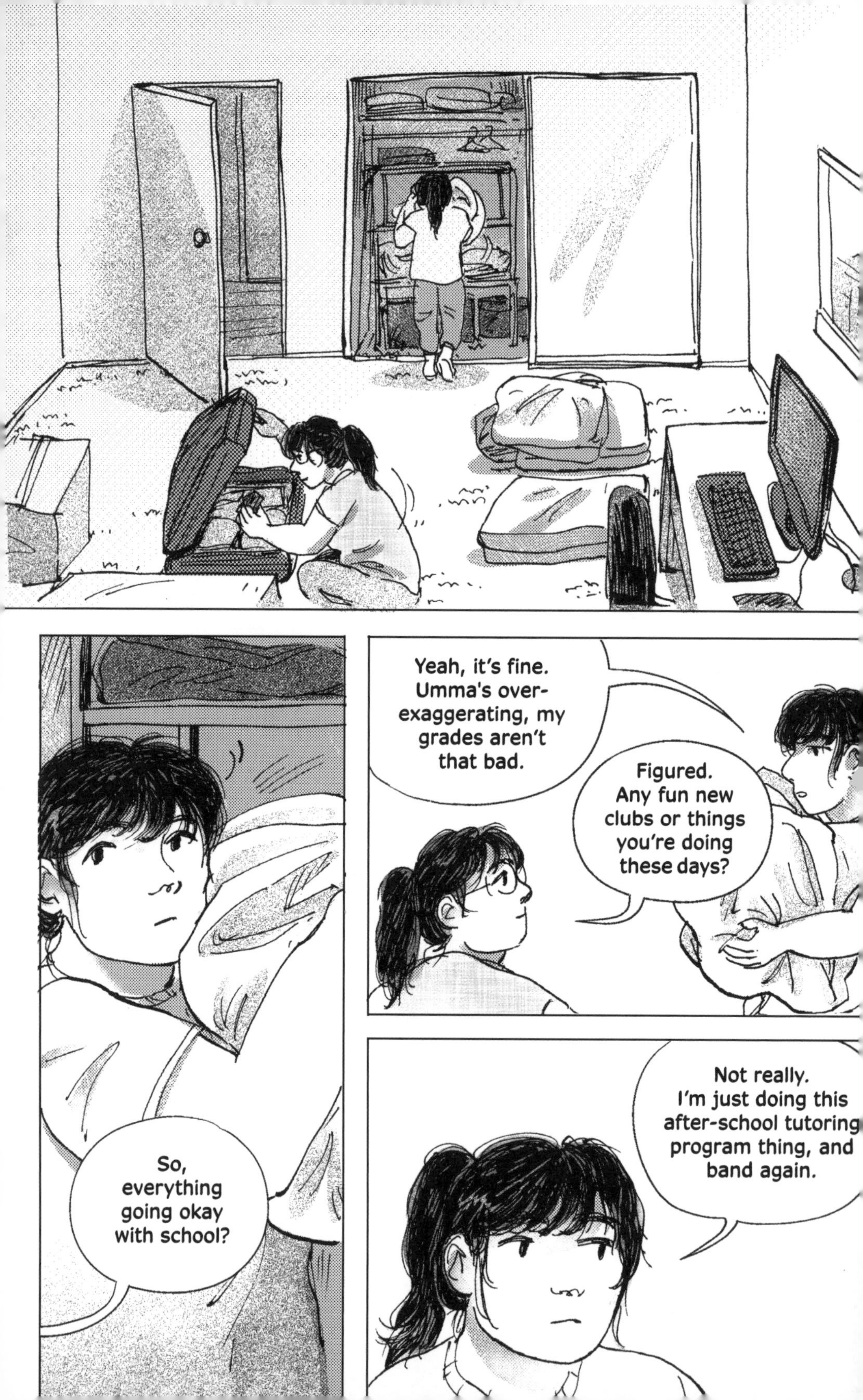
So, everything going okay with school?
Yeah, it's fine. Umma's over-exaggerating, my grades aren't that bad.
Figured. Any fun new clubs or things you're doing these days?
Not really. I'm just doing this after-school tutoring program thing, and band again.

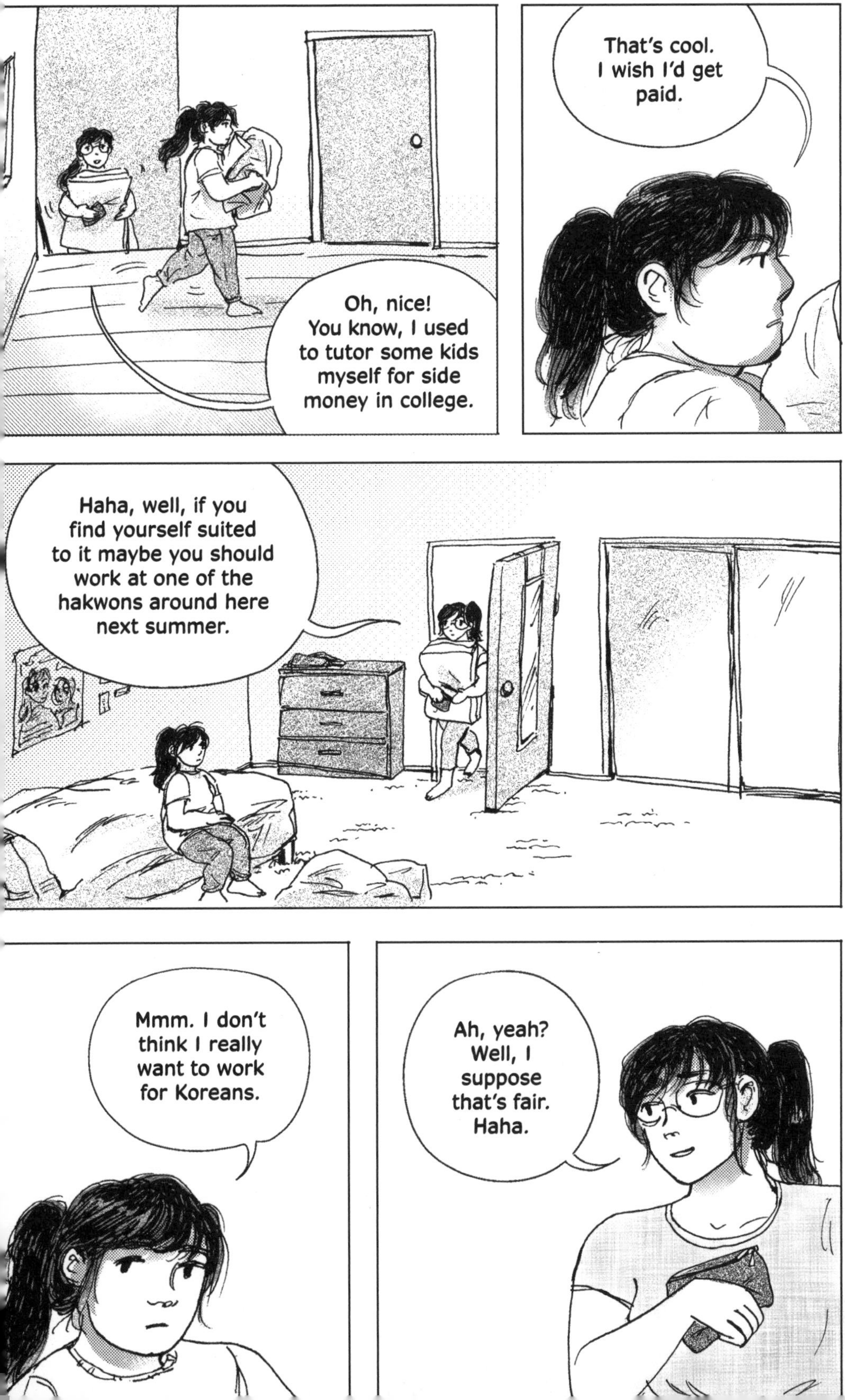
Oh, nice!
You know, I used to tutor some kids myself for side money in college.
That's cool. I wish I'd get paid.
Haha, well, if you find yourself suited to it maybe you should work at one of the hakwons around here next summer.
Mmm. I don't think I really want to work for Koreans.
Ah, yeah? Well, I suppose that's fair. Haha.

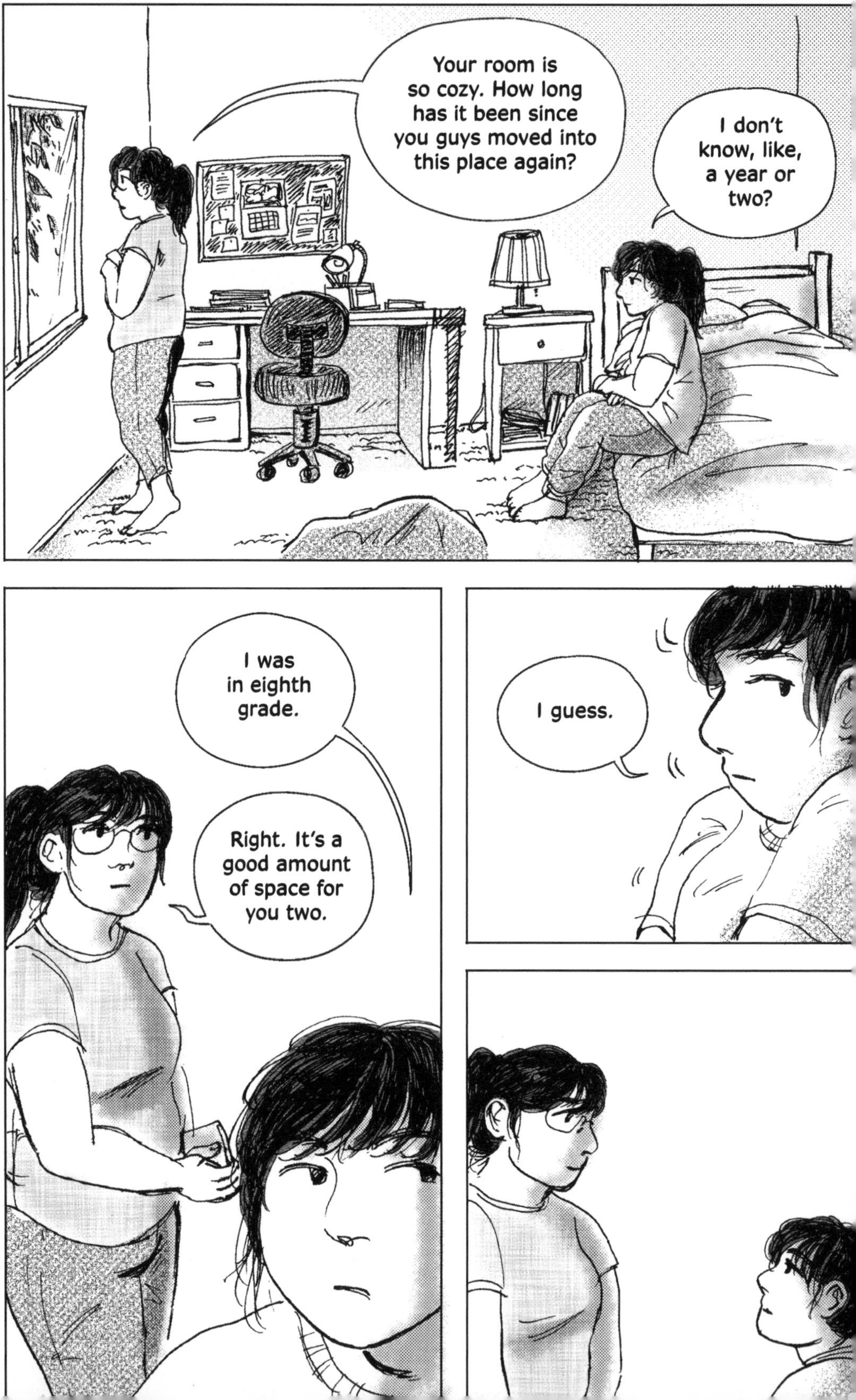
Your room is so cozy. How long has it been since you guys moved into this place again?
I don't know, like, a year or two?
I was in eighth grade.
Right. It's a good amount of space for you two.
I guess.

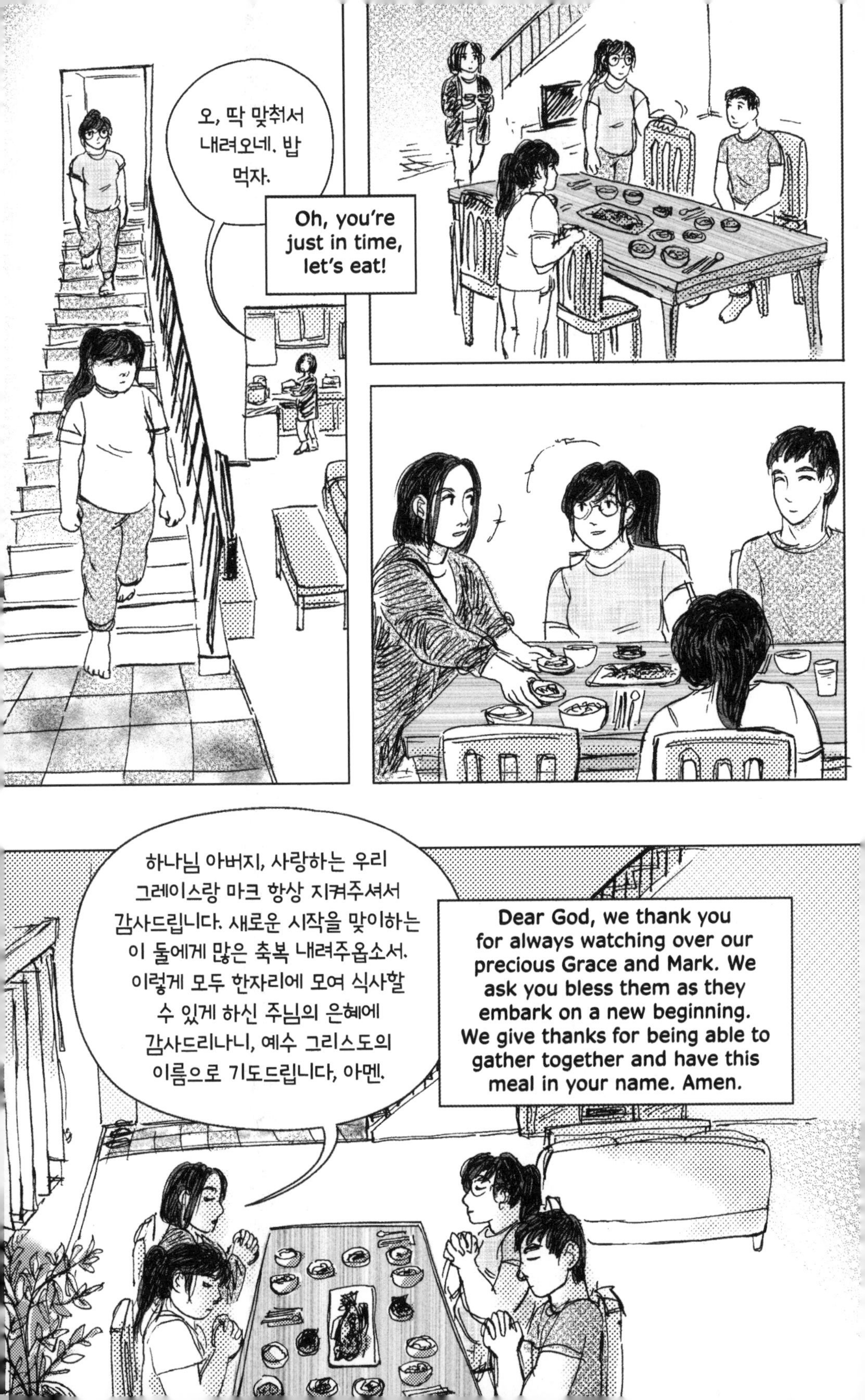
오, 딱 맞춰서 내려오네. 밥 먹자.
Oh, you're just in time, let's eat!
하나님 아버지, 사랑하는 우리 그레이스랑 마크 항상 지켜주셔서 감사드립니다. 새로운 시작을 맞이하는 이 둘에게 많은 축복 내려주옵소서. 이렇게 모두 한자리에 모여 식사할 수 있게 하신 주님의 은혜에 감사드리나니, 예수 그리스도의 이름으로 기도드립니다, 아멘.
Dear God, we thank you for always watching over our precious Grace and Mark. We ask you bless them as they embark on a new beginning. We give thanks for being able to gather together and have this meal in your name. Amen.

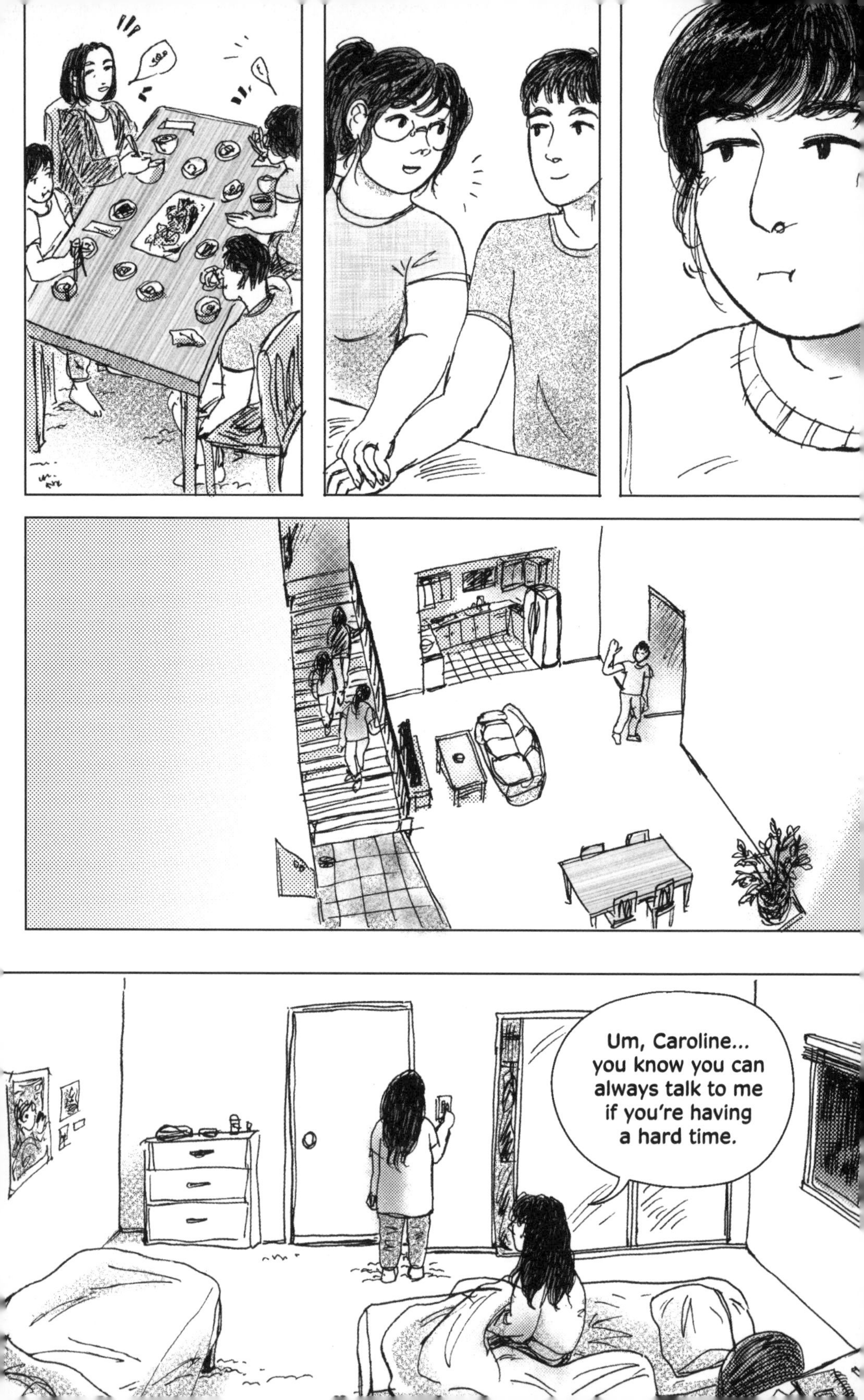
Um, Caroline...
you know you can
always talk to me
if you're having
a hard time.

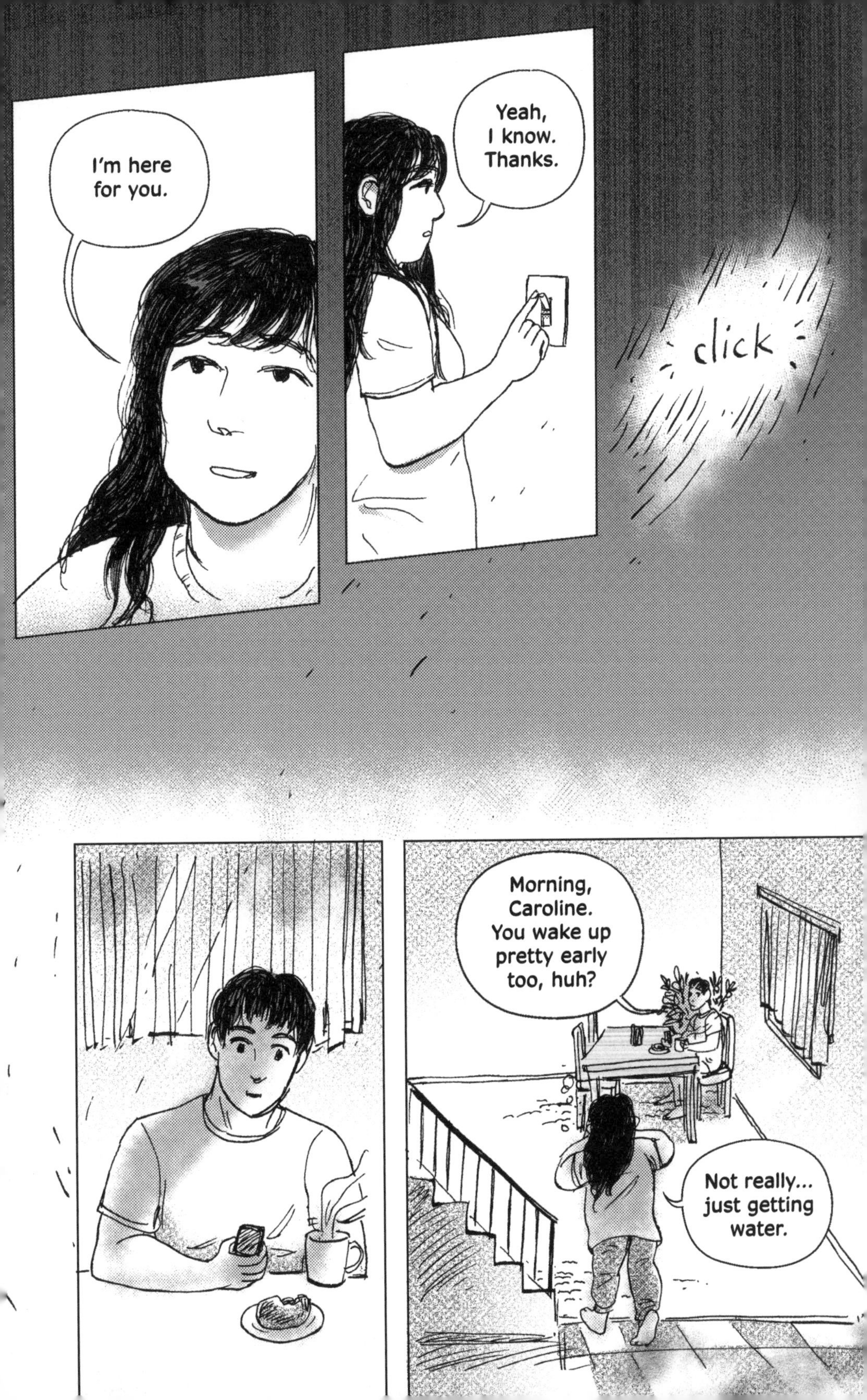
I'm here for you.
Yeah, I know. Thanks.
click
Morning, Caroline. You wake up pretty early too, huh?
Not really... just getting water.

Is Grace awake yet?

Nah.

Oh good, I'm glad one of us can sleep in after the long drive, haha.

Mhm.

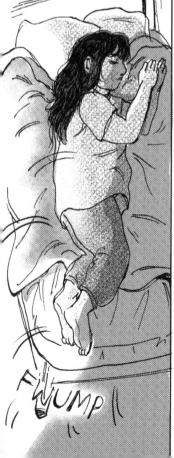

FWUMP

Caroline!

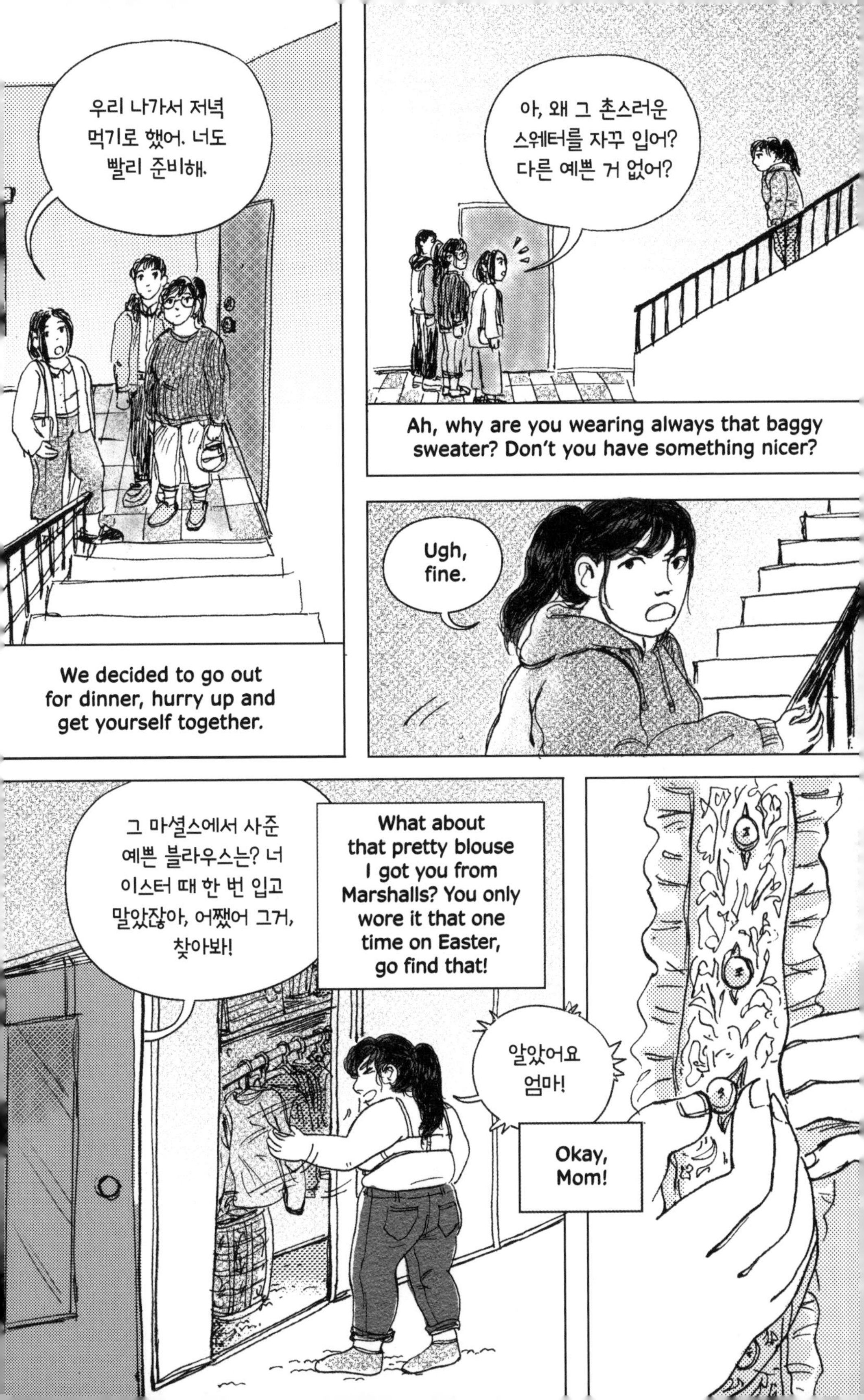
우리 나가서 저녁 먹기로 했어. 너도 빨리 준비해.
We decided to go out for dinner, hurry up and get yourself together.
아, 왜 그 촌스러운 스웨터를 자꾸 입어? 다른 예쁜 거 없어?
Ah, why are you wearing always that baggy sweater? Don't you have something nicer?
Ugh, fine.
그 마셜스에서 사준 예쁜 블라우스는? 너 이스터 때 한 번 입고 말았잖아, 어쨌어 그거, 찾아봐!
What about that pretty blouse I got you from Marshalls? You only wore it that one time on Easter, go find that!
알았어요 엄마!
Okay, Mom!

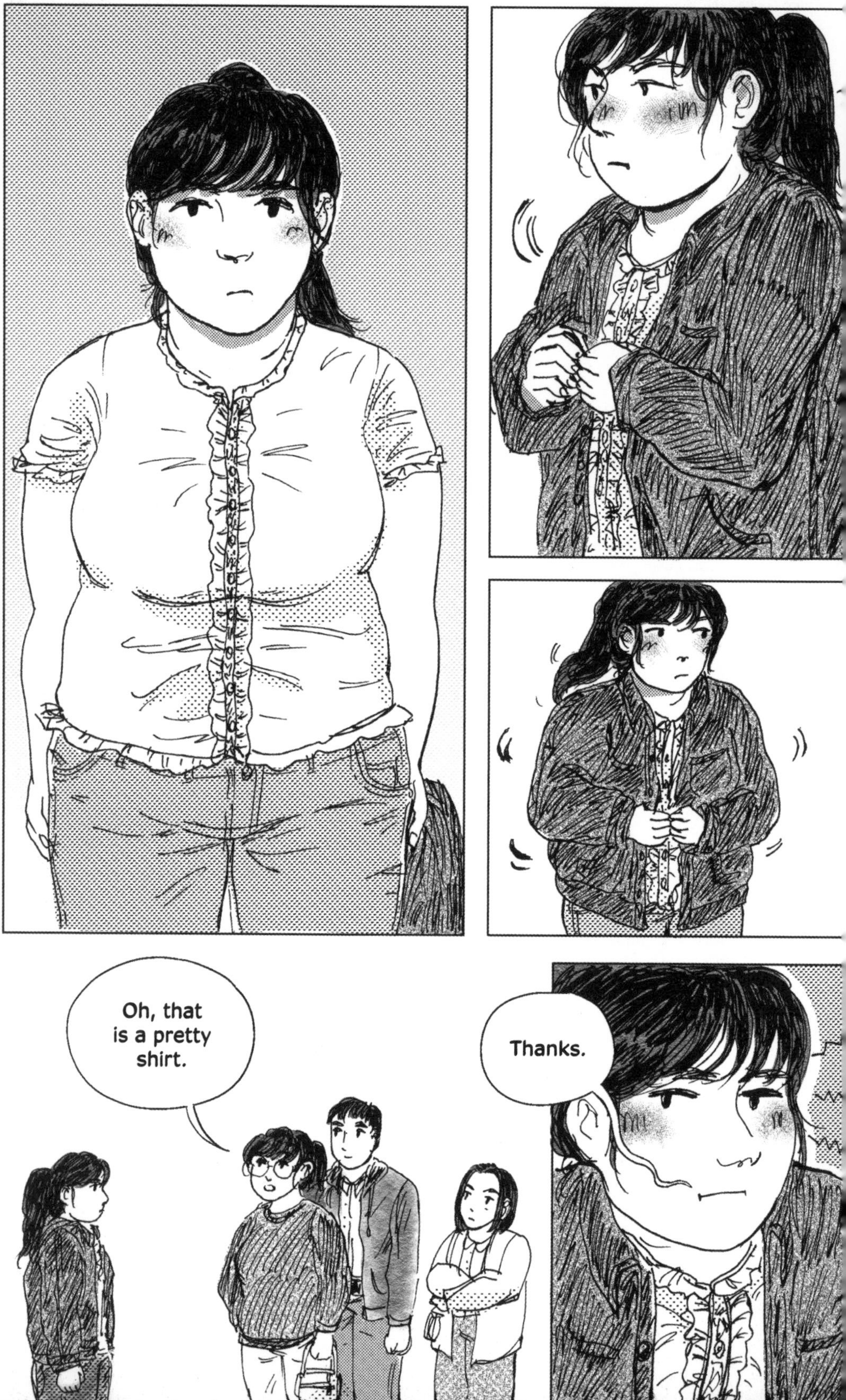
Oh, that is a pretty shirt.
Thanks.

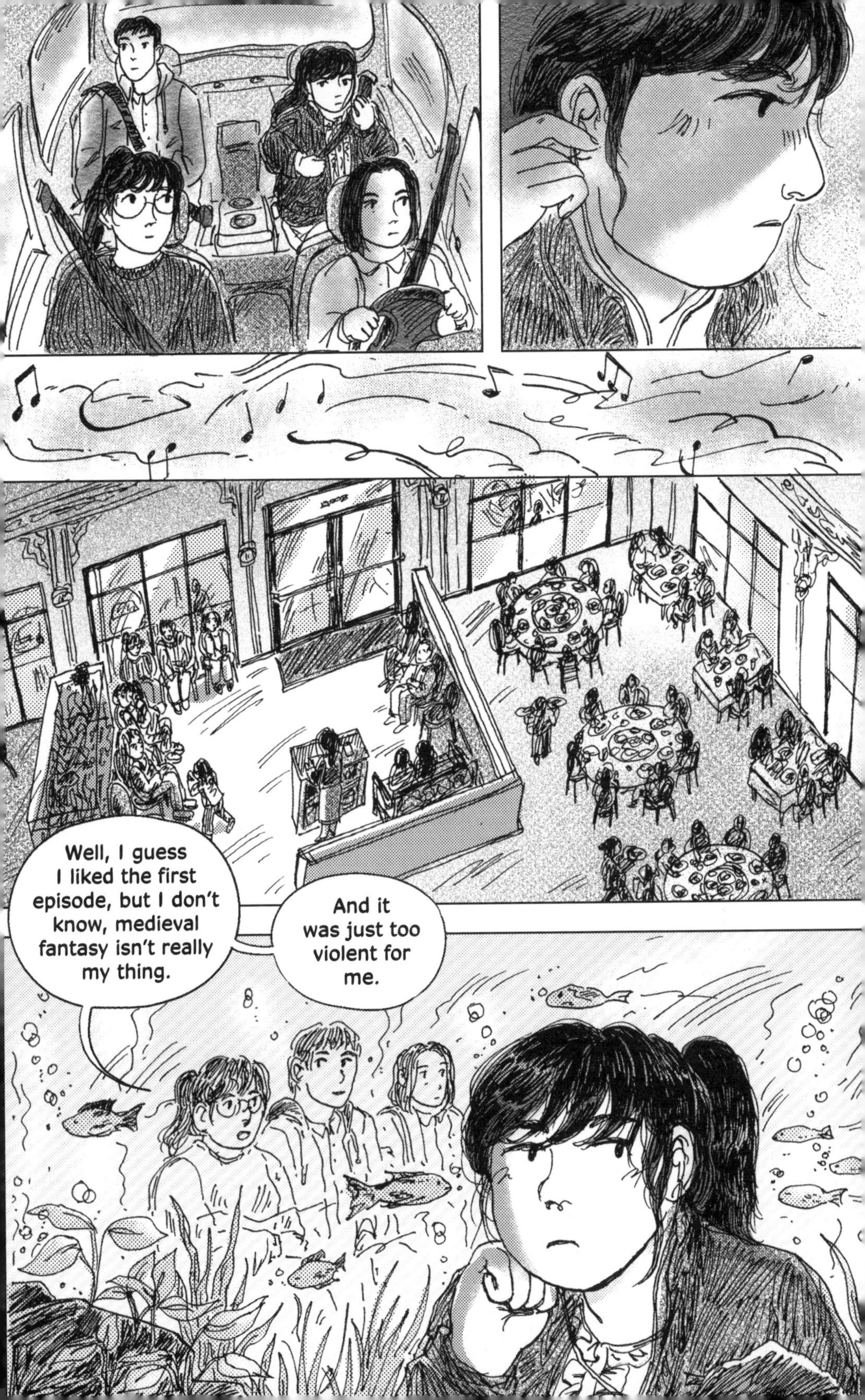
Well, I guess I liked the first episode, but I don't know, medieval fantasy isn't really my thing.
And it was just too violent for me.

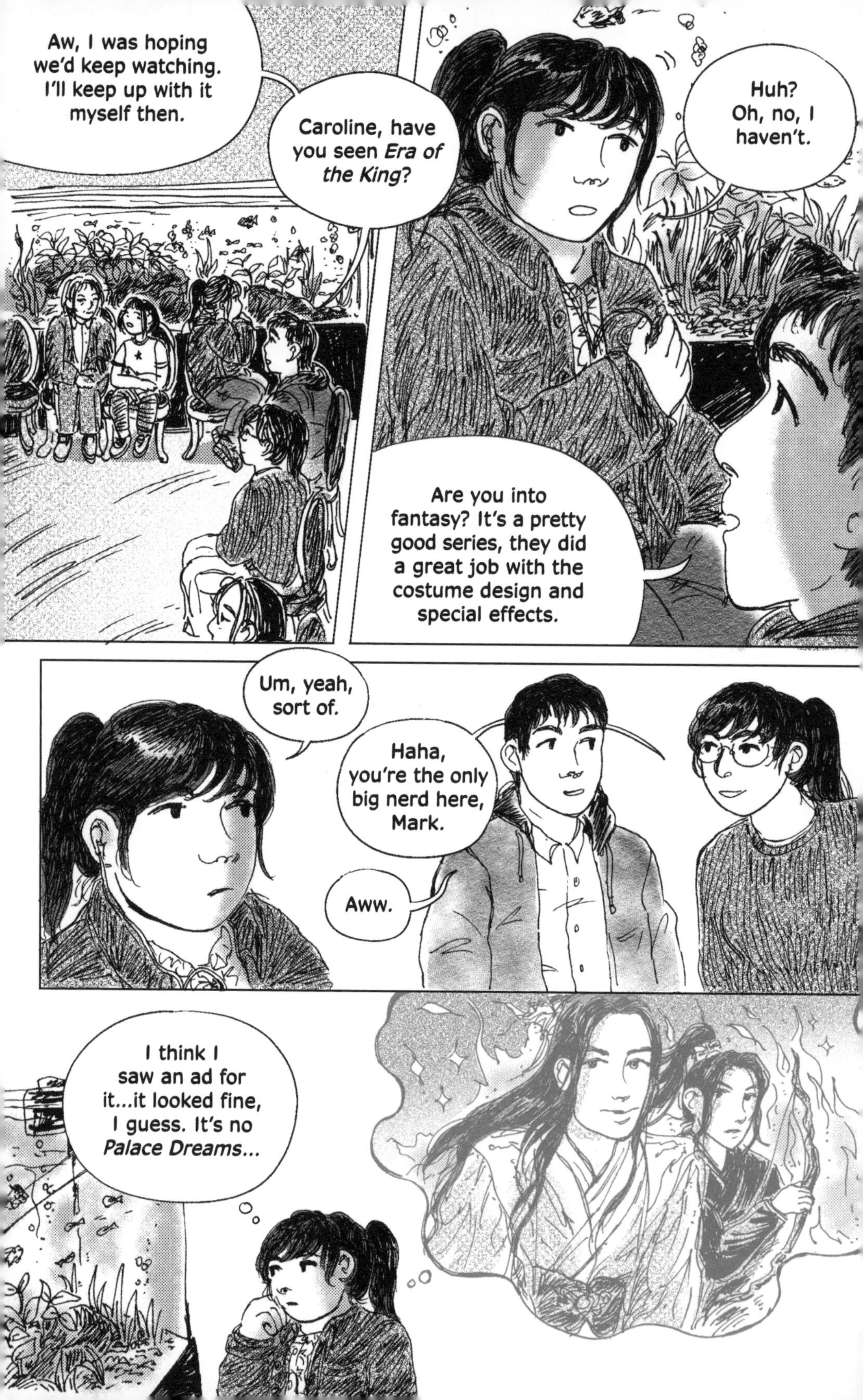
Aw, I was hoping we'd keep watching. I'll keep up with it myself then.
Caroline, have you seen *Era of the King*?
Huh? Oh, no, I haven't.
Are you into fantasy? It's a pretty good series, they did a great job with the costume design and special effects.
Um, yeah, sort of.
Haha, you're the only big nerd here, Mark.
Aww.
I think I saw an ad for it...it looked fine, I guess. It's no *Palace Dreams*...

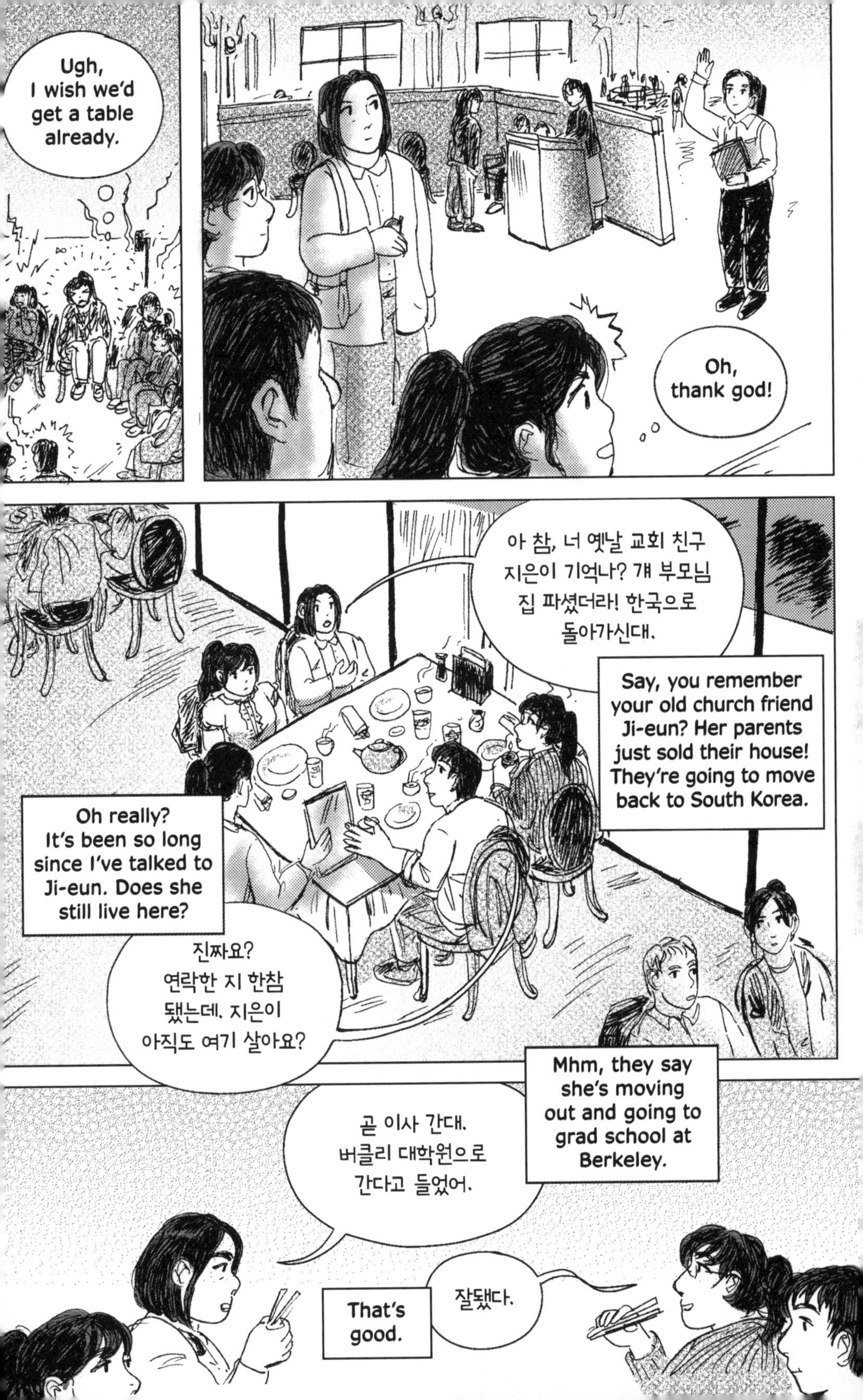
Ugh, I wish we'd get a table already.
Oh, thank god!
아 참, 너 옛날 교회 친구 지은이 기억나? 걔 부모님 집 파셨더라! 한국으로 돌아가신대.
Say, you remember your old church friend Ji-eun? Her parents just sold their house! They're going to move back to South Korea.
Oh really? It's been so long since I've talked to Ji-eun. Does she still live here?
진짜요? 연락한 지 한참 됐는데. 지은이 아직도 여기 살아요?
곧 이사 간대. 버클리 대학원으로 간다고 들었어.
Mhm, they say she's moving out and going to grad school at Berkeley.
잘됐다.
That's good.

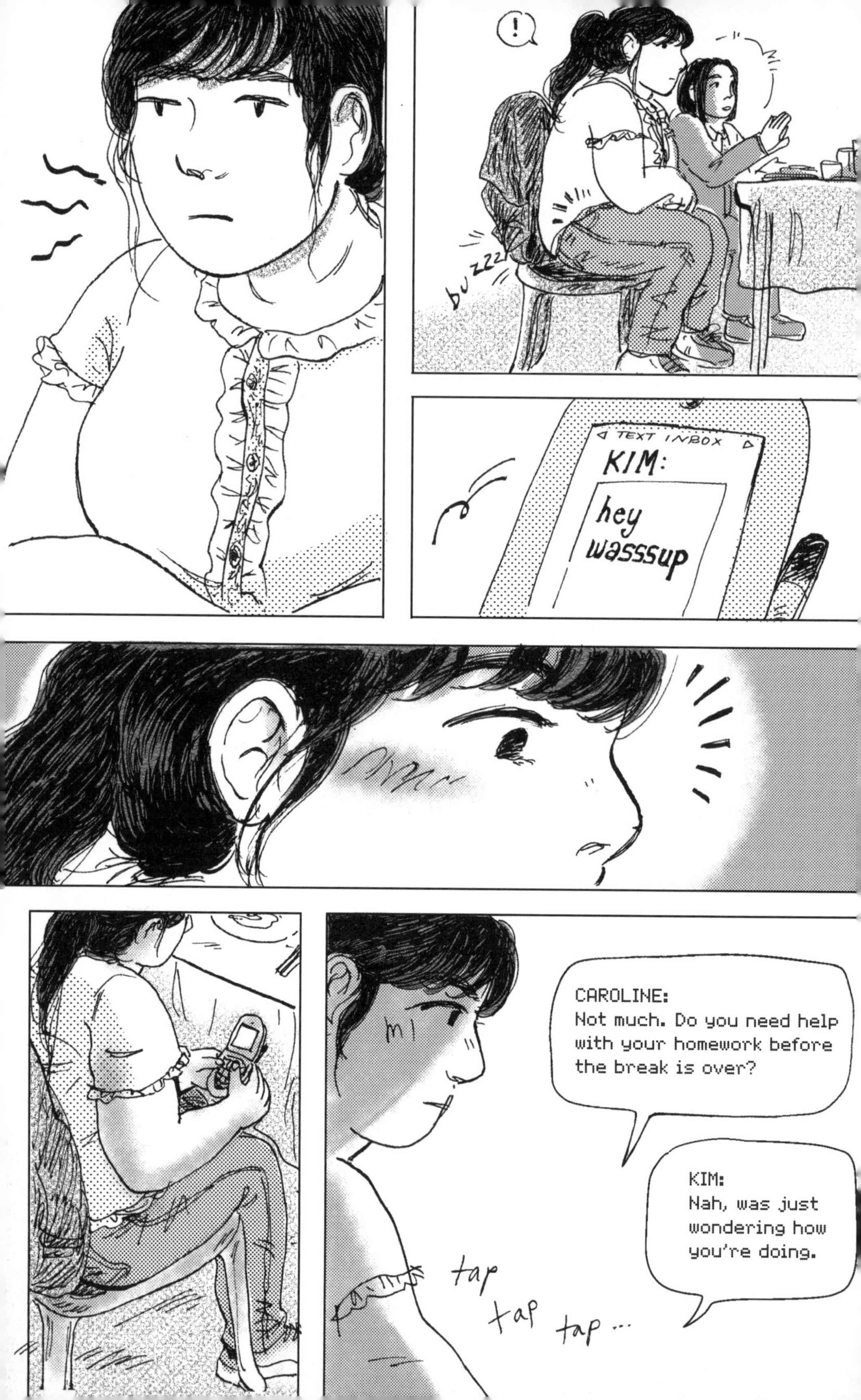
!
buzzz
TEXT INBOX
KIM:
hey wasssup
CAROLINE:
Not much. Do you need help with your homework before the break is over?
KIM:
Nah, was just wondering how you're doing.
tap tap tap ...

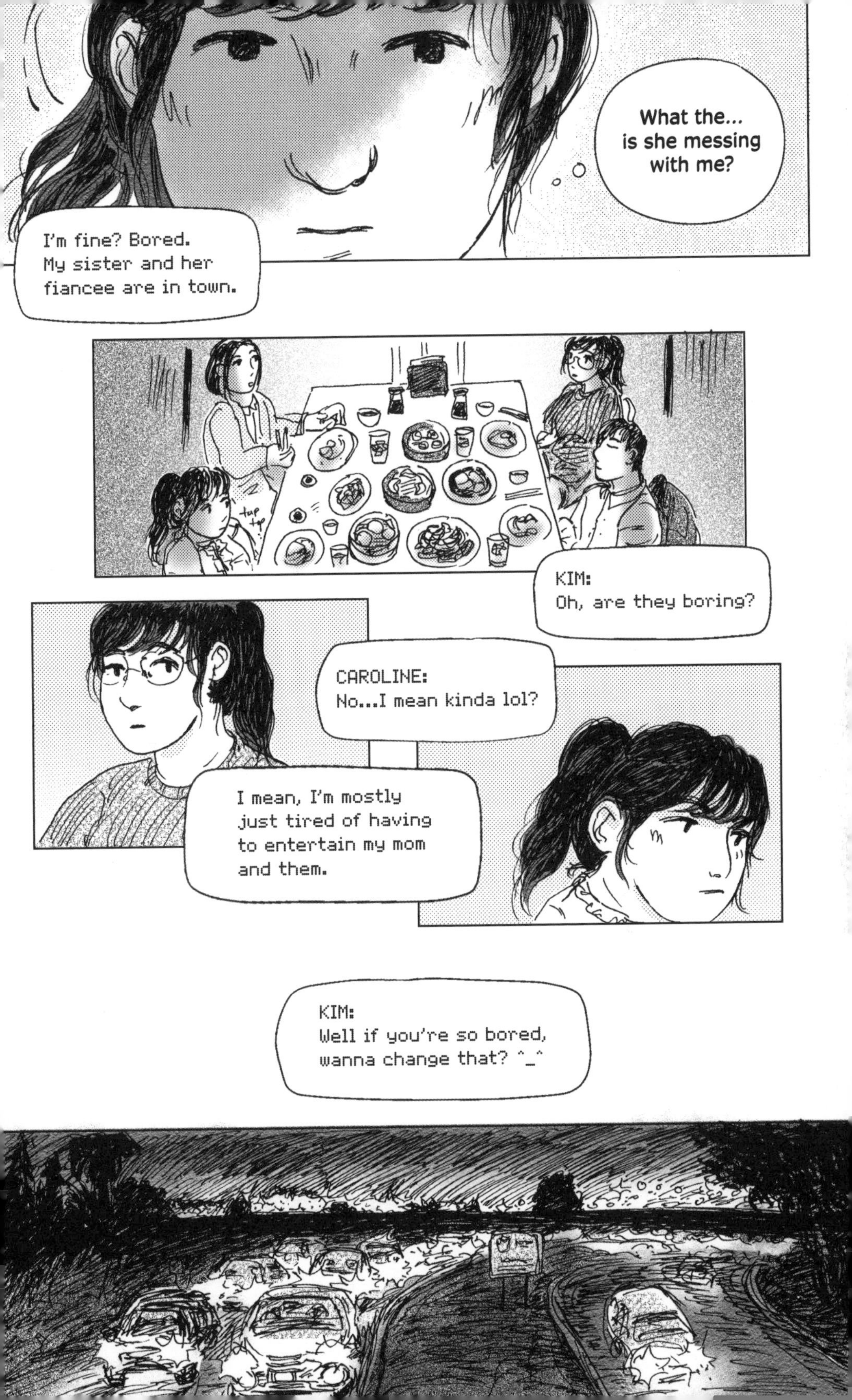
What the... is she messing with me?
I'm fine? Bored. My sister and her fiancee are in town.
tap tap
KIM: Oh, are they boring?
CAROLINE: No...I mean kinda lol?
I mean, I'm mostly just tired of having to entertain my mom and them.
KIM: Well if you're so bored, wanna change that? ^_^

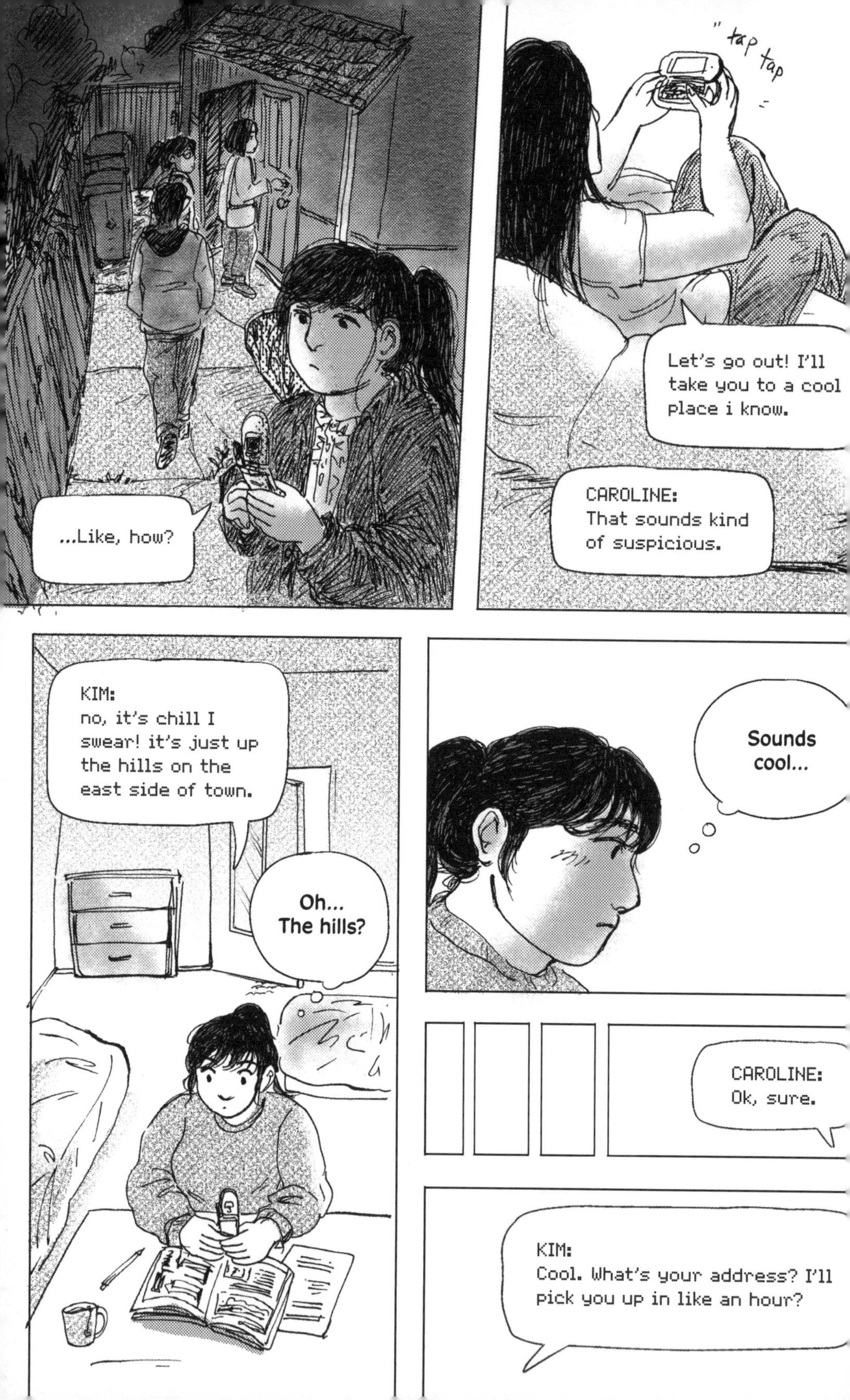
...Like, how?
tap tap
Let's go out! I'll take you to a cool place i know.
CAROLINE:
That sounds kind of suspicious.
KIM:
no, it's chill I swear! it's just up the hills on the east side of town.
Oh... The hills?
Sounds cool...
CAROLINE:
Ok, sure.
KIM:
Cool. What's your address? I'll pick you up in like an hour?

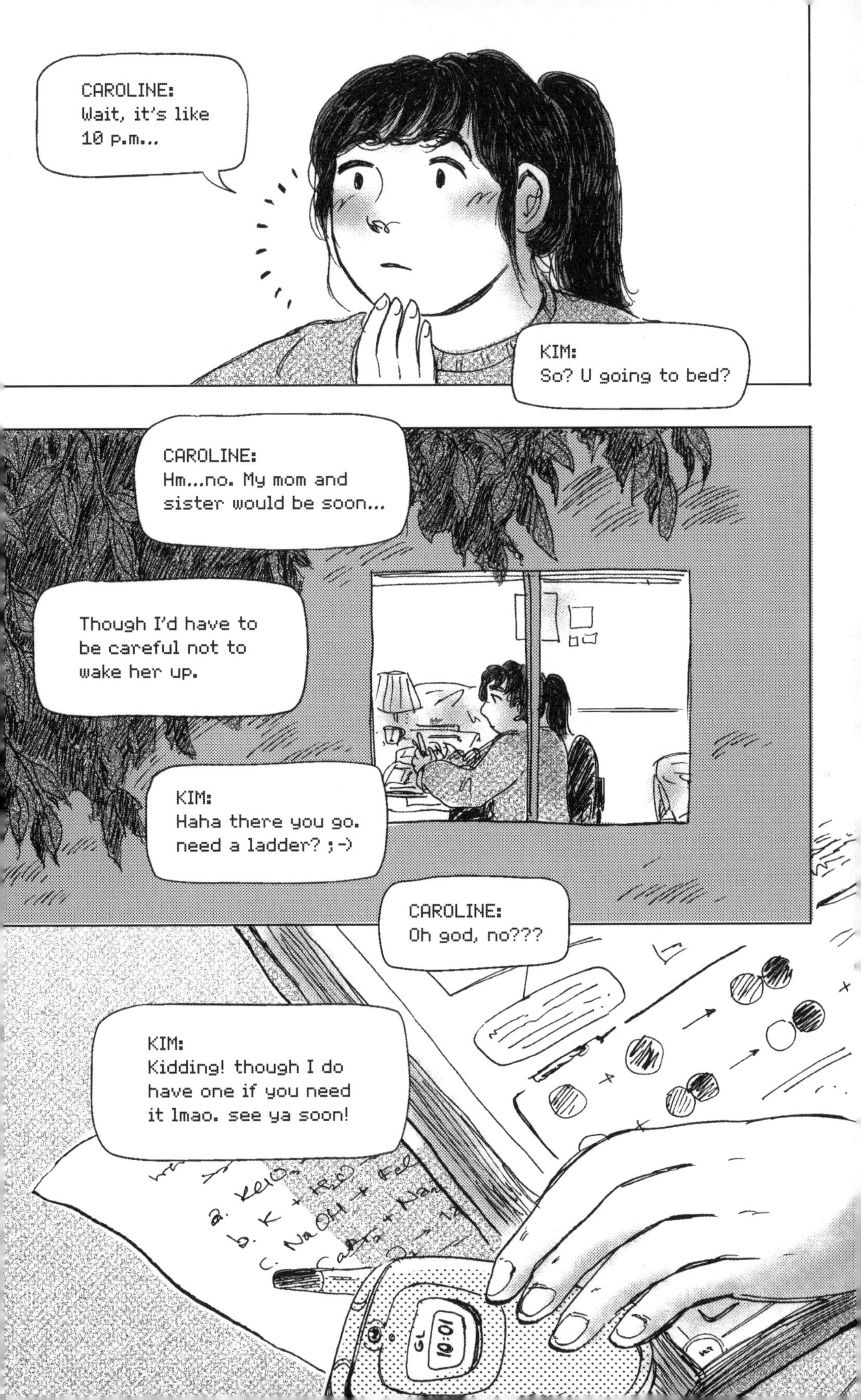
CAROLINE: Wait, it's like 10 p.m...
KIM: So? U going to bed?
CAROLINE: Hm...no. My mom and sister would be soon...
Though I'd have to be careful not to wake her up.
KIM: Haha there you go. need a ladder? ;-)
CAROLINE: Oh god, no???
KIM: Kidding! though I do have one if you need it lmao. see ya soon!
10:01

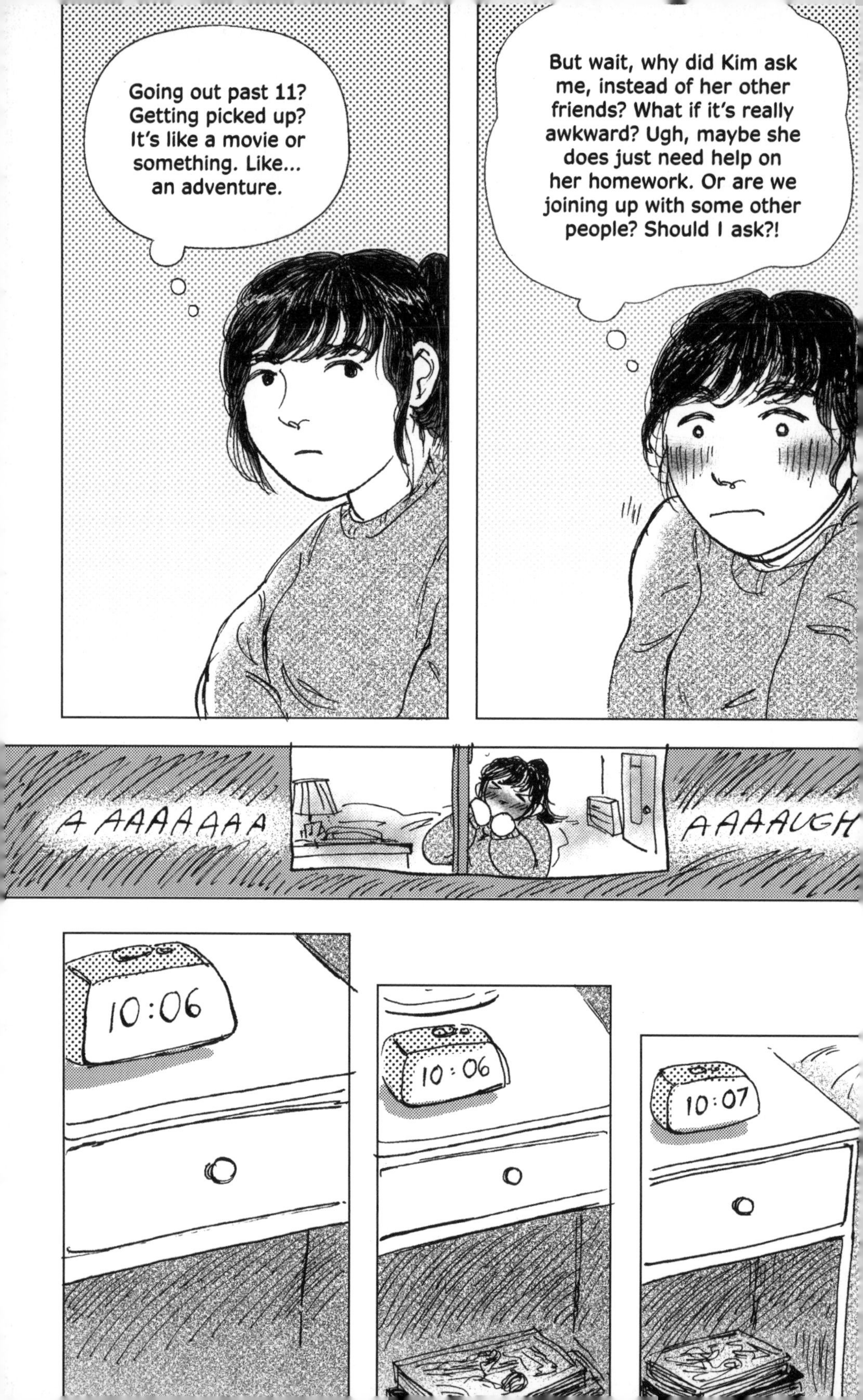
Going out past 11? Getting picked up? It's like a movie or something. Like... an adventure.
But wait, why did Kim ask me, instead of her other friends? What if it's really awkward? Ugh, maybe she does just need help on her homework. Or are we joining up with some other people? Should I ask?!
AAAAAAAA
AAAAUGH
10:06
10:06
10:07

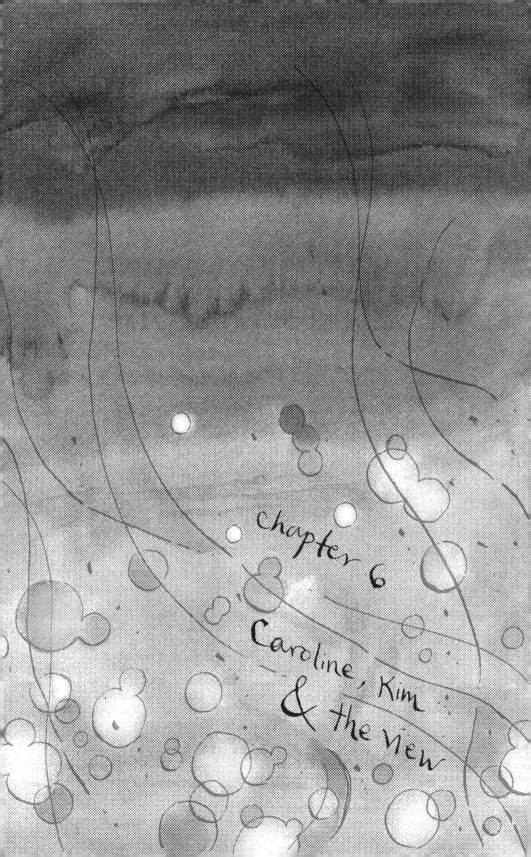

chapter 6

Caroline, Kim
& the view

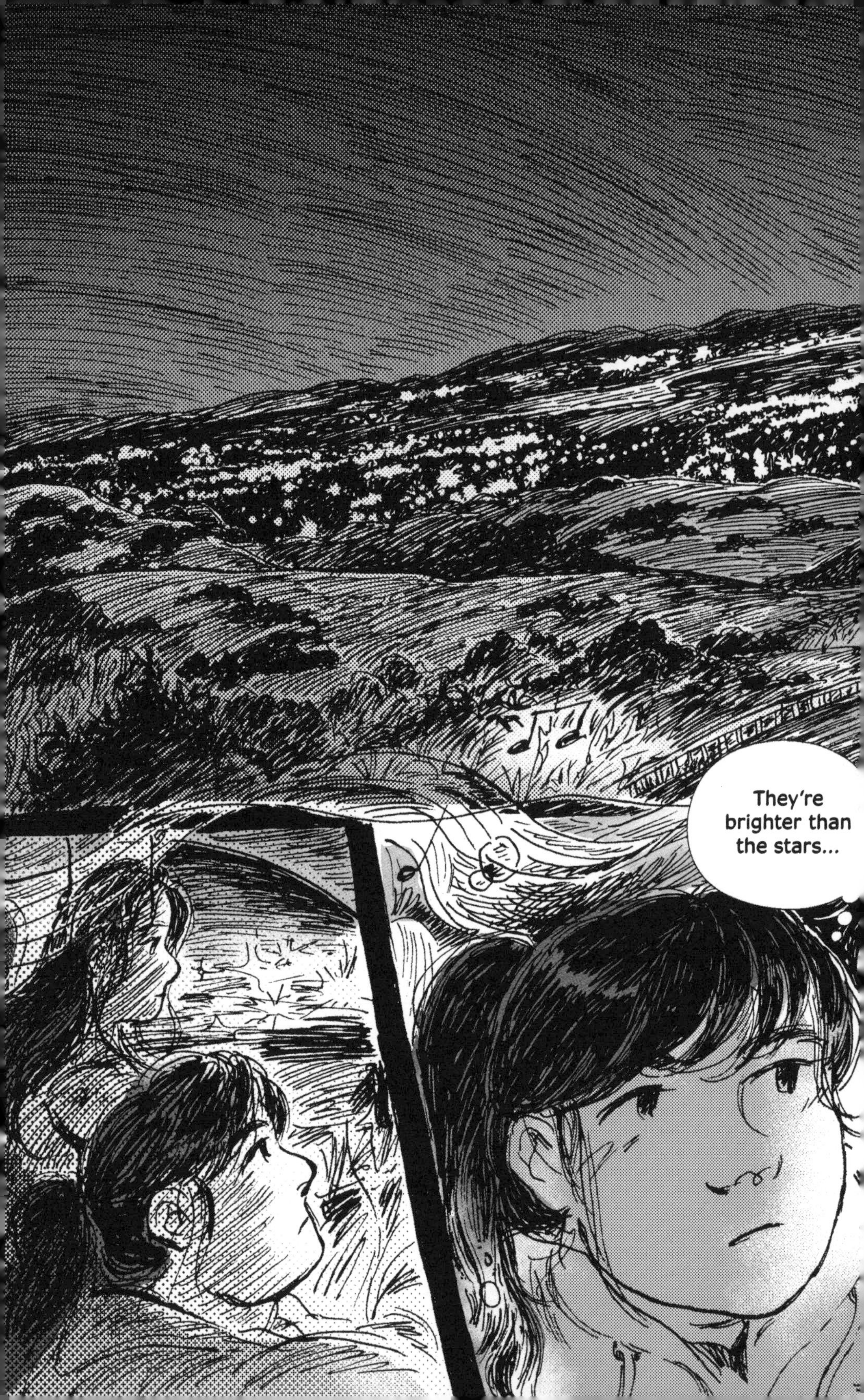
They're brighter than the stars...

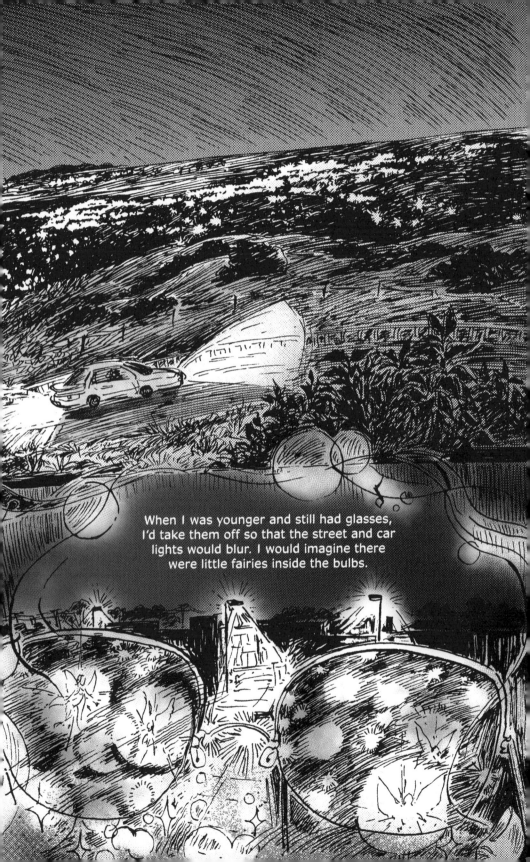

When I was younger and still had glasses,
I'd take them off so that the street and car
lights would blur. I would imagine there
were little fairies inside the bulbs.

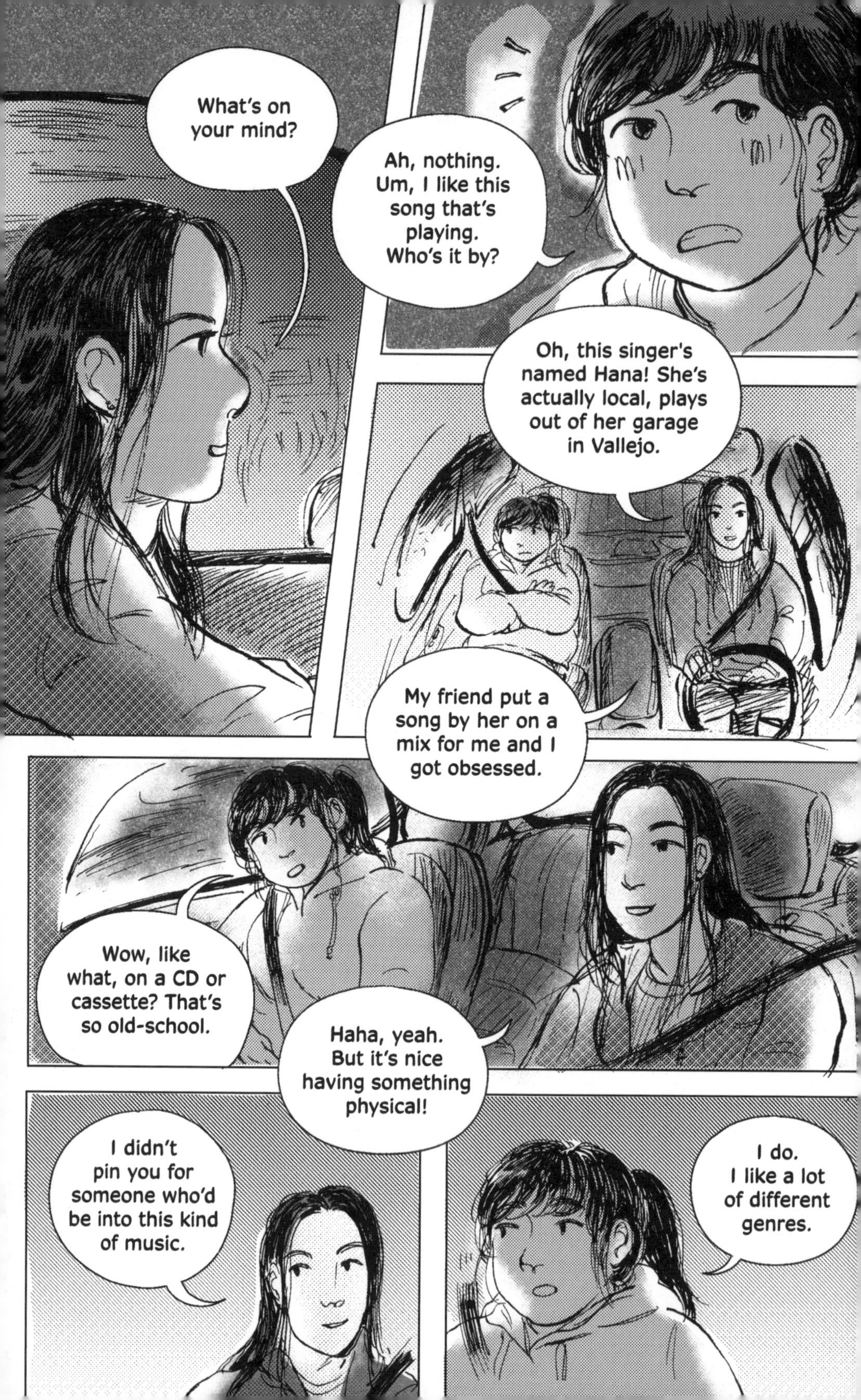
What's on your mind?
Ah, nothing. Um, I like this song that's playing. Who's it by?
Oh, this singer's named Hana! She's actually local, plays out of her garage in Vallejo.
My friend put a song by her on a mix for me and I got obsessed.
Wow, like what, on a CD or cassette? That's so old-school.
Haha, yeah. But it's nice having something physical!
I didn't pin you for someone who'd be into this kind of music.
I do. I like a lot of different genres.

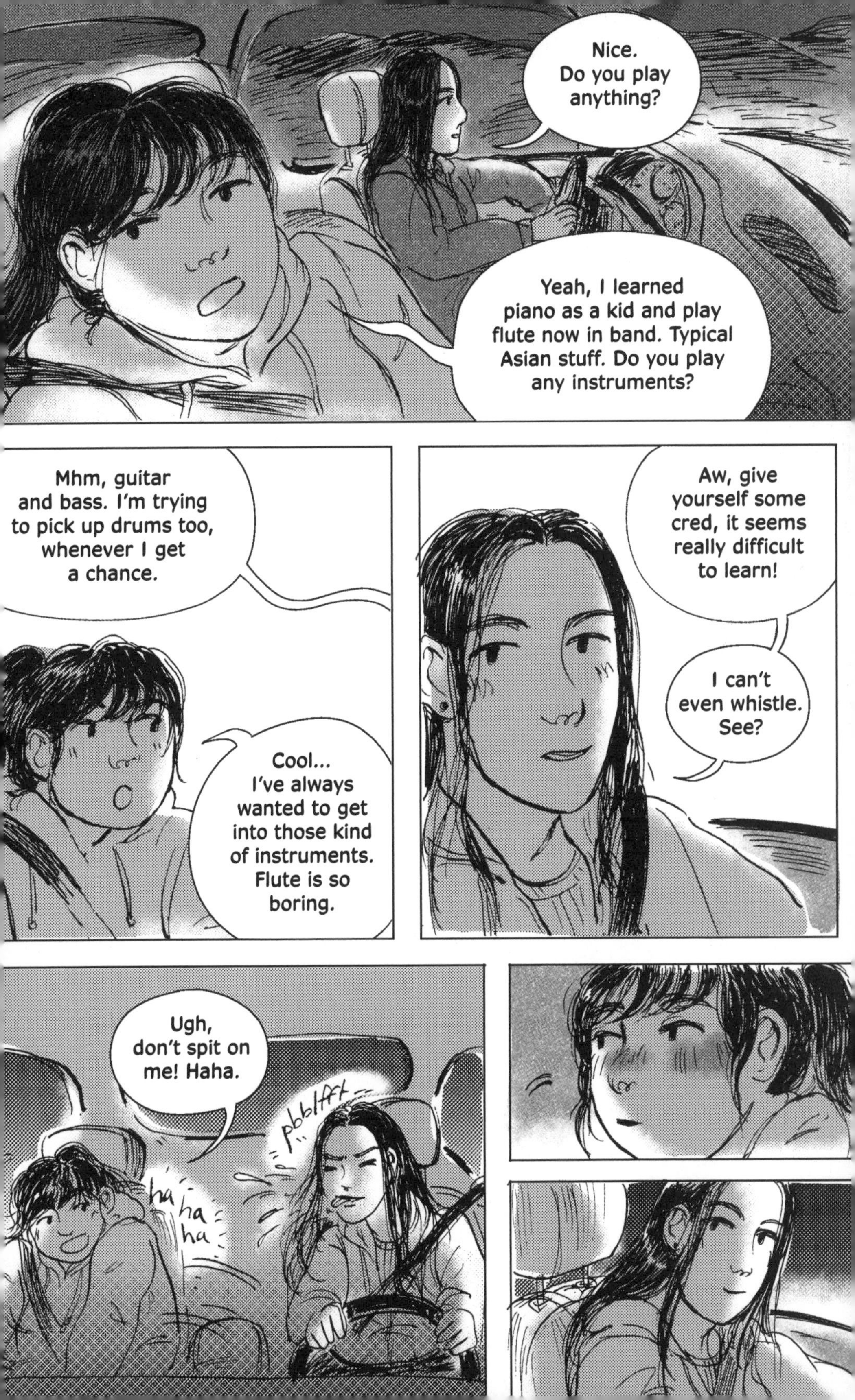
Nice.
Do you play anything?
Yeah, I learned piano as a kid and play flute now in band. Typical Asian stuff. Do you play any instruments?
Mhm, guitar and bass. I'm trying to pick up drums too, whenever I get a chance.
Cool... I've always wanted to get into those kind of instruments. Flute is so boring.
Aw, give yourself some cred, it seems really difficult to learn!
I can't even whistle. See?
Ugh, don't spit on me! Haha.
pbblfft
ha ha ha

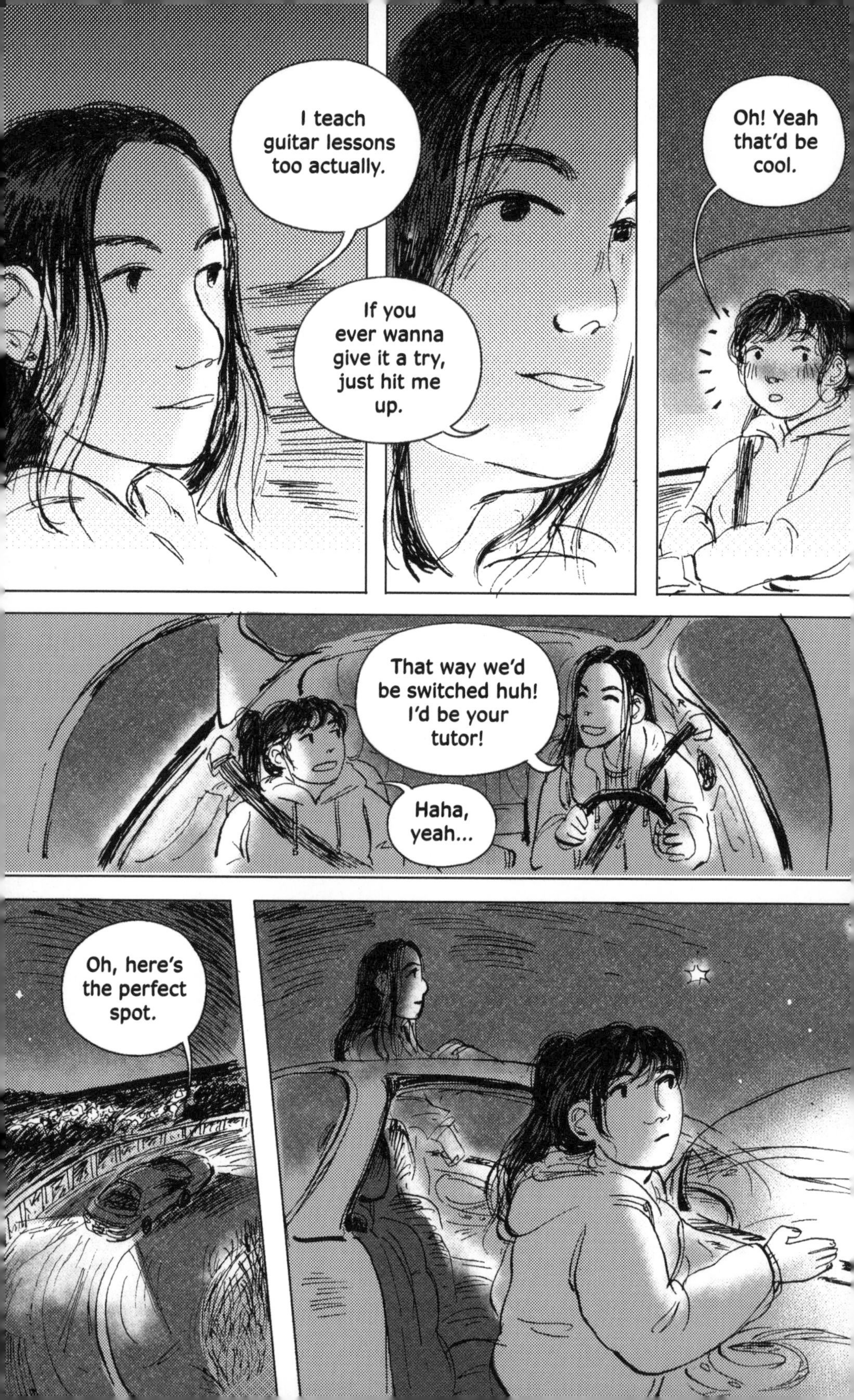
I teach guitar lessons too actually.
If you ever wanna give it a try, just hit me up.
Oh! Yeah that'd be cool.
That way we'd be switched huh! I'd be your tutor!
Haha, yeah...
Oh, here's the perfect spot.

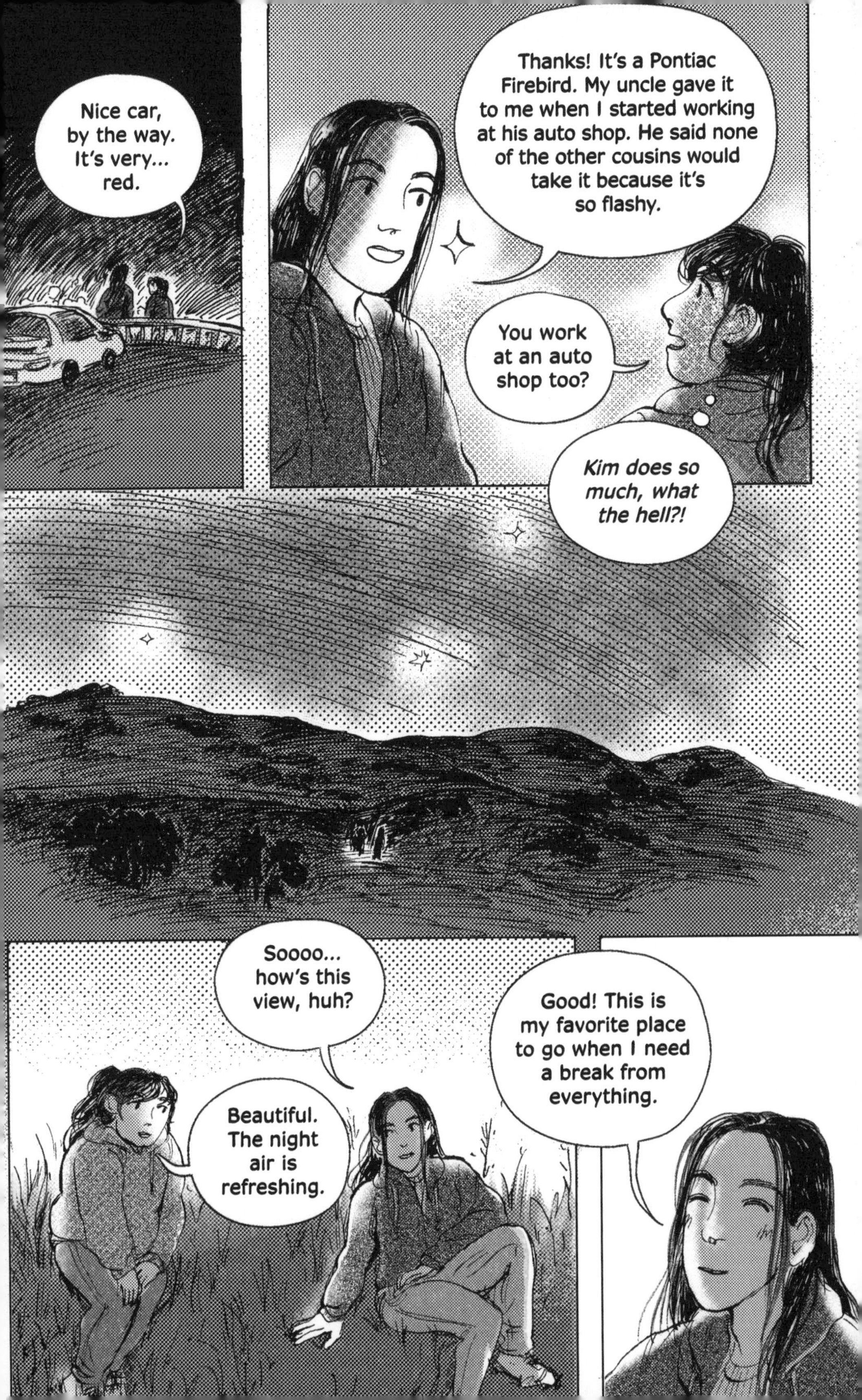

Nice car, by the way. It's very... red.
Thanks! It's a Pontiac Firebird. My uncle gave it to me when I started working at his auto shop. He said none of the other cousins would take it because it's so flashy.
You work at an auto shop too?
Kim does so much, what the hell?!
Soooo... how's this view, huh?
Beautiful. The night air is refreshing.
Good! This is my favorite place to go when I need a break from everything.

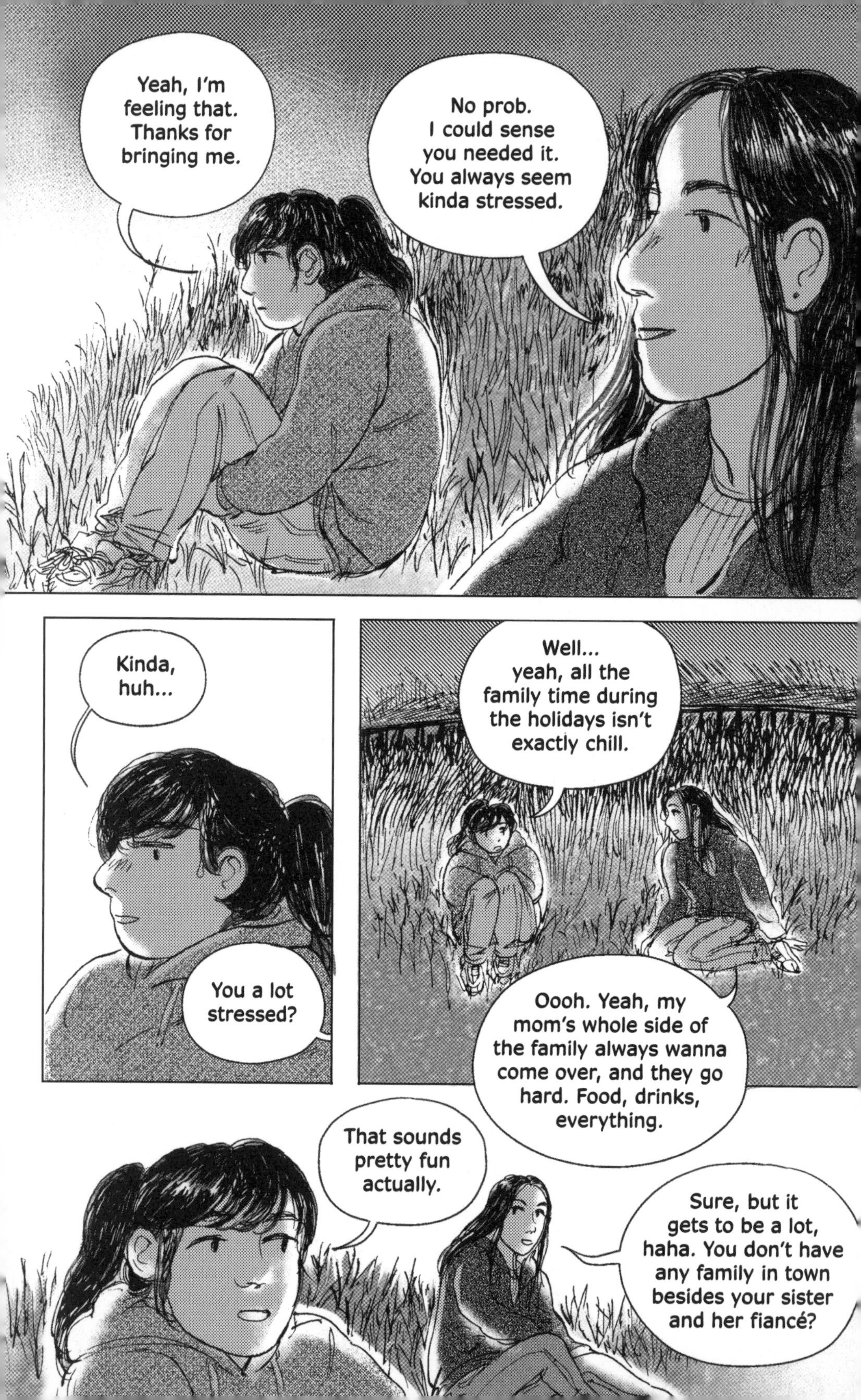
Yeah, I'm feeling that. Thanks for bringing me.
No prob. I could sense you needed it. You always seem kinda stressed.
Kinda, huh...
You a lot stressed?
Well... yeah, all the family time during the holidays isn't exactly chill.
Oooh. Yeah, my mom's whole side of the family always wanna come over, and they go hard. Food, drinks, everything.
That sounds pretty fun actually.
Sure, but it gets to be a lot, haha. You don't have any family in town besides your sister and her fiancé?

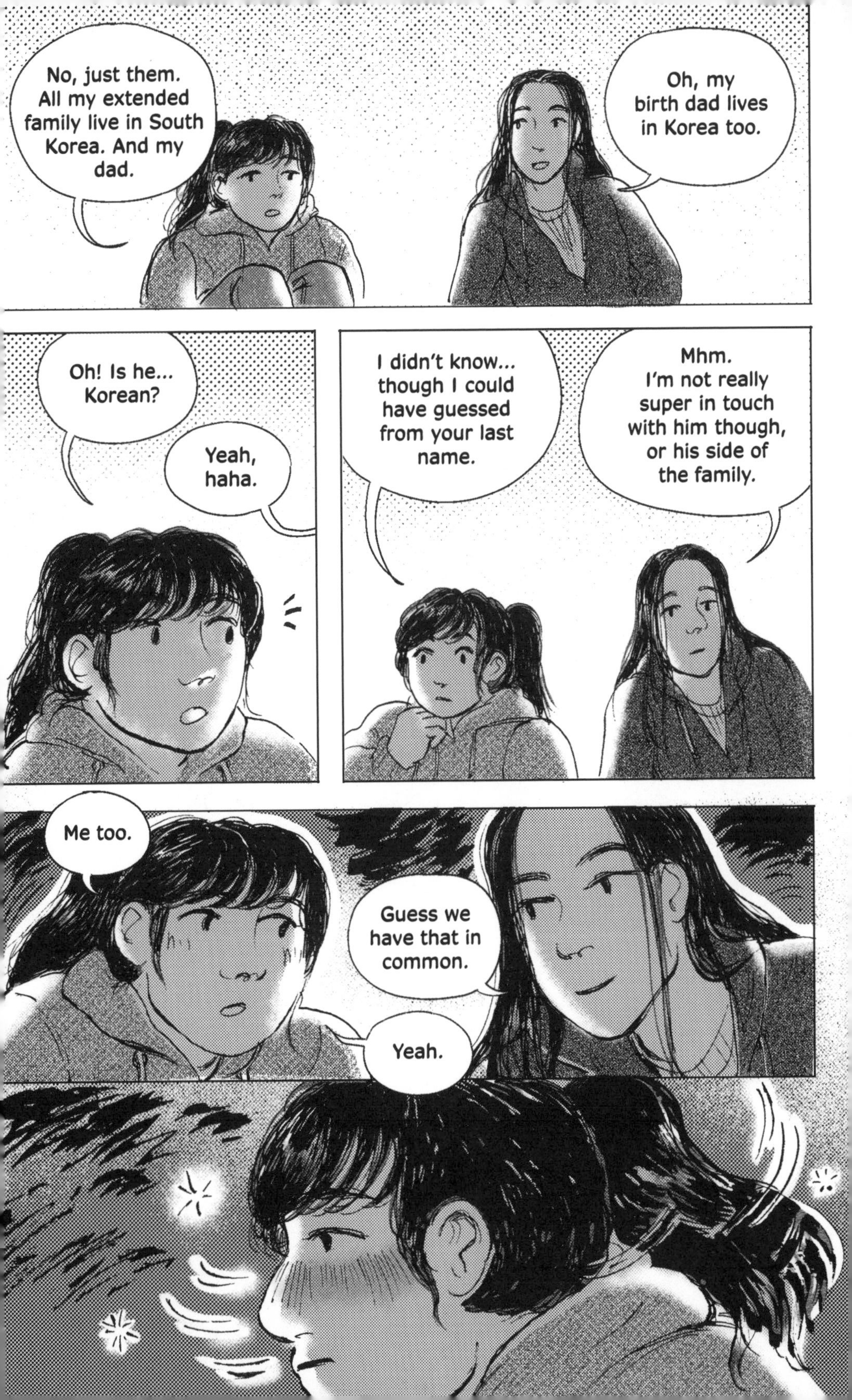
No, just them. All my extended family live in South Korea. And my dad.
Oh, my birth dad lives in Korea too.
Oh! Is he... Korean?
Yeah, haha.
I didn't know... though I could have guessed from your last name.
Mhm. I'm not really super in touch with him though, or his side of the family.
Me too.
Guess we have that in common.
Yeah.

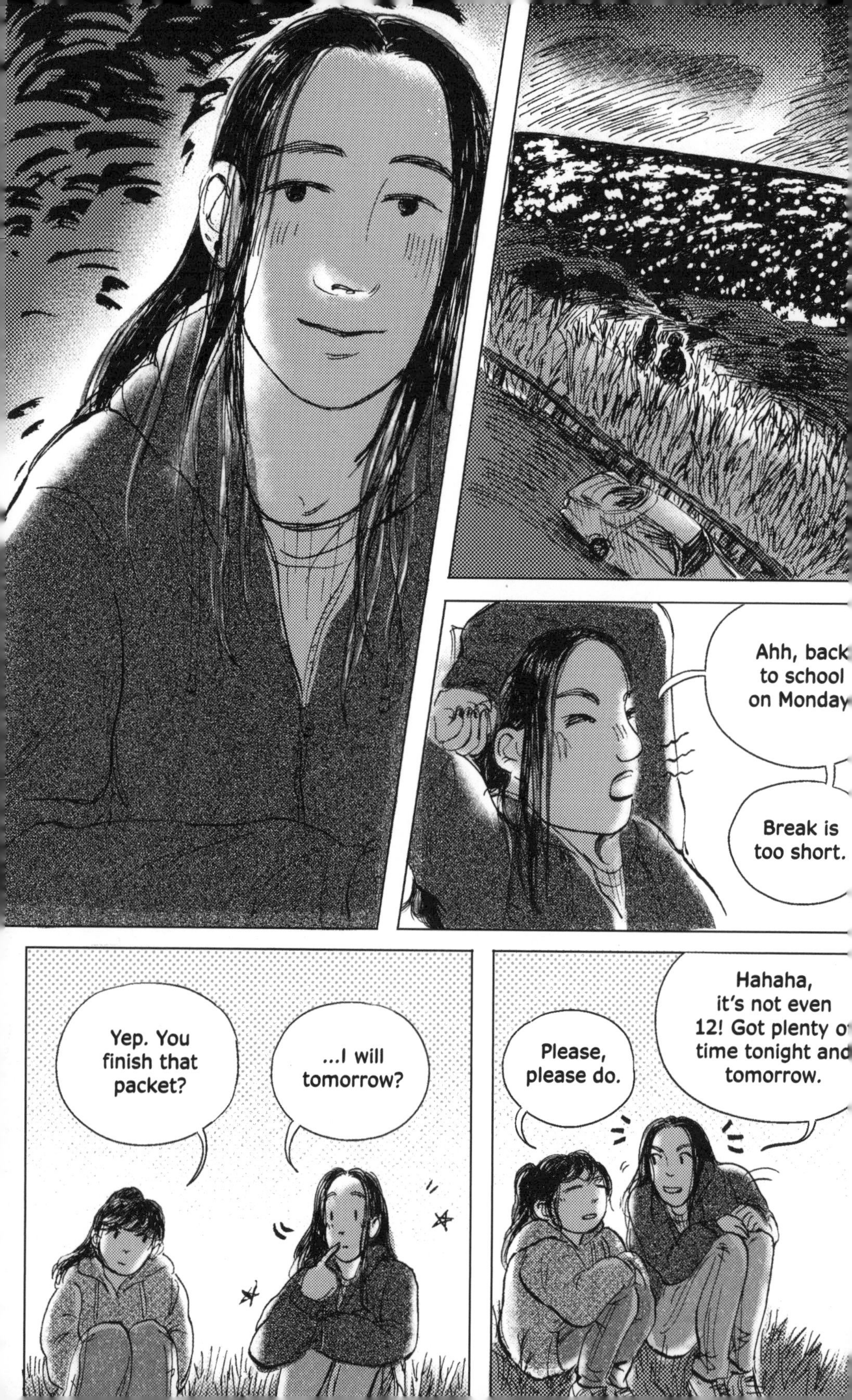
Ahh, back to school on Monday
Break is too short.
Yep. You finish that packet?
...I will tomorrow?
Hahaha, it's not even 12! Got plenty of time tonight and tomorrow.
Please, please do.

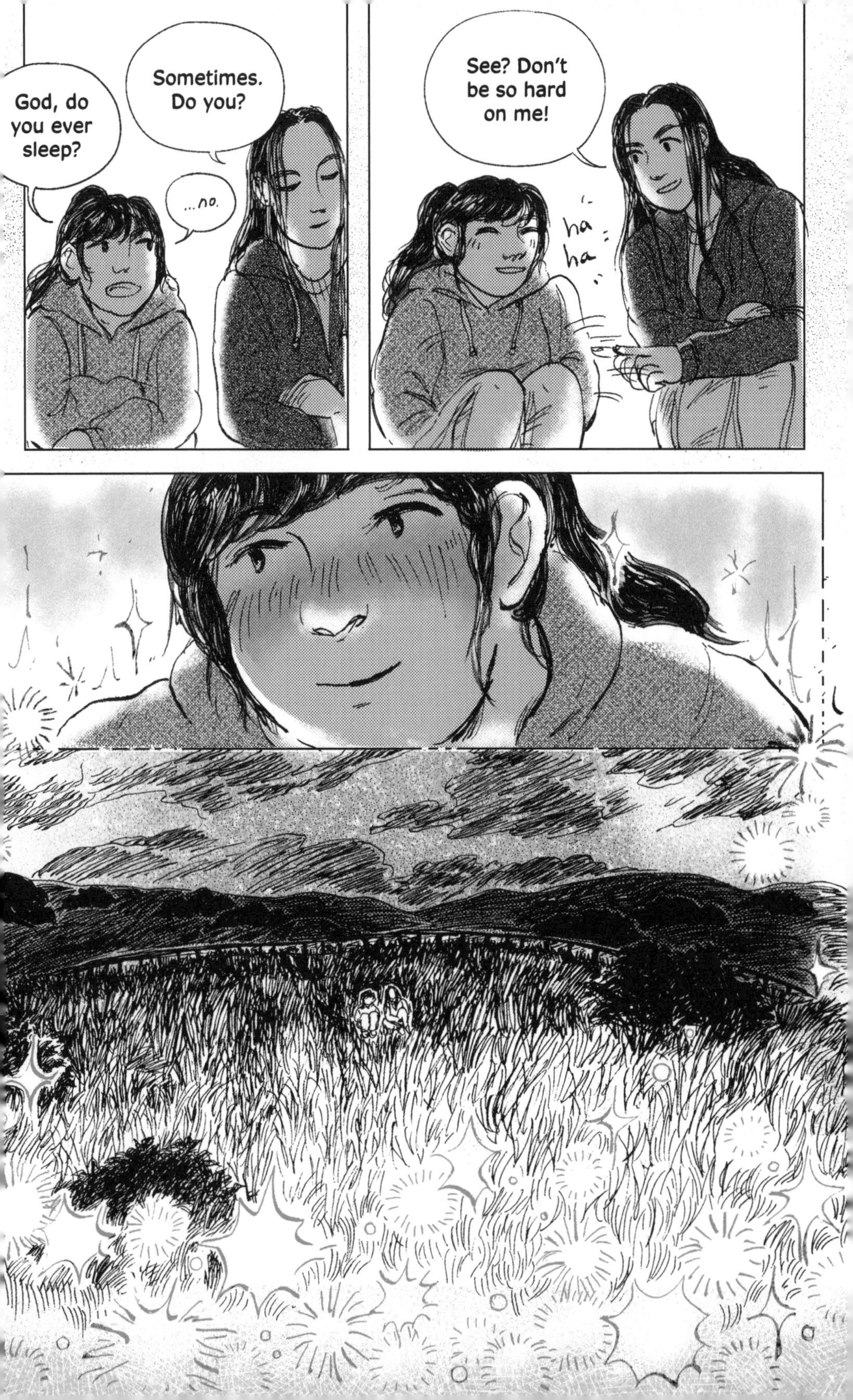
God, do you ever sleep?
Sometimes. Do you?
...no.
See? Don't be so hard on me!
ha ha

beep! beep! beep! beep! beep! beep!

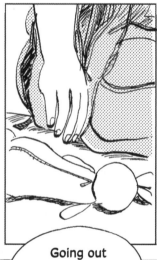

Going out with Kim was so cool...I wonder if she'd wanna hang out again.

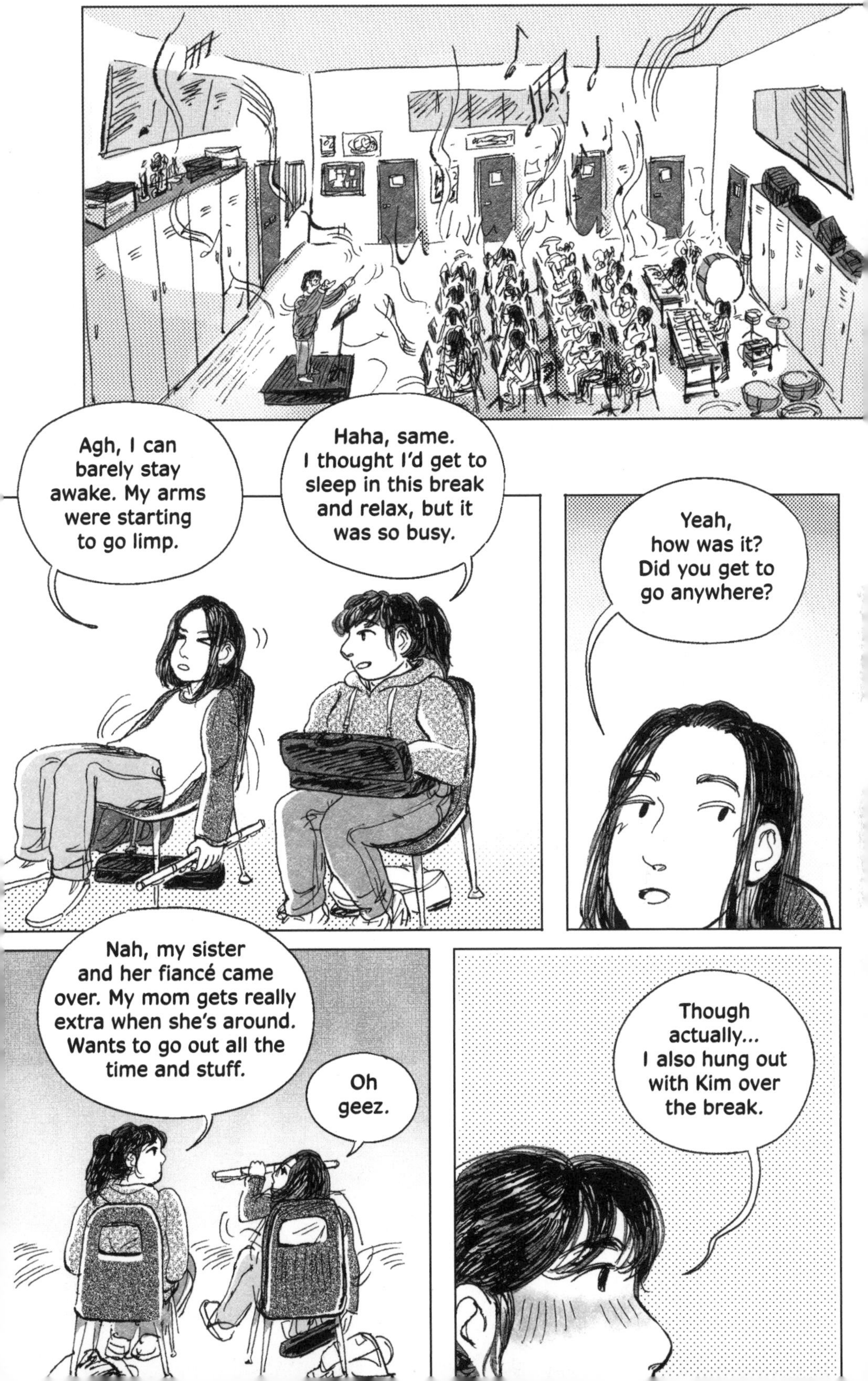
Agh, I can barely stay awake. My arms were starting to go limp.
Haha, same. I thought I'd get to sleep in this break and relax, but it was so busy.
Yeah, how was it? Did you get to go anywhere?
Nah, my sister and her fiancé came over. My mom gets really extra when she's around. Wants to go out all the time and stuff.
Oh geez.
Though actually... I also hung out with Kim over the break.

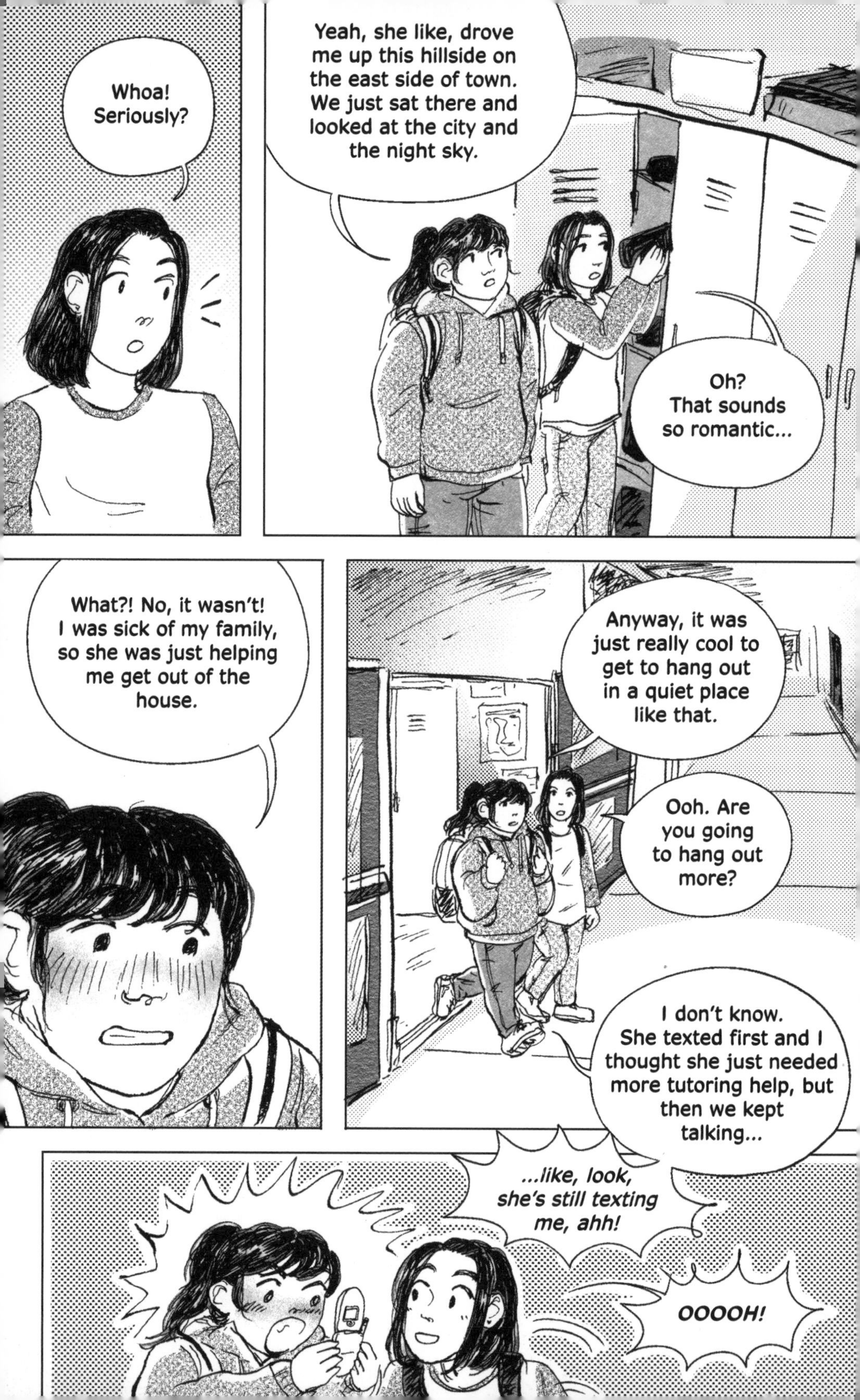

Whoa! Seriously?
Yeah, she like, drove me up this hillside on the east side of town. We just sat there and looked at the city and the night sky.
Oh? That sounds so romantic...
What?! No, it wasn't! I was sick of my family, so she was just helping me get out of the house.
Anyway, it was just really cool to get to hang out in a quiet place like that.
Ooh. Are you going to hang out more?
I don't know. She texted first and I thought she just needed more tutoring help, but then we kept talking...
...like, look, she's still texting me, ahh!
OOOOH!

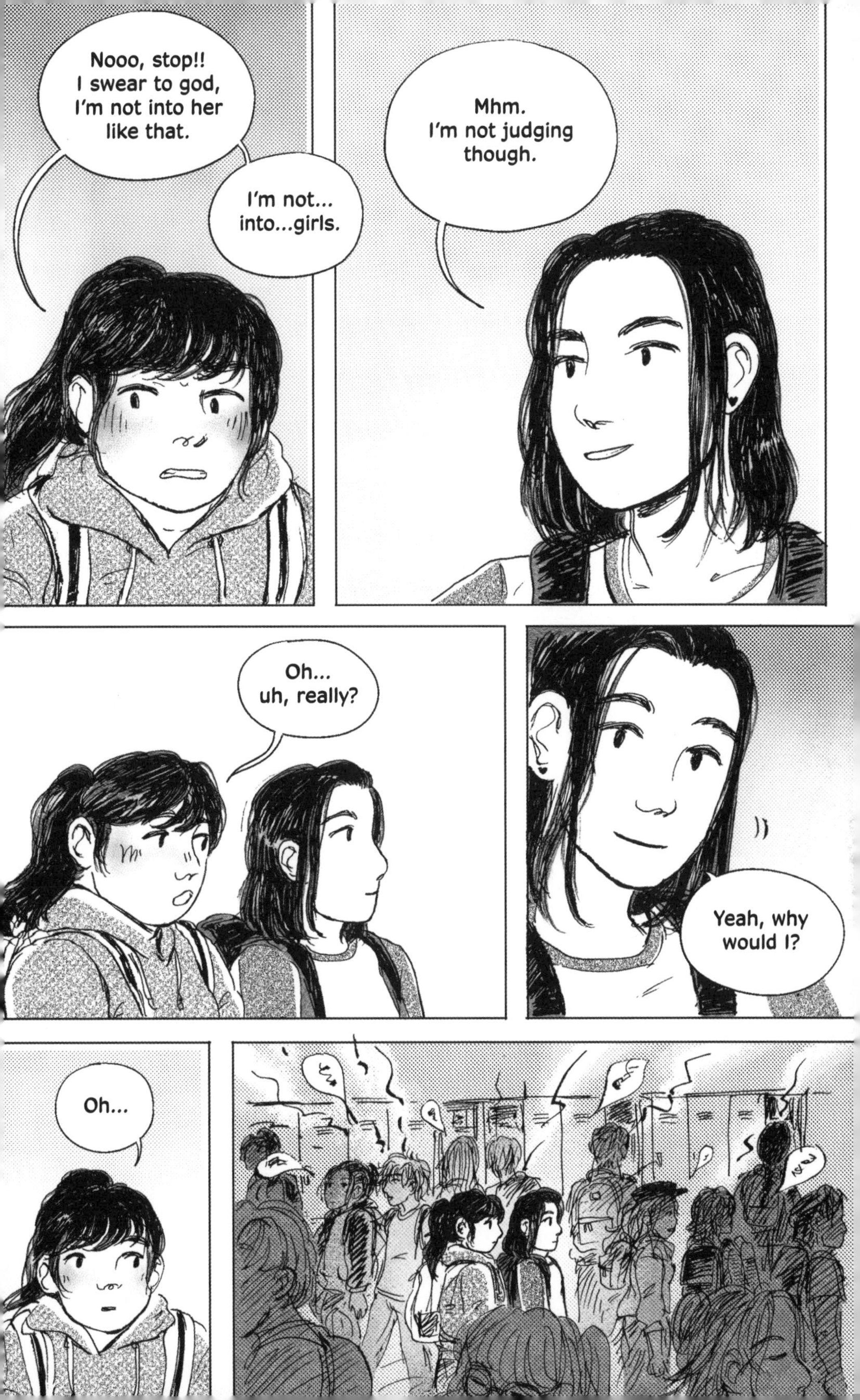
Nooo, stop!! I swear to god, I'm not into her like that.
I'm not... into...girls.
Mhm. I'm not judging though.
Oh... uh, really?
Yeah, why would I?
Oh...

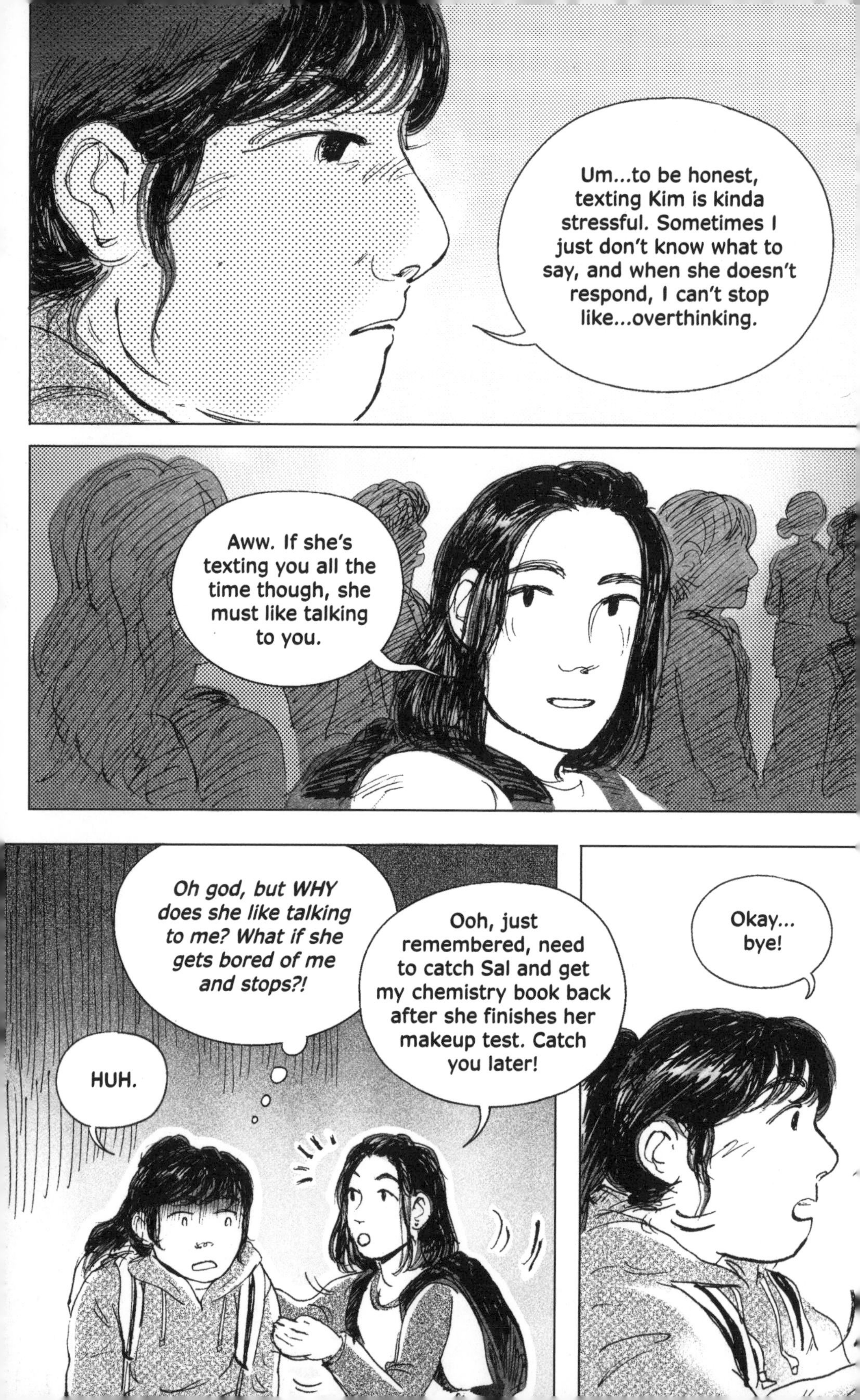
Um...to be honest, texting Kim is kinda stressful. Sometimes I just don't know what to say, and when she doesn't respond, I can't stop like...overthinking.
Aww. If she's texting you all the time though, she must like talking to you.
Oh god, but WHY does she like talking to me? What if she gets bored of me and stops?!
HUH.
Ooh, just remembered, need to catch Sal and get my chemistry book back after she finishes her makeup test. Catch you later!
Okay... bye!

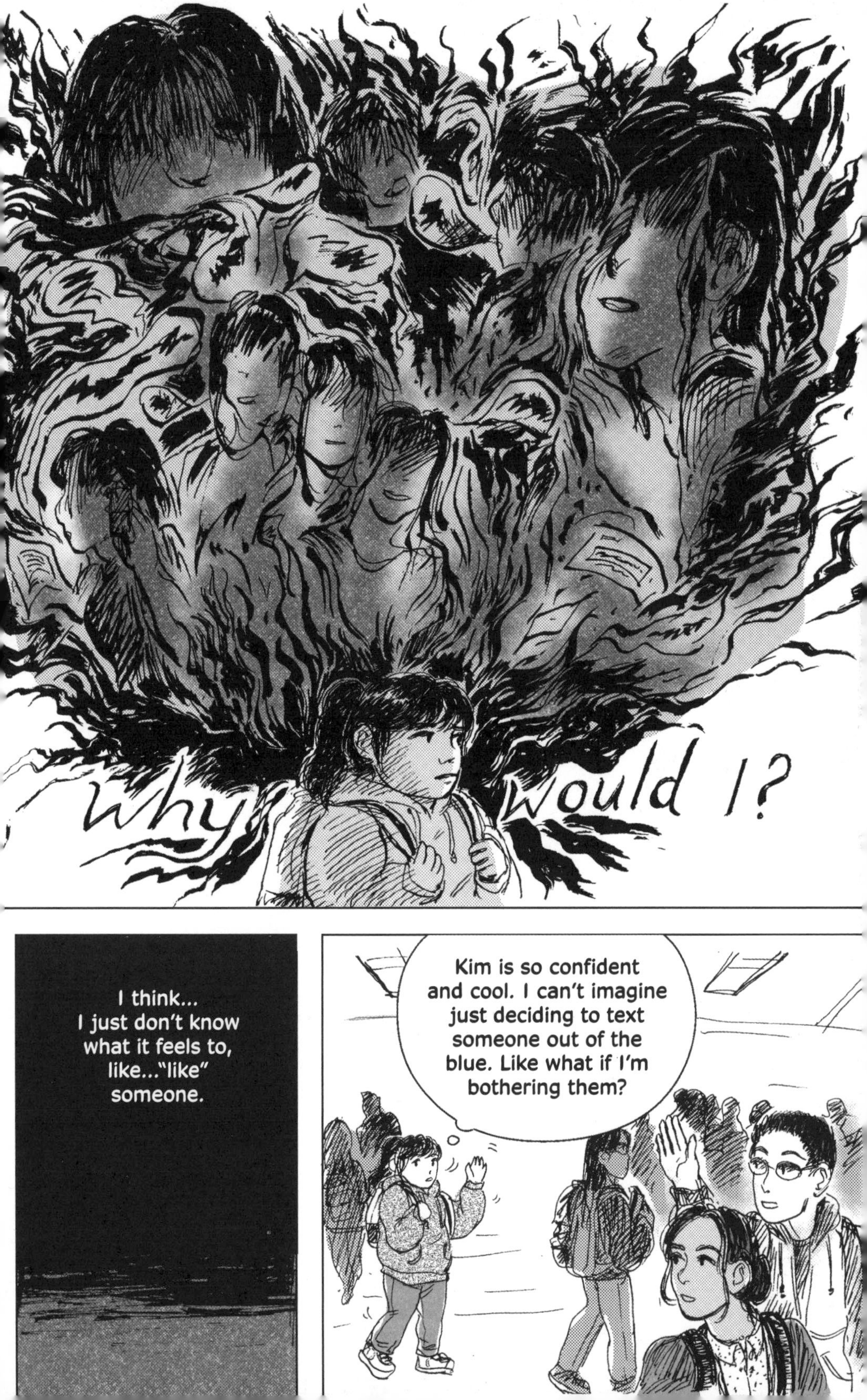
Why would I?
I think... I just don't know what it feels to, like..."like" someone.
Kim is so confident and cool. I can't imagine just deciding to text someone out of the blue. Like what if I'm bothering them?

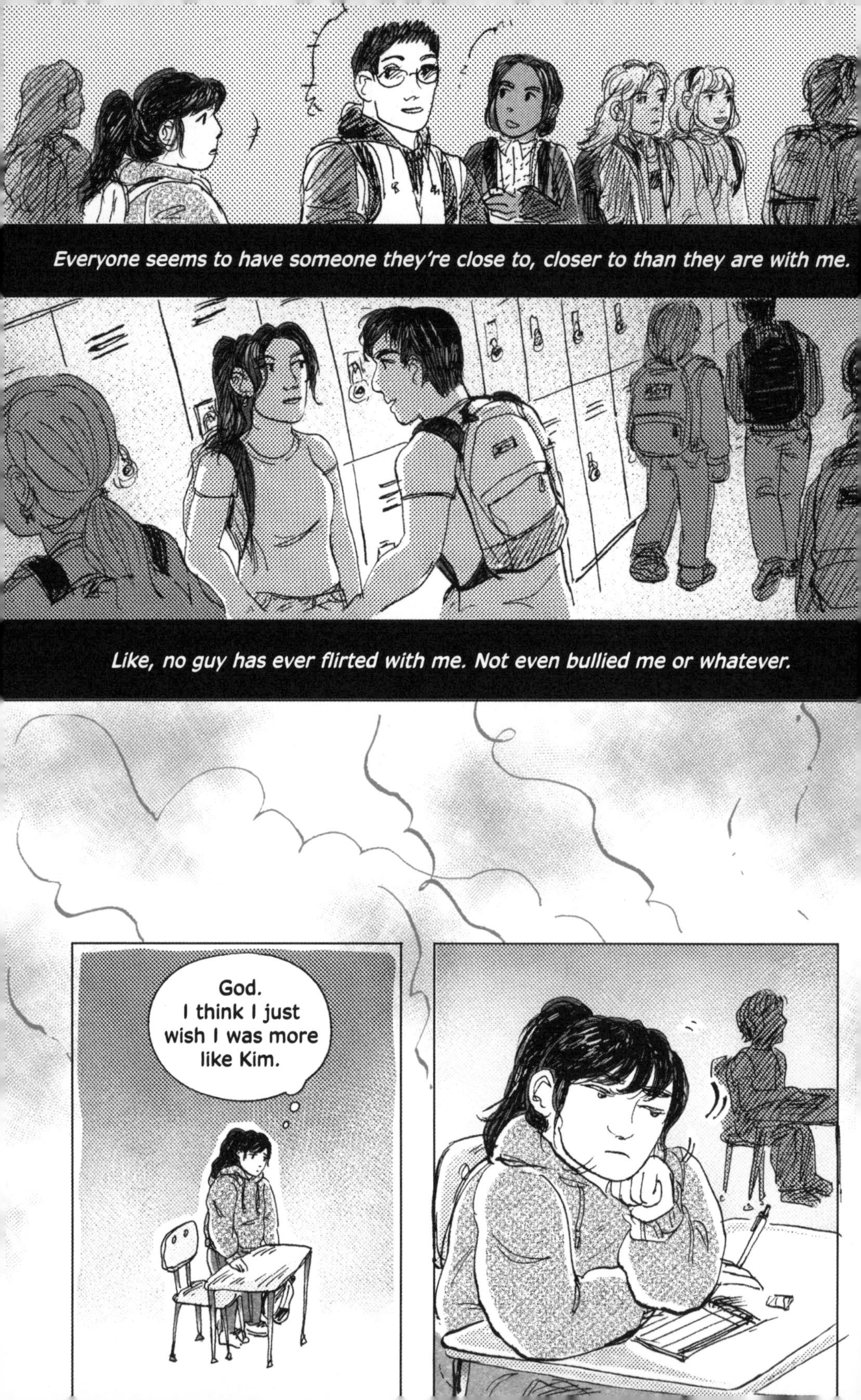
Everyone seems to have someone they're close to, closer to than they are with me.
Like, no guy has ever flirted with me. Not even bullied me or whatever.
God. I think I just wish I was more like Kim.

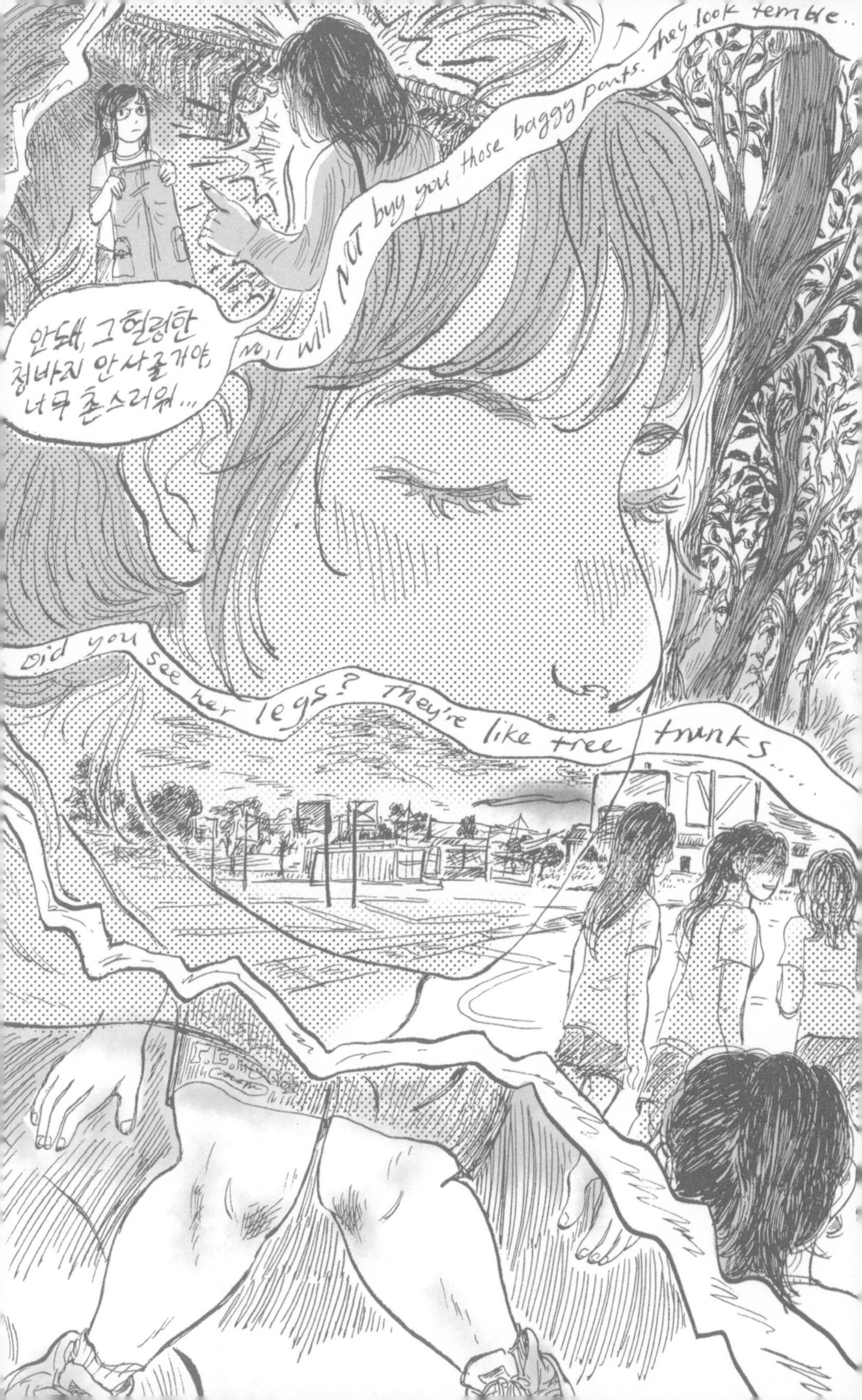
안돼, 그 헐렁한 청바지 안 사줄거야, 너무 촌스러워...
No, I will NOT buy you those baggy pants. They look terrible...
Did you see her legs? They're like tree trunks....

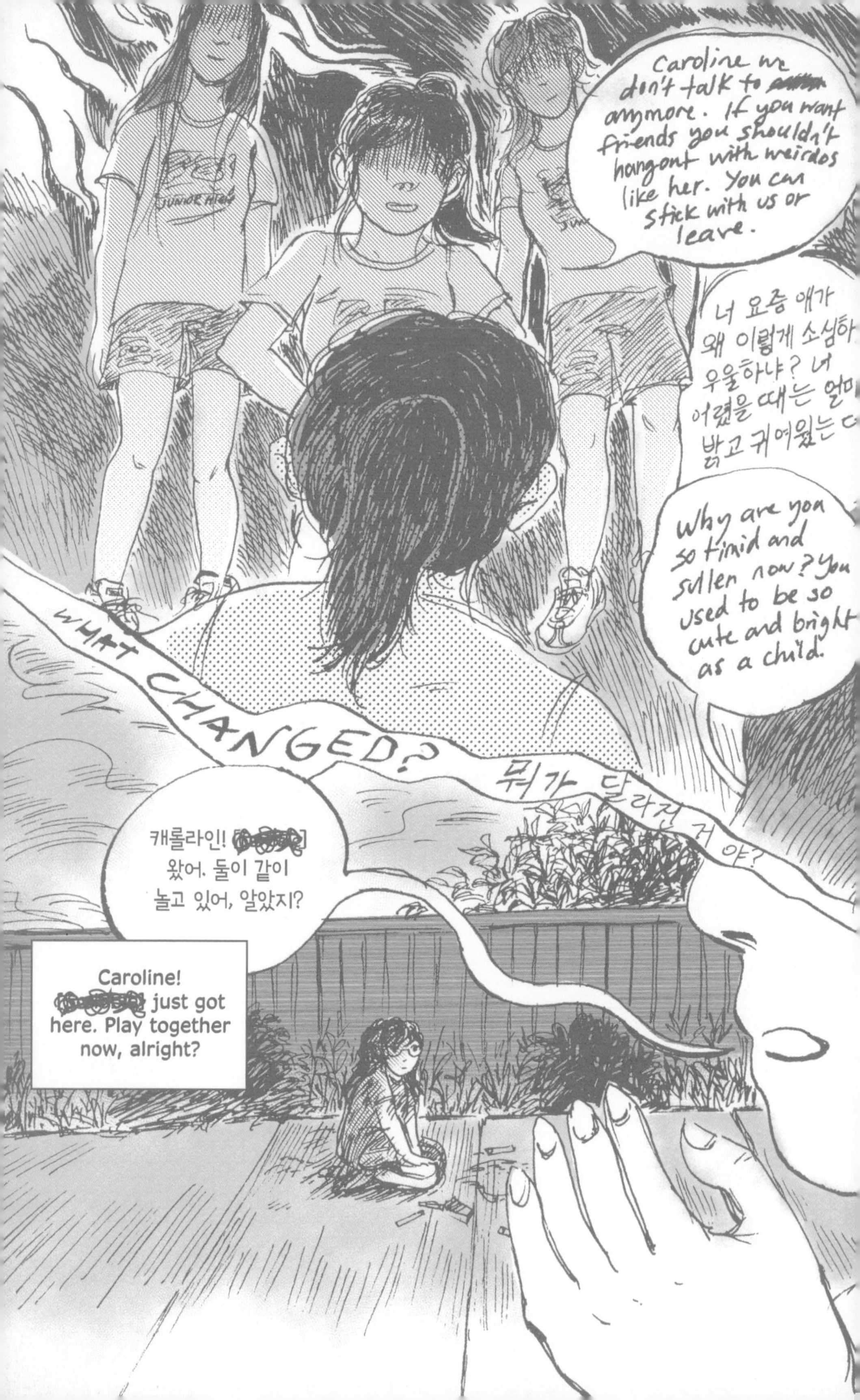
Caroline we don't talk to [redacted] anymore. If you want friends you shouldn't hangout with weirdos like her. You can stick with us or leave.
너 요즘 애가 왜 이렇게 소심하 우울하냐? 너 어렸을 때는 얼미 밝고 귀여웠는 ㄷ
Why are you so timid and sullen now? You used to be so cute and bright as a child.
WHAT CHANGED?
뭐가 달라진 거야?
캐롤라인! [redacted] 왔어. 둘이 같이 놀고 있어, 알았지?
Caroline! [redacted] just got here. Play together now, alright?

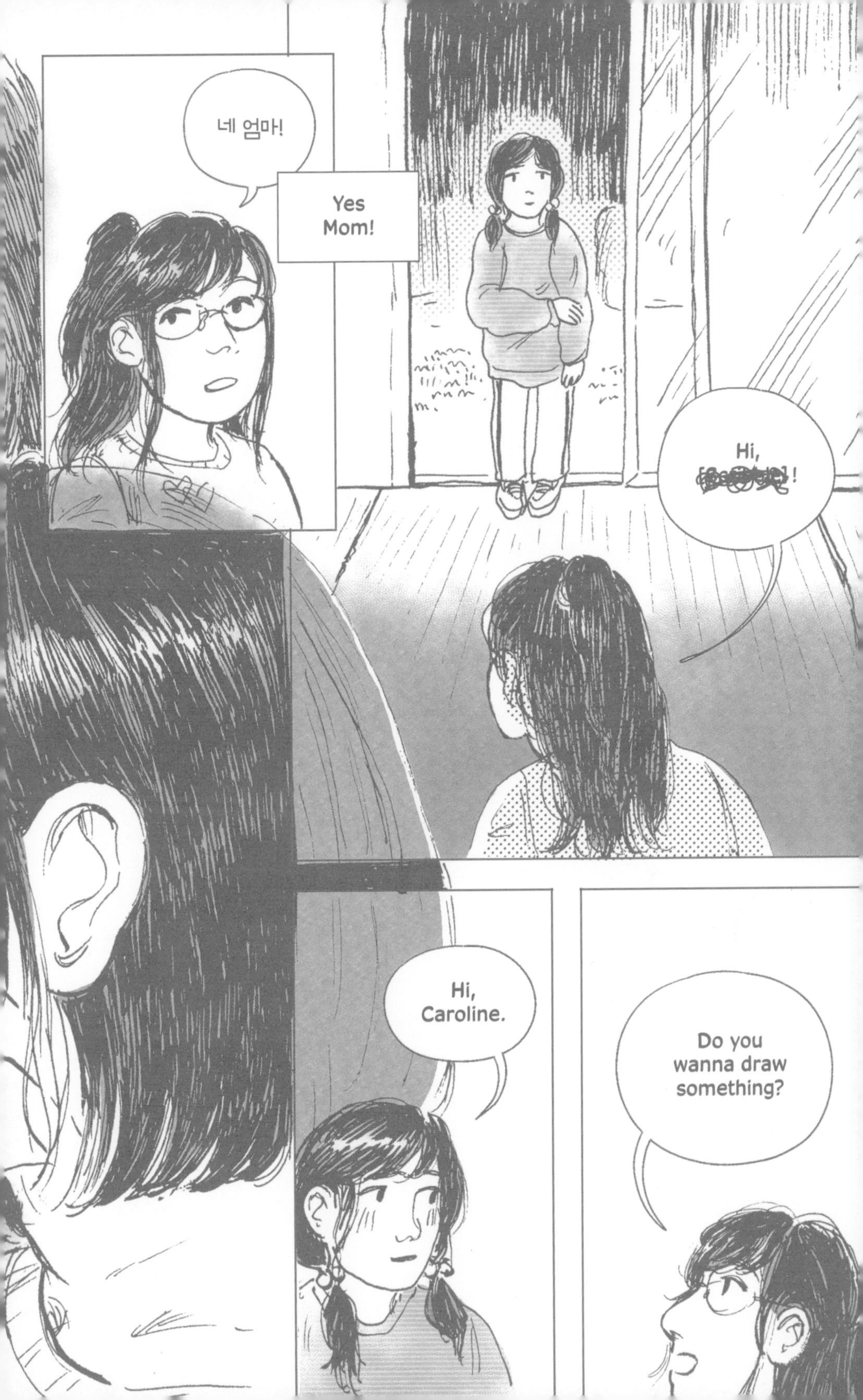
네 엄마!
Yes Mom!
Hi,
Hi, Caroline.
Do you wanna draw something?

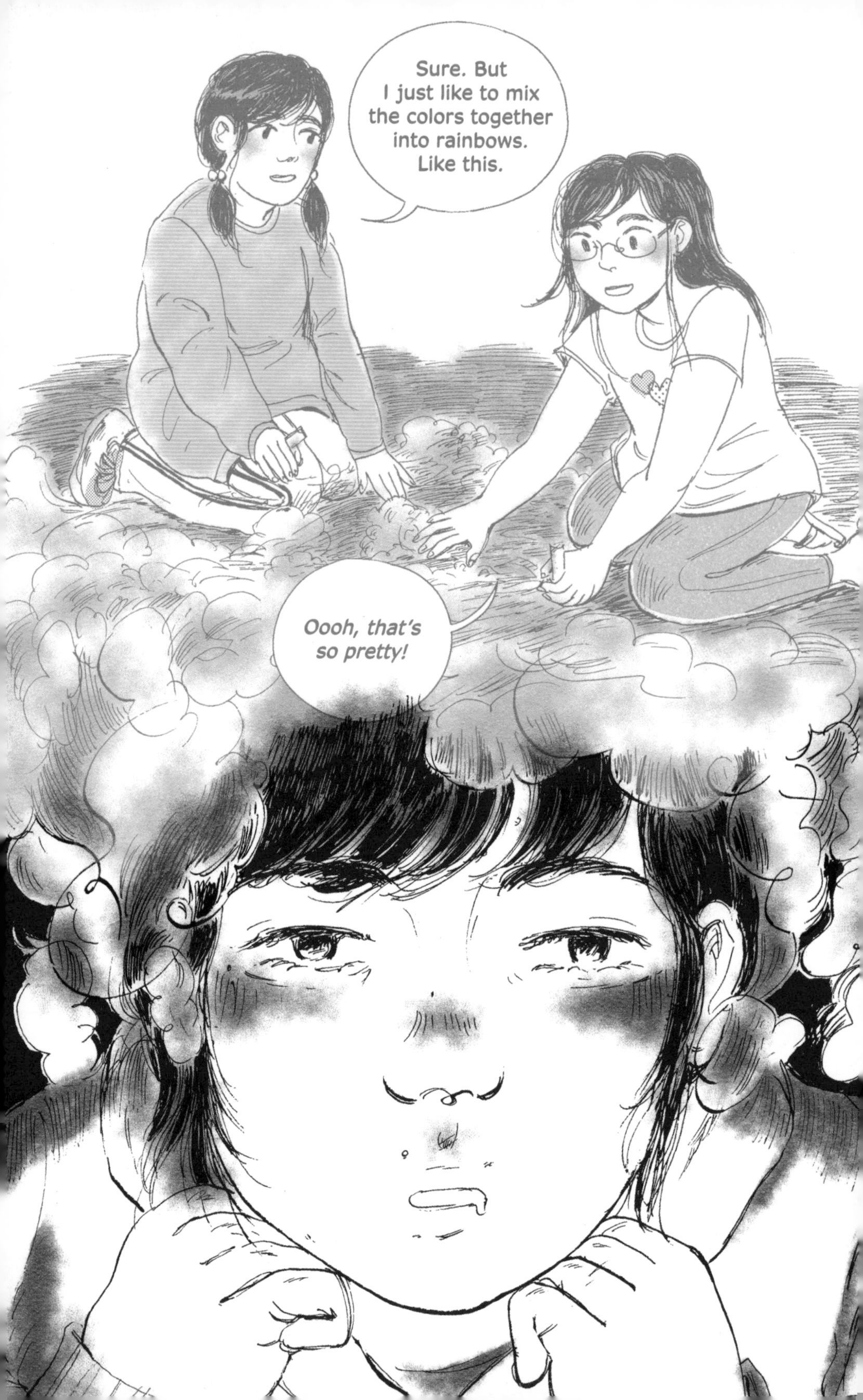
Sure. But I just like to mix the colors together into rainbows. Like this.
Oooh, that's so pretty!

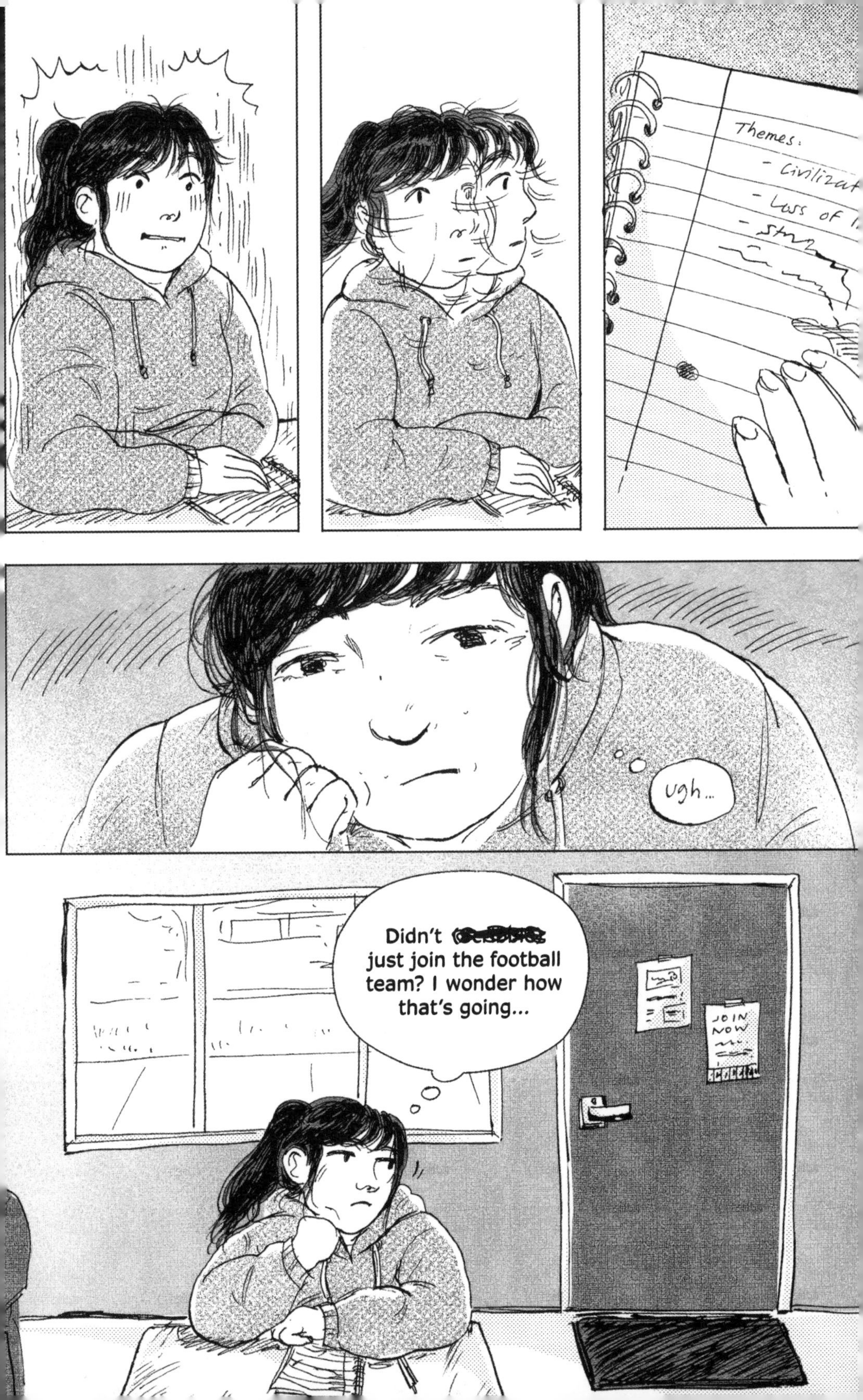
Themes:
- Civilizat
- Loss of
Ugh...
Didn't [redacted] just join the football team? I wonder how that's going...
JOIN NOW

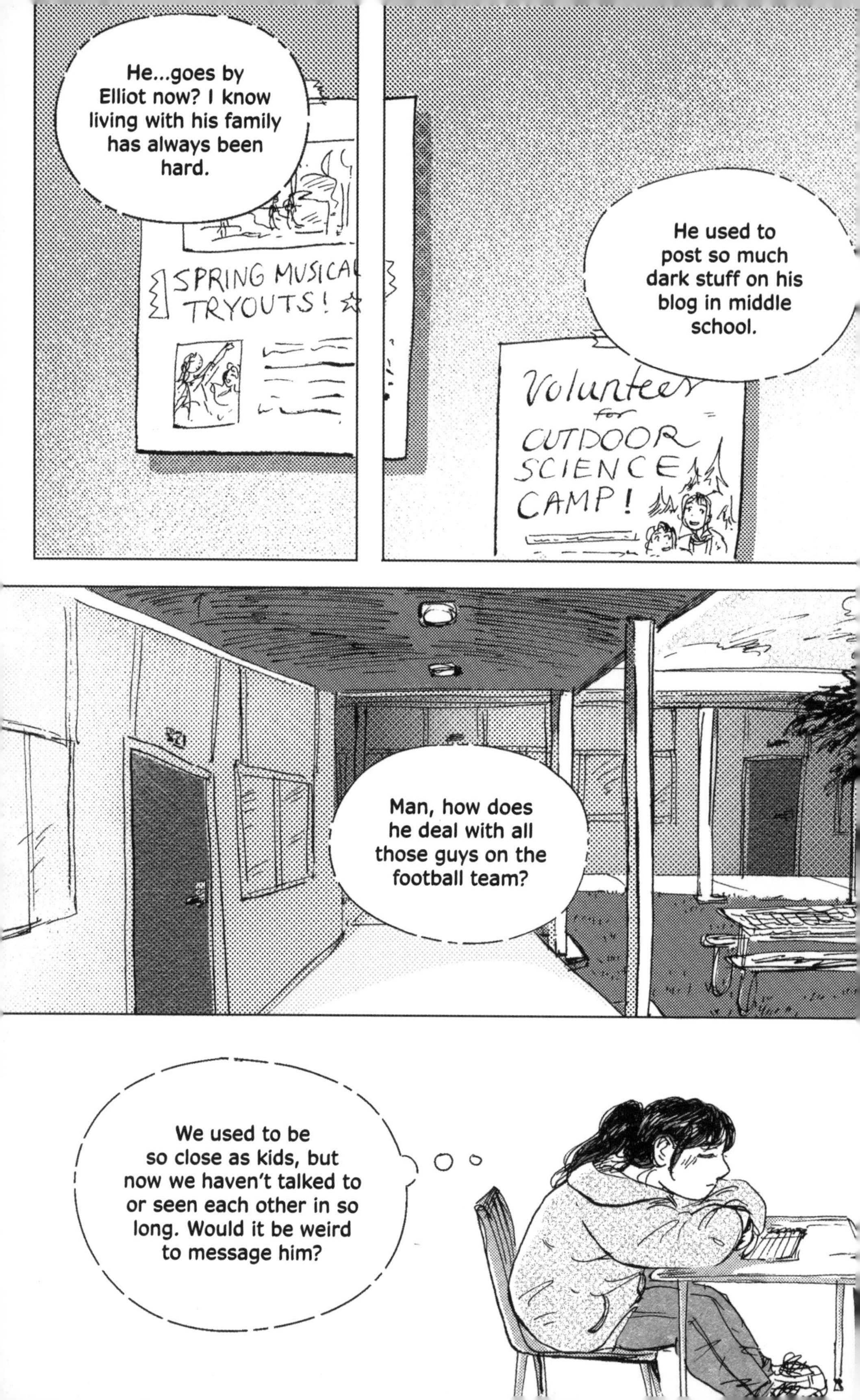
He...goes by Elliot now? I know living with his family has always been hard.
SPRING MUSICAL TRYOUTS!
He used to post so much dark stuff on his blog in middle school.
Volunteer for OUTDOOR SCIENCE CAMP!
Man, how does he deal with all those guys on the football team?
We used to be so close as kids, but now we haven't talked to or seen each other in so long. Would it be weird to message him?

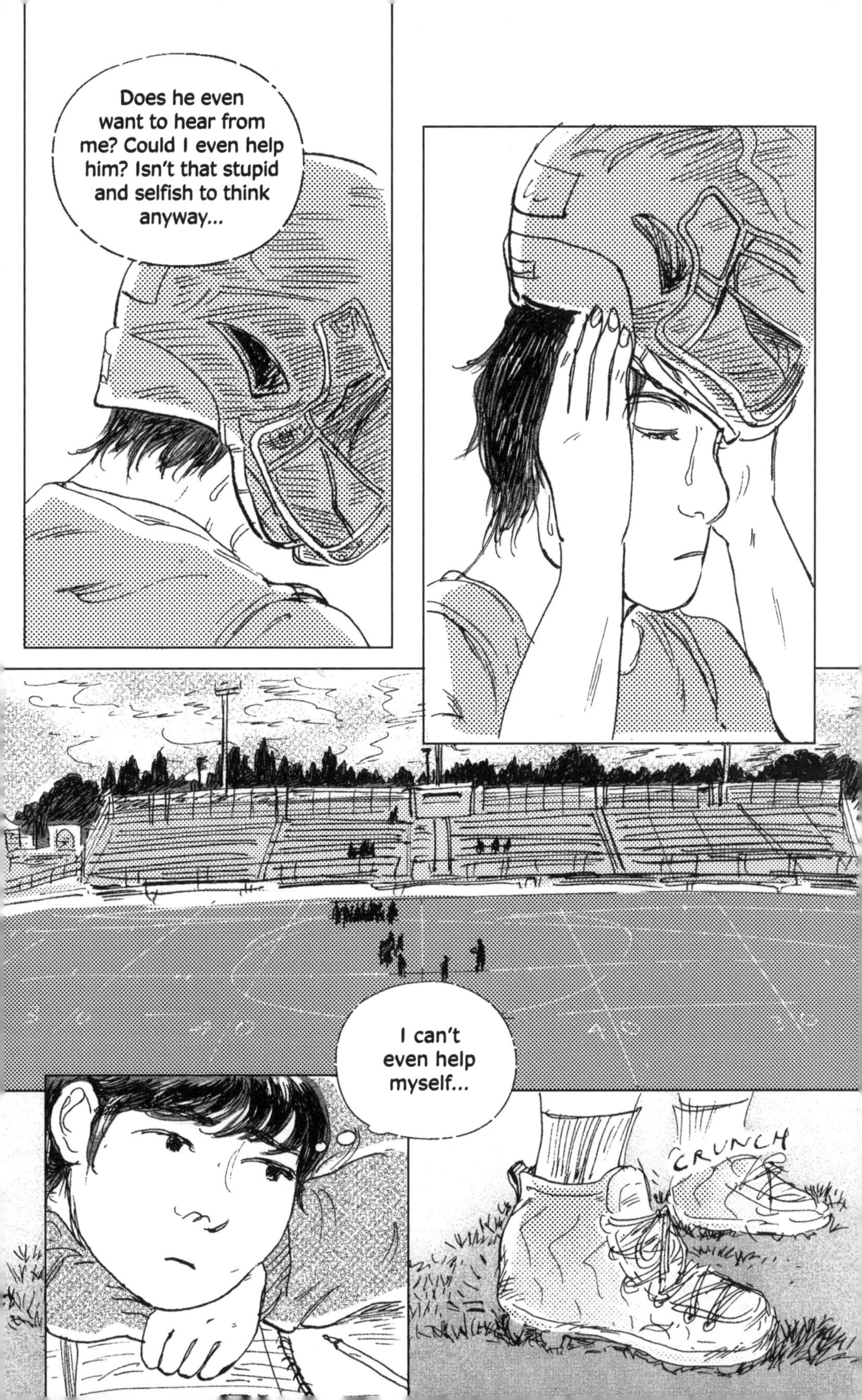
Does he even want to hear from me? Could I even help him? Isn't that stupid and selfish to think anyway...
I can't even help myself...
CRUNCH

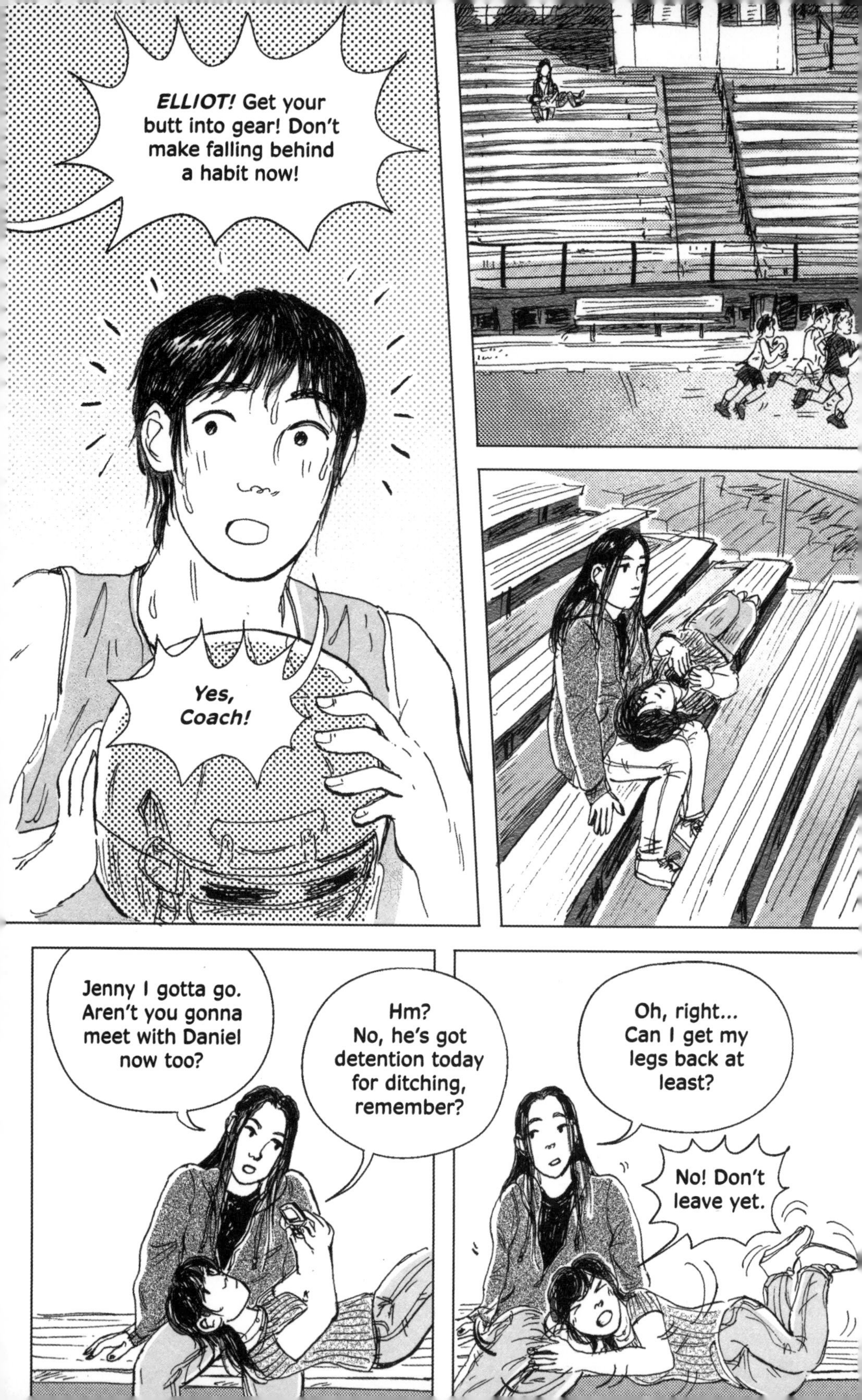
ELLIOT! Get your butt into gear! Don't make falling behind a habit now!
Yes, Coach!
Jenny I gotta go. Aren't you gonna meet with Daniel now too?
Hm? No, he's got detention today for ditching, remember?
Oh, right... Can I get my legs back at least?
No! Don't leave yet.

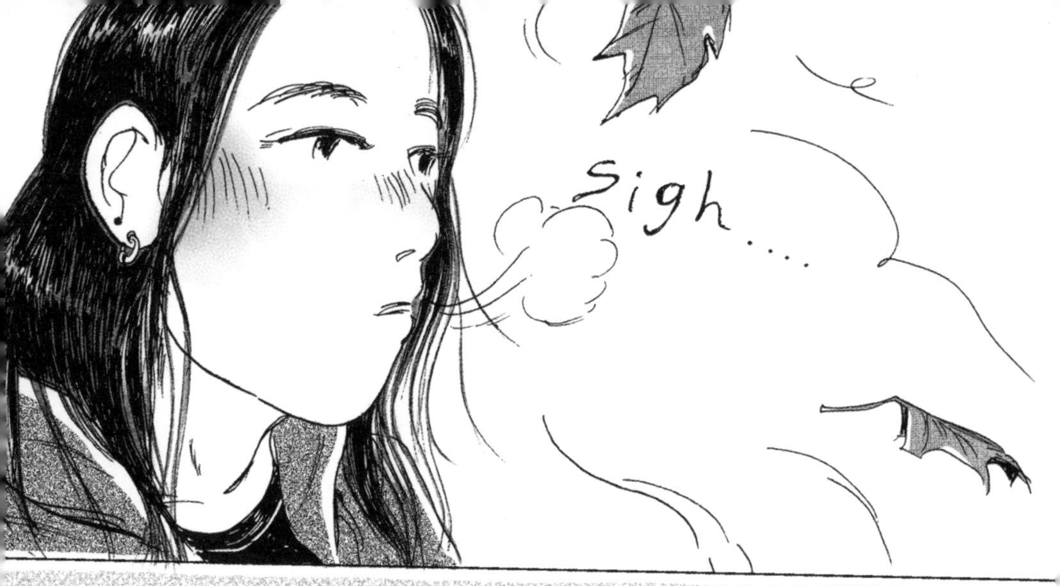
Sigh....

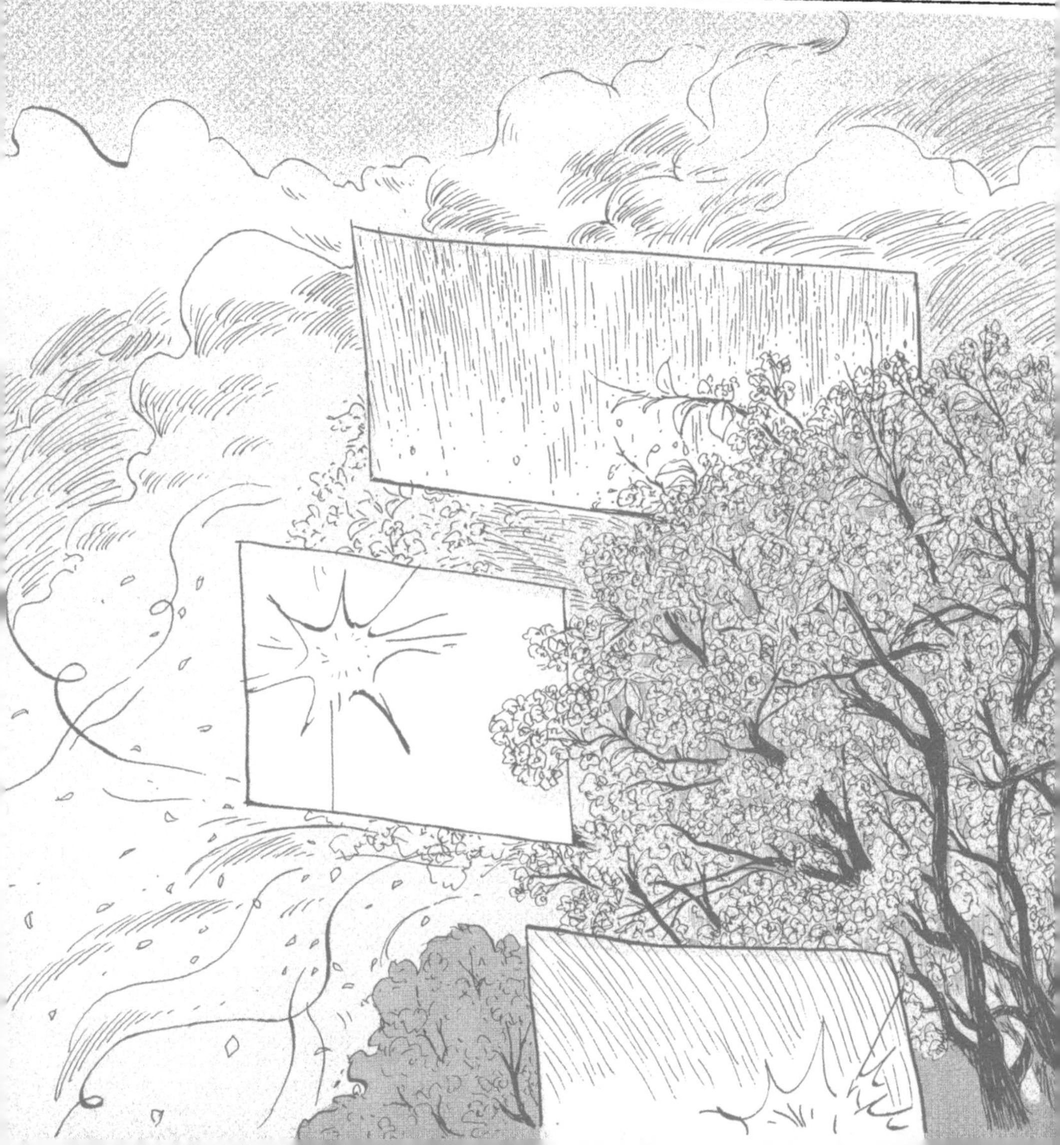

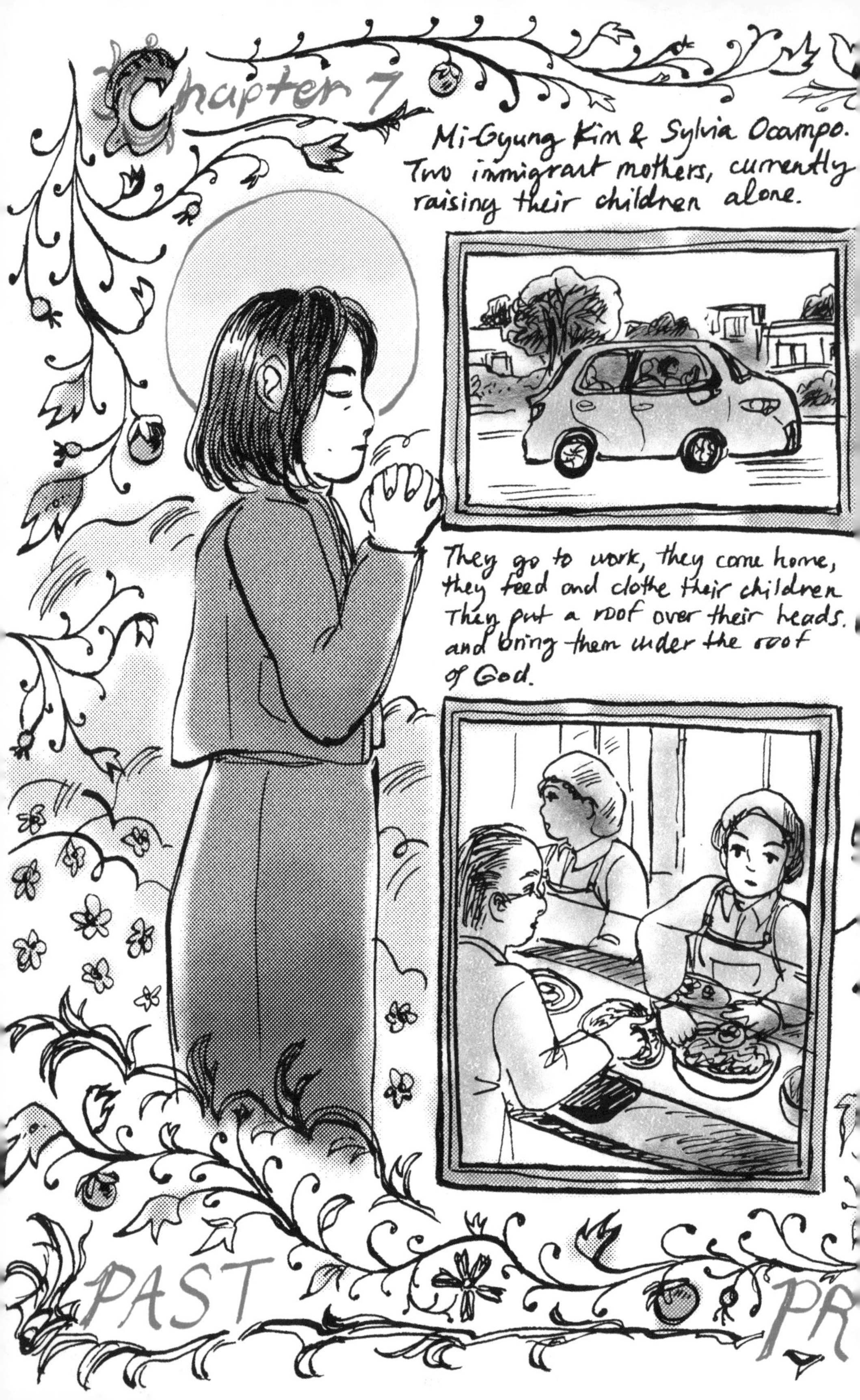
Chapter 7
Mi-Gyung Kim & Sylvia Ocampo. Two immigrant mothers, currently raising their children alone.
They go to work, they come home, they feed and clothe their children They put a roof over their heads. and bring them under the roof of God.
PAST
PR

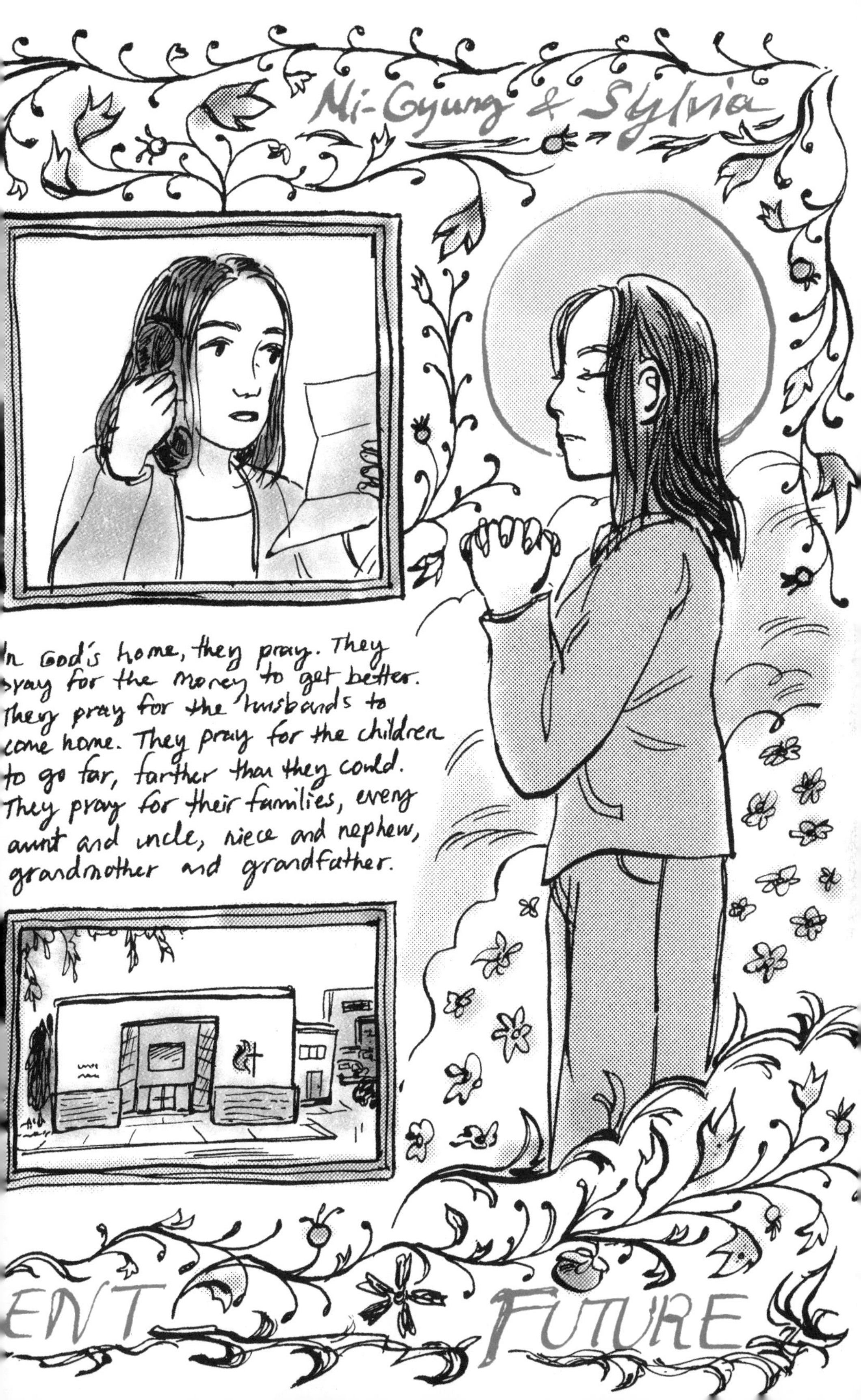

Mi-Gyung & Sylvia
In God's home, they pray. They pray for the money to get better. They pray for the husbands to come home. They pray for the children to go far, farther than they could. They pray for their families, every aunt and uncle, niece and nephew, grandmother and grandfather.
ENT
FUTURE

Here and there, week by week, month by month. Season by season, year by year passes.

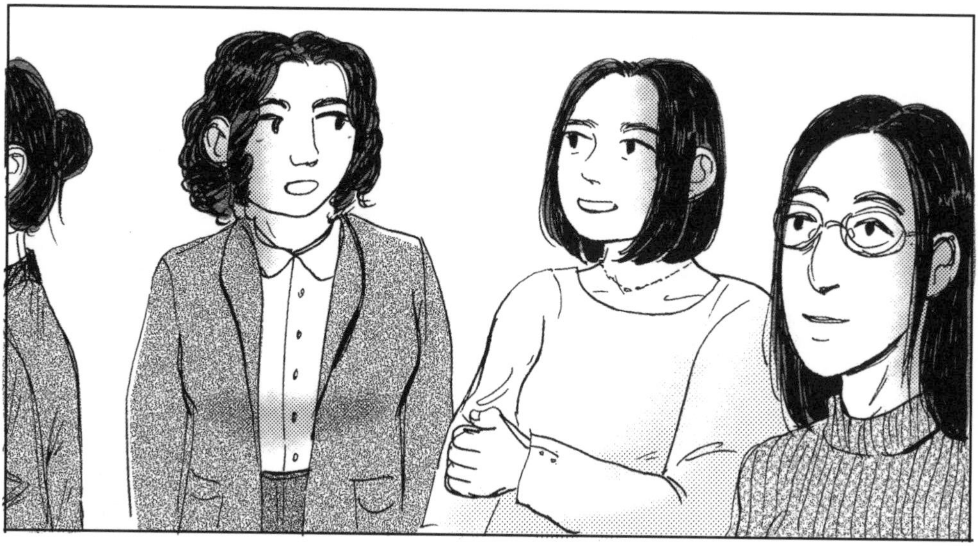

At church, they gossip with the other immigrant mothers. The women who they share with the most.

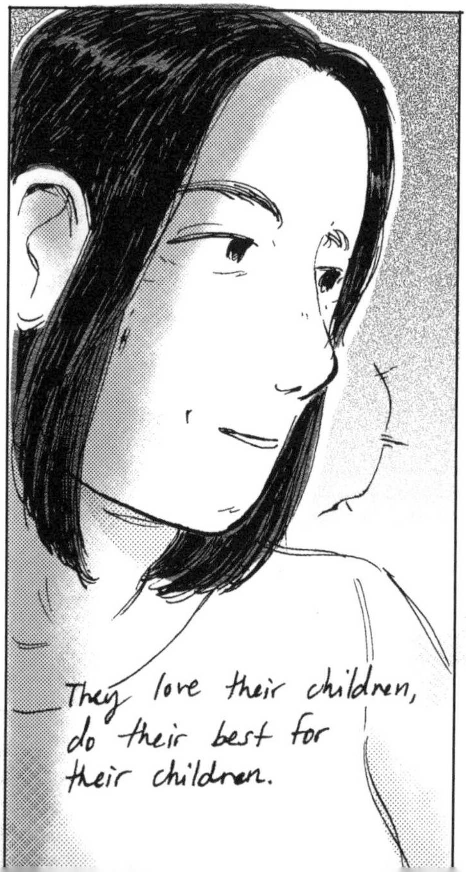
They love their children, do their best for their children.

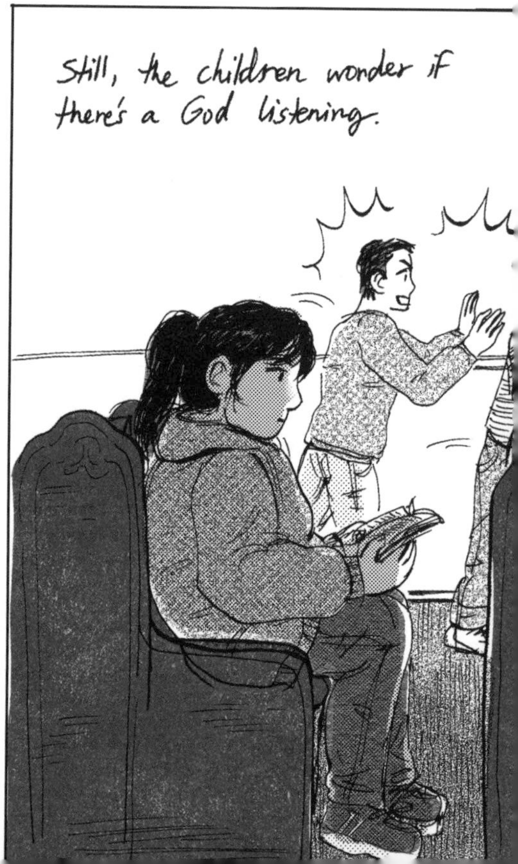
Still, the children wonder if there's a God listening.

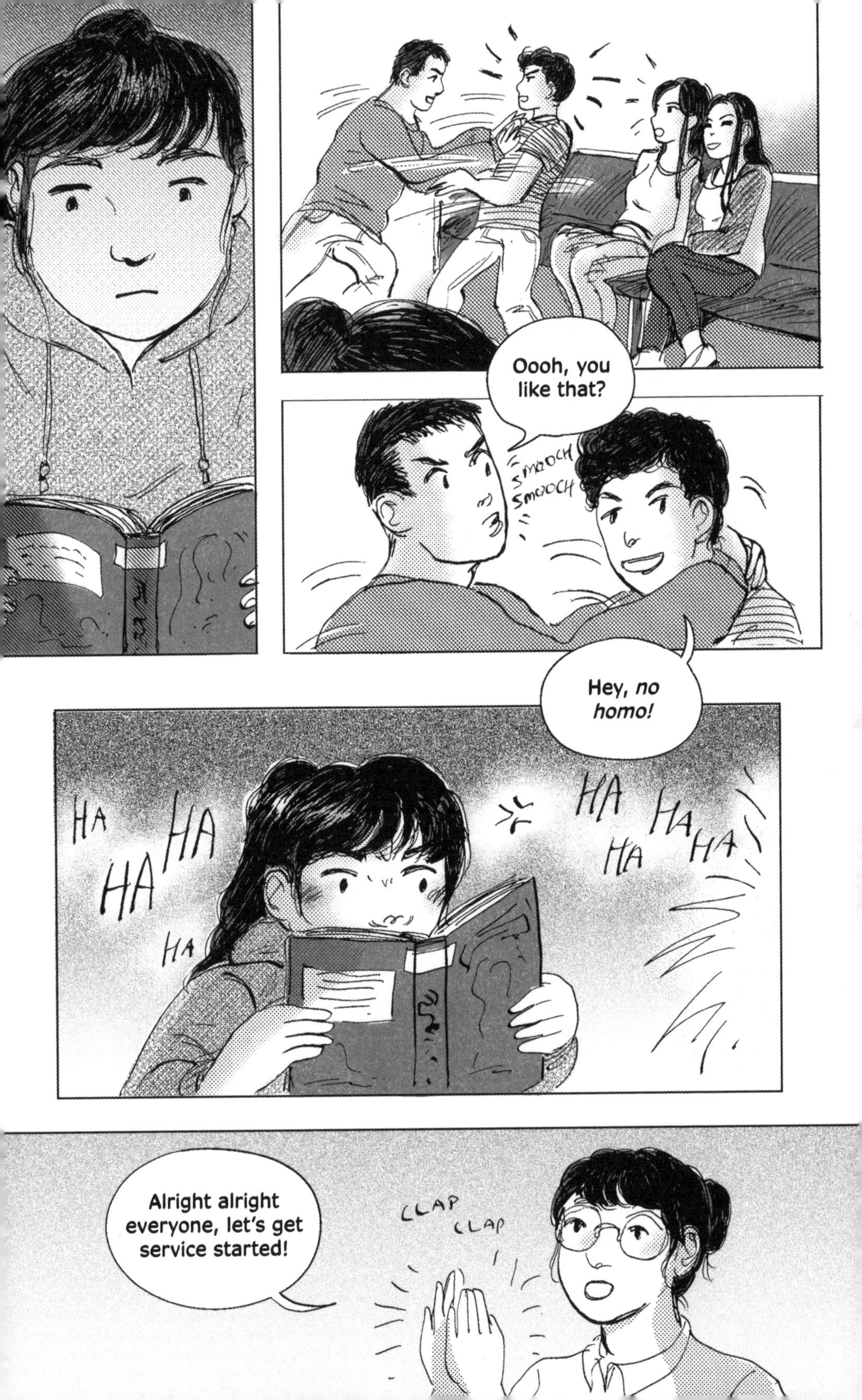
Oooh, you like that?
SMOOCH SMOOCH
Hey, *no homo!*
HA HA HA HA
HA HA HA HA HA
Alright alright everyone, let's get service started!
CLAP CLAP

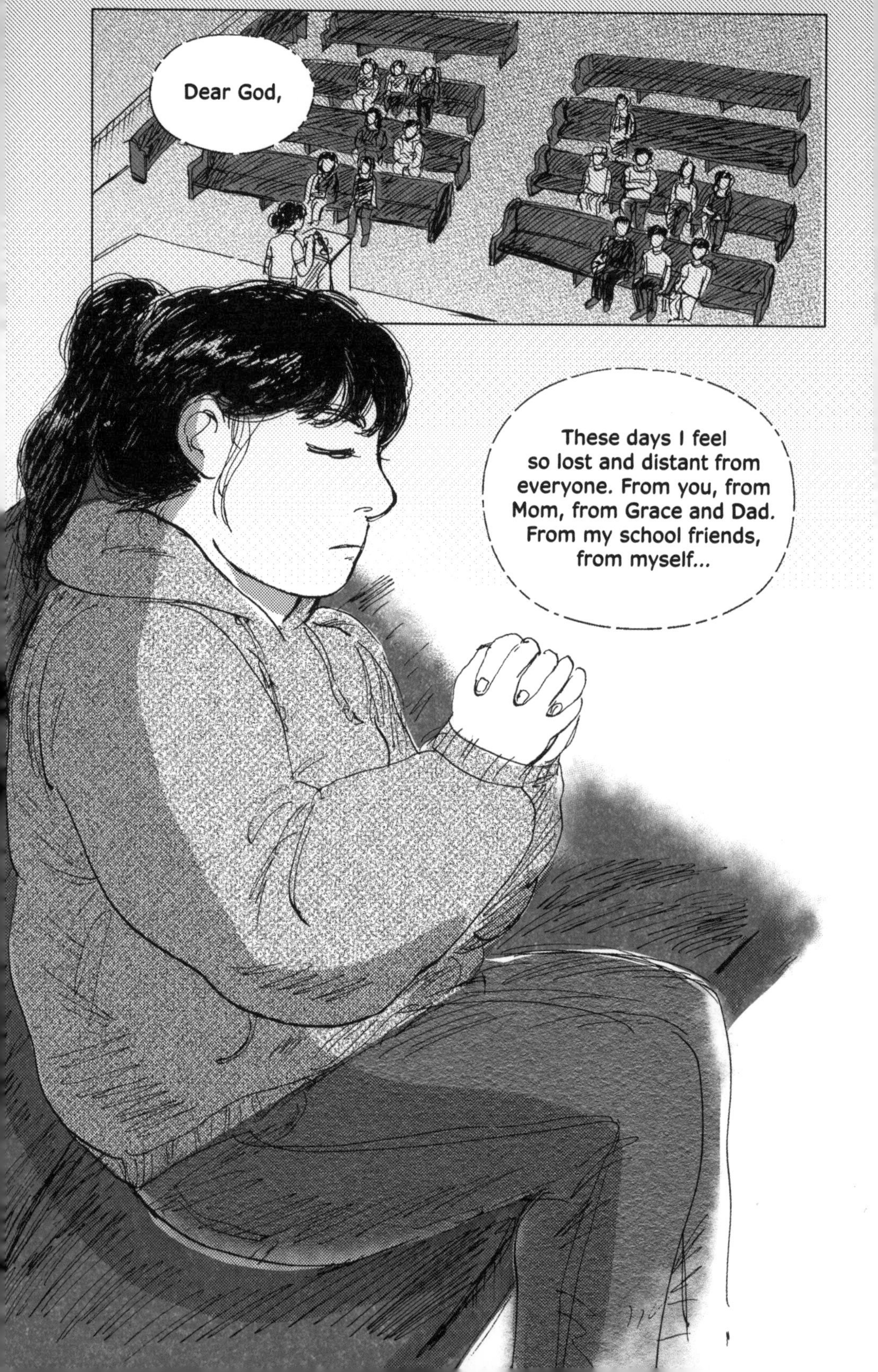
Dear God,
These days I feel so lost and distant from everyone. From you, from Mom, from Grace and Dad. From my school friends, from myself...

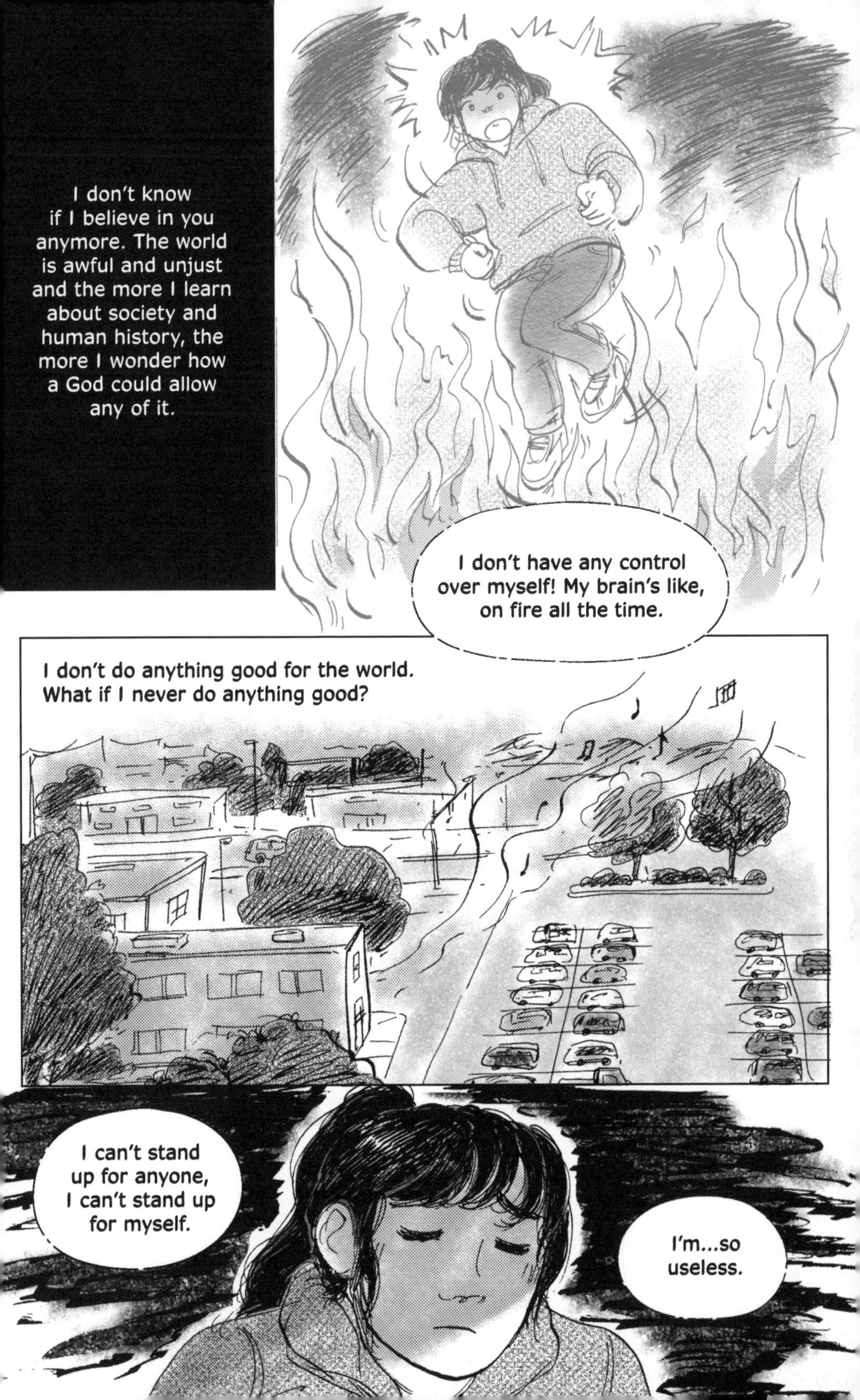
I don't know if I believe in you anymore. The world is awful and unjust and the more I learn about society and human history, the more I wonder how a God could allow any of it.
I don't have any control over myself! My brain's like, on fire all the time.
I don't do anything good for the world. What if I never do anything good?
I can't stand up for anyone, I can't stand up for myself.
I'm...so useless.

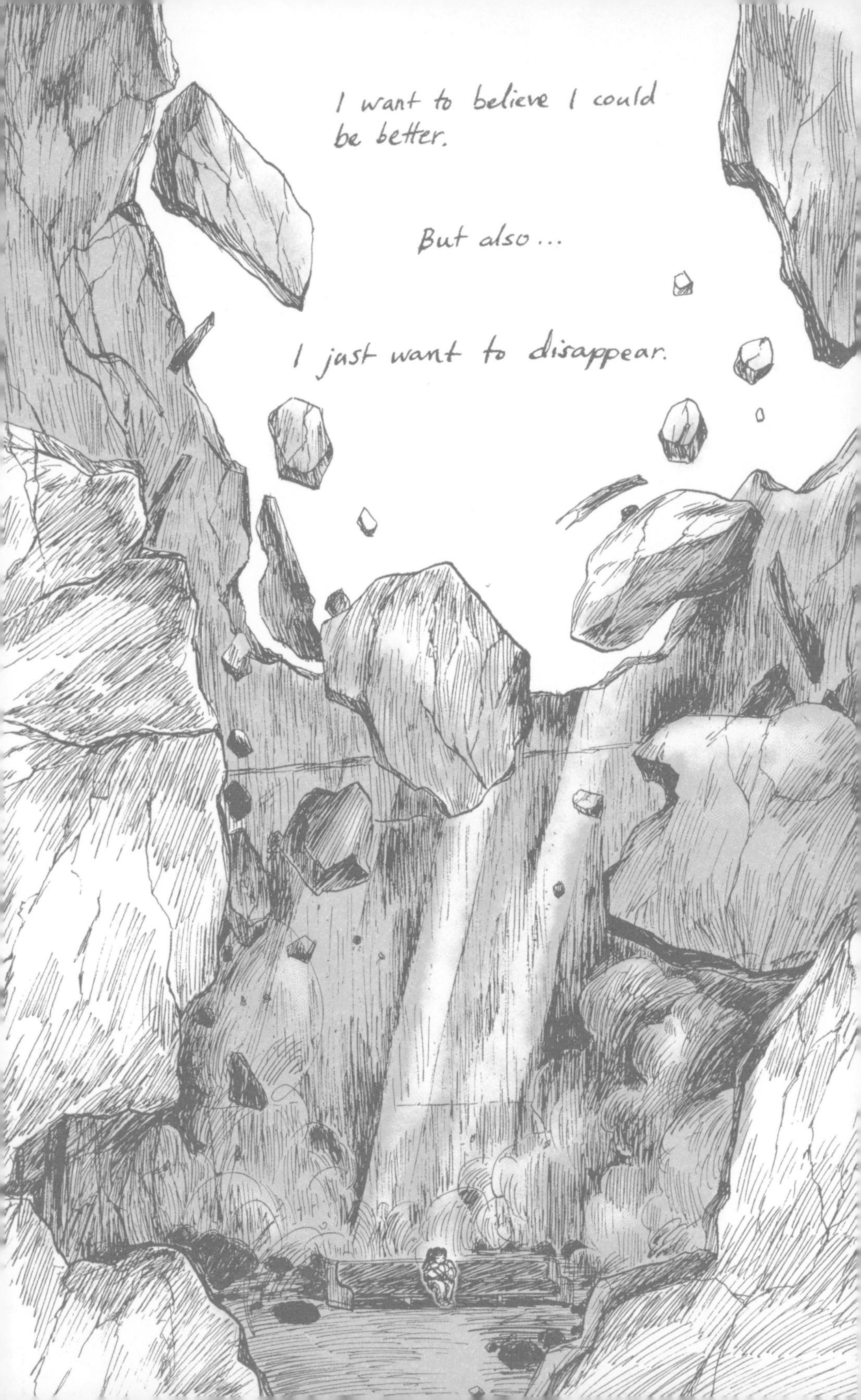
I want to believe I could be better.
But also...
I just want to disappear.

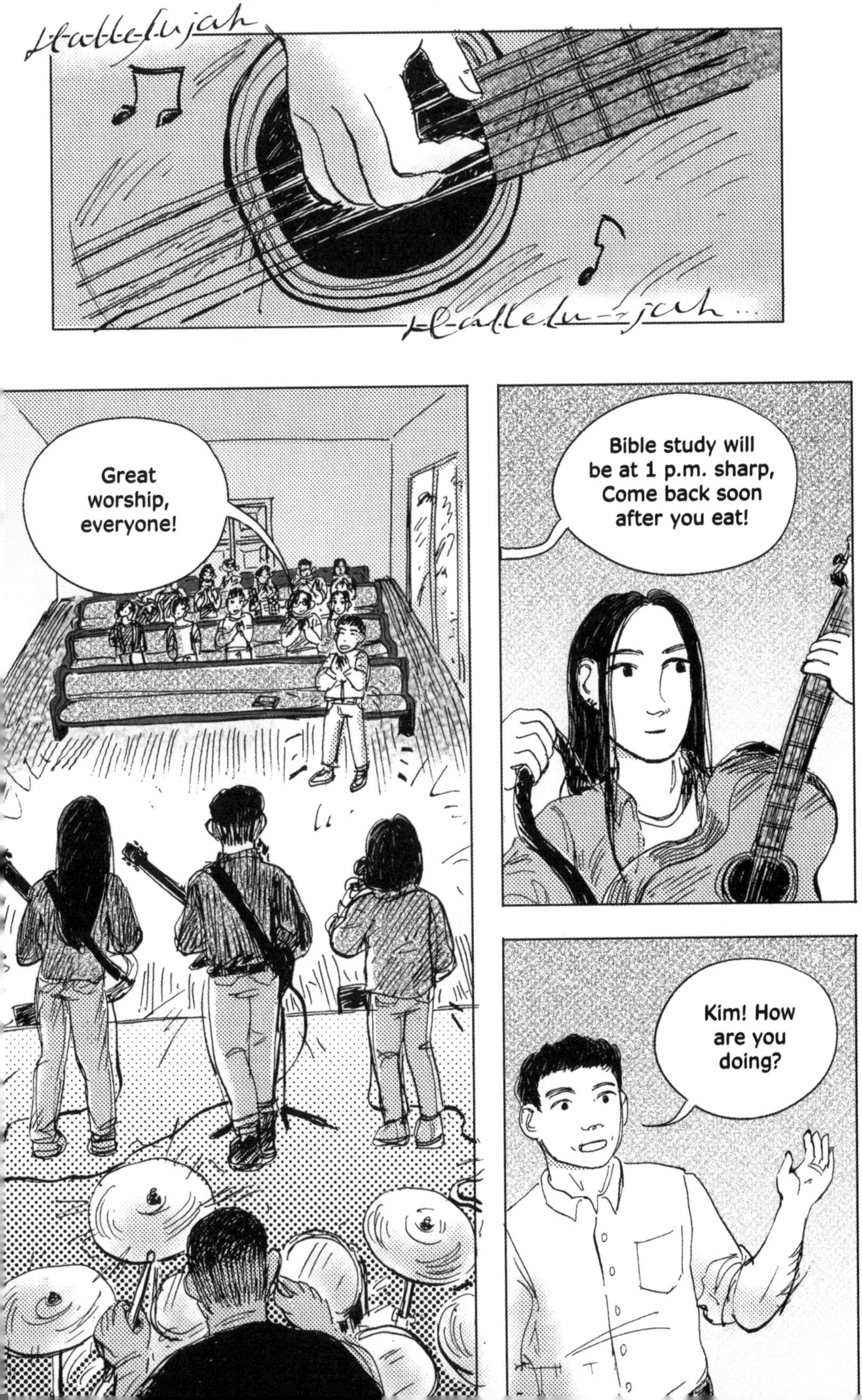
Hallelujah
Hallelu-jah..
Great worship, everyone!
Bible study will be at 1 p.m. sharp, Come back soon after you eat!
Kim! How are you doing?

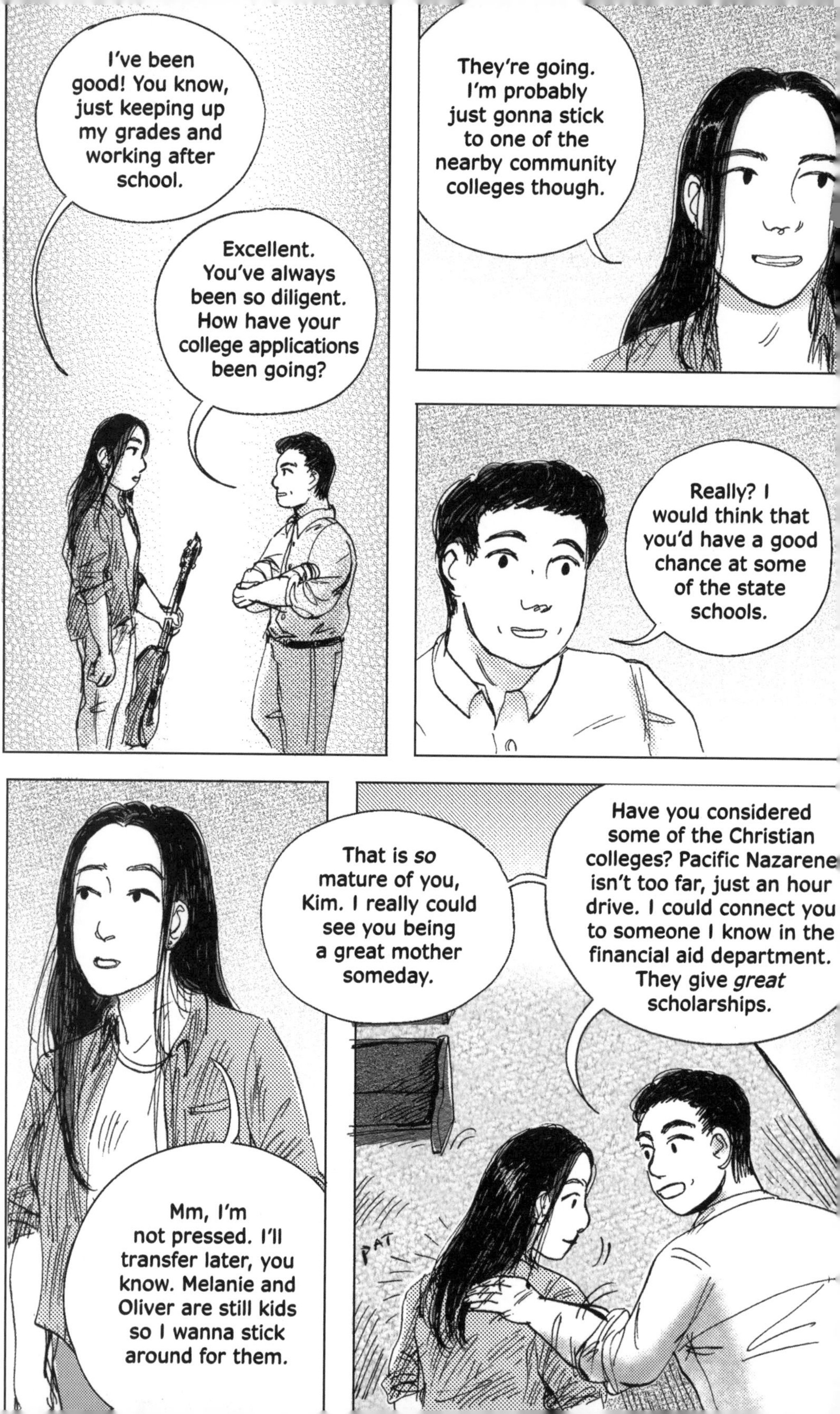

I've been good! You know, just keeping up my grades and working after school.
Excellent. You've always been so diligent. How have your college applications been going?
They're going. I'm probably just gonna stick to one of the nearby community colleges though.
Really? I would think that you'd have a good chance at some of the state schools.
Mm, I'm not pressed. I'll transfer later, you know. Melanie and Oliver are still kids so I wanna stick around for them.
That is *so* mature of you, Kim. I really could see you being a great mother someday.
Have you considered some of the Christian colleges? Pacific Nazarene isn't too far, just an hour drive. I could connect you to someone I know in the financial aid department. They give *great* scholarships.
PAT

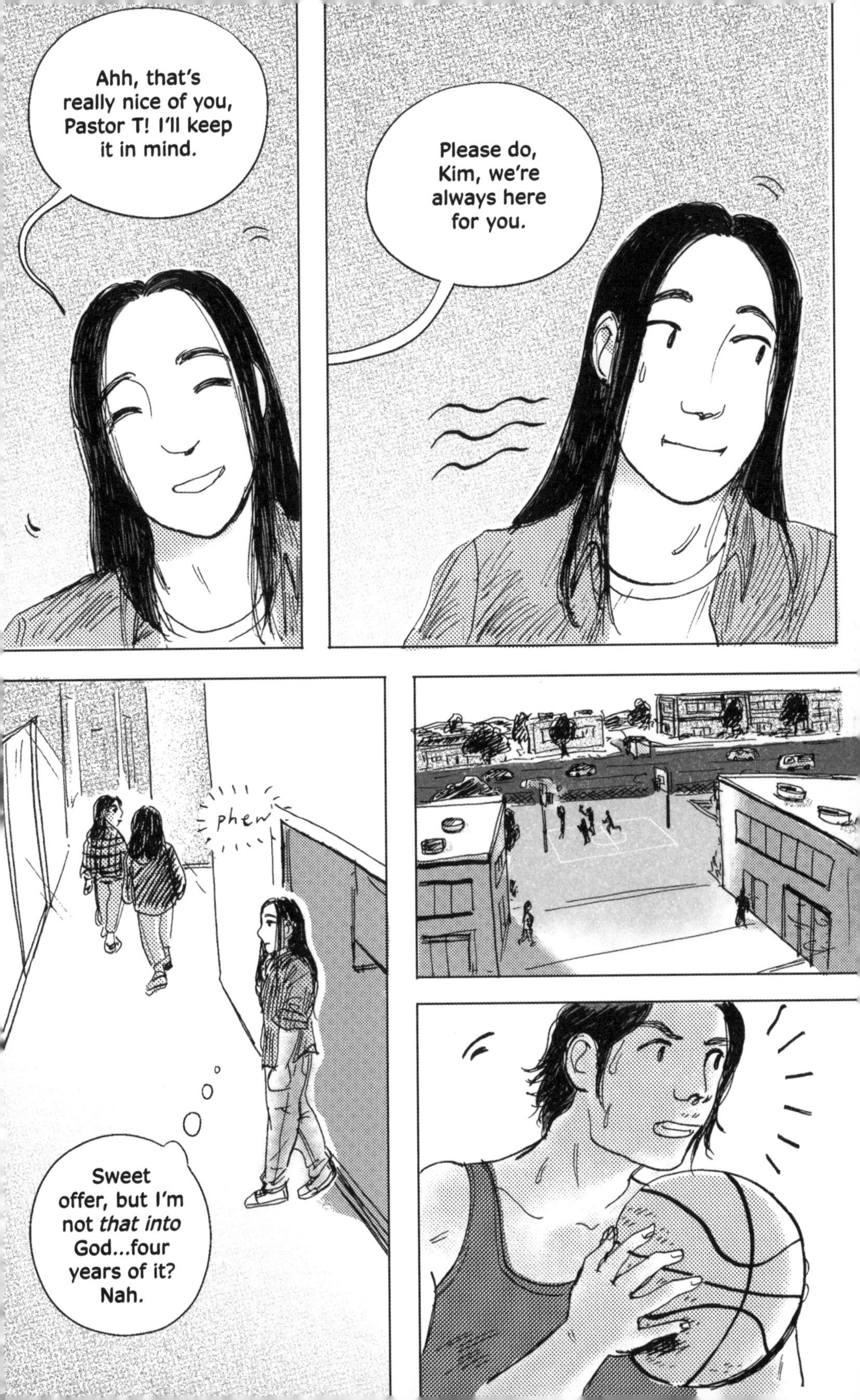
Ahh, that's really nice of you, Pastor T! I'll keep it in mind.
Please do, Kim, we're always here for you.
phew
Sweet offer, but I'm not *that into* God...four years of it? Nah.

sup

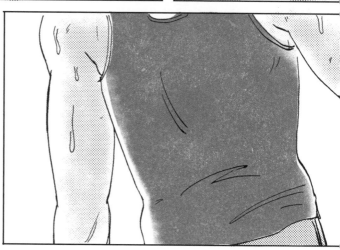

eh.

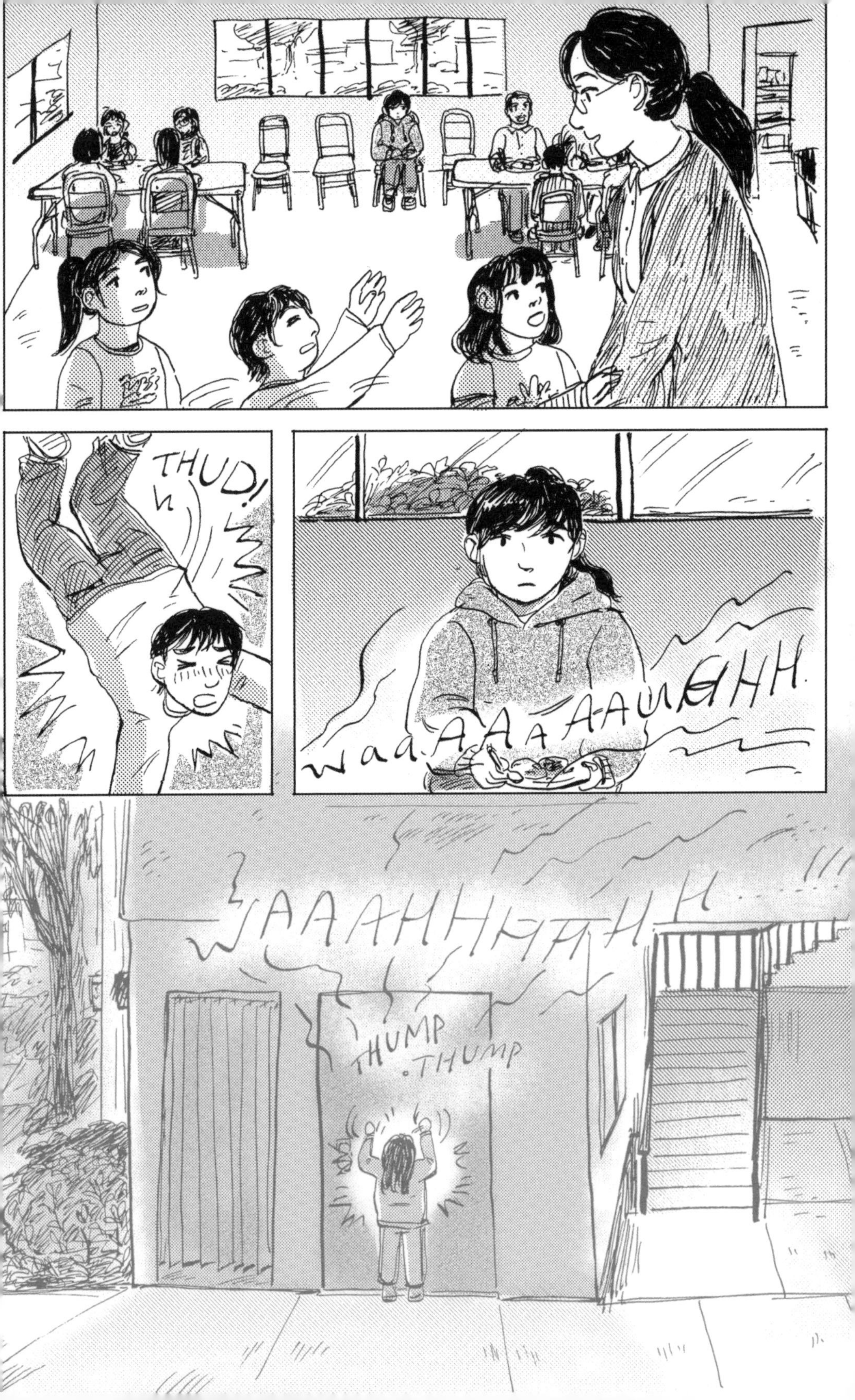
THUD!
waaAAAAAAUGHH.
WAAAHHHHHH
THUMP
THUMP

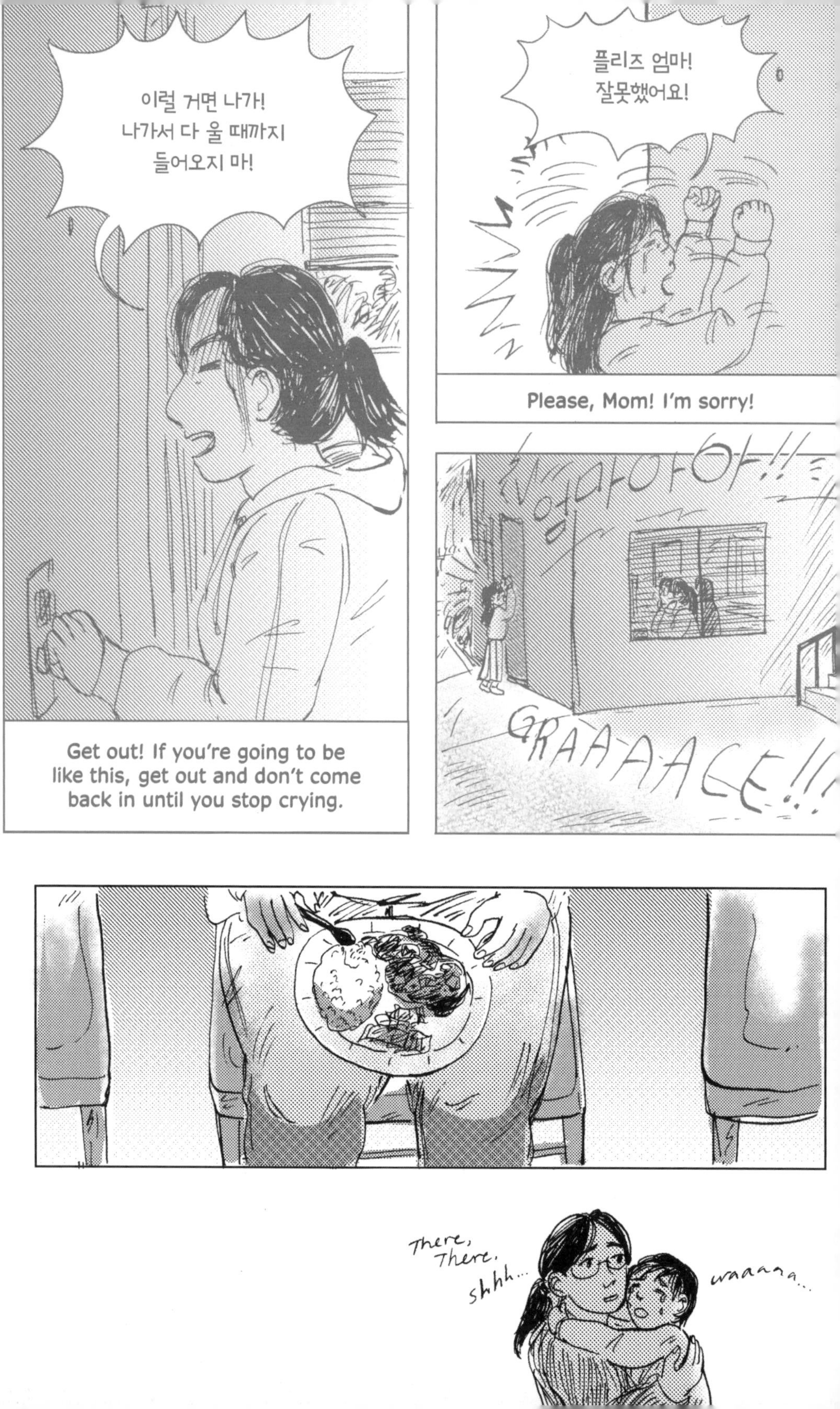

이럴 거면 나가!
나가서 다 울 때까지
들어오지 마!
Get out! If you're going to be like this, get out and don't come back in until you stop crying.
플리즈 엄마!
잘못했어요!
Please, Mom! I'm sorry!
엄마아아!!
GRAAAACE!!!
There, There. shhh...
waaaaa...

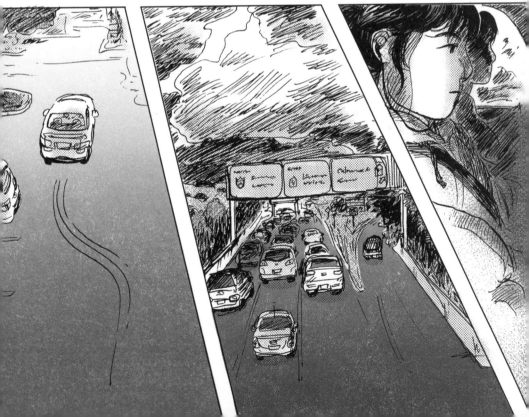

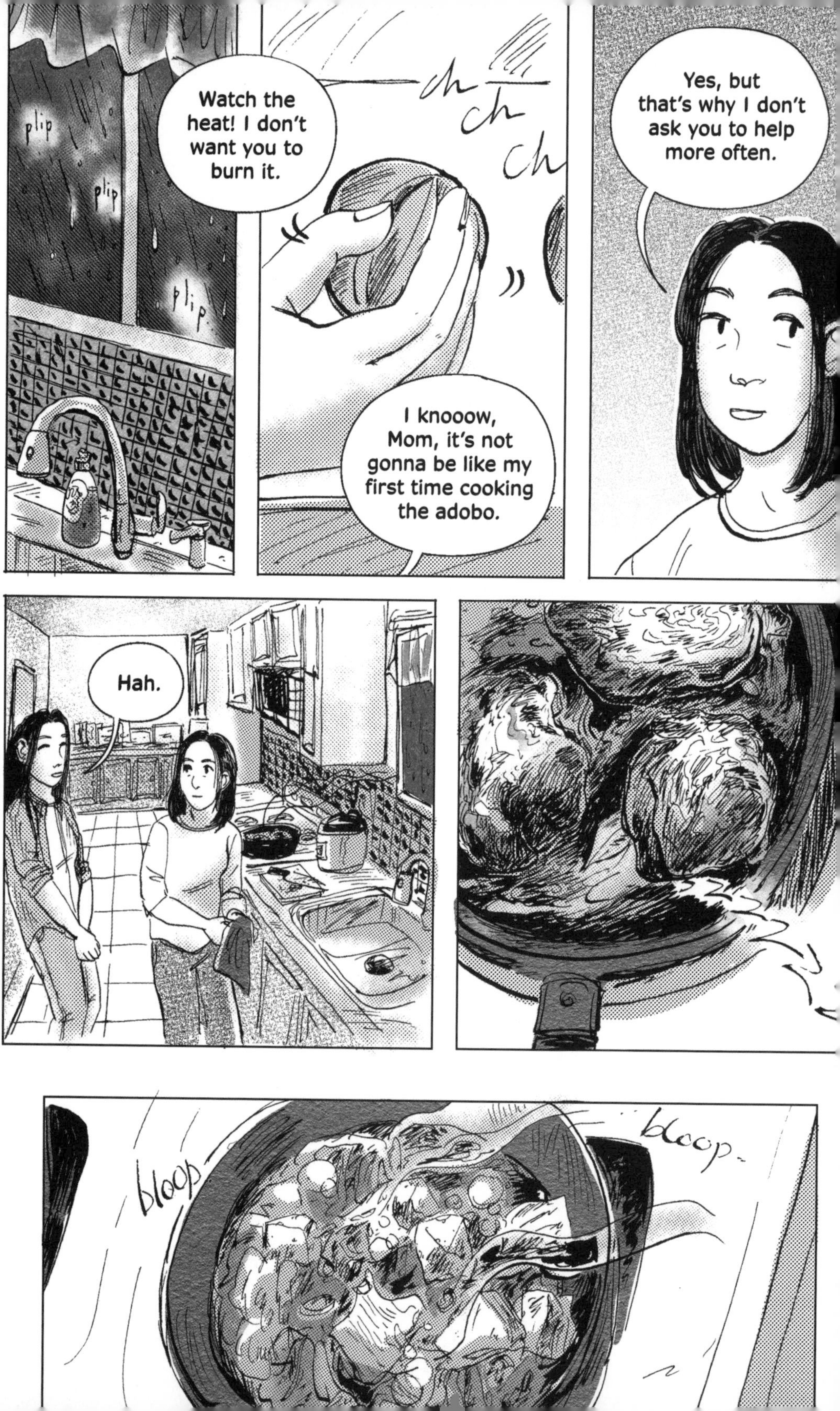
plip
plip
plip
Watch the heat! I don't want you to burn it.
ch
ch
ch
I knooow, Mom, it's not gonna be like my first time cooking the adobo.
Yes, but that's why I don't ask you to help more often.
Hah.
bloop
bloop

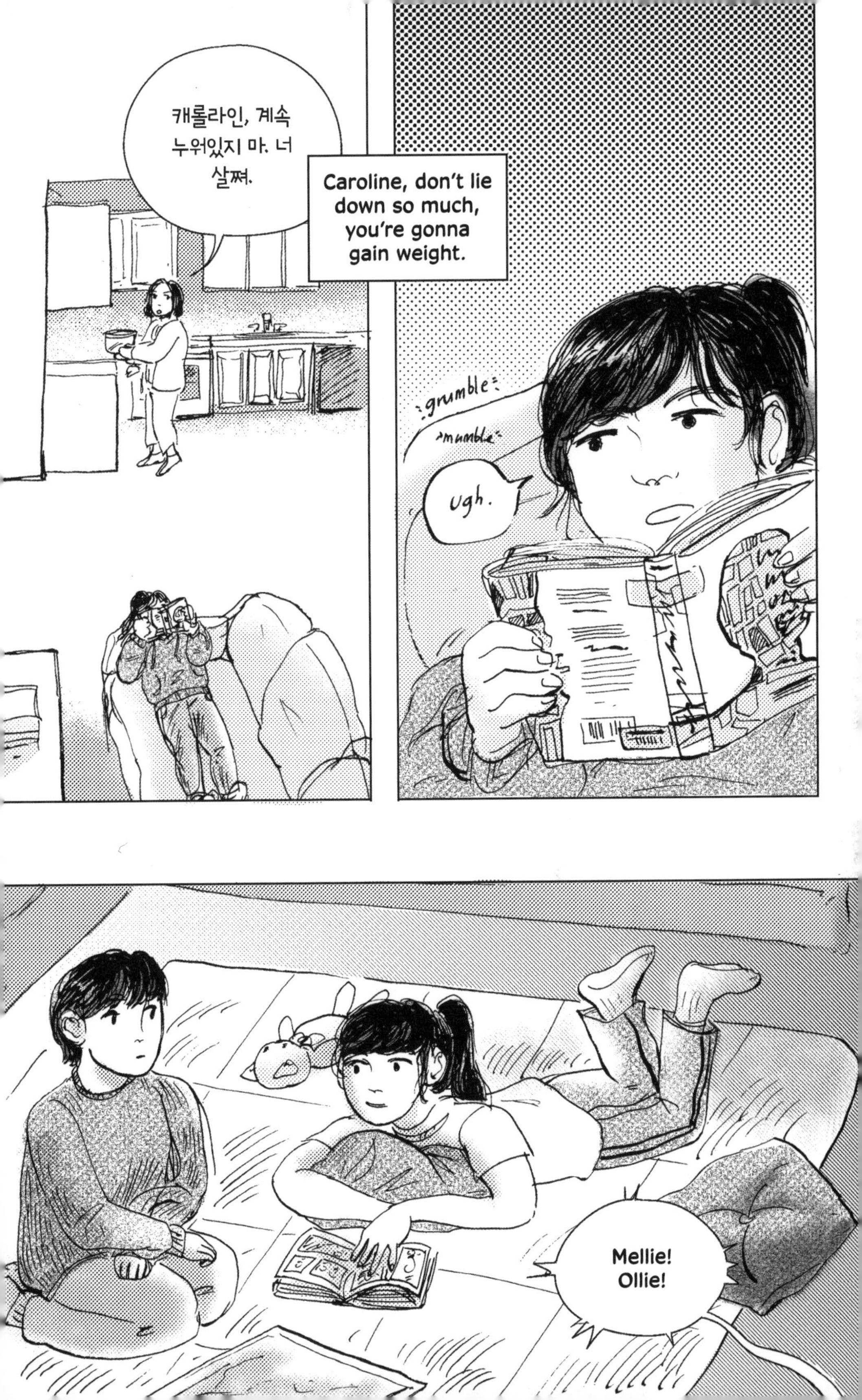
캐롤라인, 계속 누워있지 마. 너 살쪄.
Caroline, don't lie down so much, you're gonna gain weight.
grumble
mumble
Ugh.
Mellie! Ollie!

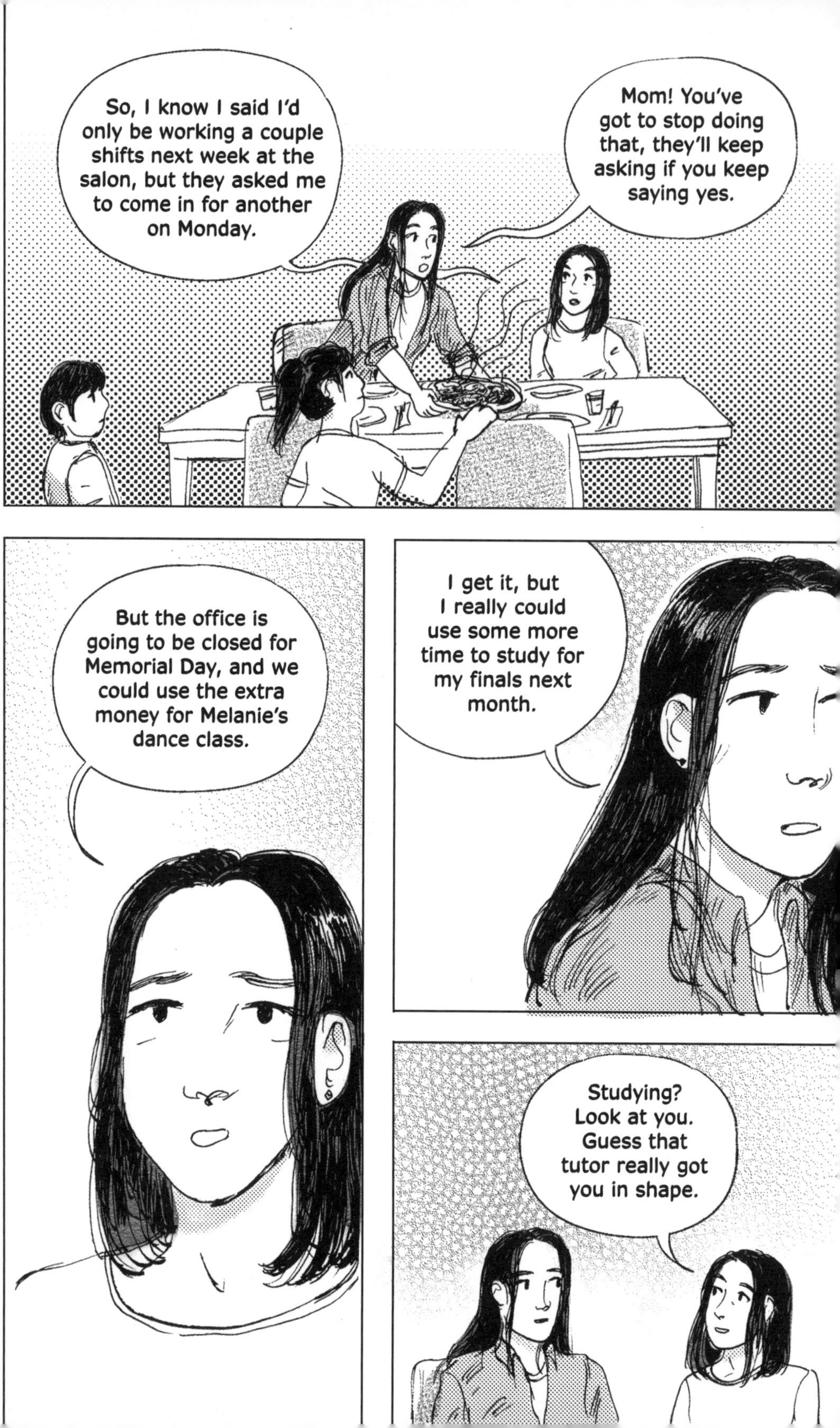
So, I know I said I'd only be working a couple shifts next week at the salon, but they asked me to come in for another on Monday.
Mom! You've got to stop doing that, they'll keep asking if you keep saying yes.
But the office is going to be closed for Memorial Day, and we could use the extra money for Melanie's dance class.
I get it, but I really could use some more time to study for my finals next month.
Studying? Look at you. Guess that tutor really got you in shape.

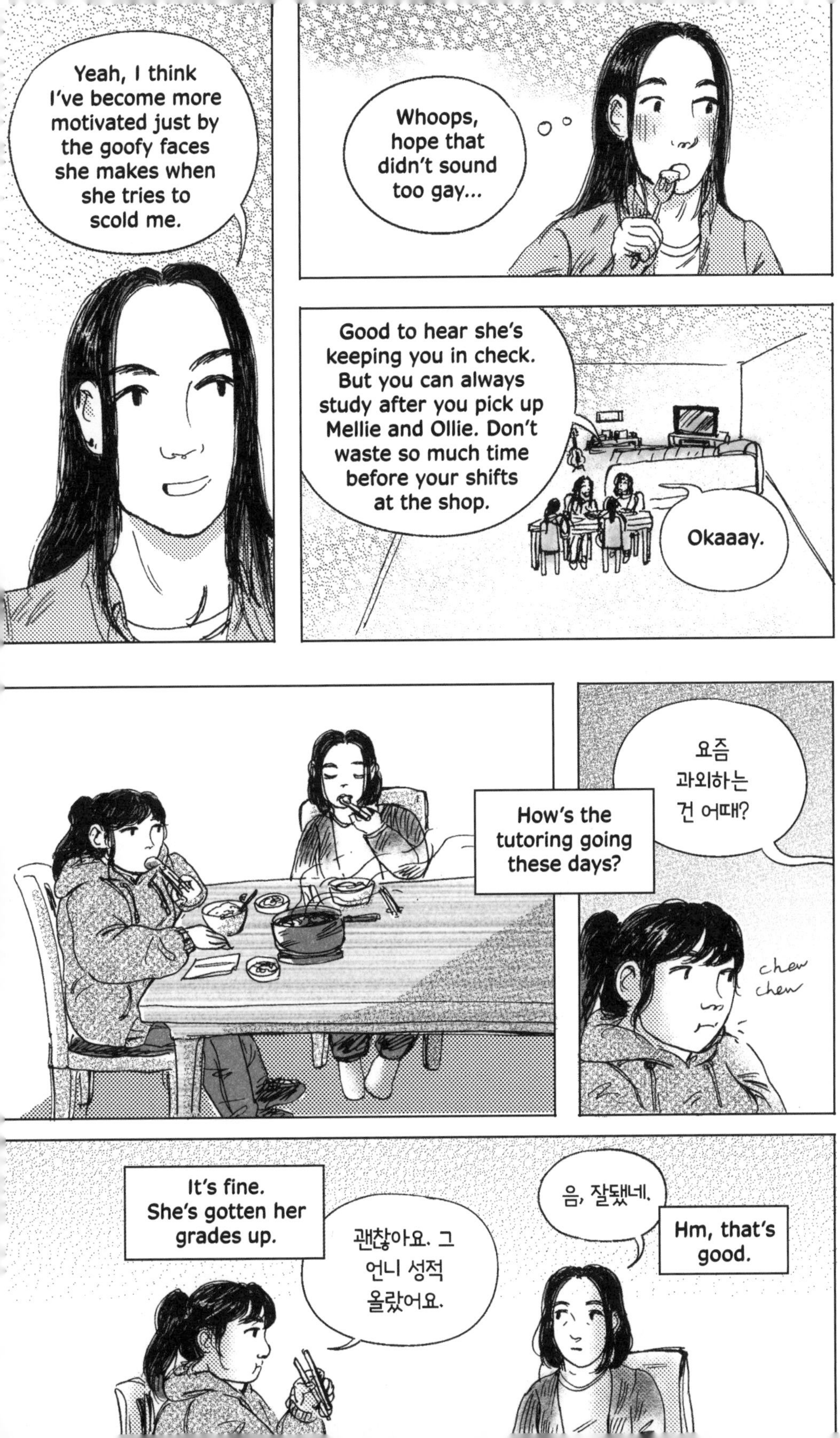

Yeah, I think I've become more motivated just by the goofy faces she makes when she tries to scold me.
Whoops, hope that didn't sound too gay...
Good to hear she's keeping you in check. But you can always study after you pick up Mellie and Ollie. Don't waste so much time before your shifts at the shop.
Okaaay.
요즘 과외하는 건 어때?
How's the tutoring going these days?
chew chew
It's fine. She's gotten her grades up.
괜찮아요. 그 언니 성적 올랐어요.
음, 잘됐네.
Hm, that's good.

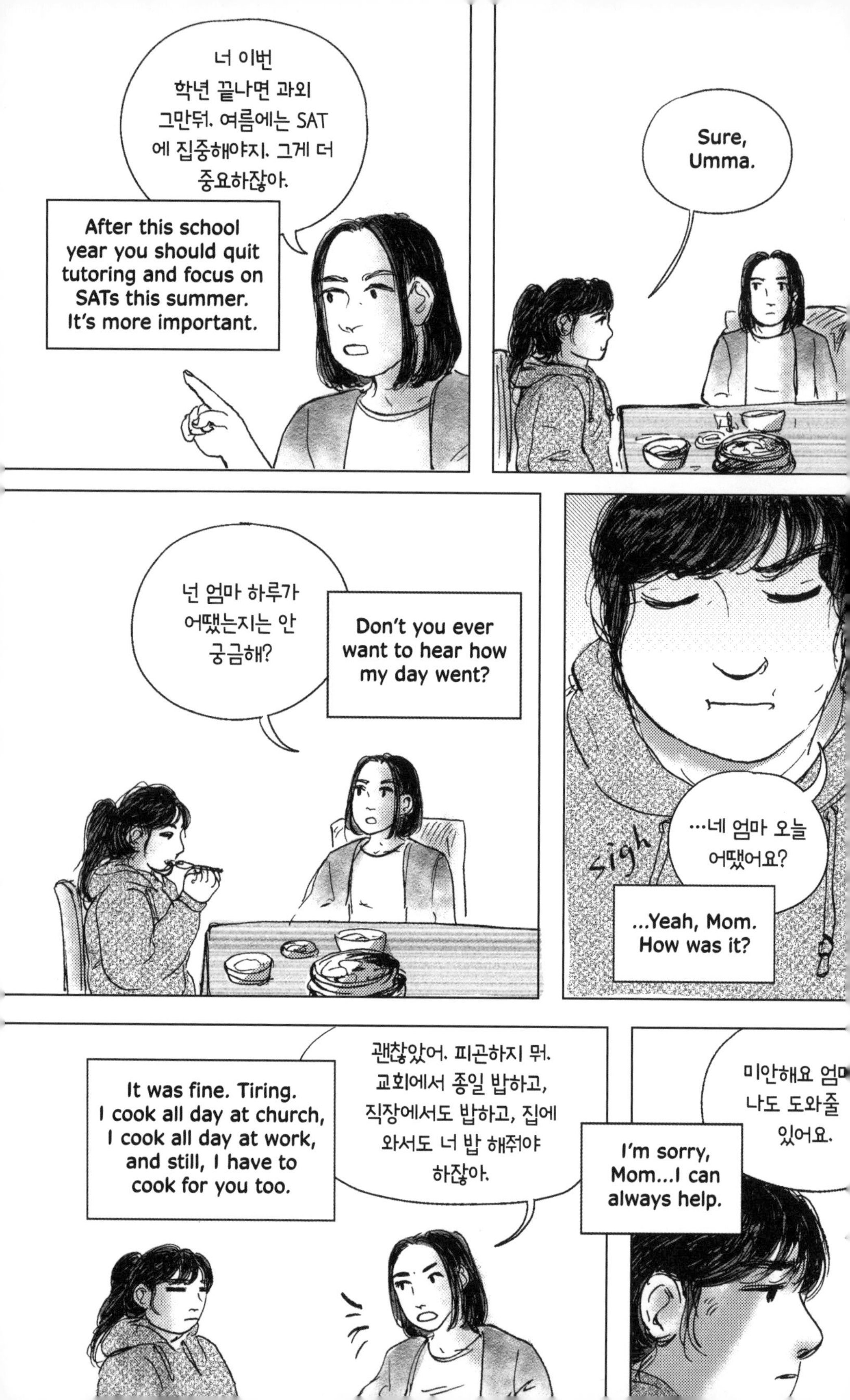
너 이번 학년 끝나면 과외 그만둬. 여름에는 SAT 에 집중해야지. 그게 더 중요하잖아.
After this school year you should quit tutoring and focus on SATs this summer. It's more important.
Sure, Umma.
넌 엄마 하루가 어땠는지는 안 궁금해?
Don't you ever want to hear how my day went?
sigh
…네 엄마 오늘 어땠어요?
...Yeah, Mom. How was it?
괜찮았어. 피곤하지 뭐. 교회에서 종일 밥하고, 직장에서도 밥하고, 집에 와서도 너 밥 해줘야 하잖아.
It was fine. Tiring. I cook all day at church, I cook all day at work, and still, I have to cook for you too.
미안해요 엄마 나도 도와줄 있어요.
I'm sorry, Mom...I can always help.

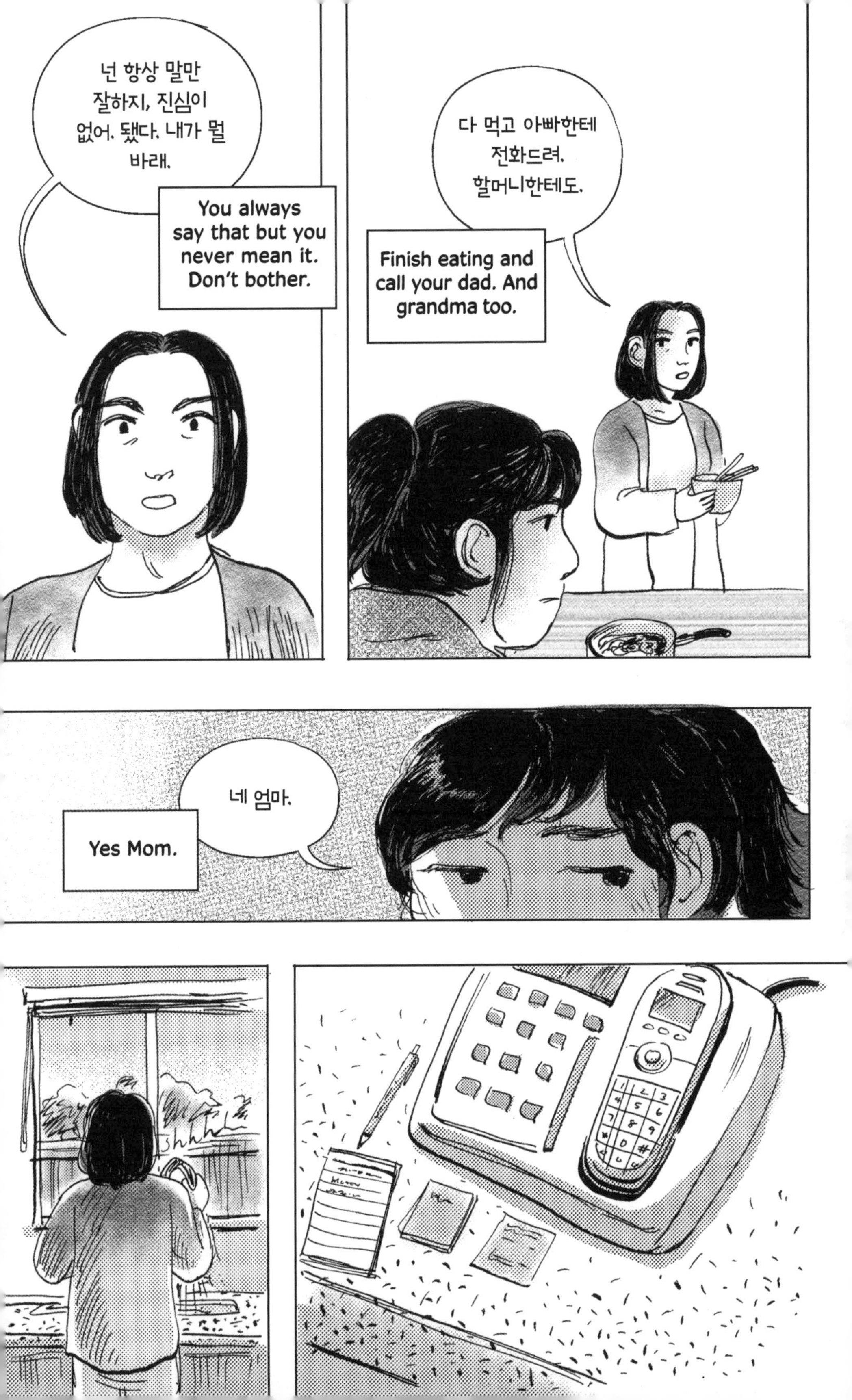
넌 항상 말만 잘하지, 진심이 없어. 됐다. 내가 뭘 바래.
You always say that but you never mean it. Don't bother.
다 먹고 아빠한테 전화드려. 할머니한테도.
Finish eating and call your dad. And grandma too.
네 엄마.
Yes Mom.

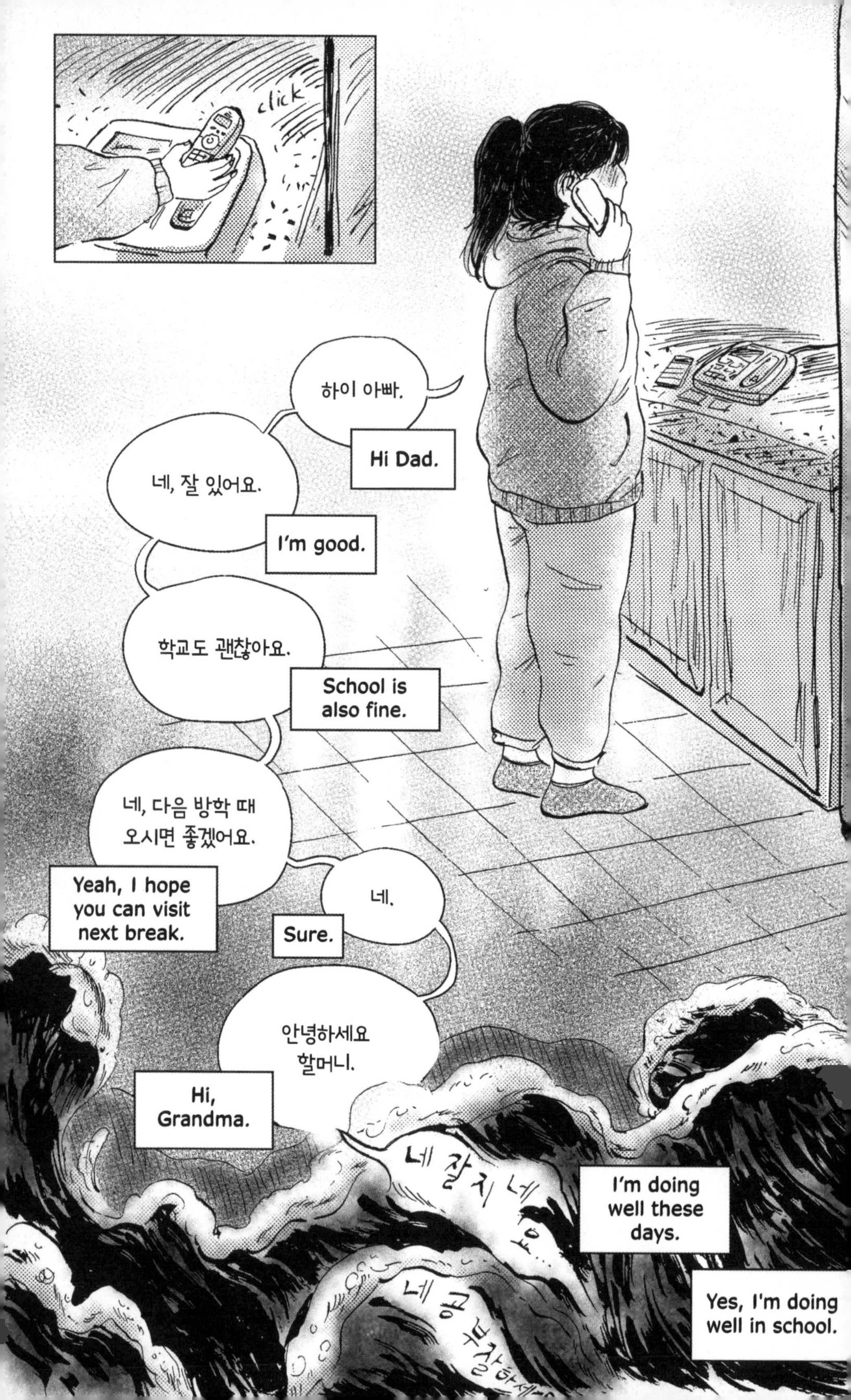
click
하이 아빠.
Hi Dad.
네, 잘 있어요.
I'm good.
학교도 괜찮아요.
School is also fine.
네, 다음 방학 때 오시면 좋겠어요.
Yeah, I hope you can visit next break.
네.
Sure.
안녕하세요 할머니.
Hi, Grandma.
네 잘지네요...
I'm doing well these days.
네 공부잘하세
Yes, I'm doing well in school.

You are on one side of the ocean
and I'm on the other.
Every year I feel myself drifting away
The waters between us growing.
건강해요
I'm healthy...
할머니도 건강하세요
stay healthy too
Grandma

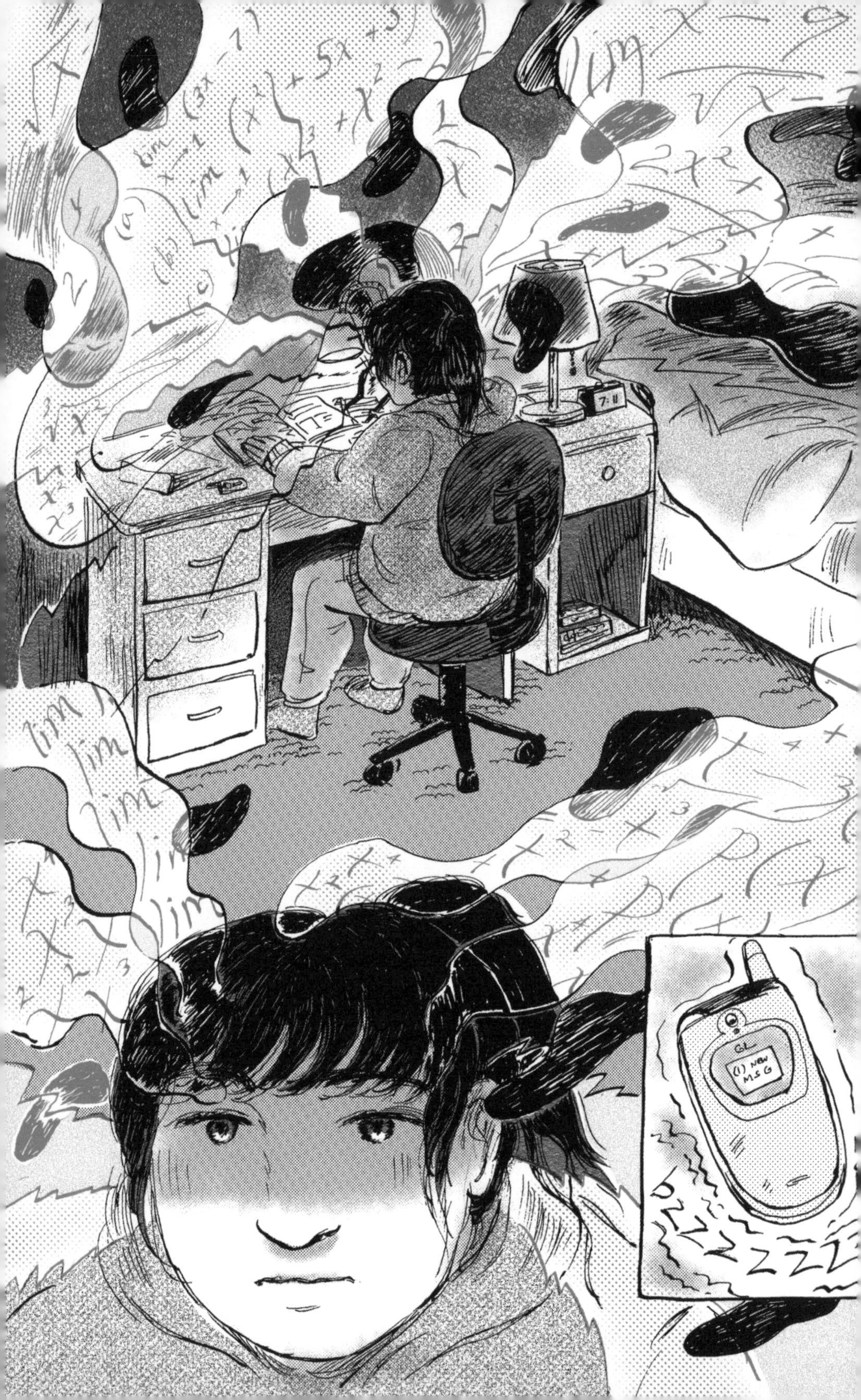
7:11
(1) NEW MSG

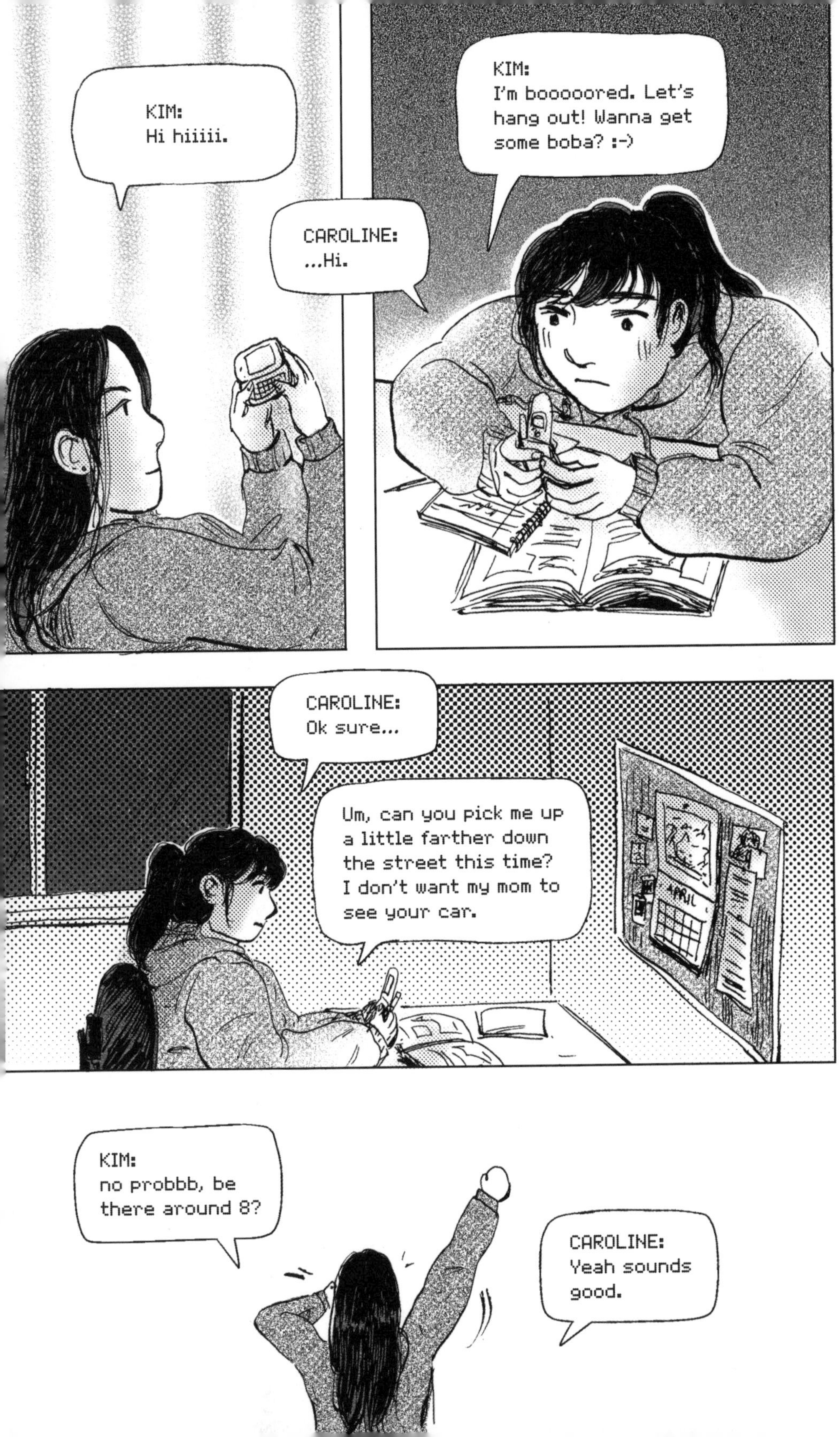
KIM:
Hi hiiiii.
CAROLINE:
...Hi.
KIM:
I'm booooored. Let's hang out! Wanna get some boba? :-)
CAROLINE:
Ok sure...
Um, can you pick me up a little farther down the street this time? I don't want my mom to see your car.
APRIL
KIM:
no probbb, be there around 8?
CAROLINE:
Yeah sounds good.

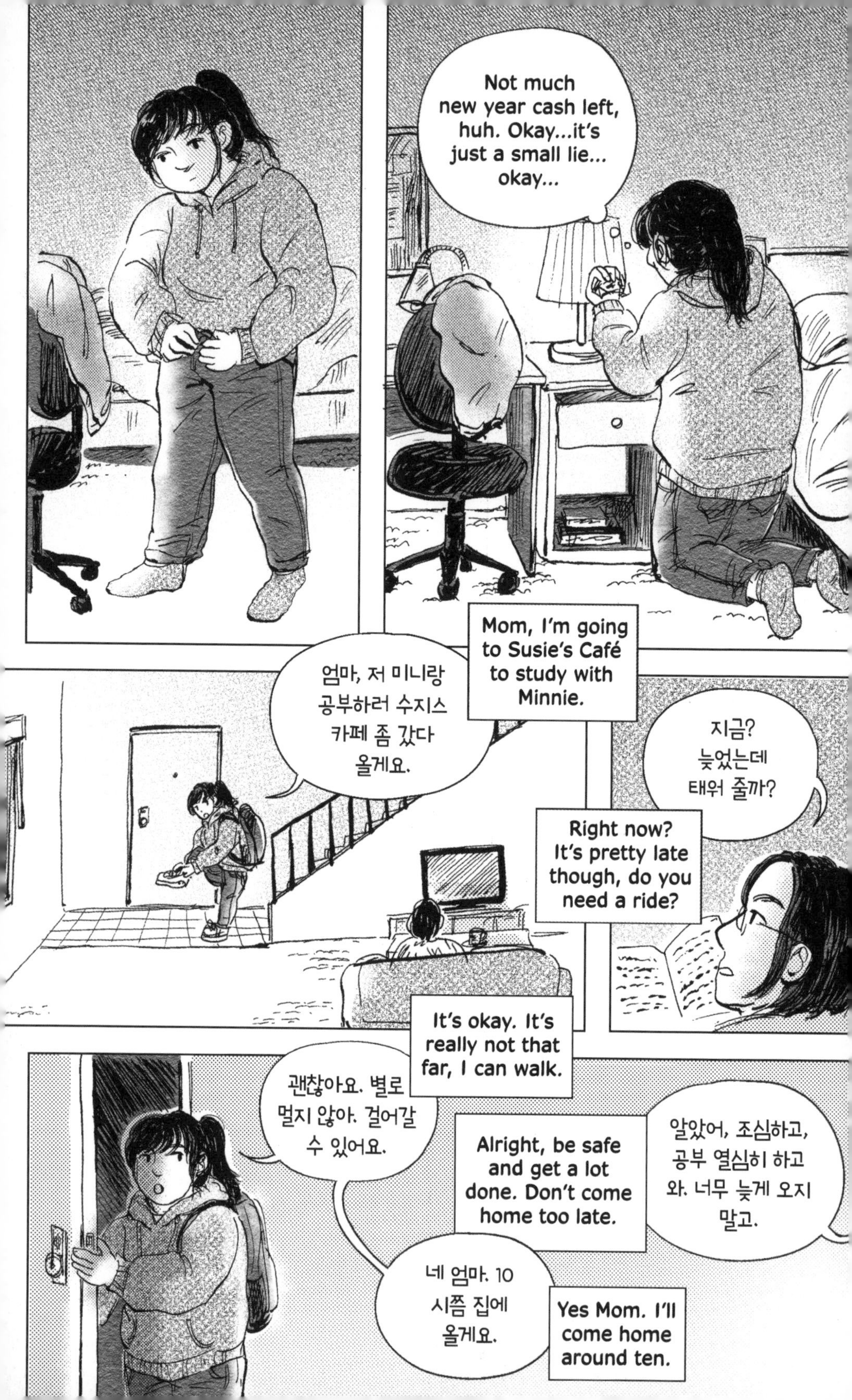
Not much new year cash left, huh. Okay...it's just a small lie... okay...
엄마, 저 미니랑 공부하러 수지스 카페 좀 갔다 올게요.
Mom, I'm going to Susie's Café to study with Minnie.
지금? 늦었는데 태워 줄까?
Right now? It's pretty late though, do you need a ride?
괜찮아요. 별로 멀지 않아. 걸어갈 수 있어요.
It's okay. It's really not that far, I can walk.
알았어, 조심하고, 공부 열심히 하고 와. 너무 늦게 오지 말고.
Alright, be safe and get a lot done. Don't come home too late.
네 엄마. 10 시쯤 집에 올게요.
Yes Mom. I'll come home around ten.

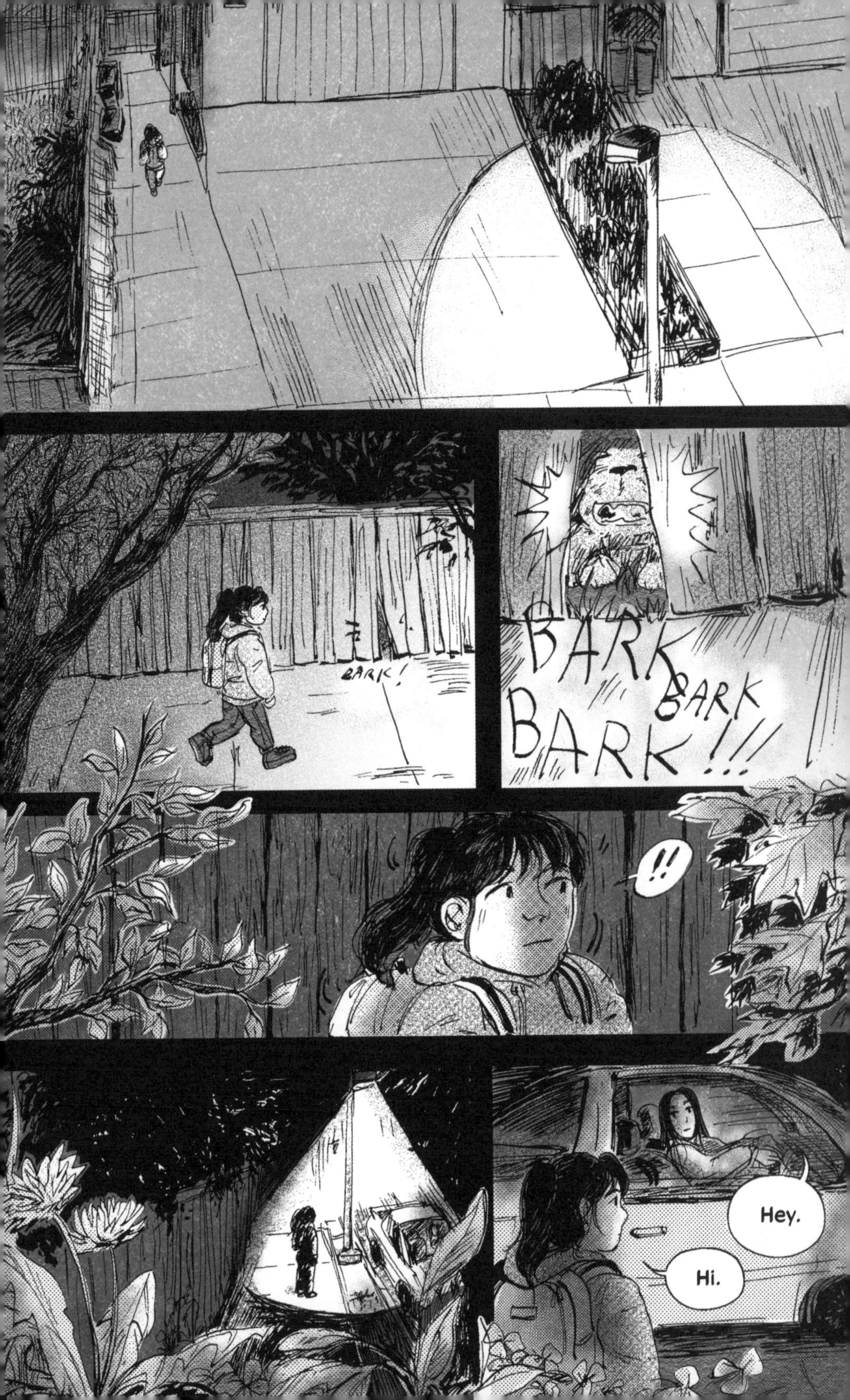
BARK!
BARK BARK BARK!!!
!!
Hey.
Hi.

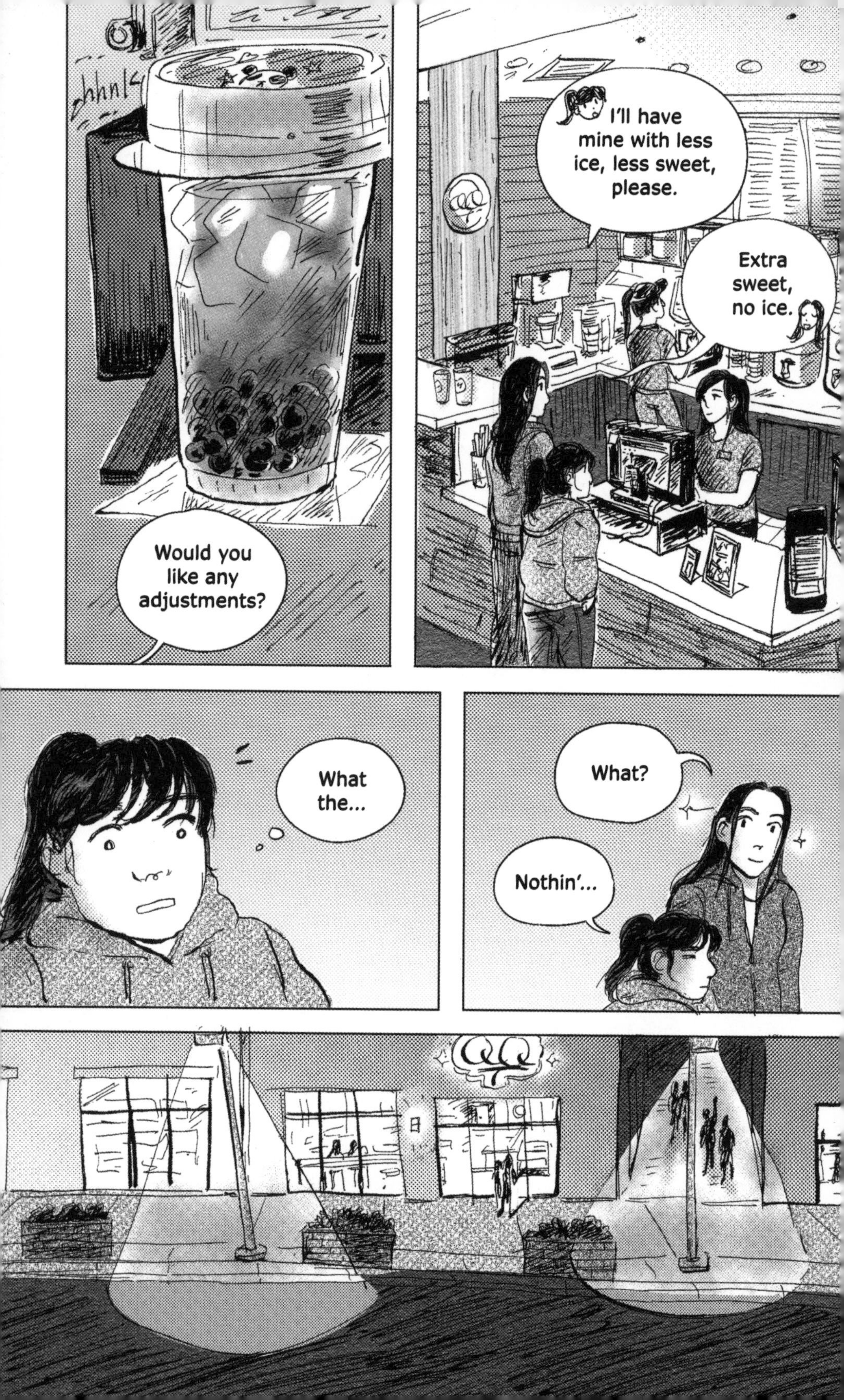
Would you like any adjustments?
I'll have mine with less ice, less sweet, please.
Extra sweet, no ice.
What the...
What?
Nothin'...

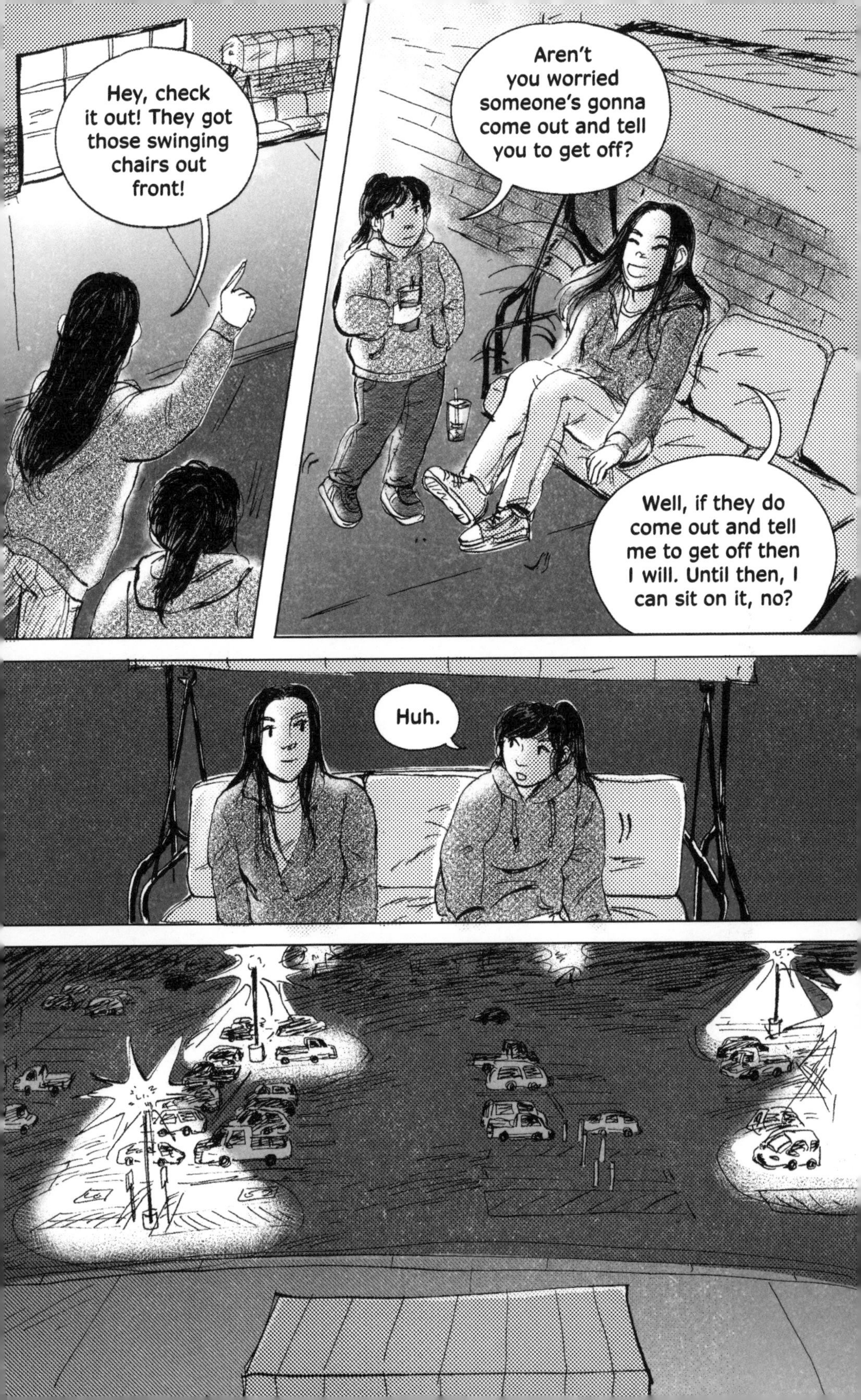
Hey, check it out! They got those swinging chairs out front!
Aren't you worried someone's gonna come out and tell you to get off?
Well, if they do come out and tell me to get off then I will. Until then, I can sit on it, no?
Huh.

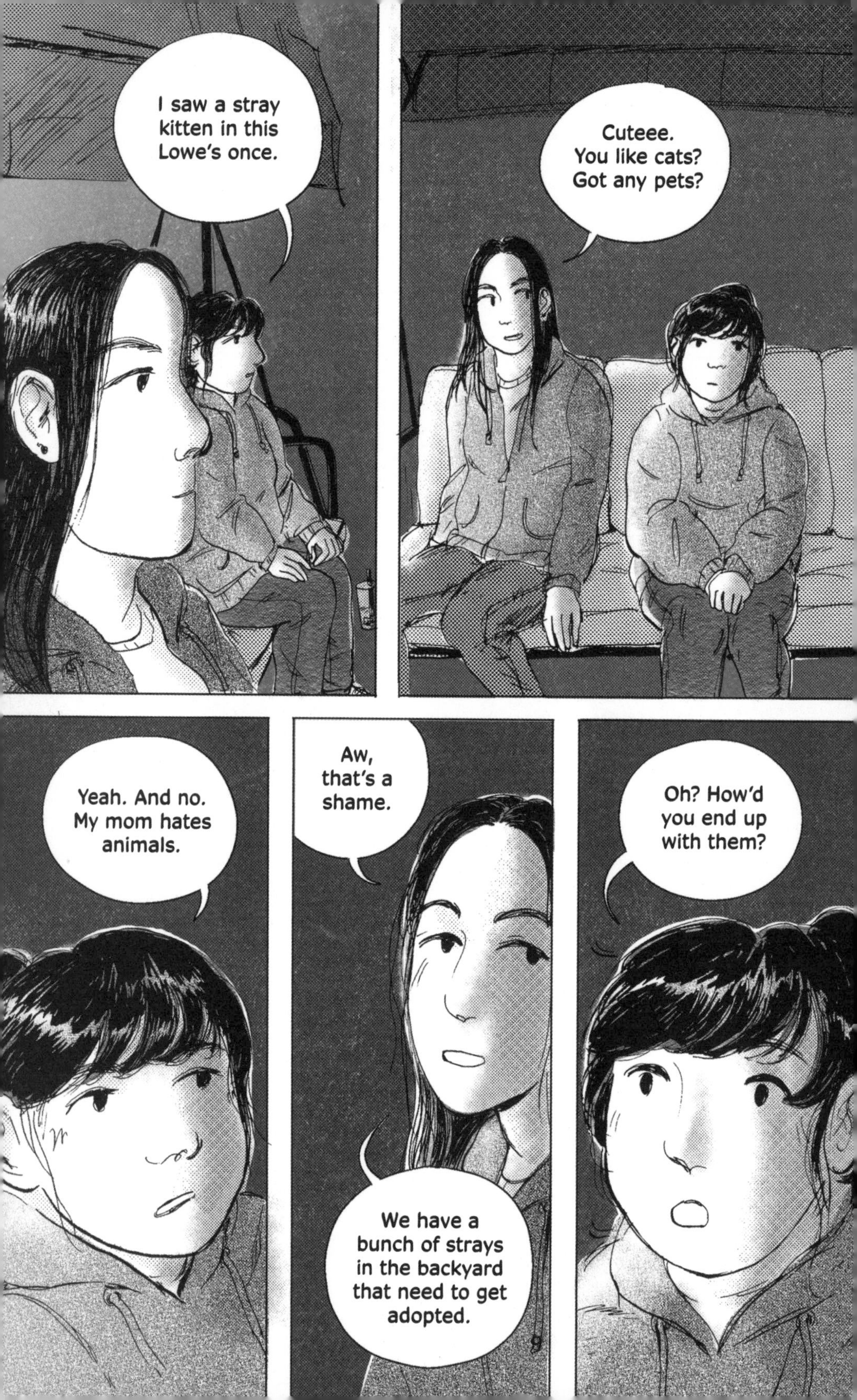
I saw a stray kitten in this Lowe's once.
Cuteee. You like cats? Got any pets?
Yeah. And no. My mom hates animals.
Aw, that's a shame.
We have a bunch of strays in the backyard that need to get adopted.
Oh? How'd you end up with them?

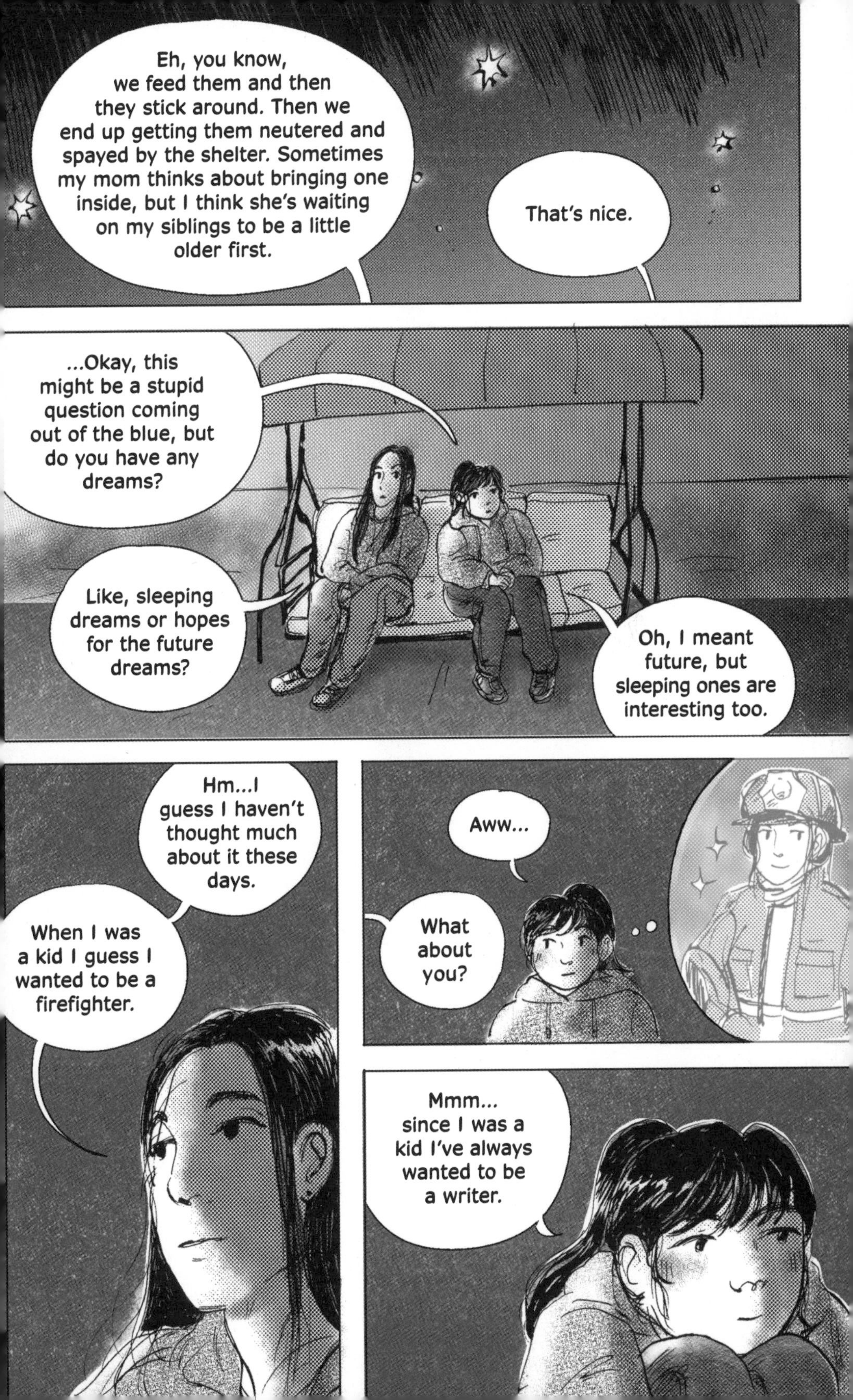
Eh, you know, we feed them and then they stick around. Then we end up getting them neutered and spayed by the shelter. Sometimes my mom thinks about bringing one inside, but I think she's waiting on my siblings to be a little older first.
That's nice.
...Okay, this might be a stupid question coming out of the blue, but do you have any dreams?
Like, sleeping dreams or hopes for the future dreams?
Oh, I meant future, but sleeping ones are interesting too.
Hm...I guess I haven't thought much about it these days.
When I was a kid I guess I wanted to be a firefighter.
Aww...
What about you?
Mmm... since I was a kid I've always wanted to be a writer.

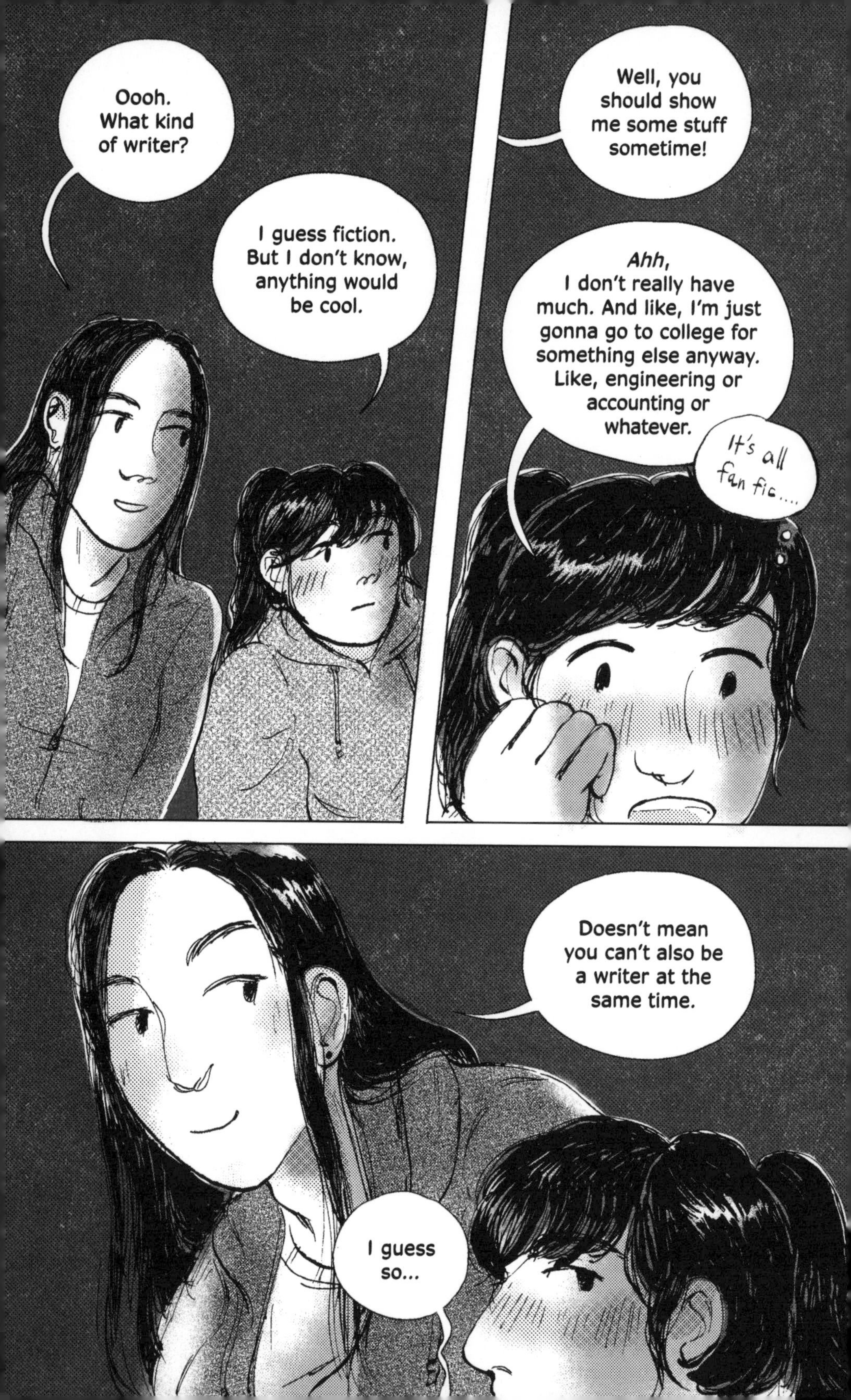
Oooh. What kind of writer?
I guess fiction. But I don't know, anything would be cool.
Well, you should show me some stuff sometime!
Ahh, I don't really have much. And like, I'm just gonna go to college for something else anyway. Like, engineering or accounting or whatever.
It's all fan fic....
Doesn't mean you can't also be a writer at the same time.
I guess so...

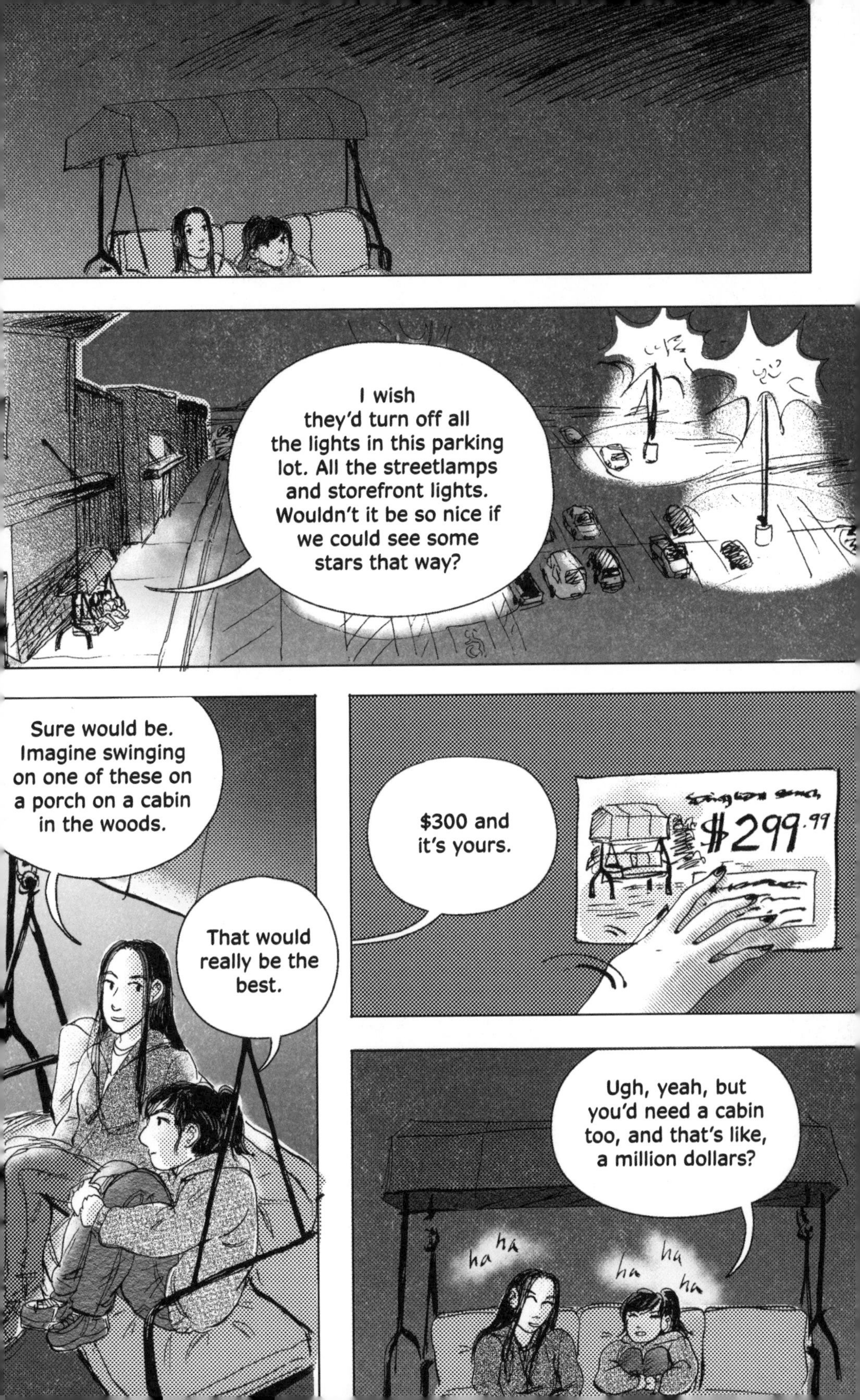
I wish they'd turn off all the lights in this parking lot. All the streetlamps and storefront lights. Wouldn't it be so nice if we could see some stars that way?
Sure would be. Imagine swinging on one of these on a porch on a cabin in the woods.
That would really be the best.
$300 and it's yours.
$299.99
Ugh, yeah, but you'd need a cabin too, and that's like, a million dollars?
ha ha
ha ha ha

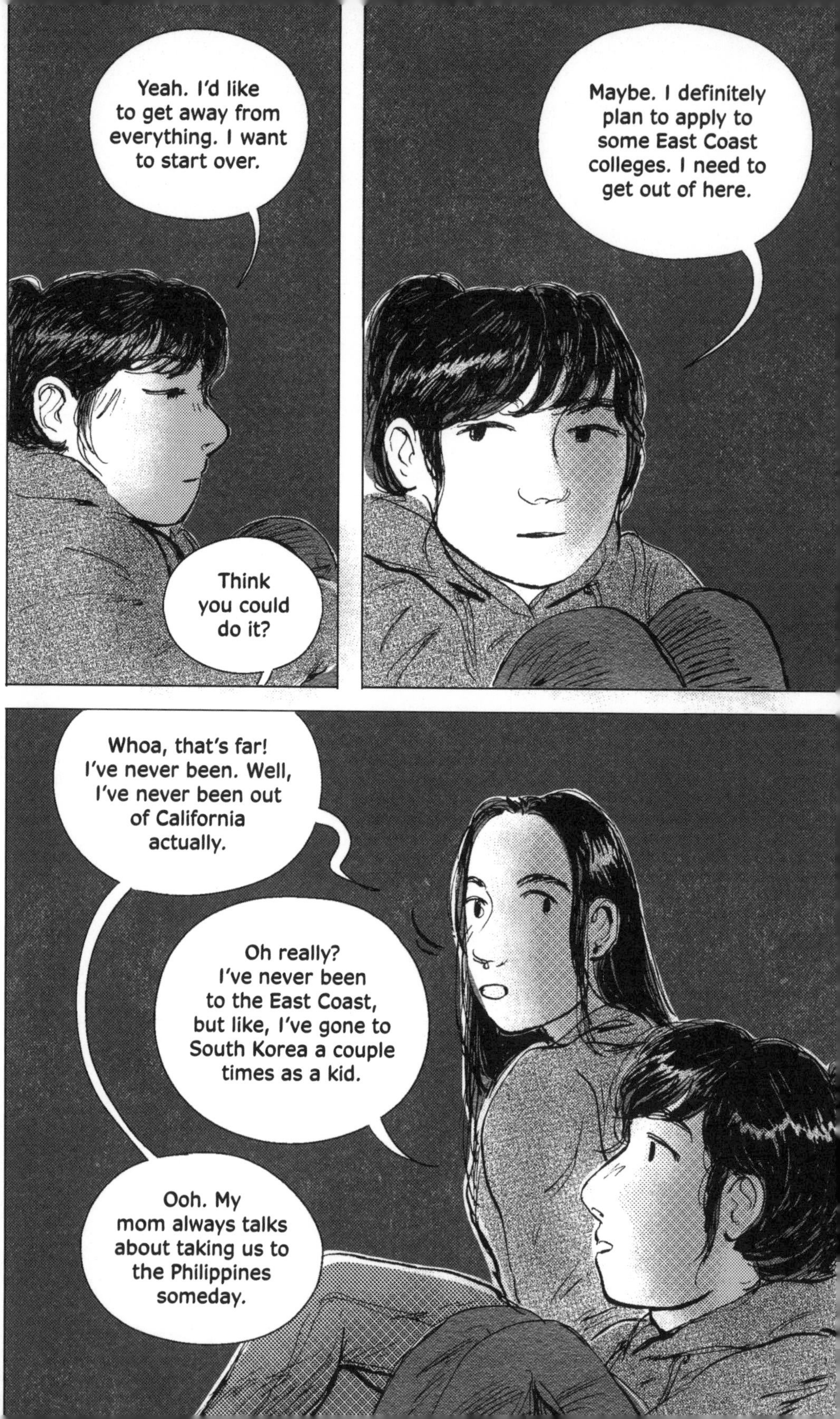
Yeah. I'd like to get away from everything. I want to start over.
Think you could do it?
Maybe. I definitely plan to apply to some East Coast colleges. I need to get out of here.
Whoa, that's far! I've never been. Well, I've never been out of California actually.
Oh really? I've never been to the East Coast, but like, I've gone to South Korea a couple times as a kid.
Ooh. My mom always talks about taking us to the Philippines someday.

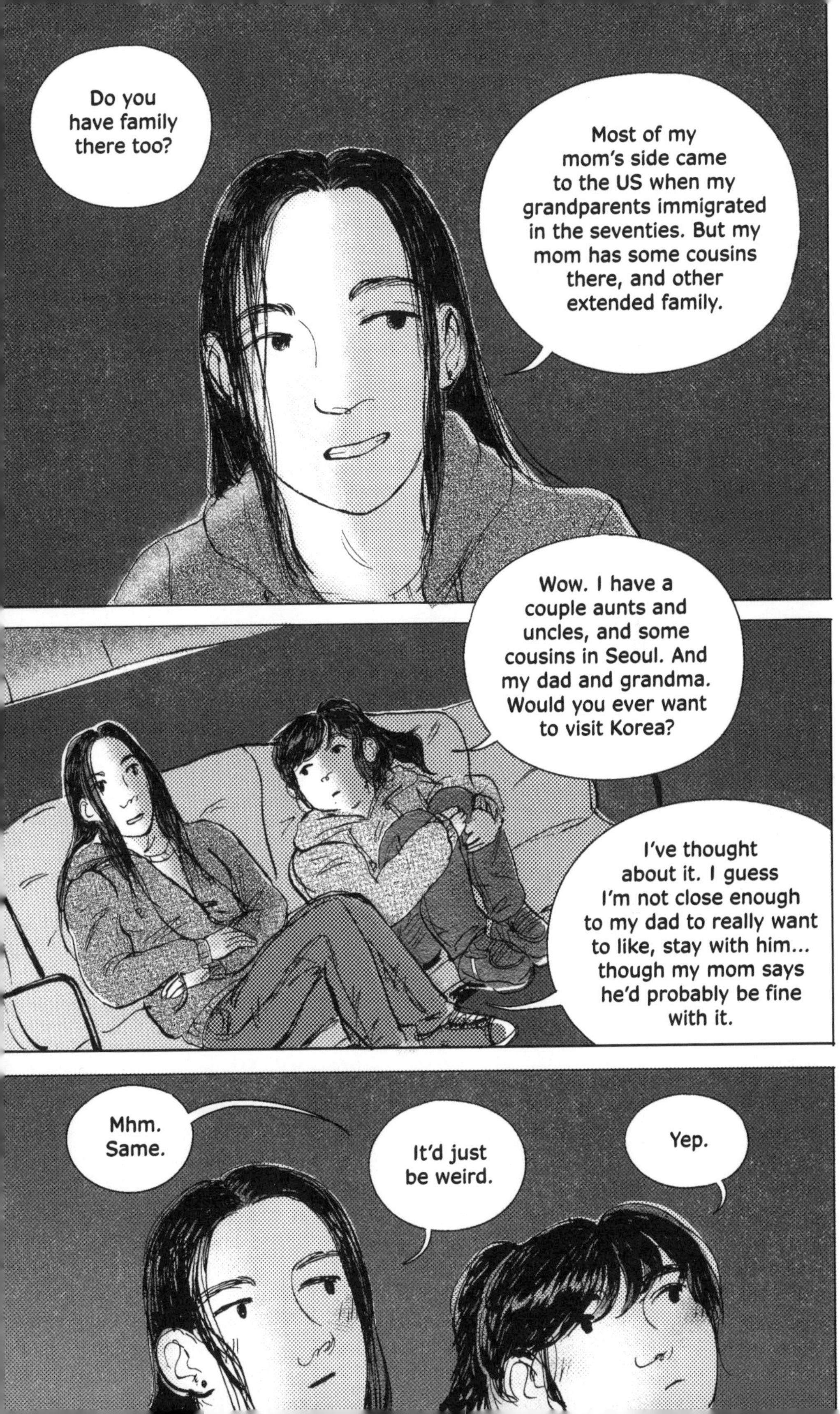
Do you have family there too?
Most of my mom's side came to the US when my grandparents immigrated in the seventies. But my mom has some cousins there, and other extended family.
Wow. I have a couple aunts and uncles, and some cousins in Seoul. And my dad and grandma. Would you ever want to visit Korea?
I've thought about it. I guess I'm not close enough to my dad to really want to like, stay with him... though my mom says he'd probably be fine with it.
Mhm. Same.
It'd just be weird.
Yep.

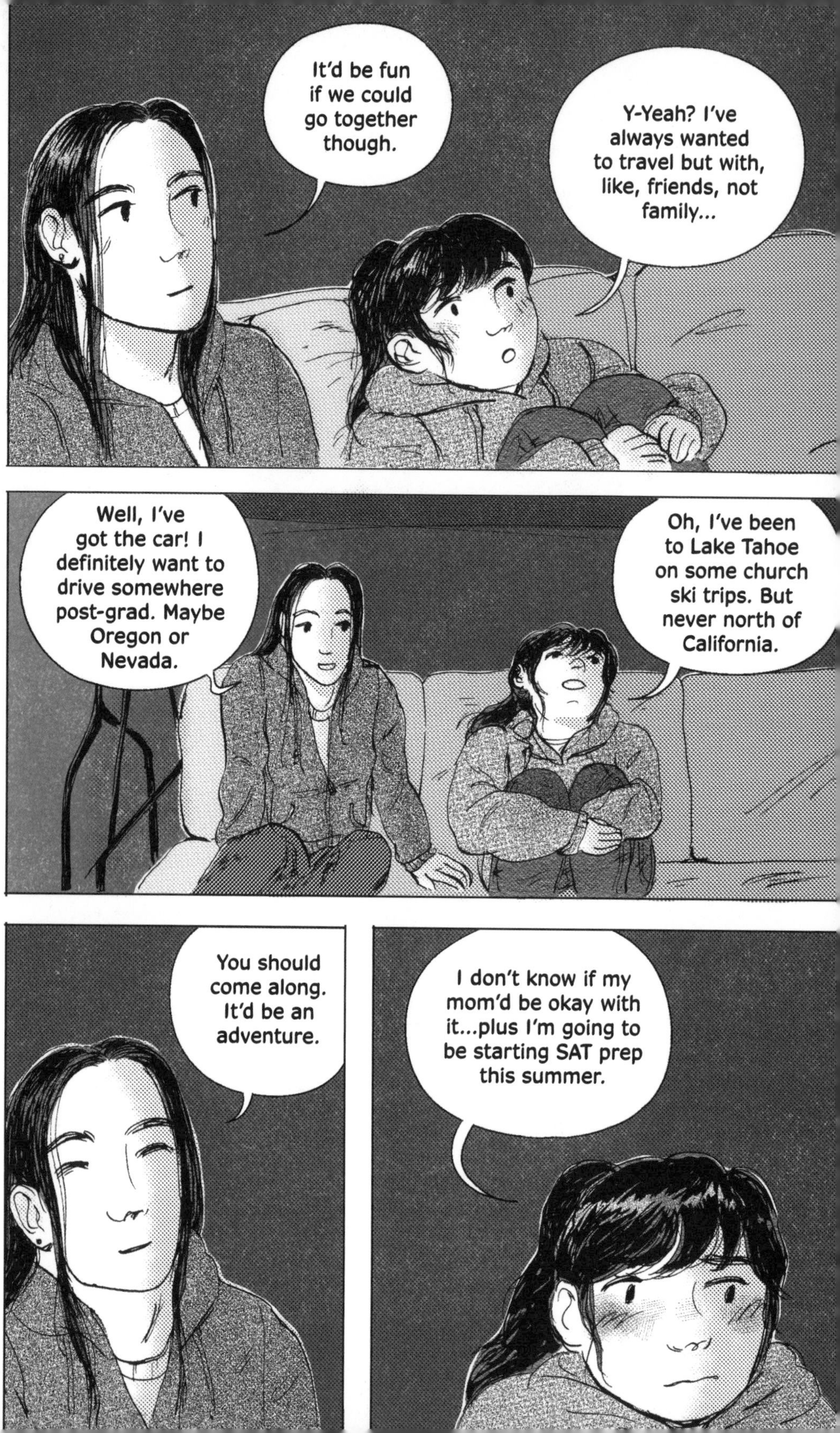
It'd be fun if we could go together though.
Y-Yeah? I've always wanted to travel but with, like, friends, not family...
Well, I've got the car! I definitely want to drive somewhere post-grad. Maybe Oregon or Nevada.
Oh, I've been to Lake Tahoe on some church ski trips. But never north of California.
You should come along. It'd be an adventure.
I don't know if my mom'd be okay with it...plus I'm going to be starting SAT prep this summer.

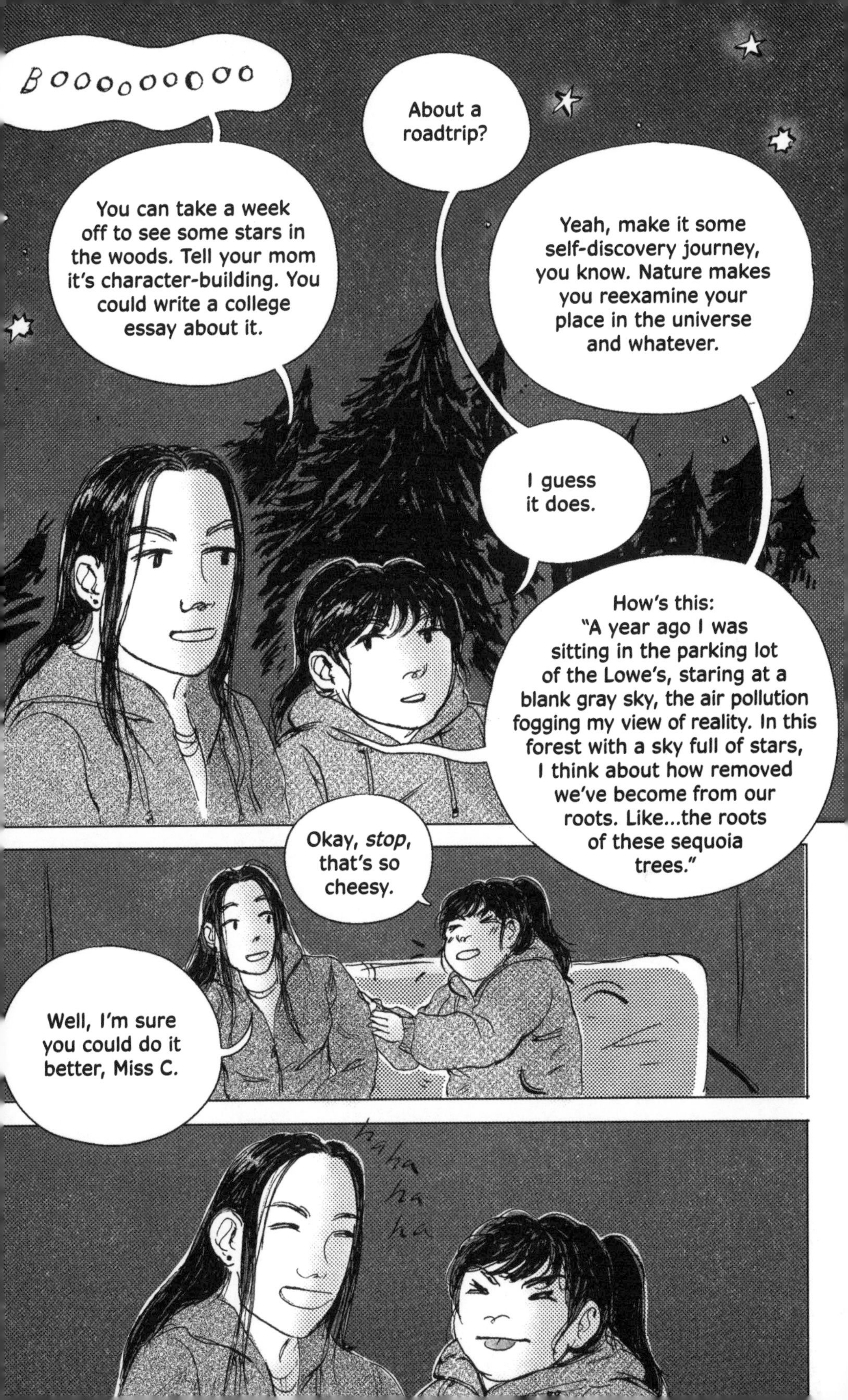
BOOOOOOOOO
You can take a week off to see some stars in the woods. Tell your mom it's character-building. You could write a college essay about it.
About a roadtrip?
Yeah, make it some self-discovery journey, you know. Nature makes you reexamine your place in the universe and whatever.
I guess it does.
How's this: "A year ago I was sitting in the parking lot of the Lowe's, staring at a blank gray sky, the air pollution fogging my view of reality. In this forest with a sky full of stars, I think about how removed we've become from our roots. Like...the roots of these sequoia trees."
Okay, *stop*, that's so cheesy.
Well, I'm sure you could do it better, Miss C.
hahahaha

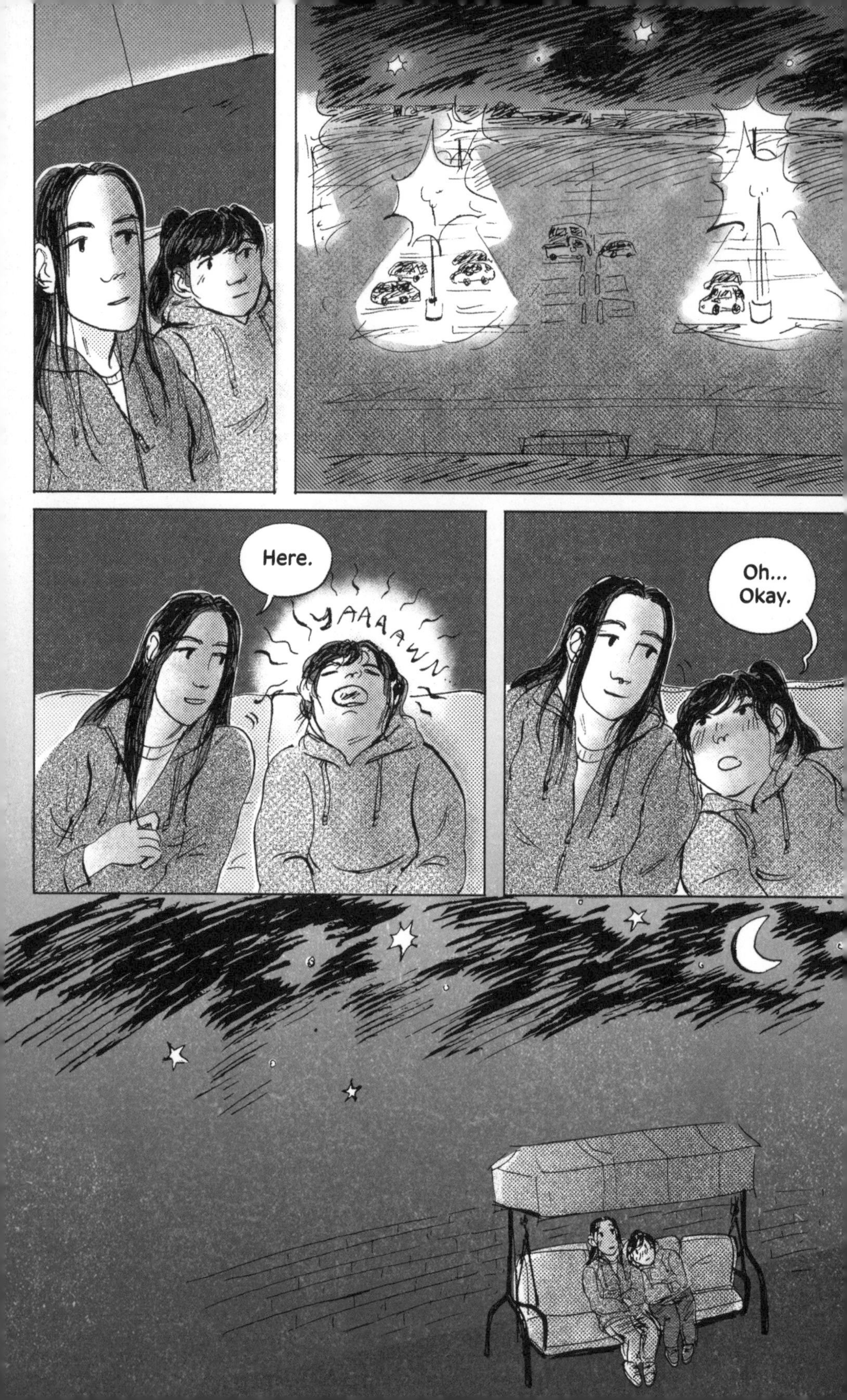
Here.
YAAAAWN
Oh... Okay.

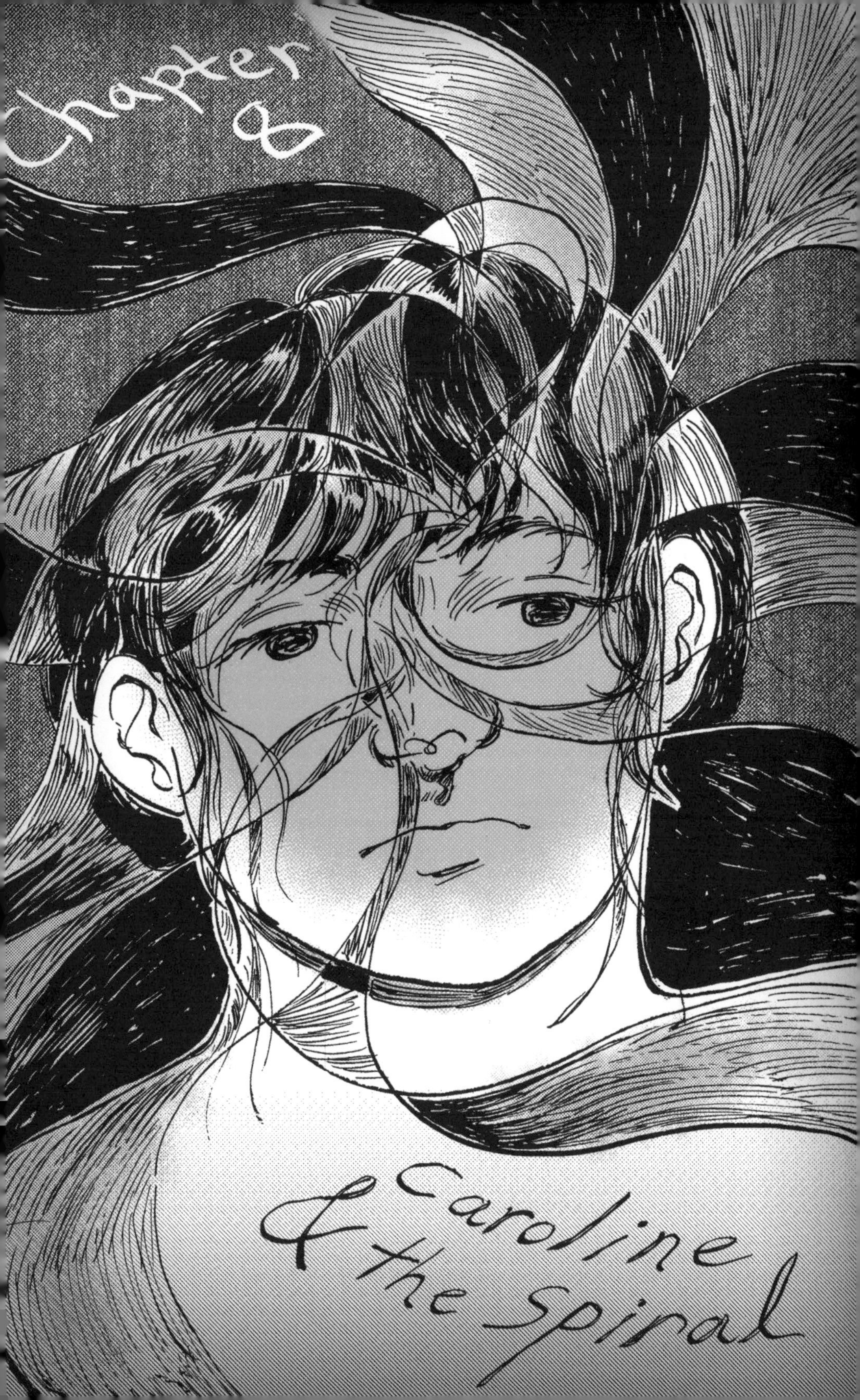
Chapter 8
Caroline & the Spiral

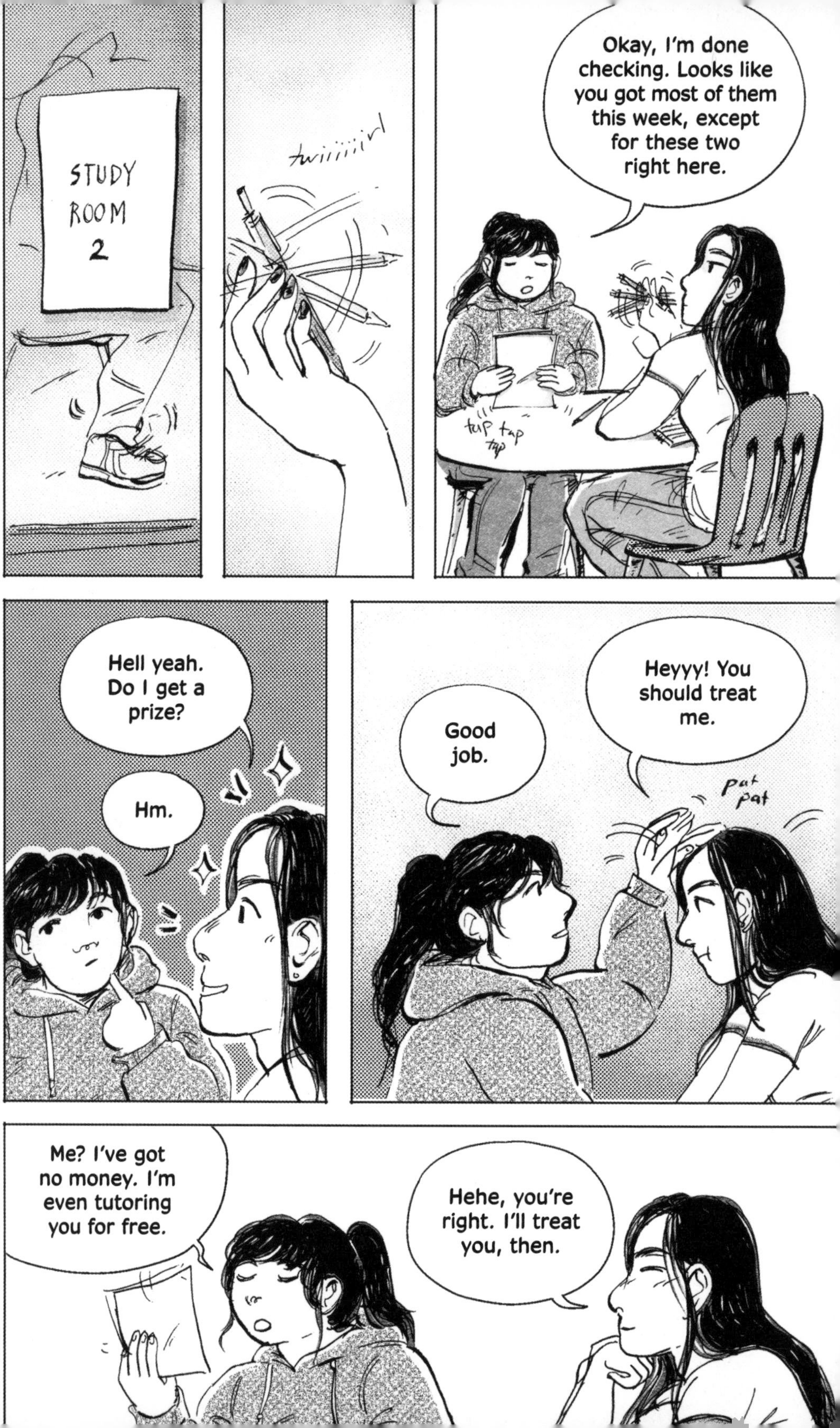
STUDY ROOM 2
twiiiiiirl
Okay, I'm done checking. Looks like you got most of them this week, except for these two right here.
tap tap tap
Hell yeah. Do I get a prize?
Hm.
Good job.
Heyyy! You should treat me.
pat pat
Me? I've got no money. I'm even tutoring you for free.
Hehe, you're right. I'll treat you, then.

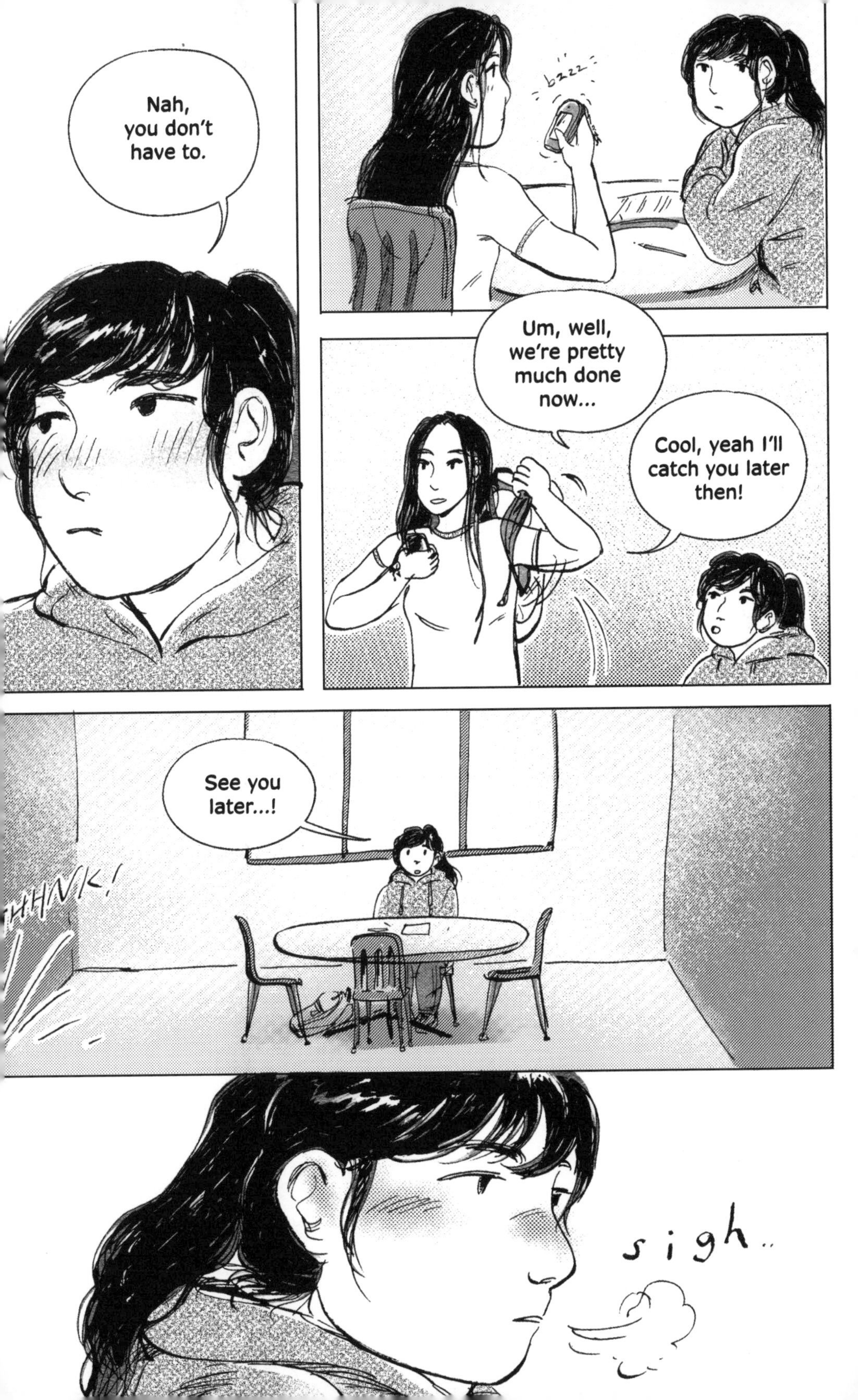
Nah, you don't have to.
bzzz
Um, well, we're pretty much done now...
Cool, yeah I'll catch you later then!
See you later...!
THNK!
sigh..

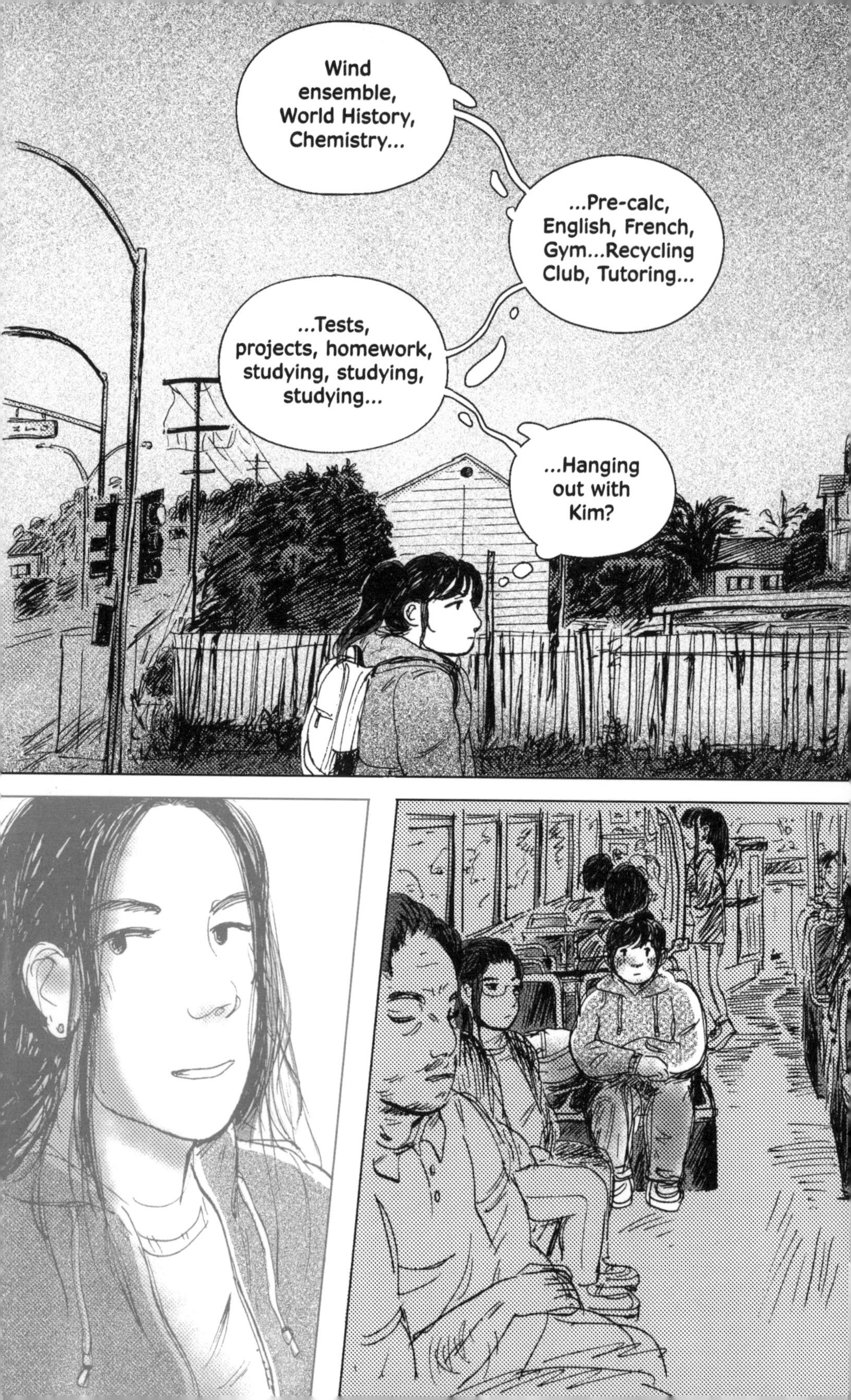
Wind ensemble, World History, Chemistry...
...Pre-calc, English, French, Gym...Recycling Club, Tutoring...
...Tests, projects, homework, studying, studying, studying...
...Hanging out with Kim?

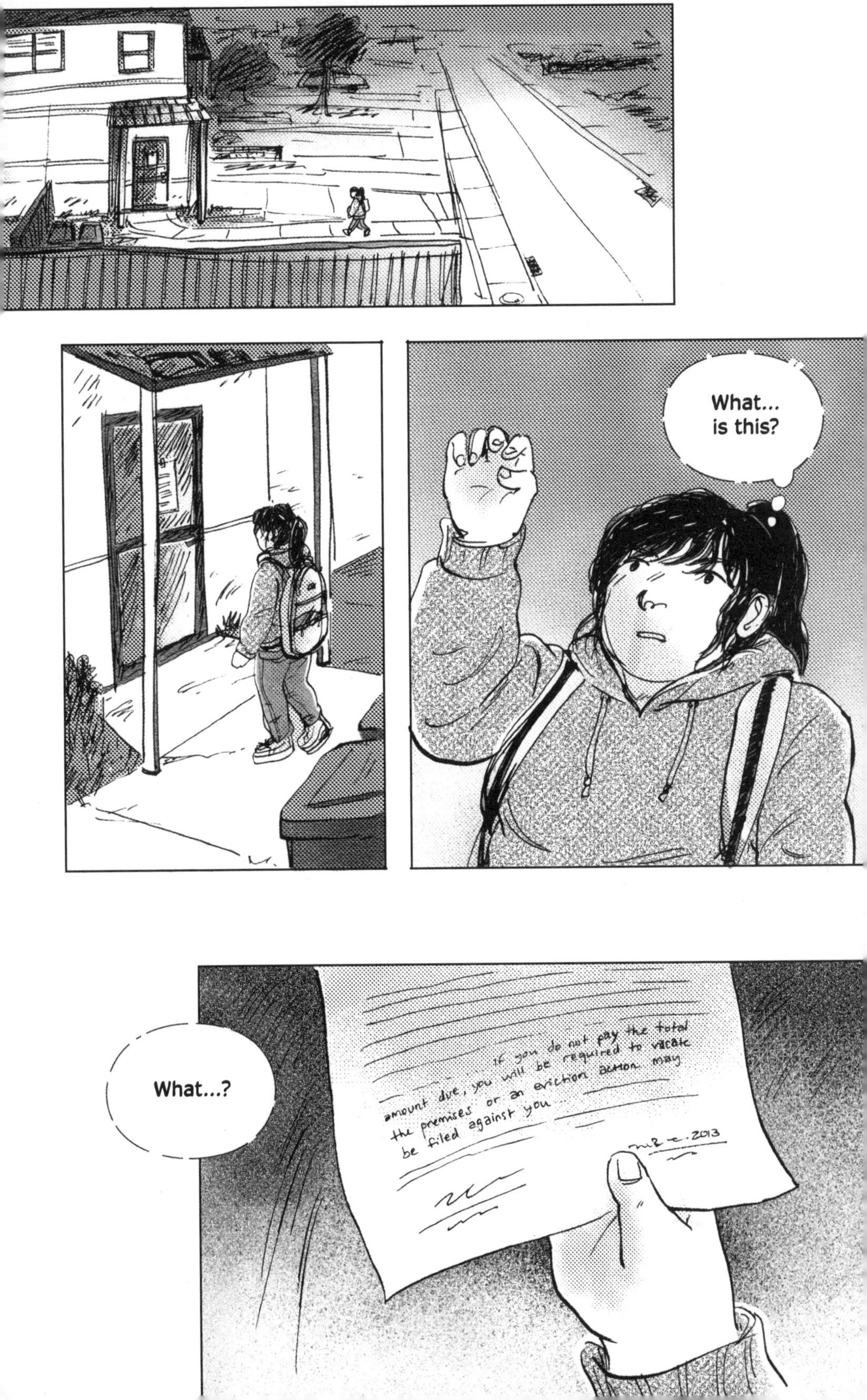
What...
is this?
If you do not pay the total amount due, you will be required to vacate the premises or an eviction action may be filed against you
What...?

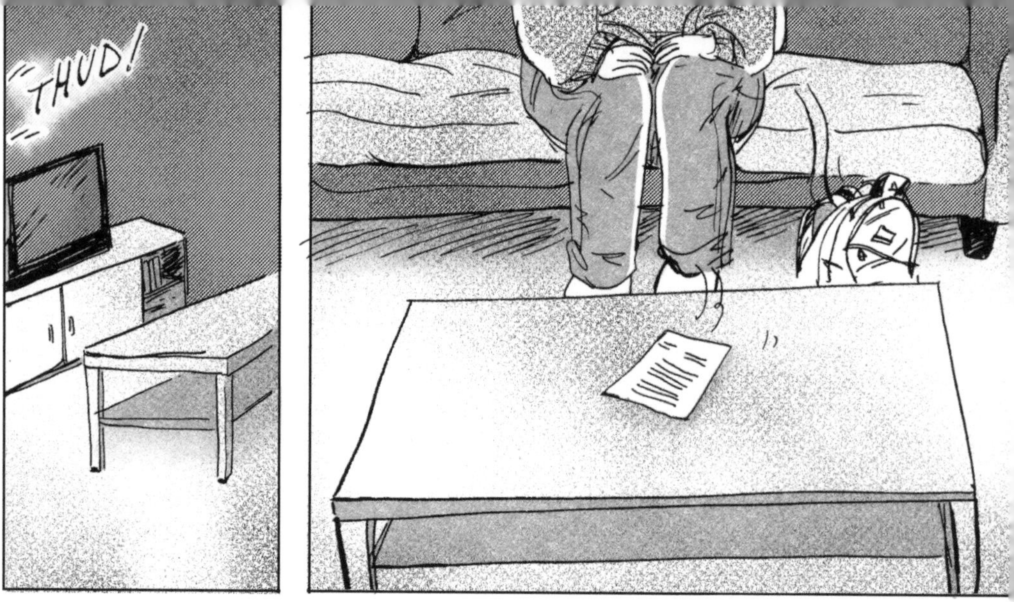
THUD!

The thing is, I don't really remember exactly what went through my head the moment after I saw the notice. All I remember is the confusion and dread.

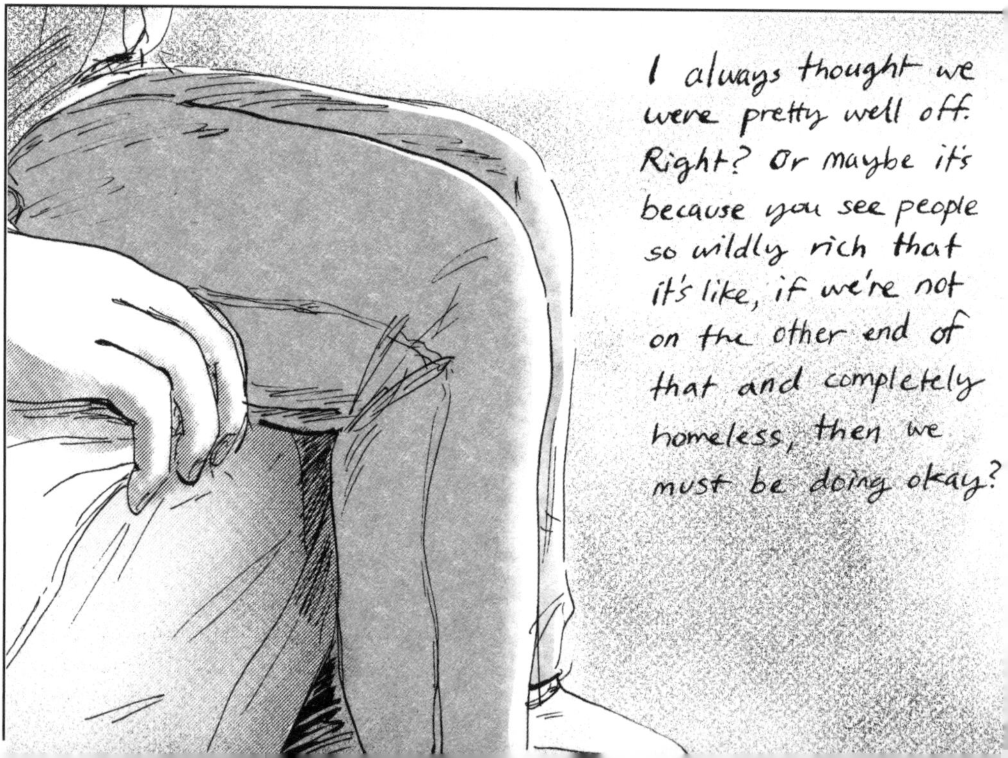
I always thought we were pretty well off. Right? Or maybe it's because you see people so wildly rich that it's like, if we're not on the other end of that and completely homeless, then we must be doing okay?

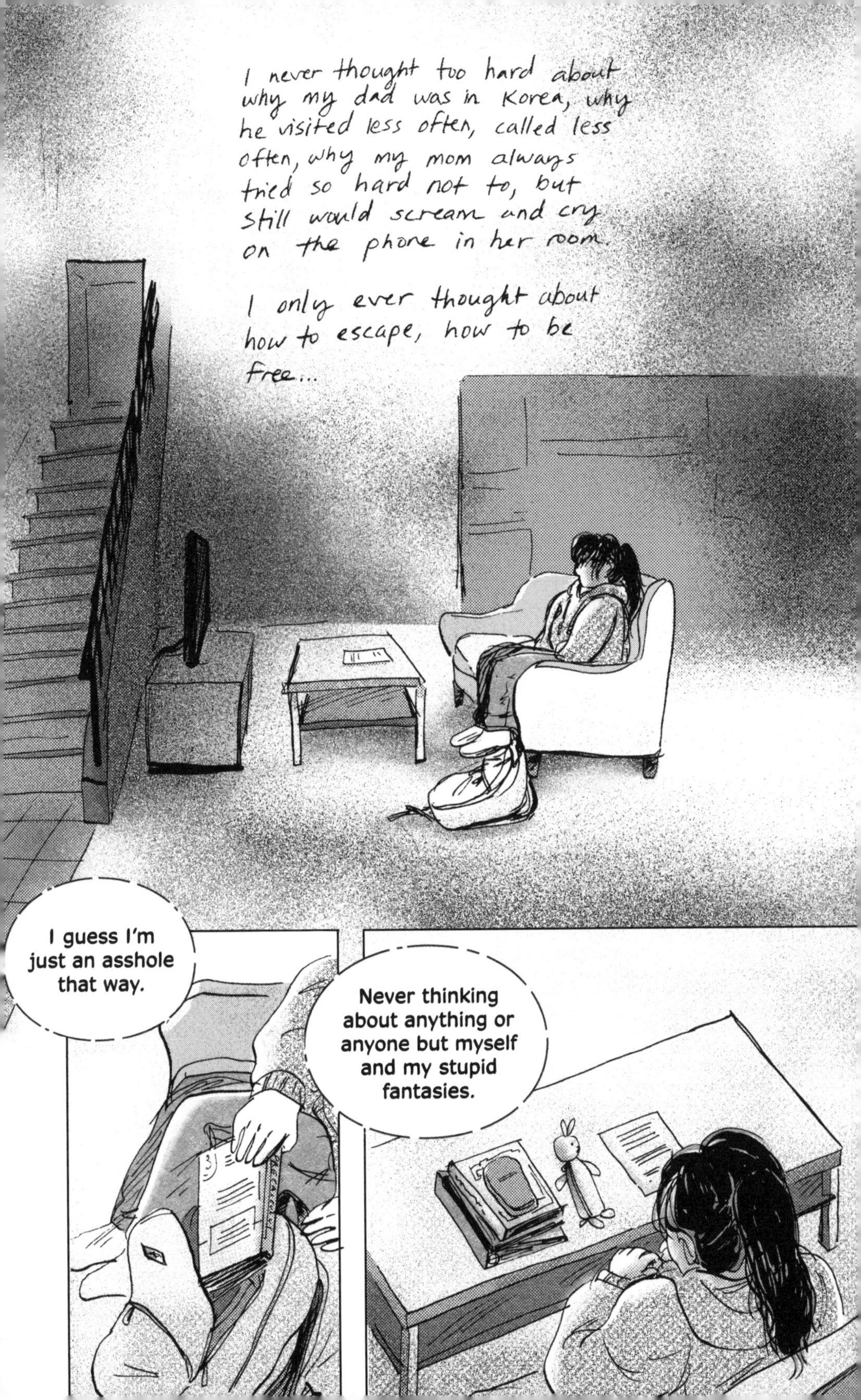
I never thought too hard about why my dad was in Korea, why he visited less often, called less often, why my mom always tried so hard not to, but still would scream and cry on the phone in her room.
I only ever thought about how to escape, how to be free...
I guess I'm just an asshole that way.
Never thinking about anything or anyone but myself and my stupid fantasies.

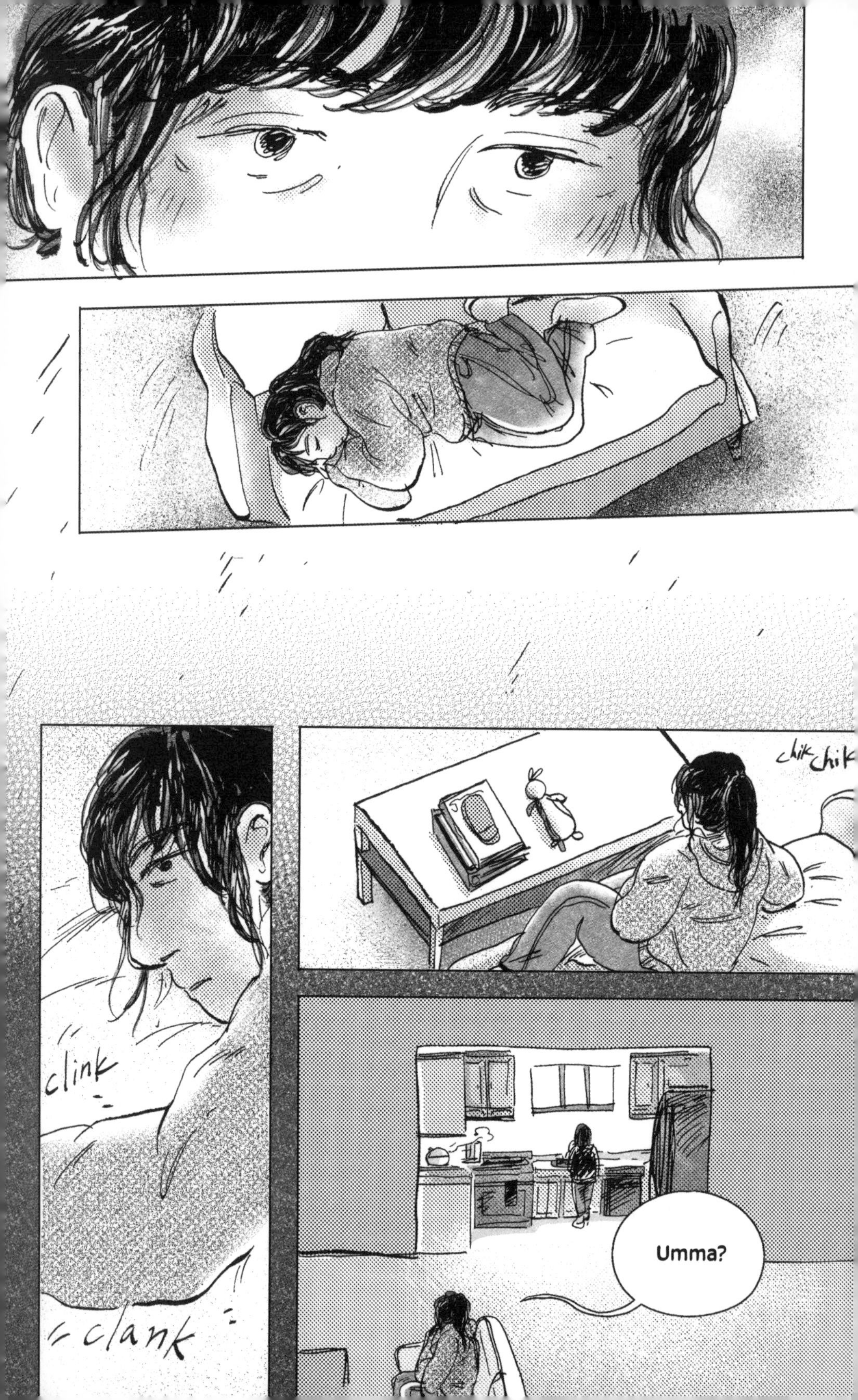
chik chik
clink
clank
Umma?

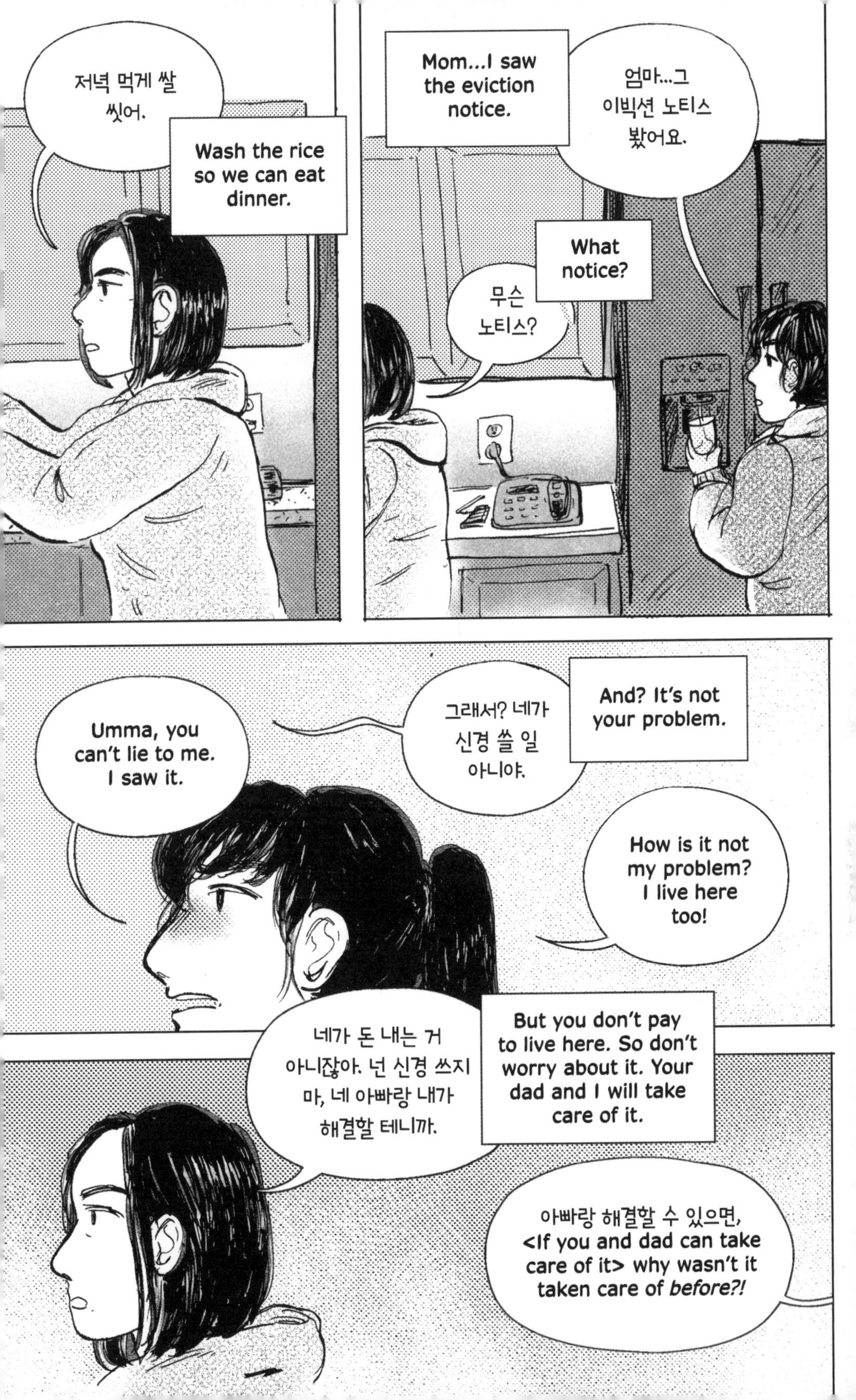
저녁 먹게 쌀 씻어.
Wash the rice so we can eat dinner.
Mom...I saw the eviction notice.
엄마...그 이빅션 노티스 봤어요.
What notice?
무슨 노티스?
Umma, you can't lie to me. I saw it.
그래서? 네가 신경 쓸 일 아니야.
And? It's not your problem.
How is it not my problem? I live here too!
네가 돈 내는 거 아니잖아. 넌 신경 쓰지 마, 네 아빠랑 내가 해결할 테니까.
But you don't pay to live here. So don't worry about it. Your dad and I will take care of it.
아빠랑 해결할 수 있으면, <If you and dad can take care of it> why wasn't it taken care of *before?!*

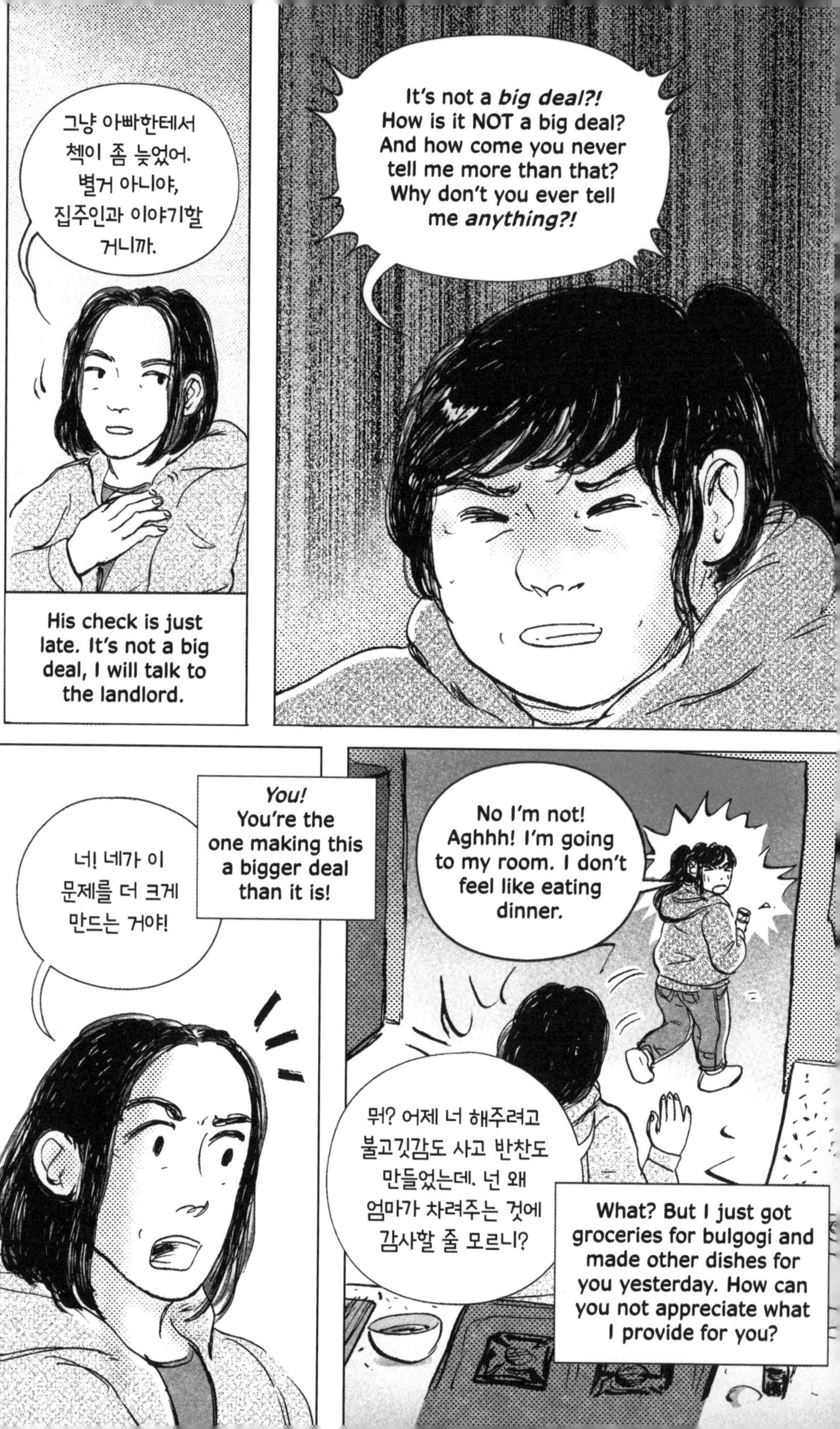
그냥 아빠한테서 첵이 좀 늦었어. 별거 아니야, 집주인과 이야기할 거니까.
His check is just late. It's not a big deal, I will talk to the landlord.
It's not a *big deal?!* How is it NOT a big deal? And how come you never tell me more than that? Why don't you ever tell me *anything?!*
너! 네가 이 문제를 더 크게 만드는 거야!
You! You're the one making this a bigger deal than it is!
No I'm not! Aghhh! I'm going to my room. I don't feel like eating dinner.
뭐? 어제 너 해주려고 불고깃감도 사고 반찬도 만들었는데. 넌 왜 엄마가 차려주는 것에 감사할 줄 모르니?
What? But I just got groceries for bulgogi and made other dishes for you yesterday. How can you not appreciate what I provide for you?

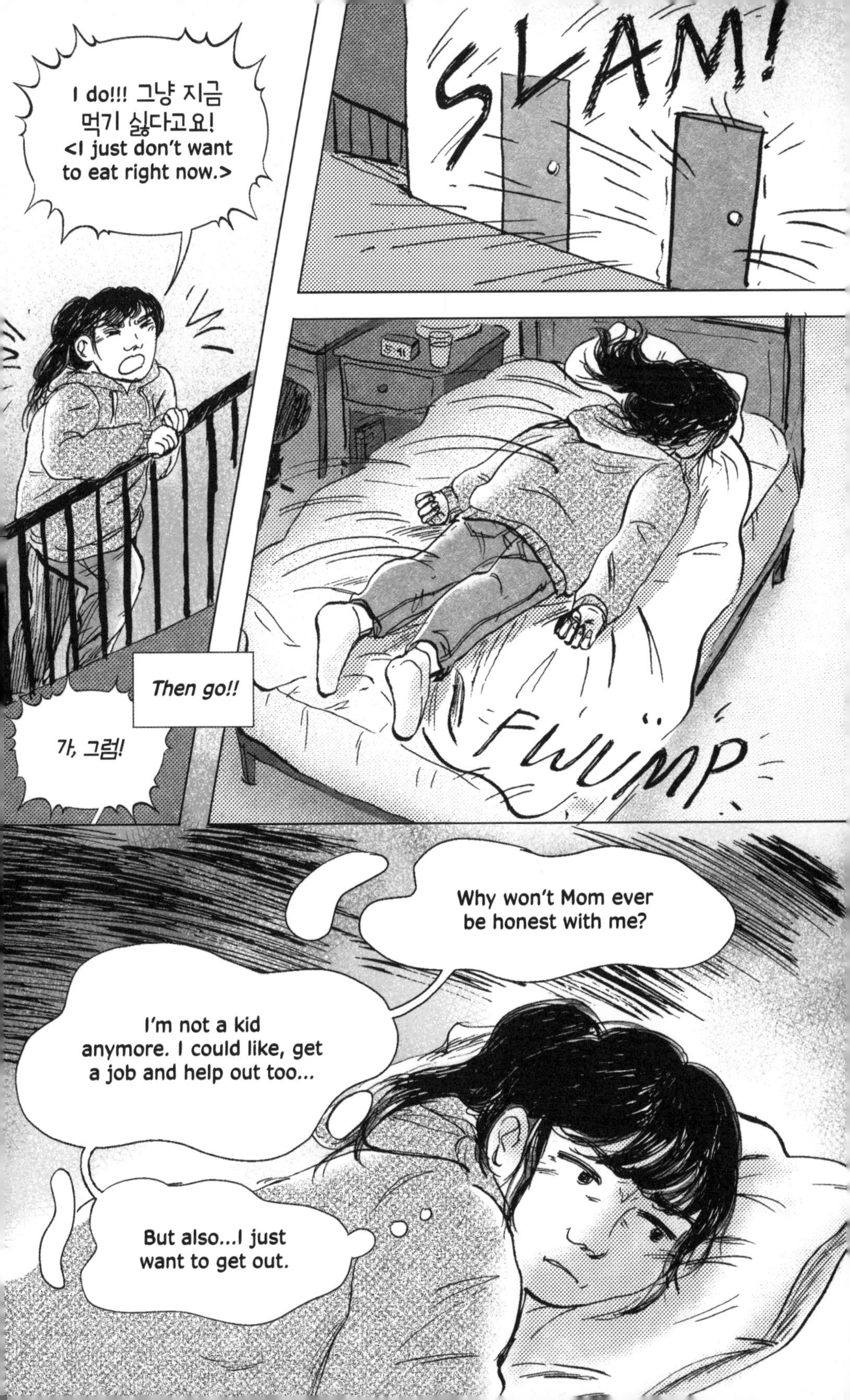
I do!!! 그냥 지금 먹기 싫다고요!
<I just don't want to eat right now.>
SLAM!
Then go!!
가, 그럼!
FWUMP
Why won't Mom ever be honest with me?
I'm not a kid anymore. I could like, get a job and help out too...
But also...I just want to get out.

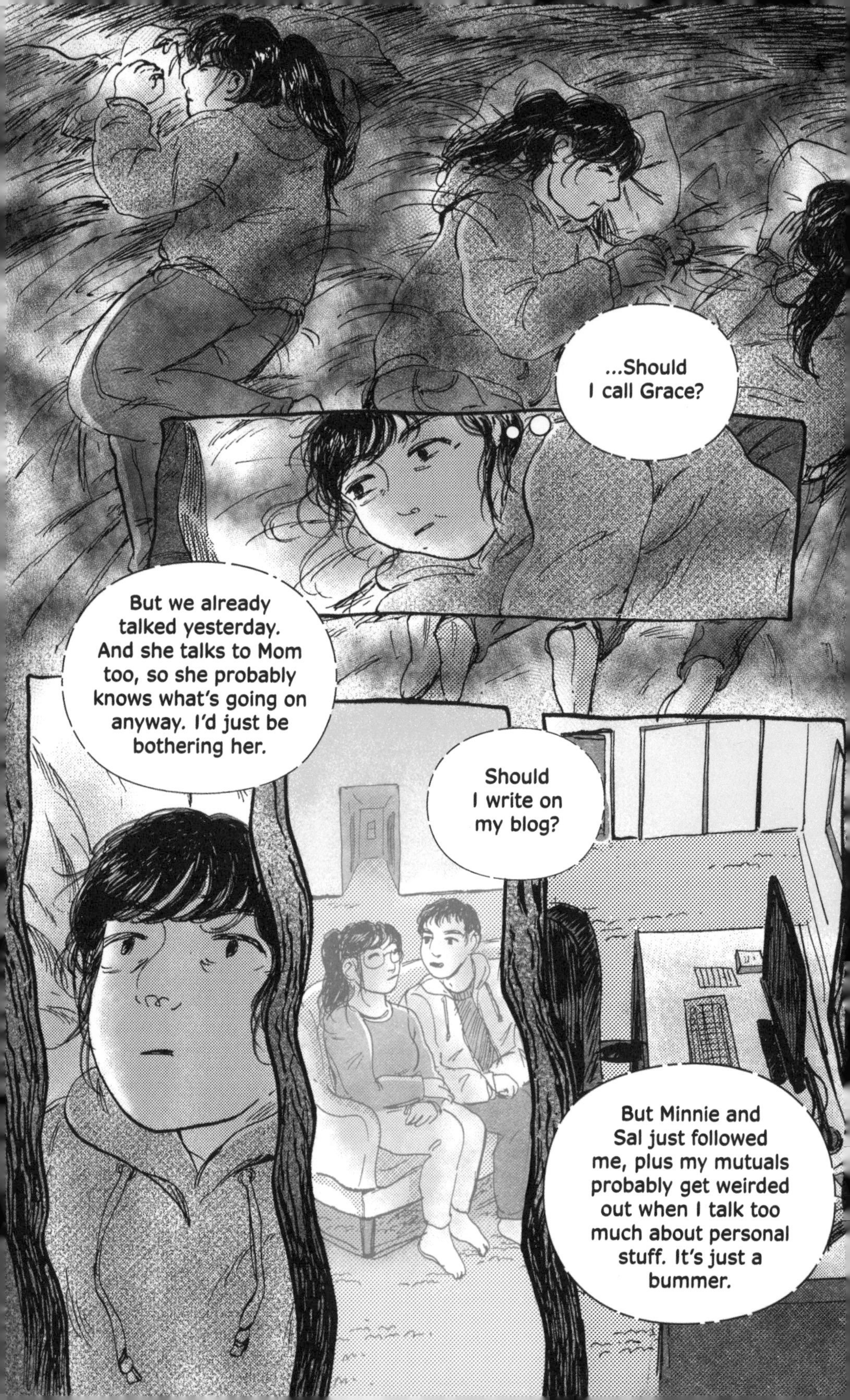
...Should I call Grace?
But we already talked yesterday. And she talks to Mom too, so she probably knows what's going on anyway. I'd just be bothering her.
Should I write on my blog?
But Minnie and Sal just followed me, plus my mutuals probably get weirded out when I talk too much about personal stuff. It's just a bummer.

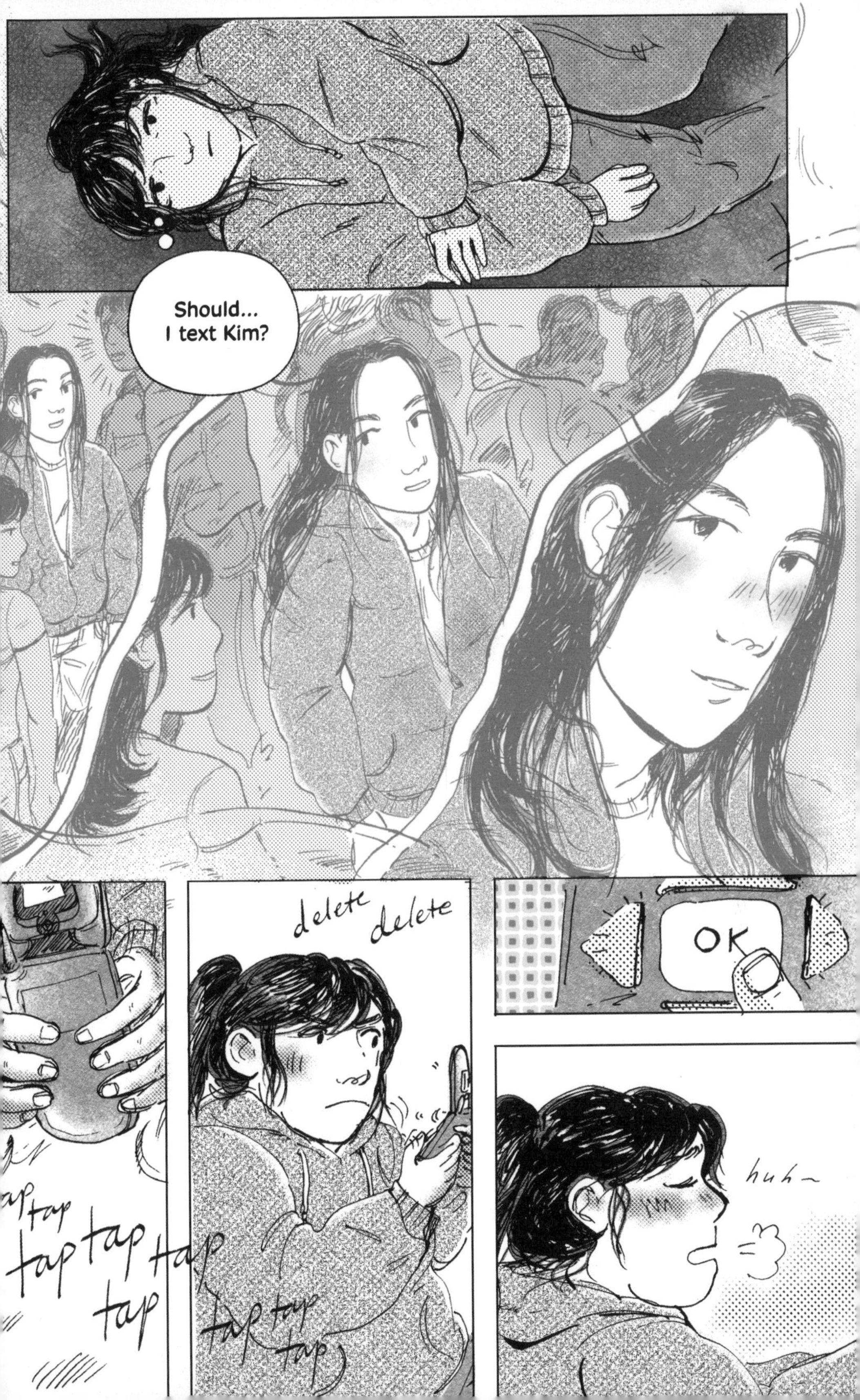
Should... I text Kim?
tap tap tap tap tap tap
delete delete
tap tap tap
OK
huh~

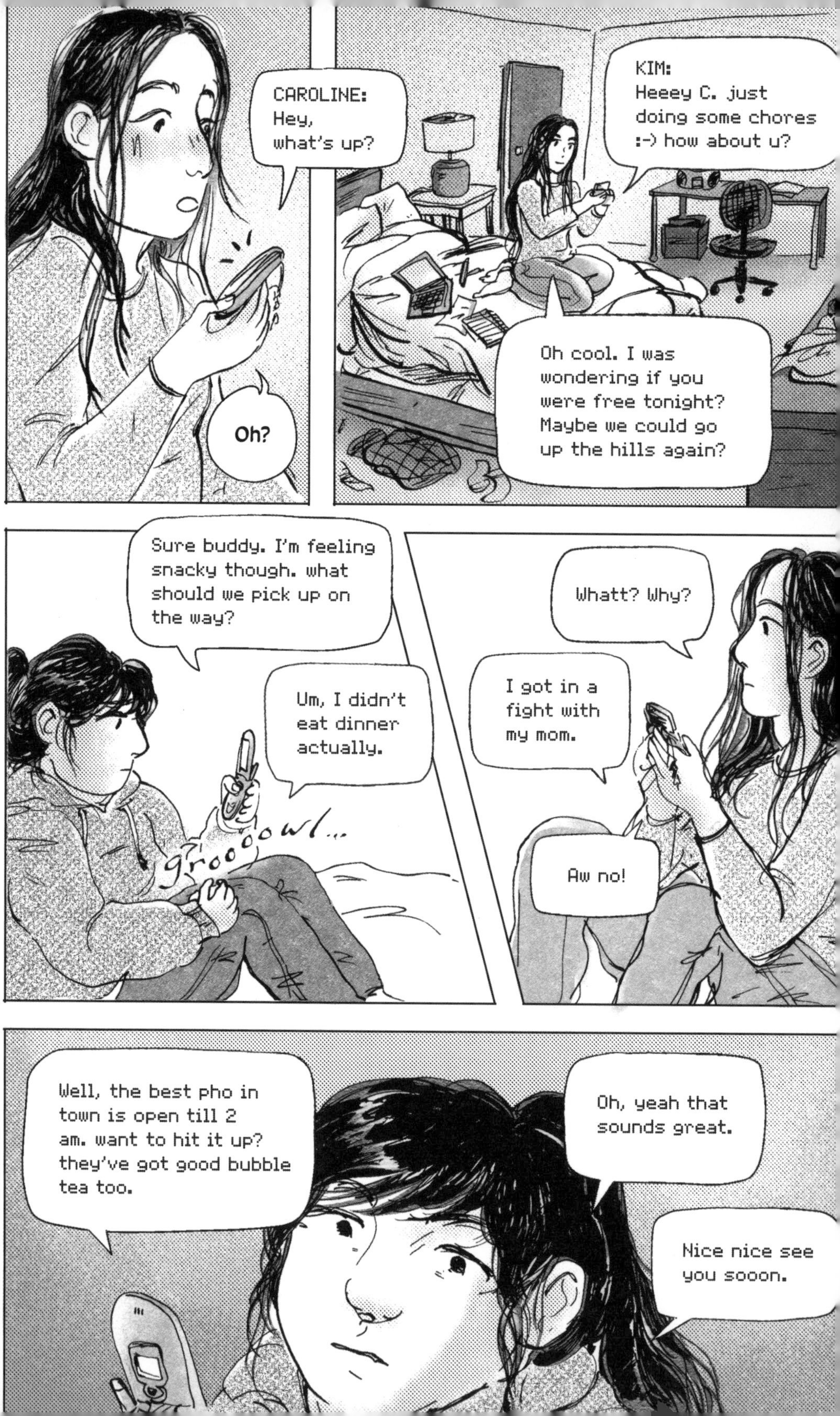
CAROLINE:
Hey,
what's up?
Oh?
KIM:
Heeey C. just doing some chores :-) how about u?
Oh cool. I was wondering if you were free tonight? Maybe we could go up the hills again?
Sure buddy. I'm feeling snacky though. what should we pick up on the way?
Um, I didn't eat dinner actually.
grooooowl...
Whatt? Why?
I got in a fight with my mom.
Aw no!
Well, the best pho in town is open till 2 am. want to hit it up? they've got good bubble tea too.
Oh, yeah that sounds great.
Nice nice see you sooon.

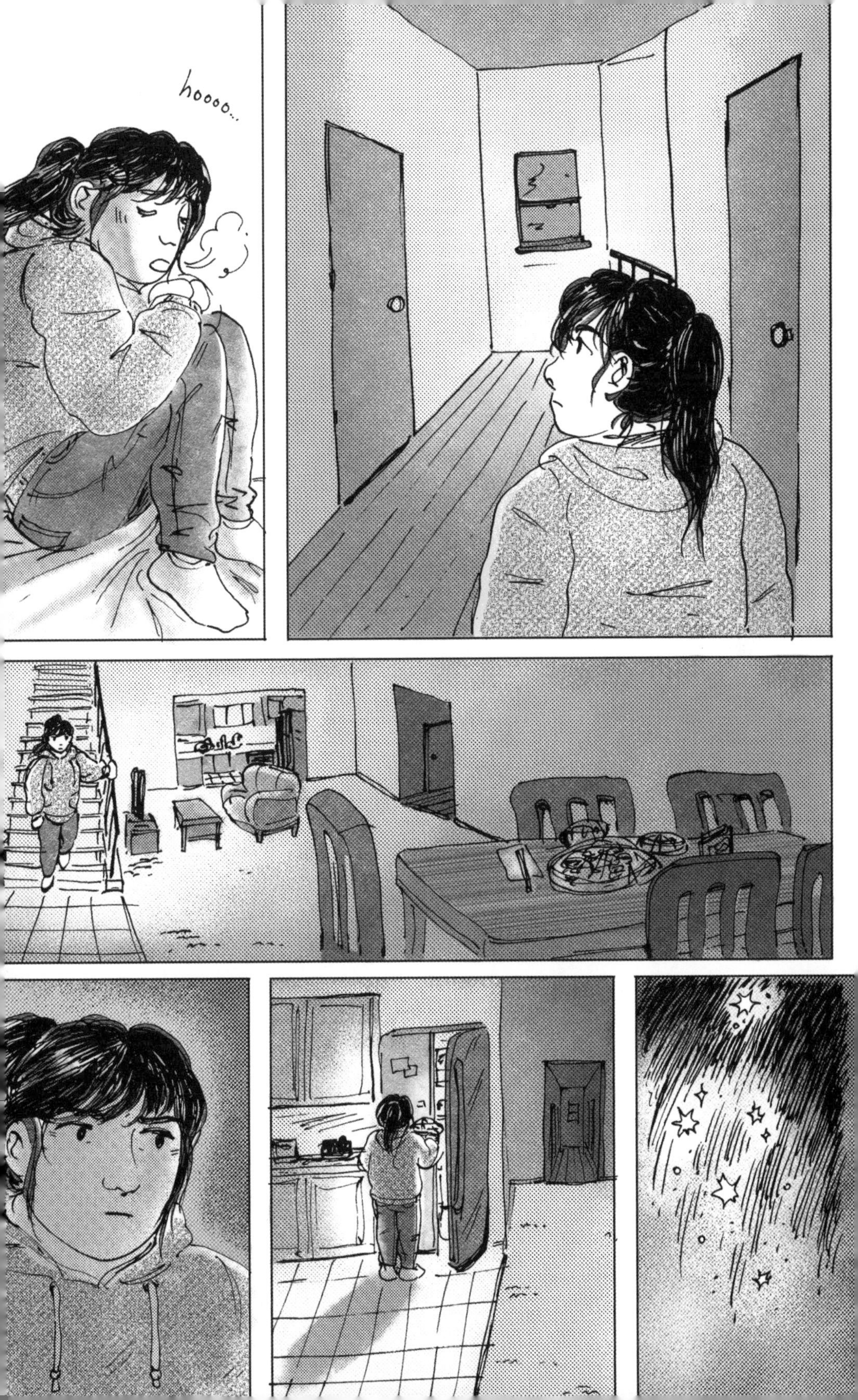
hoooo...

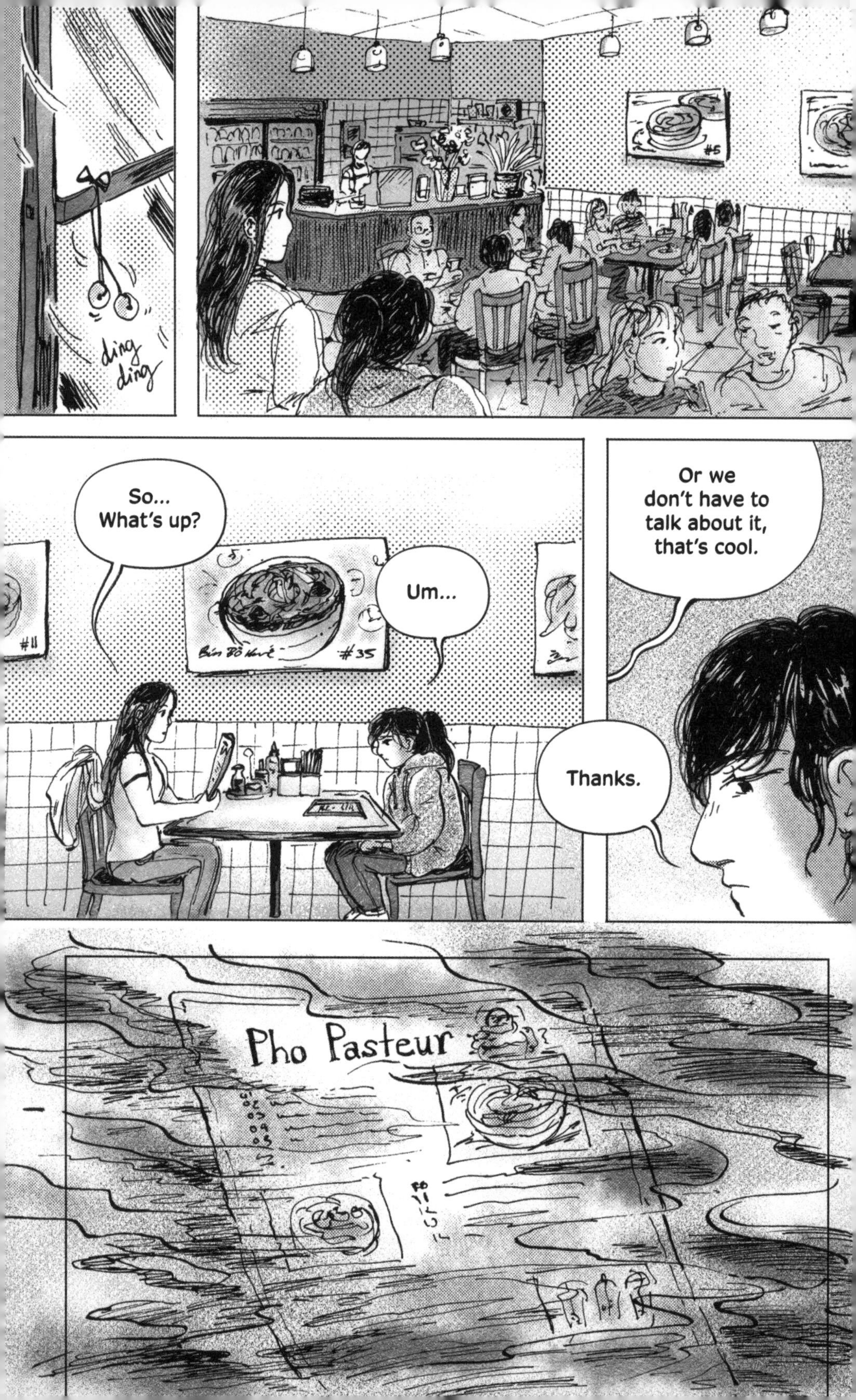
ding ding
So... What's up?
Um...
Or we don't have to talk about it, that's cool.
Thanks.
Pho Pasteur

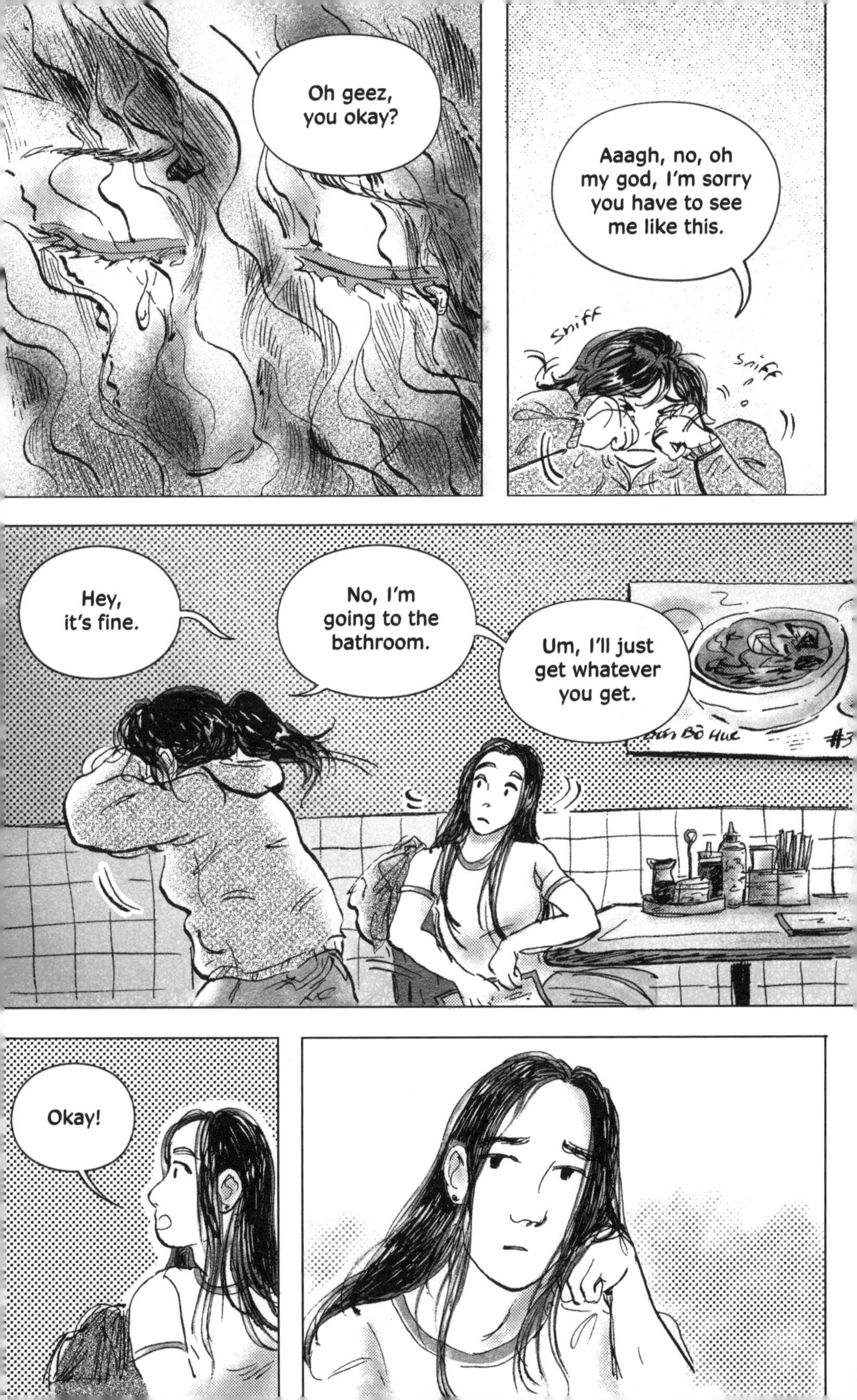
Oh geez,
you okay?
Aaagh, no, oh my god, I'm sorry you have to see me like this.
Sniff
Sniff
Hey,
it's fine.
No, I'm going to the bathroom.
Um, I'll just get whatever you get.
Okay!

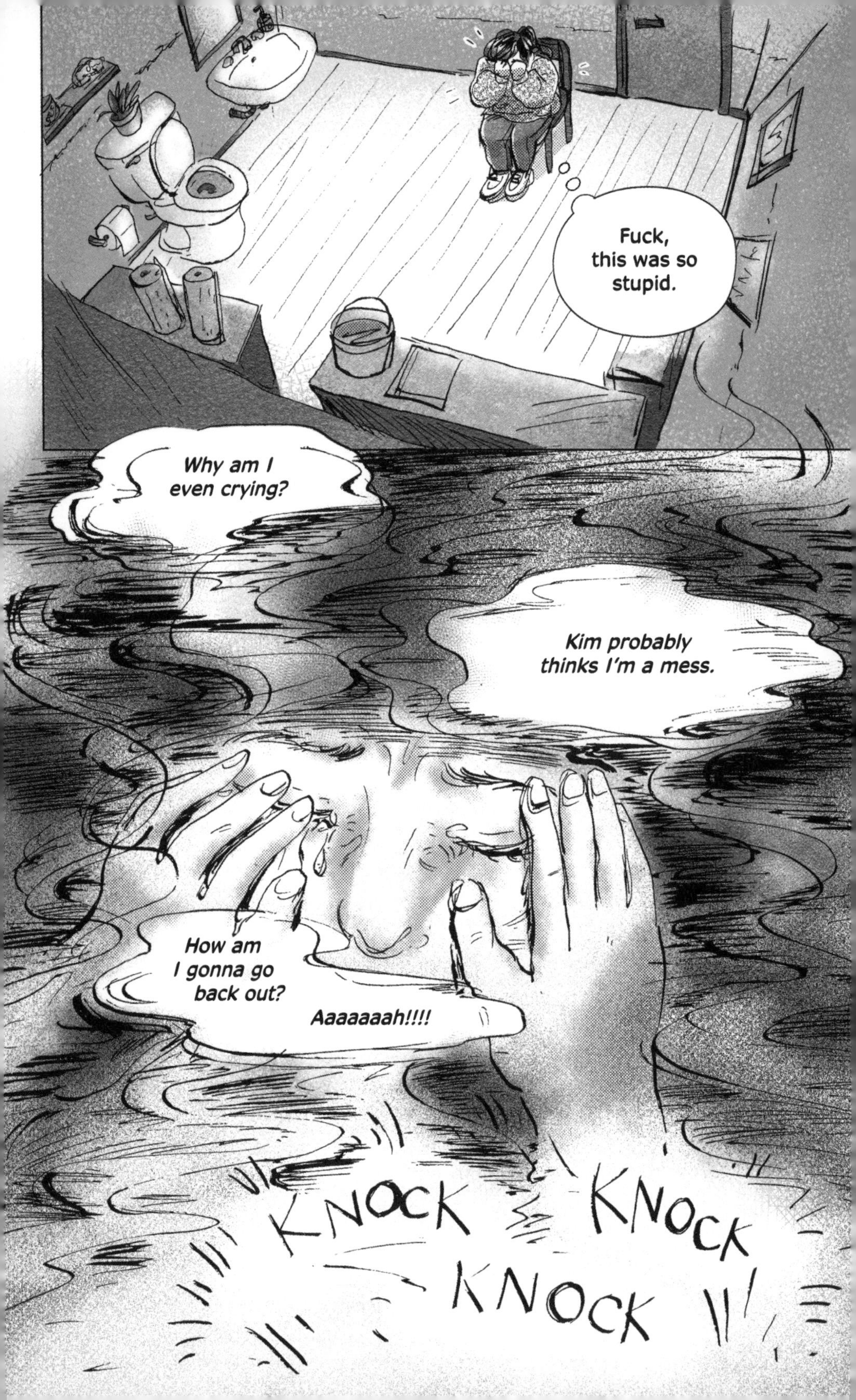
Fuck, this was so stupid.
Why am I even crying?
Kim probably thinks I'm a mess.
How am I gonna go back out?
Aaaaaaah!!!!
KNOCK KNOCK KNOCK

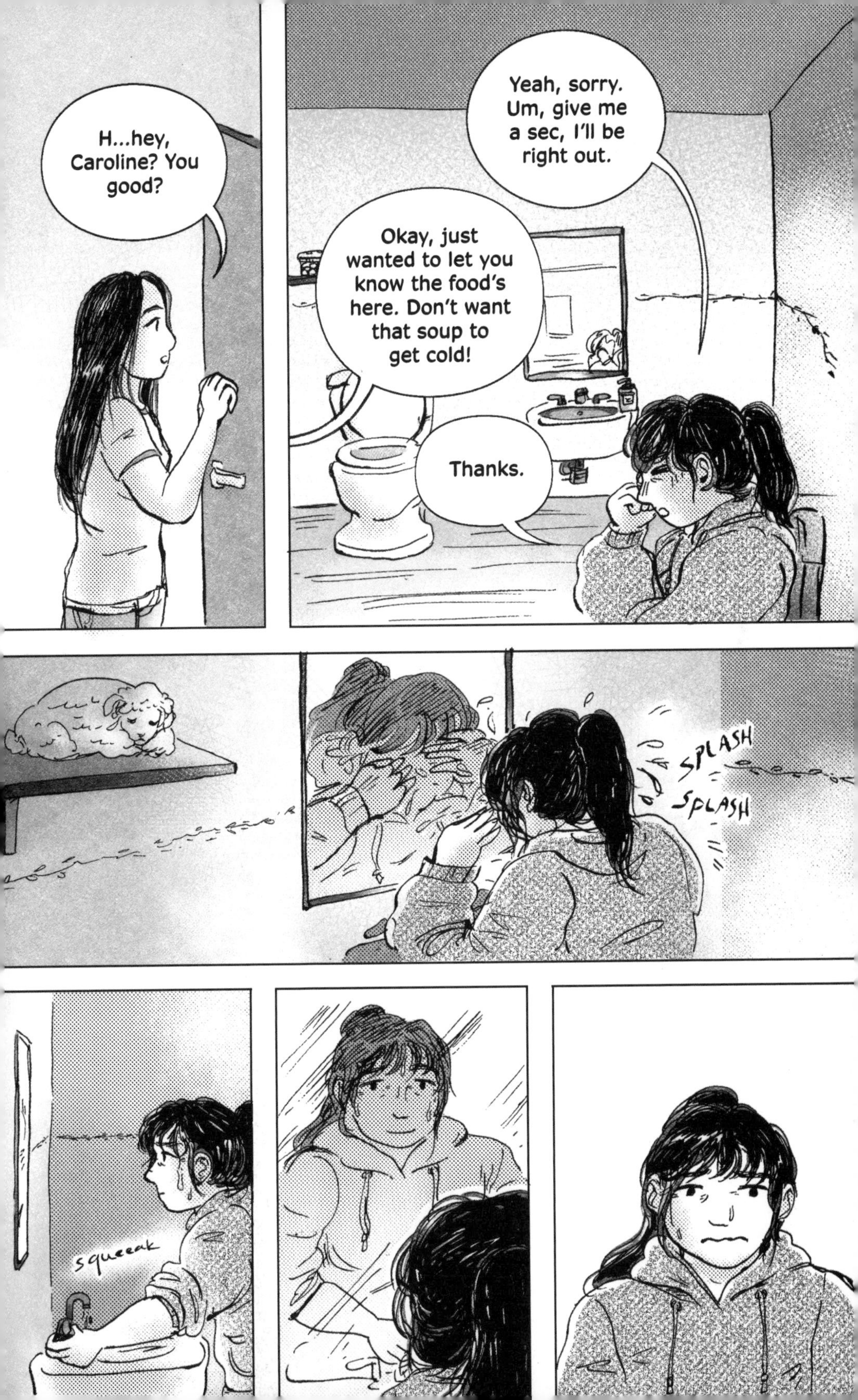
H...hey, Caroline? You good?
Yeah, sorry. Um, give me a sec, I'll be right out.
Okay, just wanted to let you know the food's here. Don't want that soup to get cold!
Thanks.
SPLASH
SPLASH
squeeak

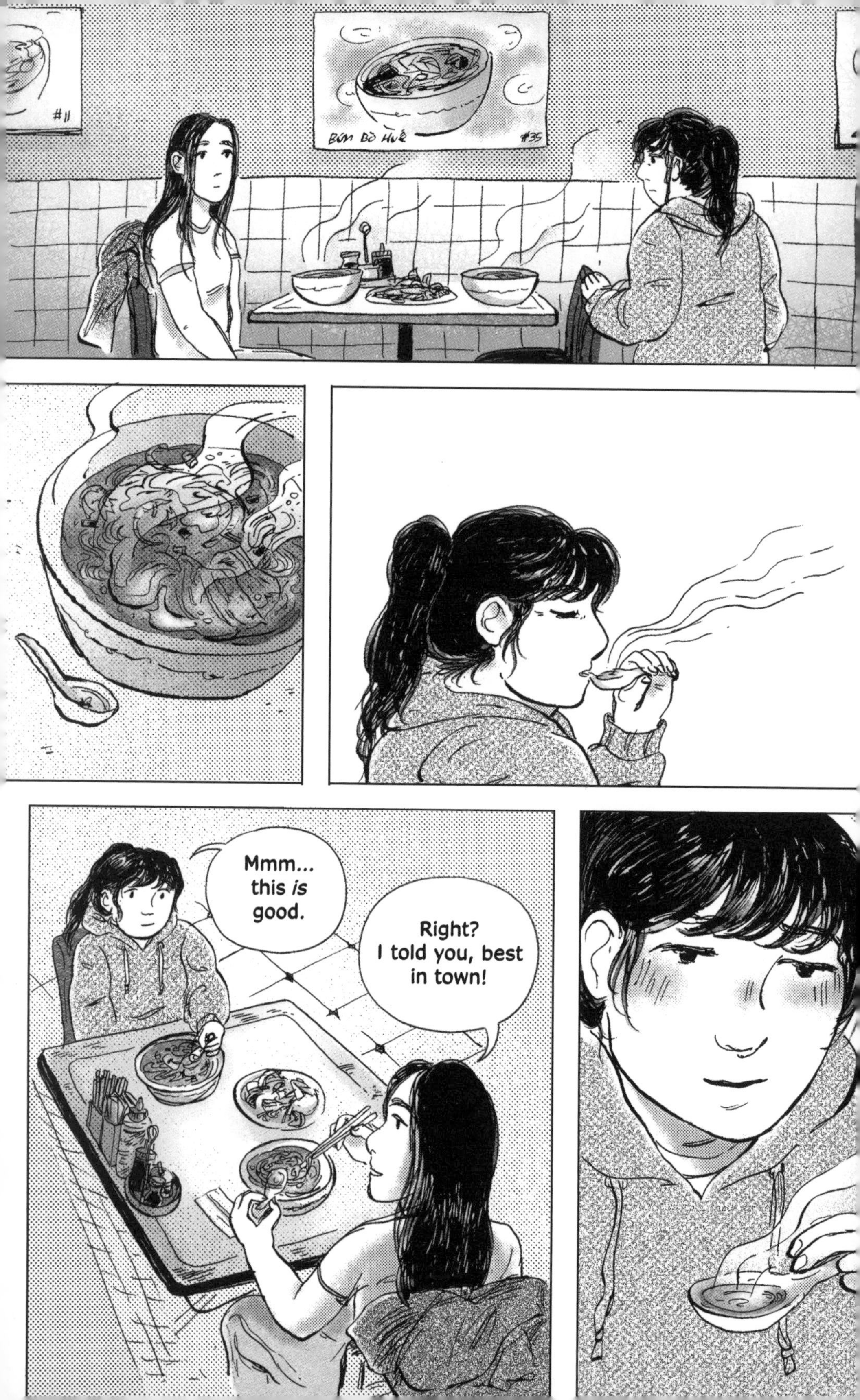
#11
Bún Bò Huế
#35
Mmm... this *is* good.
Right? I told you, best in town!

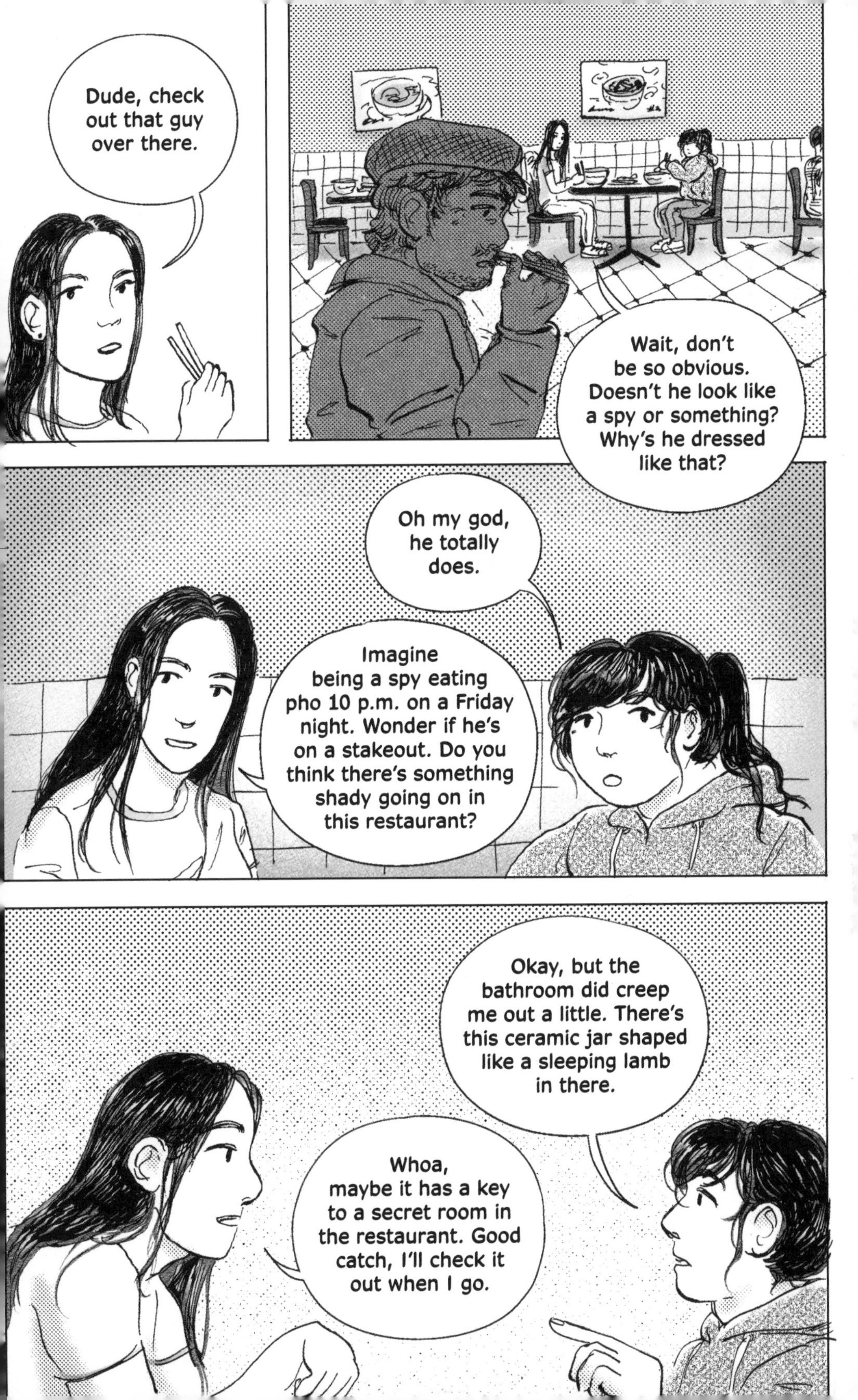
Dude, check out that guy over there.
Wait, don't be so obvious. Doesn't he look like a spy or something? Why's he dressed like that?
Oh my god, he totally does.
Imagine being a spy eating pho 10 p.m. on a Friday night. Wonder if he's on a stakeout. Do you think there's something shady going on in this restaurant?
Okay, but the bathroom did creep me out a little. There's this ceramic jar shaped like a sleeping lamb in there.
Whoa, maybe it has a key to a secret room in the restaurant. Good catch, I'll check it out when I go.

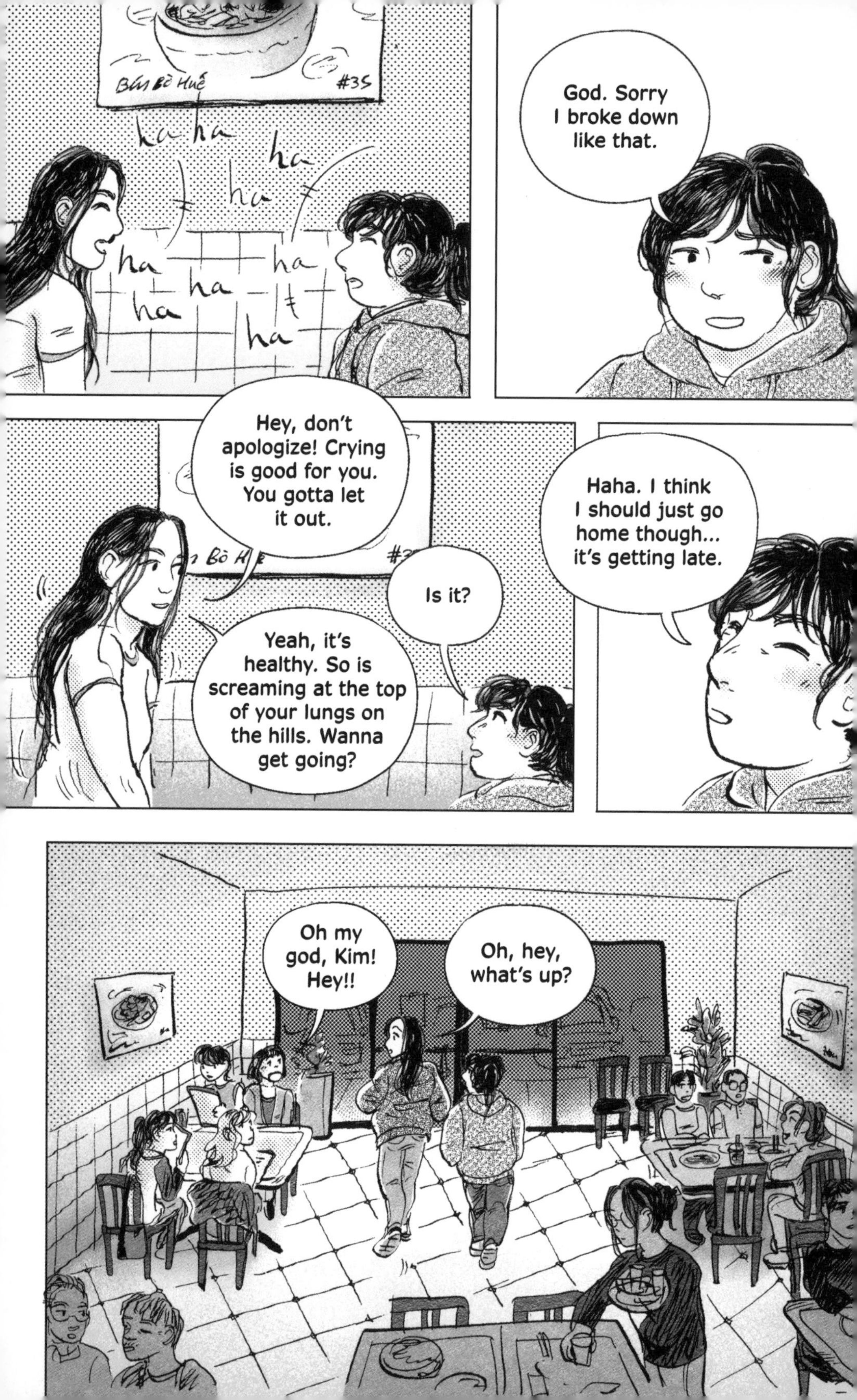
Bún Bò Huế
#35
ha ha ha ha ha ha ha ha ha
God. Sorry I broke down like that.
Hey, don't apologize! Crying is good for you. You gotta let it out.
Yeah, it's healthy. So is screaming at the top of your lungs on the hills. Wanna get going?
Is it?
Haha. I think I should just go home though... it's getting late.
Oh my god, Kim! Hey!!
Oh, hey, what's up?

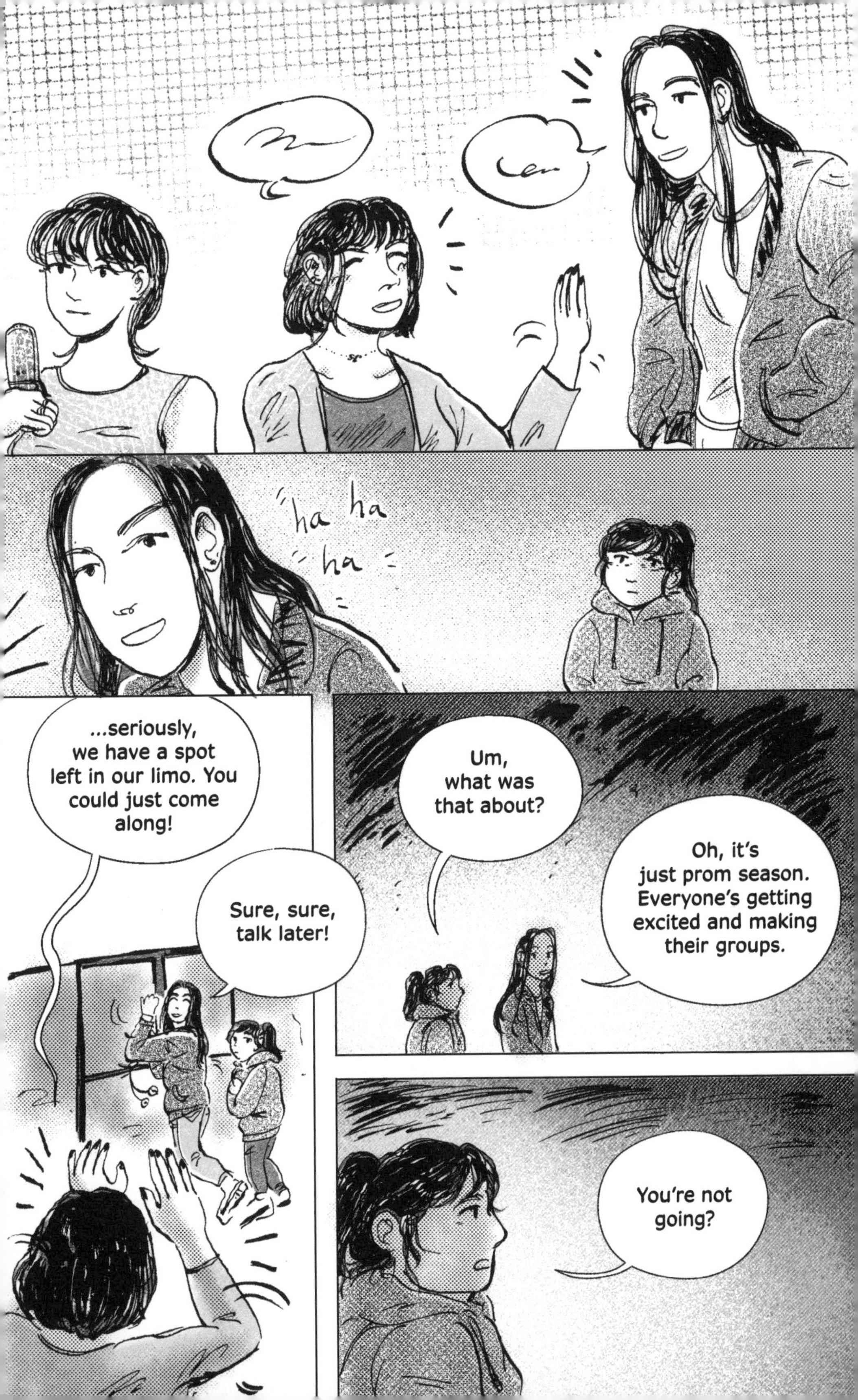
ha ha
ha
...seriously, we have a spot left in our limo. You could just come along!
Sure, sure, talk later!
Um, what was that about?
Oh, it's just prom season. Everyone's getting excited and making their groups.
You're not going?

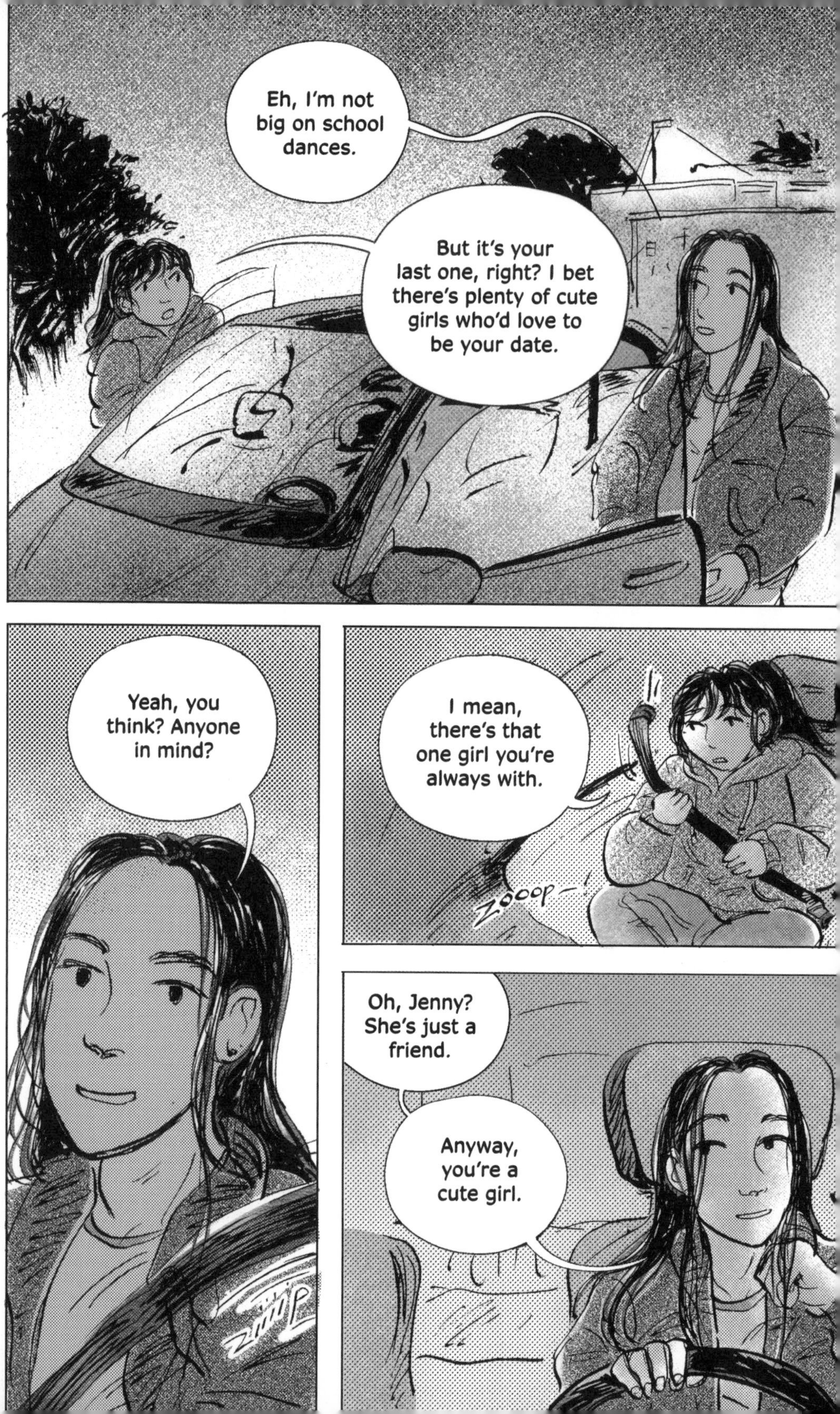
Eh, I'm not big on school dances.
But it's your last one, right? I bet there's plenty of cute girls who'd love to be your date.
Yeah, you think? Anyone in mind?
I mean, there's that one girl you're always with.
ZOOOP—!
Oh, Jenny? She's just a friend.
Anyway, you're a cute girl.

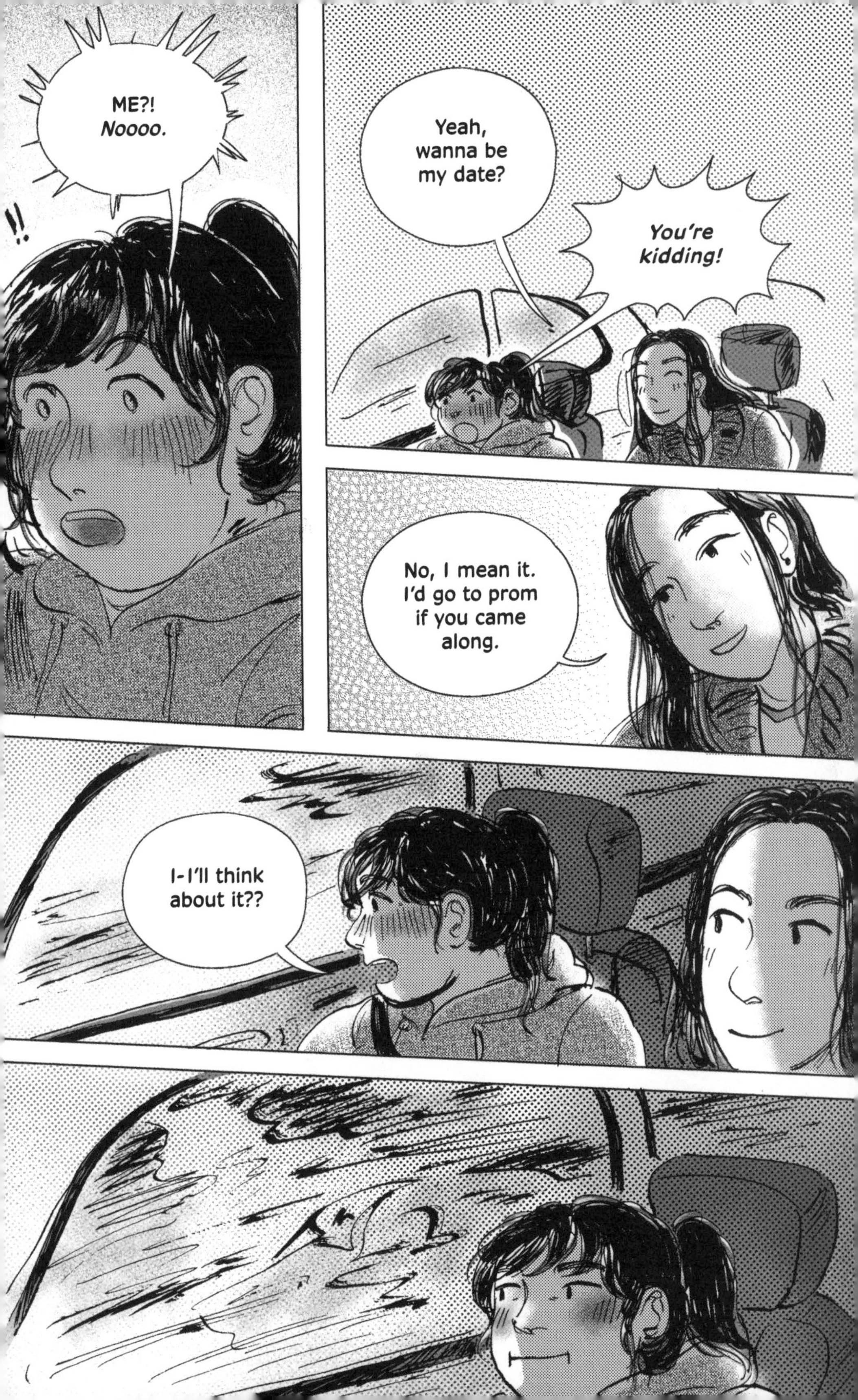
ME?! *Noooo.*
!!
Yeah, wanna be my date?
You're kidding!
No, I mean it. I'd go to prom if you came along.
I-I'll think about it??

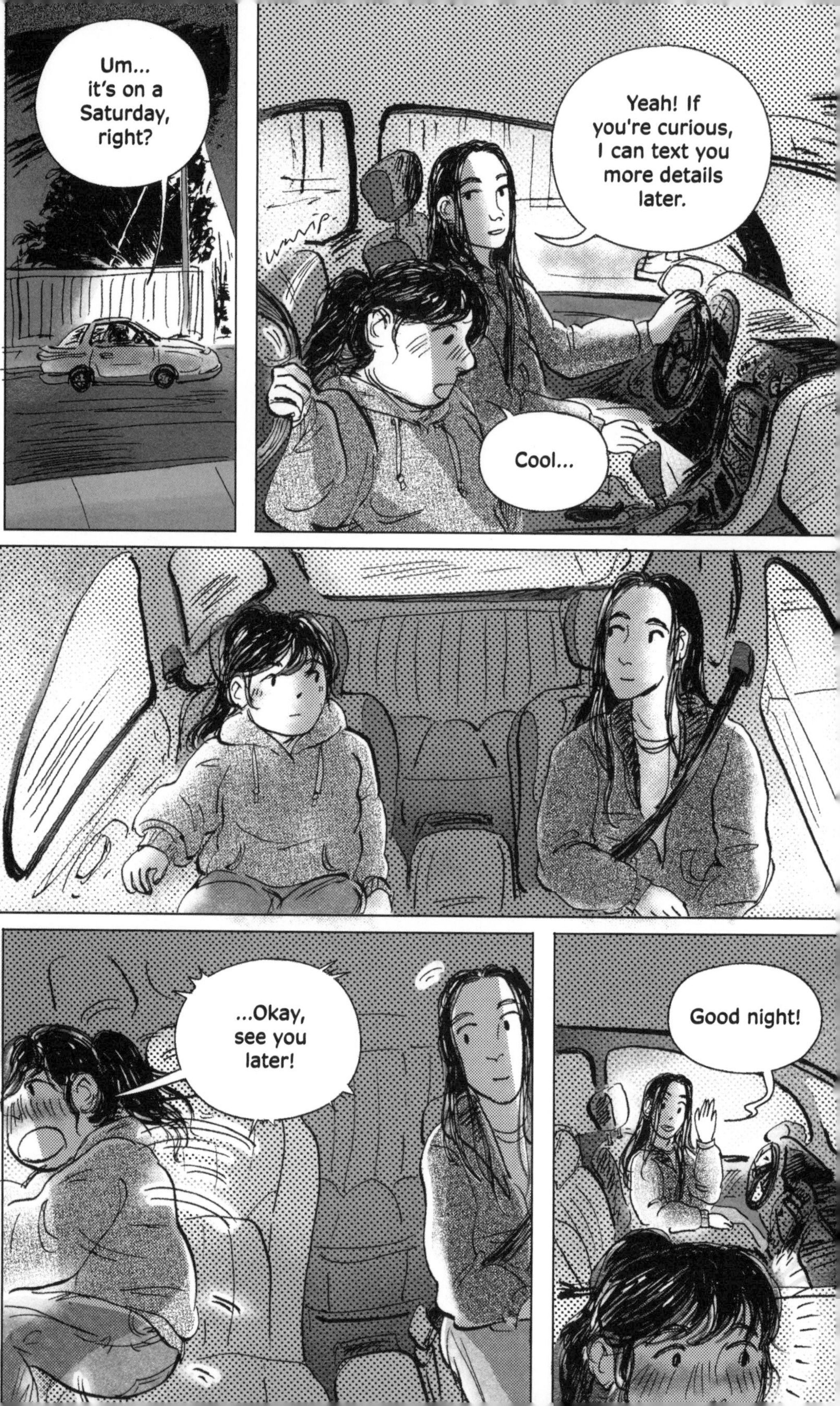
Um... it's on a Saturday, right?
Yeah! If you're curious, I can text you more details later.
Cool...
...Okay, see you later!
Good night!

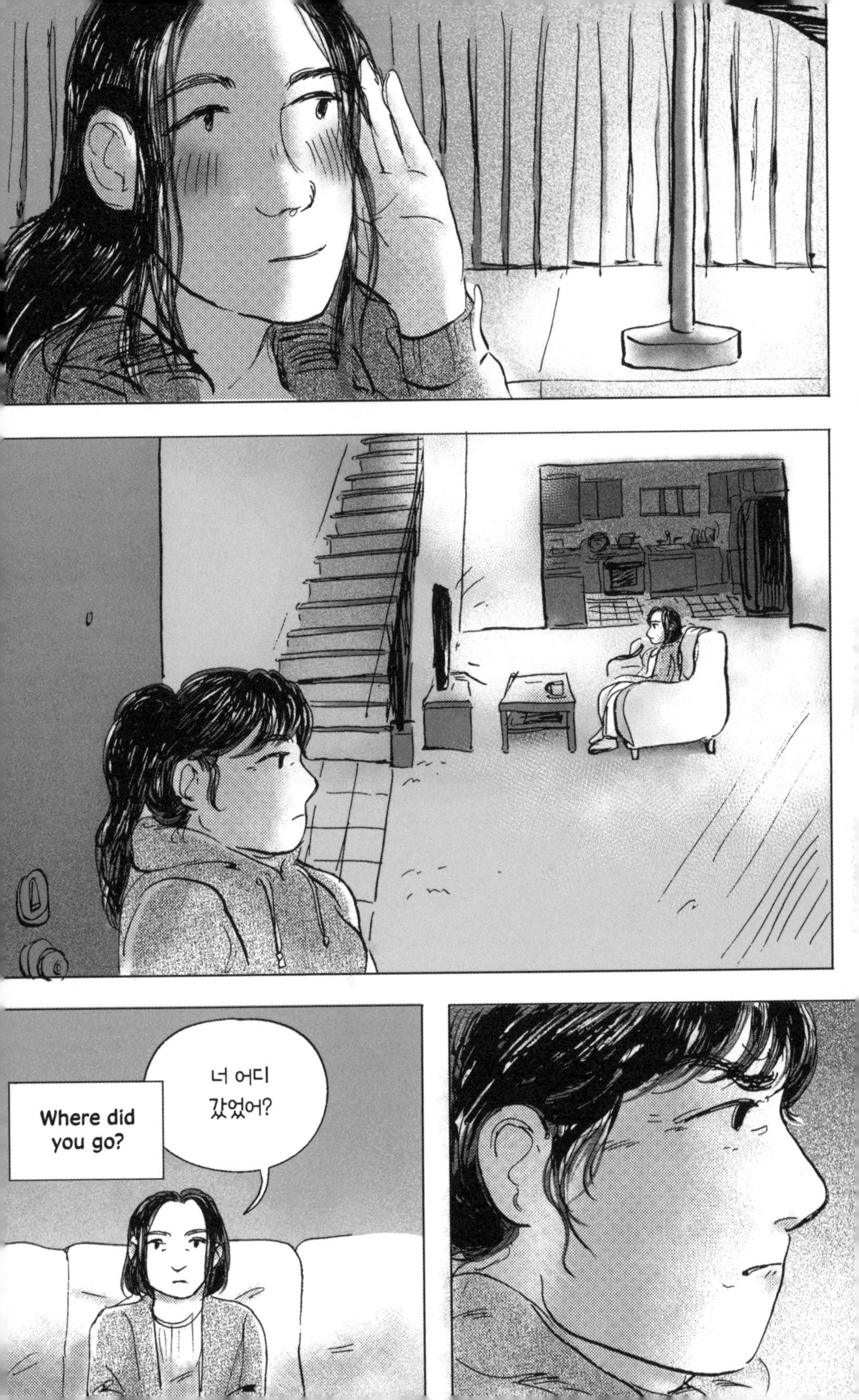
너 어디 갔었어?
Where did you go?

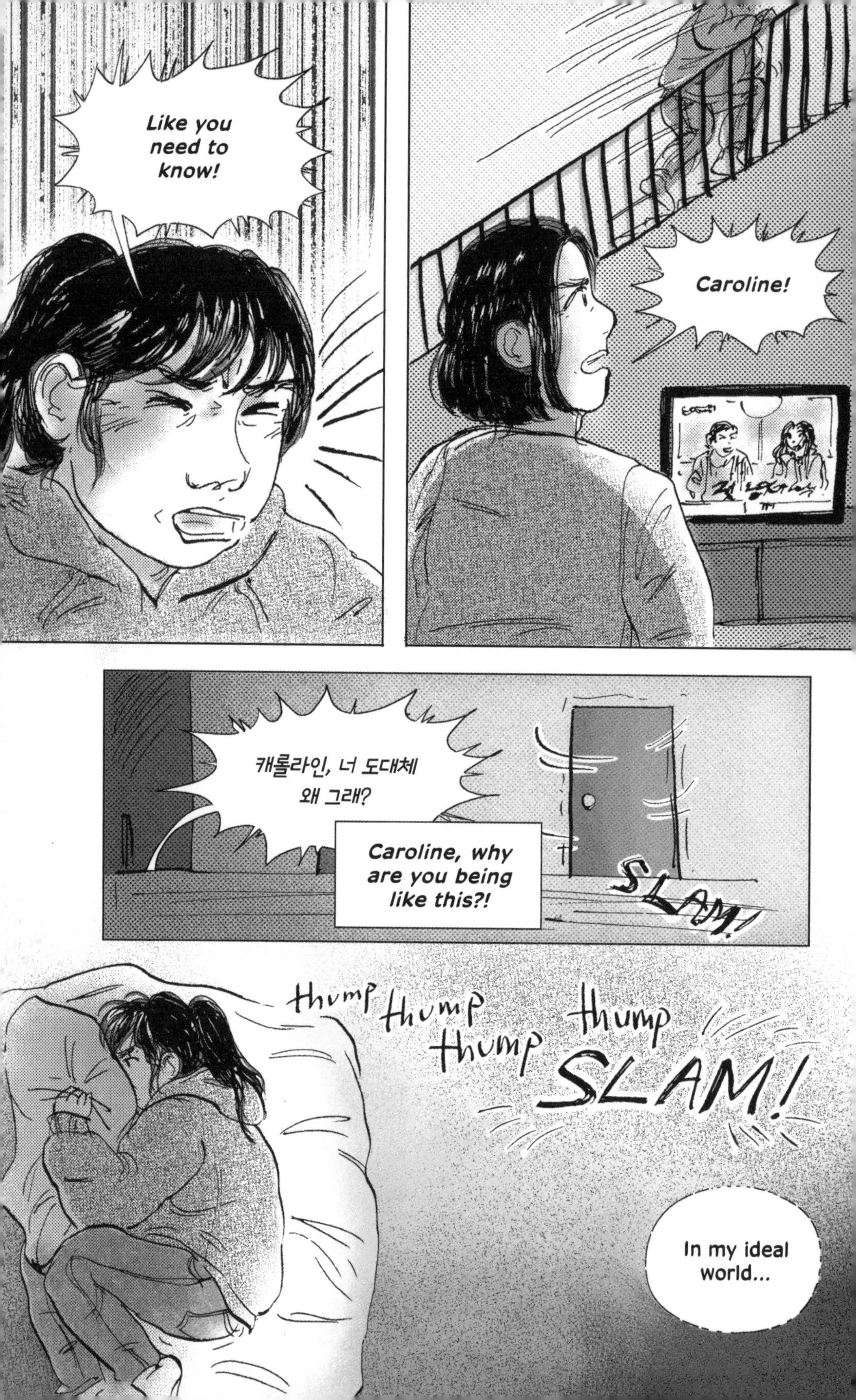
Like you need to know!
Caroline!
캐롤라인, 너 도대체 왜 그래?
Caroline, why are you being like this?!
SLAM!
thump thump thump thump
SLAM!
In my ideal world...

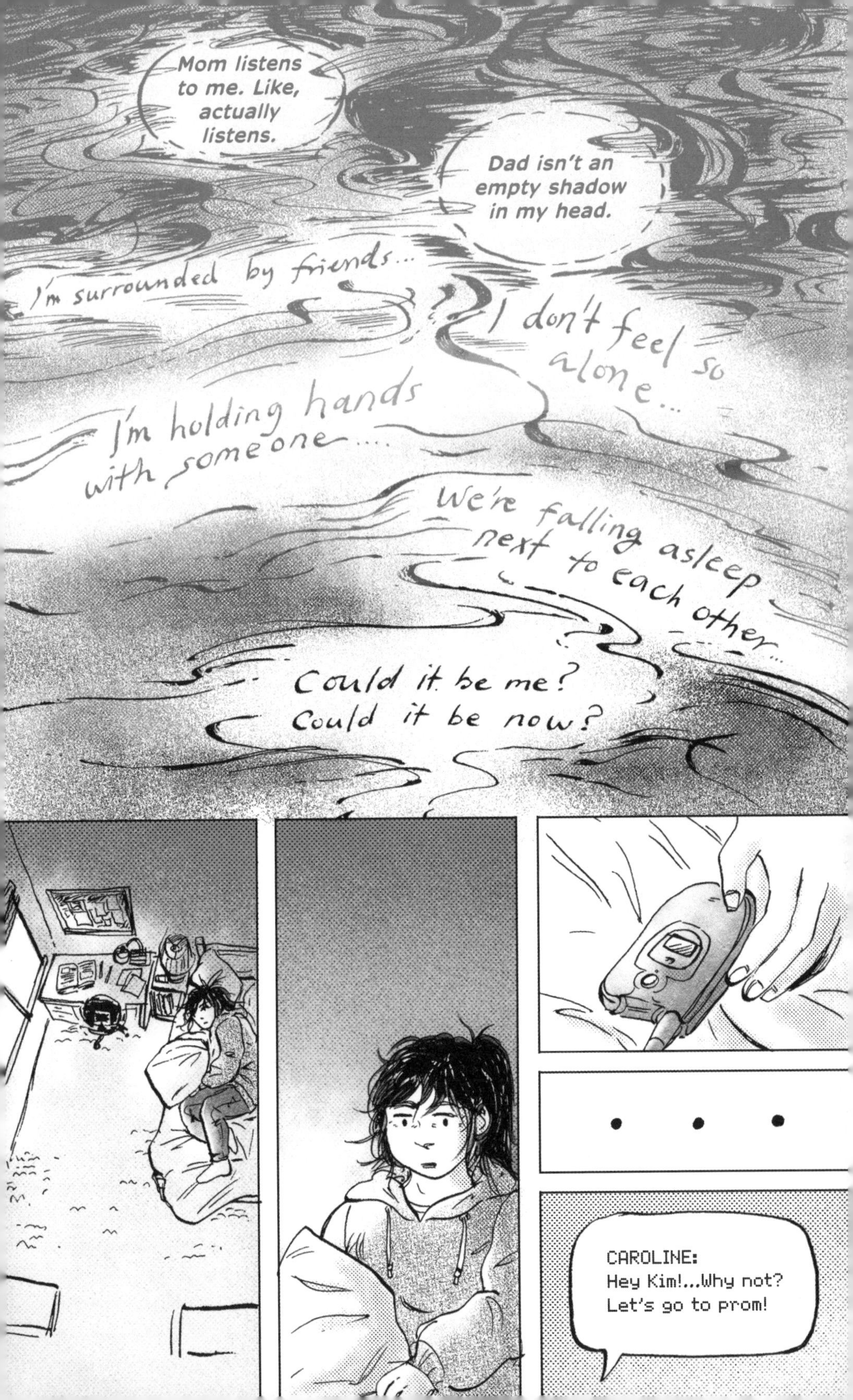
Mom listens to me. Like, actually listens.
Dad isn't an empty shadow in my head.
I'm surrounded by friends...
I don't feel so alone...
I'm holding hands with someone...
We're falling asleep next to each other...
Could it be me? Could it be now?
CAROLINE:
Hey Kim!...Why not? Let's go to prom!

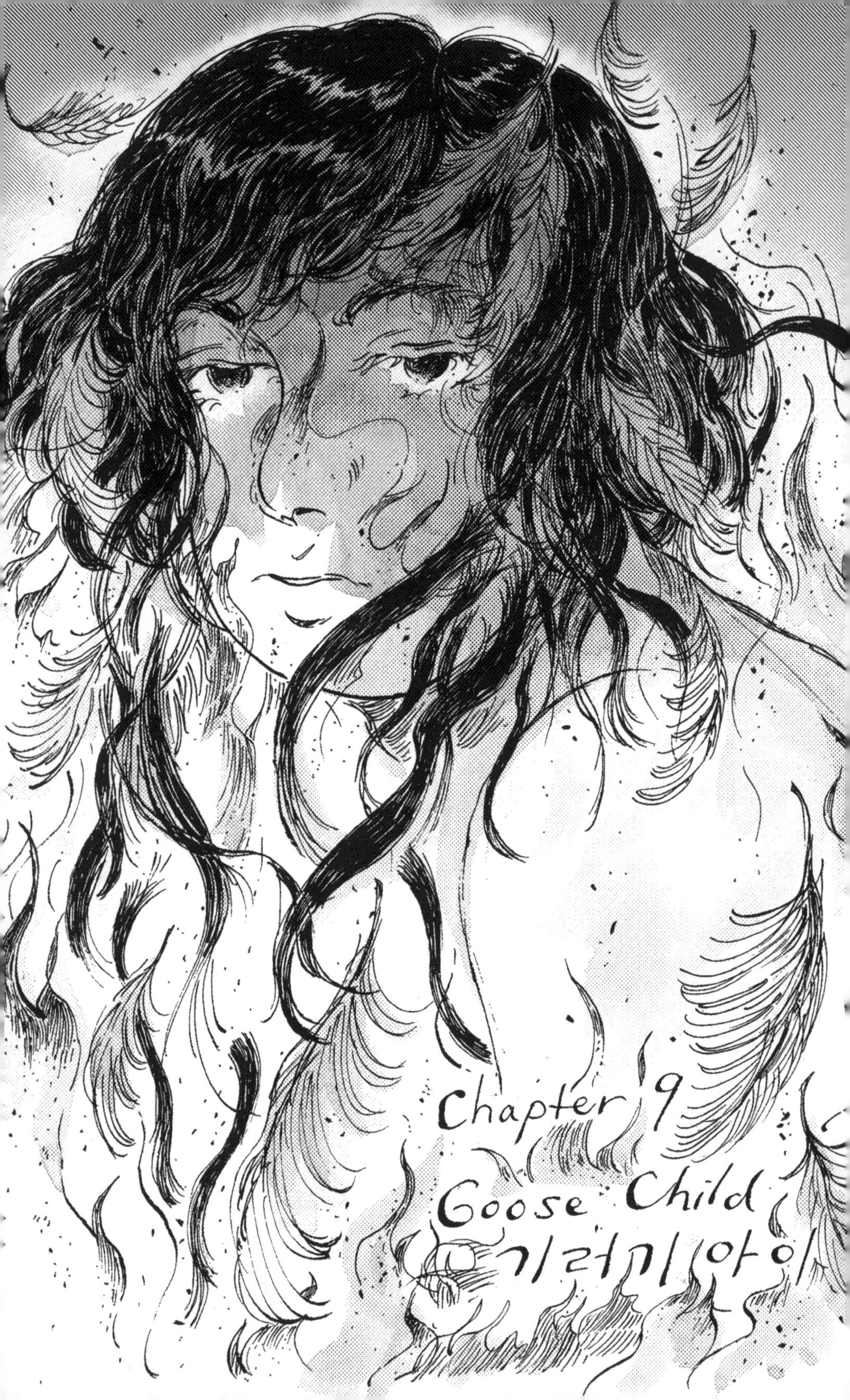

Chapter 9
Goose Child
기러기 아이

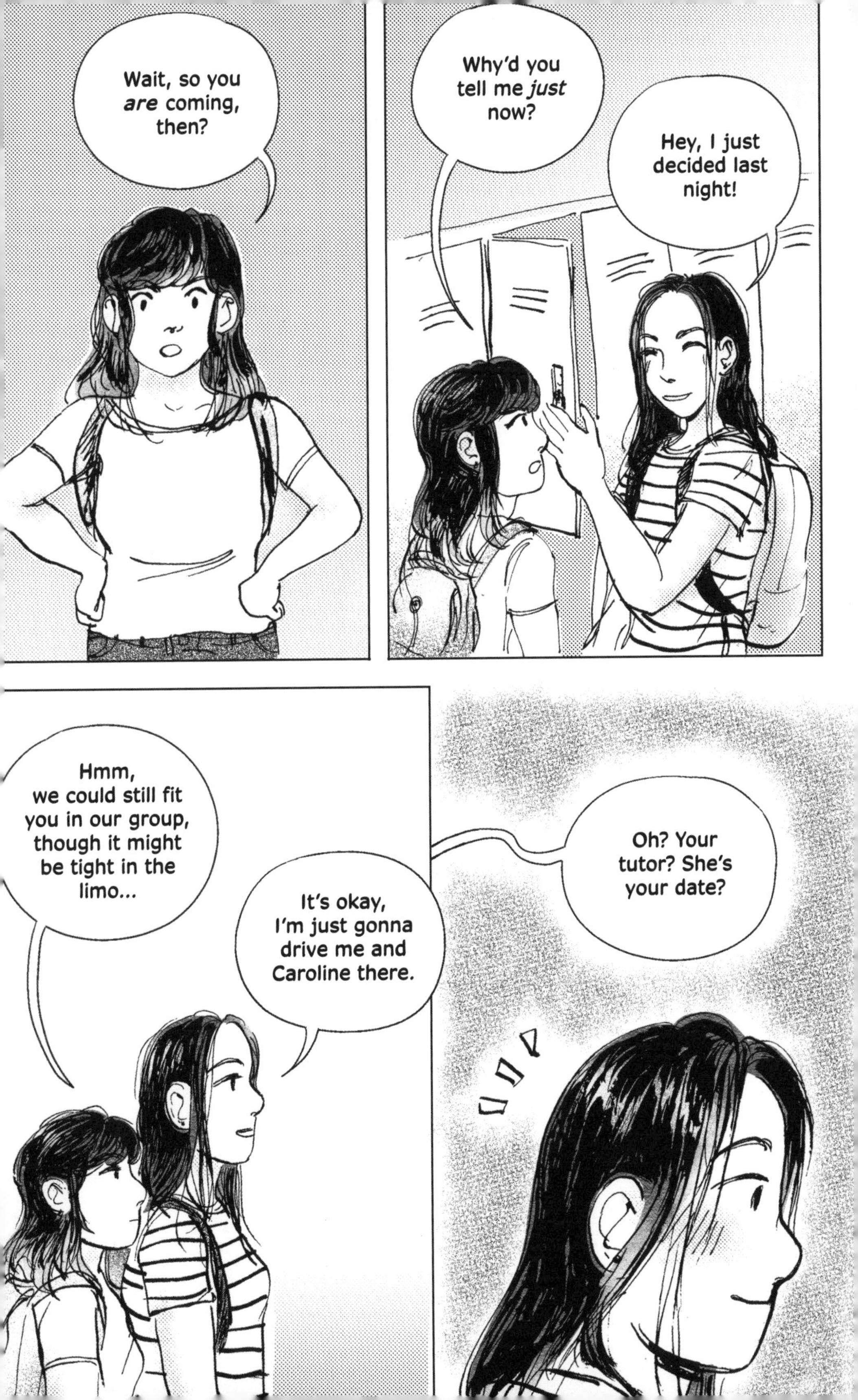
Wait, so you *are* coming, then?
Why'd you tell me *just* now?
Hey, I just decided last night!
Hmm, we could still fit you in our group, though it might be tight in the limo...
It's okay, I'm just gonna drive me and Caroline there.
Oh? Your tutor? She's your date?

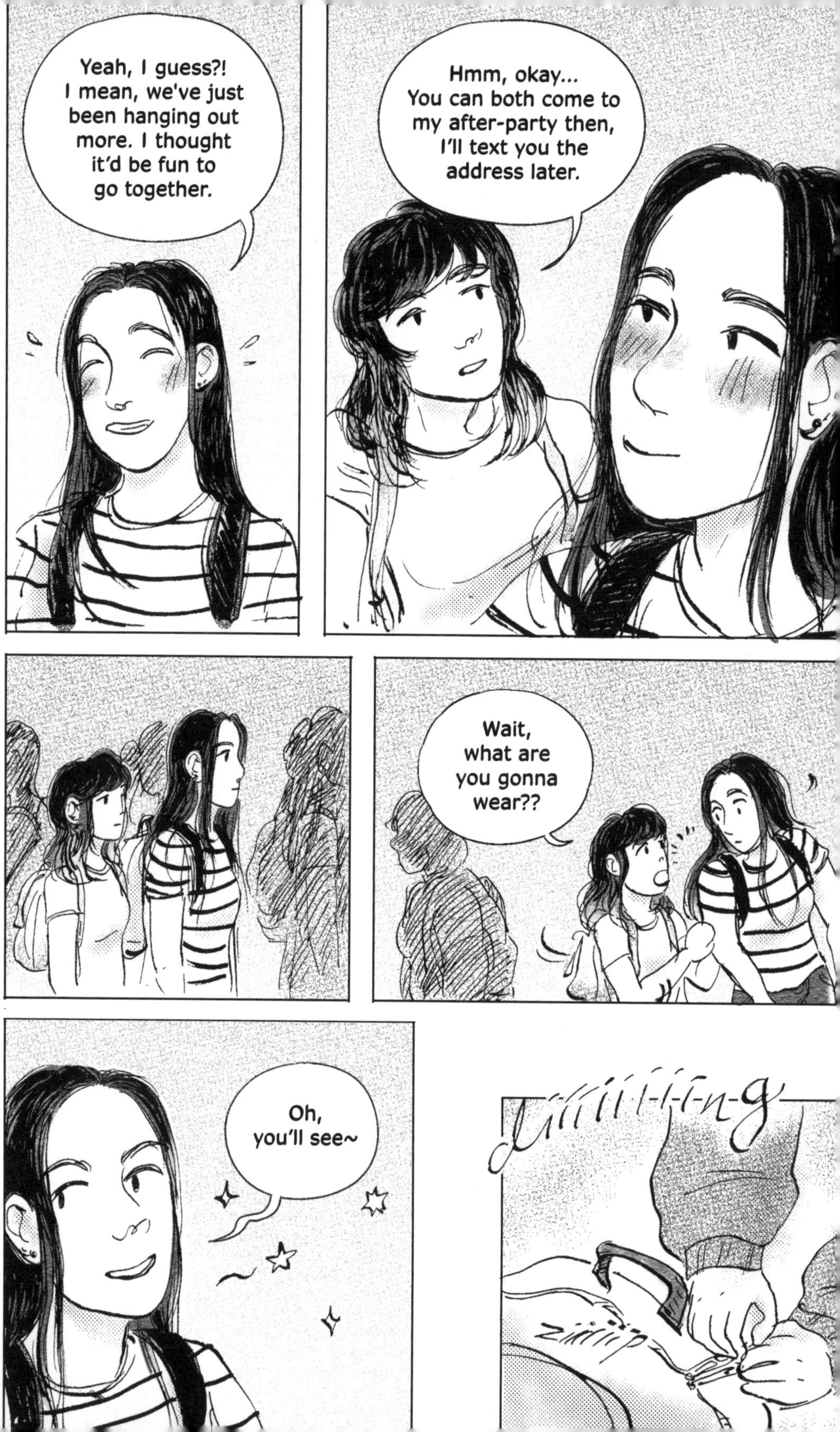
Yeah, I guess?! I mean, we've just been hanging out more. I thought it'd be fun to go together.
Hmm, okay... You can both come to my after-party then, I'll text you the address later.
Wait, what are you gonna wear??
Oh, you'll see~

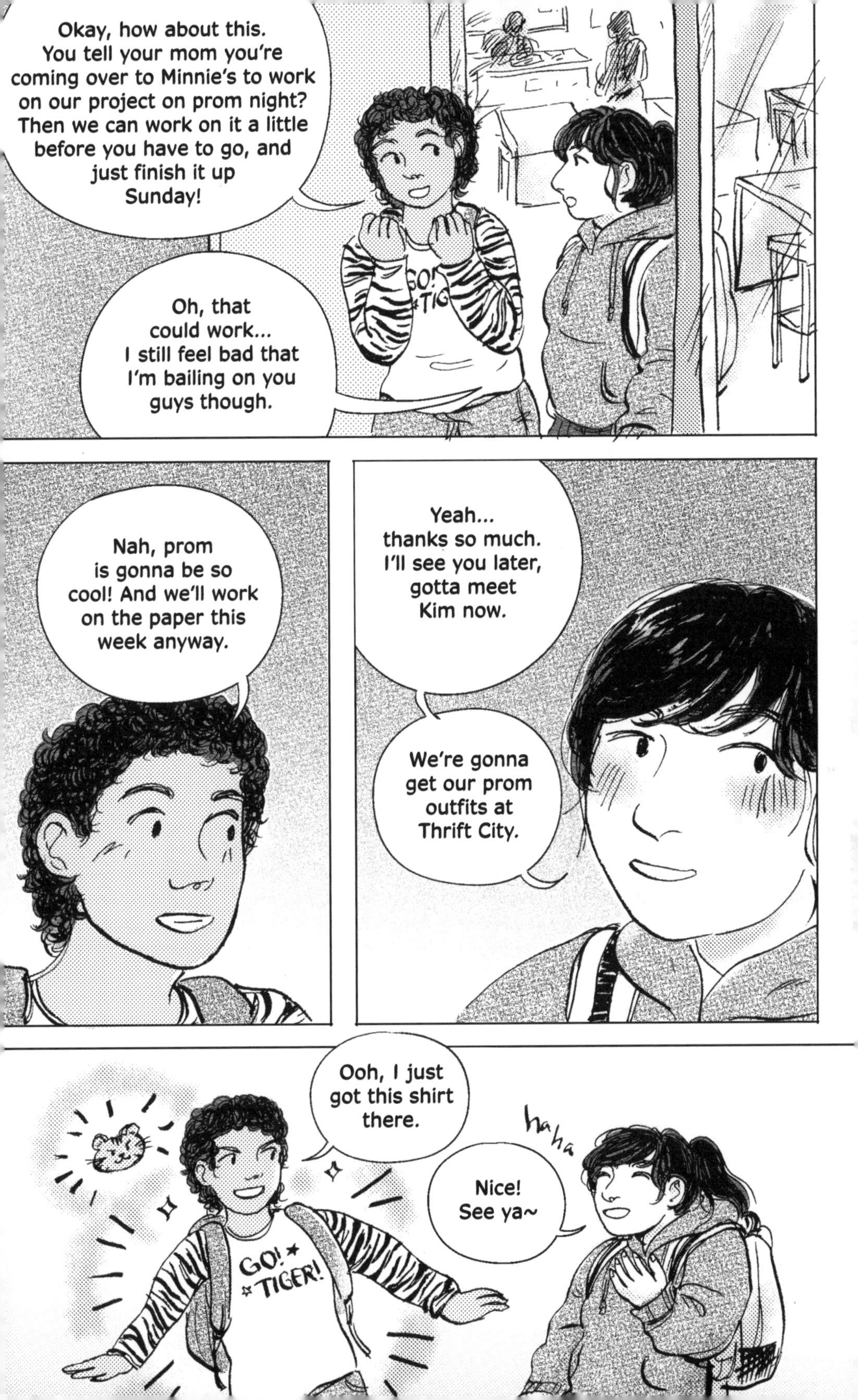
Okay, how about this. You tell your mom you're coming over to Minnie's to work on our project on prom night? Then we can work on it a little before you have to go, and just finish it up Sunday!
Oh, that could work... I still feel bad that I'm bailing on you guys though.
Nah, prom is gonna be so cool! And we'll work on the paper this week anyway.
Yeah... thanks so much. I'll see you later, gotta meet Kim now.
We're gonna get our prom outfits at Thrift City.
Ooh, I just got this shirt there.
haha
Nice! See ya~
GO! TIGER!

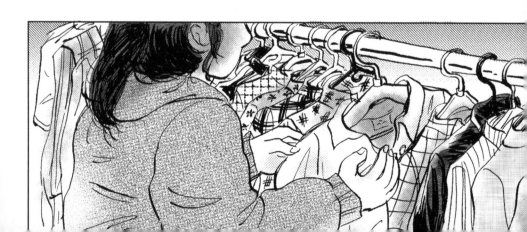

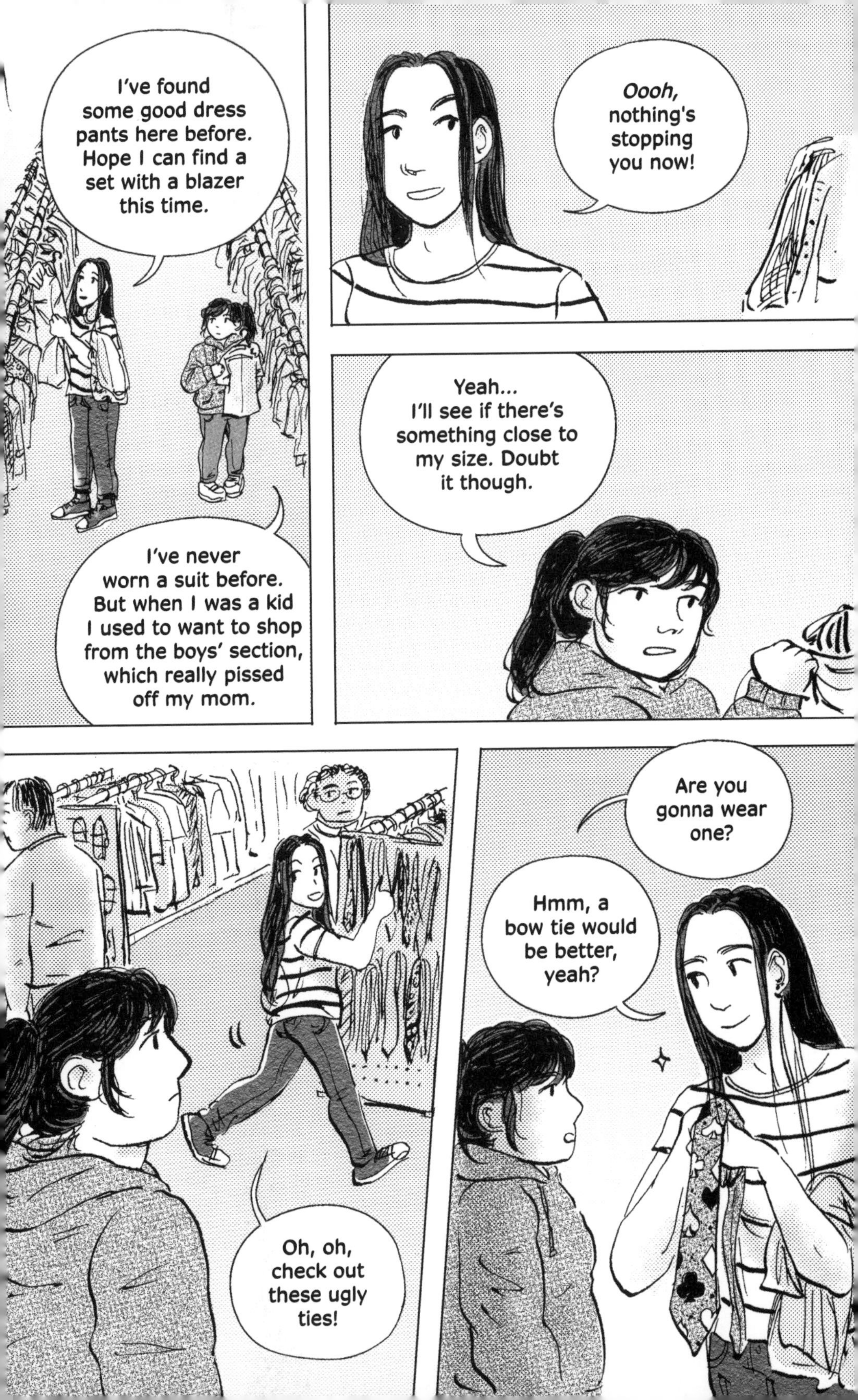
I've found some good dress pants here before. Hope I can find a set with a blazer this time.
I've never worn a suit before. But when I was a kid I used to want to shop from the boys' section, which really pissed off my mom.
Oooh, nothing's stopping you now!
Yeah... I'll see if there's something close to my size. Doubt it though.
Oh, oh, check out these ugly ties!
Are you gonna wear one?
Hmm, a bow tie would be better, yeah?

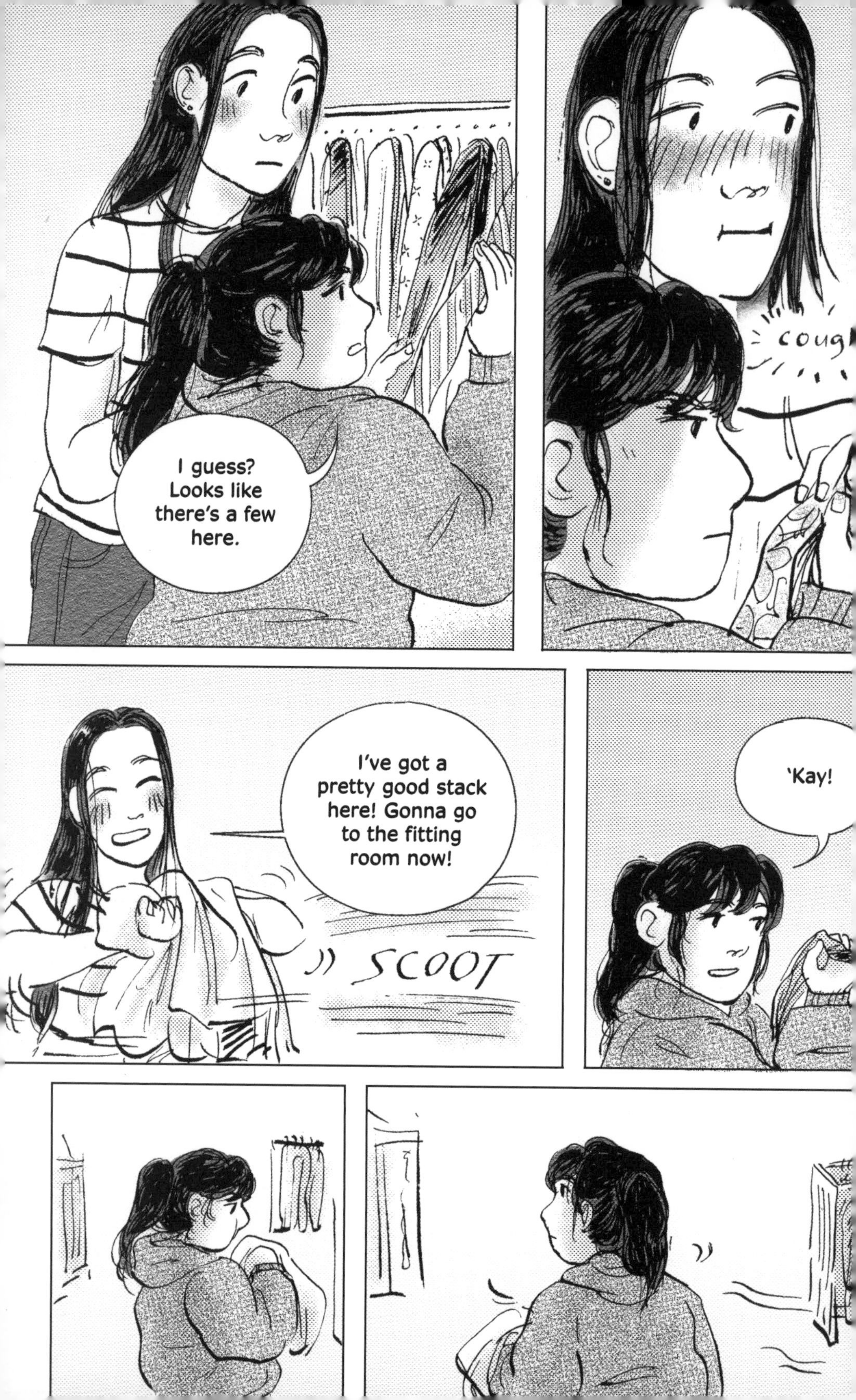
I guess? Looks like there's a few here.
COUGH
I've got a pretty good stack here! Gonna go to the fitting room now!
SCOOT
'Kay!

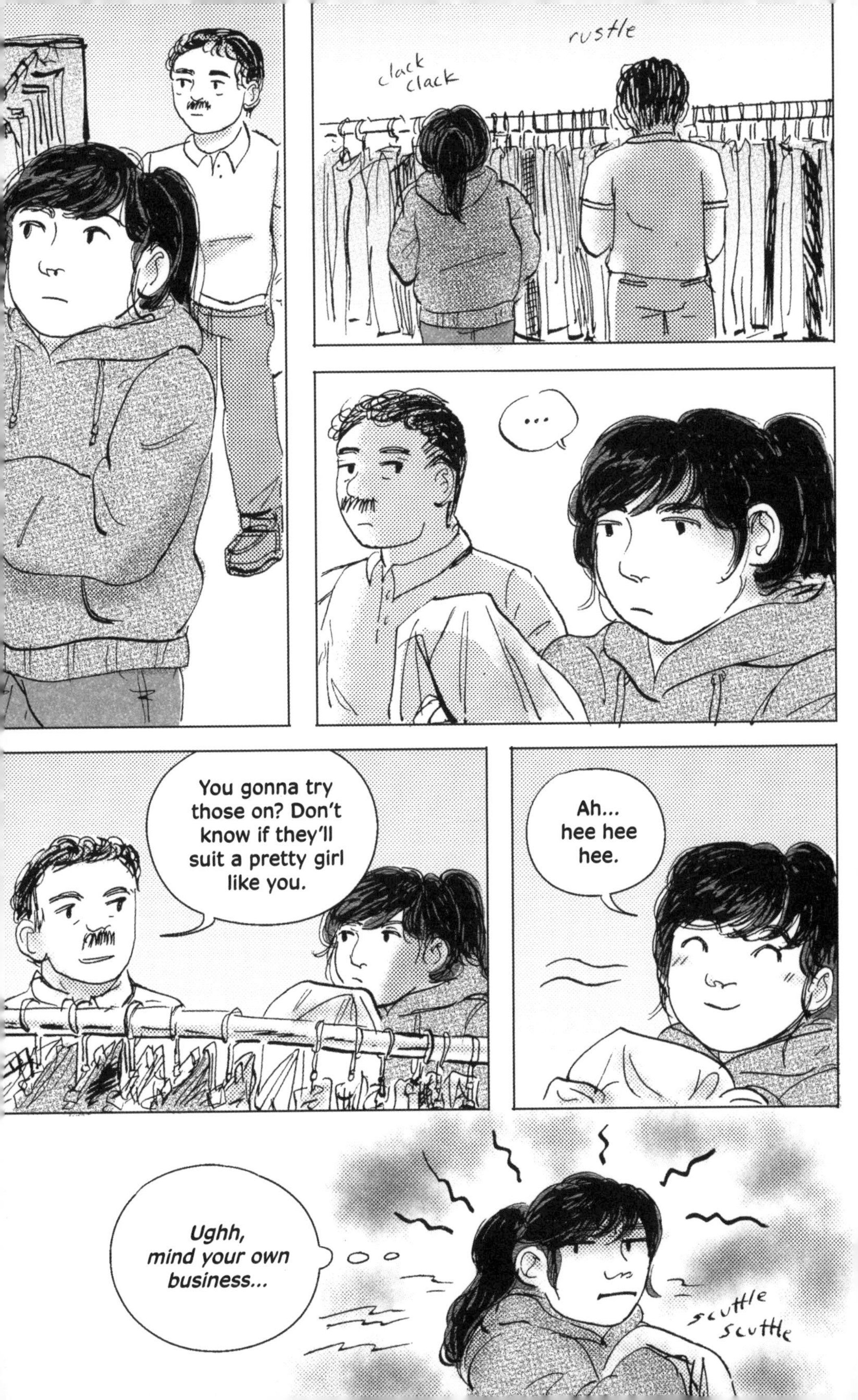
rustle
clack clack
...
You gonna try those on? Don't know if they'll suit a pretty girl like you.
Ah... hee hee hee.
Ughh, mind your own business...
scuttle scuttle

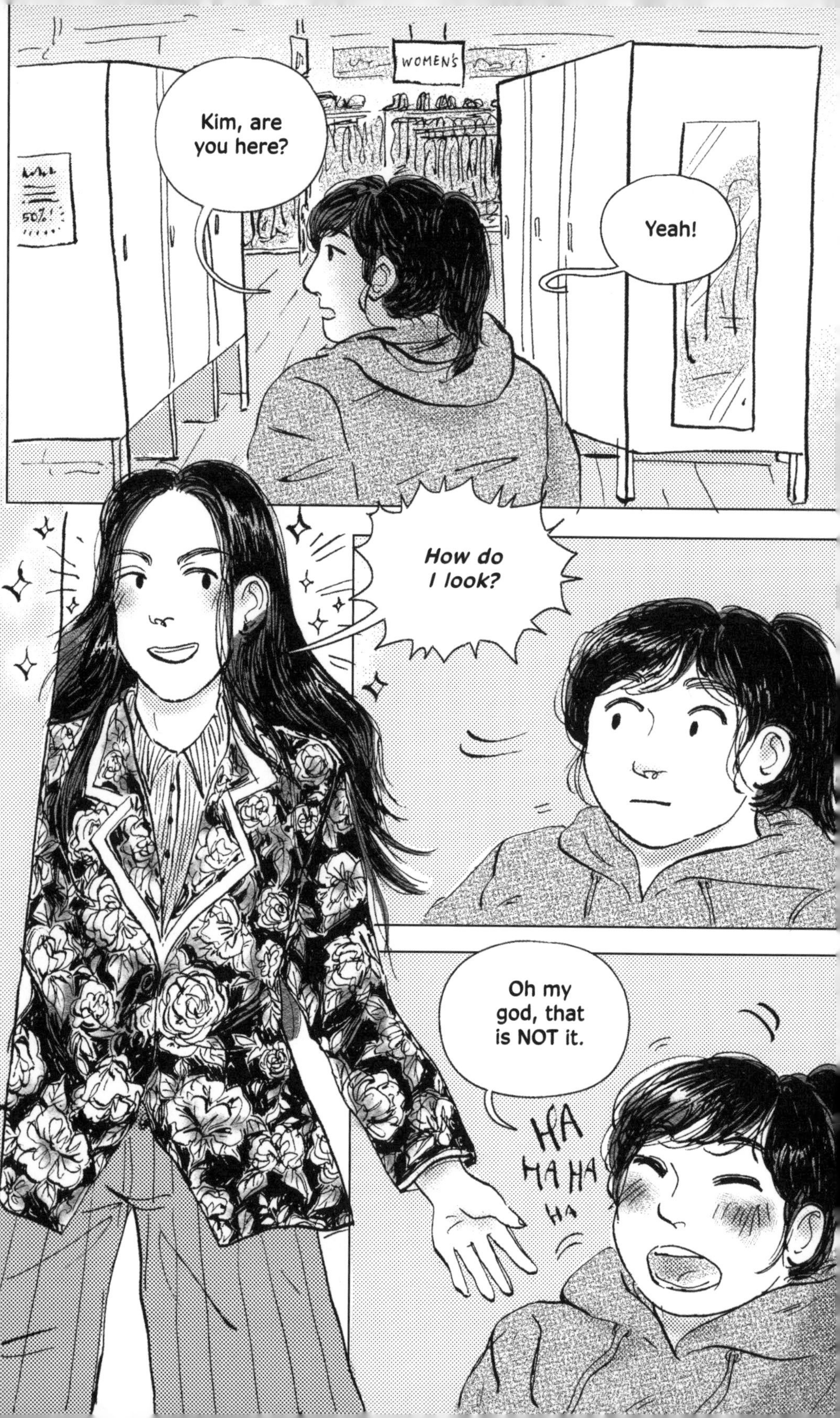

WOMEN'S
50%!
Kim, are you here?
Yeah!
How do I look?
Oh my god, that is NOT it.
HA HA HA HA

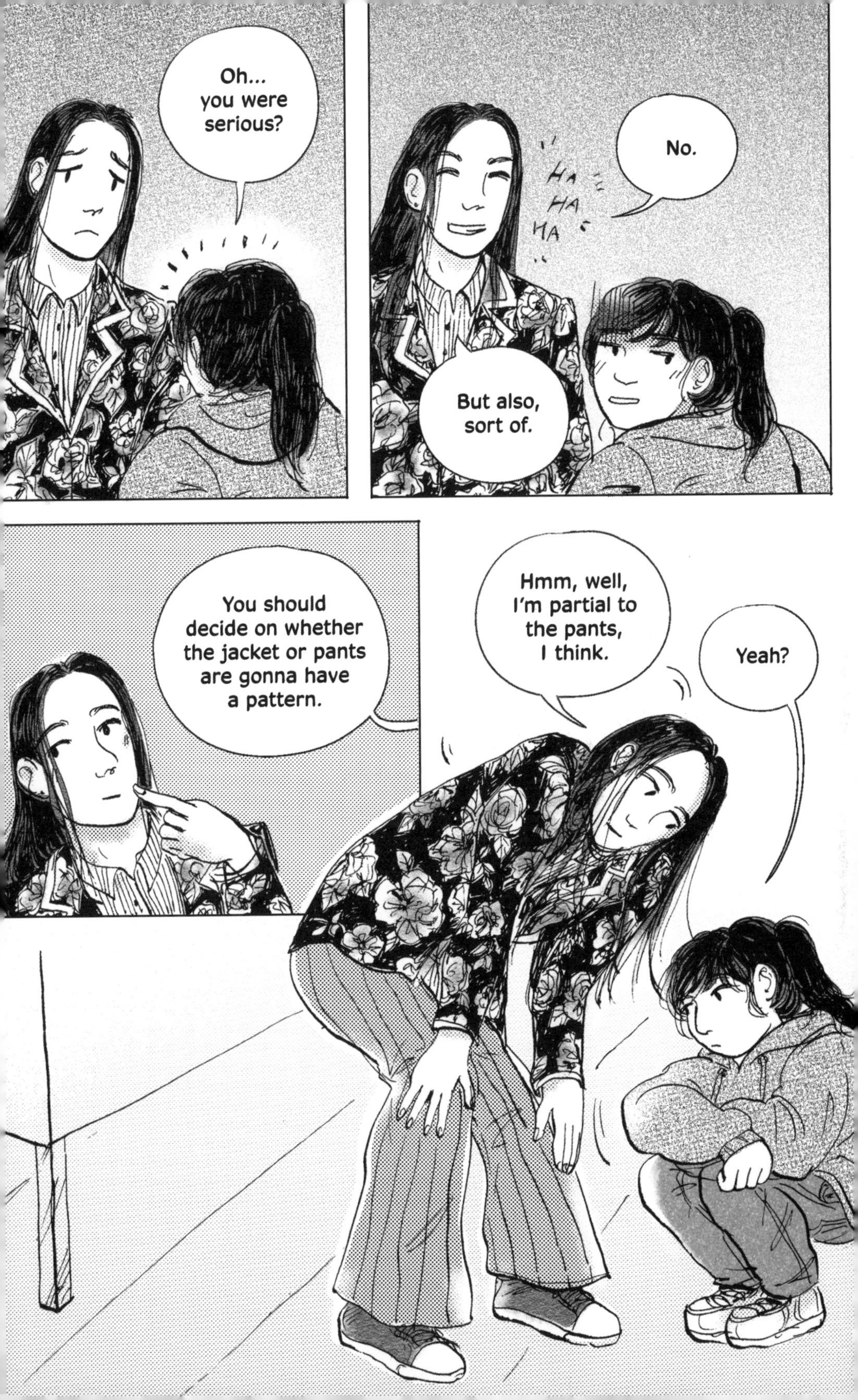
Oh...
you were
serious?
HA
HA
HA
No.
But also,
sort of.
You should
decide on whether
the jacket or pants
are gonna have
a pattern.
Hmm, well,
I'm partial to
the pants,
I think.
Yeah?

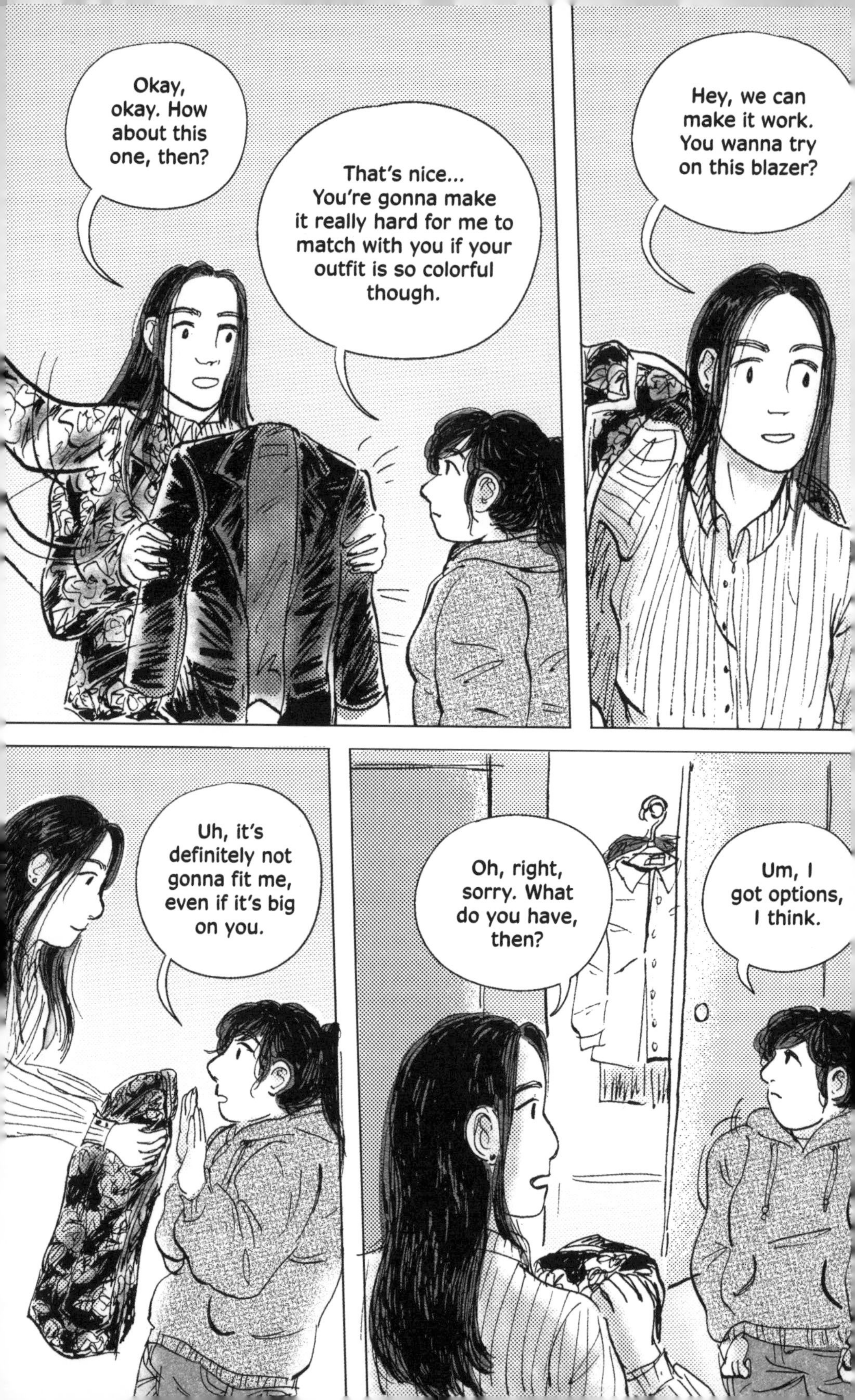
Okay, okay. How about this one, then?
That's nice... You're gonna make it really hard for me to match with you if your outfit is so colorful though.
Hey, we can make it work. You wanna try on this blazer?
Uh, it's definitely not gonna fit me, even if it's big on you.
Oh, right, sorry. What do you have, then?
Um, I got options, I think.

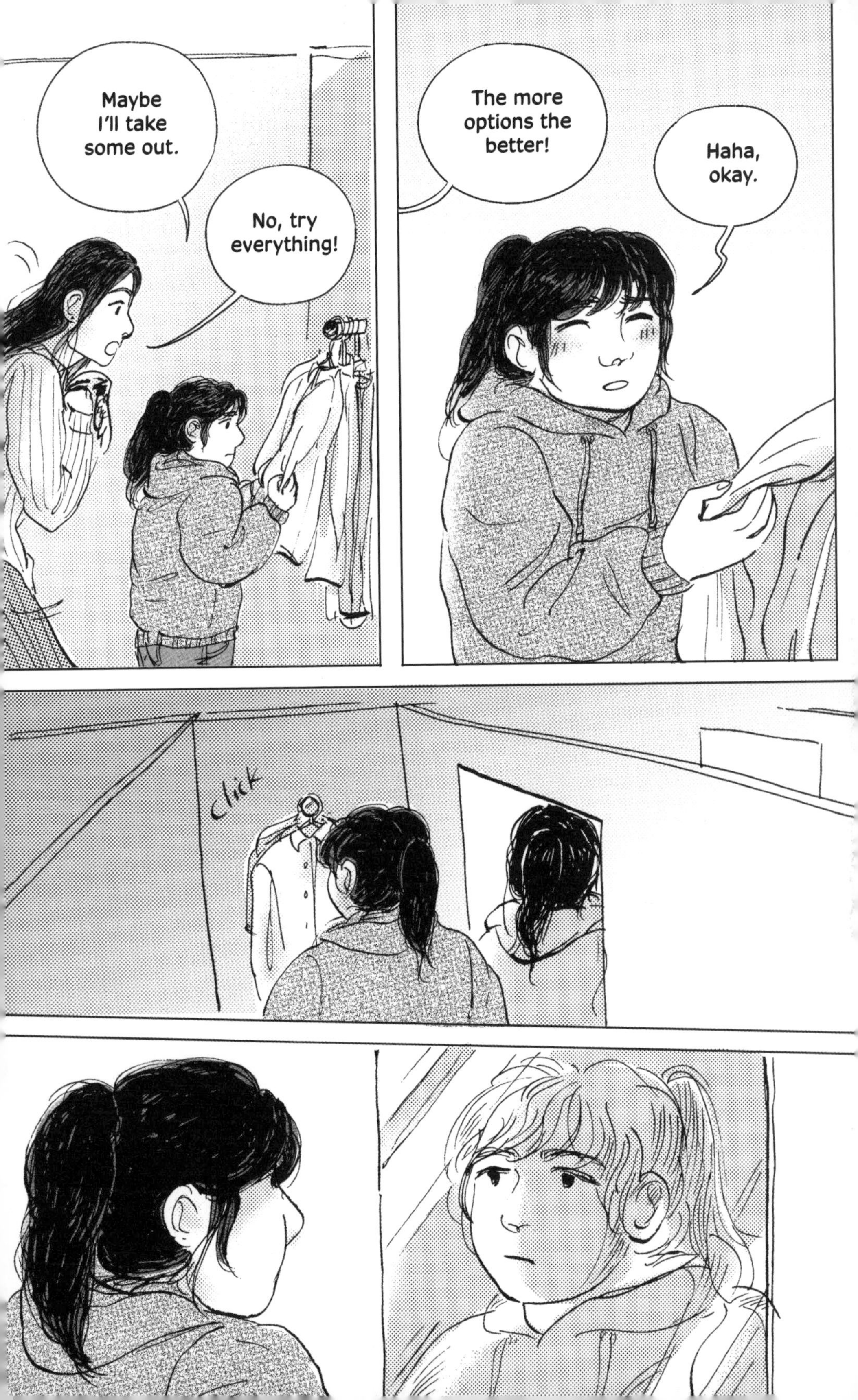
Maybe I'll take some out.
No, try everything!
The more options the better!
Haha, okay.
click

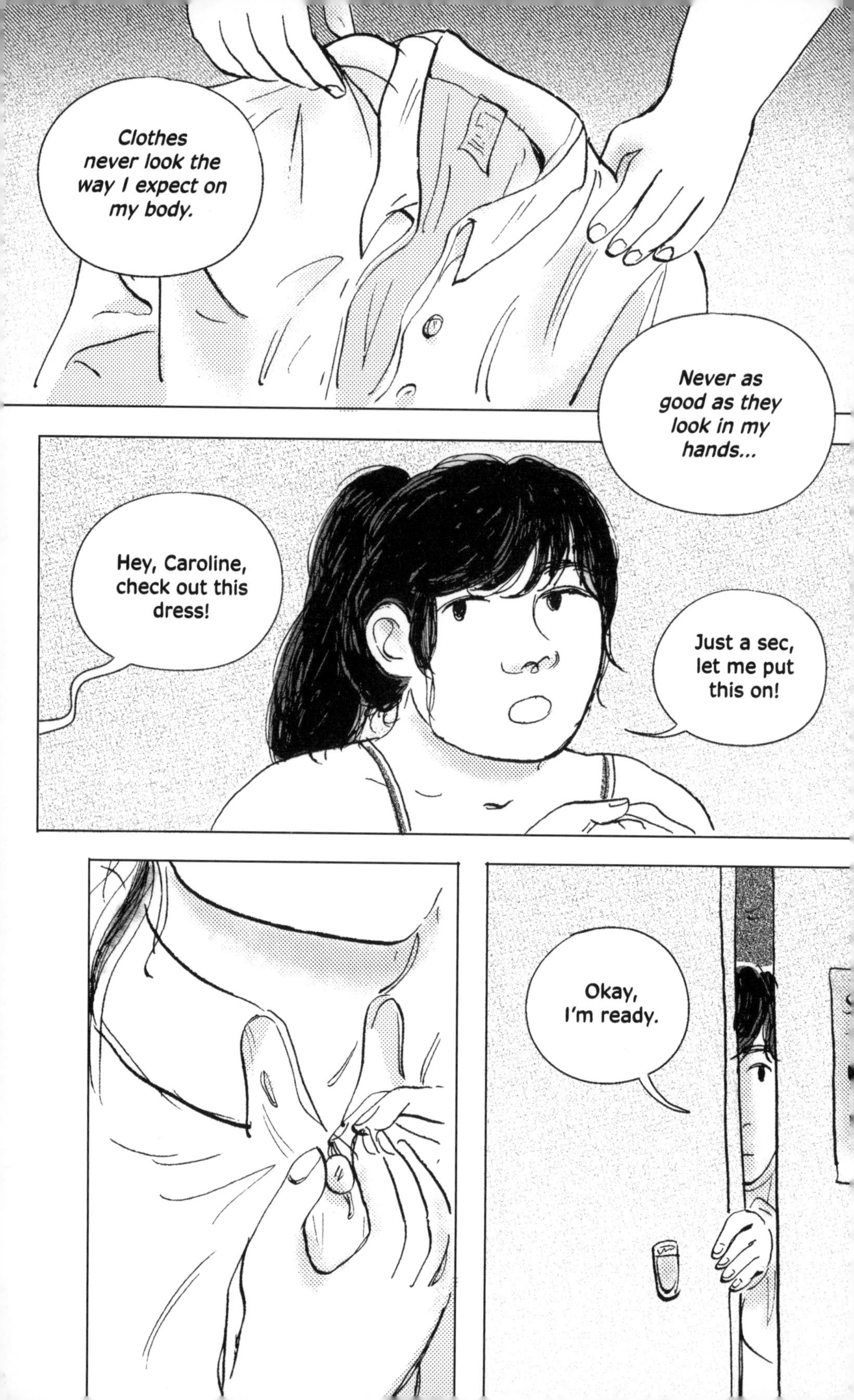

Clothes never look the way I expect on my body.
Never as good as they look in my hands...
Hey, Caroline, check out this dress!
Just a sec, let me put this on!
Okay, I'm ready.

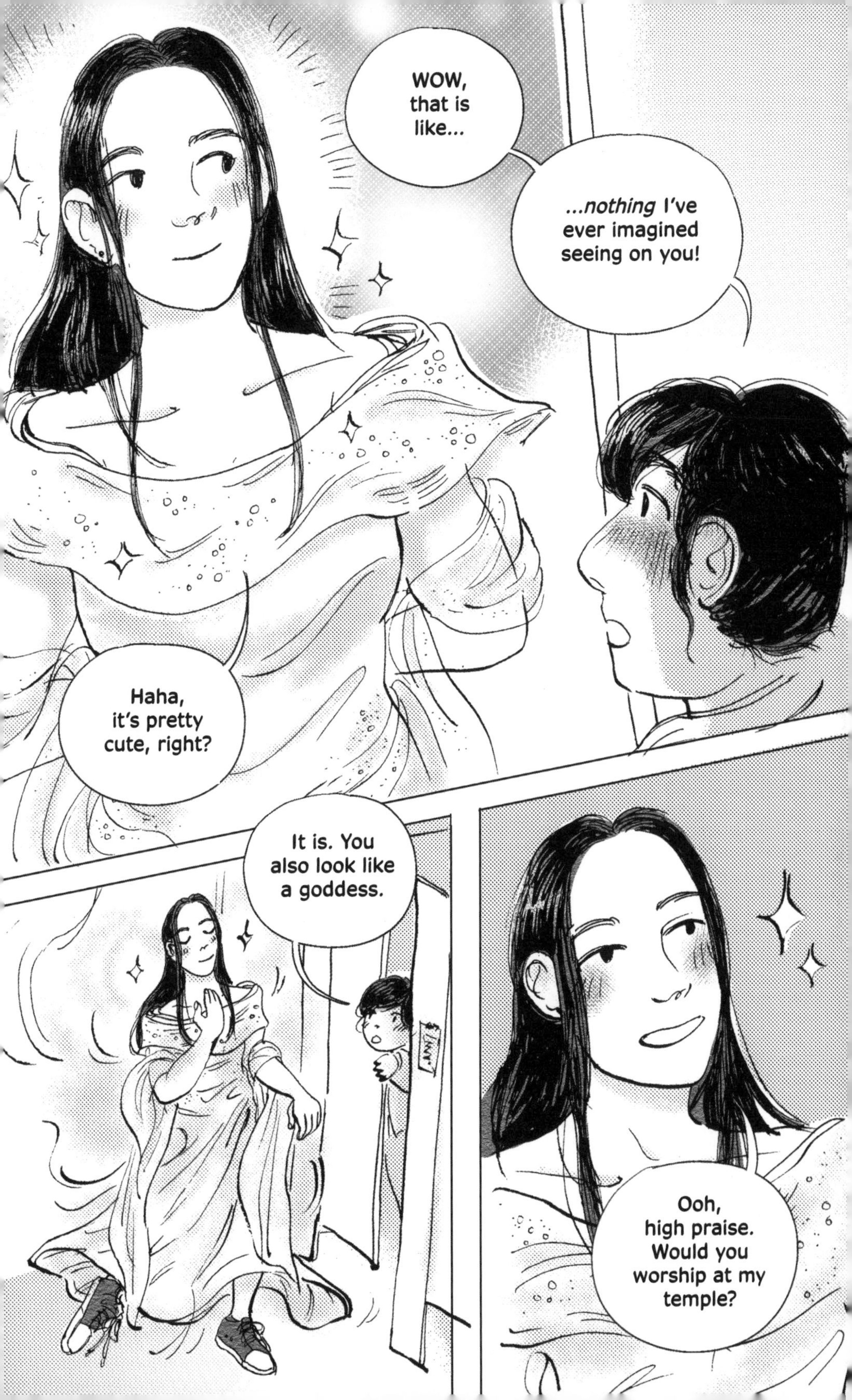
WOW, that is like...
...*nothing* I've ever imagined seeing on you!
Haha, it's pretty cute, right?
It is. You also look like a goddess.
Ooh, high praise. Would you worship at my temple?

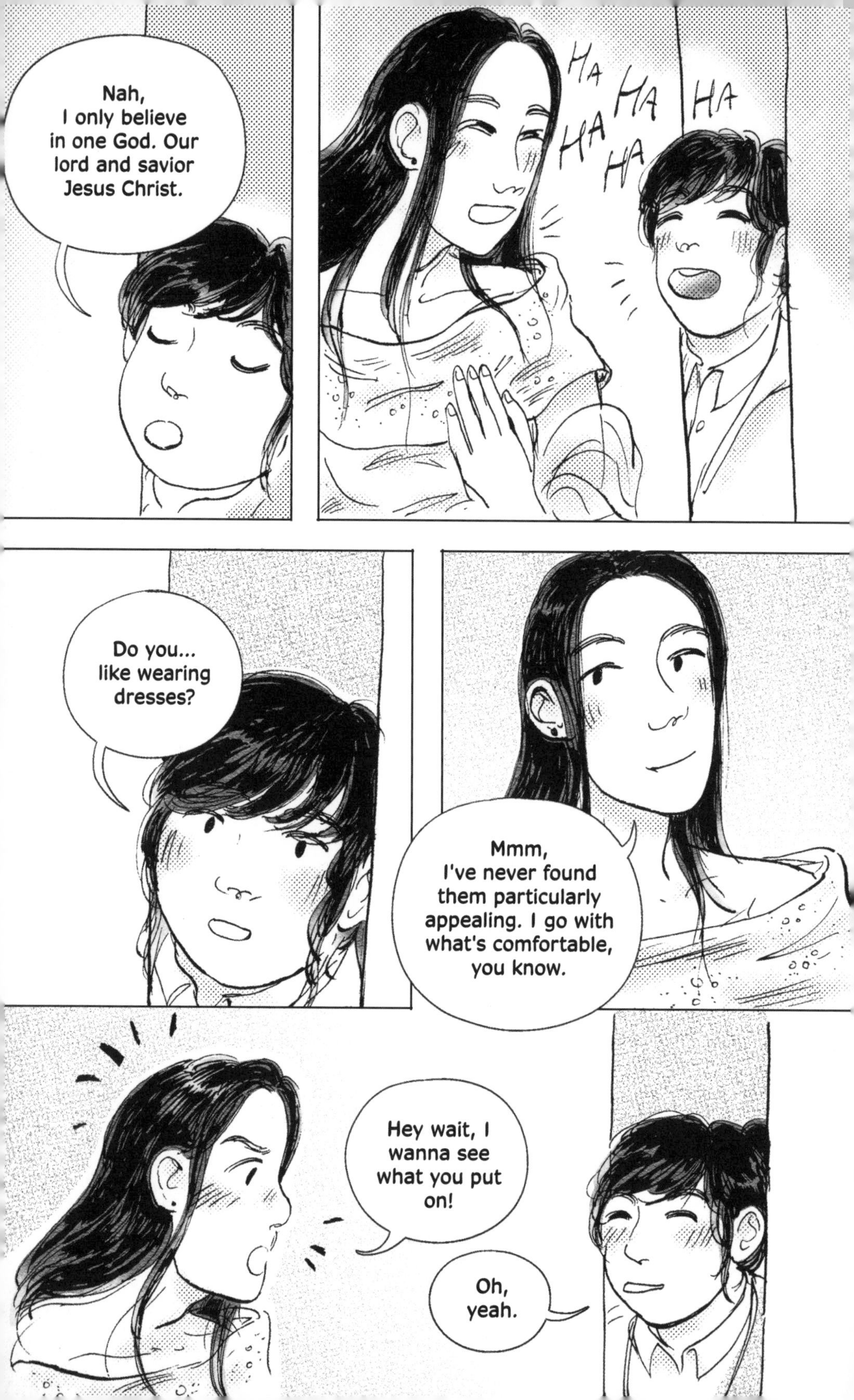
Nah, I only believe in one God. Our lord and savior Jesus Christ.
HA HA HA HA HA HA
Do you... like wearing dresses?
Mmm, I've never found them particularly appealing. I go with what's comfortable, you know.
Hey wait, I wanna see what you put on!
Oh, yeah.

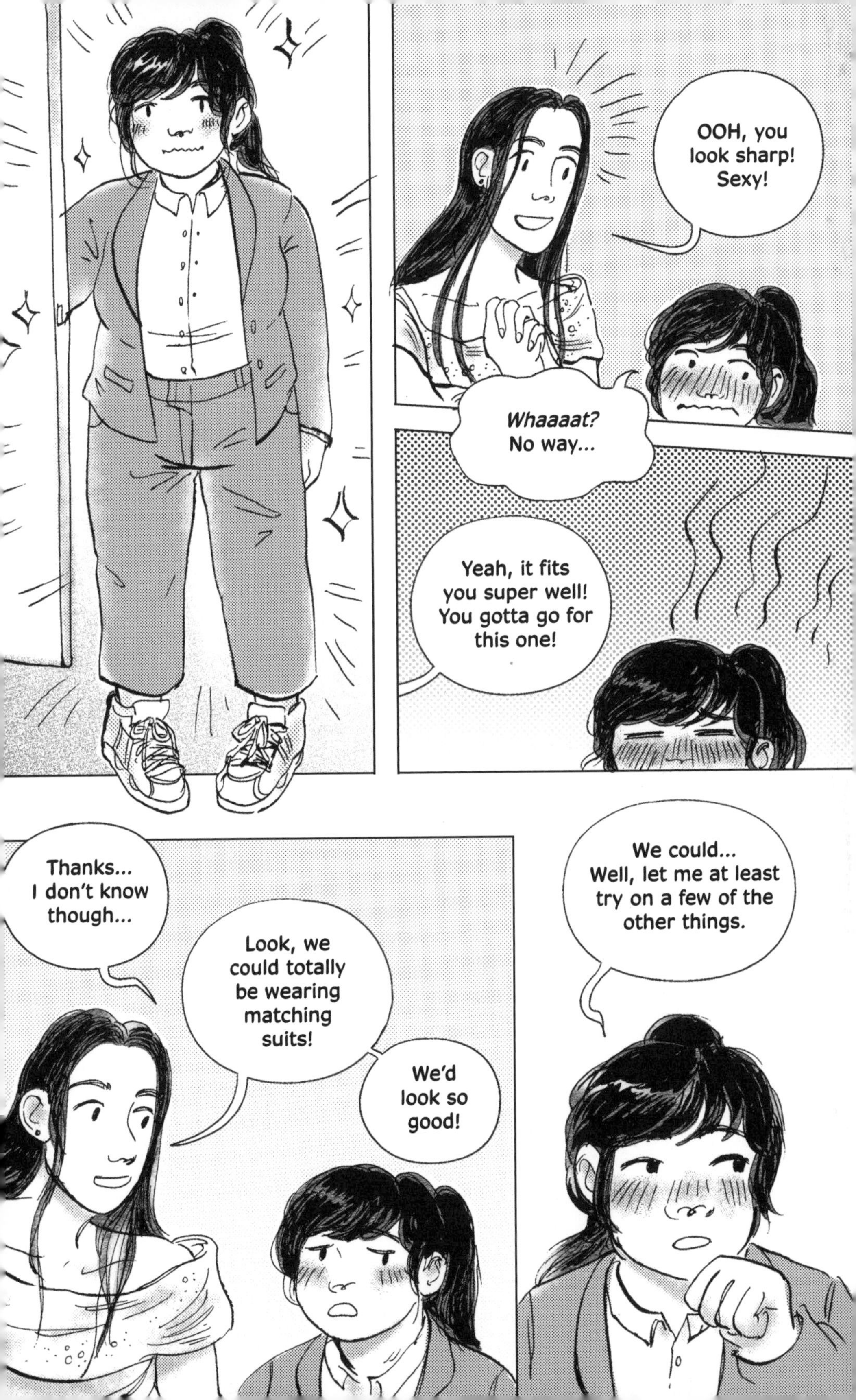
OOH, you look sharp! Sexy!
Whaaaat? No way...
Yeah, it fits you super well! You gotta go for this one!
Thanks... I don't know though...
Look, we could totally be wearing matching suits!
We'd look so good!
We could... Well, let me at least try on a few of the other things.

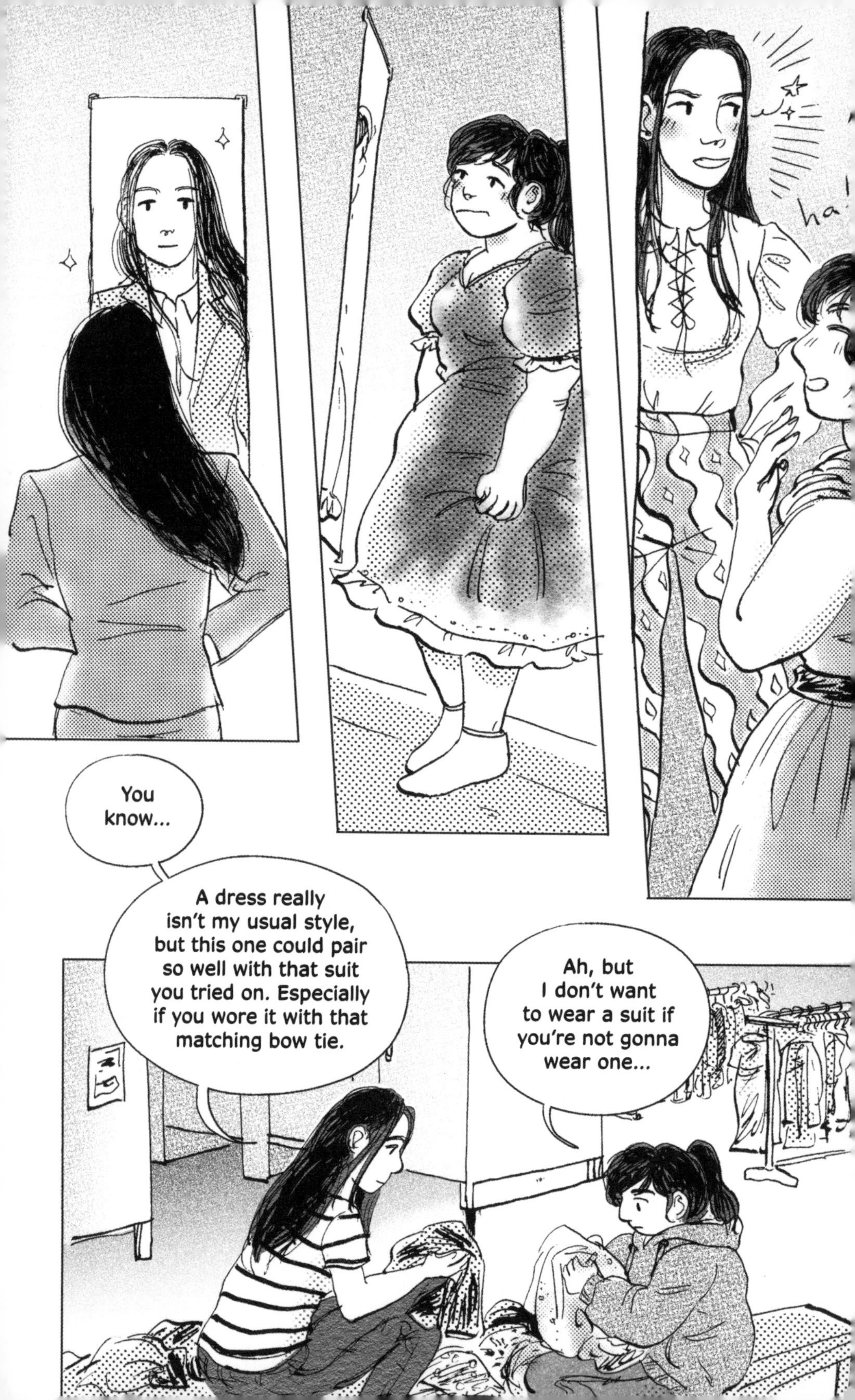
ha!
You know...
A dress really isn't my usual style, but this one could pair so well with that suit you tried on. Especially if you wore it with that matching bow tie.
Ah, but I don't want to wear a suit if you're not gonna wear one...

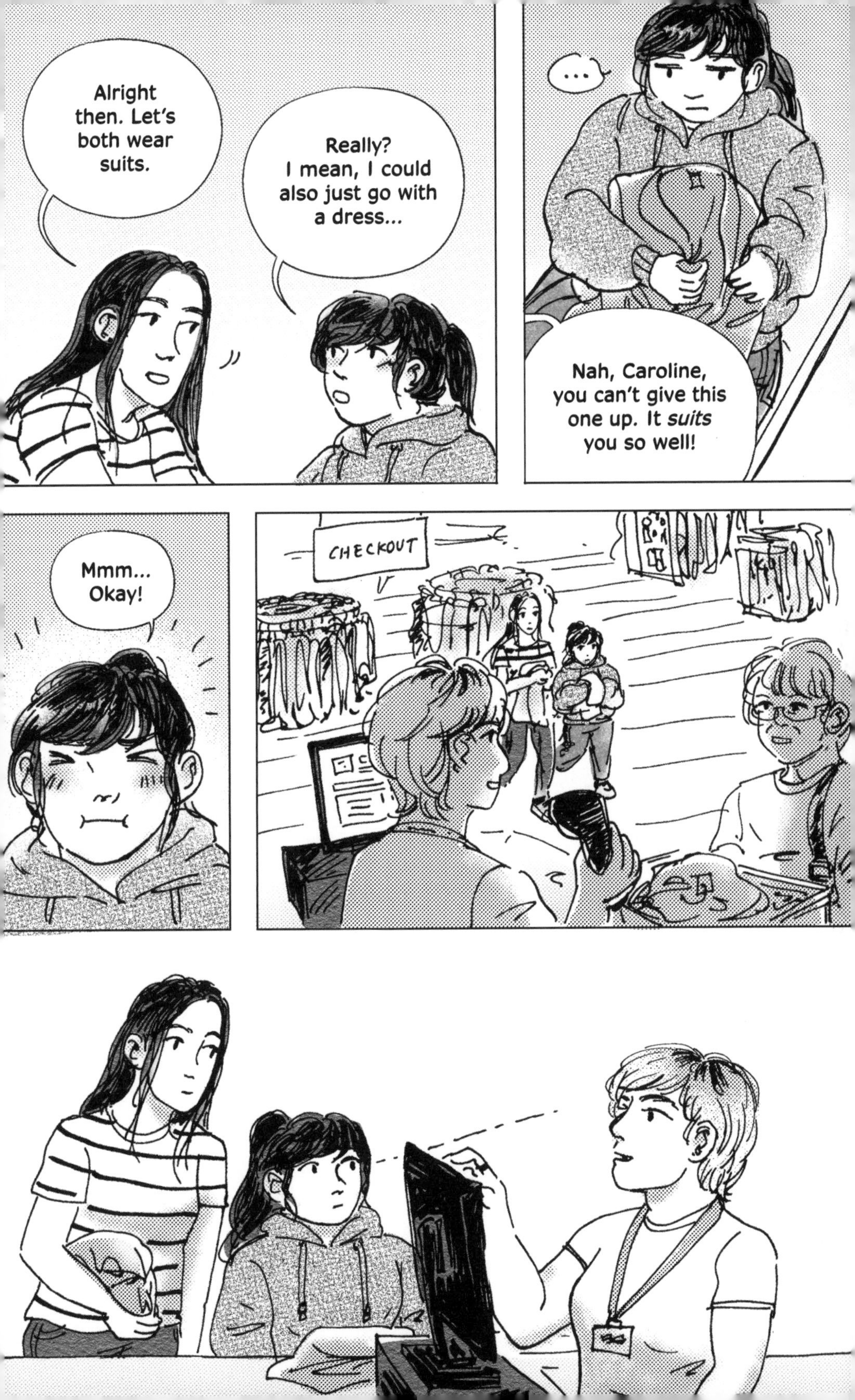
Alright then. Let's both wear suits.
Really? I mean, I could also just go with a dress...
...
Nah, Caroline, you can't give this one up. It *suits* you so well!
Mmm... Okay!
CHECKOUT

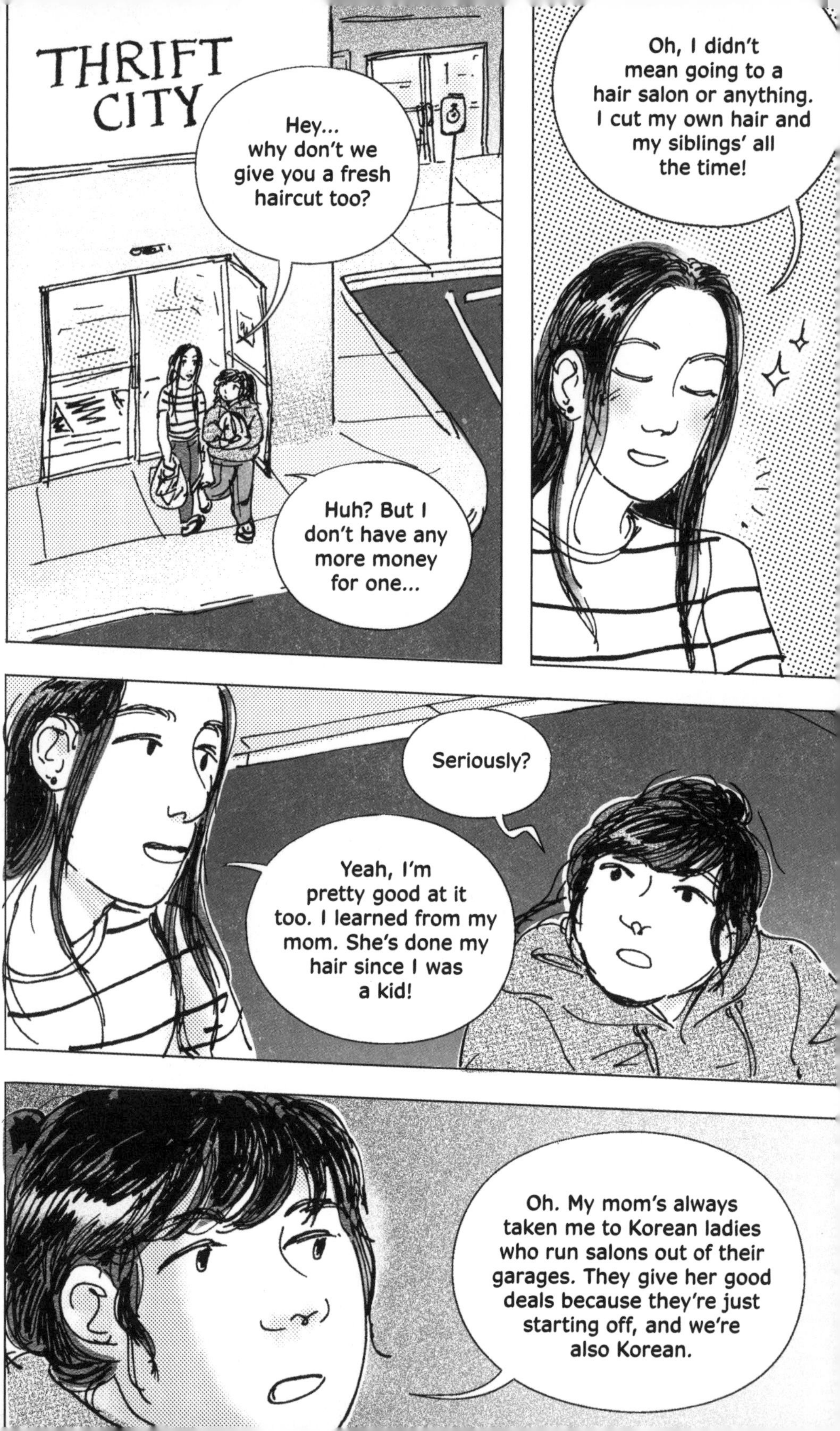
THRIFT CITY
Hey... why don't we give you a fresh haircut too?
Huh? But I don't have any more money for one...
Oh, I didn't mean going to a hair salon or anything. I cut my own hair and my siblings' all the time!
Seriously?
Yeah, I'm pretty good at it too. I learned from my mom. She's done my hair since I was a kid!
Oh. My mom's always taken me to Korean ladies who run salons out of their garages. They give her good deals because they're just starting off, and we're also Korean.

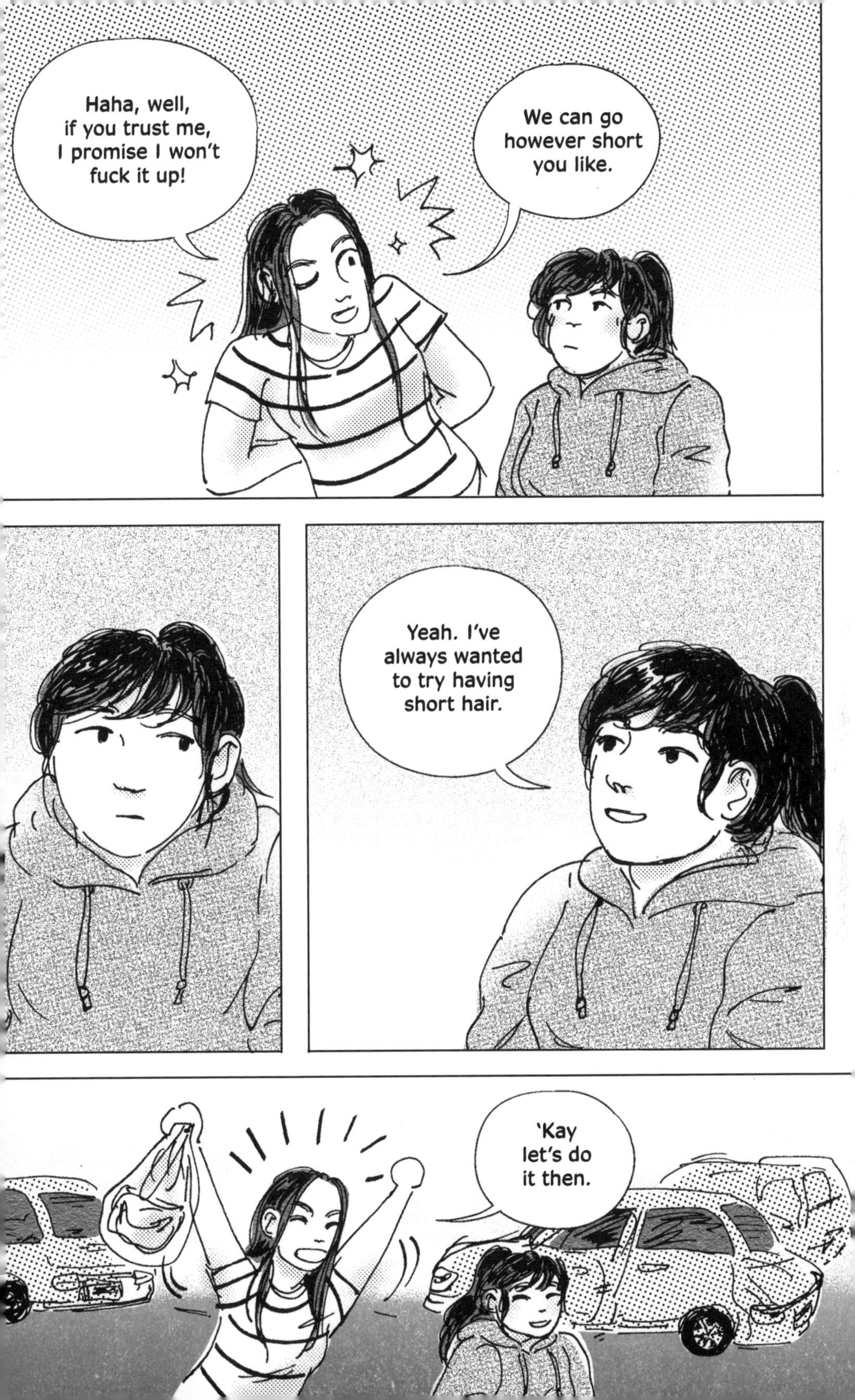
Haha, well, if you trust me, I promise I won't fuck it up!
We can go however short you like.
Yeah. I've always wanted to try having short hair.
'Kay let's do it then.

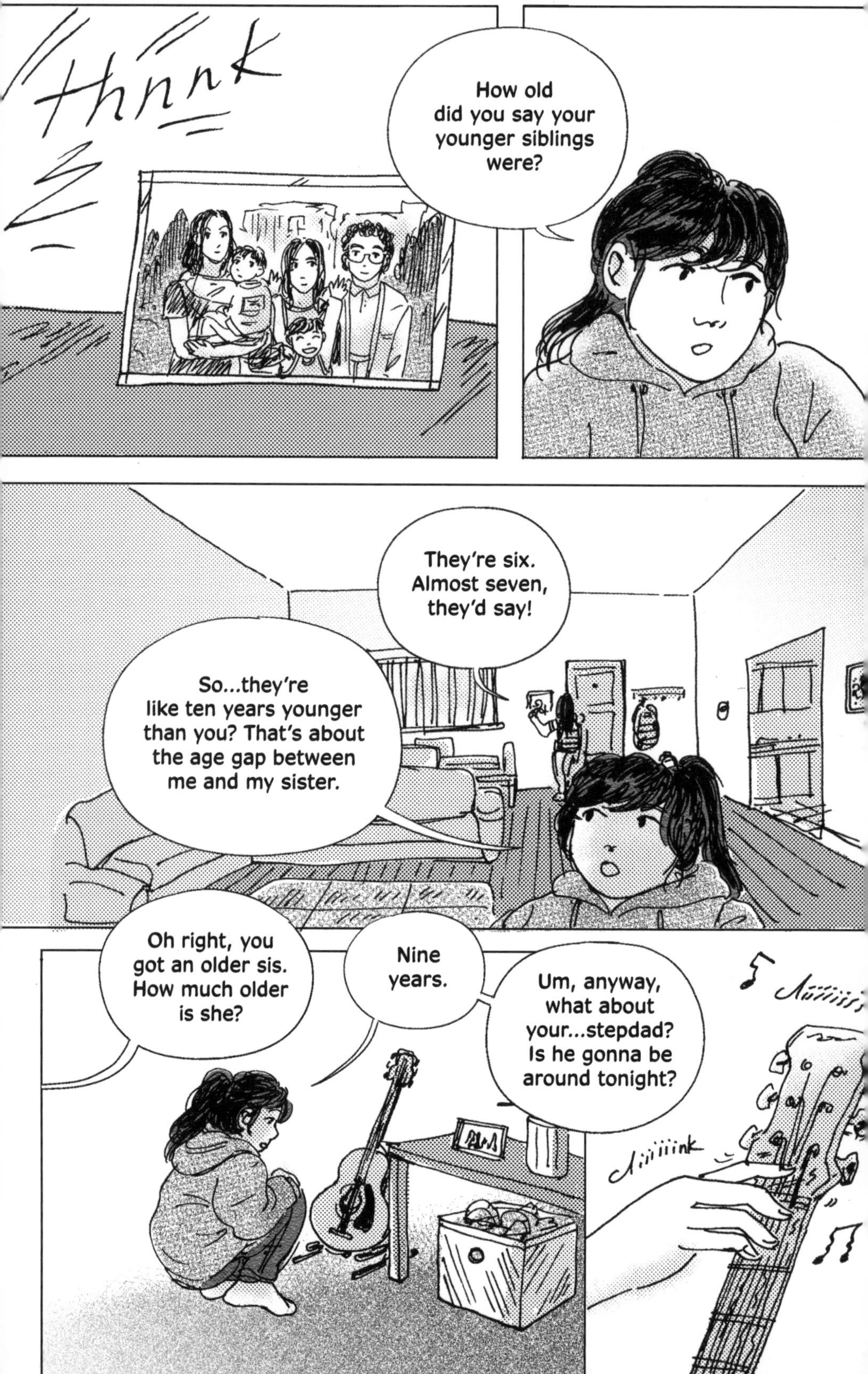
thnnk
How old did you say your younger siblings were?
They're six. Almost seven, they'd say!
So...they're like ten years younger than you? That's about the age gap between me and my sister.
Oh right, you got an older sis. How much older is she?
Nine years.
Um, anyway, what about your...stepdad? Is he gonna be around tonight?
tiiiiink

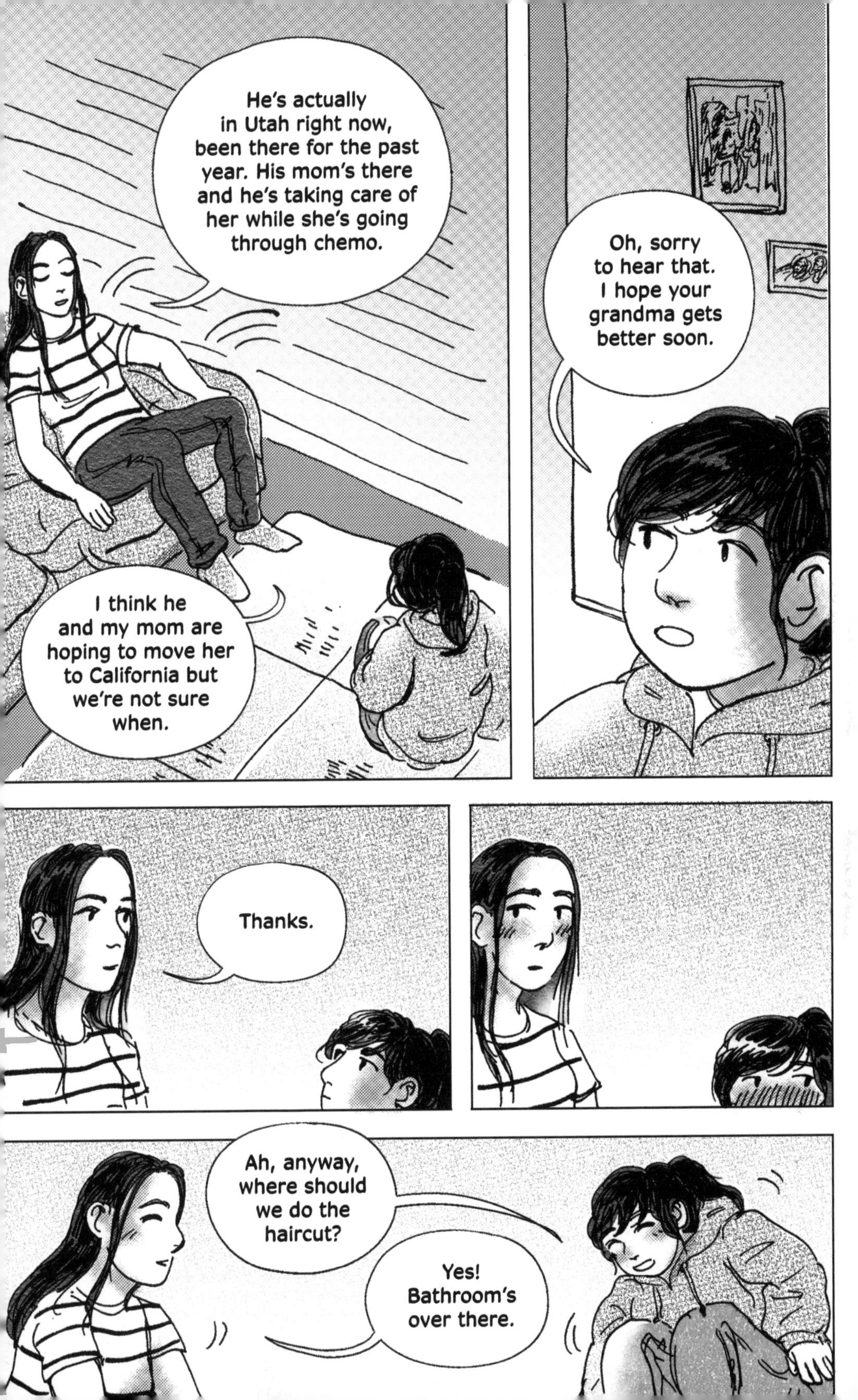
He's actually in Utah right now, been there for the past year. His mom's there and he's taking care of her while she's going through chemo.
I think he and my mom are hoping to move her to California but we're not sure when.
Oh, sorry to hear that. I hope your grandma gets better soon.
Thanks.
Ah, anyway, where should we do the haircut?
Yes! Bathroom's over there.

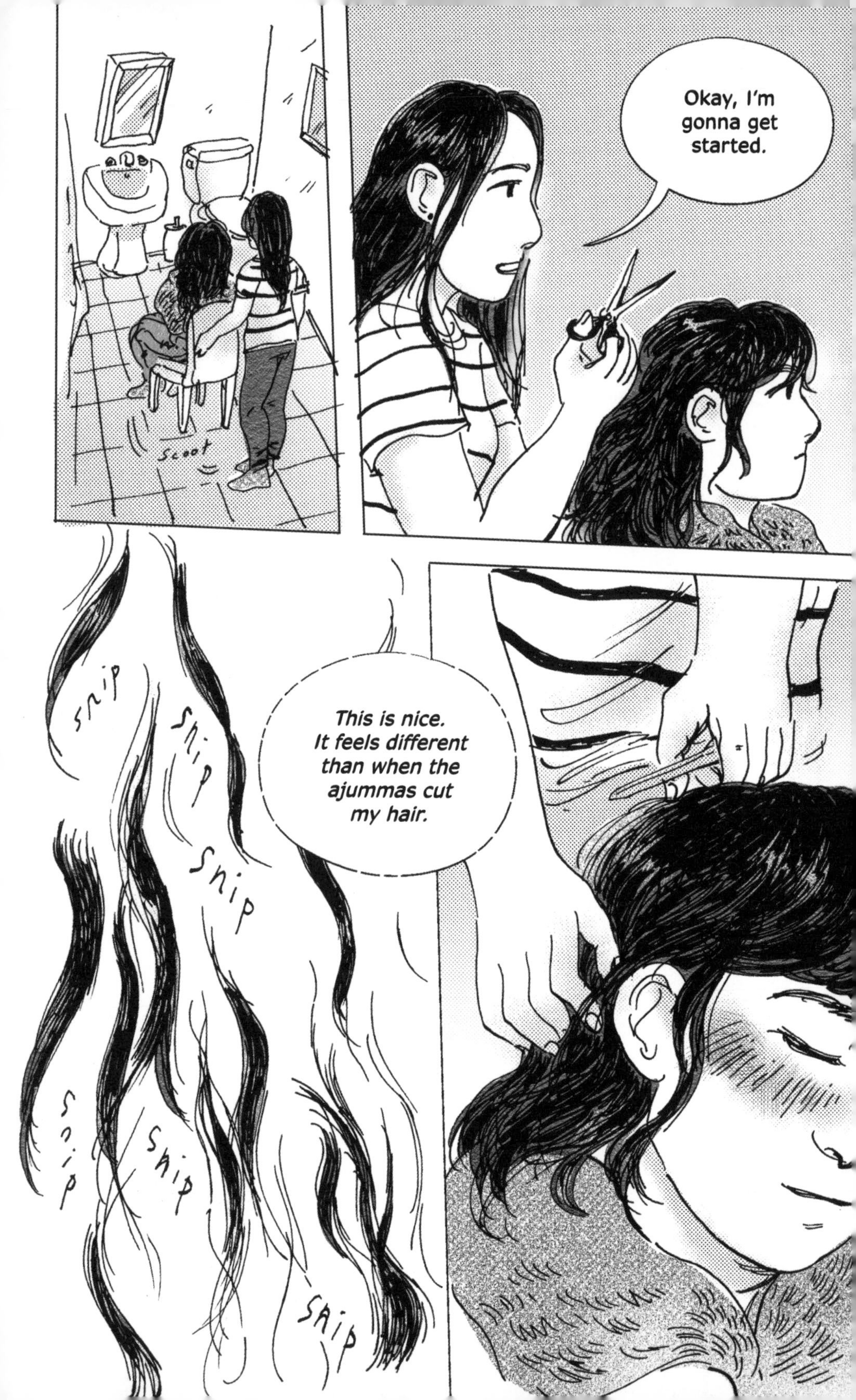
scoot
Okay, I'm gonna get started.
snip
snip
snip
This is nice. It feels different than when the ajummas cut my hair.
snip
snip
snip

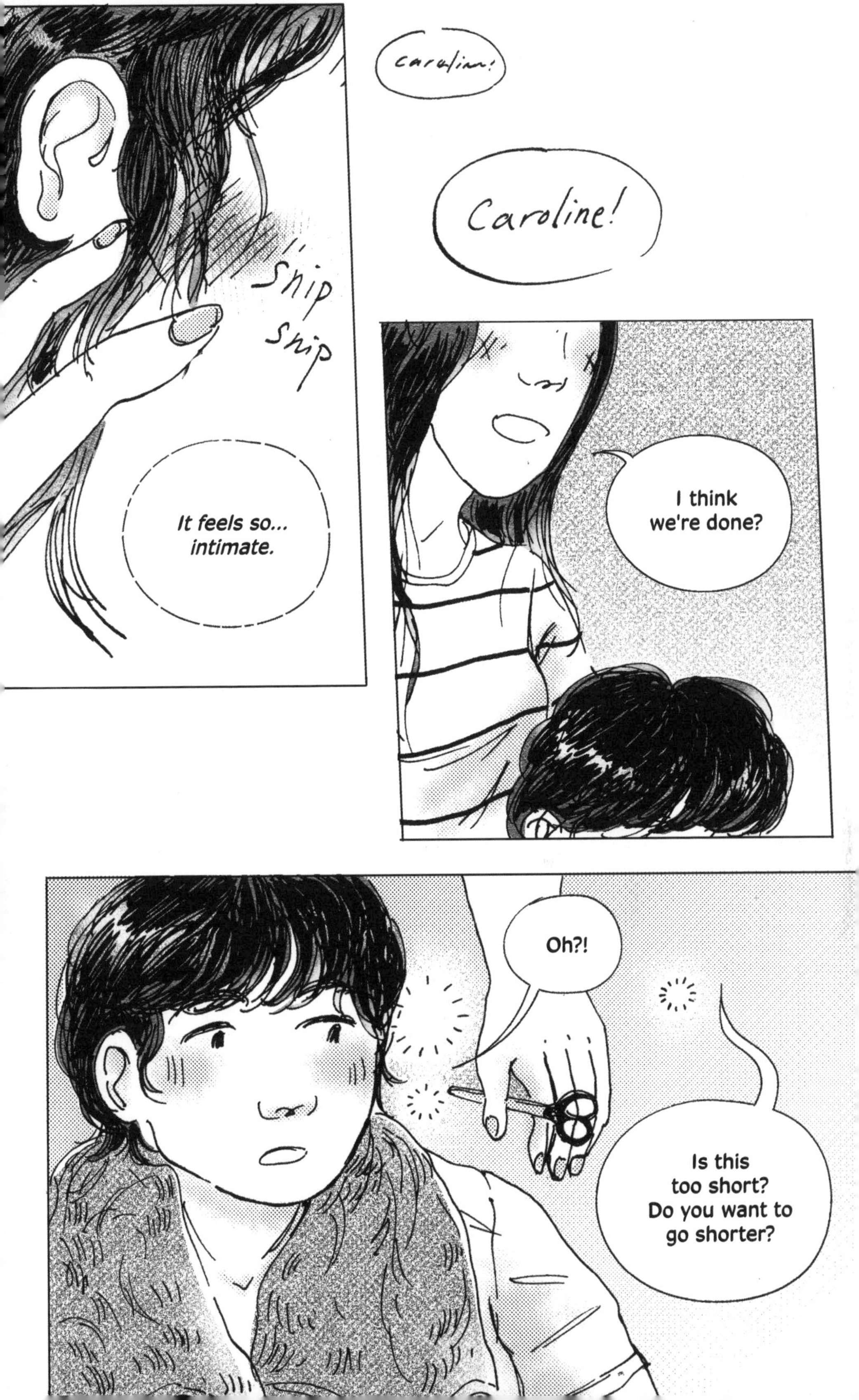
Caroline!
Snip snip
It feels so... intimate.
I think we're done?
Oh?!
Is this too short? Do you want to go shorter?

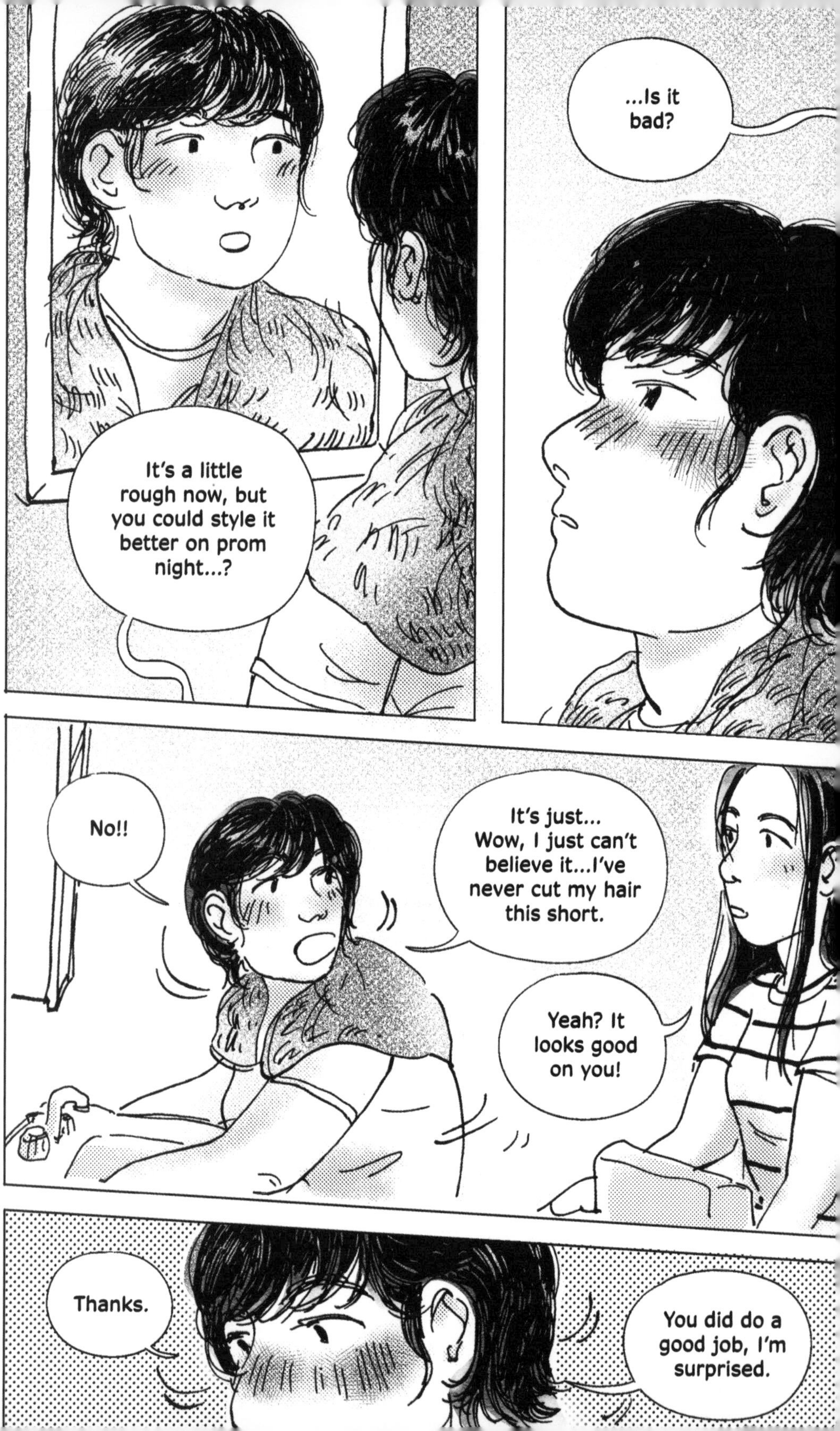
...Is it bad?
It's a little rough now, but you could style it better on prom night...?
No!!
It's just... Wow, I just can't believe it...I've never cut my hair this short.
Yeah? It looks good on you!
Thanks.
You did do a good job, I'm surprised.

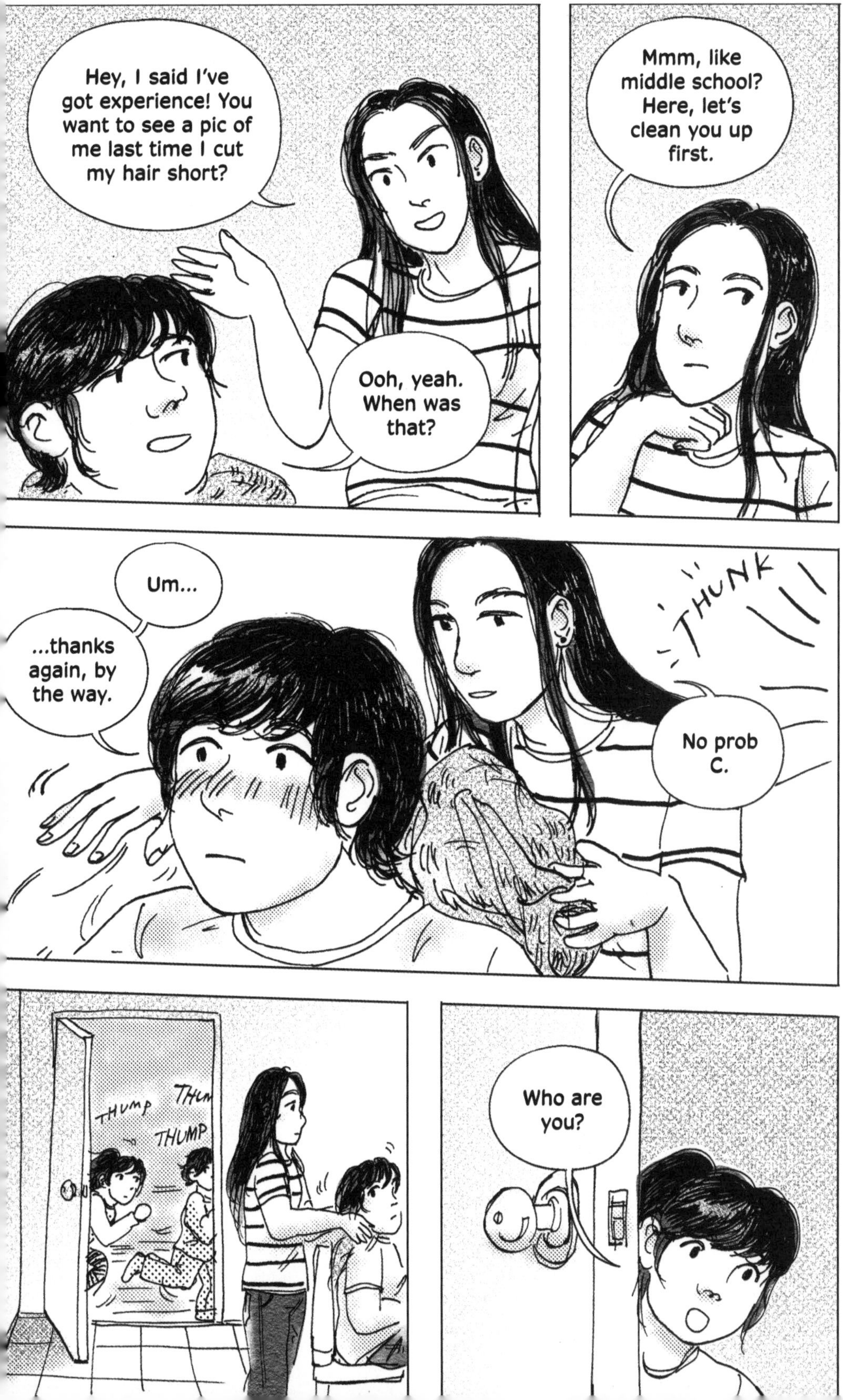
Hey, I said I've got experience! You want to see a pic of me last time I cut my hair short?
Ooh, yeah. When was that?
Mmm, like middle school? Here, let's clean you up first.
Um...
...thanks again, by the way.
THUNK
No prob C.
THUMP
THUM
THUMP
Who are you?

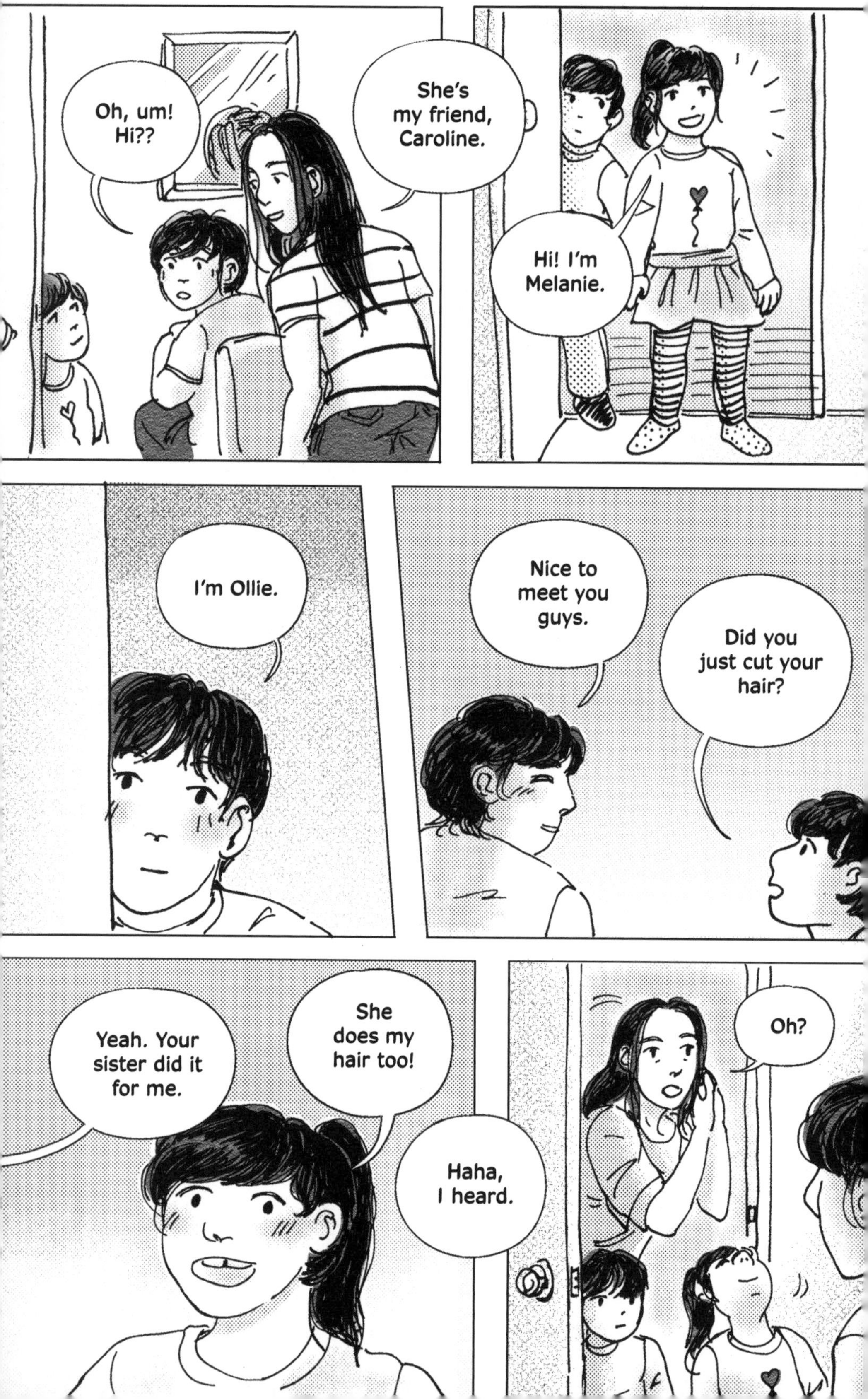
Oh, um!
Hi??
She's my friend, Caroline.
Hi! I'm Melanie.
I'm Ollie.
Nice to meet you guys.
Did you just cut your hair?
Yeah. Your sister did it for me.
She does my hair too!
Haha, I heard.
Oh?

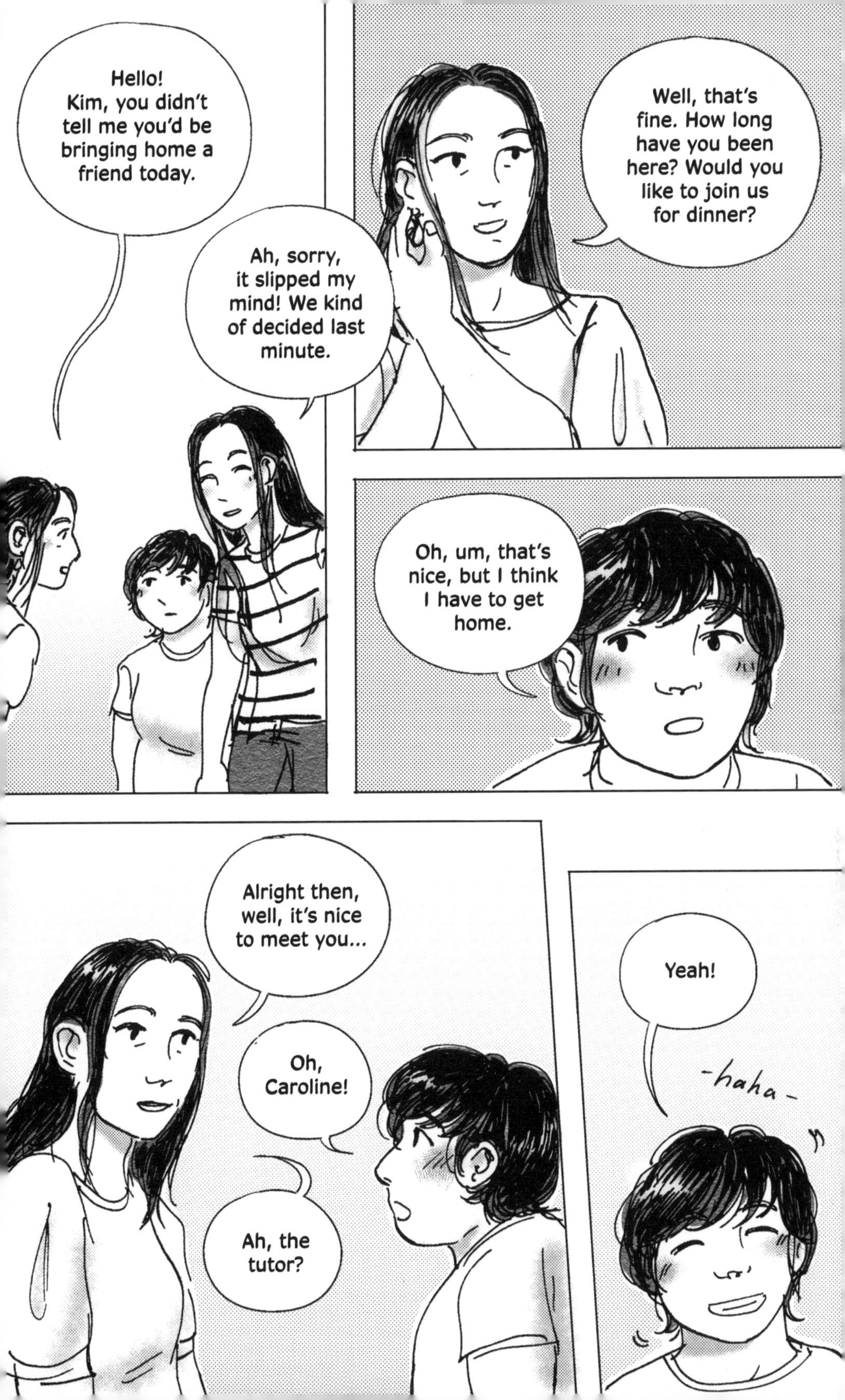
Hello! Kim, you didn't tell me you'd be bringing home a friend today.
Ah, sorry, it slipped my mind! We kind of decided last minute.
Well, that's fine. How long have you been here? Would you like to join us for dinner?
Oh, um, that's nice, but I think I have to get home.
Alright then, well, it's nice to meet you...
Oh, Caroline!
Ah, the tutor?
Yeah!
-haha-

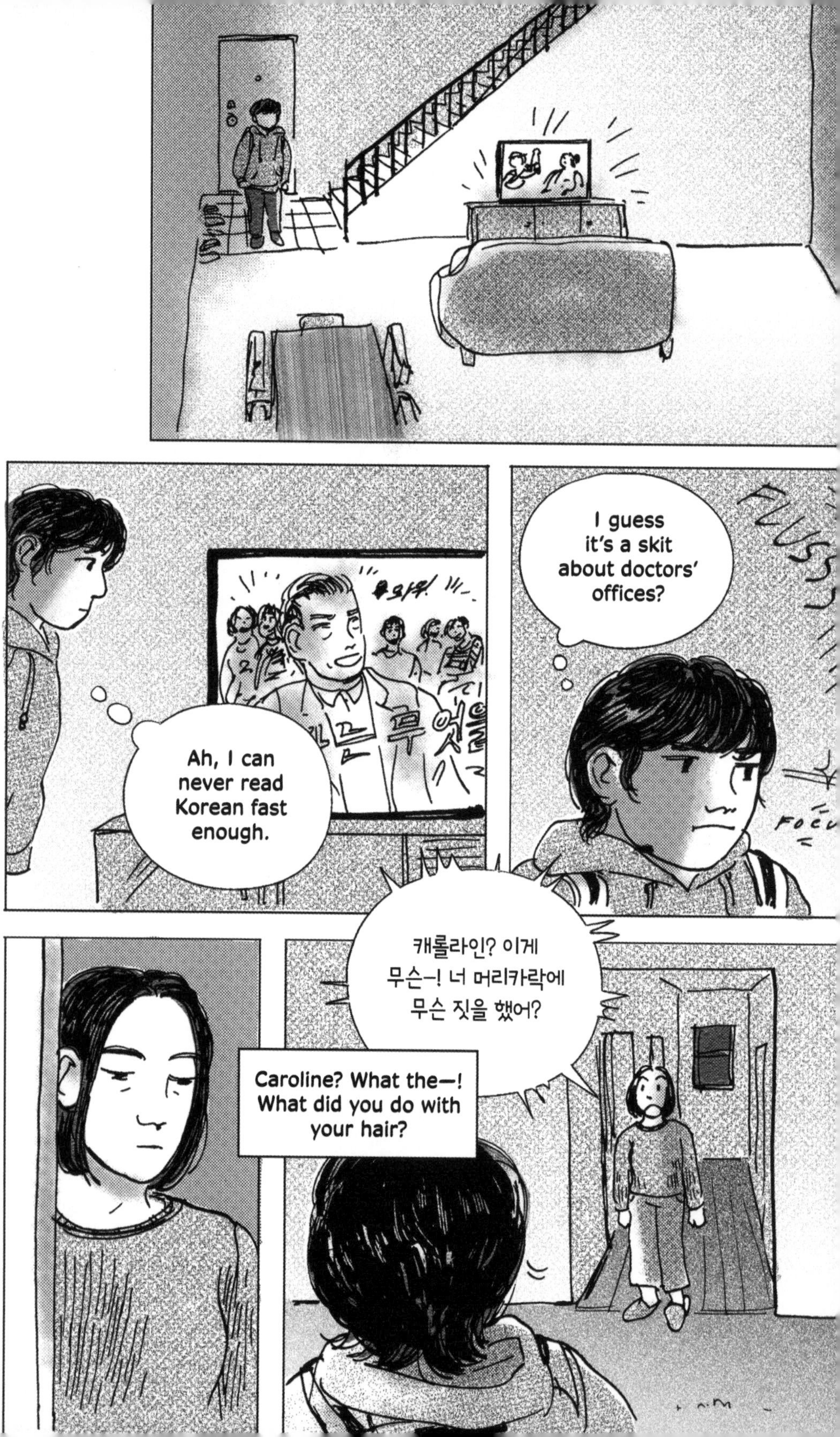
Ah, I can never read Korean fast enough.
I guess it's a skit about doctors' offices?
캐롤라인? 이게 무슨—! 너 머리카락에 무슨 짓을 했어?
Caroline? What the—! What did you do with your hair?

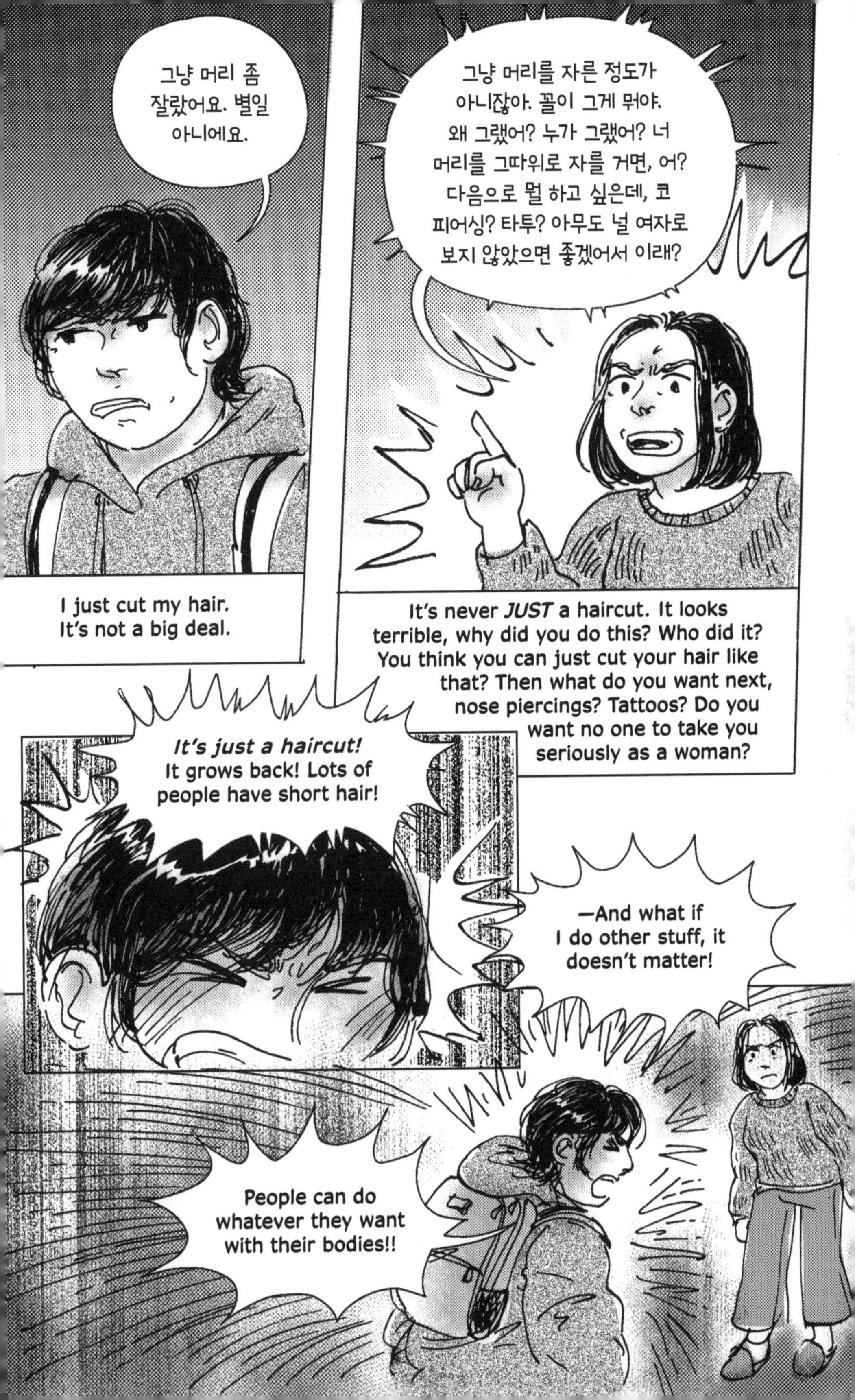
그냥 머리 좀 잘랐어요. 별일 아니에요.
I just cut my hair. It's not a big deal.
그냥 머리를 자른 정도가 아니잖아. 꼴이 그게 뭐야. 왜 그랬어? 누가 그랬어? 너 머리를 그따위로 자를 거면, 어? 다음으로 뭘 하고 싶은데, 코 피어싱? 타투? 아무도 널 여자로 보지 않았으면 좋겠어서 이래?
It's never *JUST* a haircut. It looks terrible, why did you do this? Who did it? You think you can just cut your hair like that? Then what do you want next, nose piercings? Tattoos? Do you want no one to take you seriously as a woman?
It's just a haircut! It grows back! Lots of people have short hair!
—And what if I do other stuff, it doesn't matter!
People can do whatever they want with their bodies!!

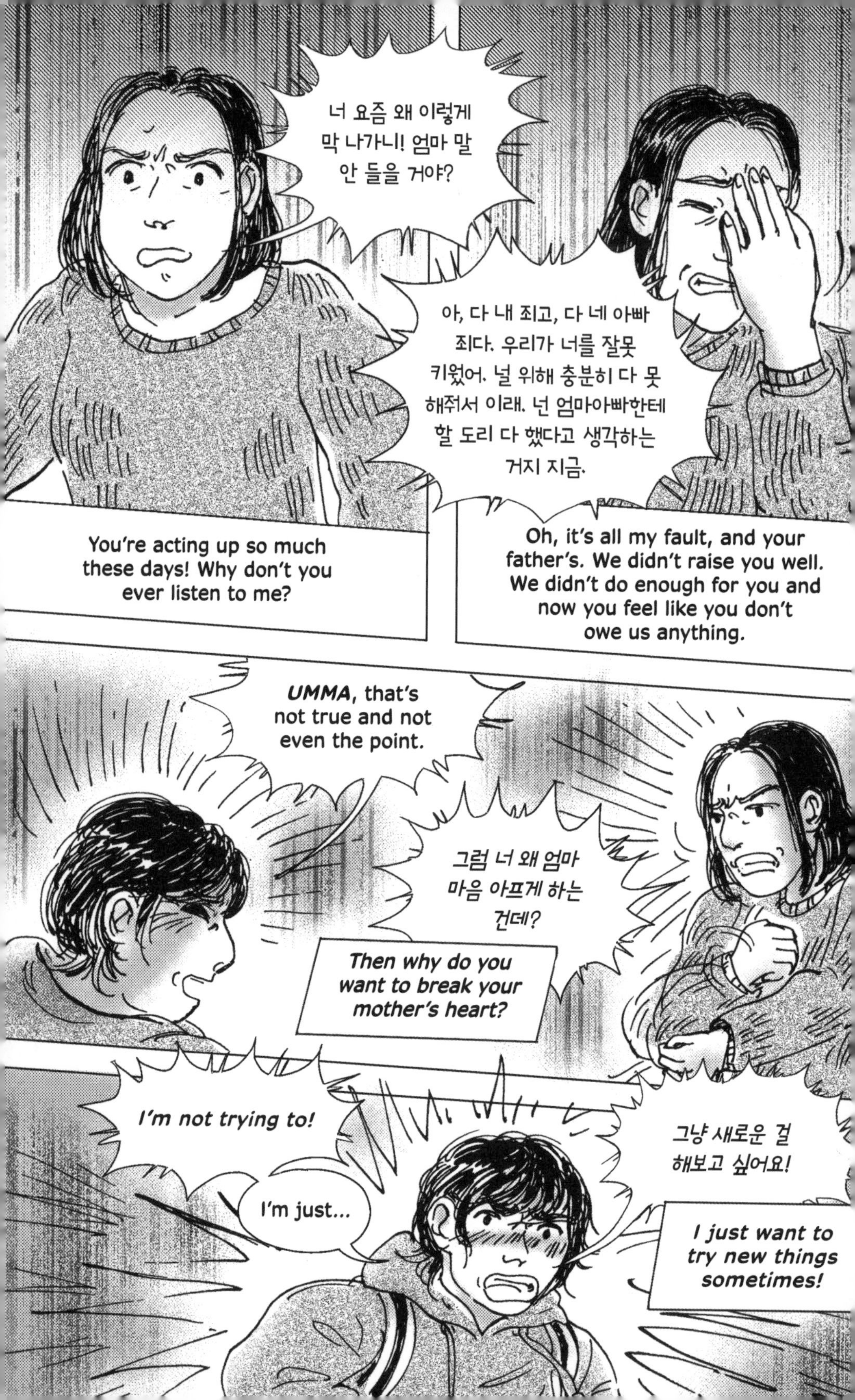

너 요즘 왜 이렇게 막 나가니! 엄마 말 안 들을 거야?
아, 다 내 죄고, 다 네 아빠 죄다. 우리가 너를 잘못 키웠어. 널 위해 충분히 다 못 해줘서 이래. 넌 엄마아빠한테 할 도리 다 했다고 생각하는 거지 지금.
You're acting up so much these days! Why don't you ever listen to me?
Oh, it's all my fault, and your father's. We didn't raise you well. We didn't do enough for you and now you feel like you don't owe us anything.
UMMA, that's not true and not even the point.
그럼 너 왜 엄마 마음 아프게 하는 건데?
Then why do you want to break your mother's heart?
I'm not trying to!
I'm just...
그냥 새로운 걸 해보고 싶어요!
I just want to try new things sometimes!

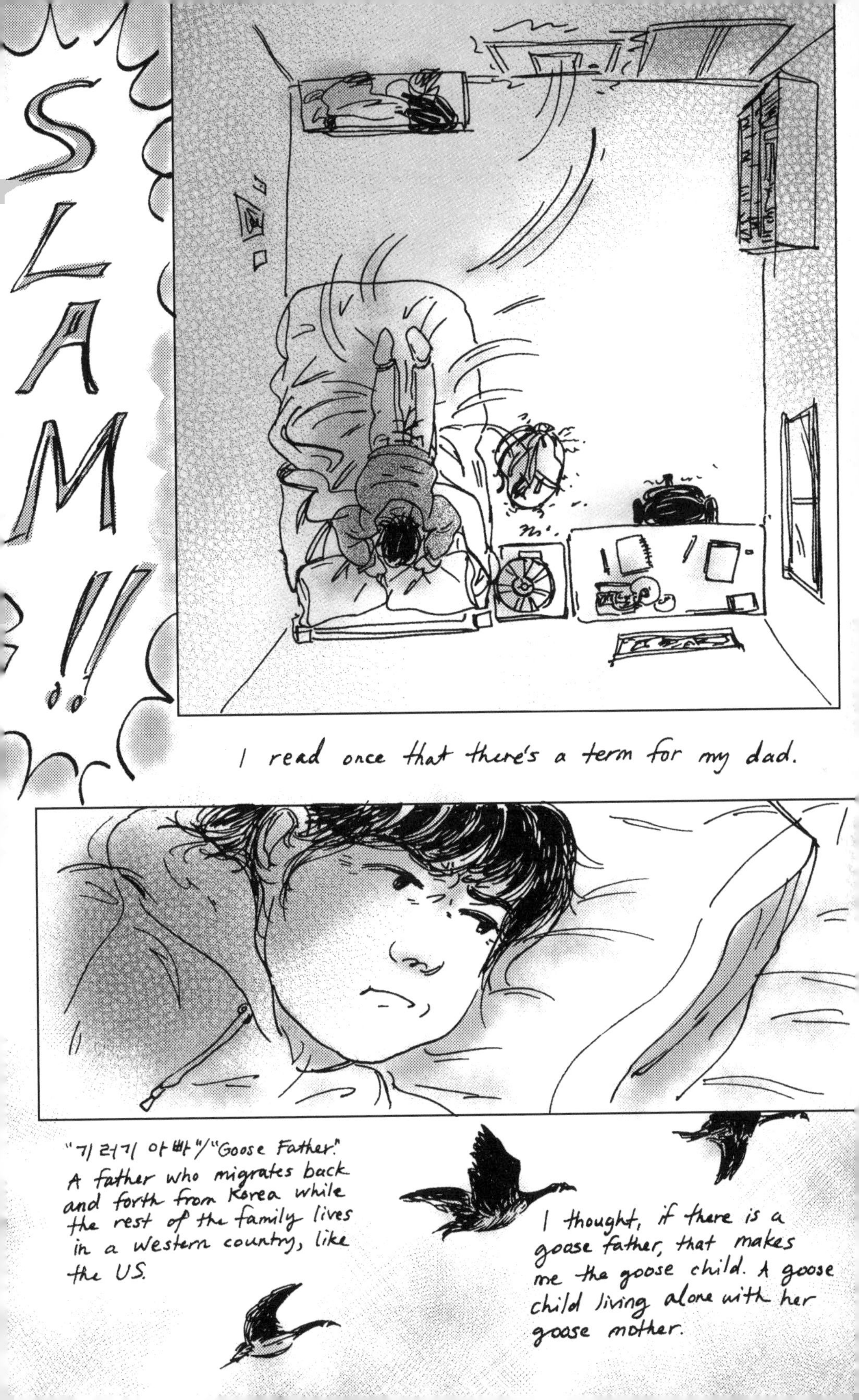
SLAM!!
I read once that there's a term for my dad.
"기러기 아빠"/"Goose Father."
A father who migrates back and forth from Korea while the rest of the family lives in a Western country, like the US.
I thought, if there is a goose father, that makes me the goose child. A goose child living alone with her goose mother.

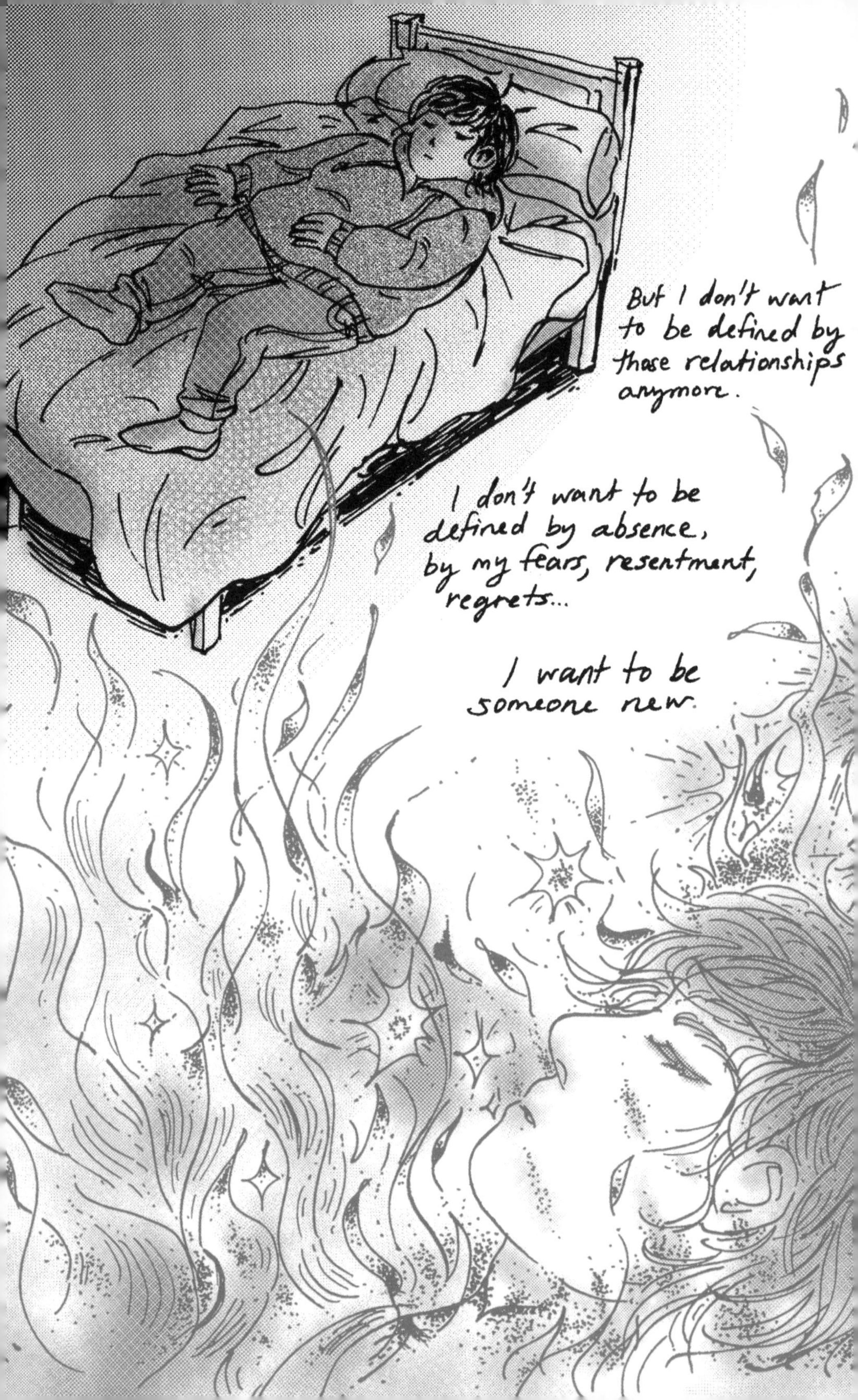
But I don't want to be defined by those relationships anymore.
I don't want to be defined by absence, by my fears, resentment, regrets...
I want to be someone new.

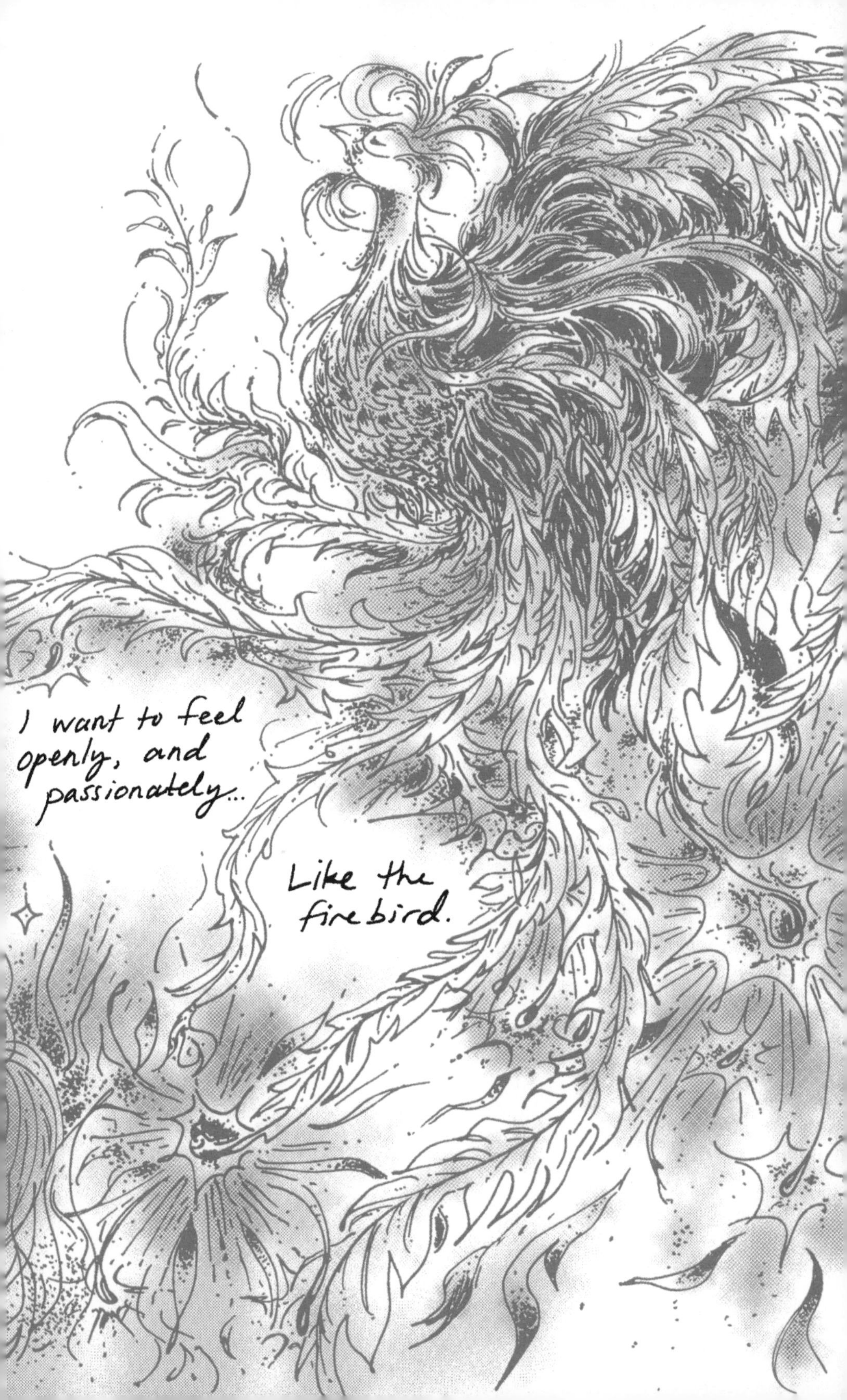
I want to feel openly, and passionately...
Like the firebird.

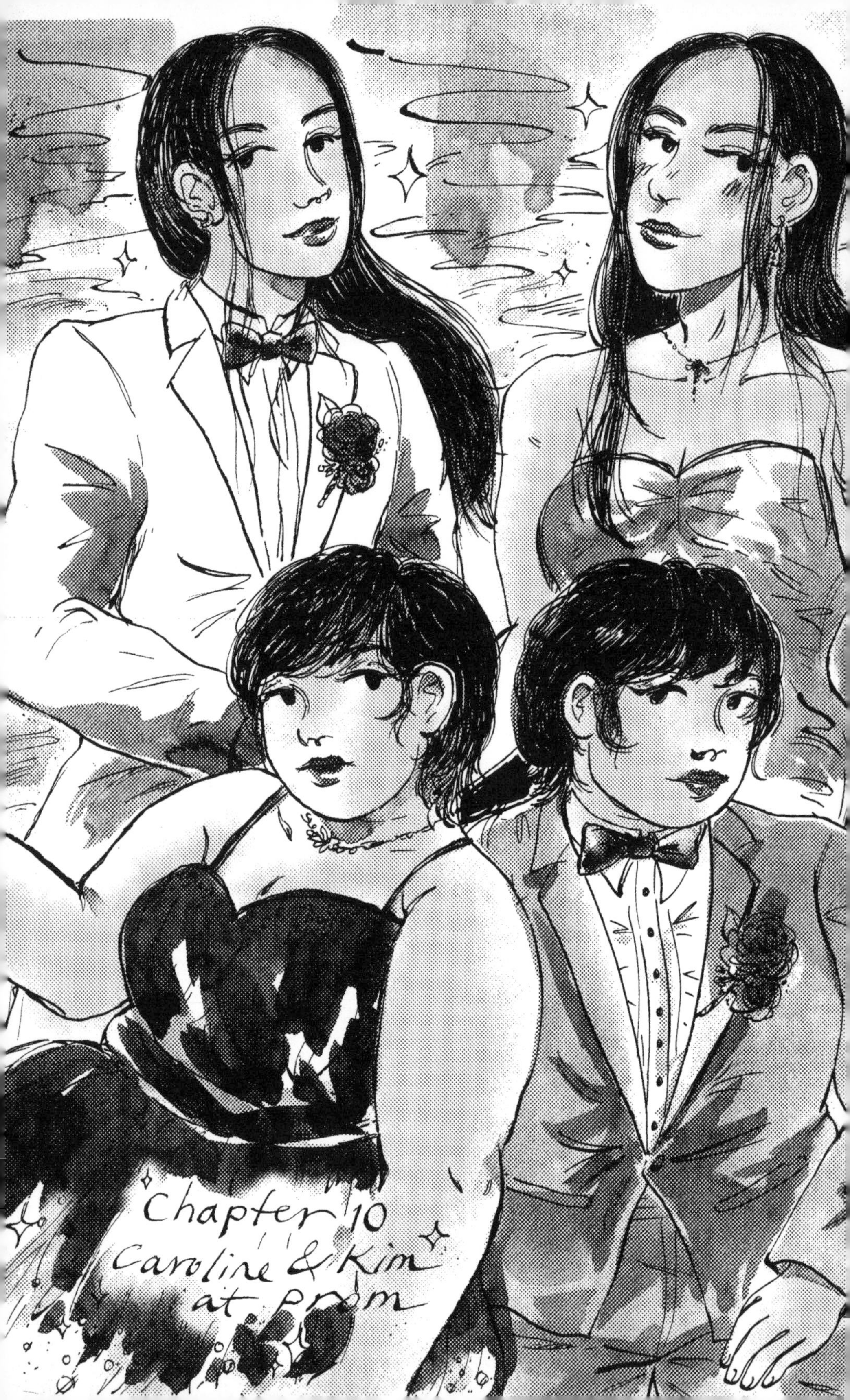
Chapter 10
Caroline & Kim at prom

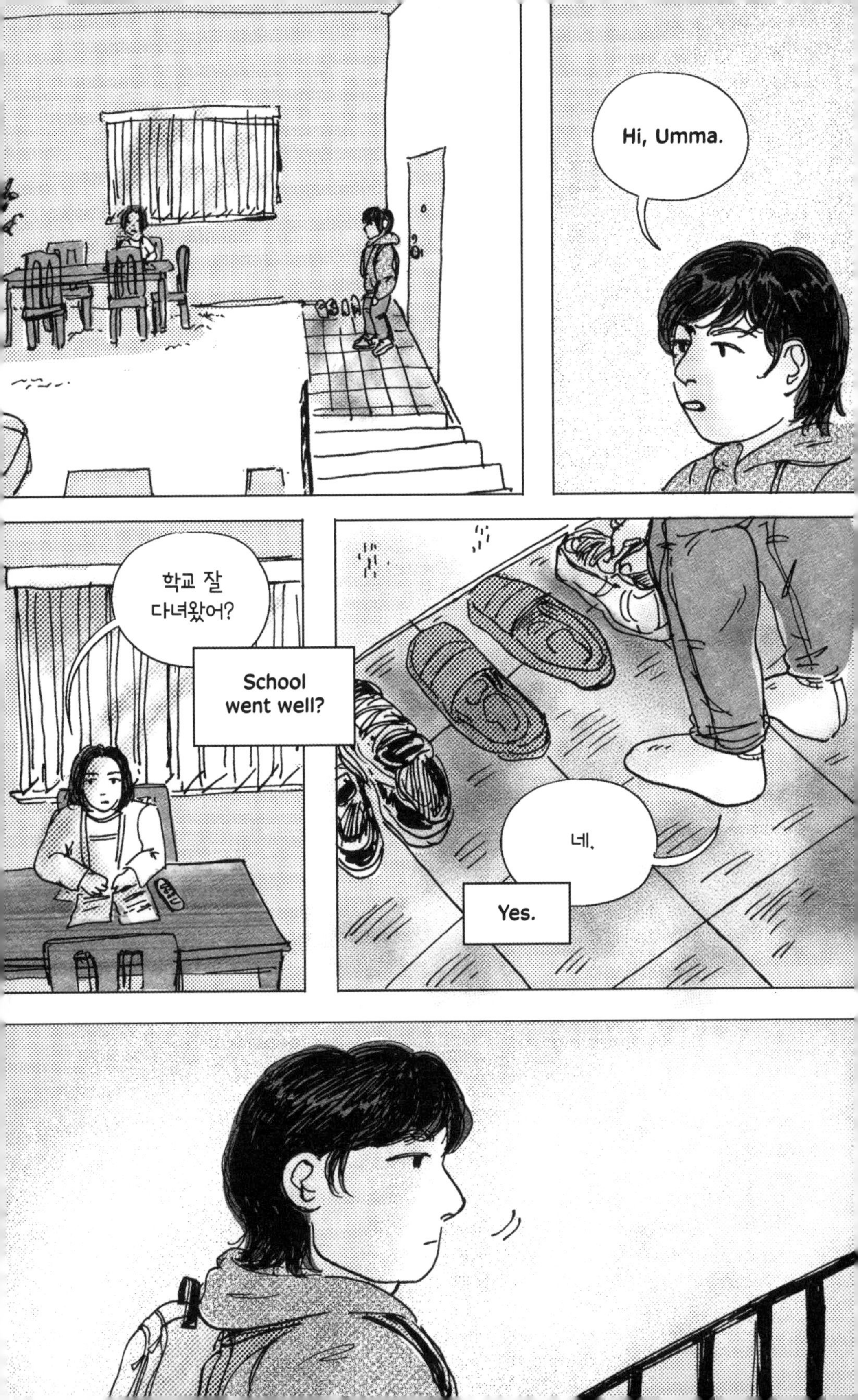
Hi, Umma.
학교 잘 다녀왔어?
School went well?
네.
Yes.

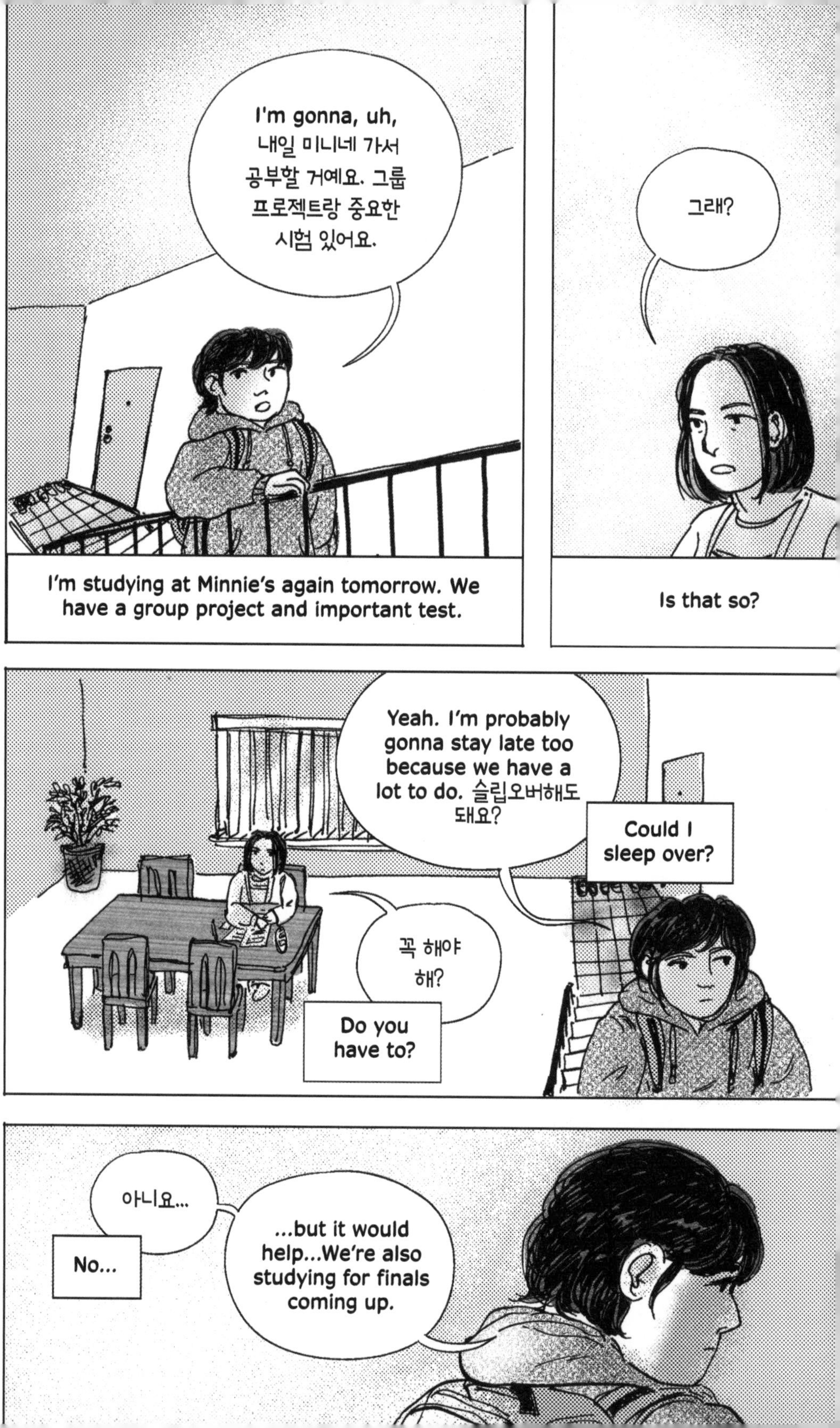
I'm gonna, uh, 내일 미니네 가서 공부할 거예요. 그룹 프로젝트랑 중요한 시험 있어요.
I'm studying at Minnie's again tomorrow. We have a group project and important test.
그래?
Is that so?
Yeah. I'm probably gonna stay late too because we have a lot to do. 슬립오버해도 돼요?
Could I sleep over?
꼭 해야 해?
Do you have to?
아니요...
No...
...but it would help...We're also studying for finals coming up.

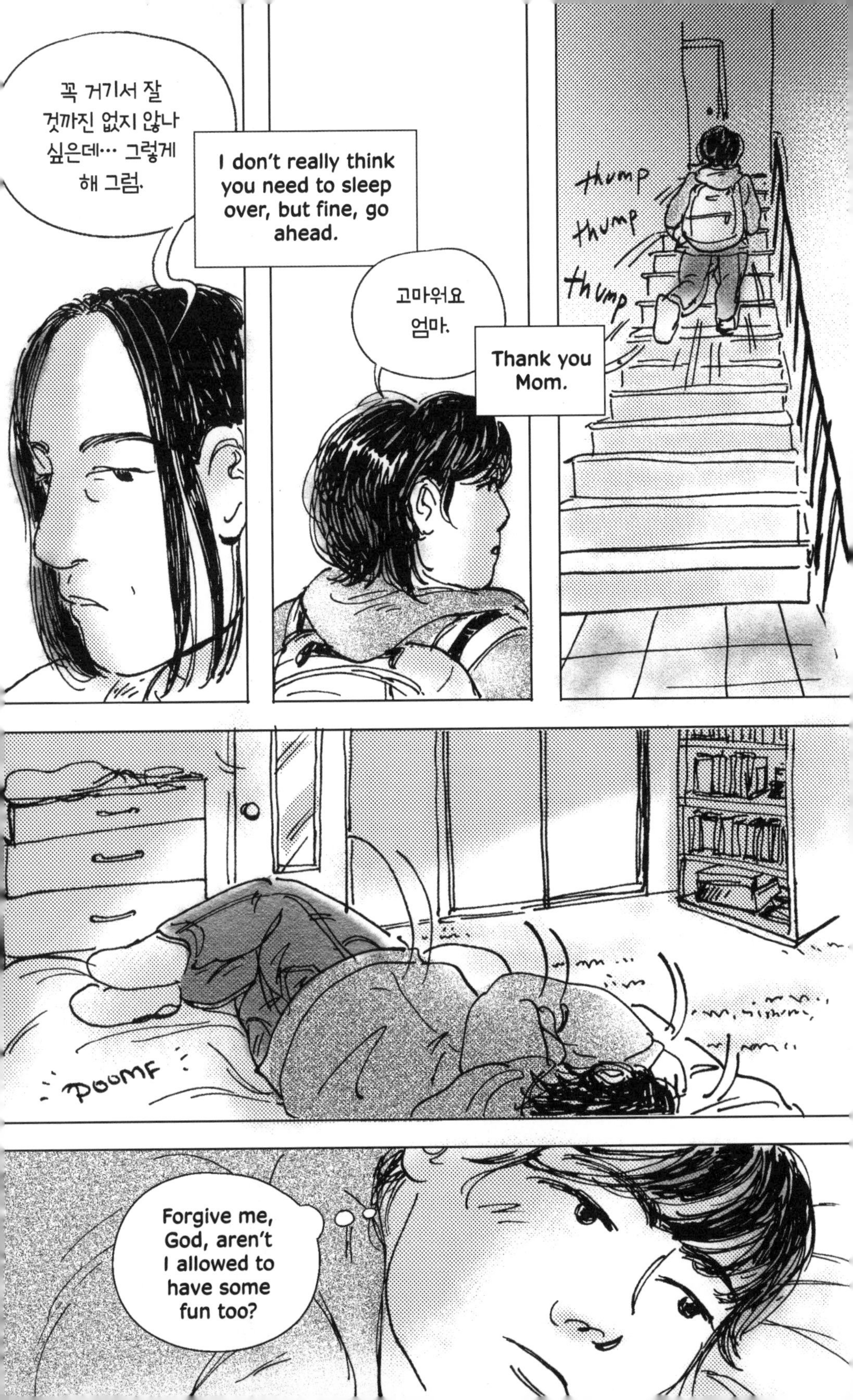
꼭 거기서 잘 것까진 없지 않나 싶은데… 그렇게 해 그럼.
I don't really think you need to sleep over, but fine, go ahead.
고마워요 엄마.
Thank you Mom.
thump
thump
thump
DOOMF
Forgive me, God, aren't I allowed to have some fun too?

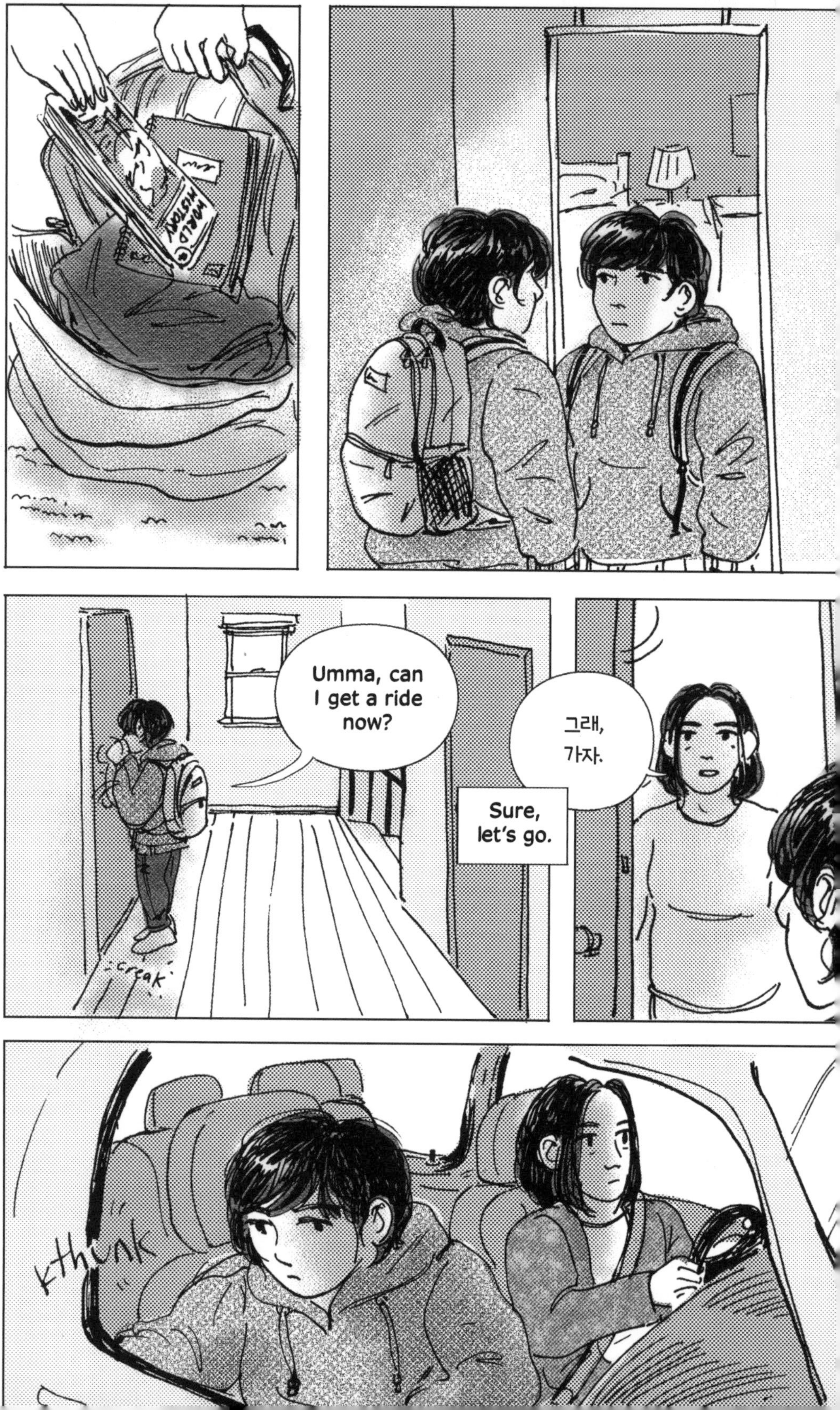
WORLD HISTORY
Umma, can I get a ride now?
creak
그래, 가자.
Sure, let's go.
kthunk

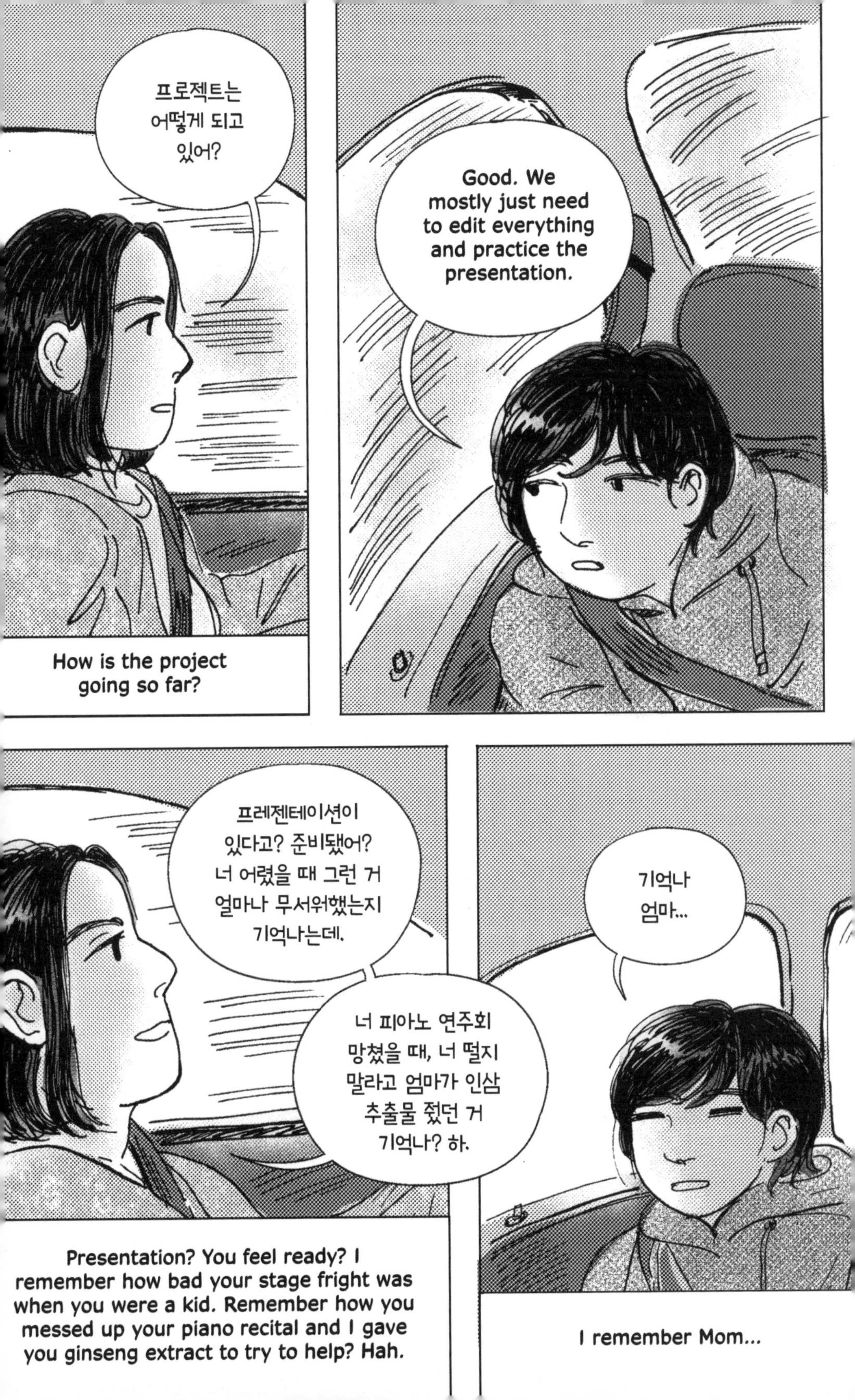
프로젝트는 어떻게 되고 있어?
How is the project going so far?
Good. We mostly just need to edit everything and practice the presentation.
프레젠테이션이 있다고? 준비됐어? 너 어렸을 때 그런 거 얼마나 무서워했는지 기억나는데.
너 피아노 연주회 망쳤을 때, 너 떨지 말라고 엄마가 인삼 추출물 줬던 거 기억나? 하.
Presentation? You feel ready? I remember how bad your stage fright was when you were a kid. Remember how you messed up your piano recital and I gave you ginseng extract to try to help? Hah.
기억나 엄마...
I remember Mom...

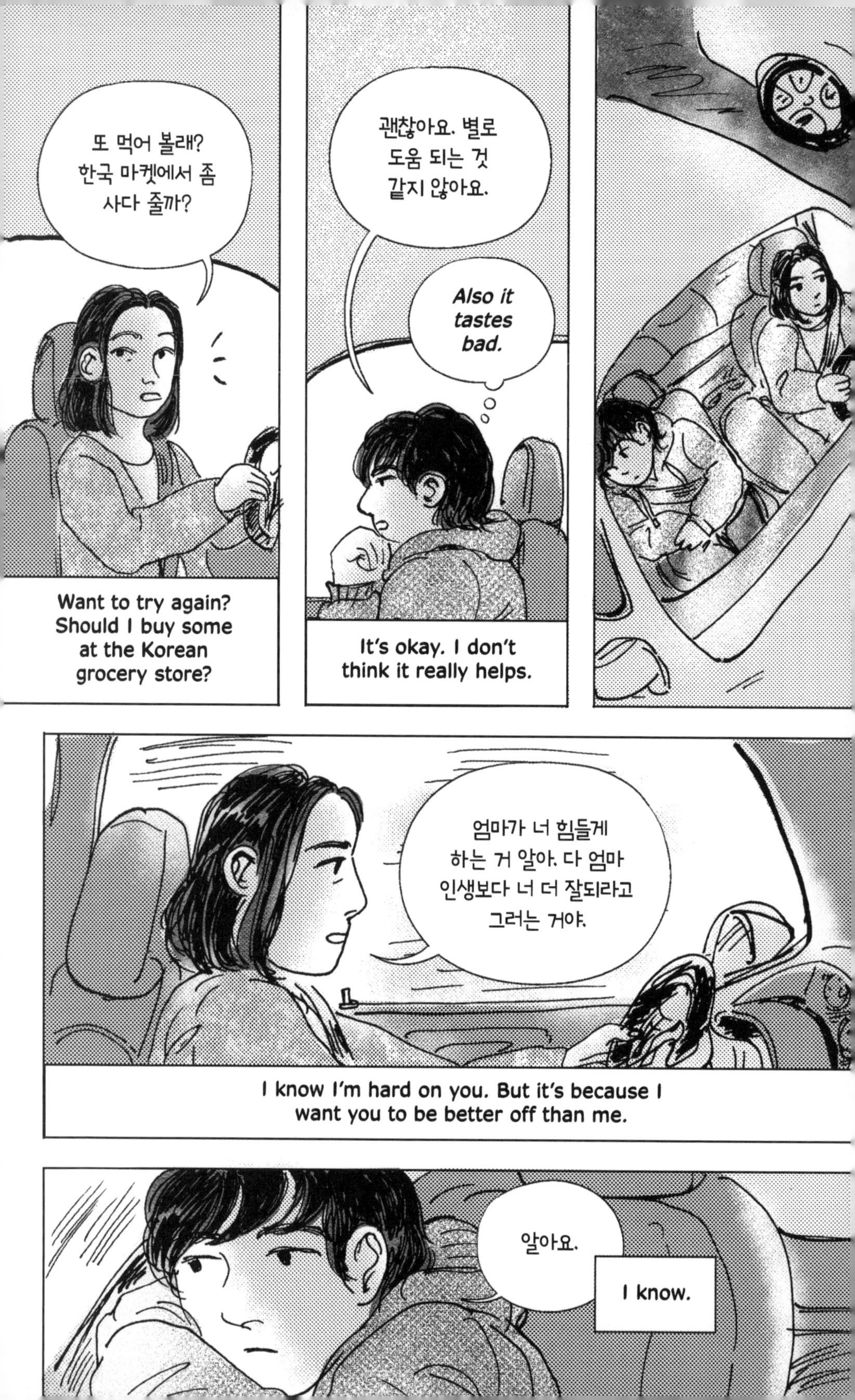
또 먹어 볼래? 한국 마켓에서 좀 사다 줄까?
Want to try again? Should I buy some at the Korean grocery store?
괜찮아요. 별로 도움 되는 것 같지 않아요.
Also it tastes bad.
It's okay. I don't think it really helps.
엄마가 너 힘들게 하는 거 알아. 다 엄마 인생보다 너 더 잘되라고 그러는 거야.
I know I'm hard on you. But it's because I want you to be better off than me.
알아요.
I know.

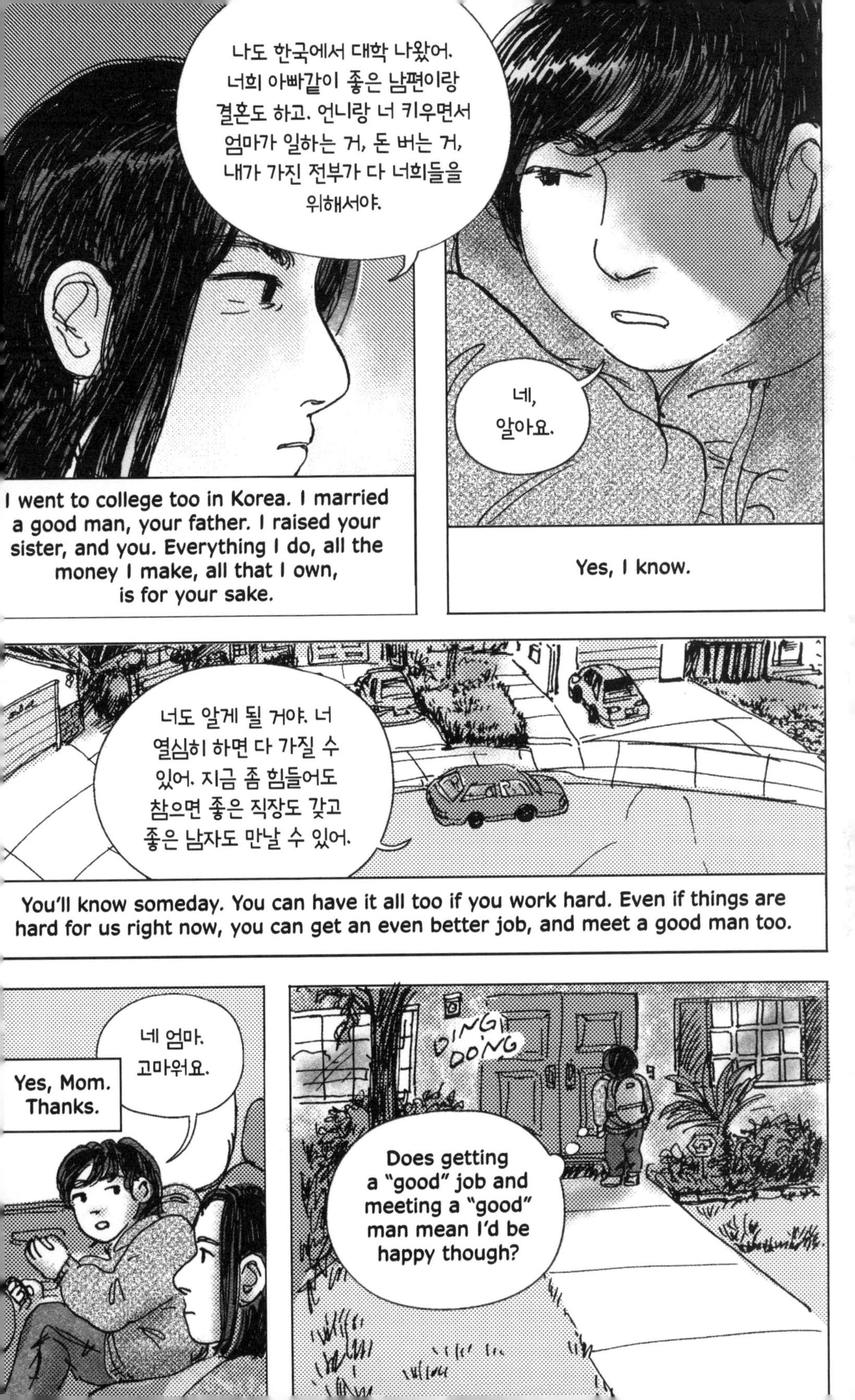
나도 한국에서 대학 나왔어. 너희 아빠같이 좋은 남편이랑 결혼도 하고. 언니랑 너 키우면서 엄마가 일하는 거, 돈 버는 거, 내가 가진 전부가 다 너희들을 위해서야.
I went to college too in Korea. I married a good man, your father. I raised your sister, and you. Everything I do, all the money I make, all that I own, is for your sake.
네, 알아요.
Yes, I know.
너도 알게 될 거야. 너 열심히 하면 다 가질 수 있어. 지금 좀 힘들어도 참으면 좋은 직장도 갖고 좋은 남자도 만날 수 있어.
You'll know someday. You can have it all too if you work hard. Even if things are hard for us right now, you can get an even better job, and meet a good man too.
네 엄마. 고마워요.
Yes, Mom. Thanks.
DING DONG
Does getting a "good" job and meeting a "good" man mean I'd be happy though?

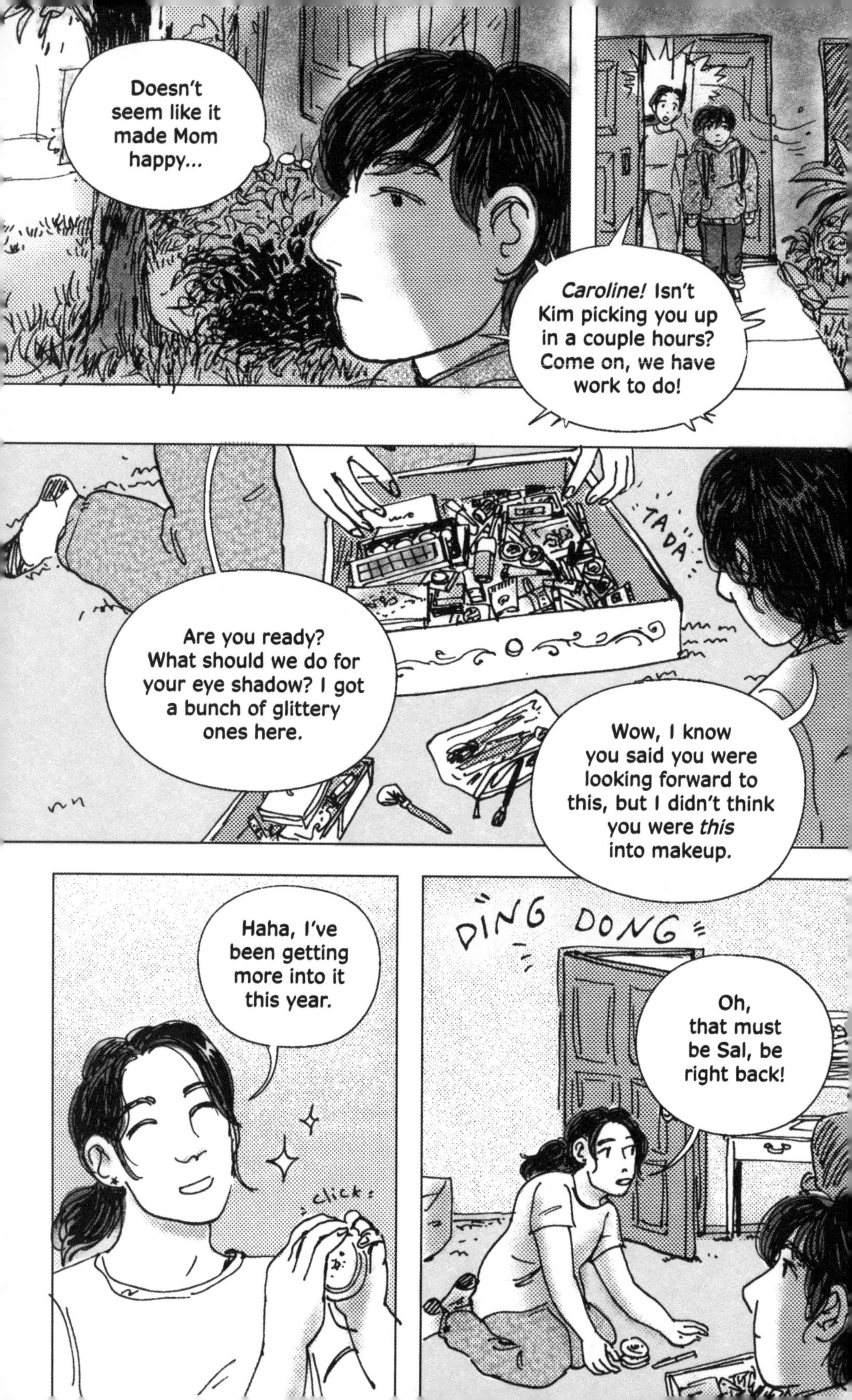
Doesn't seem like it made Mom happy...
Caroline! Isn't Kim picking you up in a couple hours? Come on, we have work to do!
TADA
Are you ready? What should we do for your eye shadow? I got a bunch of glittery ones here.
Wow, I know you said you were looking forward to this, but I didn't think you were *this* into makeup.
Haha, I've been getting more into it this year.
click
DING DONG
Oh, that must be Sal, be right back!

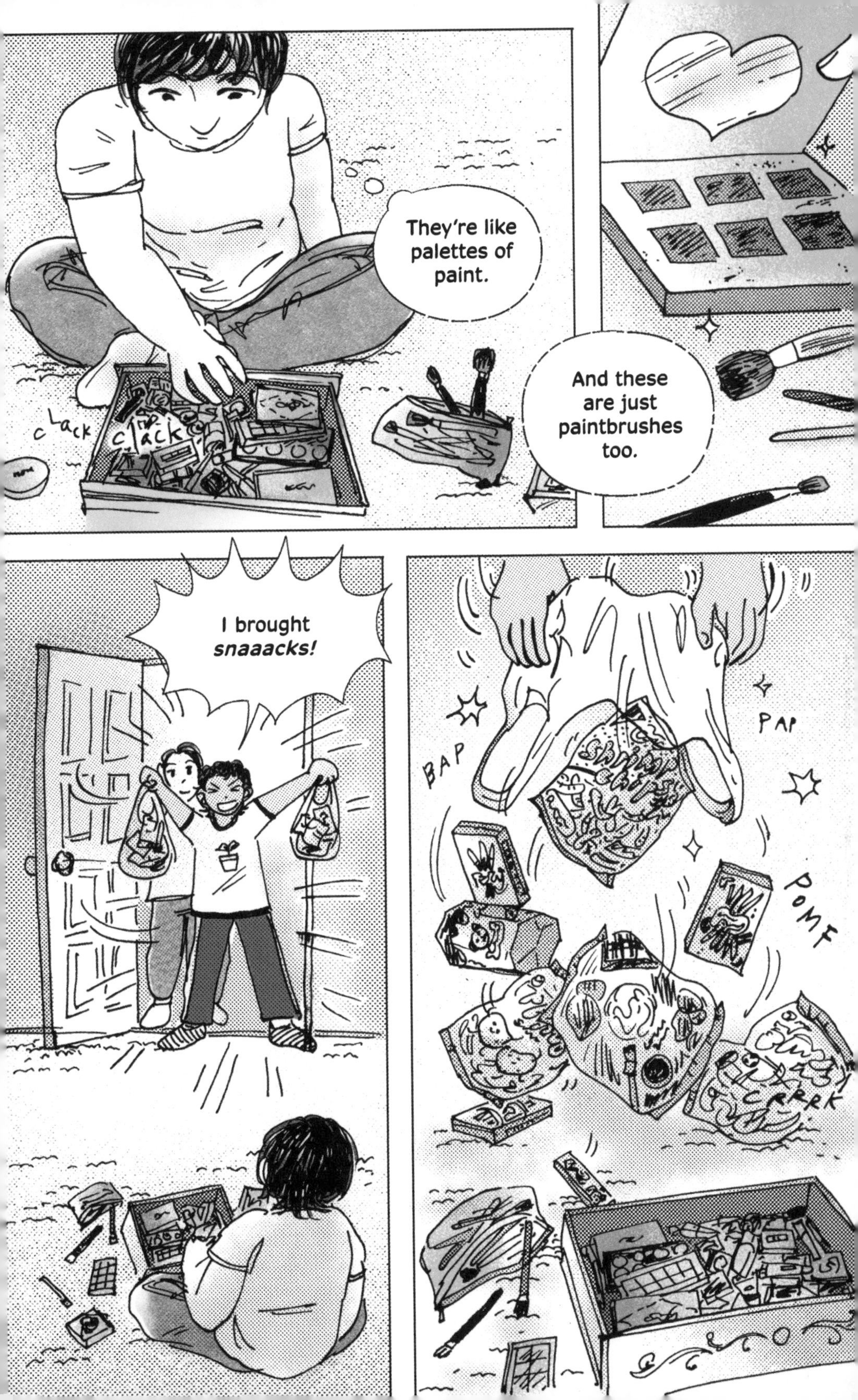
They're like palettes of paint.
CLACK
CLACK
And these are just paintbrushes too.
I brought *snaaacks!*
BAP
PAP
POMF
CRRRK

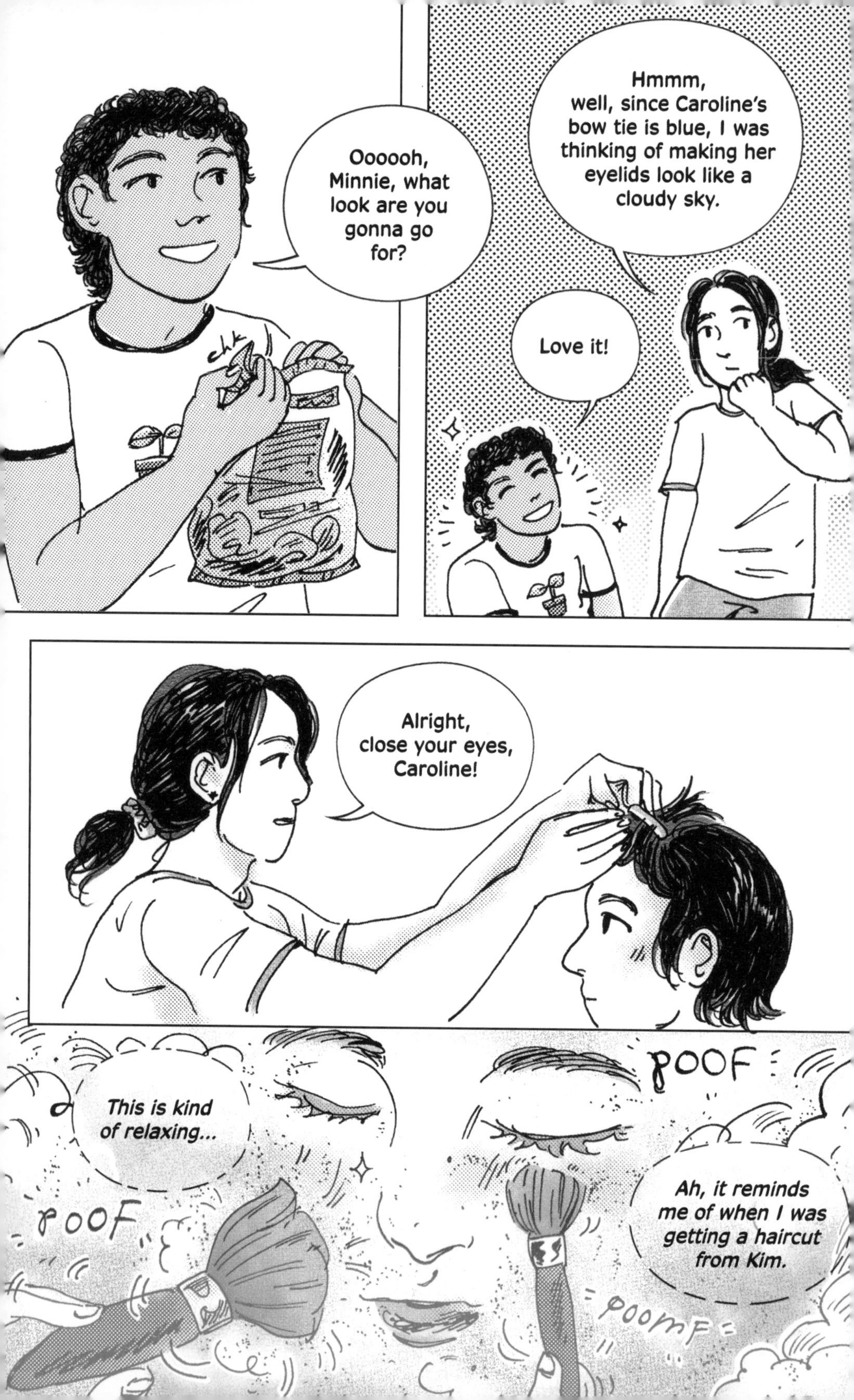
chk
Oooooh, Minnie, what look are you gonna go for?
Hmmm, well, since Caroline's bow tie is blue, I was thinking of making her eyelids look like a cloudy sky.
Love it!
Alright, close your eyes, Caroline!
This is kind of relaxing...
POOF
POOF
Ah, it reminds me of when I was getting a haircut from Kim.
POOMF

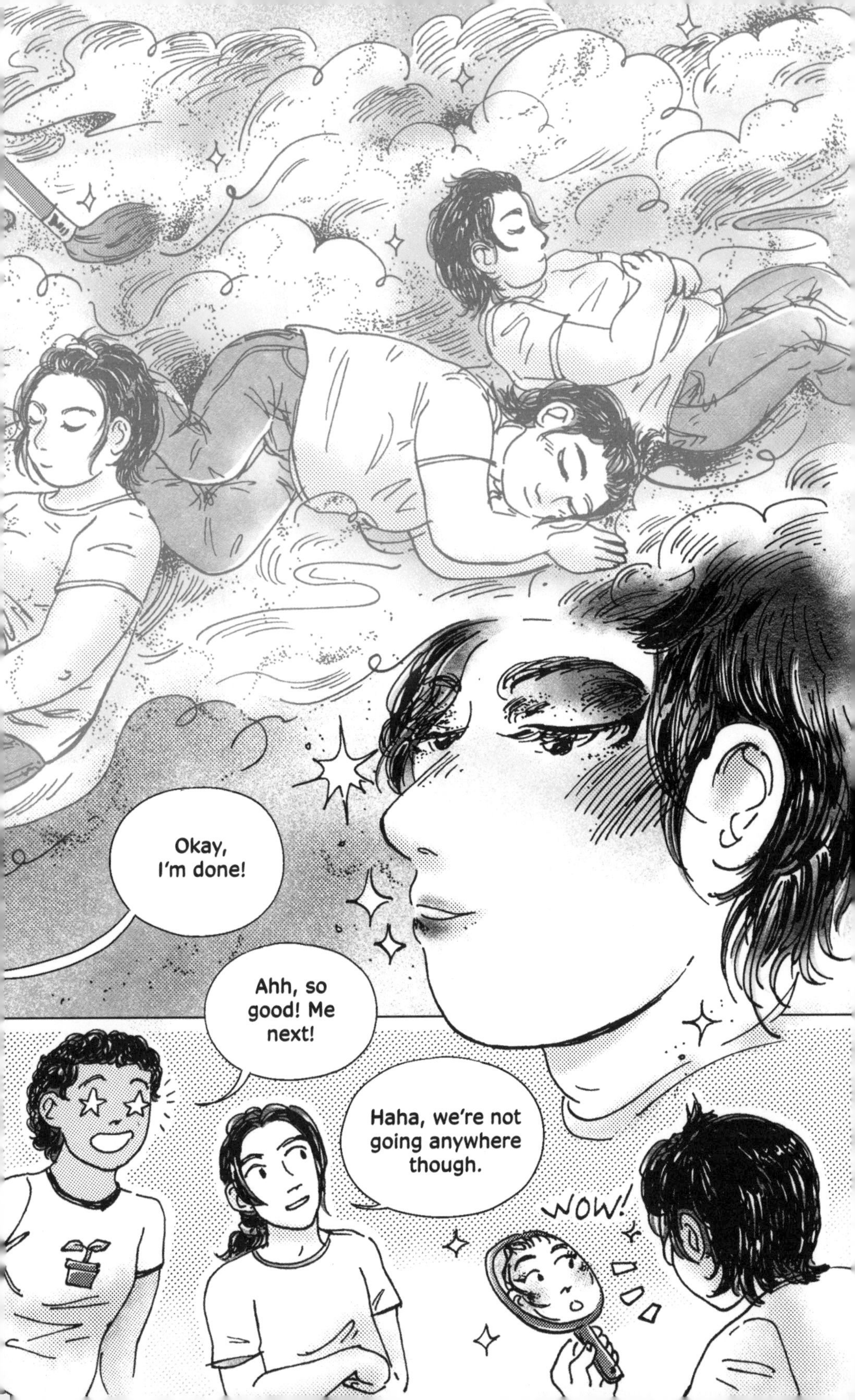
Okay, I'm done!
Ahh, so good! Me next!
Haha, we're not going anywhere though.
WOW!

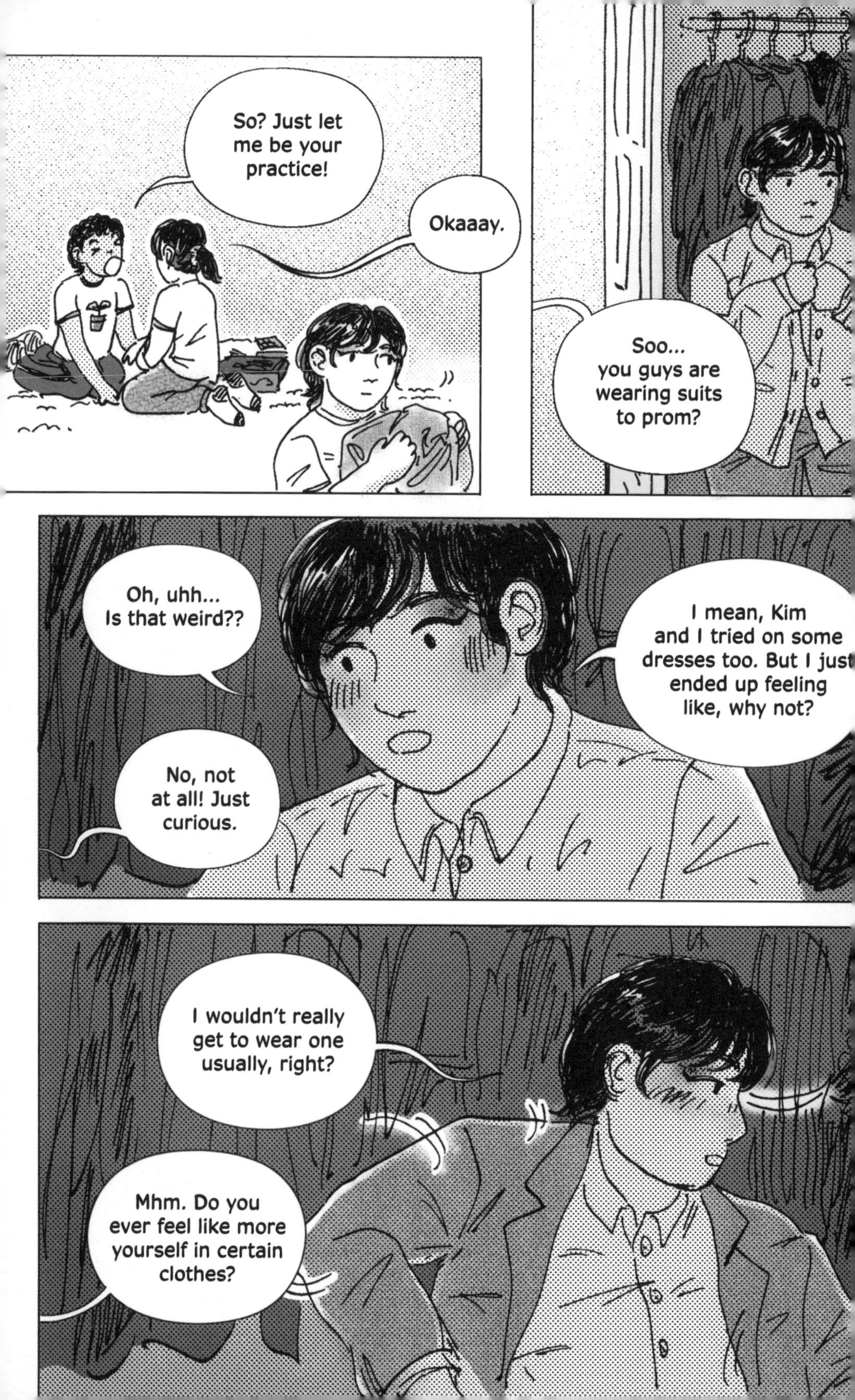
So? Just let me be your practice!
Okaaay.
Soo... you guys are wearing suits to prom?
Oh, uhh... Is that weird??
No, not at all! Just curious.
I mean, Kim and I tried on some dresses too. But I just ended up feeling like, why not?
I wouldn't really get to wear one usually, right?
Mhm. Do you ever feel like more yourself in certain clothes?

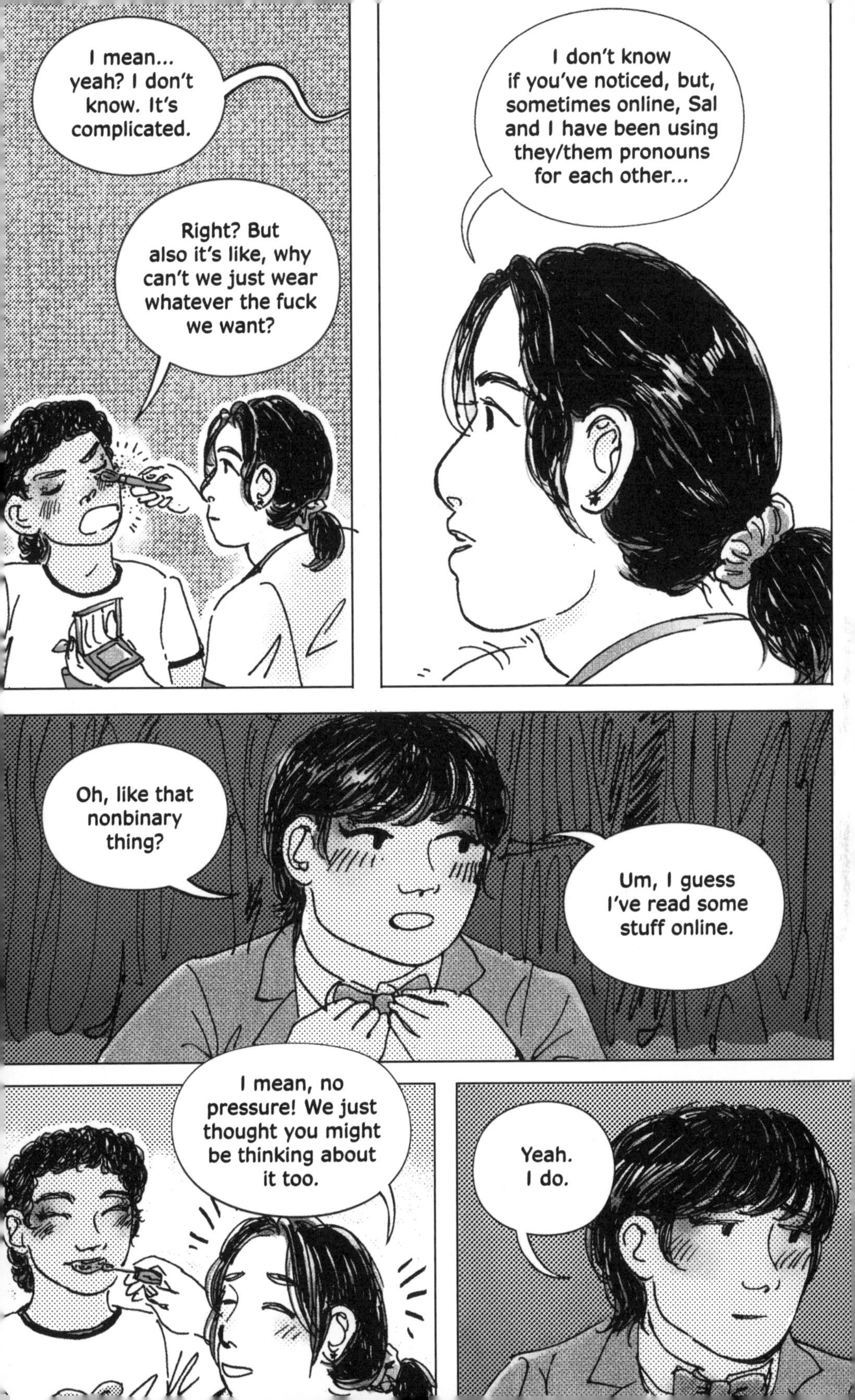
I mean... yeah? I don't know. It's complicated.
Right? But also it's like, why can't we just wear whatever the fuck we want?
I don't know if you've noticed, but, sometimes online, Sal and I have been using they/them pronouns for each other...
Oh, like that nonbinary thing?
Um, I guess I've read some stuff online.
I mean, no pressure! We just thought you might be thinking about it too.
Yeah. I do.

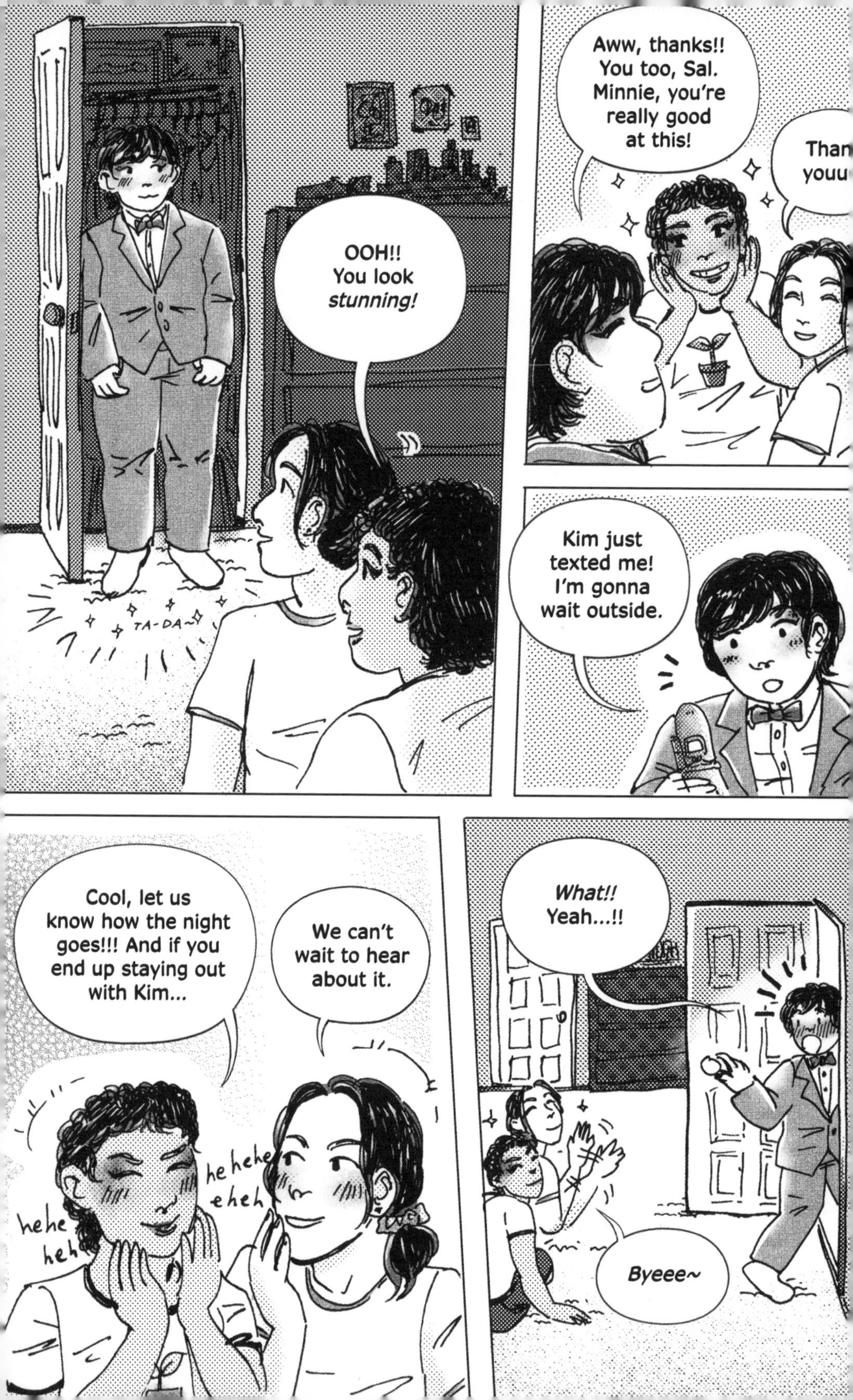
TA-DA~
OOH!! You look *stunning!*
Aww, thanks!! You too, Sal. Minnie, you're really good at this!
Than youuu
Kim just texted me! I'm gonna wait outside.
Cool, let us know how the night goes!!! And if you end up staying out with Kim...
We can't wait to hear about it.
hehe heh
hehehe eheh
What!! Yeah...!!
Byeee~

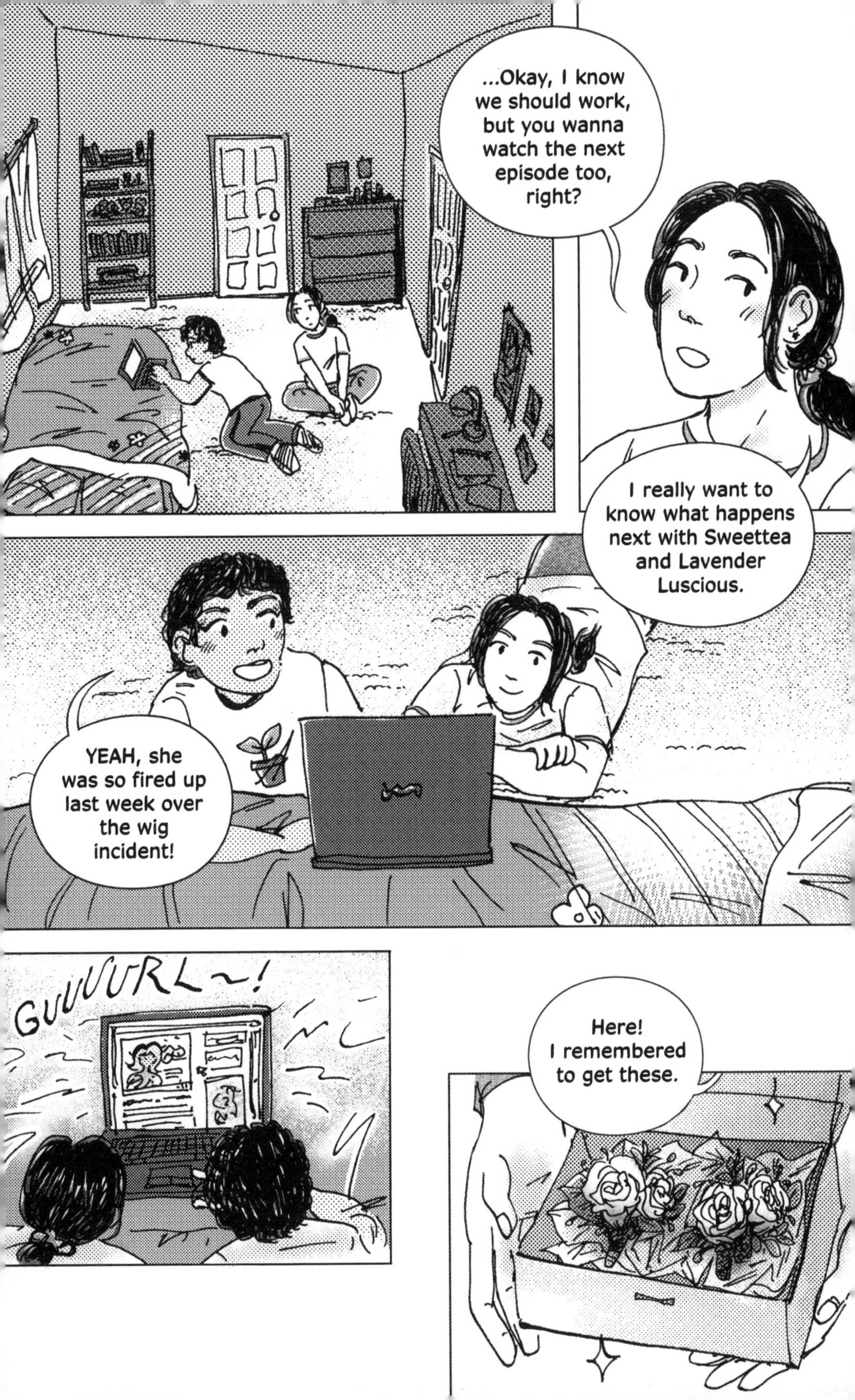
...Okay, I know we should work, but you wanna watch the next episode too, right?
I really want to know what happens next with Sweettea and Lavender Luscious.
YEAH, she was so fired up last week over the wig incident!
GUUUURL~!
Here! I remembered to get these.

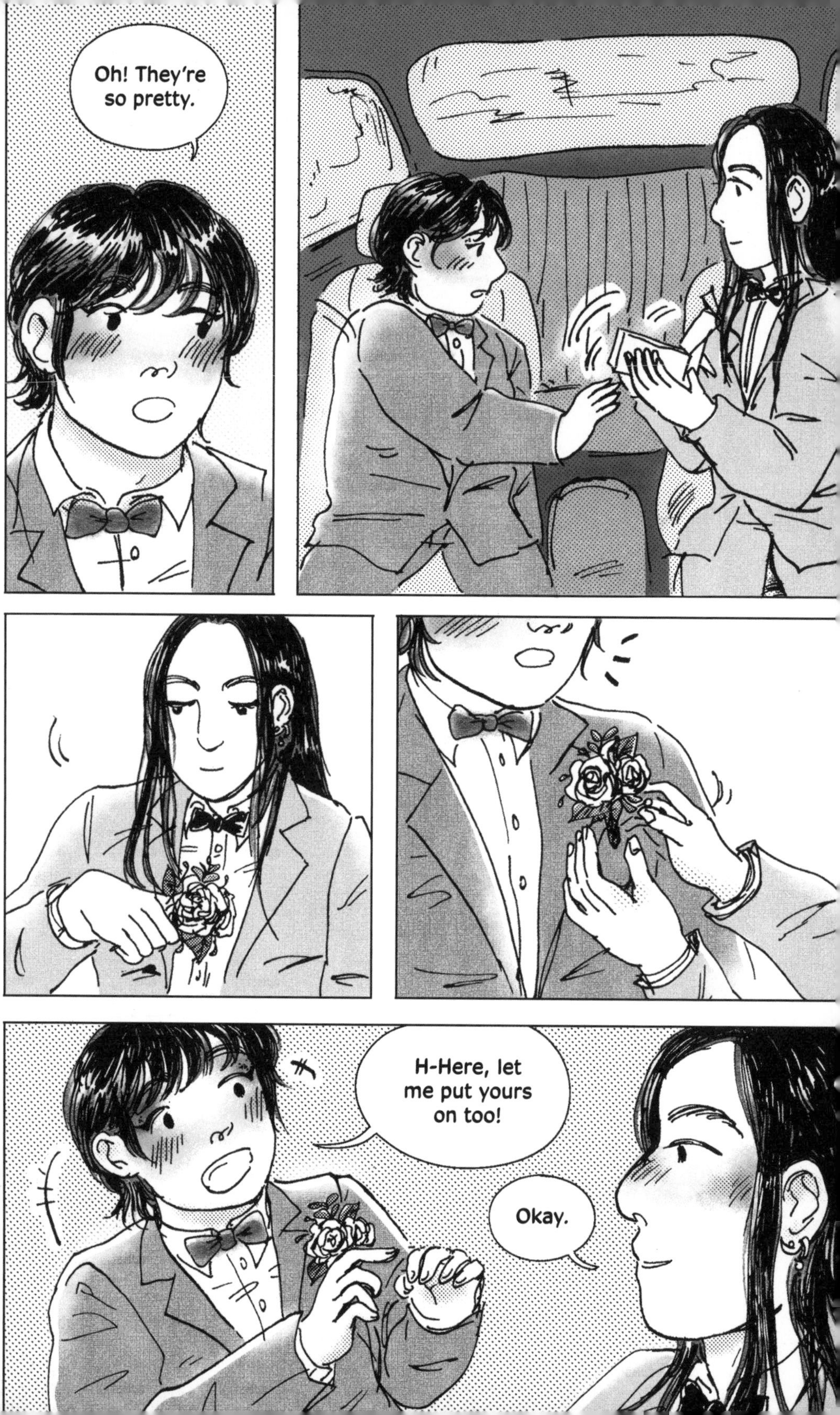
Oh! They're so pretty.
H-Here, let me put yours on too!
Okay.

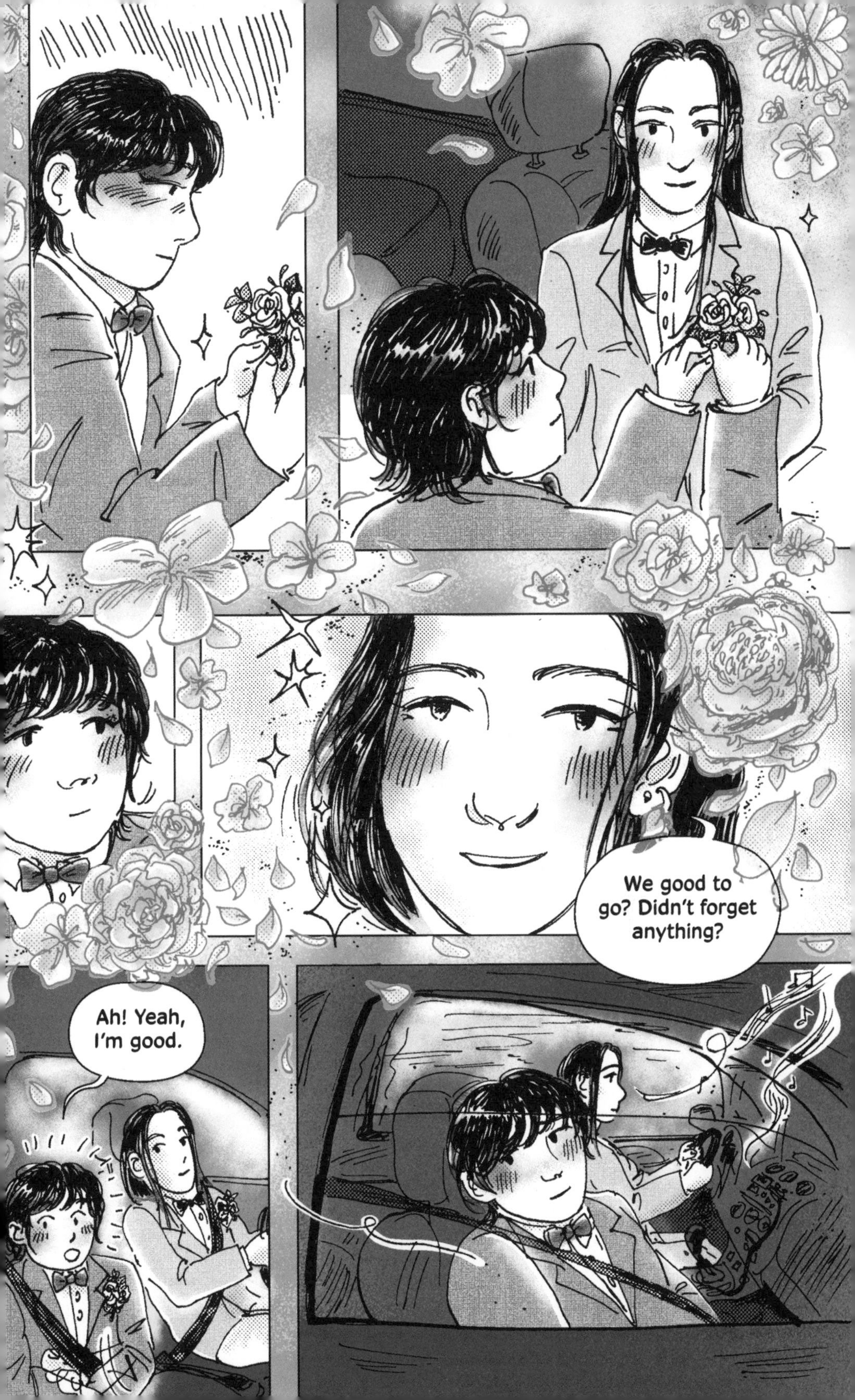
We good to go? Didn't forget anything?
Ah! Yeah, I'm good.

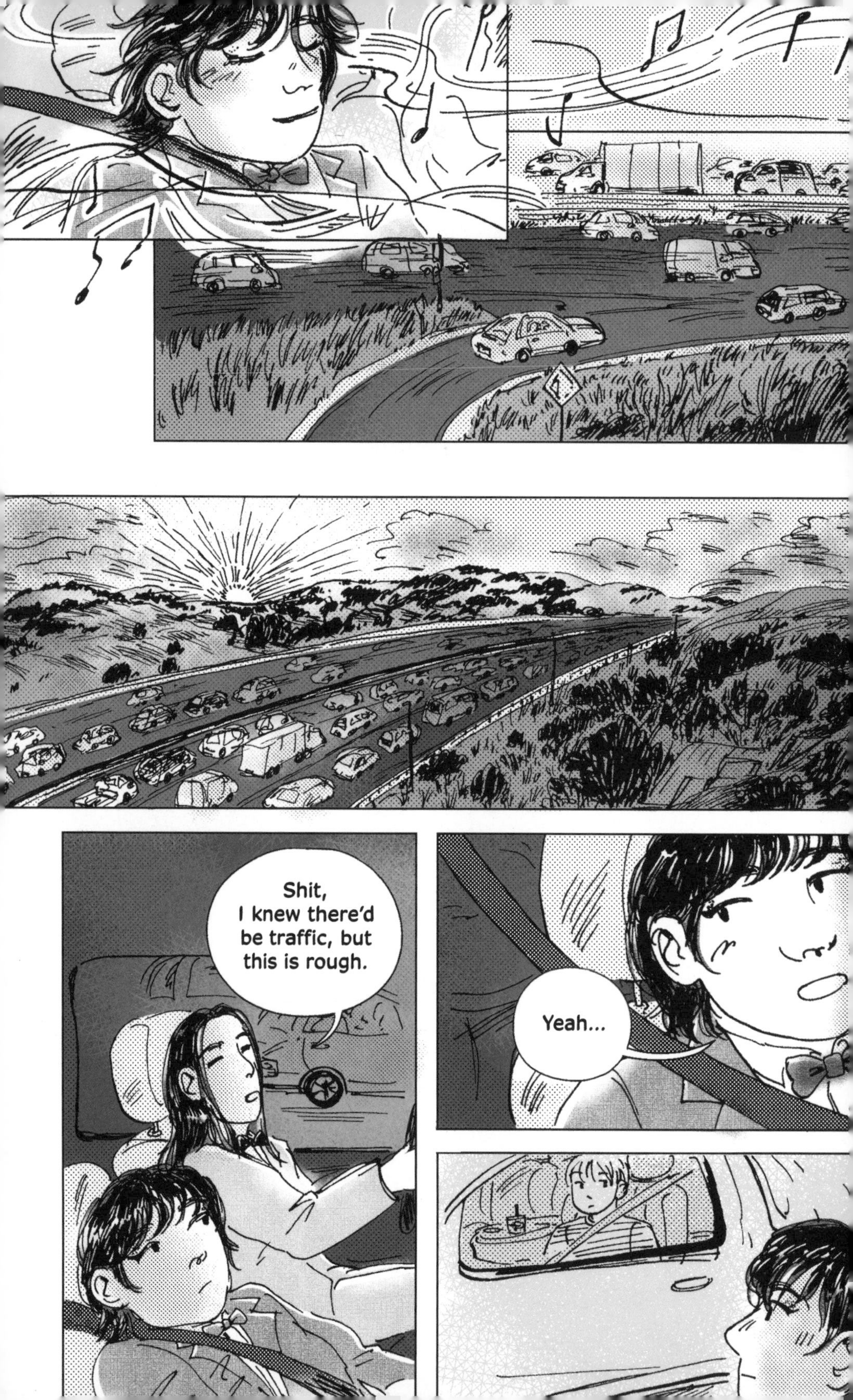
Shit,
I knew there'd
be traffic, but
this is rough.
Yeah...

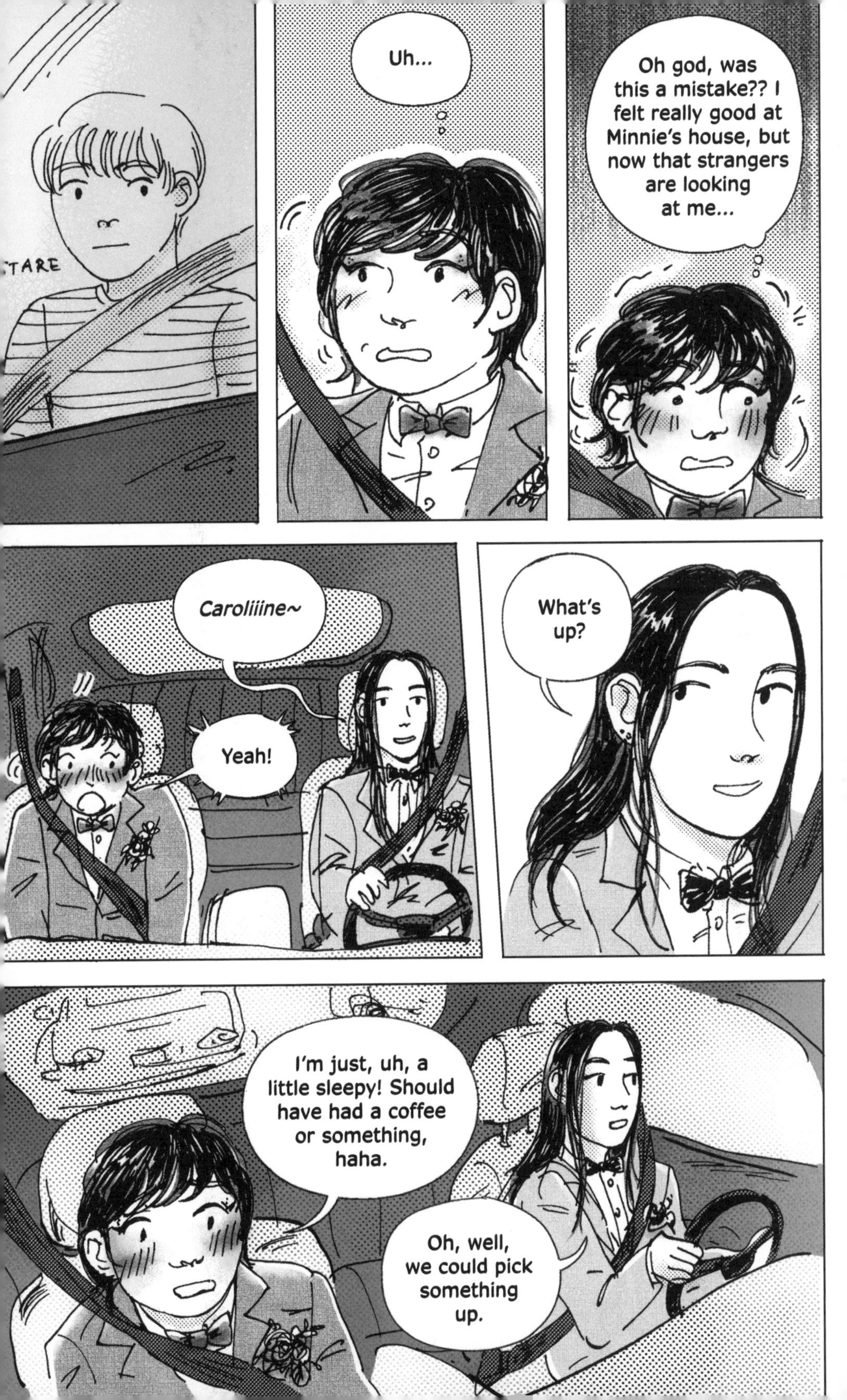
STARE
Uh...
Oh god, was this a mistake?? I felt really good at Minnie's house, but now that strangers are looking at me...
Caroliiine~
Yeah!
What's up?
I'm just, uh, a little sleepy! Should have had a coffee or something, haha.
Oh, well, we could pick something up.

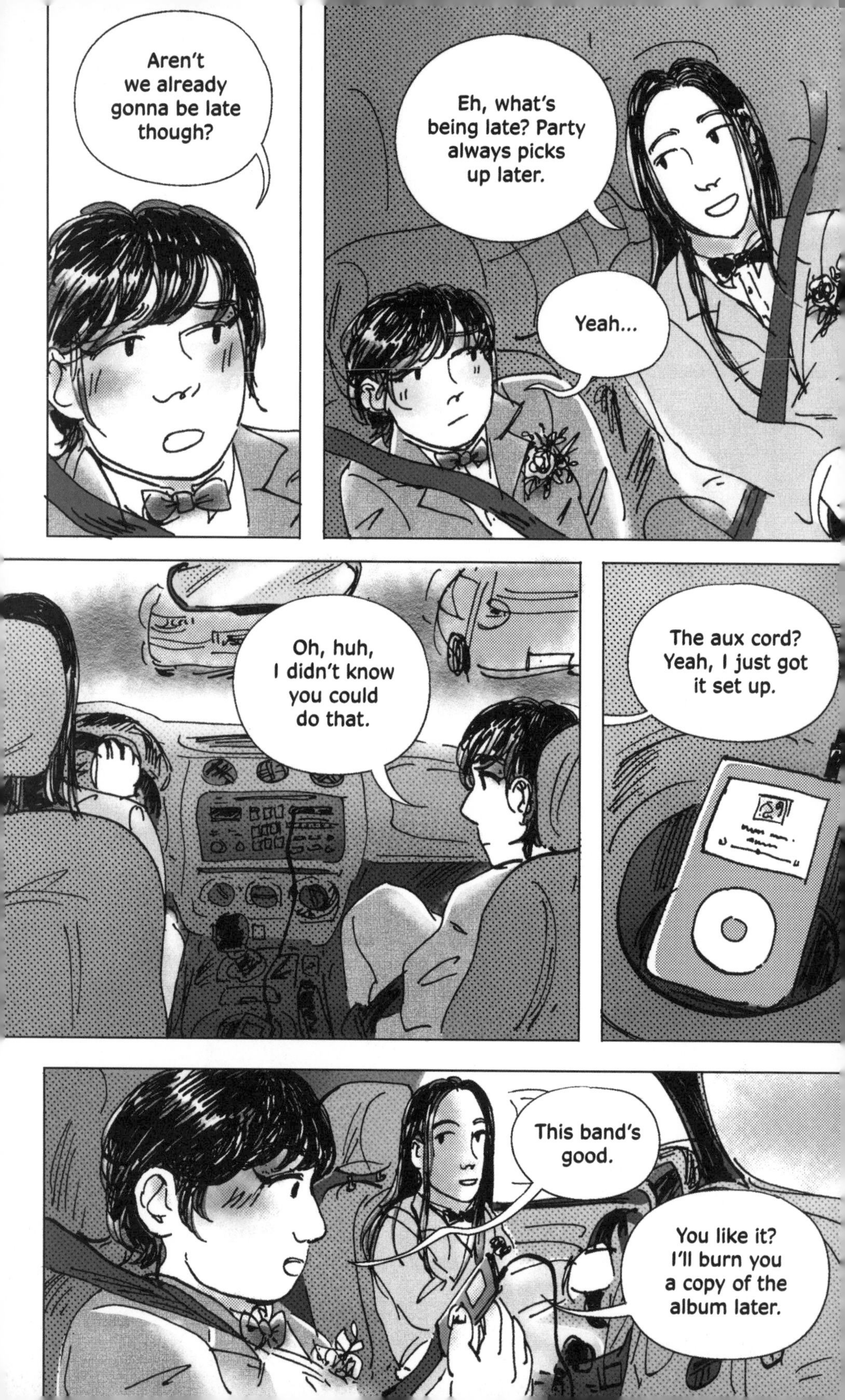
Aren't we already gonna be late though?
Eh, what's being late? Party always picks up later.
Yeah...
Oh, huh, I didn't know you could do that.
The aux cord? Yeah, I just got it set up.
This band's good.
You like it? I'll burn you a copy of the album later.

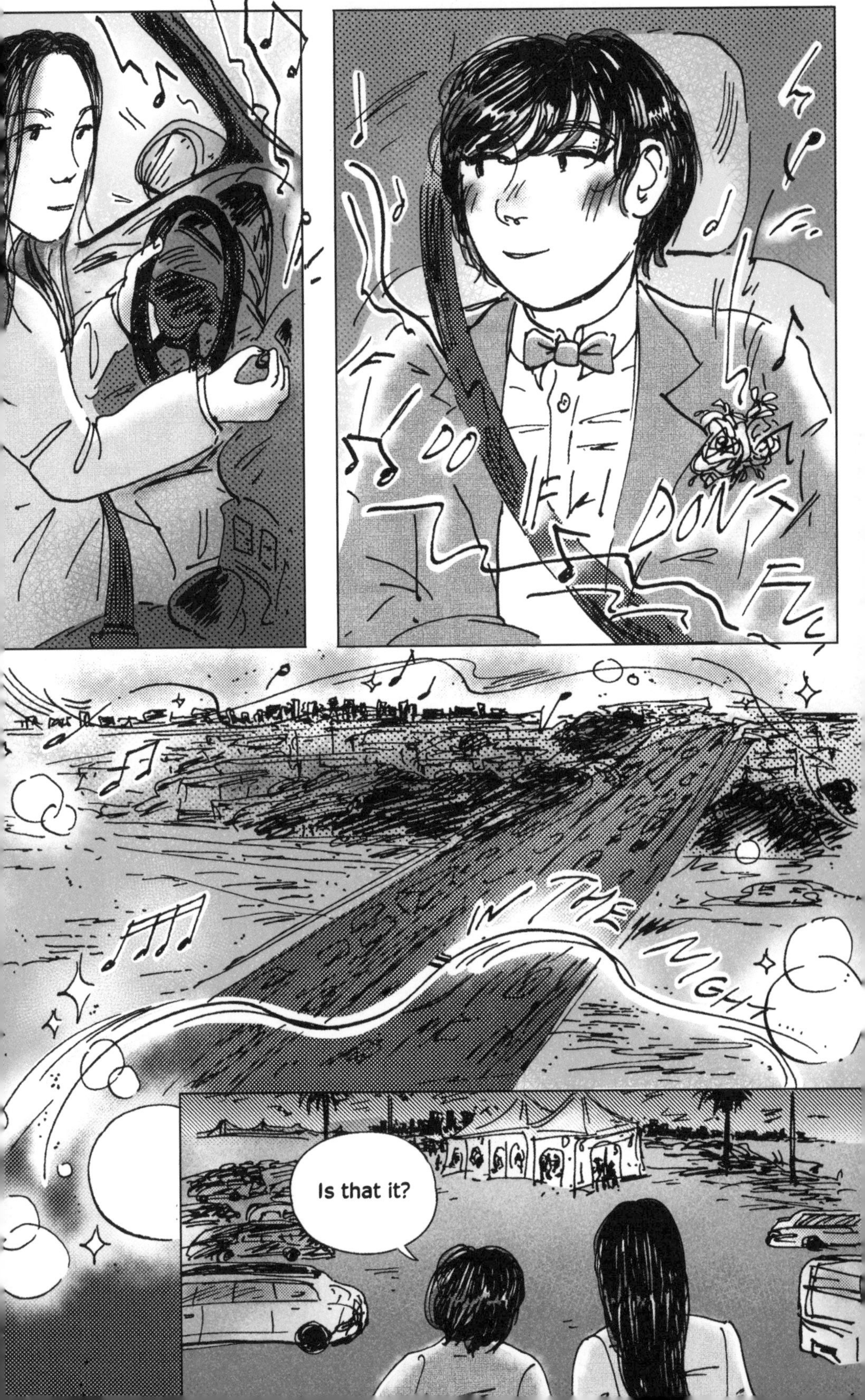

I DO
IF I
DON'T
IN THE NIGHT.....
Is that it?

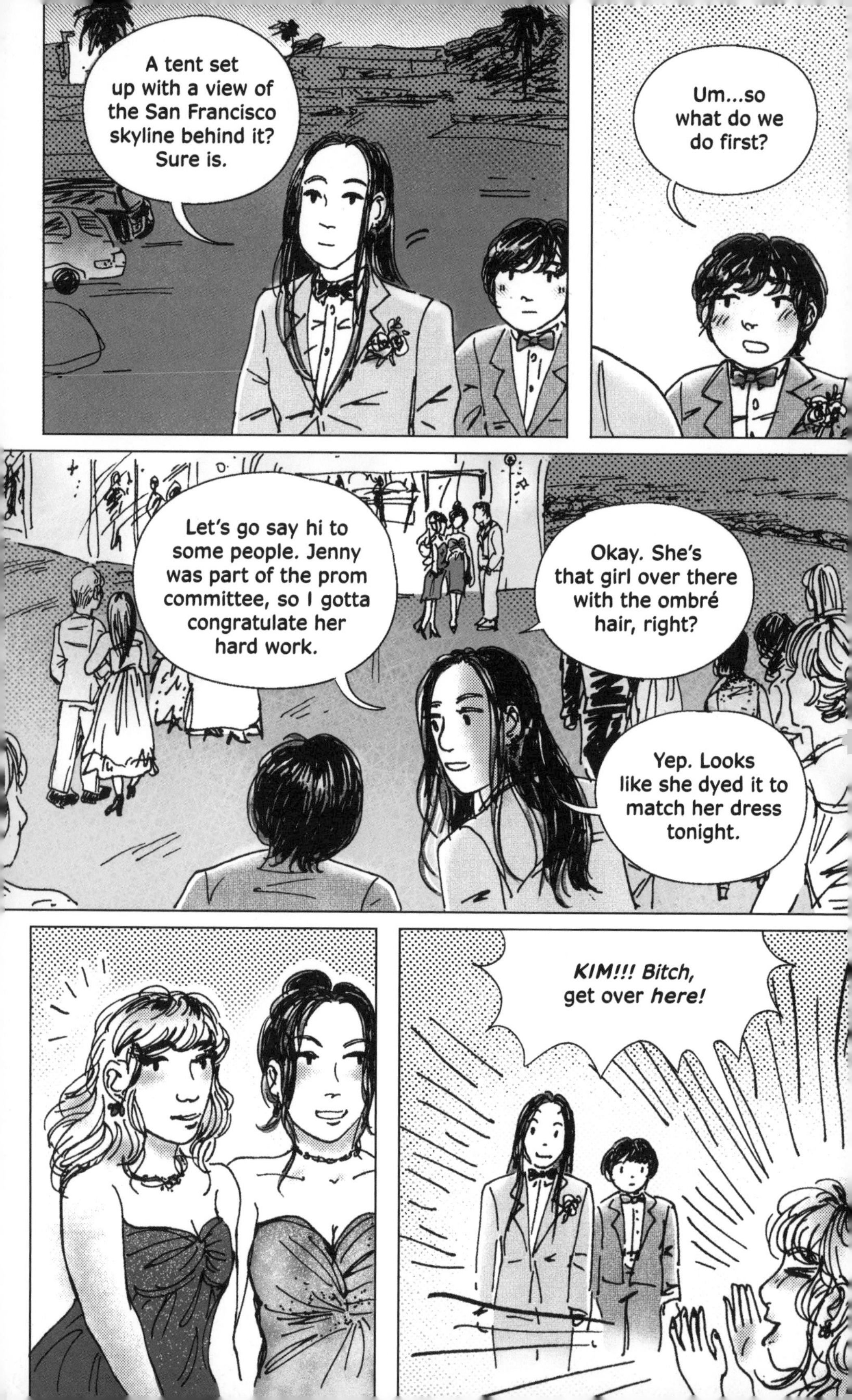
A tent set up with a view of the San Francisco skyline behind it? Sure is.
Um...so what do we do first?
Let's go say hi to some people. Jenny was part of the prom committee, so I gotta congratulate her hard work.
Okay. She's that girl over there with the ombré hair, right?
Yep. Looks like she dyed it to match her dress tonight.
KIM!!! Bitch, get over *here!*

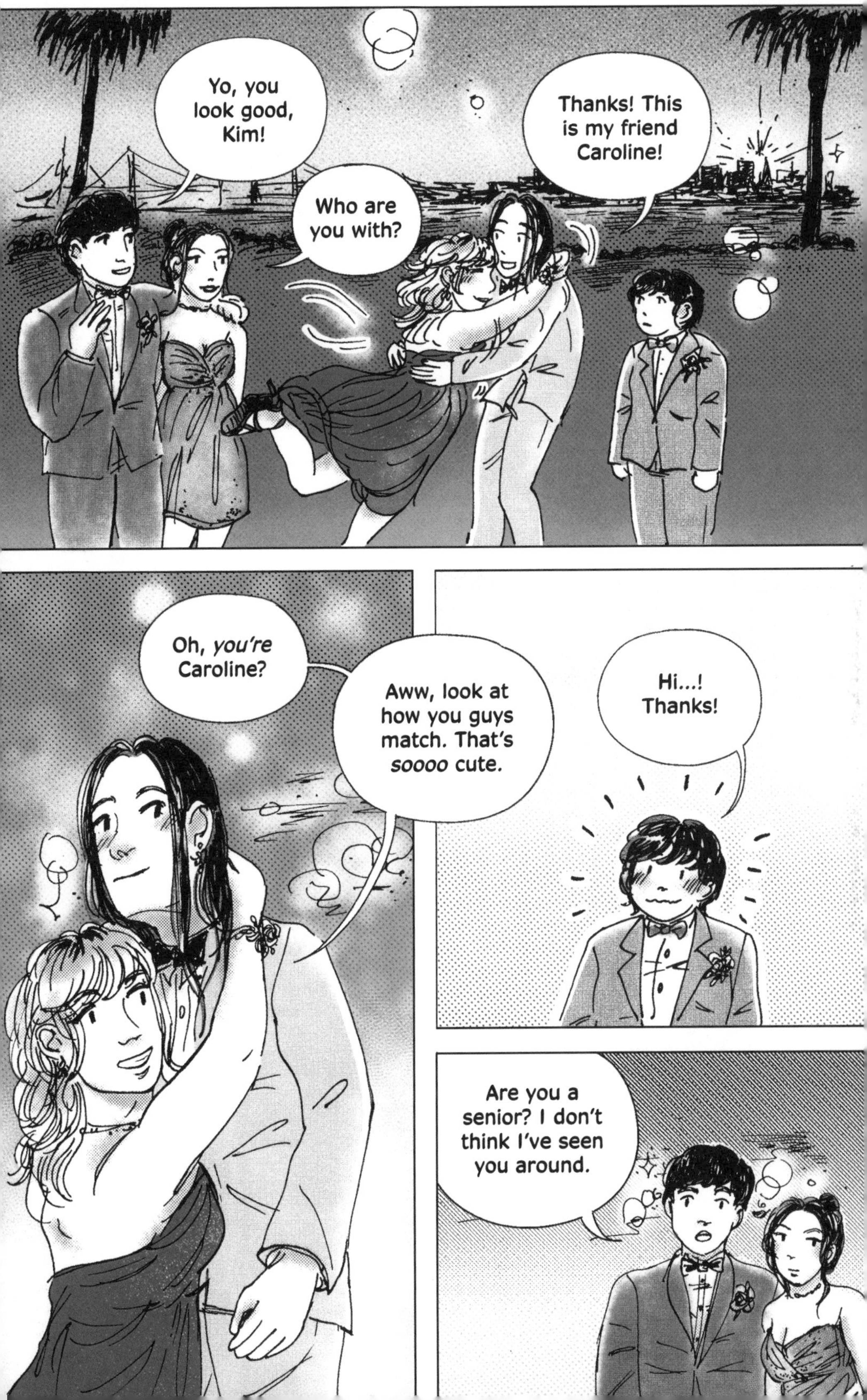
Yo, you look good, Kim!
Who are you with?
Thanks! This is my friend Caroline!
Oh, *you're* Caroline?
Aww, look at how you guys match. That's *soooo* cute.
Hi...! Thanks!
Are you a senior? I don't think I've seen you around.

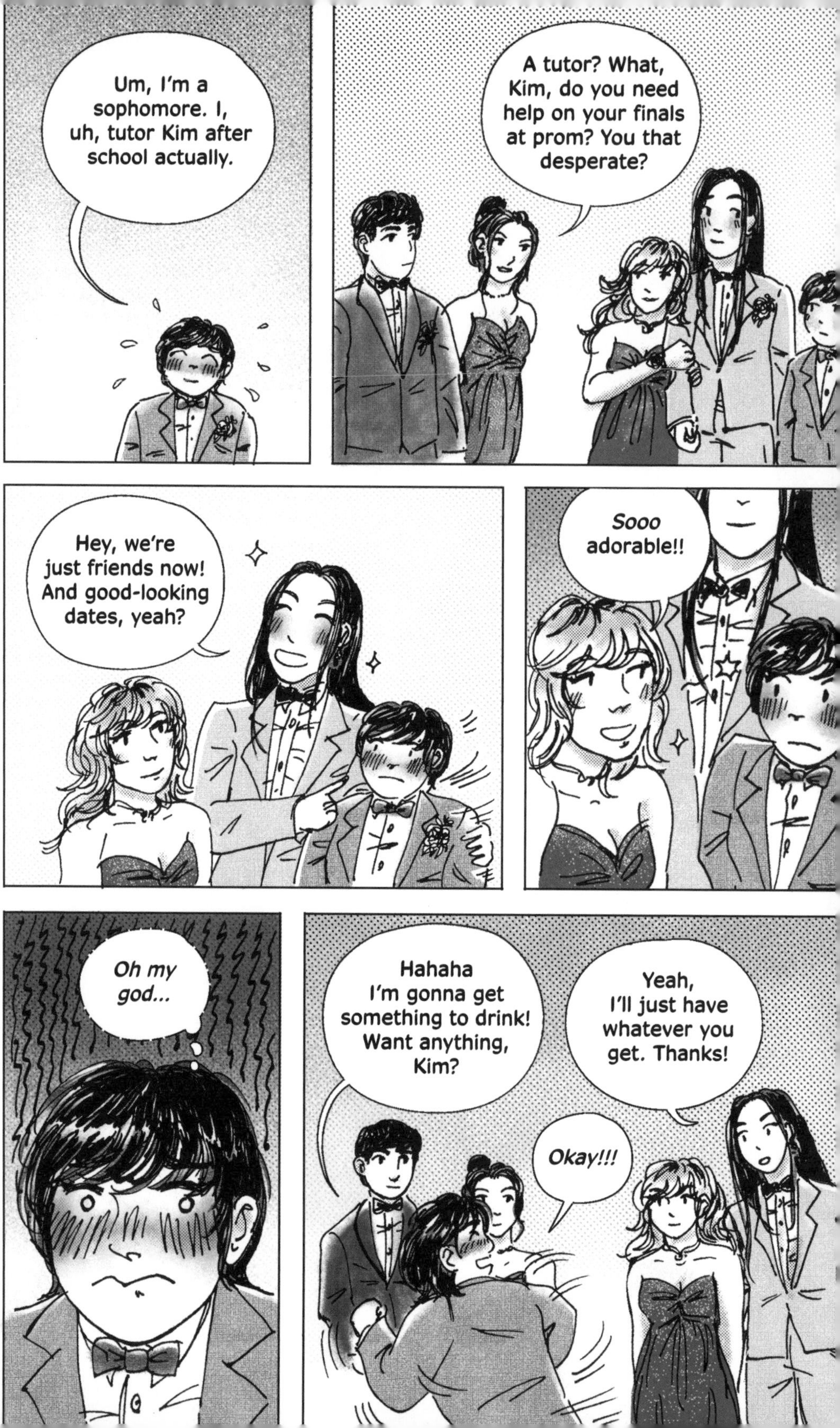
Um, I'm a sophomore. I, uh, tutor Kim after school actually.
A tutor? What, Kim, do you need help on your finals at prom? You that desperate?
Hey, we're just friends now! And good-looking dates, yeah?
Sooo adorable!!
Oh my god...
Hahaha I'm gonna get something to drink! Want anything, Kim?
Yeah, I'll just have whatever you get. Thanks!
Okay!!!

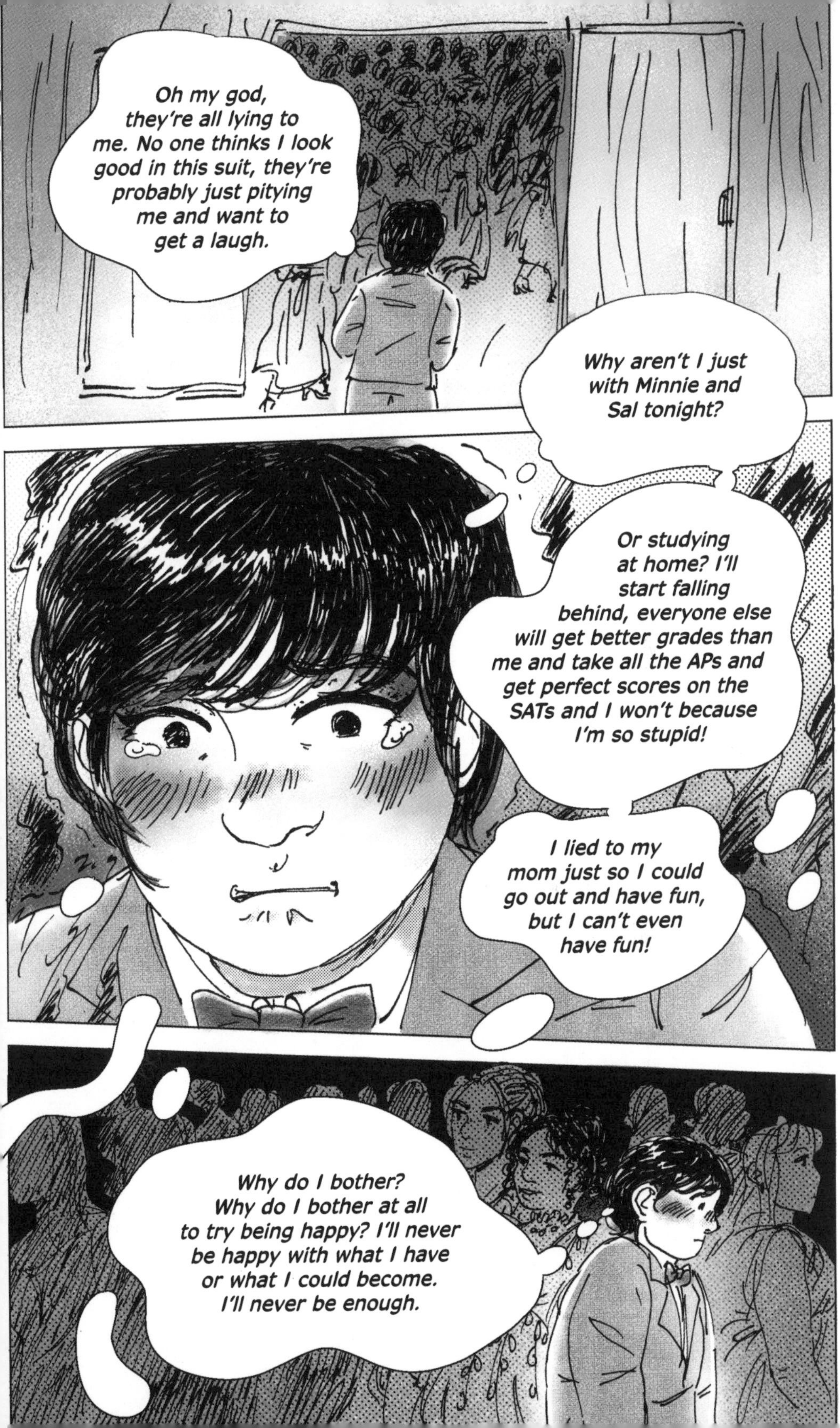
Oh my god, they're all lying to me. No one thinks I look good in this suit, they're probably just pitying me and want to get a laugh.
Why aren't I just with Minnie and Sal tonight?
Or studying at home? I'll start falling behind, everyone else will get better grades than me and take all the APs and get perfect scores on the SATs and I won't because I'm so stupid!
I lied to my mom just so I could go out and have fun, but I can't even have fun!
Why do I bother? Why do I bother at all to try being happy? I'll never be happy with what I have or what I could become. I'll never be enough.

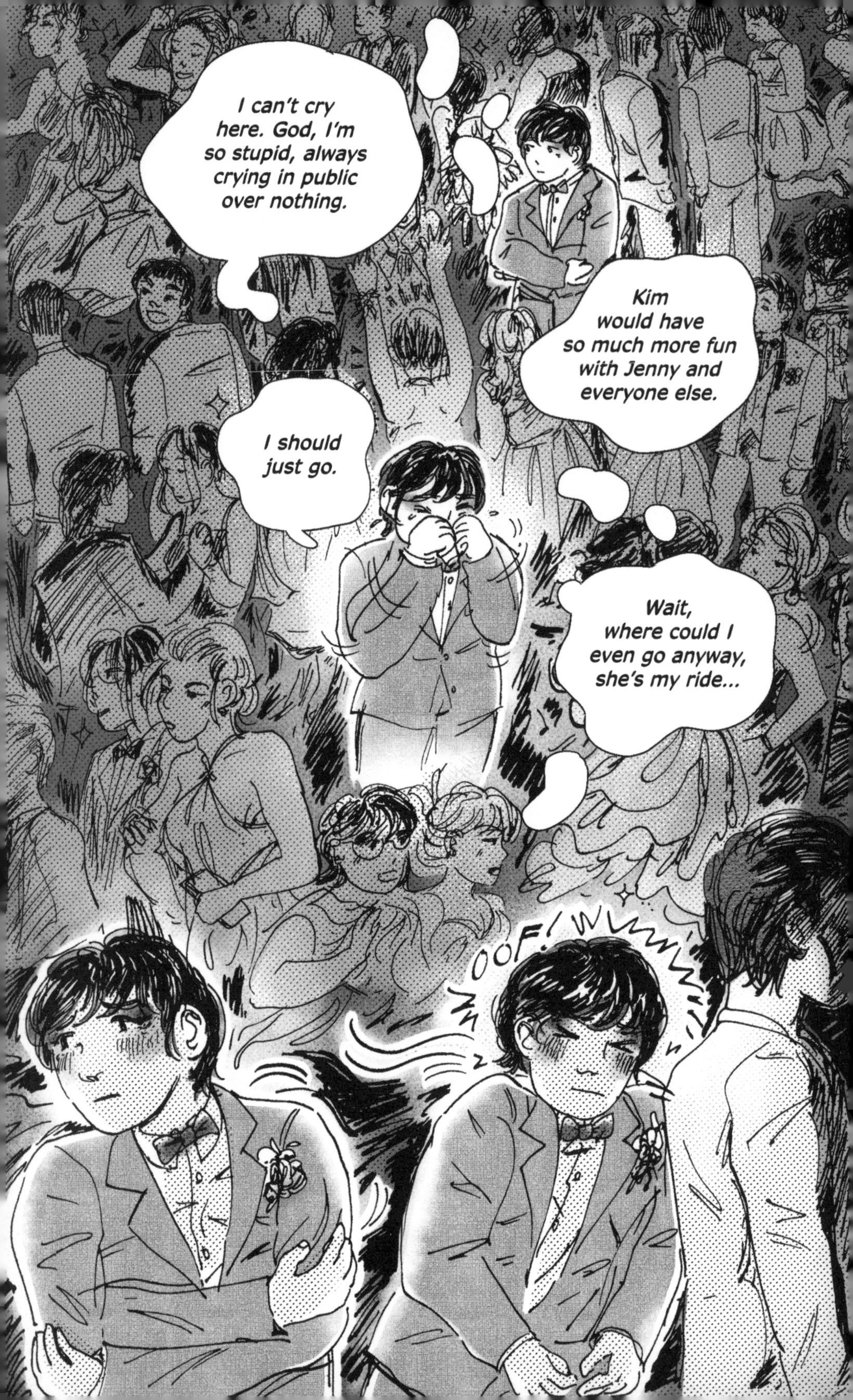
I can't cry here. God, I'm so stupid, always crying in public over nothing.
Kim would have so much more fun with Jenny and everyone else.
I should just go.
Wait, where could I even go anyway, she's my ride...
OOF!
WUMMM

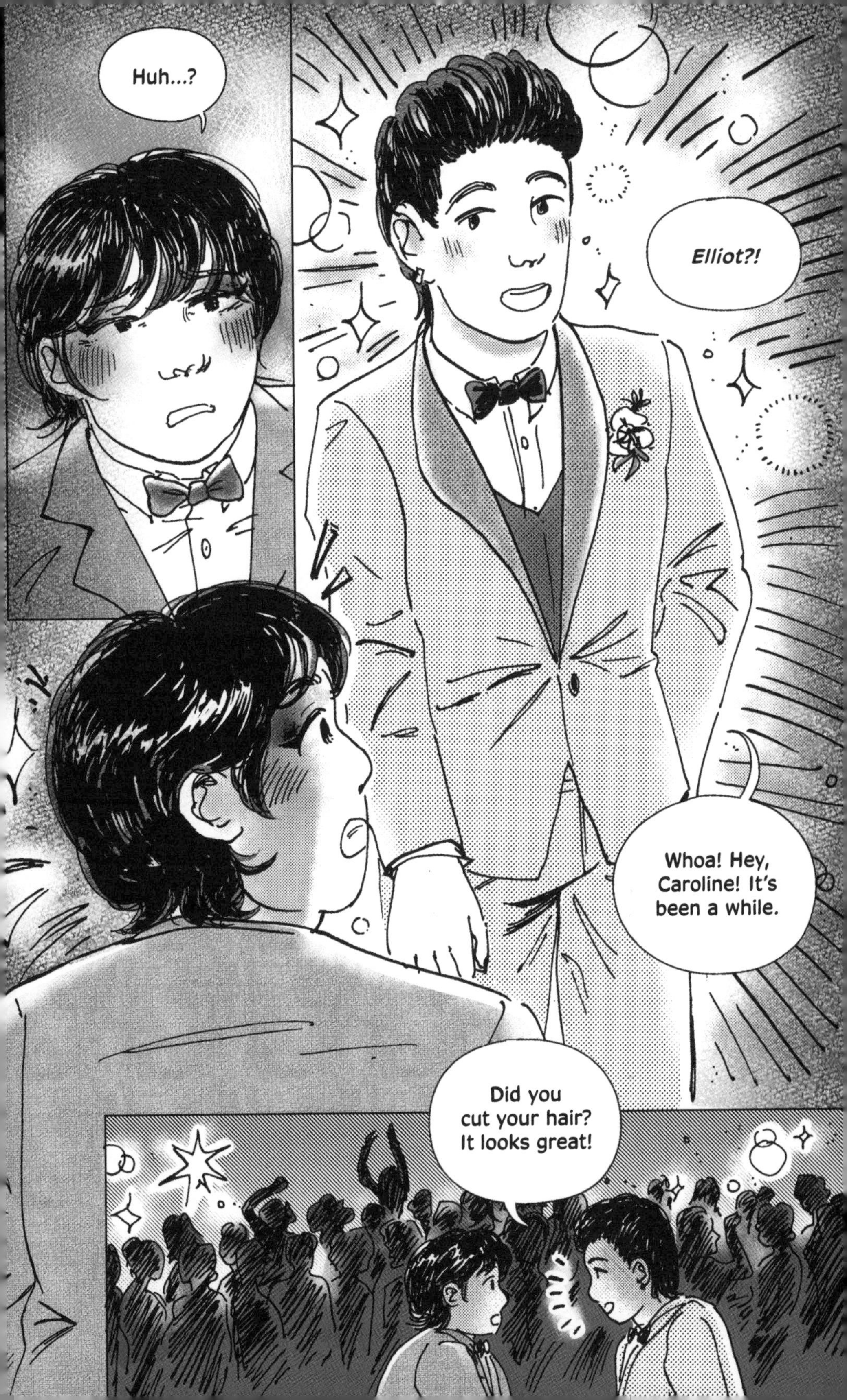
Huh...?
Elliot?!
Whoa! Hey, Caroline! It's been a while.
Did you cut your hair? It looks great!

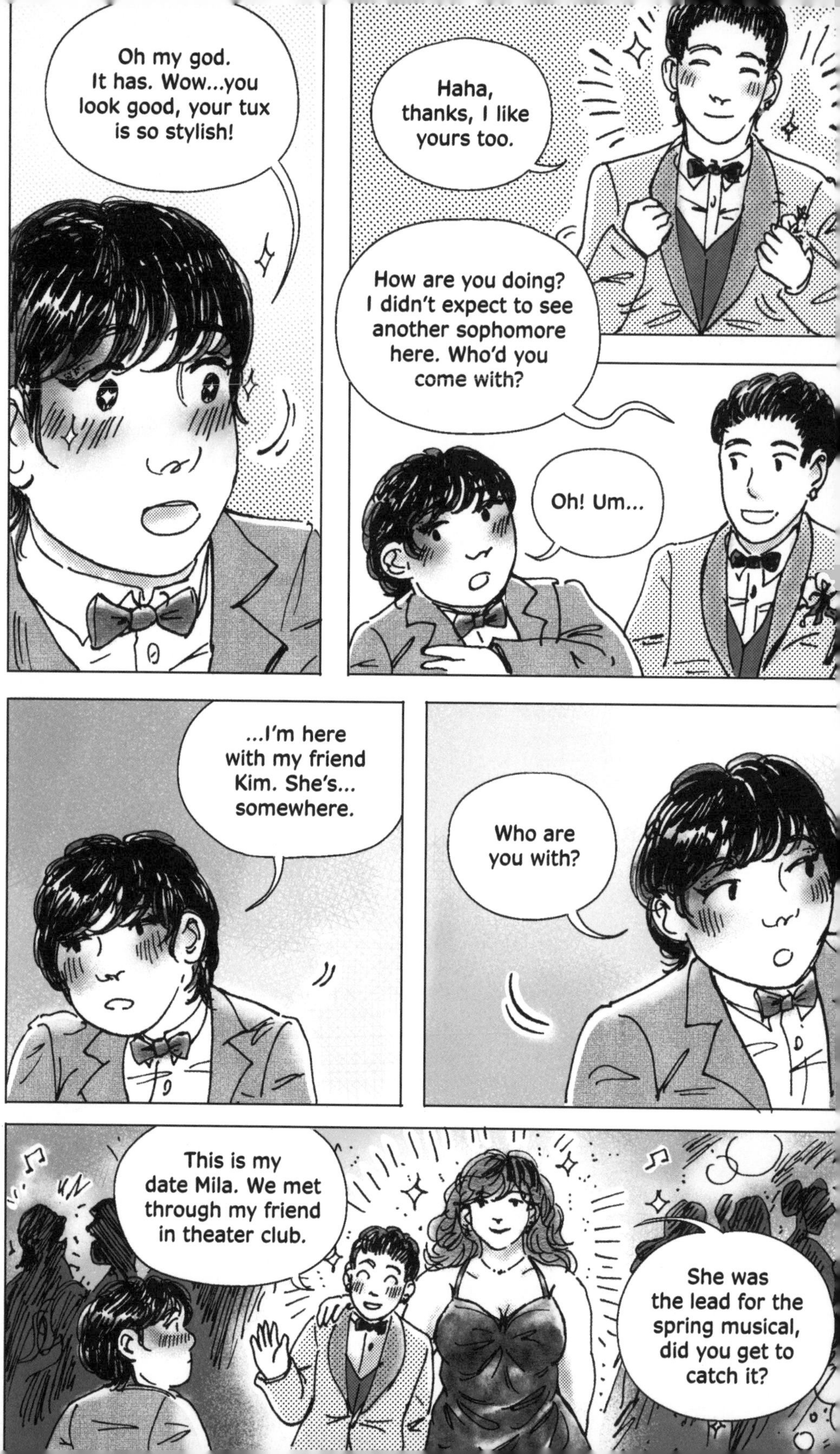
Oh my god. It has. Wow...you look good, your tux is so stylish!
Haha, thanks, I like yours too.
How are you doing? I didn't expect to see another sophomore here. Who'd you come with?
Oh! Um...
...I'm here with my friend Kim. She's... somewhere.
Who are you with?
This is my date Mila. We met through my friend in theater club.
She was the lead for the spring musical, did you get to catch it?

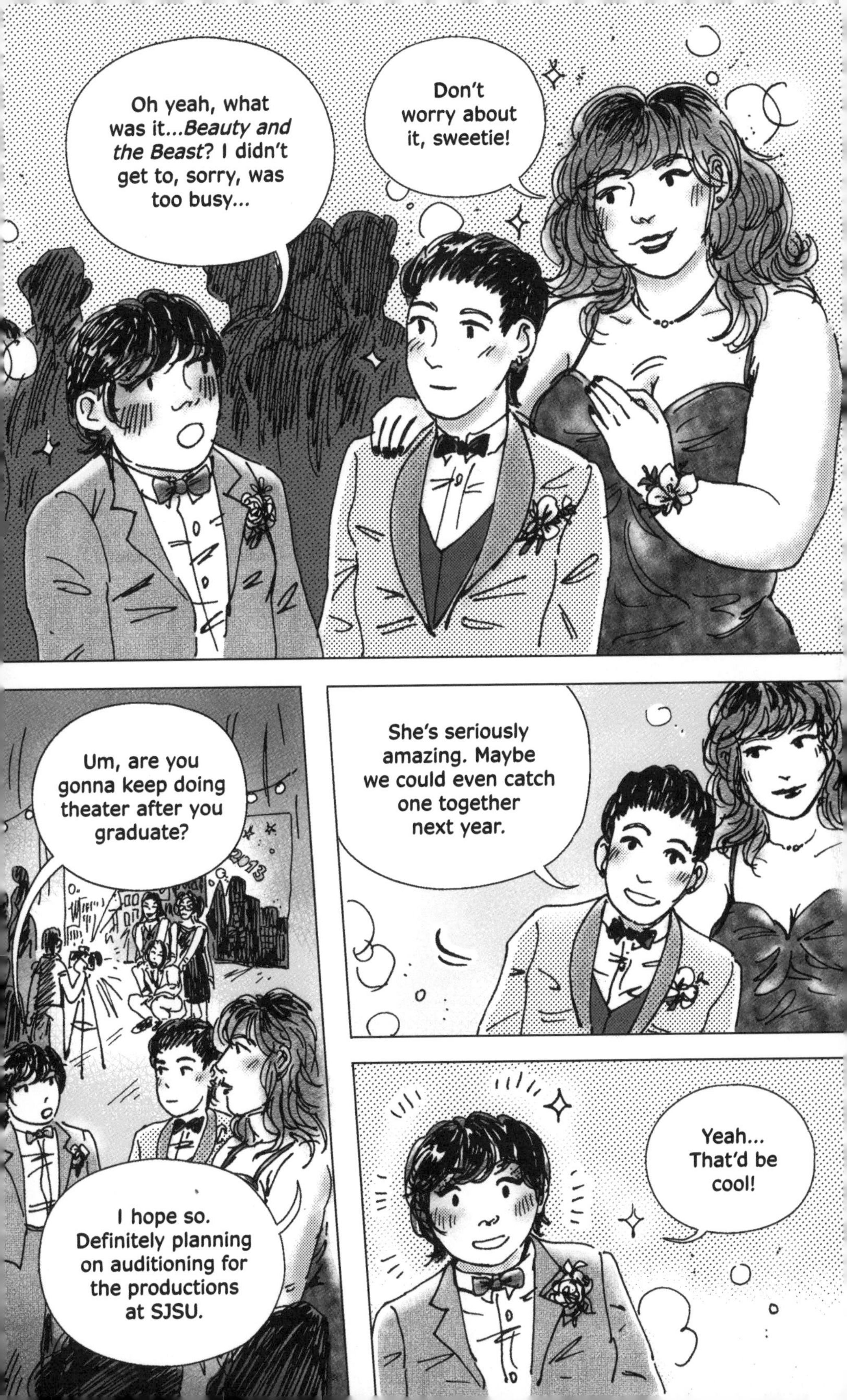
Oh yeah, what was it...*Beauty and the Beast*? I didn't get to, sorry, was too busy...
Don't worry about it, sweetie!
Um, are you gonna keep doing theater after you graduate?
I hope so. Definitely planning on auditioning for the productions at SJSU.
She's seriously amazing. Maybe we could even catch one together next year.
Yeah... That'd be cool!

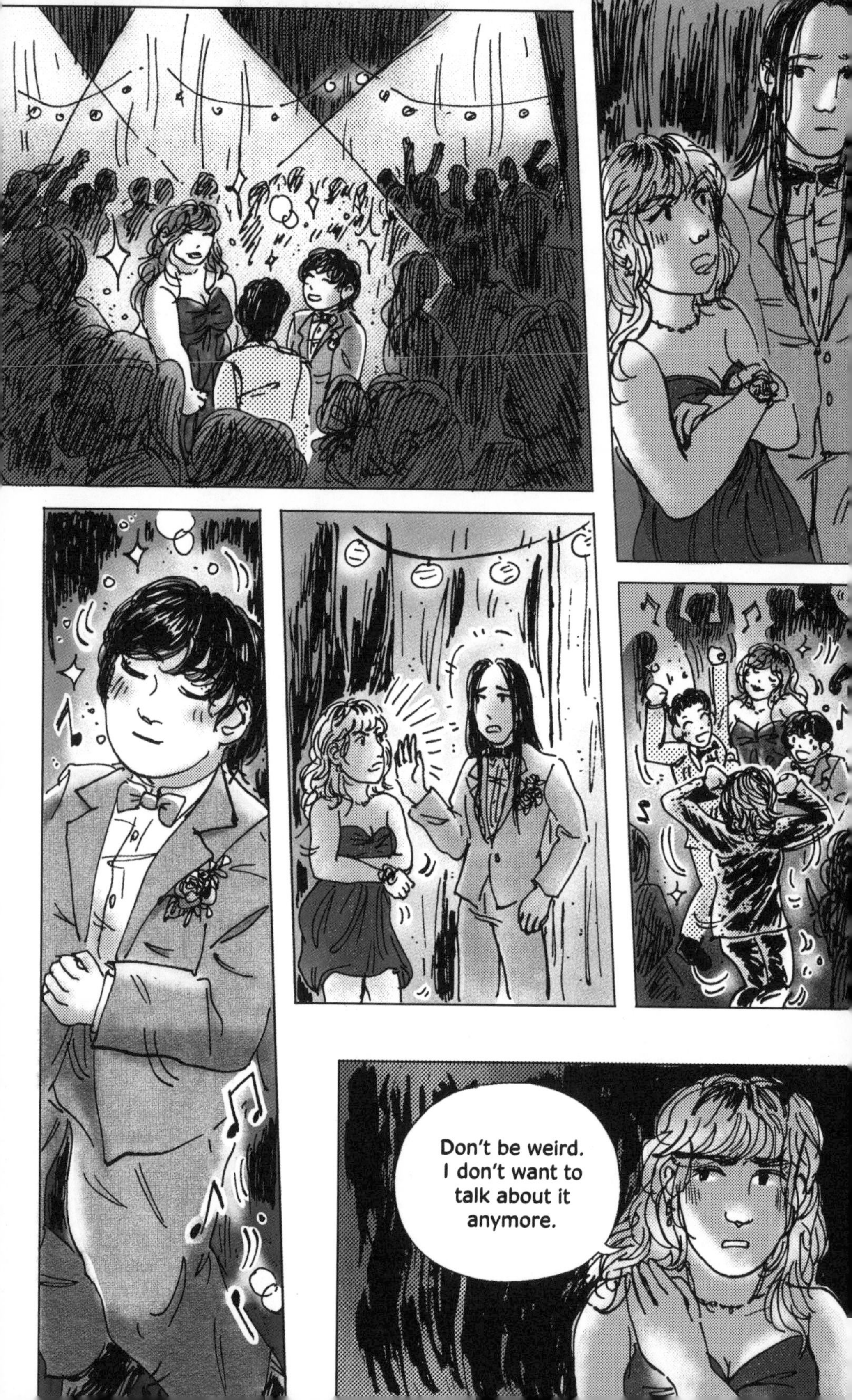
Don't be weird. I don't want to talk about it anymore.

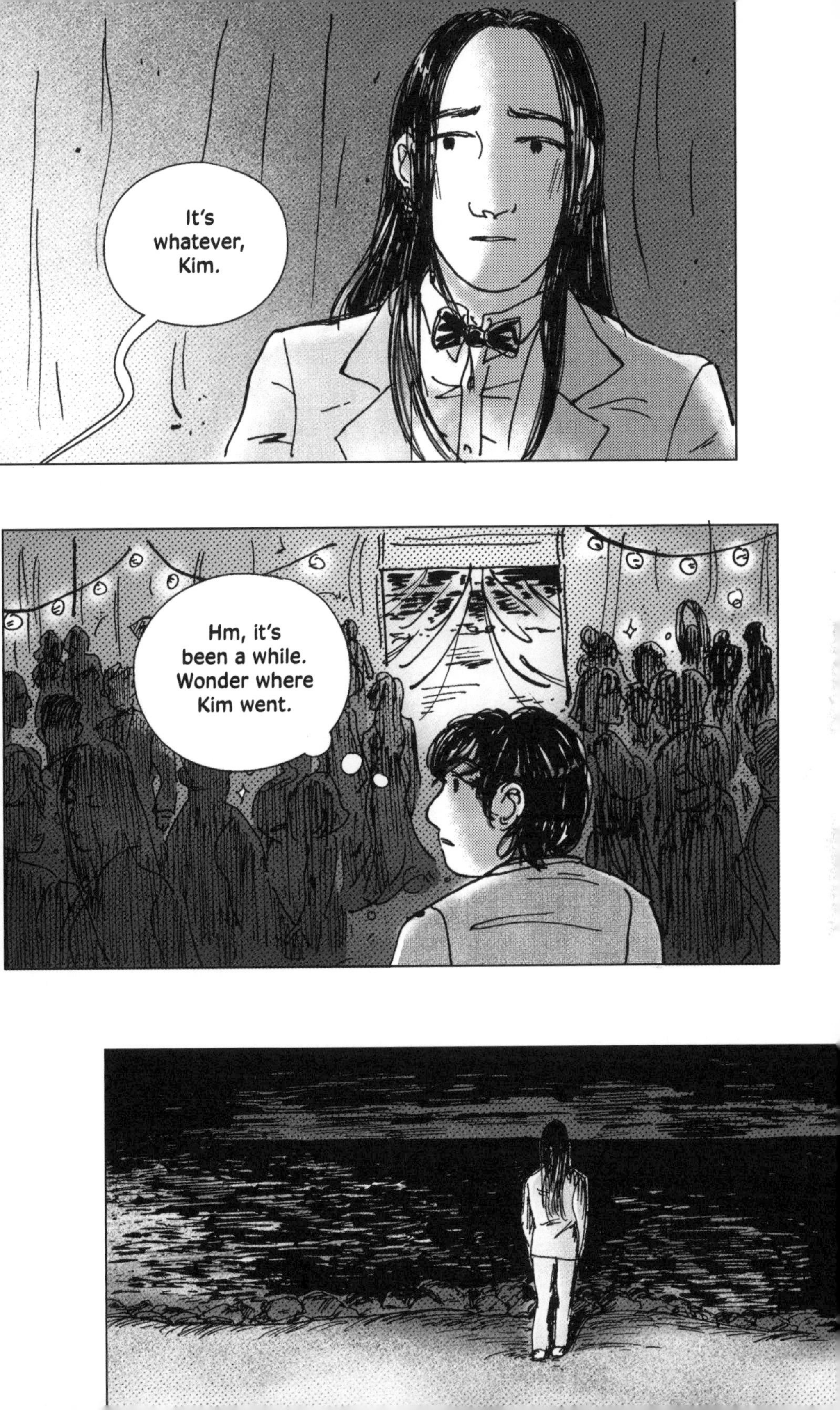

It's whatever, Kim.
Hm, it's been a while. Wonder where Kim went.

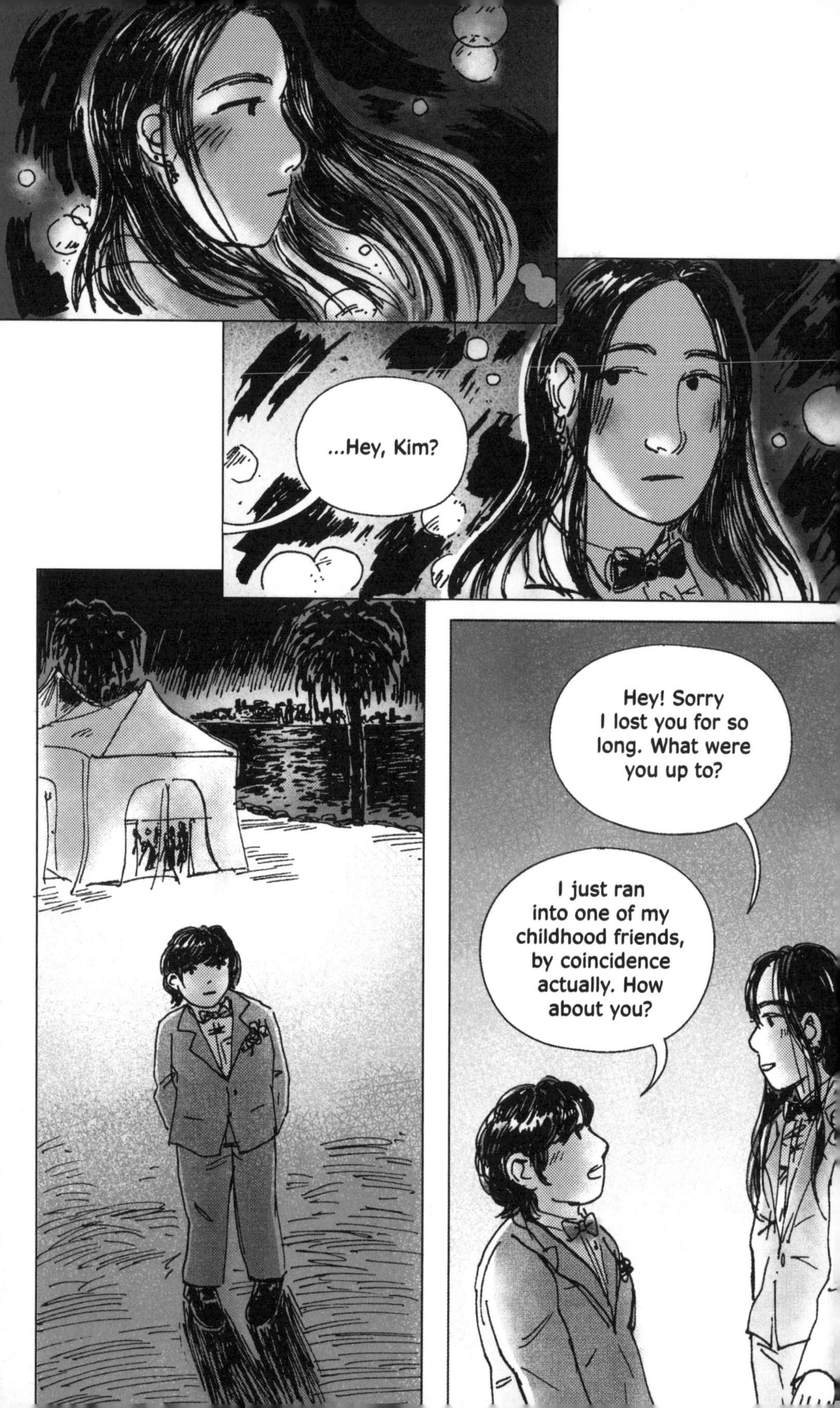
...Hey, Kim?
Hey! Sorry I lost you for so long. What were you up to?
I just ran into one of my childhood friends, by coincidence actually. How about you?

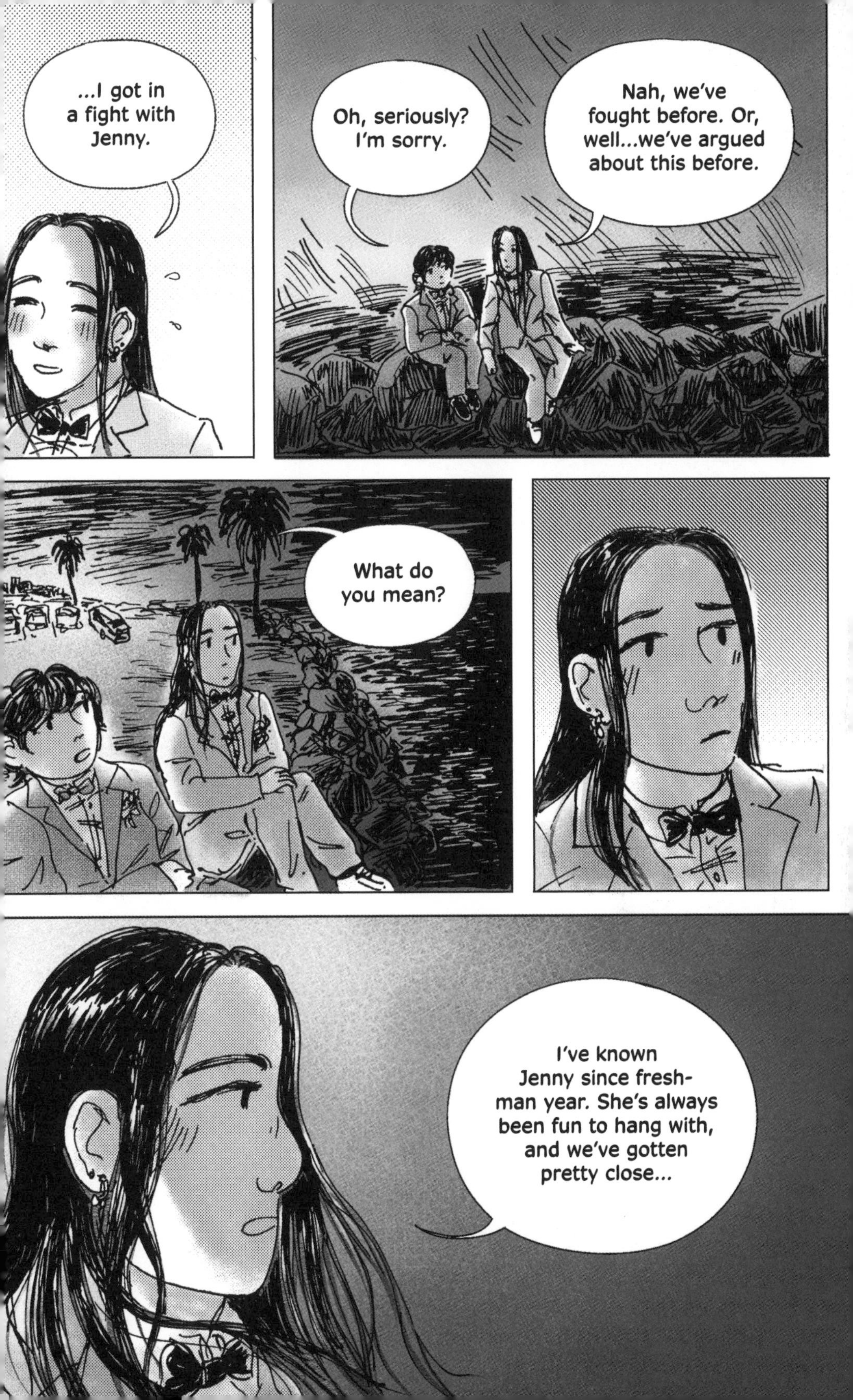
...I got in a fight with Jenny.
Oh, seriously? I'm sorry.
Nah, we've fought before. Or, well...we've argued about this before.
What do you mean?
I've known Jenny since fresh-man year. She's always been fun to hang with, and we've gotten pretty close...

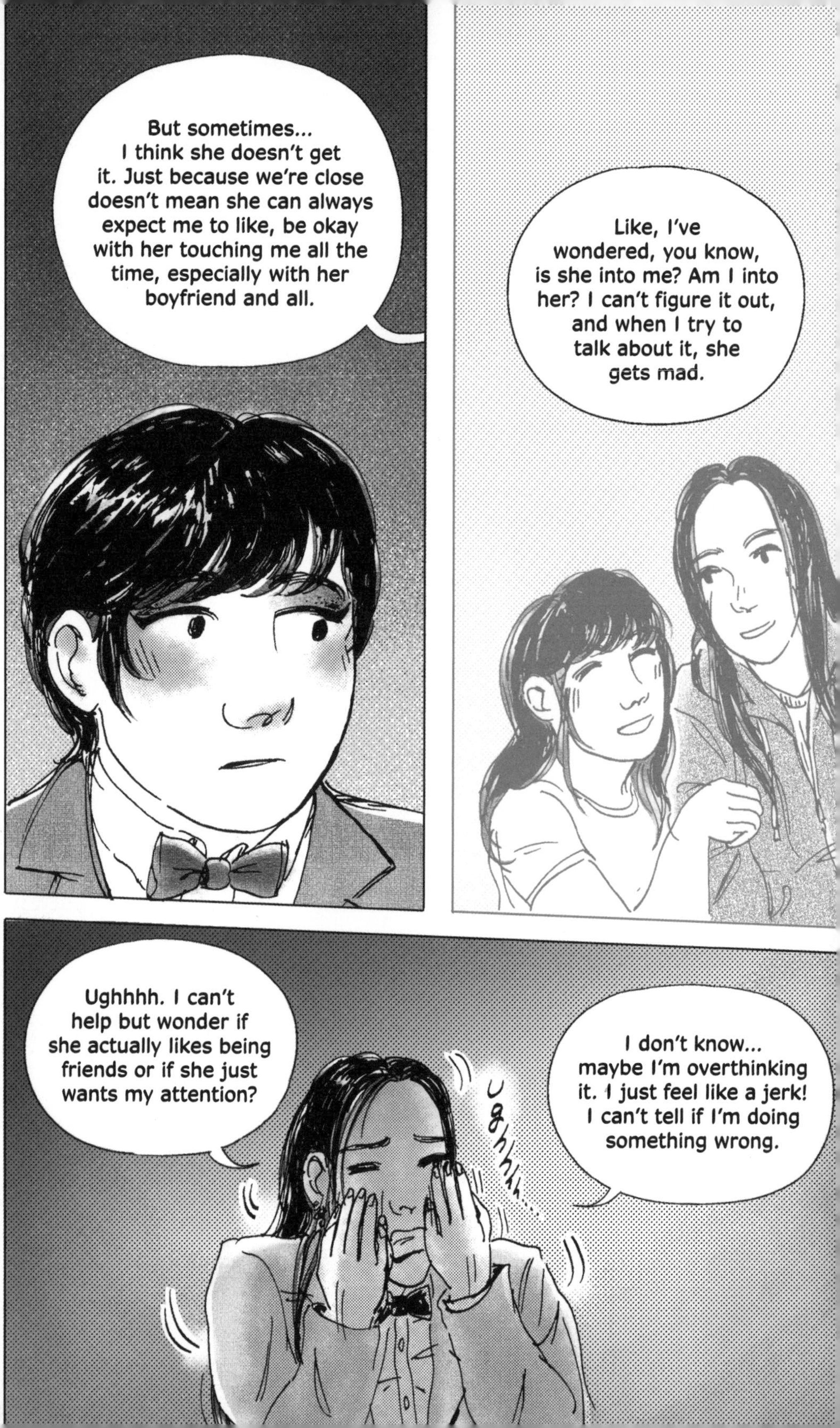
But sometimes... I think she doesn't get it. Just because we're close doesn't mean she can always expect me to like, be okay with her touching me all the time, especially with her boyfriend and all.
Like, I've wondered, you know, is she into me? Am I into her? I can't figure it out, and when I try to talk about it, she gets mad.
Ughhhh. I can't help but wonder if she actually likes being friends or if she just wants my attention?
I don't know... maybe I'm overthinking it. I just feel like a jerk! I can't tell if I'm doing something wrong.

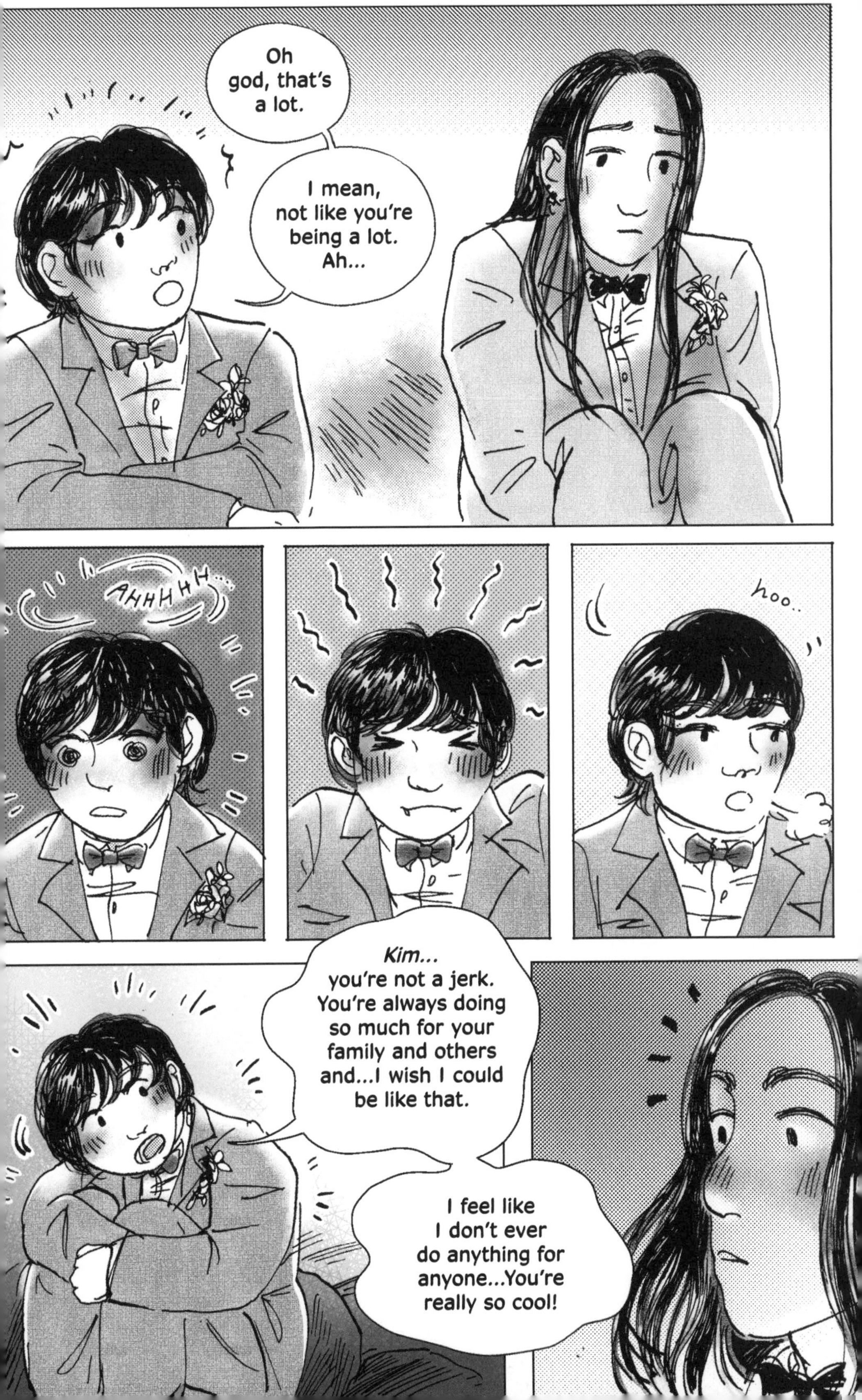
Oh god, that's a lot.
I mean, not like you're being a lot. Ah...
AHHHHH...
hoo..
Kim... you're not a jerk. You're always doing so much for your family and others and...I wish I could be like that.
I feel like I don't ever do anything for anyone...You're really so cool!

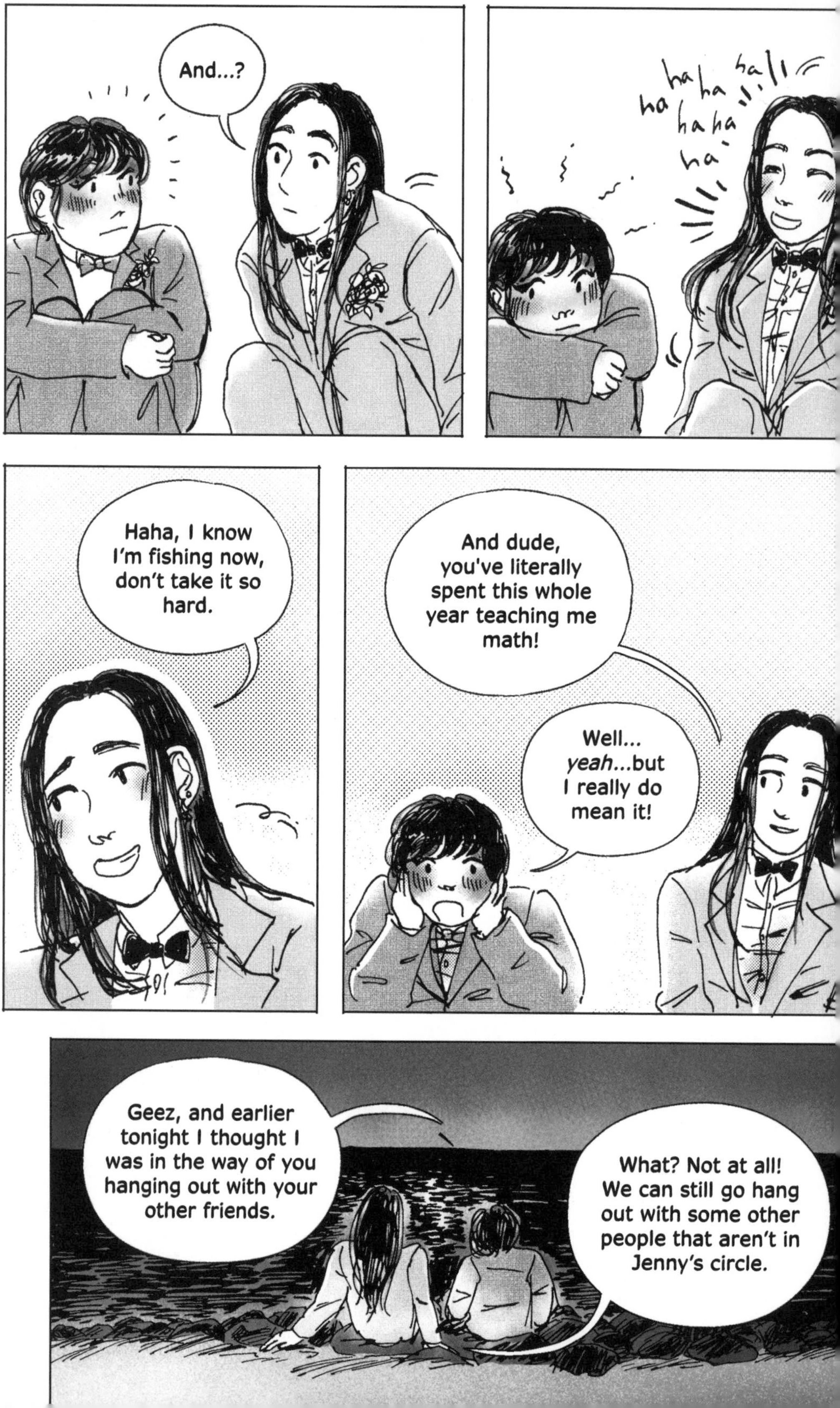
And...?
ha ha ha ha ha ha ha ha!
Haha, I know I'm fishing now, don't take it so hard.
And dude, you've literally spent this whole year teaching me math!
Well... *yeah*...but I really do mean it!
Geez, and earlier tonight I thought I was in the way of you hanging out with your other friends.
What? Not at all! We can still go hang out with some other people that aren't in Jenny's circle.

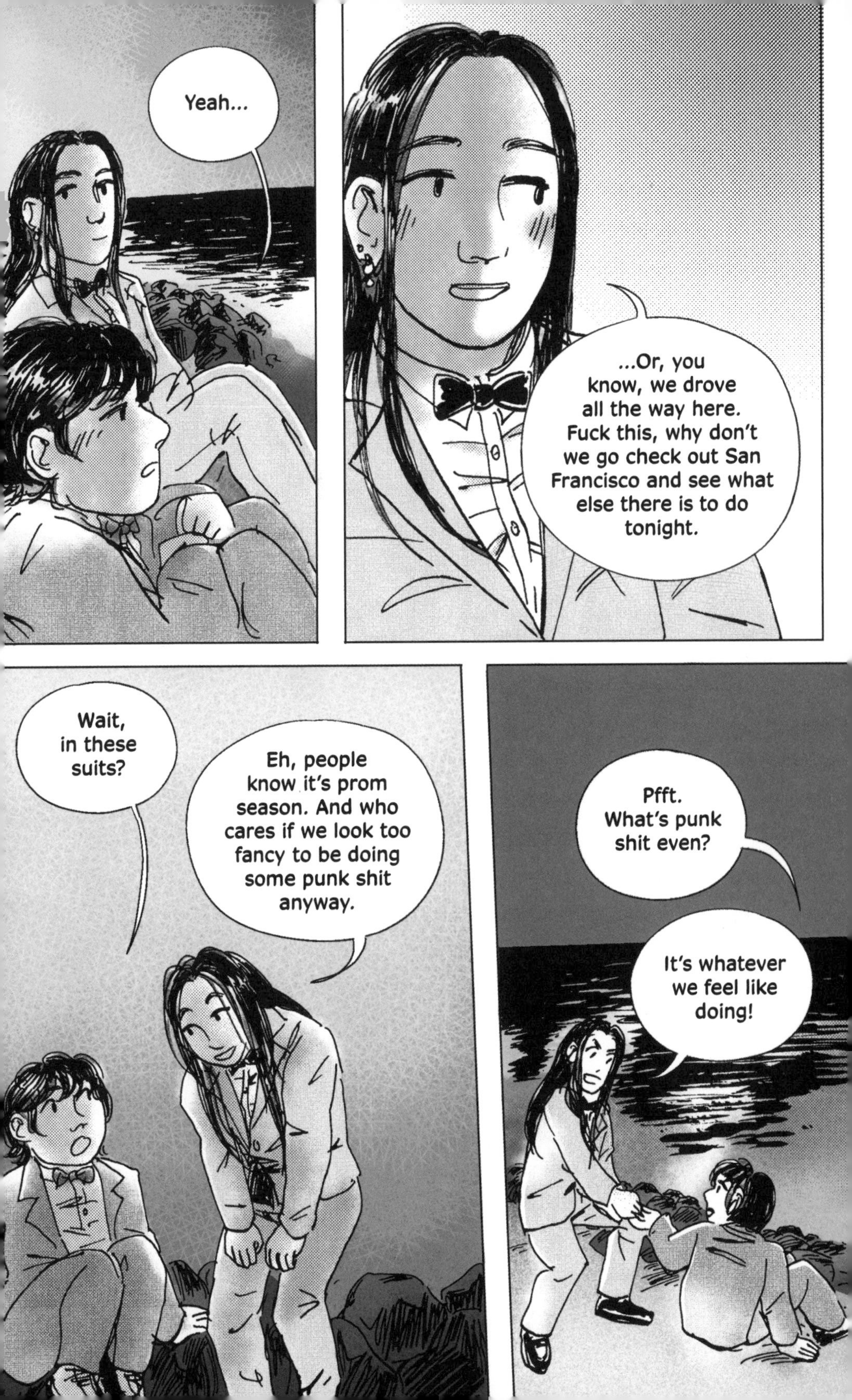
Yeah...
...Or, you know, we drove all the way here. Fuck this, why don't we go check out San Francisco and see what else there is to do tonight.
Wait, in these suits?
Eh, people know it's prom season. And who cares if we look too fancy to be doing some punk shit anyway.
Pfft. What's punk shit even?
It's whatever we feel like doing!

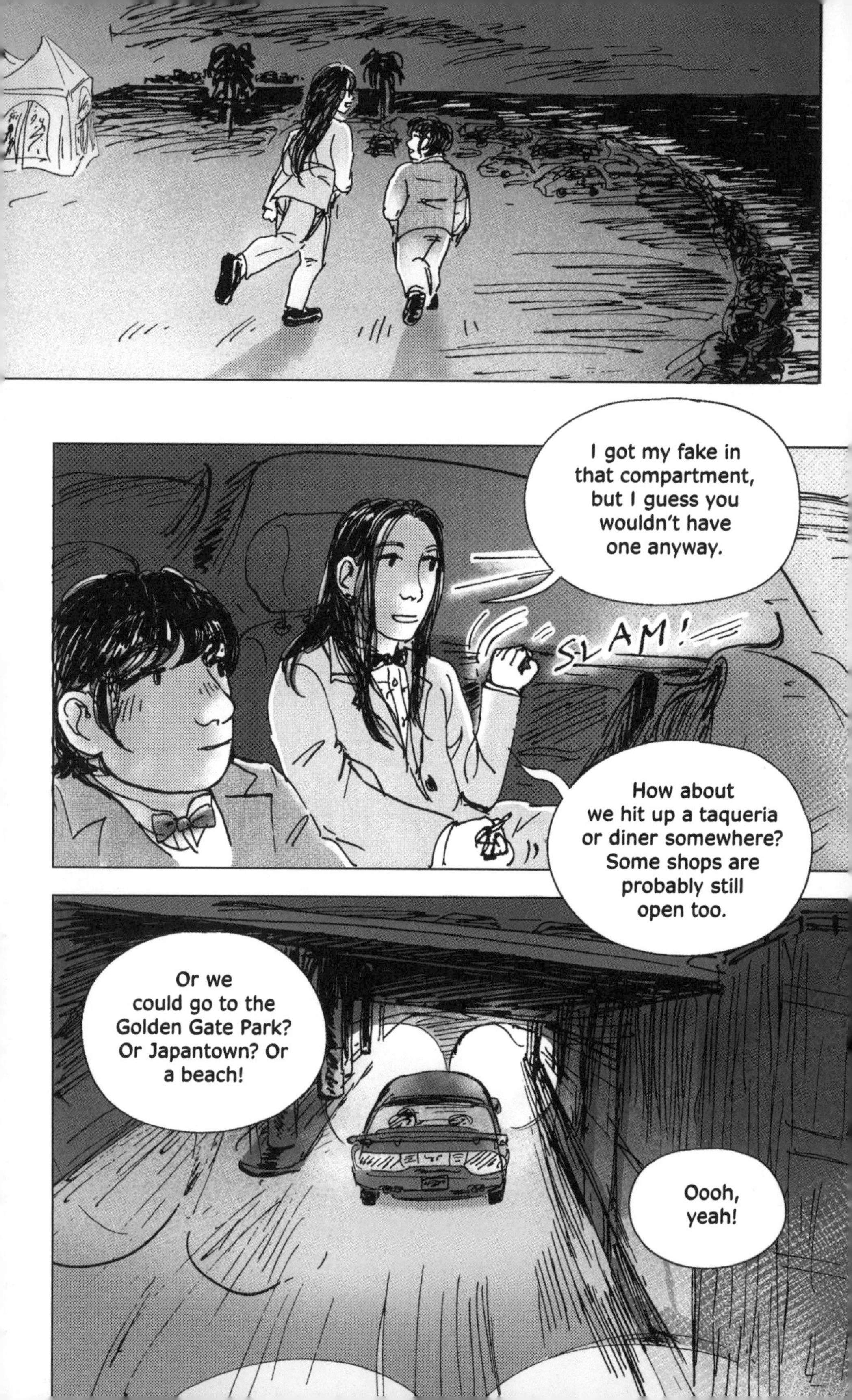

I got my fake in that compartment, but I guess you wouldn't have one anyway.
SLAM!
How about we hit up a taqueria or diner somewhere? Some shops are probably still open too.
Or we could go to the Golden Gate Park? Or Japantown? Or a beach!
Oooh, yeah!

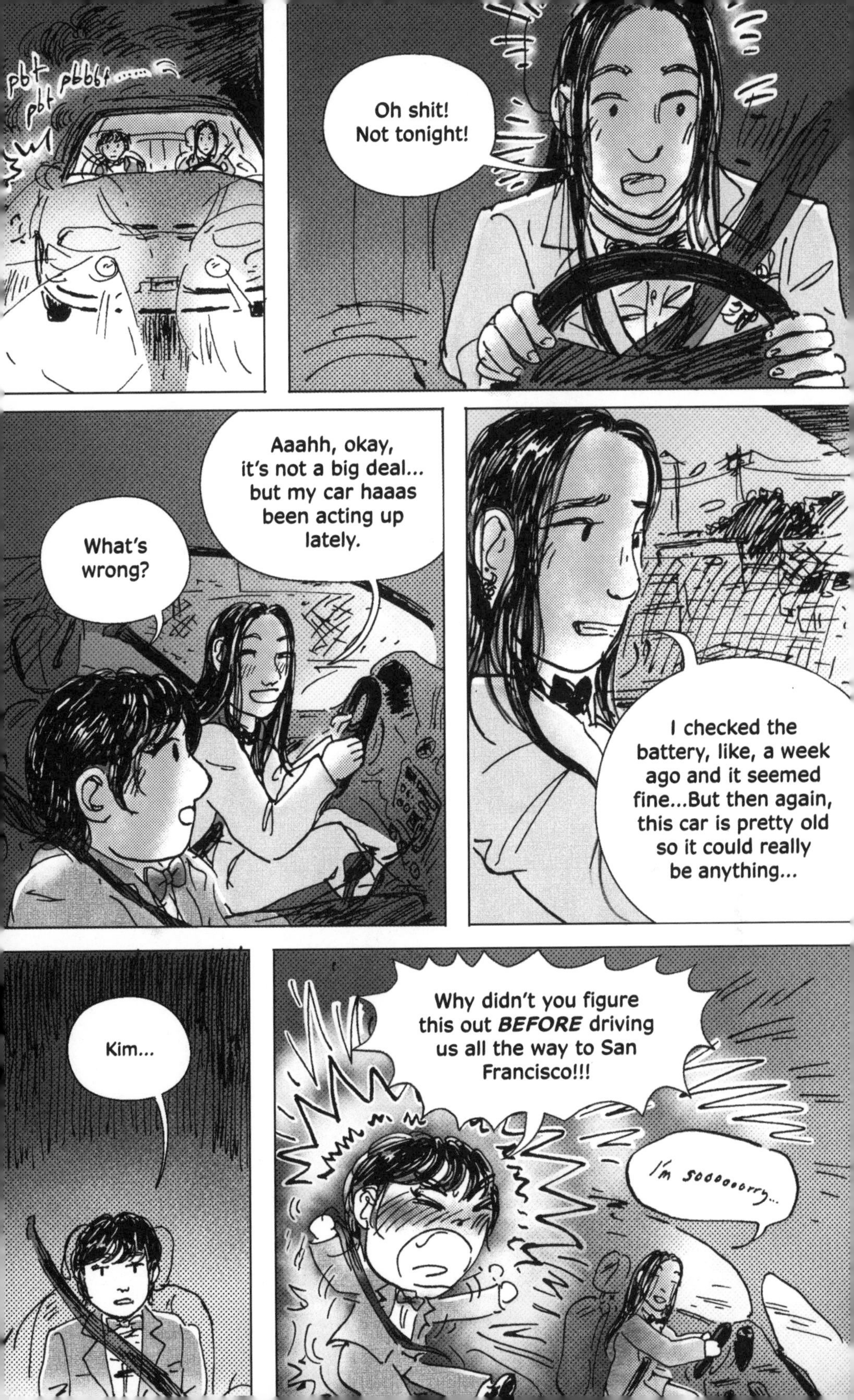
pbt pbt pbbbt.....
Oh shit! Not tonight!
What's wrong?
Aaahh, okay, it's not a big deal... but my car haaas been acting up lately.
I checked the battery, like, a week ago and it seemed fine...But then again, this car is pretty old so it could really be anything...
Kim...
Why didn't you figure this out *BEFORE* driving us all the way to San Francisco!!!
I'm soooooorry...

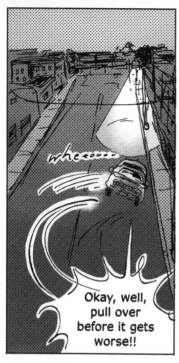

whe<ooo>

Okay, well, pull over before it gets worse!!

Man. Okay...let's see if Dylan can help us out.

Brrriiiiing Brrrriiiing

rrriiiiing rrriiiiing

pff...

HA HA HA HA HA HA HA HA

What's so funny?!

Hahahaha, I don't know!! This night has been so unpredictable.

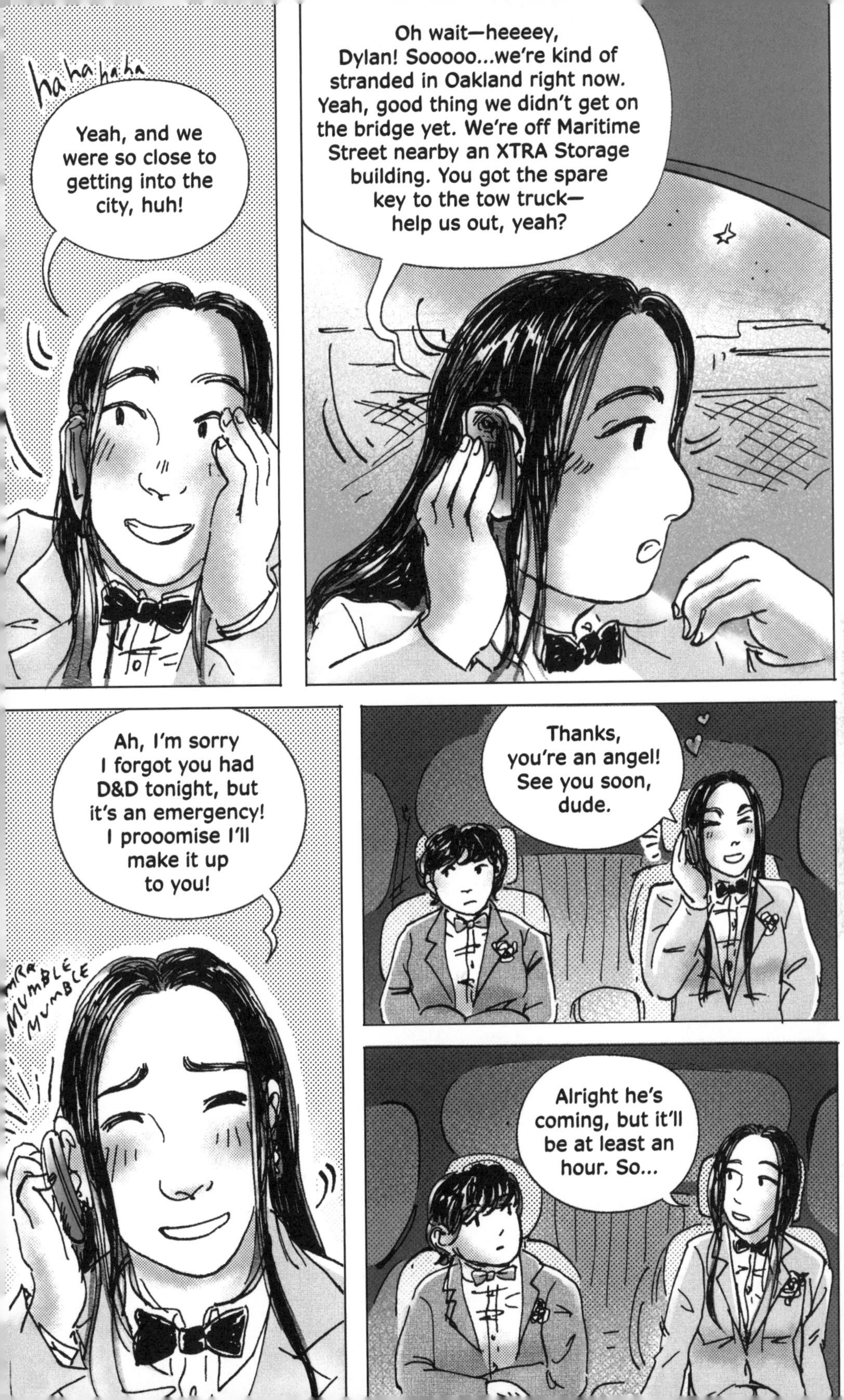
ha ha ha ha
Yeah, and we were so close to getting into the city, huh!
Oh wait—heeeey, Dylan! Sooooo...we're kind of stranded in Oakland right now. Yeah, good thing we didn't get on the bridge yet. We're off Maritime Street nearby an XTRA Storage building. You got the spare key to the tow truck—help us out, yeah?
Ah, I'm sorry I forgot you had D&D tonight, but it's an emergency! I prooomise I'll make it up to you!
MUMBLE MUMBLE
Thanks, you're an angel! See you soon, dude.
Alright he's coming, but it'll be at least an hour. So...

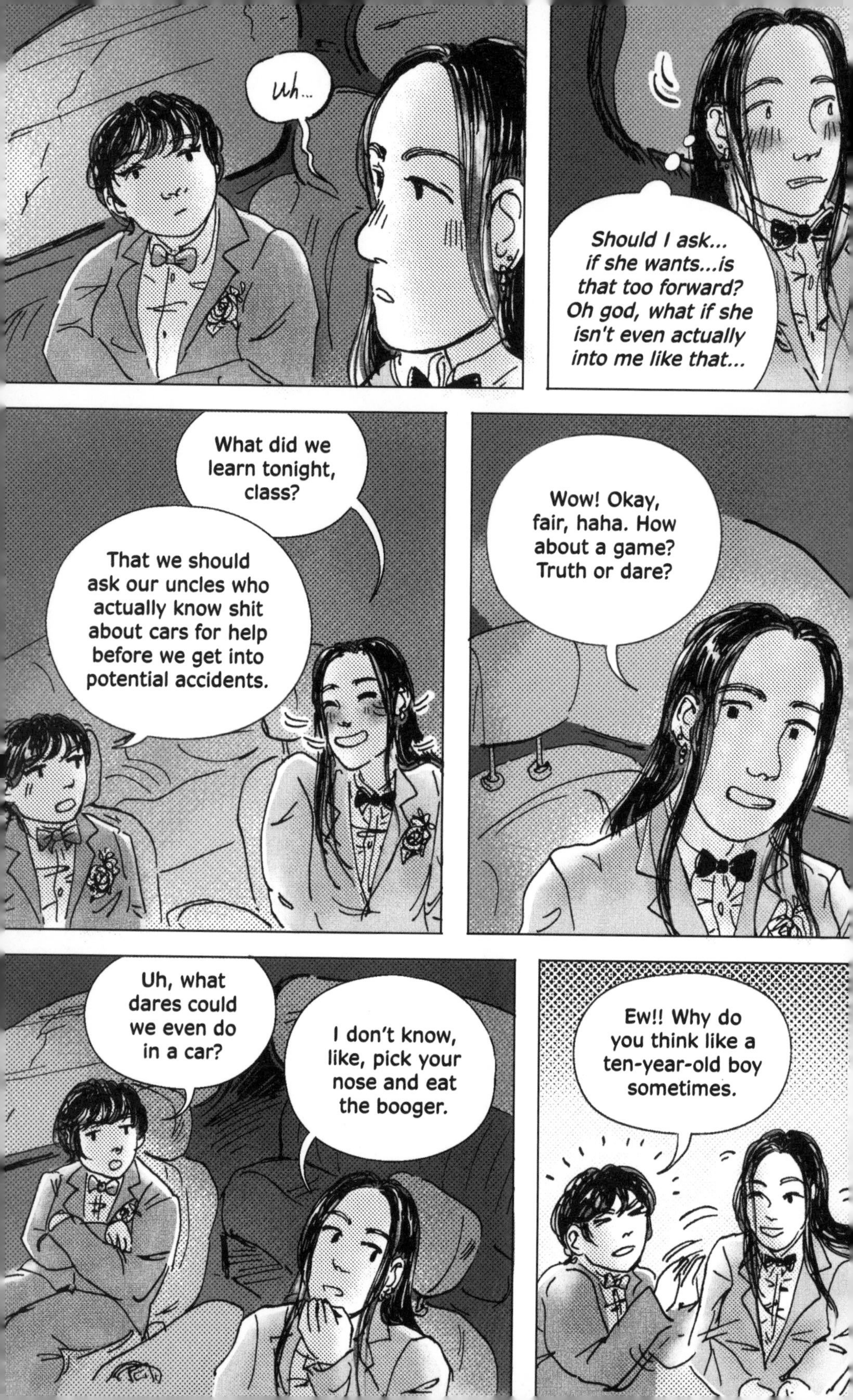
Uh...
Should I ask... if she wants...is that too forward? Oh god, what if she isn't even actually into me like that...
What did we learn tonight, class?
That we should ask our uncles who actually know shit about cars for help before we get into potential accidents.
Wow! Okay, fair, haha. How about a game? Truth or dare?
Uh, what dares could we even do in a car?
I don't know, like, pick your nose and eat the booger.
Ew!! Why do you think like a ten-year-old boy sometimes.

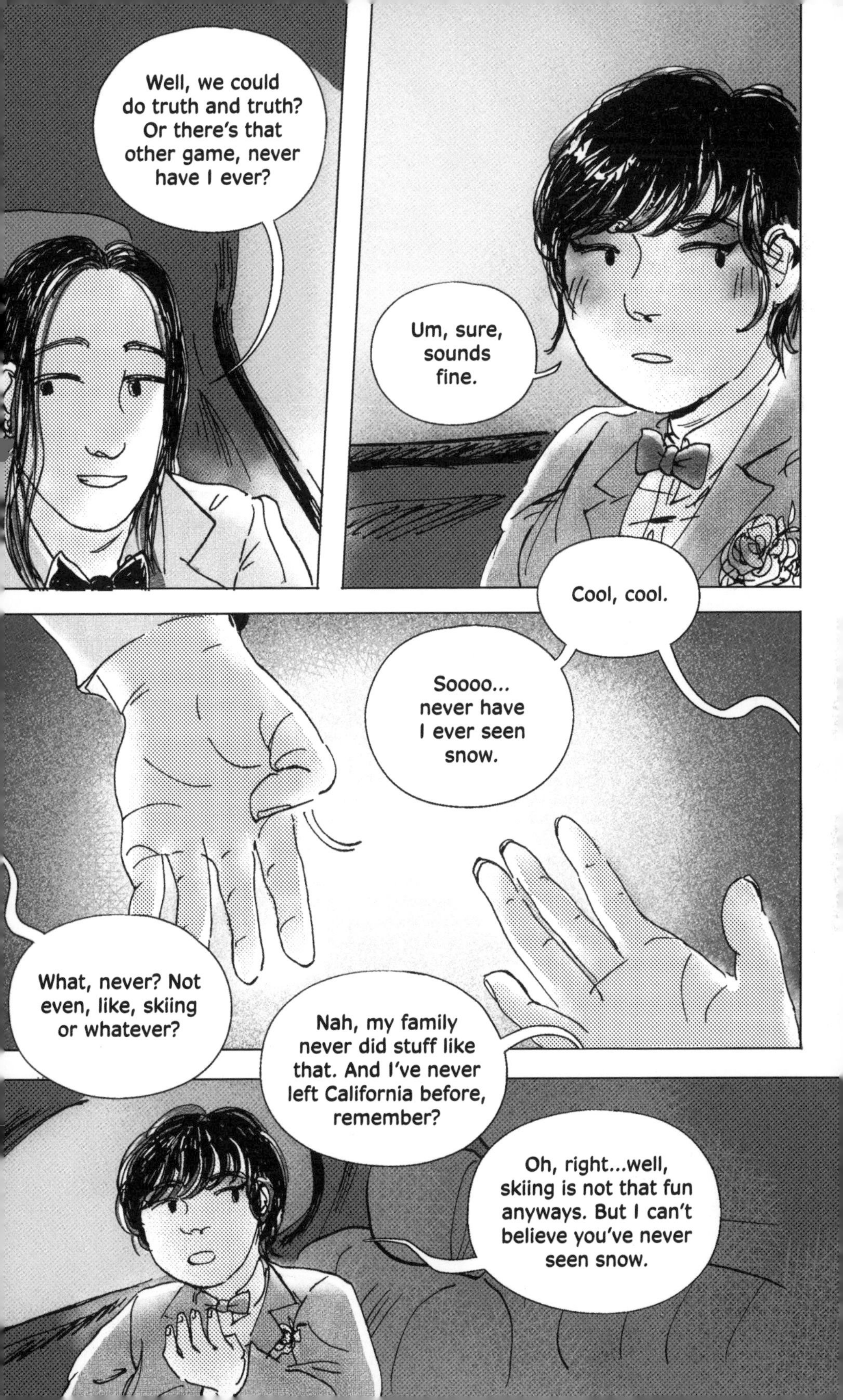

Well, we could do truth and truth? Or there's that other game, never have I ever?
Um, sure, sounds fine.
Cool, cool.
Soooo... never have I ever seen snow.
What, never? Not even, like, skiing or whatever?
Nah, my family never did stuff like that. And I've never left California before, remember?
Oh, right...well, skiing is not that fun anyways. But I can't believe you've never seen snow.

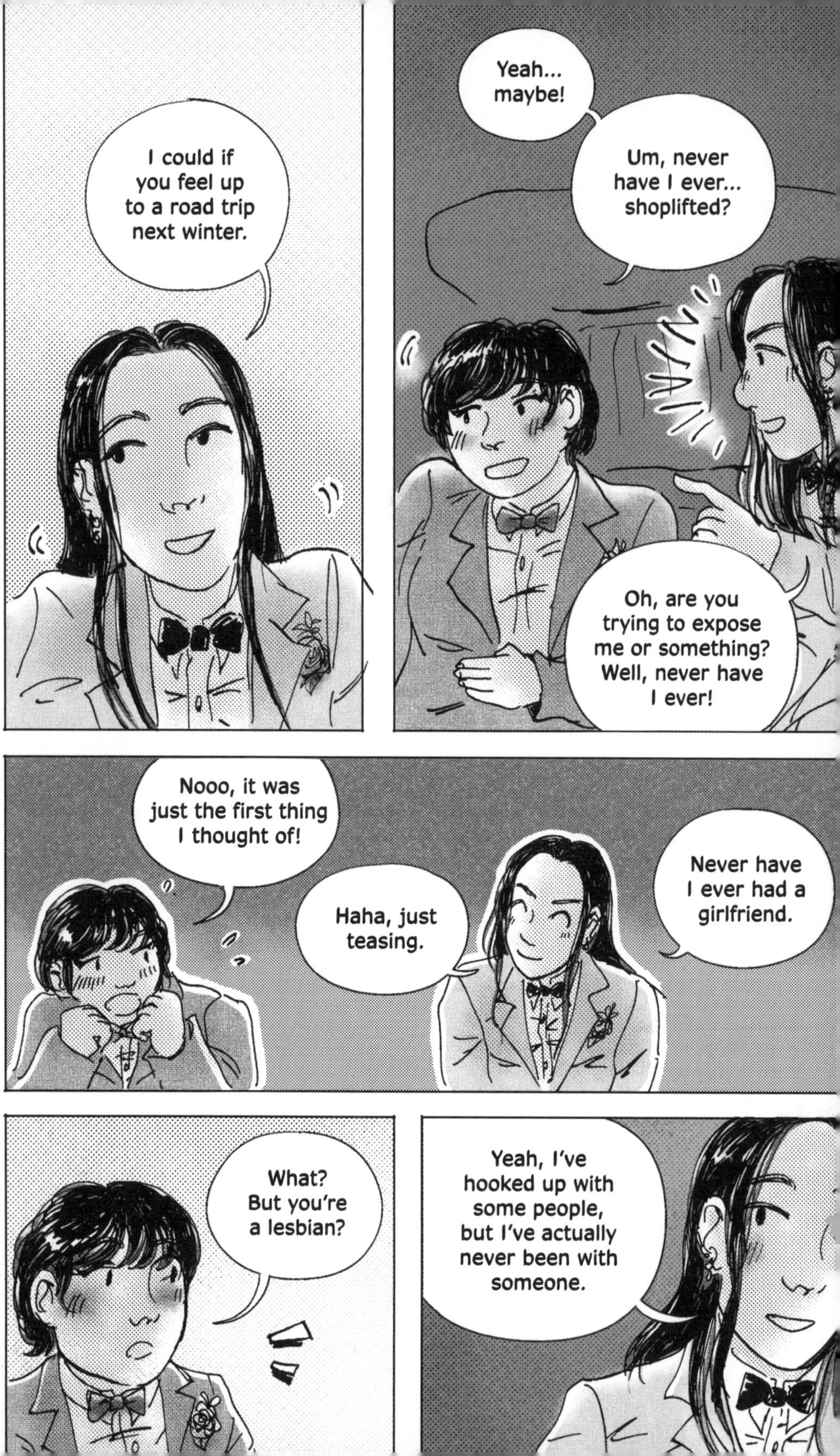
I could if you feel up to a road trip next winter.
Yeah... maybe!
Um, never have I ever... shoplifted?
Oh, are you trying to expose me or something? Well, never have I ever!
Nooo, it was just the first thing I thought of!
Haha, just teasing.
Never have I ever had a girlfriend.
What? But you're a lesbian?
Yeah, I've hooked up with some people, but I've actually never been with someone.

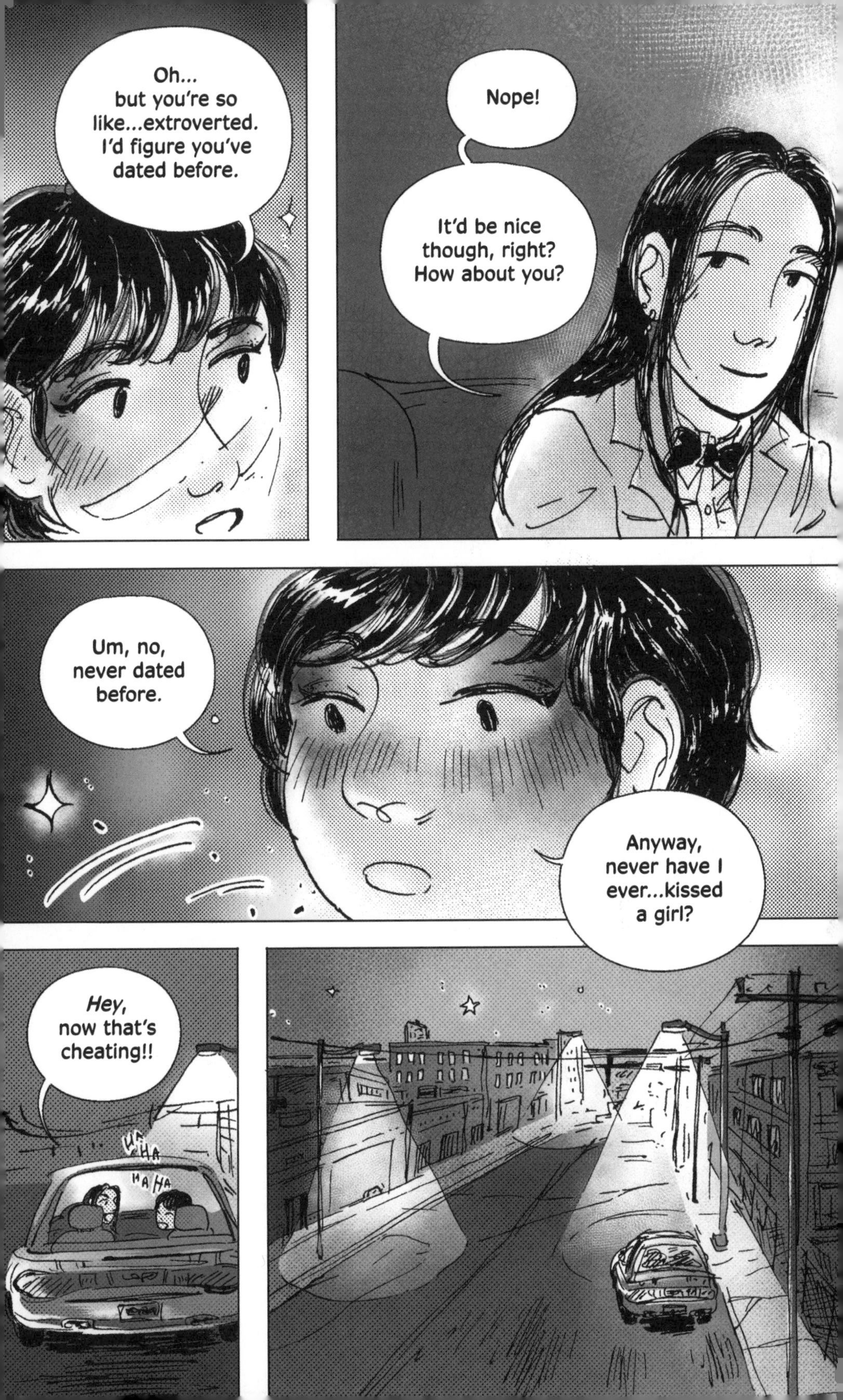
Oh... but you're so like...extroverted. I'd figure you've dated before.
Nope!
It'd be nice though, right? How about you?
Um, no, never dated before.
Anyway, never have I ever...kissed a girl?
Hey, now that's cheating!!
HA HA
HA HA

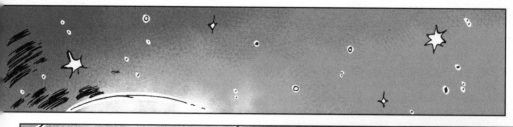

Dylan! Our hero!

Yes, yes, I'm here. Kim, you're gonna have to get out and help me after I pull up in front of you.

You got it.

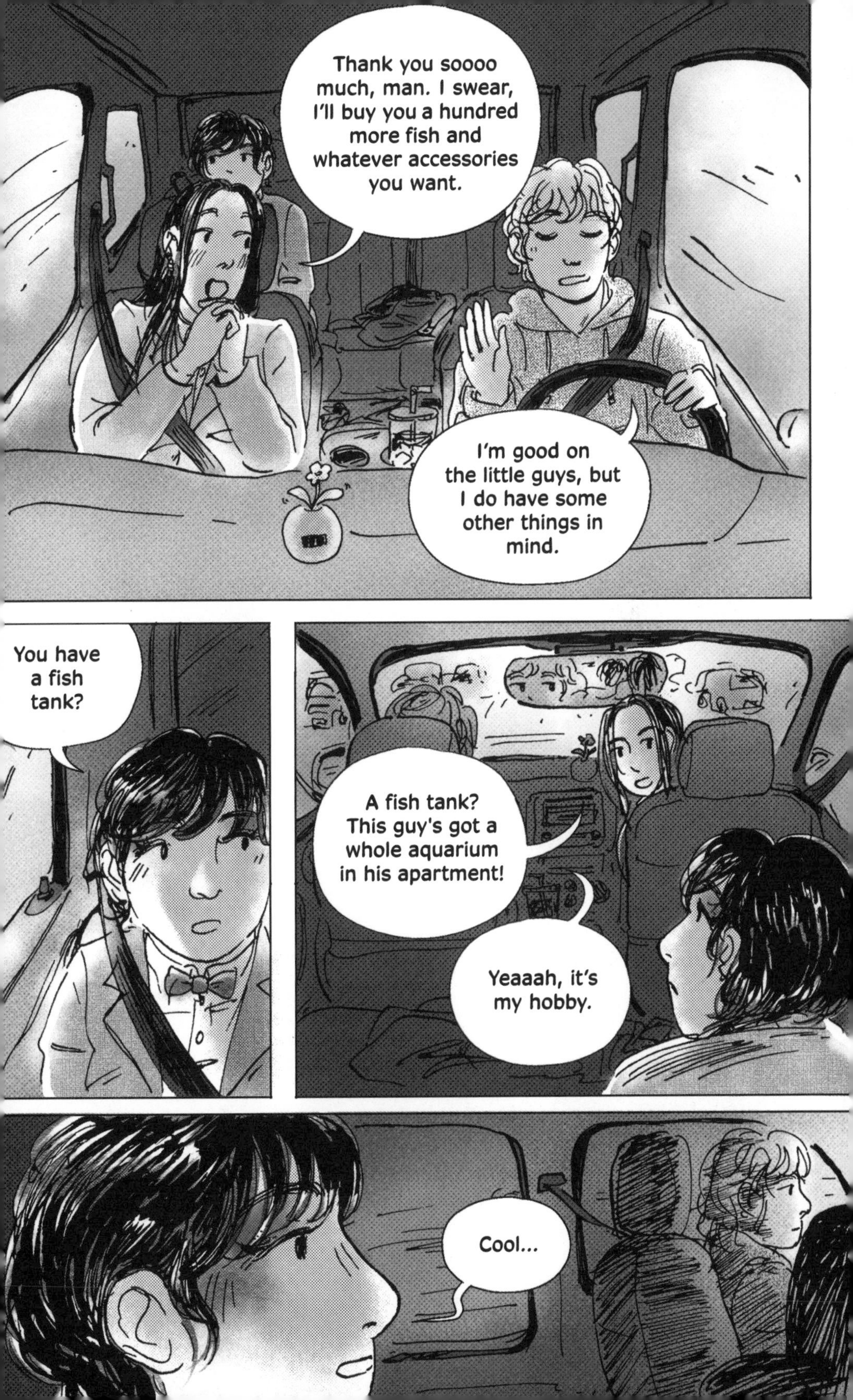

Thank you soooo much, man. I swear, I'll buy you a hundred more fish and whatever accessories you want.
I'm good on the little guys, but I do have some other things in mind.
You have a fish tank?
A fish tank? This guy's got a whole aquarium in his apartment!
Yeaaah, it's my hobby.
Cool...

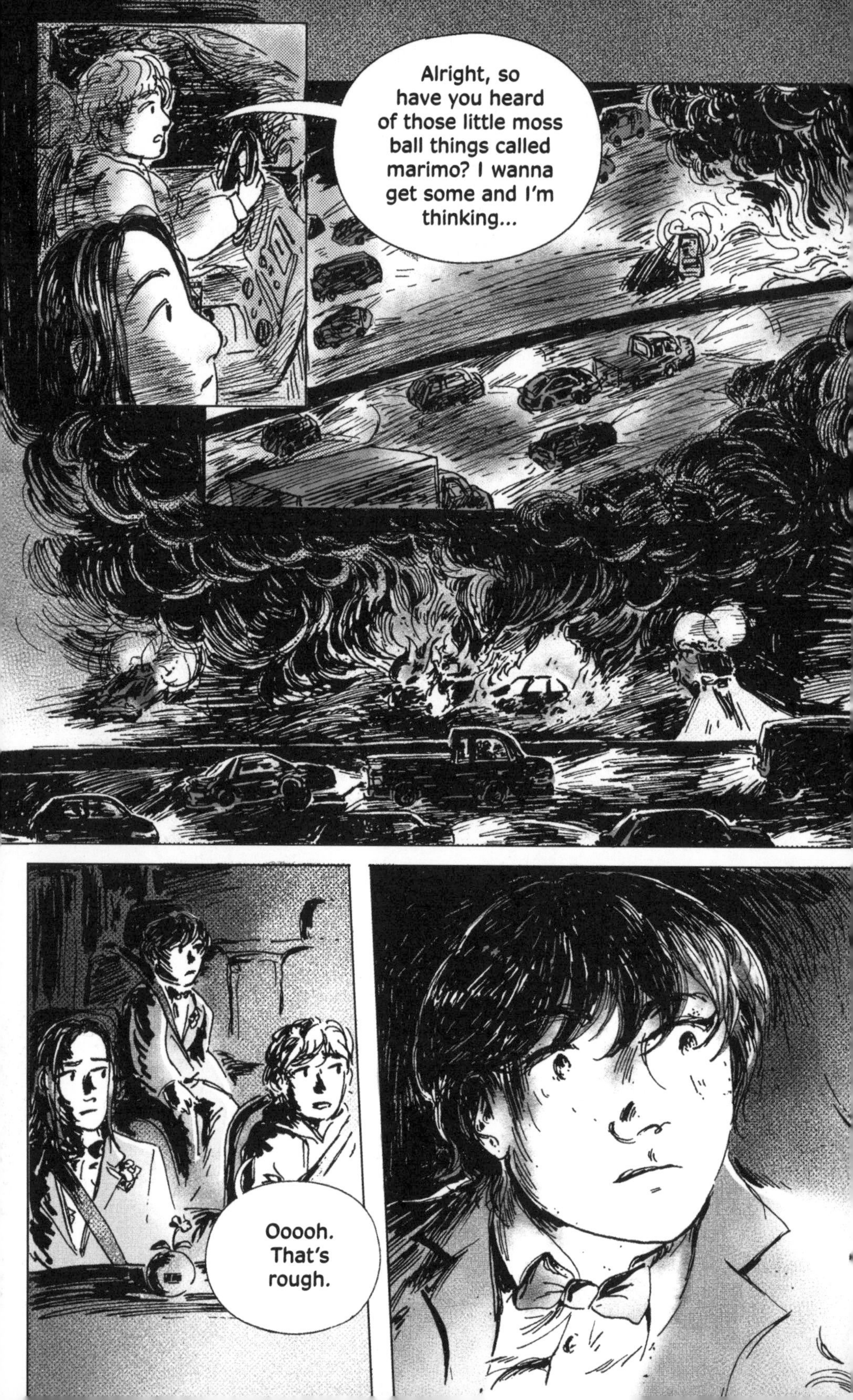
Alright, so have you heard of those little moss ball things called marimo? I wanna get some and I'm thinking...
Ooooh. That's rough.

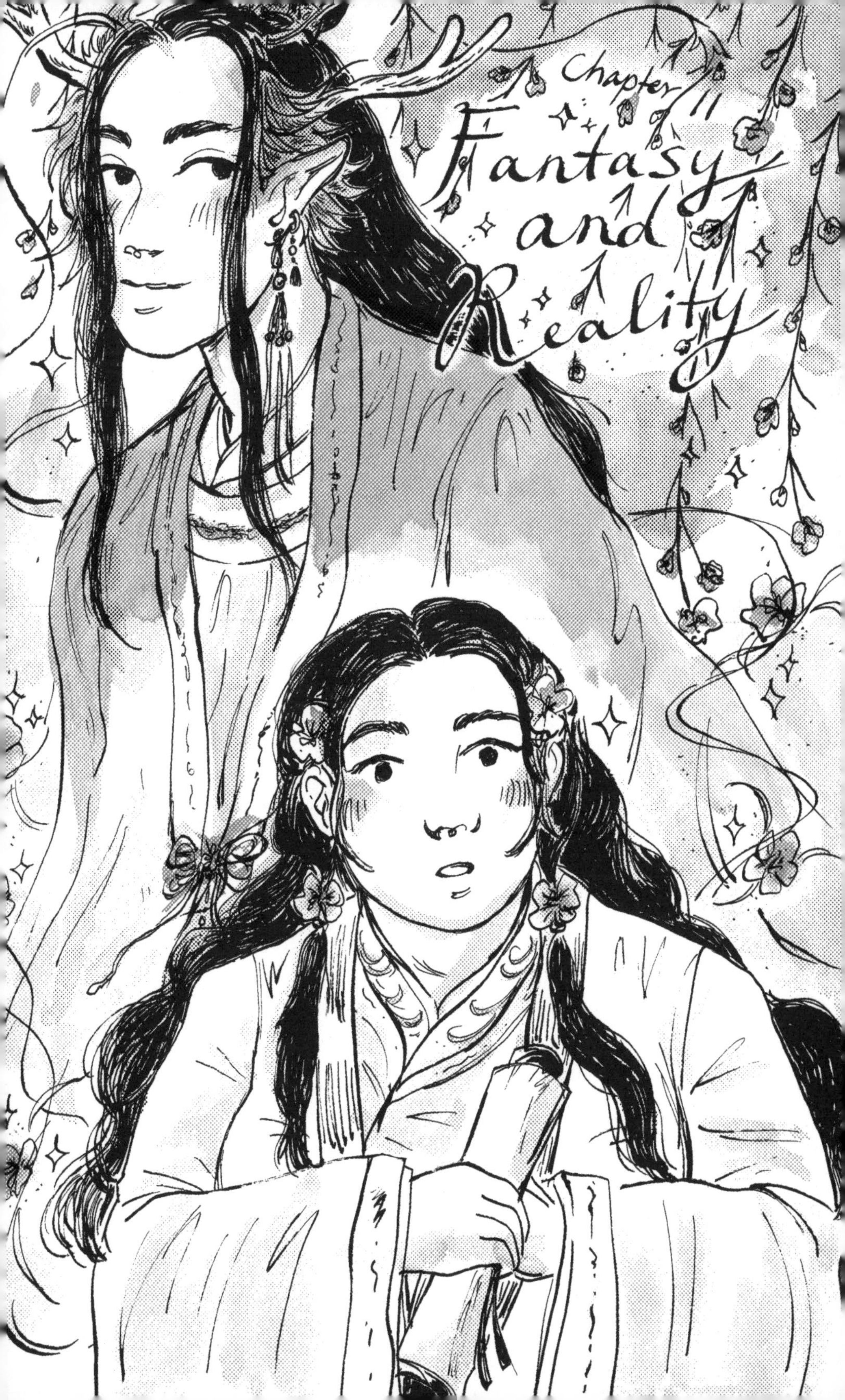
Chapter
Fantasy
and
Reality

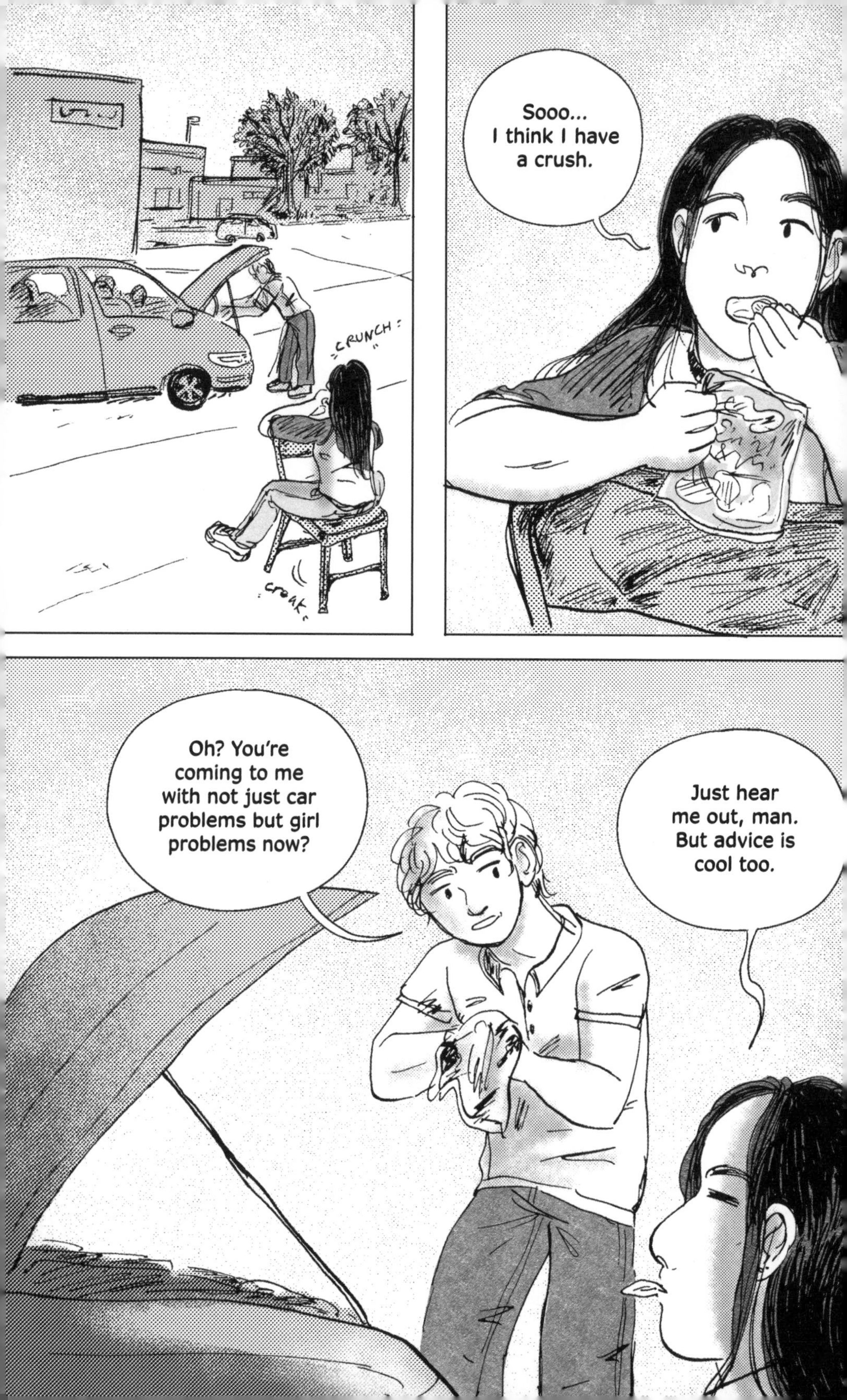
CRUNCH
croak
Sooo... I think I have a crush.
Oh? You're coming to me with not just car problems but girl problems now?
Just hear me out, man. But advice is cool too.

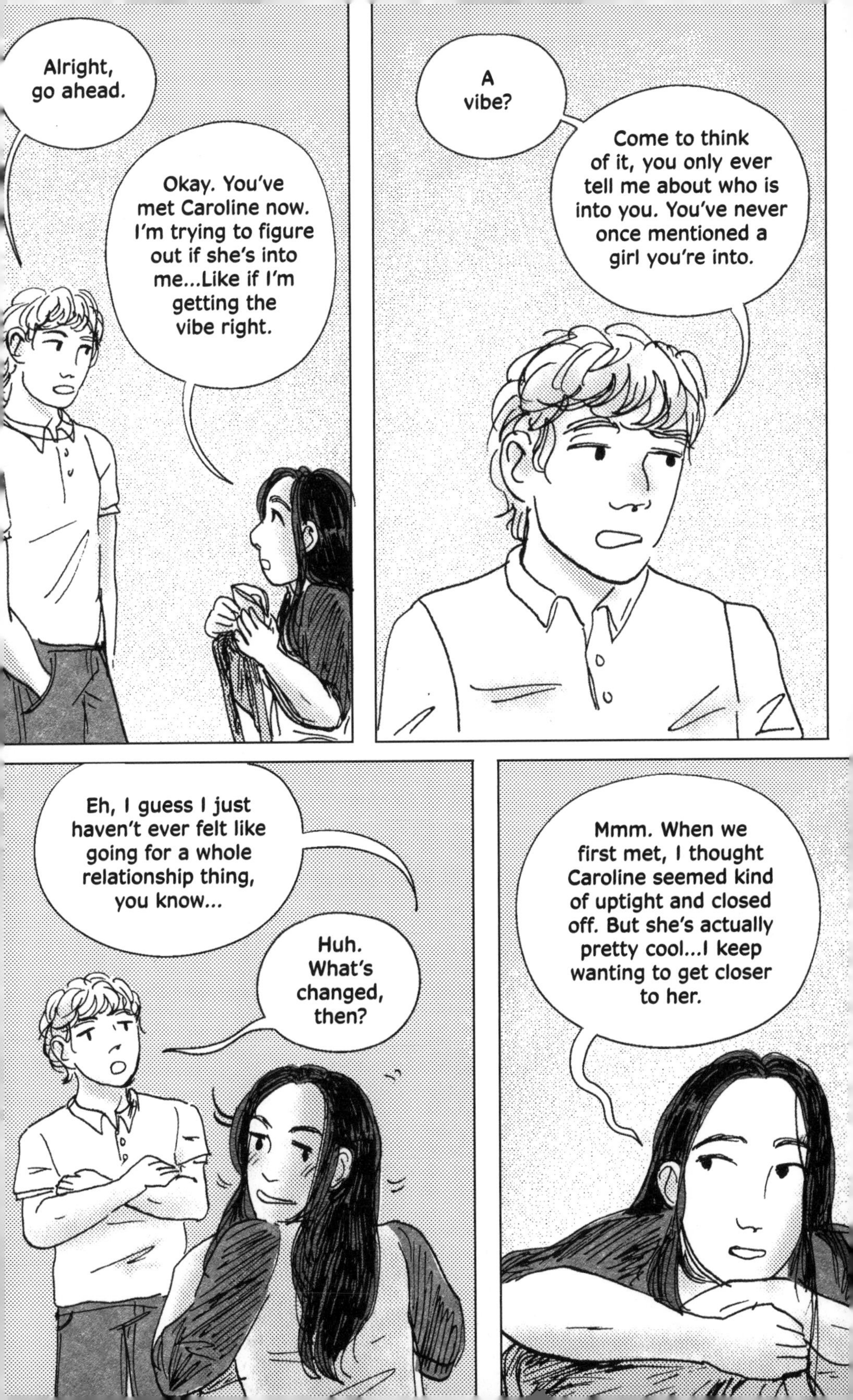
Alright, go ahead.
Okay. You've met Caroline now. I'm trying to figure out if she's into me...Like if I'm getting the vibe right.
A vibe?
Come to think of it, you only ever tell me about who is into you. You've never once mentioned a girl you're into.
Eh, I guess I just haven't ever felt like going for a whole relationship thing, you know...
Huh. What's changed, then?
Mmm. When we first met, I thought Caroline seemed kind of uptight and closed off. But she's actually pretty cool...I keep wanting to get closer to her.

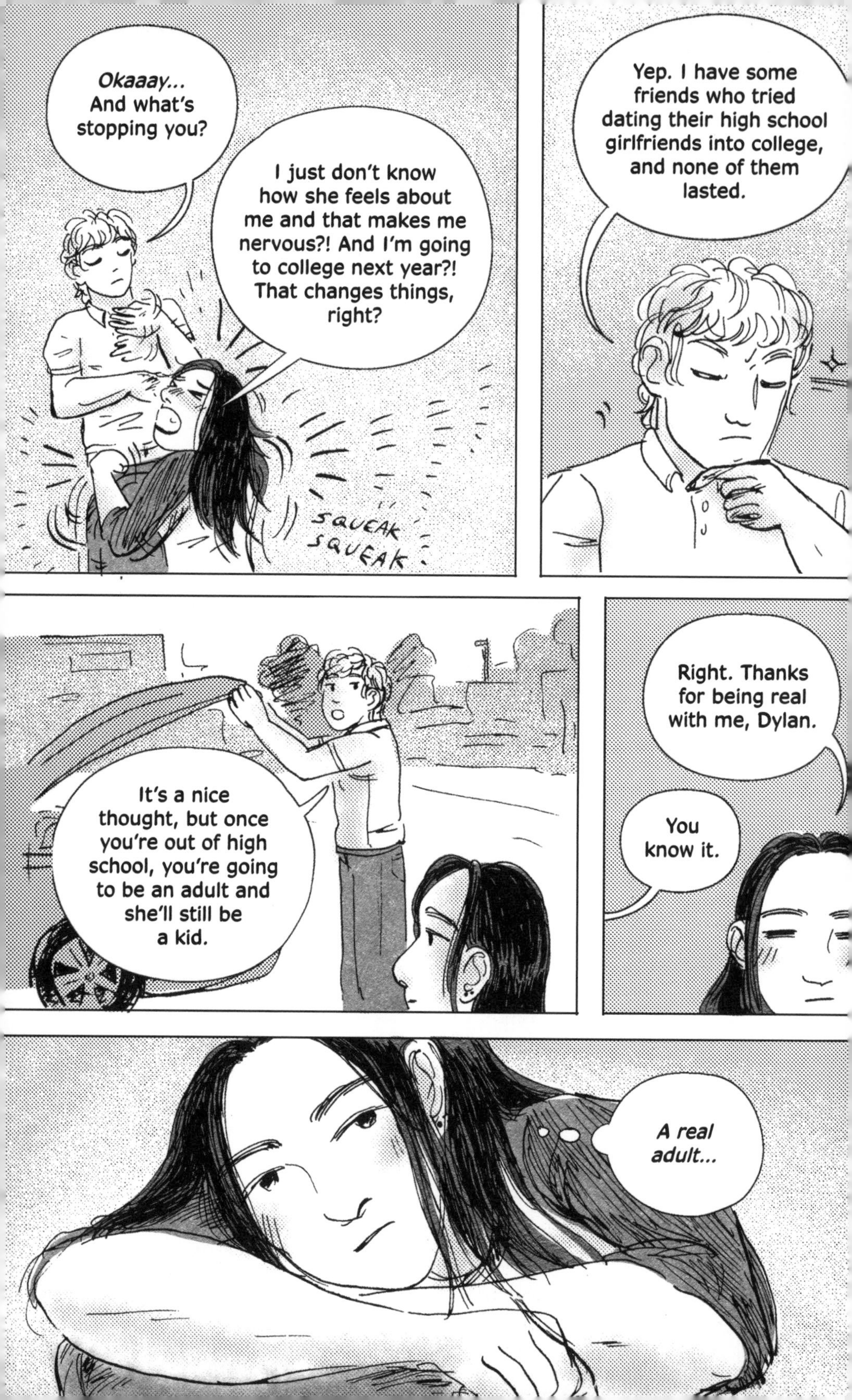
Okaaay... And what's stopping you?
I just don't know how she feels about me and that makes me nervous?! And I'm going to college next year?! That changes things, right?
SQUEAK SQUEAK
Yep. I have some friends who tried dating their high school girlfriends into college, and none of them lasted.
It's a nice thought, but once you're out of high school, you're going to be an adult and she'll still be a kid.
Right. Thanks for being real with me, Dylan.
You know it.
A real adult...

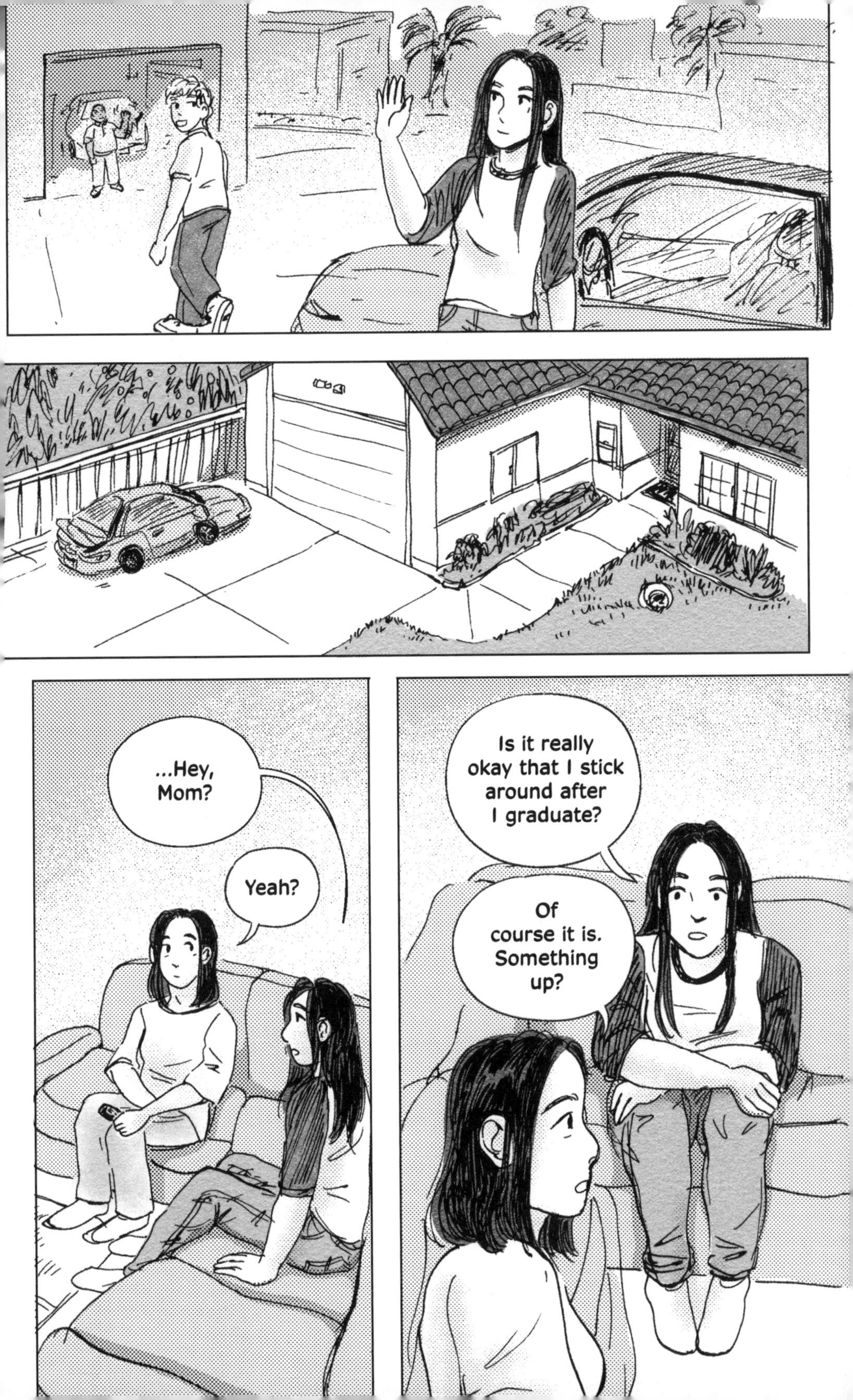
...Hey, Mom?
Yeah?
Is it really okay that I stick around after I graduate?
Of course it is. Something up?

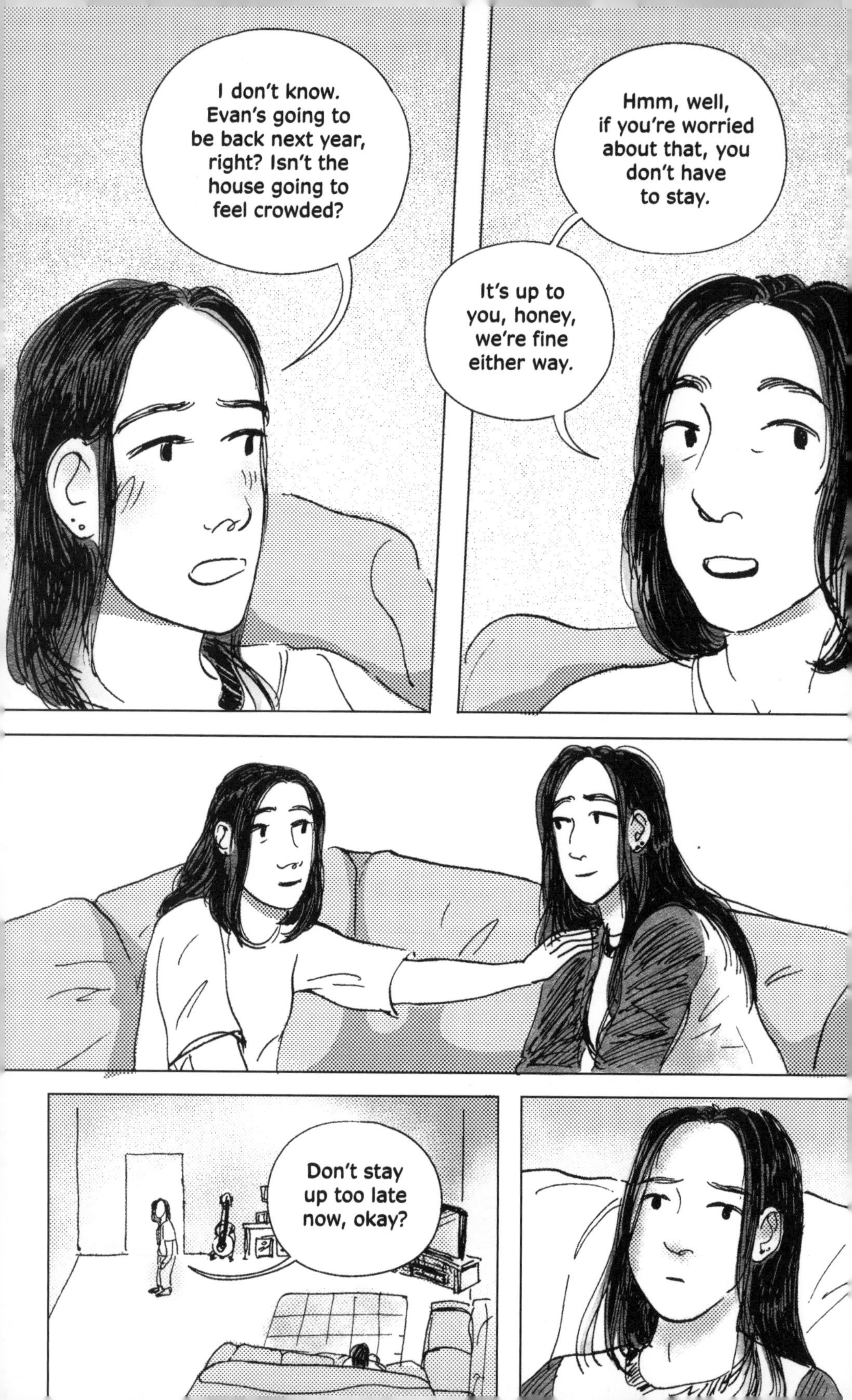
I don't know. Evan's going to be back next year, right? Isn't the house going to feel crowded?
Hmm, well, if you're worried about that, you don't have to stay.
It's up to you, honey, we're fine either way.
Don't stay up too late now, okay?

BRIIIIIIIIIIIIING!!!!!
Alright, I will be grading these tonight and posting final results on the online portal.
See you in class next Monday and congrats on finishing your final exam!
KIM: hey carolineee, I'm doooone!
CAROLINE: Wow, congrats! How do you feel?
KIM: pretty good! hope I passed or else, well, off to summer school I goooo.

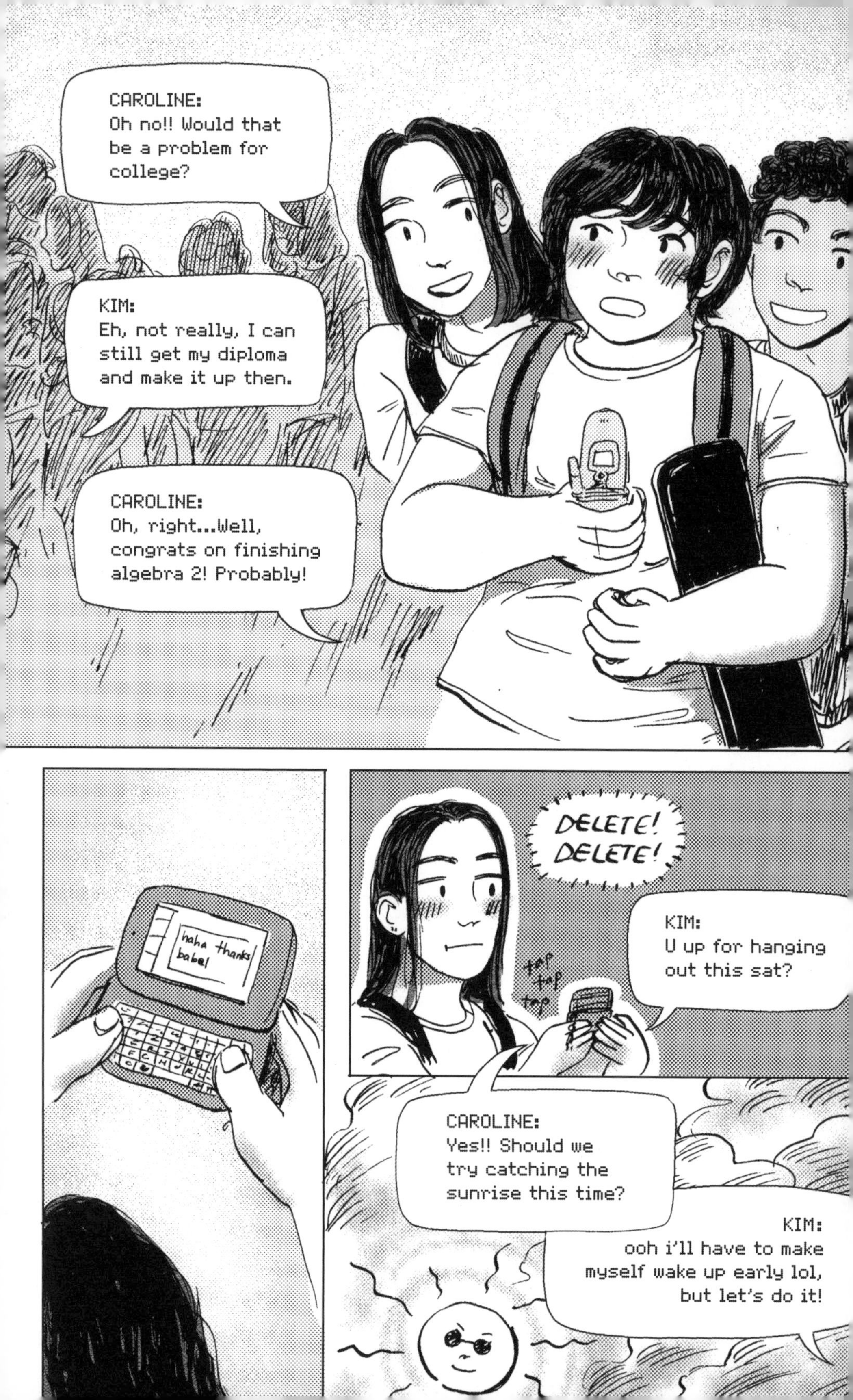
CAROLINE: Oh no!! Would that be a problem for college?
KIM: Eh, not really, I can still get my diploma and make it up then.
CAROLINE: Oh, right...Well, congrats on finishing algebra 2! Probably!
haha thanks babe!
DELETE! DELETE!
tap tap tap
KIM: U up for hanging out this sat?
CAROLINE: Yes!! Should we try catching the sunrise this time?
KIM: ooh i'll have to make myself wake up early lol, but let's do it!

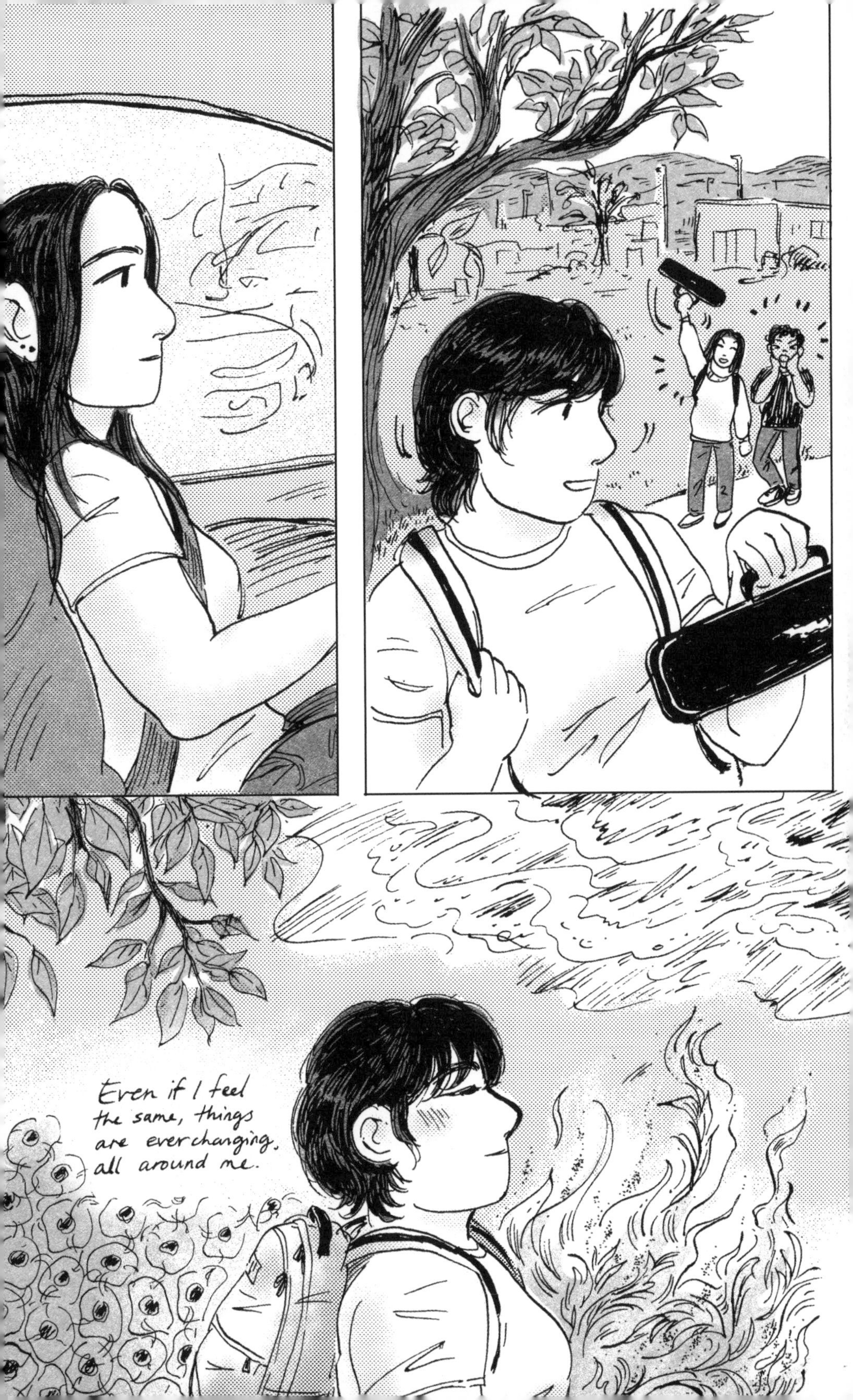
Even if I feel the same, things are everchanging all around me.

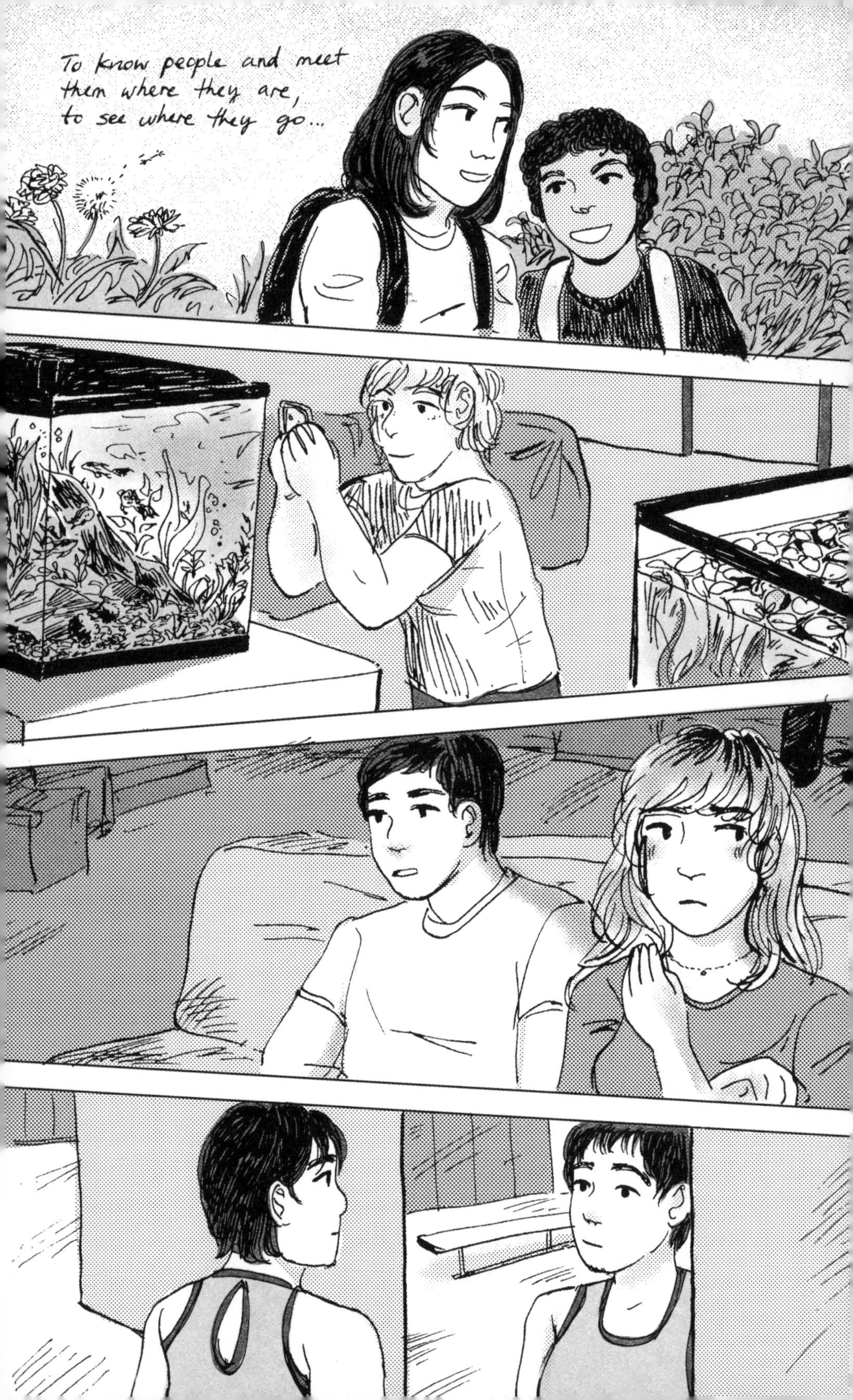
To know people and meet them where they are, to see where they go...

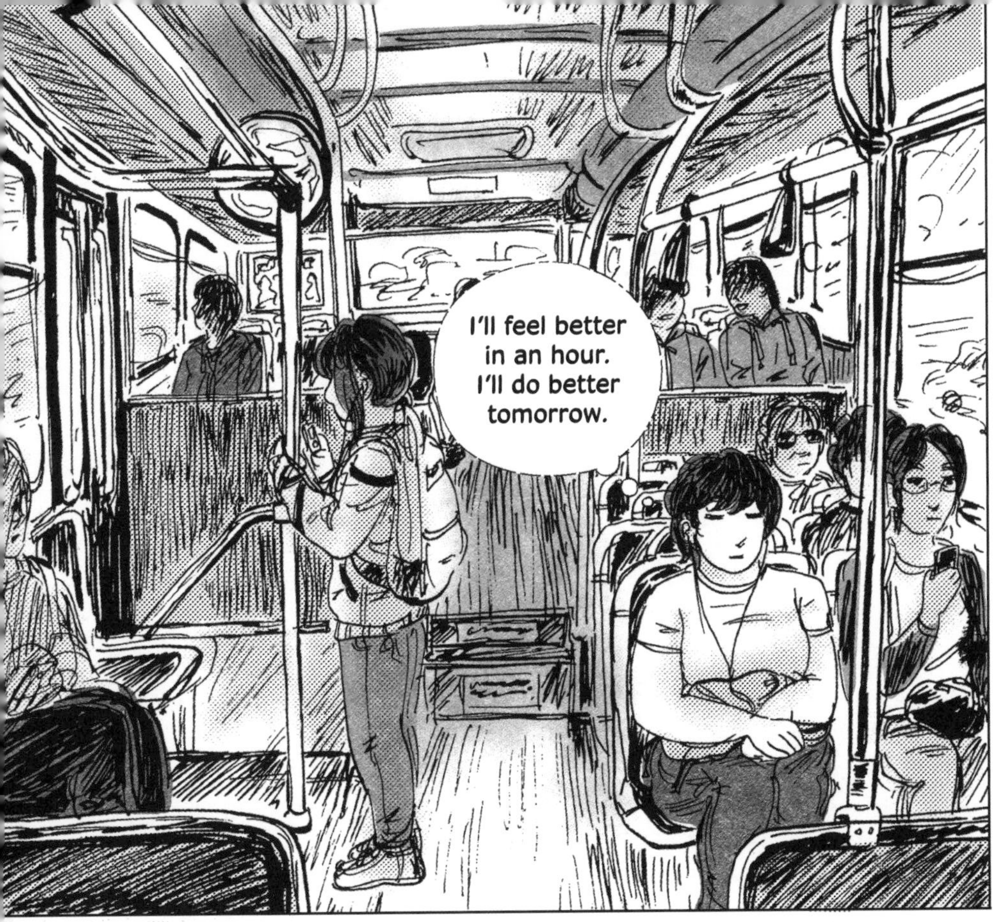
I'll feel better
in an hour.
I'll do better
tomorrow.

I'm okay right now.

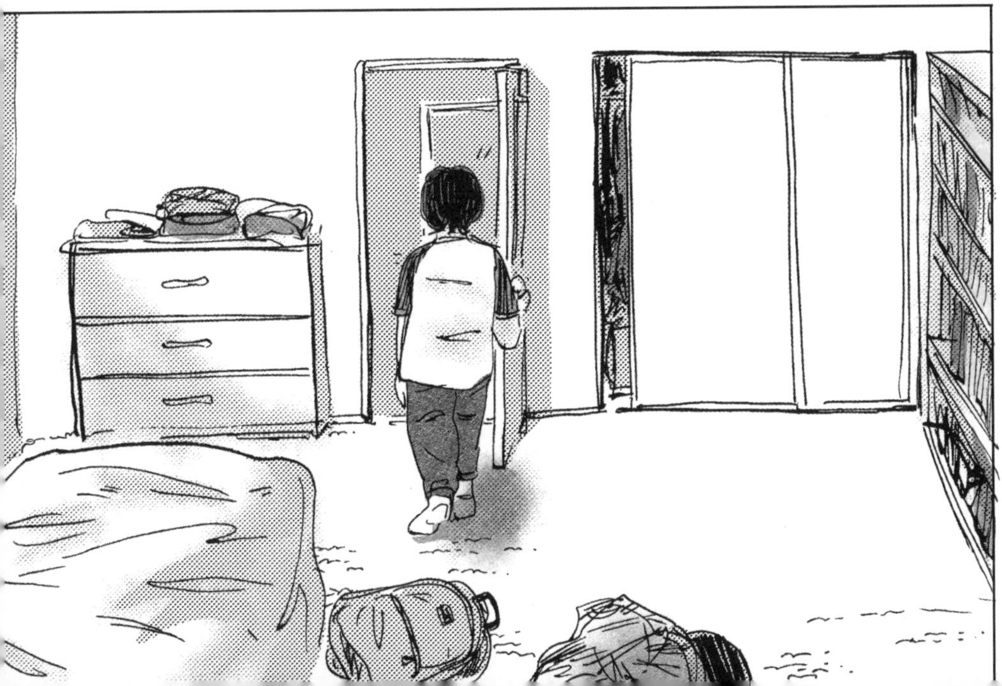

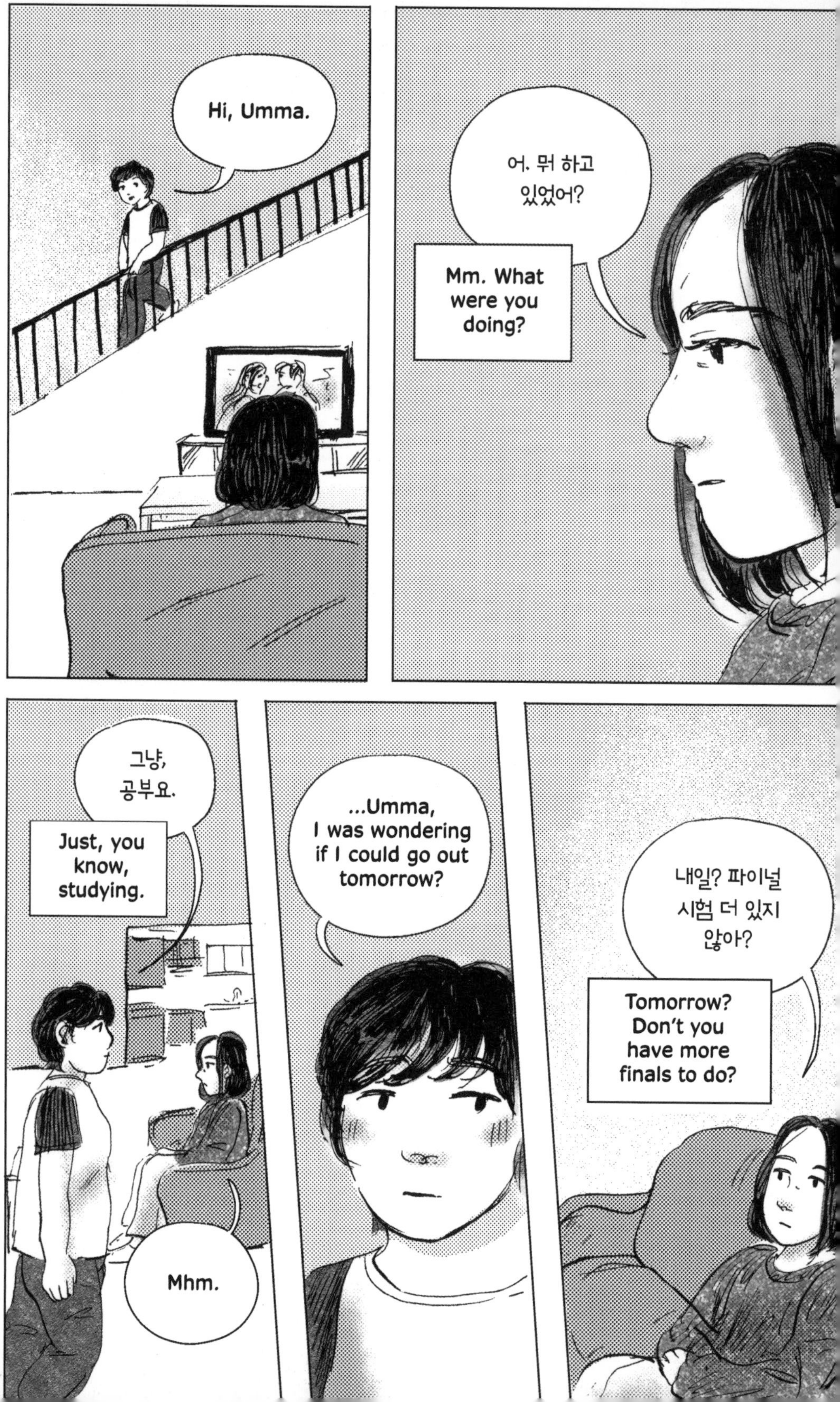
Hi, Umma.
어. 뭐 하고 있었어?
Mm. What were you doing?
그냥, 공부요.
Just, you know, studying.
Mhm.
...Umma, I was wondering if I could go out tomorrow?
내일? 파이널 시험 더 있지 않아?
Tomorrow? Don't you have more finals to do?

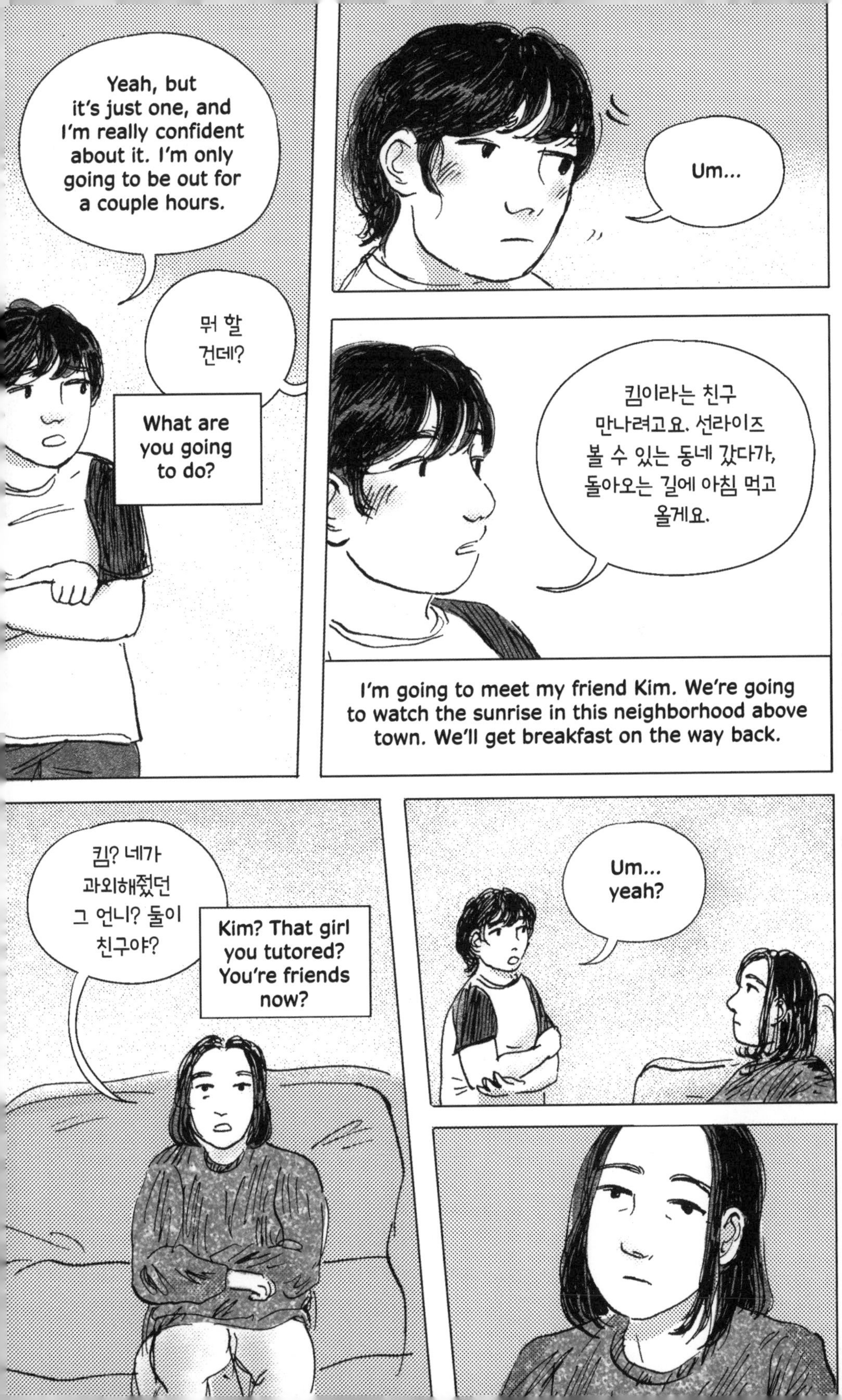
Yeah, but it's just one, and I'm really confident about it. I'm only going to be out for a couple hours.
Um...
뭐 할 건데?
What are you going to do?
킴이라는 친구 만나려고요. 선라이즈 볼 수 있는 동네 갔다가, 돌아오는 길에 아침 먹고 올게요.
I'm going to meet my friend Kim. We're going to watch the sunrise in this neighborhood above town. We'll get breakfast on the way back.
킴? 네가 과외해줬던 그 언니? 둘이 친구야?
Kim? That girl you tutored? You're friends now?
Um... yeah?

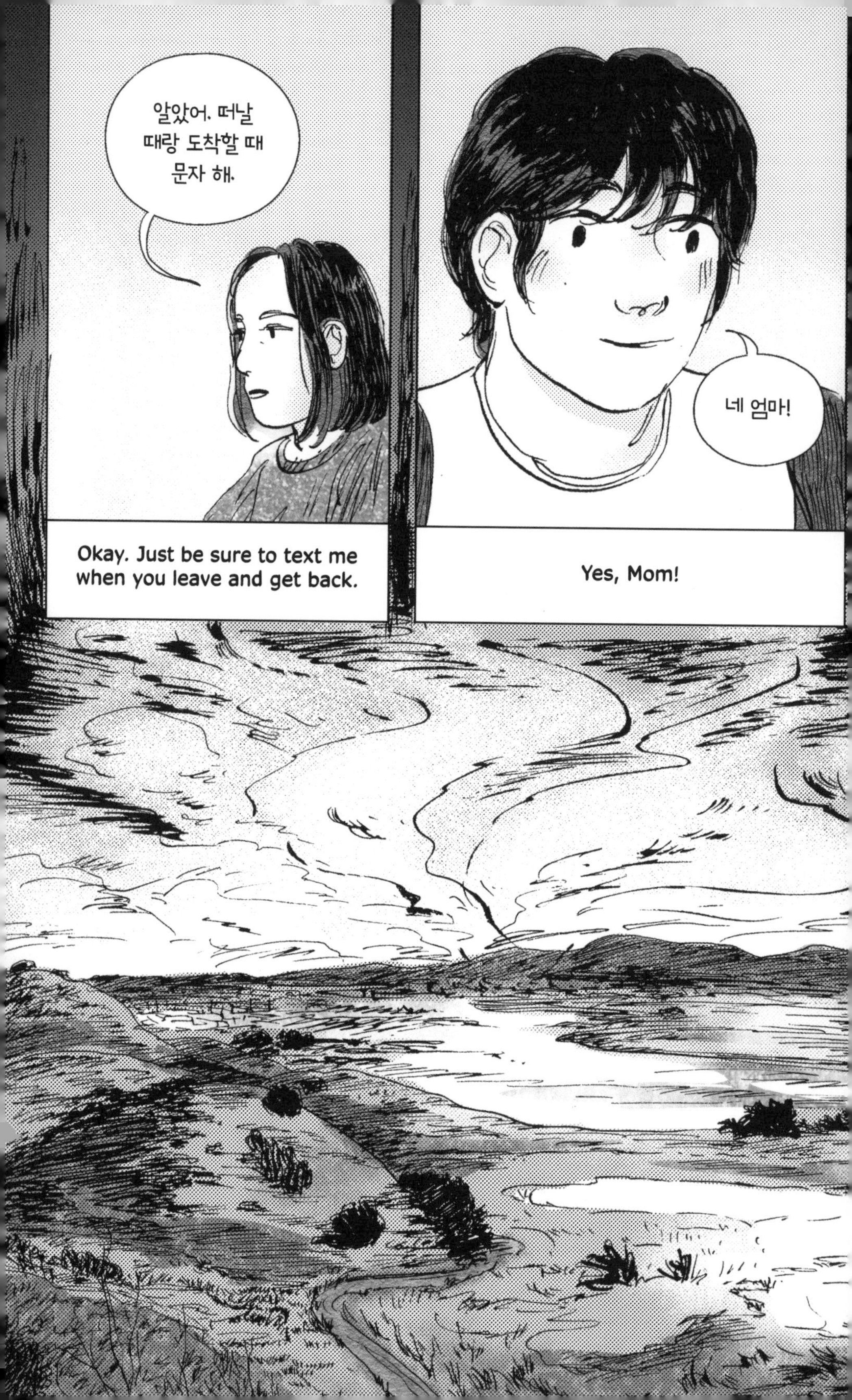
알았어. 떠날 때랑 도착할 때 문자 해.
Okay. Just be sure to text me when you leave and get back.
네 엄마!
Yes, Mom!

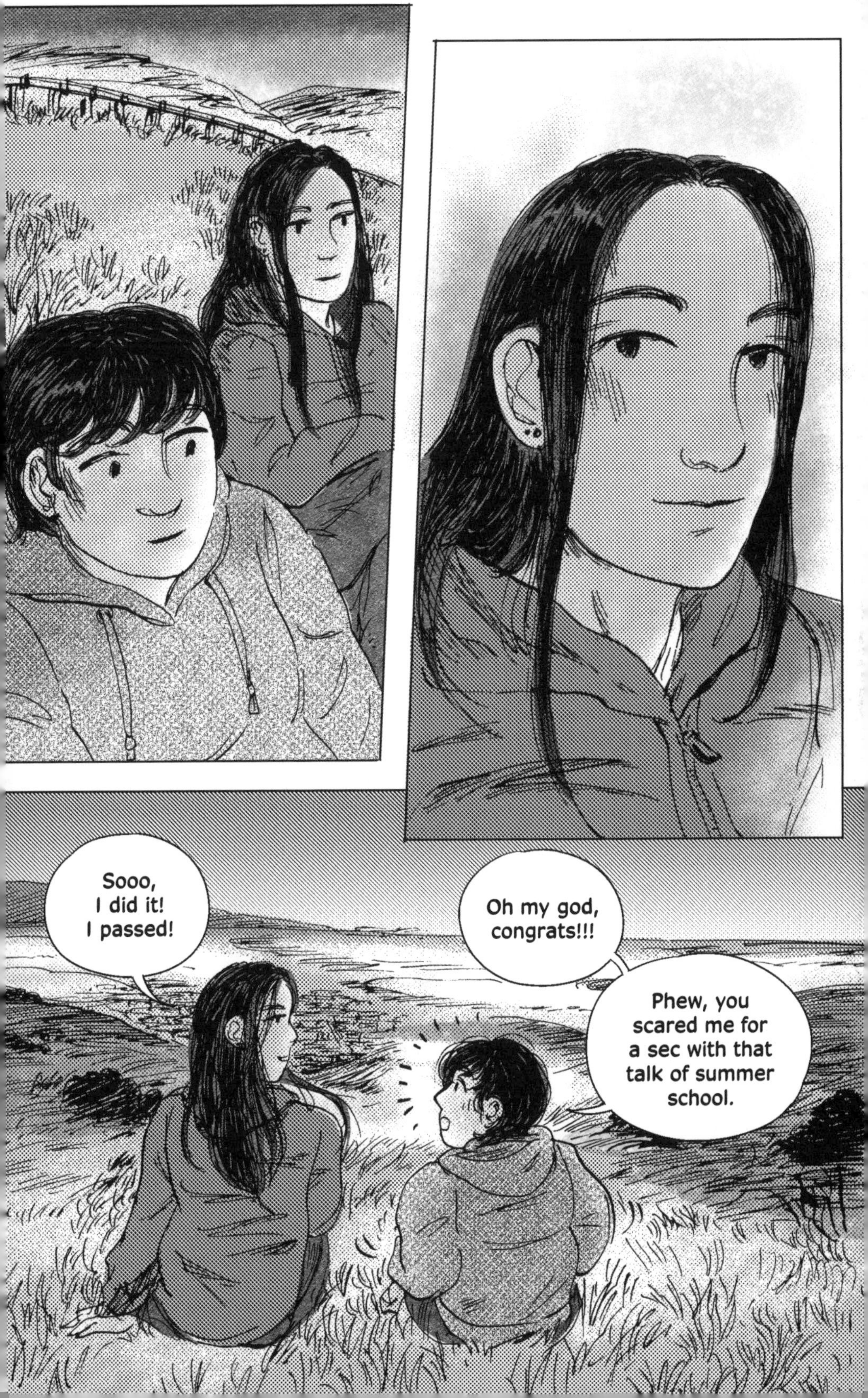
Sooo,
I did it!
I passed!
Oh my god,
congrats!!!
Phew, you
scared me for
a sec with that
talk of summer
school.

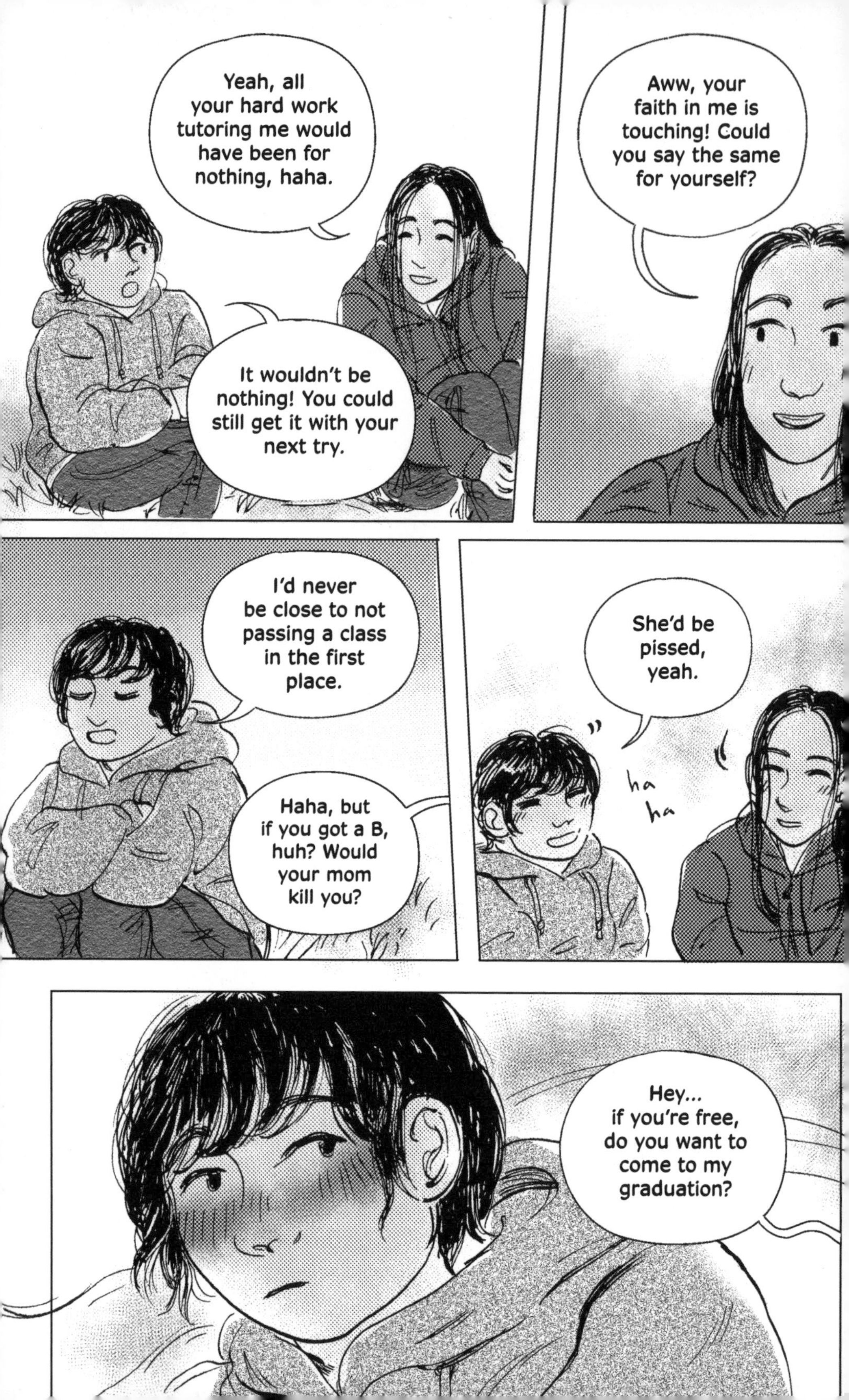
Yeah, all your hard work tutoring me would have been for nothing, haha.
It wouldn't be nothing! You could still get it with your next try.
Aww, your faith in me is touching! Could you say the same for yourself?
I'd never be close to not passing a class in the first place.
Haha, but if you got a B, huh? Would your mom kill you?
She'd be pissed, yeah.
ha ha
Hey... if you're free, do you want to come to my graduation?

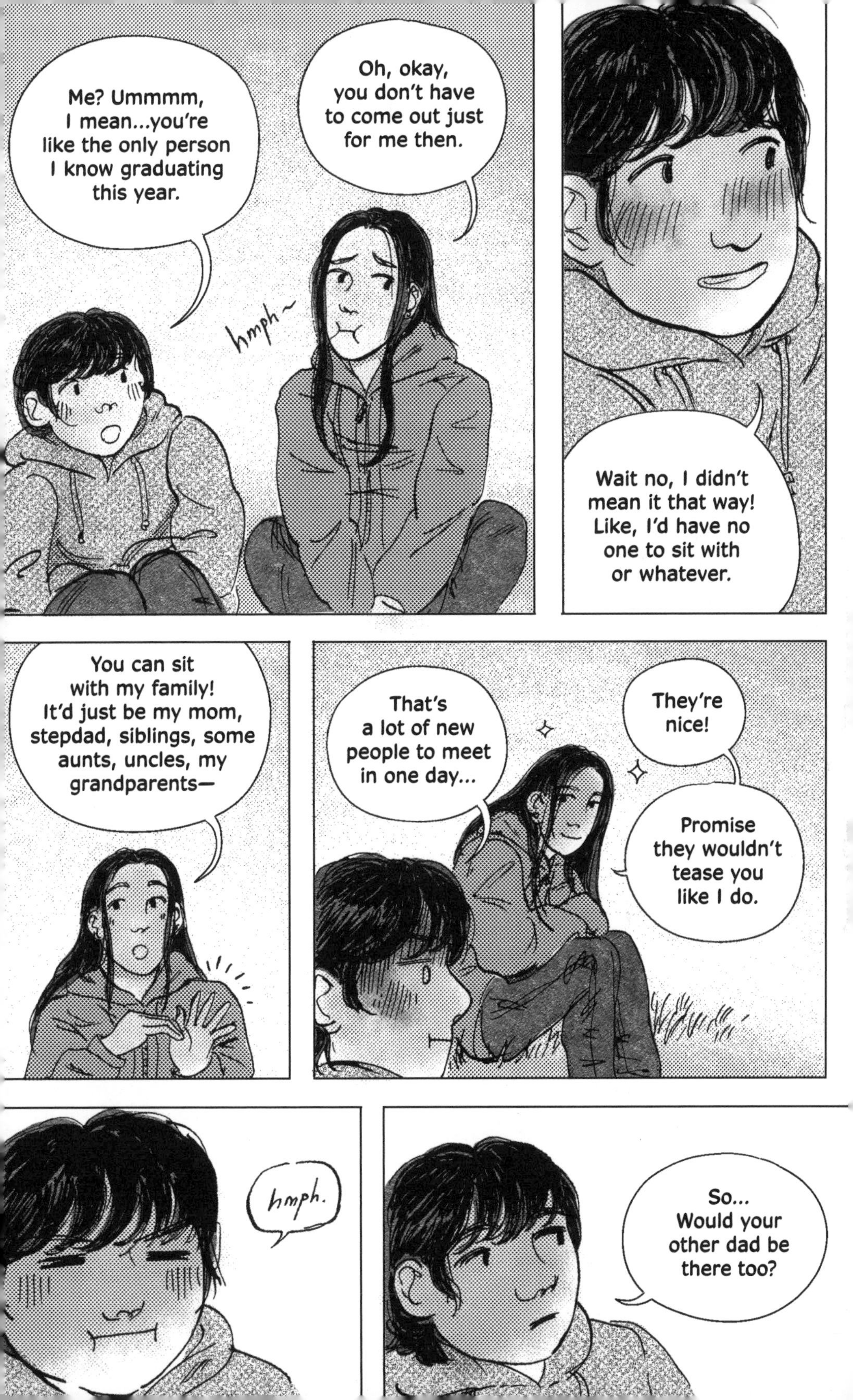
Me? Ummmm, I mean...you're like the only person I know graduating this year.
Oh, okay, you don't have to come out just for me then.
hmph~
Wait no, I didn't mean it that way! Like, I'd have no one to sit with or whatever.
You can sit with my family! It'd just be my mom, stepdad, siblings, some aunts, uncles, my grandparents—
That's a lot of new people to meet in one day...
They're nice!
Promise they wouldn't tease you like I do.
hmph.
So... Would your other dad be there too?

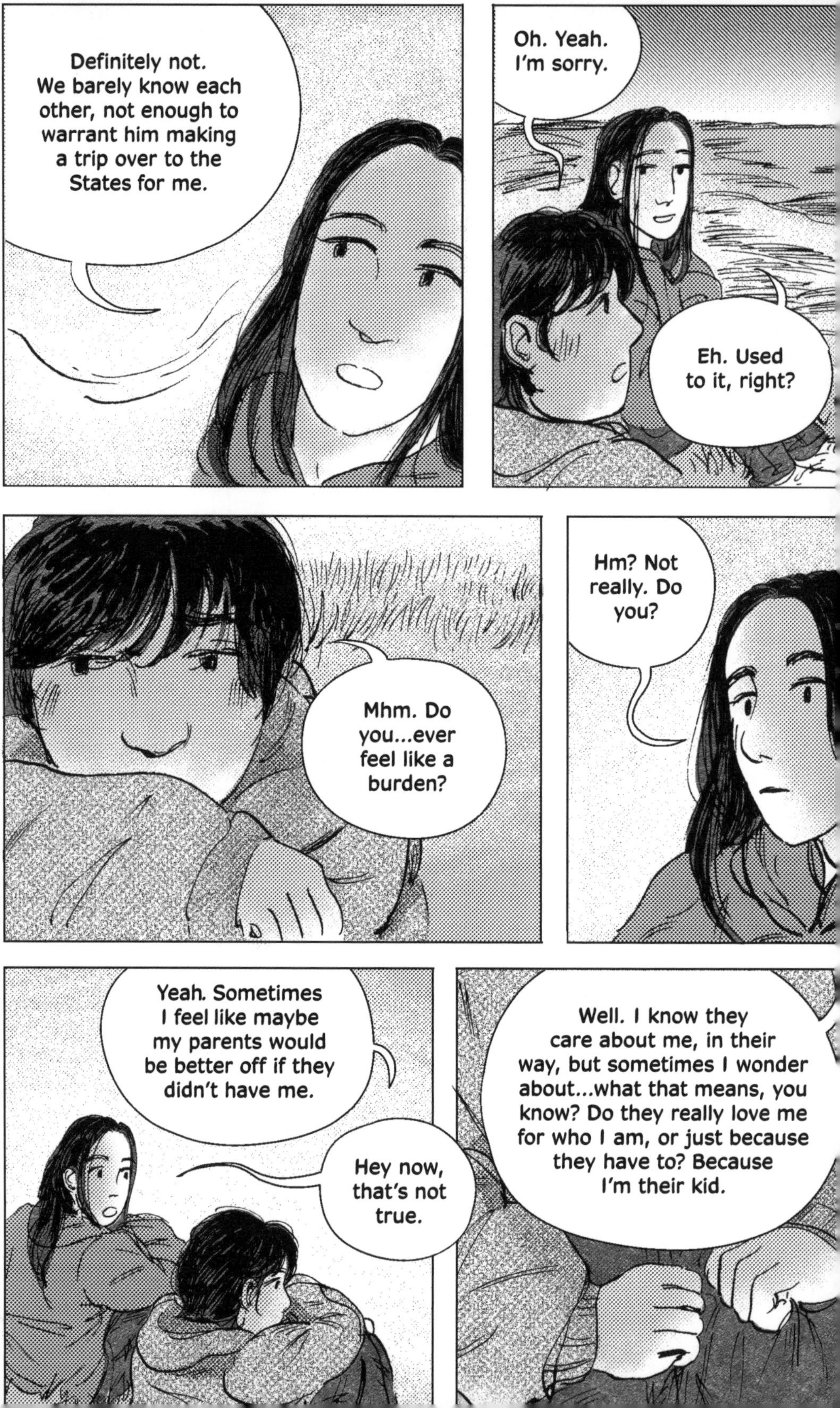
Definitely not. We barely know each other, not enough to warrant him making a trip over to the States for me.
Oh. Yeah. I'm sorry.
Eh. Used to it, right?
Mhm. Do you...ever feel like a burden?
Hm? Not really. Do you?
Yeah. Sometimes I feel like maybe my parents would be better off if they didn't have me.
Hey now, that's not true.
Well. I know they care about me, in their way, but sometimes I wonder about...what that means, you know? Do they really love me for who I am, or just because they have to? Because I'm their kid.

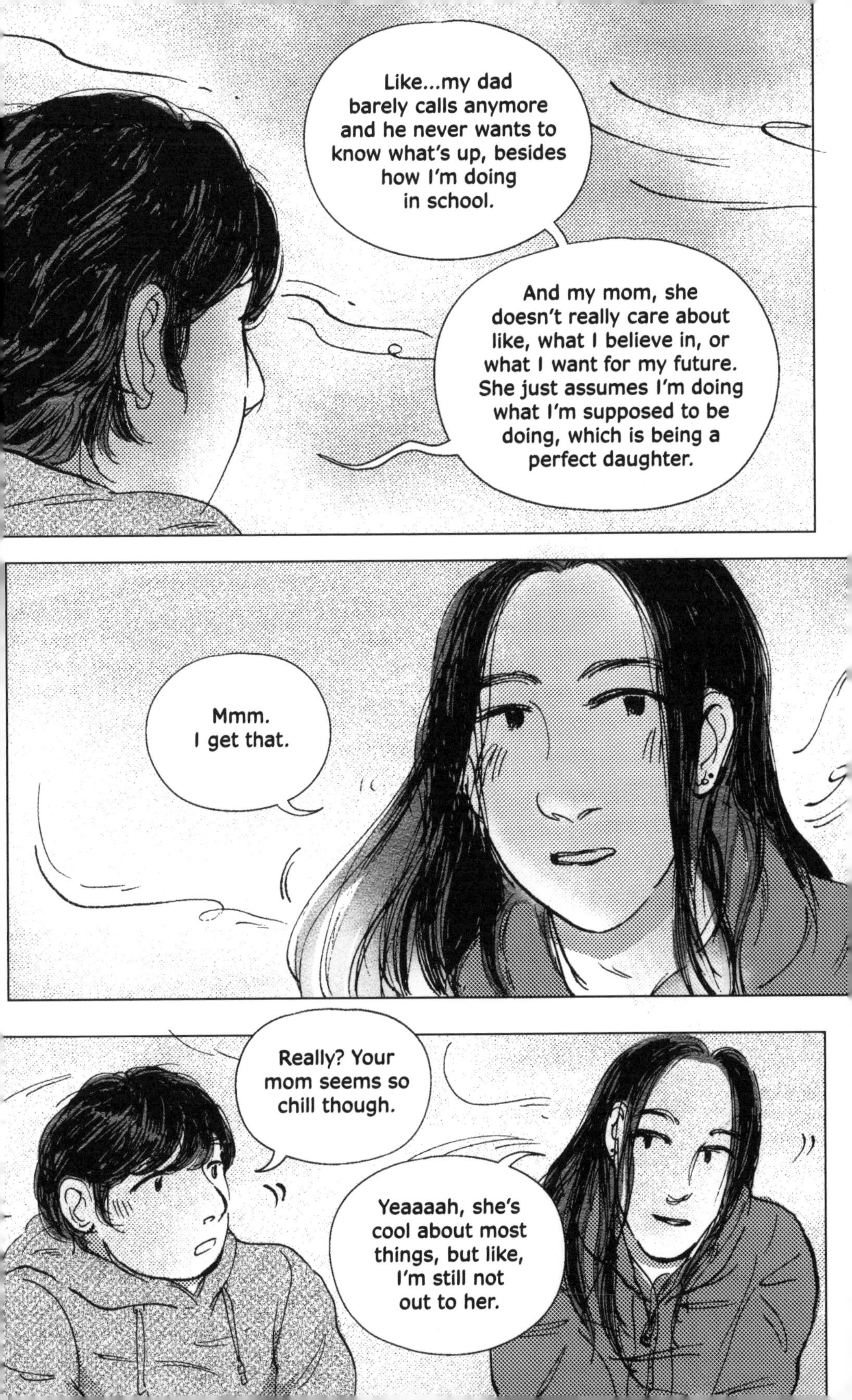
Like...my dad barely calls anymore and he never wants to know what's up, besides how I'm doing in school.
And my mom, she doesn't really care about like, what I believe in, or what I want for my future. She just assumes I'm doing what I'm supposed to be doing, which is being a perfect daughter.
Mmm. I get that.
Really? Your mom seems so chill though.
Yeaaaah, she's cool about most things, but like, I'm still not out to her.

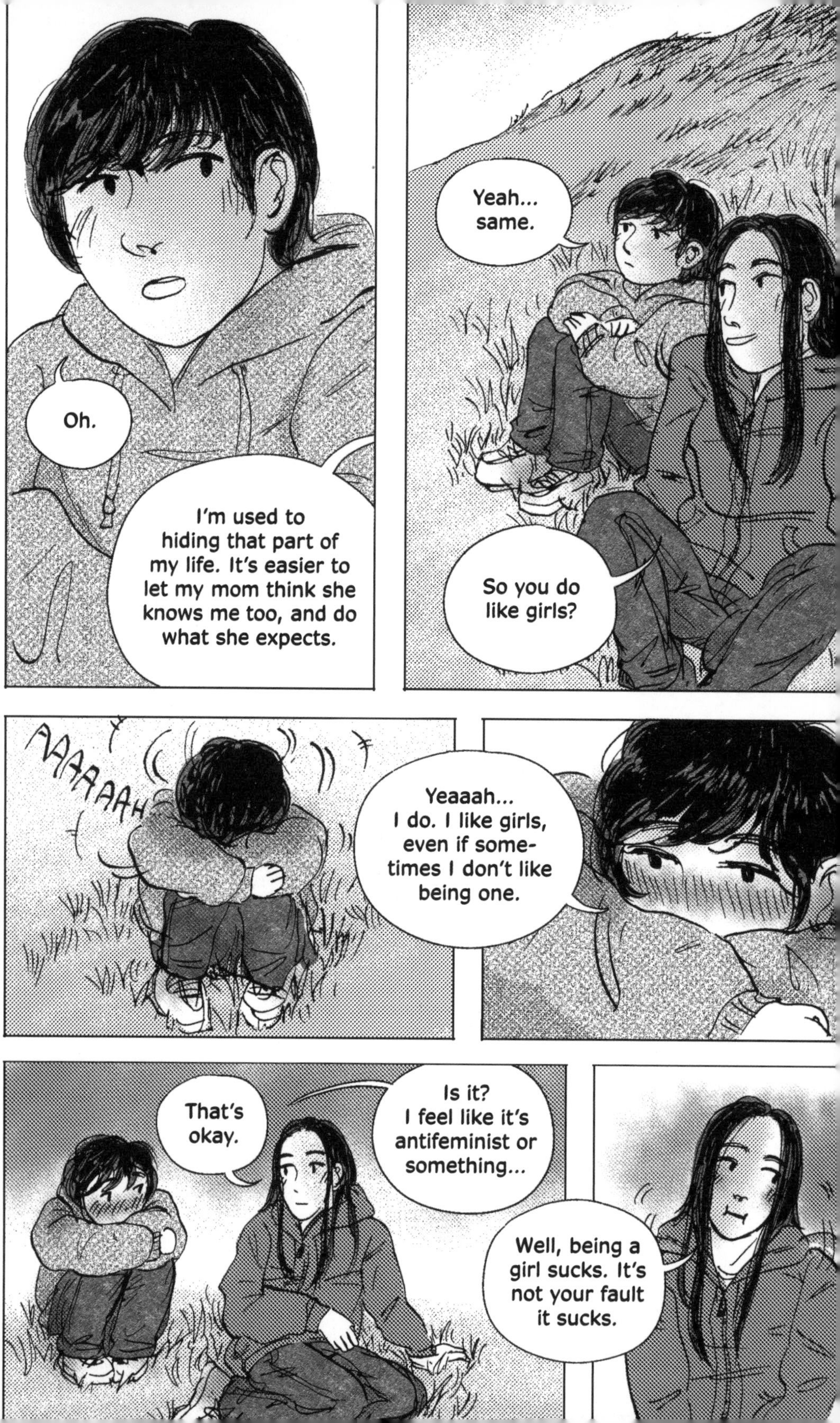
Oh.
I'm used to hiding that part of my life. It's easier to let my mom think she knows me too, and do what she expects.
Yeah... same.
So you do like girls?
AAAAAAH
Yeaaah... I do. I like girls, even if some-times I don't like being one.
That's okay.
Is it? I feel like it's antifeminist or something...
Well, being a girl sucks. It's not your fault it sucks.

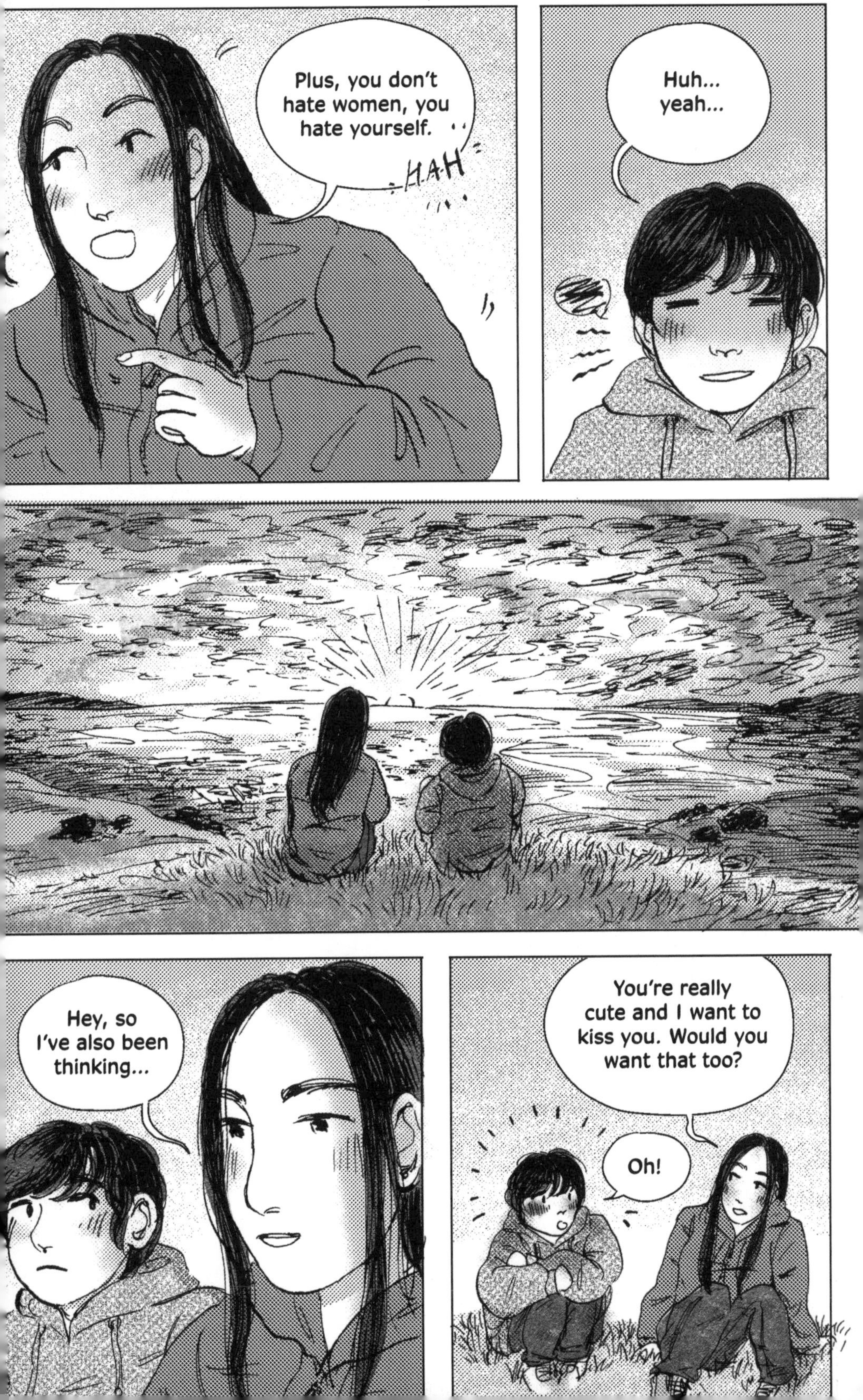
Plus, you don't hate women, you hate yourself.
HAH
Huh... yeah...
Hey, so I've also been thinking...
You're really cute and I want to kiss you. Would you want that too?
Oh!

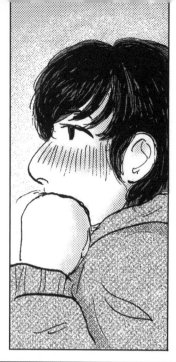

Okay.
Yes.

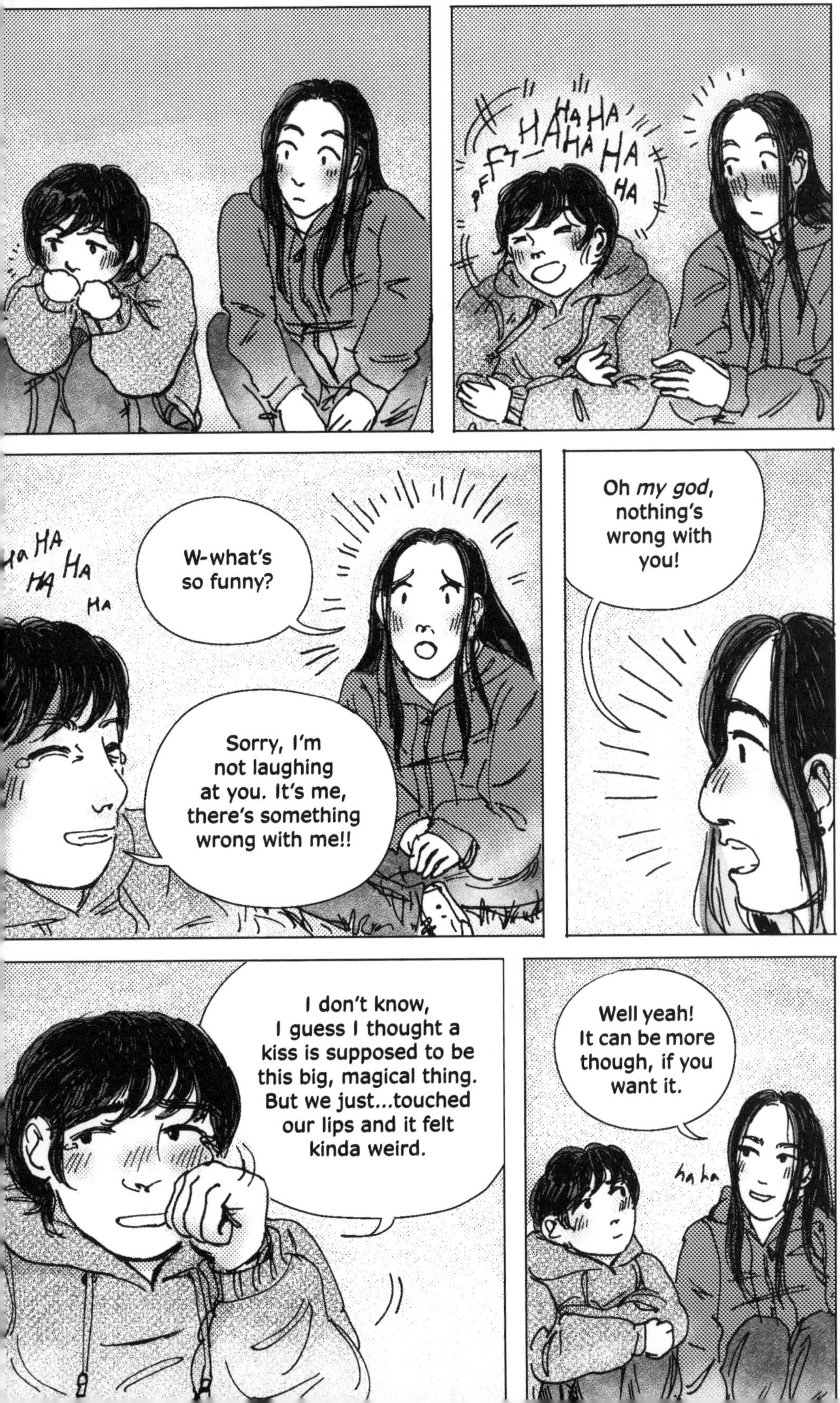

HA HA
HA HA HA
HA
HA HA
HA HA
HA
W-what's so funny?
Sorry, I'm not laughing at you. It's me, there's something wrong with me!!
Oh *my god*, nothing's wrong with you!
I don't know, I guess I thought a kiss is supposed to be this big, magical thing. But we just...touched our lips and it felt kinda weird.
Well yeah! It can be more though, if you want it.
ha ha

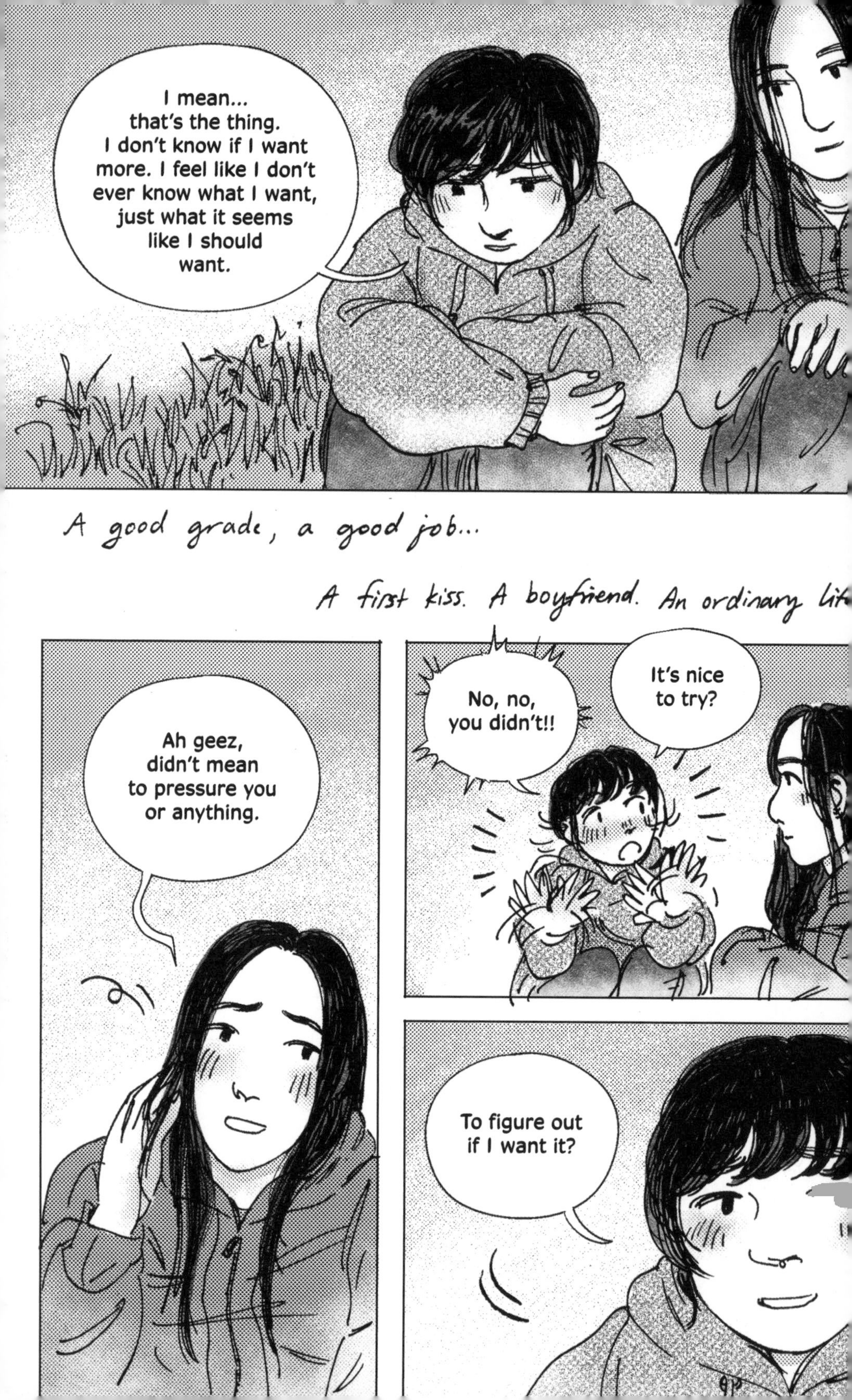
I mean... that's the thing. I don't know if I want more. I feel like I don't ever know what I want, just what it seems like I should want.
A good grade, a good job...
A first kiss. A boyfriend. An ordinary lif
Ah geez, didn't mean to pressure you or anything.
No, no, you didn't!!
It's nice to try?
To figure out if I want it?

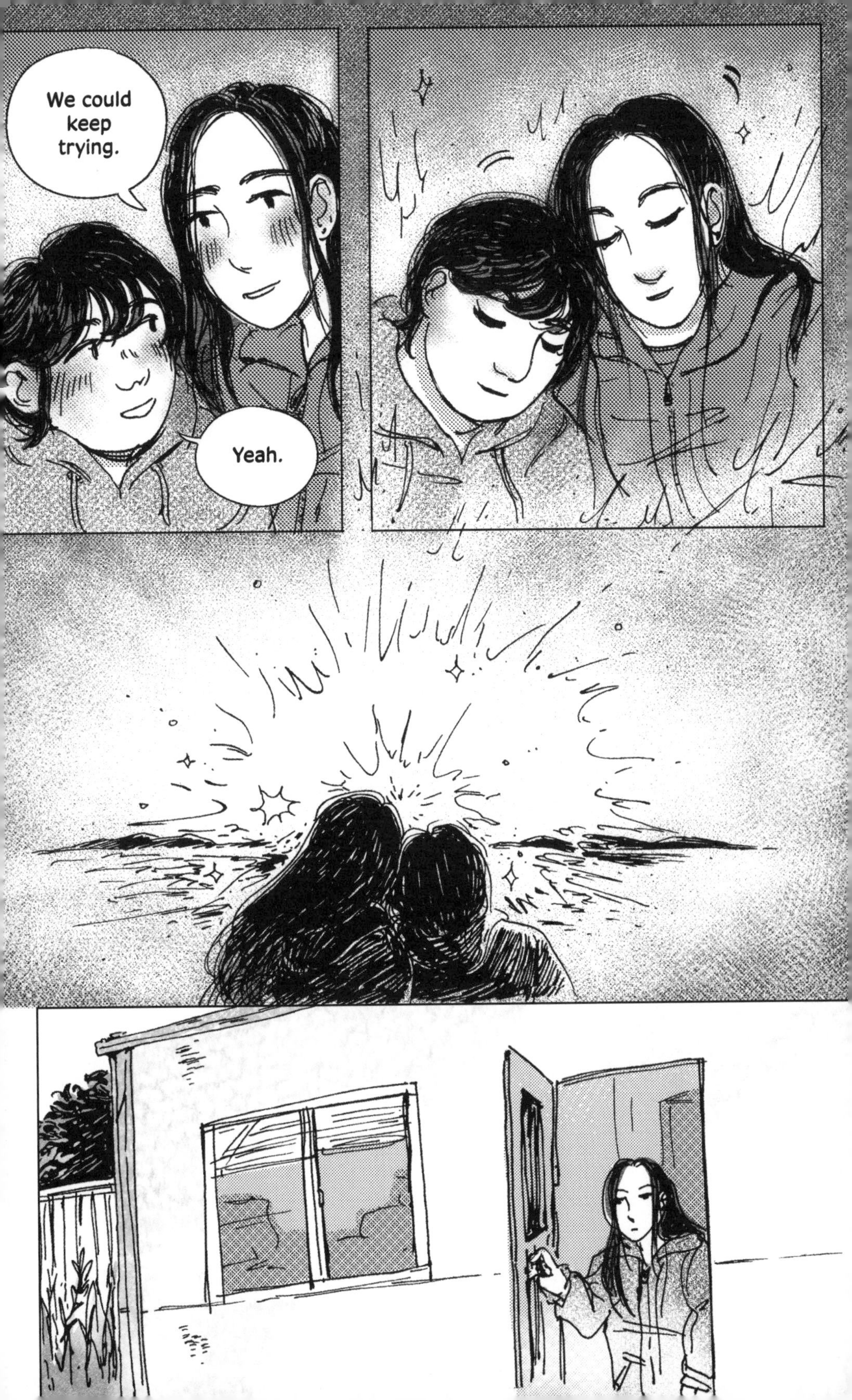
We could keep trying.
Yeah.

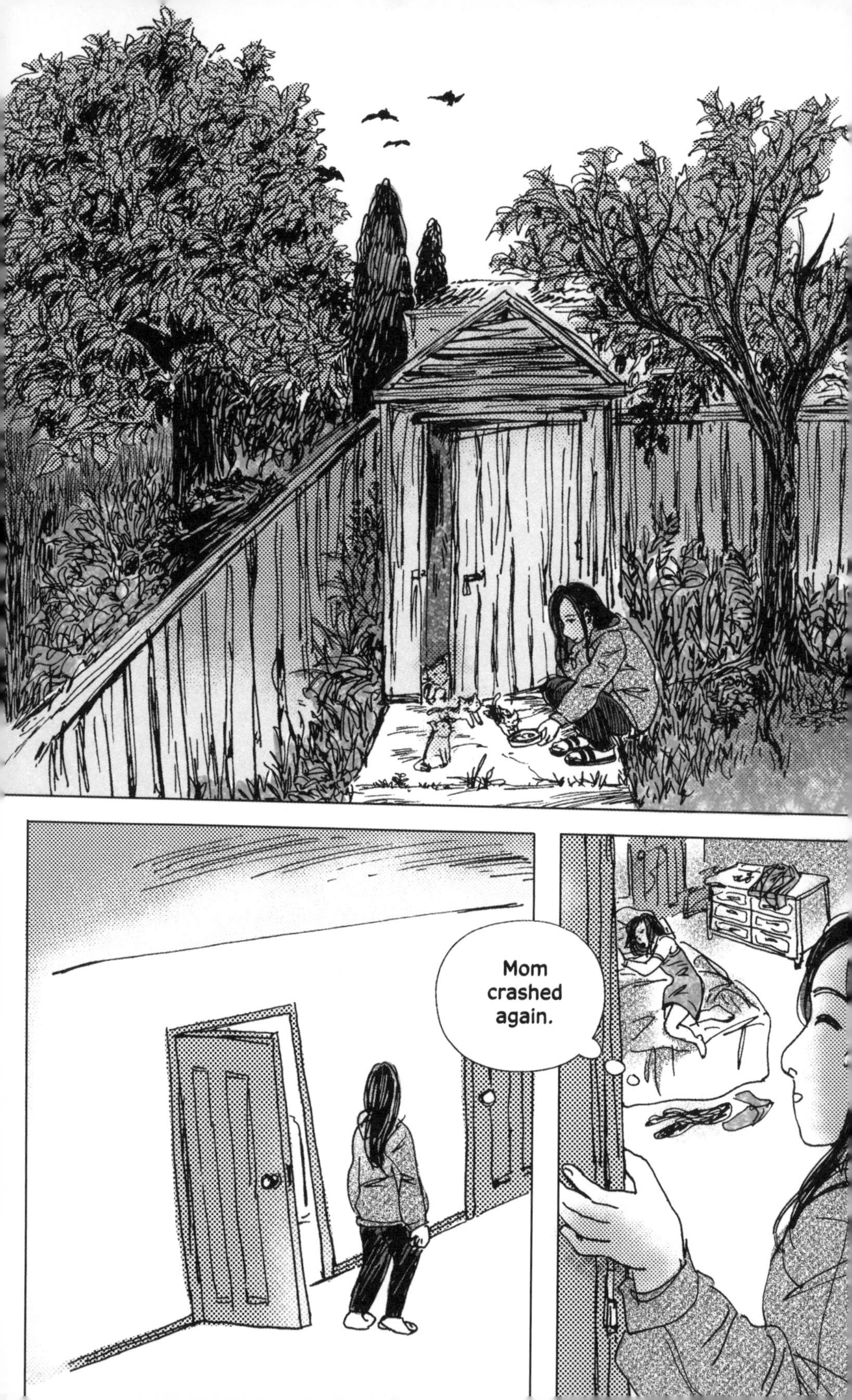
Mom
crashed
again.

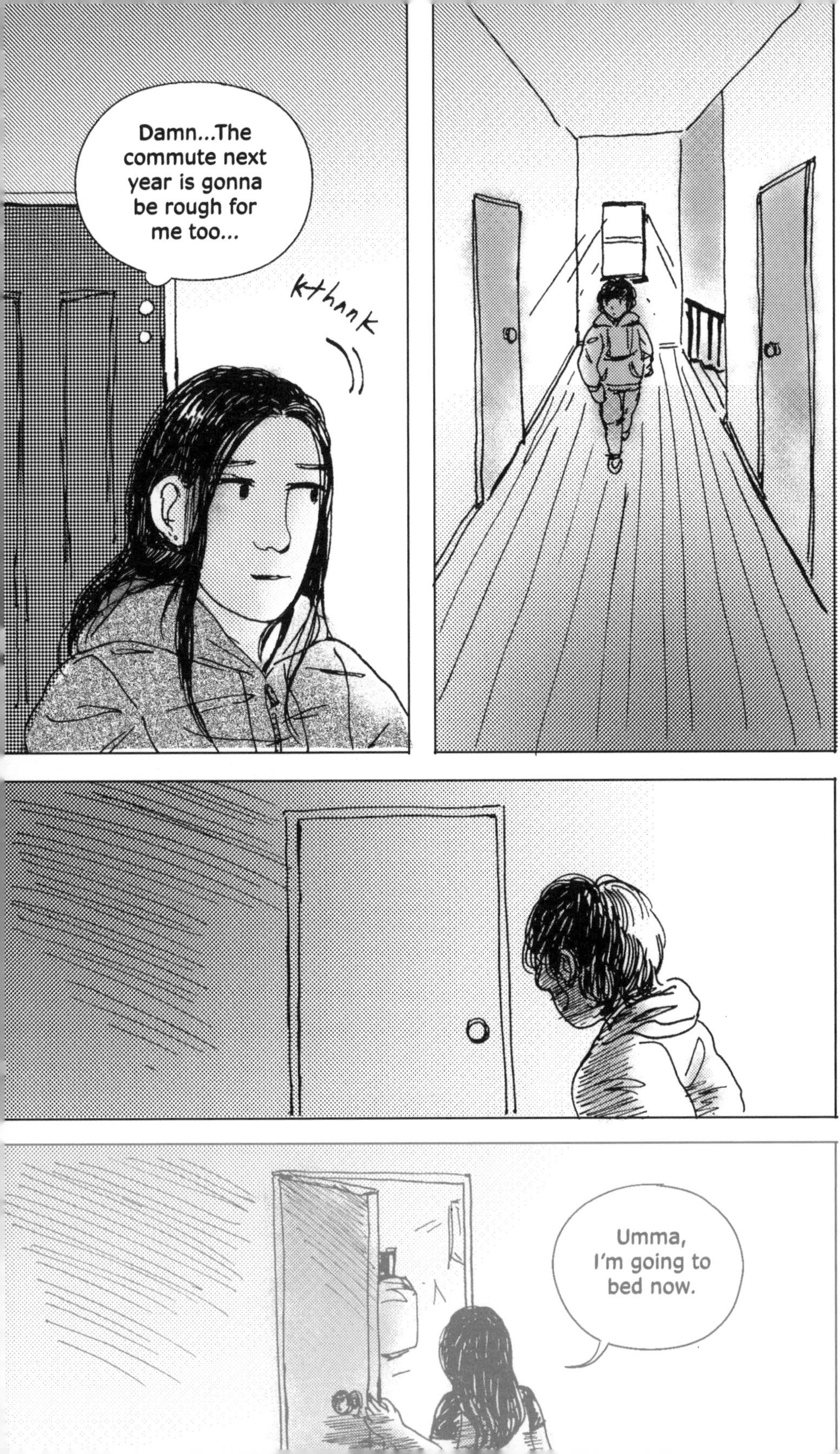
Damn...The commute next year is gonna be rough for me too...
kthank
Umma, I'm going to bed now.

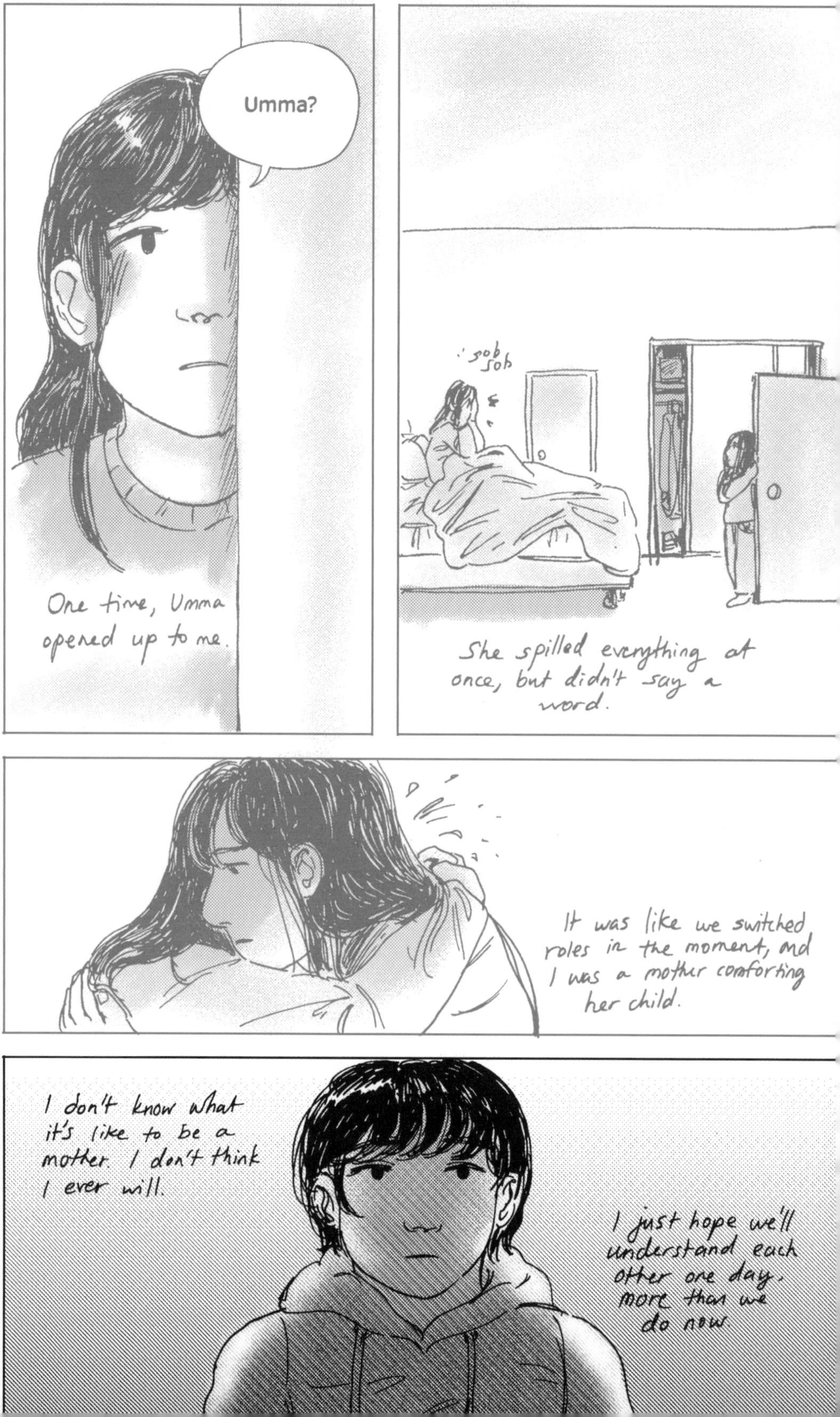
Umma?
One time, Umma opened up to me.
sob sob
She spilled everything at once, but didn't say a word.
It was like we switched roles in the moment, and I was a mother comforting her child.
I don't know what it's like to be a mother. I don't think I ever will.
I just hope we'll understand each other one day, more than we do now.

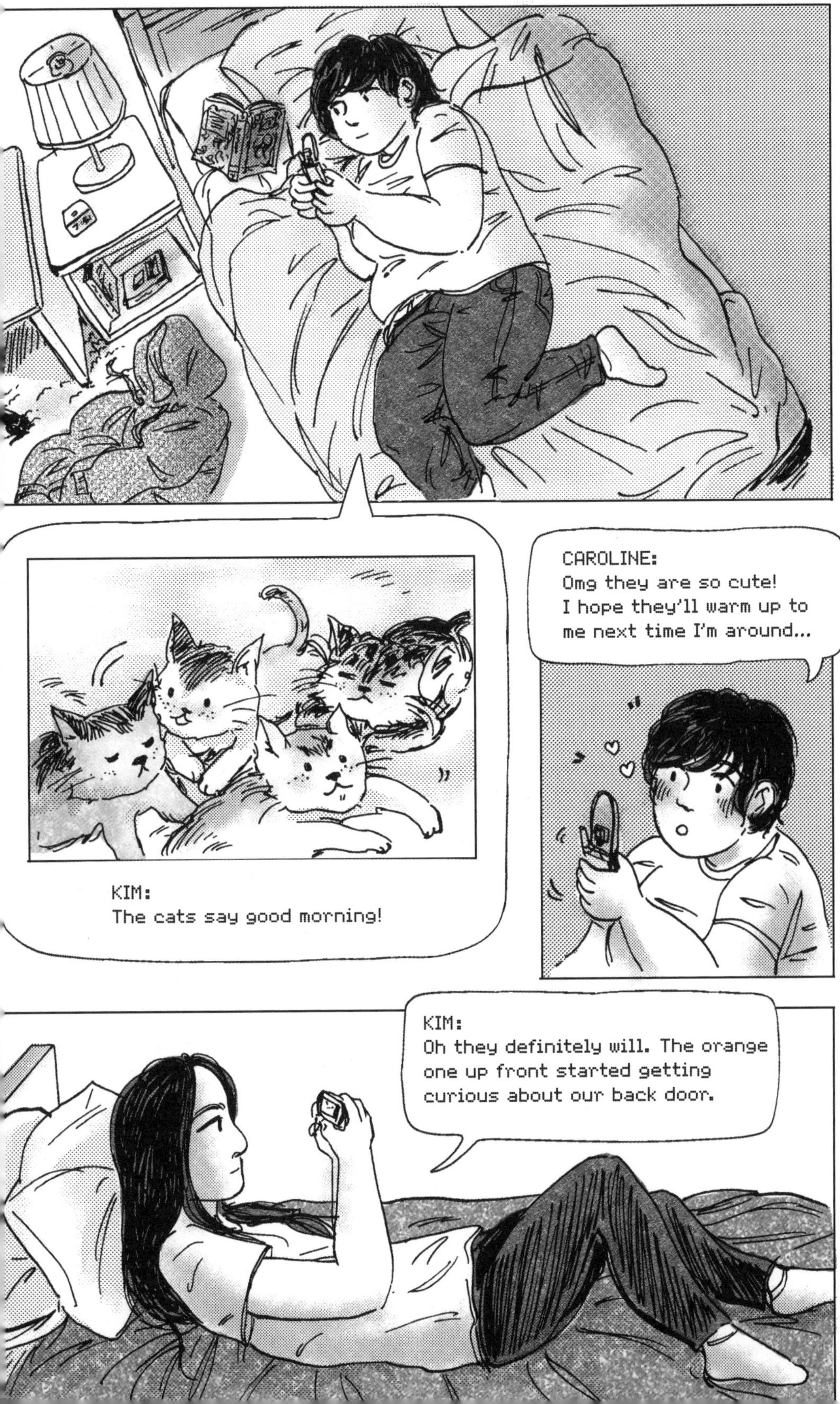
KIM:
The cats say good morning!
CAROLINE:
Omg they are so cute!
I hope they'll warm up to me next time I'm around...
KIM:
Oh they definitely will. The orange one up front started getting curious about our back door.

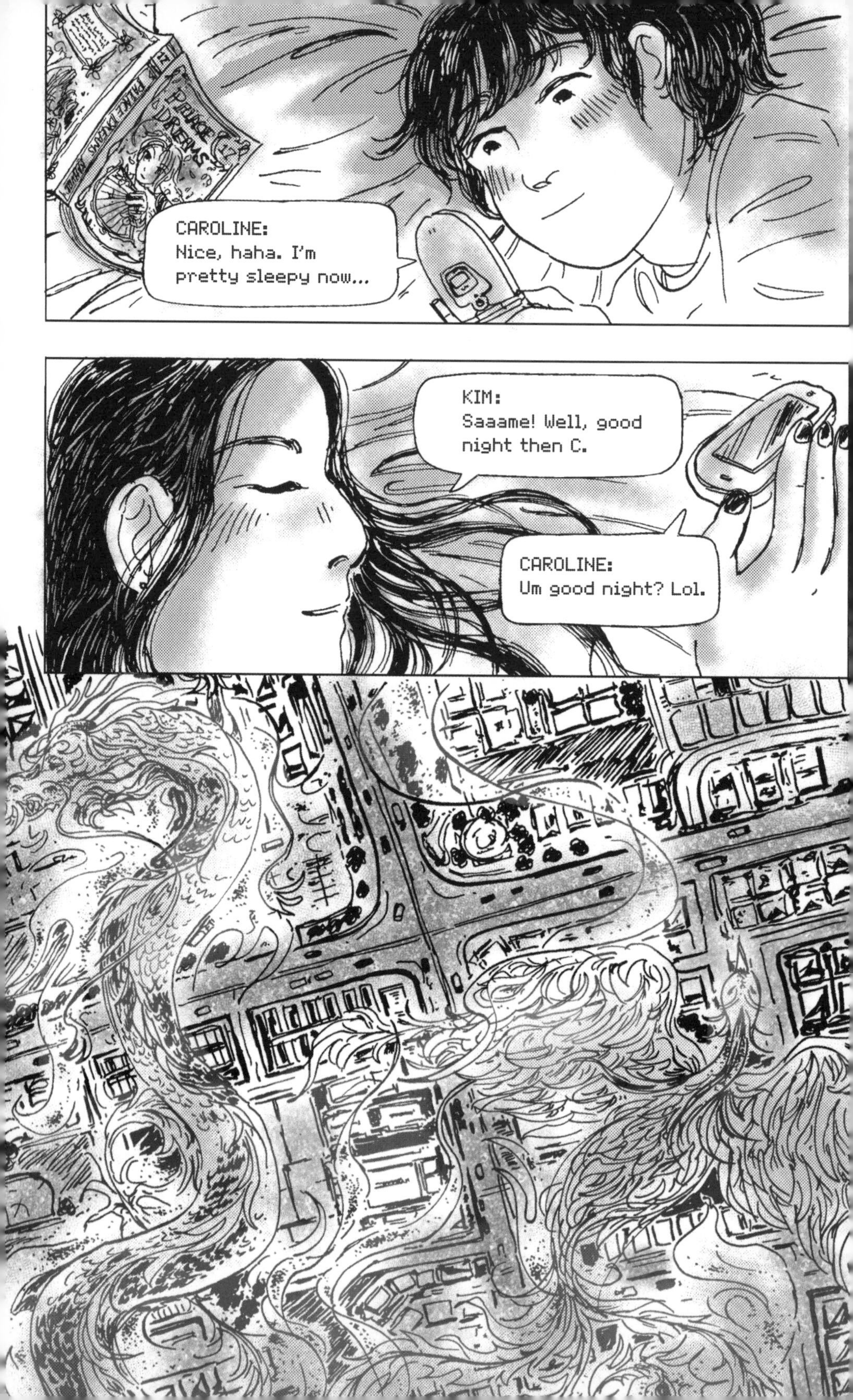
CAROLINE: Nice, haha. I'm pretty sleepy now...
KIM: Saaame! Well, good night then C.
CAROLINE: Um good night? Lol.

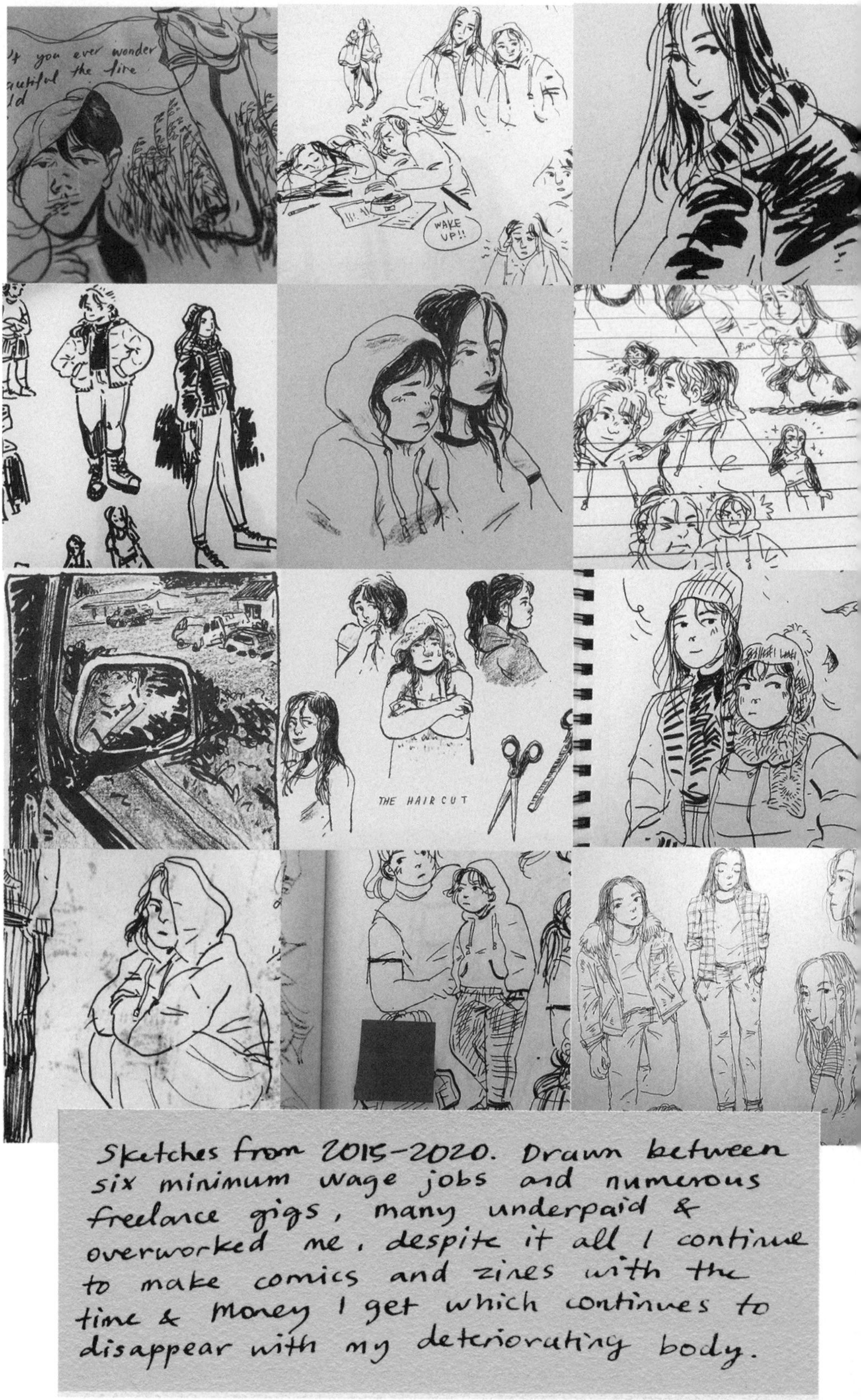
you ever wonder
WAKE UP!!
THE HAIR CUT

Sketches from 2015–2020. Drawn between six minimum wage jobs and numerous freelance gigs, many underpaid & overworked me. despite it all I continue to make comics and zines with the time & money I get which continues to disappear with my deteriorating body.

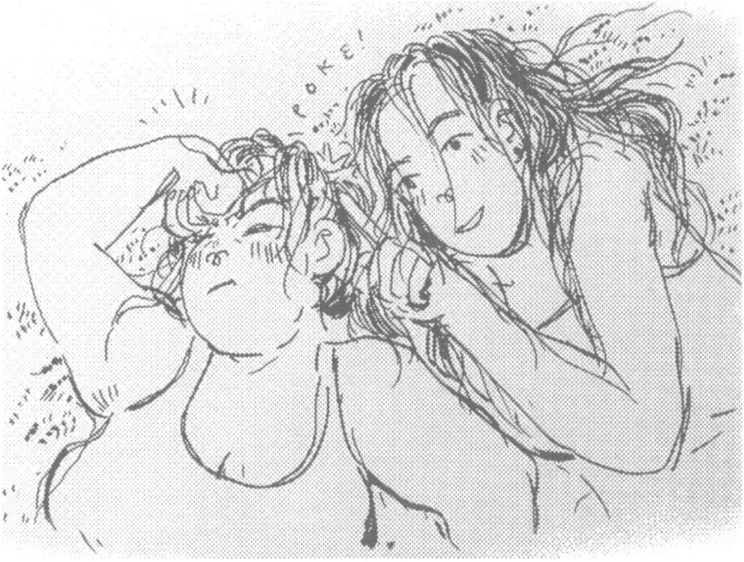
POKE!

Thank you to my HarperAlley team, my agent Susan, my Korean editor Seola, my assistants Raven, Sarah & Syd, the printers overseas, the dock workers, the freight haulers, the booksellers and librarians, for all your hard work now and to come. My homes: Mar, Ashanti, Binglei, Ann, Jules, our animals. My mentors, peers, collaborators (wish I could list you all): Ryan, Carta, Paloma, my Lucky Pocket Press pals, your families and our friends — "movies to cry to," "Stuck Inside Watching Shit," "Art & Labor", "Kuorum", "Gal Pals," "Secret BBS," "Anime Convent," "Baltimore Asian Resistance In Solidarity," "Hidden Harvest Farm," 엄마, 아빠, 에디, 가족들, 우리 볼티모어에 퀴어 친구들/our queer Baltimore friends. This book was written and drawn on Piscataway Land and its story takes place on Ohlone Land.

— SUNMI
ㅅㅓㄴㅁㅣ

Dedicated to my friends

HarperAlley is an imprint of HarperCollins Publishers.
Firebird. Copyright © 2023 by Sunmi. All rights reserved. Manufactured in Italy.
No part of this book may be used or reproduced in any manner whatsoever without
written permission except in the case of brief quotations embodied in critical articles
and reviews. For information address HarperCollins Children's Books, a division of
HarperCollins Publishers, 195 Broadway, New York, NY 10007. www.harperalley.com
ISBN 978-0-06-298151-6 This book was drawn with the following fountain pens: Pilot
Parallel 1.5-4.0mm, Lamy Joy 1.1 mm, Pilot Explorer Fine, with black Lamy and Parker ink.
Digitally toned with Clip Studio Paint. Typography by Sunmi and Erica De Chavez Wong
23 24 25 26 27   RTLO   10 9 8 7 6 5 4 3 2 1
❖ First Edition